PANTERROR!

The Epic Babysitting Adventures of Rachel Pugsley

Also by Gregory Saur

Royal Pains and Angels in the Outhouse: One Big Little League Story That Goes a Bit Foul

Otherworld: Orcish Delight (as G. D. Saur)

Stuck in the Past (with Jack Irish)

The Pond Scum Gang

Soccer Star

Diving Catch

PANTERROR!

The Epic Babysitting Adventures of Rachel Pugsley

Gregory Saur

A Saur & Saur Publishing Project

ISBN (hc) 978–0-9964245–0-9

First Edition

All characters in this book are fictitious, and any resemblance to real persons, living or dead, is coincidental.

Book Design by RS and GS

We gratefully acknowledge the use of the following images for the cover:
Hand Mirror © <href='http://www.123rf.com/profile_thanapun'> / 123RF Stock Photo</a>
Table © Copyright: <a href='http://www.123rf.com/profile_scyther5'>scyther5 / 123RF Stock Photo</a>
Various children and wizard:
© Pascal Broze/ONOKY/Getty images
© Fabrice Lerouge/ONOKY/Getty Images
© Yuganov Konstantin/Shutterstock.com
©iStock.com /FlairImages
Thank you to all involved for the excellent photography.

Printed in the United States of America

Dedicated to

Priscilla Outland. I will always miss you. Thank you for all your kindness and patience. May your memory be eternal.

Humility is the only thing we need; one can still fall having virtues other than humility—but with humility one does not fall.

Elder Herman of Mount Athos

Prologue

In a far-off land ...

The hot sun spilled from the sky like a golden liquid, flooding the land with a sweltering heat. Most animals with good sense had long before found shelter in shade. Most animals didn't have guard duty.

Perched closest to the radiating furnace, the armored guard leaned tiredly against his spear and sighed heavily. He wiped rivulets of sweat from his helmed brow and looked down from the ramparts before him.

The Fortress of Belford stood over fifteen floors at its highest point—the center turret overlooking the walls of black stone mined from the mountain it guarded. The lone guard stood in the center of this turret, which gave him a good view of the road leading to the village below him. He traced it with his eyes, watching the smooth, hard-packed dirt twisting away from the fortress before vanishing into the forest. It appeared very peaceful, like a river on a calm day. If only that were the truth.

In truth, no peace could be found in this forsaken land. Instead, fear reigned, and that alone kept the land so still and silent. As still as a graveyard. The king had vanished and was rumored to be dead. All his heirs were scattered and lost. And the wizard …… Well, the wizard had left many moons before, without a word and without a trace. And that was for the best. Now the kingdom was starting to crumble like an ill-fired clay pot left to the elements. City-states were sprouting as the larger cities abandoned hope of a monarch and began establishing their own rule. Smaller villages grew tighter and fiercer as fear of strangers set in. Without the King's Guard patrolling the roads, thieves and murderers grew like weeds. Yes, in this day and age strangers became enemies until proven otherwise. Even with the land bathed in sunlight, hope dimmed as a prosperous future seemed farther and farther away.

The guard should have been happy in his position—he was part of a strong force stationed behind thick walls with lots of food and drink close by. The only problem, his family was stuck in the village down the silent road, where most of the food and drink came from. Times were getting hard, but not in the fortress. People there were growing fat and content while those outside were getting hungrier and angrier. Something in the air whispered of a change coming … it had to come. But would it be for the better, or for the worse? Everyone past their twelfth year knew the answer. Nothing got better since the king's death.

"What we need," mumbled the guard to himself, "is a hero."

Blinking away sweat, he focused his gaze on the quiet road, willing himself to see a giant black charger galloping into view, carrying a tall, noble knight with a gleaming shield and long, pointed lance. Perhaps a wizard full of power and wisdom would arrive instead, floating on a cloud and wielding a staff. He didn't care that if this ever actually happened, his job would most likely be to fight against the hero. He imagined it would be a halfhearted attempt on his part and the hero would spare his life. Or, if he did die, then at least his family would be able to live in peace and his children would never have to hold a spear for the rest of their days …

All he saw, like every other day, was sun-drenched dirt, and all he got was a bad case of sunburn. It was a long day and many more were to follow.

"Heroes," mumbled the guard, "are the wishes of fools."

In his heart he knew a hero would have to be the biggest fool of all. In this land you either had to fight for power or follow somebody fighting for power. Otherwise you were stuck in the middle. Standing up for the poor and weak meant falling into an early grave. To fight for the people … that only led to certain, and painful, death.

Not so far away …
A power settled … Darkness had settled and it would be hours before the sun stretched its arms over the horizon. This was the in-between time, the time when all should be quiet … when all should be safe. Children were long tucked in and parents were finally receiving well-deserved rest. This is when it comes … this is when nightmares rise.

A house stands on top of a hill. There is a deadly silence within the dark. Not even the crickets dare make a sound as the stillness stretches over the house like a giant hand about to pounce. The world holds its breath as darkness darker than night creeps forward.

"*Welcome …*" A soft, high-pitched purr wafted through the fog. "*You have been waiting for me for a veerrry long time …*"

The small boy shifted uncomfortably in his bed, but did not stir from sleep.

"*And finally you are mine,*" continued the voice. "*Mine to do with as we please!*"

The voice rose in volume and turned into a cackle that sounded like a hen being scalded. This twisted laughter brought the boy to semiconsciousness. His eyelids started to flutter and he murmured something unintelligible.

"*Yes … wakey, wakey!*" said the voice.

All at once his body went rigid. His eyelids squeezed shut and a terrible pain pulsed in his head. Just as he was about to call out, a terrible pressure suddenly pushed down on his chest and arms. His ribs threatened to crack and his breath went out in a whoosh.

"*Yes!*" cried the voice, turning from a bird-sized pip to the roar from an angry lion. "*You are mine!*"

Now fully awake, the boy's entire body went into a panic. Arms and legs thrashed wildly as he sought to escape. His breath flew from his lungs as the terrible pressure remained. It felt as if he'd been zapped with electricity. Both eyes remained tightly shut.

If he couldn't see it, his mind reasoned, maybe *it* didn't exist. Above him, though, he knew with all his heart, lurked an evil, dark, and terrible presence. It waited for him to open his eyes, and then it would destroy him. But as long as his eyes remained closed, just maybe it was all a part of his imagination …

"*You will never escape me*!" hissed the voice just above him. "*Look upon me! Look*!"

NO! The boy jerked his head violently away and grimaced in terror. His thin arms desperately retreated to his chest to meet his trembling knees. Never before had this evil spoken to him. Before it had been just a shadow watching him … Now the terror had become all too real.

Fear surged into the boy and took completely over. With all his strength, he pressed upward with his hands and thrashed wildly to escape the heavy weight.

Terrible laughter answered his attempts.

Suddenly his covers, his only barrier from the horror above, were ripped from him. Still the weight pressed down.

Now the boy's breath came in gasps. His feet kicked weakly, it felt as if he was moving underwater. The pressure started to descend little by little, suffocating him, snuffing him out.

"*It's time, Little One! It's time you come to me*!"

An intense flash suddenly exploded before the boy's eyes and he went limp as a deep darkness took over. Everything ceased and the boy knew nothing for a long time.

The small, thin body lay exposed to the dark. Waiting.

The boy cracked open an eye only to have it burn against a hot, bright light. Wincing, he turned his head and gulped deep breaths of air. It had to be a dream, he thought. Just a dream. The horrible presence no longer loomed over him but an intense fear remained. Sweat bathed his skin and soaked his clothes. *Was it really all a dream?*

His heart thumped against his sore ribs like a frightened animal trapped in a cage. Probing with his bare toes, he felt for his bedsheet and came up empty. This did not feel right …

His heart nearly stopped completely. He couldn't move. His feet were locked in place at the ankles. So were his wrists. Intense heat washed over his body and sweat and tears ran down his face.

Turning his head, he managed to crack open an eye. A single, naked light loomed menacingly over him. Like a giant, lidless eyeball, it stared down with no mercy.

Escaping the glare proved impossible. Lifting his neck, his eyes widened in horror. His wrists and ankles were tied firmly to his bed, only it wasn't his bed anymore. Now he lay on a flat examination table. He tried jerking his limbs free with no success. Now desperate, he tried crying out, but barely managed a whimper.

The light grew even brighter, as if mocking him.

What was happening? What was this? His mind went into a whirl.

Then a dark presence loomed just beyond the light, staring at him. Dread filled the boy's belly. Whimpering, he put down his head and looked the other way. All he had seen was a dark shadow, but it had been enough. The nightmare was real. It had not left.

"*You wakes, do you?*" breathed a nasty voice in the darkness. "*It is time we begins.*"

That terrible voice, like a snake from the bowels of darkness, slithered into the boy's head and down to his heart.

Gripped with the worst kind of fear he had ever experienced, the boy once again did all he could to escape … Arching his back, he gritted his teeth and tugged at his bonds. Pain flared in his ankles and wrists, but they remained in place.

"*You are quite trapped,*" cackled the voice.

A soft jangling sounded just beyond the boy's head—almost like bells.

His throat dry, the boy opened his eyes. All he saw were the blades.

Descending, like a twisted wind chime from the unseen ceiling next to the glaring lamp, was a host of glittering butcher knives, saws, and many other sharp objects best kept away from children. All were well sharpened. Pausing a foot over his wide-eyed face, they danced in an invisible breeze. Their menacing jangle sent shivers down the boy's spine.

"*Lets us see,*" purred the voice like a garbage disposal. "*This wills do nicely.*"

A dark, shadowy hand moved into the light and grabbed a wicked-looking hacksaw next to a sharp, pointed poker.

"N-No," croaked the boy. "Please, no …" he begged. This could not be happening. He forced his gaze to where the arm came from. His lips trembled in time with his knees. A great shadowy figure stood next to him—featureless, but oozing with evil. Even in the light, the figure remained all shadow.

Turning on the boy, the shadowy face suddenly lit up with a smile of fire. Orange flame appeared in the place of eyes and mouth.

"You remembers me, boy, don't you?"

The boy couldn't speak again. It had been years since he last saw the terrible shadowman. He'd been told by his parents that it was just his imagination—a bad dream. No such thing existed. Nothing to be frightened of, because, after all, the shadowman could never harm him. It had never done so before, right?

Physically, no. Not yet, at least.

The boy forced his eyes on the shadow. "I-I'm not afraid," he whispered, finally finding his voice. "You can't hurt me." This is what his parents told him to say … what the doctors told him to say. It was like whistling to stop a bullet. The terror kept coming.

"*Hurts you? Who said anything about hurting* you?" Laughing like a jagged shard of glass, the shadowman advanced on the boy. Putting a single finger on the boy's white T-shirt caused a short burst of pain and then a flash of smoke.

It happened so fast the boy could not even cry out. His shirt vanished into gray ash that shot away into the darkness.

An angry welt festered on the boy's bony chest, just over where his heart continued to crash against his ribs. Feeling a burning pain there, the boy took rapid, shallow breaths.

"*That's where I stabs you when it's time. Not time yet, boy. Not yet.*" Stepping back, the shadowman flung out its arm that was gripping the jagged saw. The lamp threw a bolt of light that lit up the other side of the room.

The boy sucked in his breath in horror. Across the room he saw another examination table, similar to the one that held him. On this table lay a young girl only a few years older than the boy.

Similarly strapped down, she had bright red hair and appeared to be asleep. She had to be asleep … Wearing a white robe, it was the boy's sister … and her eyes were open. Open, but seeing nothing.

"*You see, I don't wants to spoil your skin, boy … just your soul. Watch closely as I guts your sister, slicing hers into tiny bits and then crams them down your little throat*!!!"

Snarling like a beast, the shadowman lunged toward the unmoving girl. The saw swung with wild abandon.

The boy screamed as the blade swung toward the unprotected neck. He screamed and screamed.

Steven jerked awake, gasping for a breath. Darkness instantly embraced him, destroying the terrible image. This darkness was different and held no shadowy figure. Yet the feeling of fear and terror remained ever present. A hand roughly shook his shoulder.

"Steven!" whispered a frightened voice over him. "Steven, you're dreaming again! Snap out of it!"

Gulping deep breaths of air, Steven's entire body shuddered. Ever so carefully, he tried to relax. His eyes remained closed.

It was his sister's voice. She was alive and unharmed.

It was just a dream, he thought. *Just another stupid dream.*

Somewhere above him a light flicked on; one much gentler than the lamp in the dream. He was home in bed … everything was okay …

"What is it?" asked his mother, sounding concerned and tense.

"Another nightmare," his sister nearly spat. Very much alive and not strapped to a terrible table, she sounded trapped between helplessness and anger. "It must have been bad this time. Worse than usual."

"Look at him—he's soaked with sweat!" said his father's voice. The cool, strong hands of his father pulled Steven to a sitting position.

The boy pressed back against his father's muscular arm and kept his eyes shut.

"Get his shirt off and bring him downstairs." His mother sighed. "I'll put on a pot of coffee and warm milk."

"Careful, Dad," Lisa said. "Remember this morning's accident."

"I got it! I thought these nights were over," his father said with real irritation. Then his voice went soft and kind. "Hey, relax, guy. I'm here to help. It's going to be okay. I promise."

At the sound of the irritation, Steven had gone rigid. But he didn't resist his dad's touch and allowed the shirt sticking to his skin to be peeled up and over his shoulders. Briefly, he cracked his eyes open to make sure there were no burns on his skin. His stomach, flat and tight against his bones, remained brown and unmarked. With a sigh, he leaned his head against his father's chest as he felt strong hands gently scoop him up into safety.

"I got you, guy," murmured his father. "It's over now."

But the boy knew it wasn't over. The shadowman lived on … lived inside of him. It was the shadowman who controlled the monster. It would be back … like always.

"Lisa," said his mother, "get to bed. Your brother will be fine."

"Will he?" Real anger lived in Lisa's voice. "Why can't we do something to stop this!"

"Just get to bed, honey," her mother's voice said gently. "We'll talk in the morning."

"I don't want to go to bed!"

"Lisa," her father said softly. "I think it's best if we don't argue."

"Can she stay with me?" asked a frightened voice from the bed across the room.

Lisa immediately stifled a sob. "Oh, Robbie, I'm sorry. We woke you! Of course I'll stay with you … if that's okay with you, Mom."

"Yes, that'll be fine … and, if you two don't mind a crowd, I'll even come up and join you."

"Thanks," Robbie's small voice said. Usually he barely tolerated his sister's touch or presence. Usually his older brother didn't wake with blood-curdling screams in the middle of the night.

"Just make sure everyone goes back to sleep," mumbled their father, heading to the door with his limp load cradled closely to his chest.

Sleep did come to the family … eventually. Darkness once again overtook the house, but now it was a good, restful darkness. A steady breeze caressed the house, and a host of crickets broke the silence. The shadowman wouldn't be back until another night.

Earlier in the day our story really begins …

PART I—*The Babysitter Is Born*

Chapter One

For a long time, Lisa Winter sat in her bed, staring dourly at the reflection staring dourly right back. On the lamp stand to her right, her alarm clock switched from 5:30 a.m. to 5:31 a.m.

The girl in the reflection crossed her arms and made a face.

"Hhmmphed." Air shot from Lisa's lower lip and up her face, throwing her bangs into an unruly mess. Who knew finding a new friend would be so hard and so dangerous? Who knew finding a friend would only lead to an enemy? She hated people sometimes.

It'd all started the day before when the girl, Lisa's potential friend now turned archenemy, walked by the house in such a lonely manner that Lisa longed to call out to her.

"Hey," she wanted to say. "Want to come in and go swimming?" Lack of confidence stopped her, tying her tongue in a knot. So Lisa only watched.

About Lisa's age, tall and sinewy, the girl had skin the color of rich coffee and tight hair as black as night. Carrying a basketball under a crooked elbow, the girl slouched low. Her head drooped and bobbed so it was often lower than her bony shoulders. Her free arm hung limply at her side like a deflated balloon. Still, she moved with an athletic grace that reminded Lisa of a cat on the prowl.

Hidden from view behind the thorny hedges that lined her driveway and small front yard, Lisa watched her pass by and then continued to stare. The girl kept her eyes glued to the road and never once looked up.

Lisa felt a longing to meet the girl—to run after her and introduce herself. They could become best friends … Lisa was an idiot.

Who knew the girl had a disgusting hoodlum brother and lived in a rundown shack that probably had more cockroaches than occupants? Lisa didn't … not then.

So Lisa counted to twenty and then ran for her bicycle in the garage—the flashy pink bike she hadn't used in almost a month, the day before she declared it too ugly to ride in public. Once on her bike, which had been covered with a thin layer of dust, Lisa pedaled furiously down the driveway before skidding to a stop.

Should I go on? she asked herself. She looked back at the empty garage and then at the retreating girl. Biting her lower lip, she gripped the handlebars tightly. "Stay here and be bored … or maybe find a best friend?"

The girl neared the new neighbor's house some distance away and maintained her rolling gait. Lisa tried imagining what this girl would be like. As she did so, she started pedaling at a slow pace, following. New details had emerged about this girl.

She must be poor, Lisa thought, *but definitely nice. I bet she's lonely too.*

The girl had her dark hair bunched in tight curls. They dripped sweat on a well-worn, gray tank top. Hanging loosely from her waist, faded blue athletic shorts extended to the girl's calves. On her feet were battered sneakers with ankle socks barely visible.

From the back, Lisa suddenly thought ruefully, *she could pass for a boy*. She almost turned back … but the longing for a friend kept her pedaling onward. *I'm not really following her … just going on a small bike ride … in the same direction as this poor, lonely girl.*

Not surprisingly, the girl reached the end of the street—where the freshly paved road abruptly ended and the wild tangles of high grass took over—and continued without slowing. Finding a path through the high grass that easily came to her waist, she headed into the clump of trees that stood from the grass, acting like a great wall intending to keep people out.

Lisa jammed her brakes and skidded to a stop for a second time. Now she really had to make a decision. She bit back a bad word. The grass and trees were warning signs. A gust of wind shot toward her, bending the branches of the trees and stalks of the grass so they looked to be shooing her away. *GO BACK… GO BACK WHERE YOU BELONG.*

No kid from her neighborhood had ever ignored this warning before. This was because the trees hid another world, a dark, dangerous world. It was a world where the other people lived and where the dark-skinned girl must live, too.

"I'm not afraid," Lisa said aloud, pushing her foot off the hard pavement and back on the pedal, propelling her bike forward. "I don't care."

Another gust of wind blew disapproval in her face. Still, high above, the sun shone brightly down and warmed Lisa's head as well as her outlook.

"It will be okay," she told herself softly. "I'll just see where she lives. Maybe next time I can play basketball with her."

Fantasizing about a day in the park, shooting hoops and talking about girl stuff, Lisa made it through the grass without a hitch. She easily found the well-used hard dirt path through the woods and soon entered another world.

Where Lisa came from, the houses were like castles compared to what she saw now. In a matter of feet, she completely left the town of Dougarsville and the upscale neighborhood of Camelot Acres, where every house had a swimming pool and at least an acre of carefully trimmed, vibrant green lawn. Emerging from the trees, she entered what she quickly labeled as Poopersville, Dismalot Fakers.

In this new land, every house was about the size of Lisa's garage and surrounded by a few feet of sick-looking earth. Tufts of weeds surrounded by gray dirt made up the best lawns here. The street sign at the corner actually read Flamingo Street, but Lisa doubted any flamingo would be caught dead on this side of town. And if they did try to come anyway, they'd probably be shot dead and eaten for supper. Swallowing her fear and distaste, Lisa forced herself to pedal. She scanned the area for the girl. Longing for a friend proved too great to back out now.

Turning right, her bike met hard, cracked pavement dotted with potholes. The path through the woods was smoother than the actual road here. Twice she nearly fell. No cars or people were in sight. Still, it felt as if a million hidden eyes were watching her.

Lisa shuddered as she rode between the rows of silent houses. She felt very much like a scared girl doing something horribly wrong. The sun now seemed to be glaring down at her, and the wind puffed at her face as if laughing at her.

She knew she didn't belong in this world.

Being stubborn, Lisa refused to retreat now. Even if she did live in a fancy neighborhood with everything she wanted, she still lacked one thing. She lacked a friend who lived close by.

To find a friend, you have to be a friend. That was what her mother told her.

"First I have to find her …"

Pedaling slowly, Lisa could not spot the girl but felt this was the way she had gone. Besides, maybe it was best that she didn't find her … but if she did …

Lisa started to imagine all the things the two of them could do together. They could go swimming in Lisa's pool after shooting baskets at the park. Sure, she hadn't ever played basketball, but she could learn. The girl could teach—

"Hey!" barked an ugly voice from the left. "What are you doing, strawberry cake?"

The voice came so fast and hard it caused Lisa's startled feet to drop from the pedals. Skidding to a stop, she nearly wrecked her bike in the shallow ditch. Only her shin barking painfully into her right pedal kept her from falling.

Gritting her teeth, she whipped her head to find the voice.

The girl Lisa had been following stepped from behind a decrepit-looking oak tree in front of a decrepit-looking house.

"Why you following me?" the girl snapped. The basketball had moved in front of her and was gripped in both hands like it was about to become a weapon. A sneer twisted her otherwise good-looking face.

"Oh, I, I …" Lisa sputtered to find the right words. She'd rehearsed this speech in her head over three times while pedaling, but now her voice ran and hid from her. Heart thumping wildly,

Lisa felt the onset of panic quickly approaching—like the time William Pendler told her that she had a booger in her nose in front of the entire gym class. Lisa had slapped him then, but this time such an action seemed totally inappropriate.

"You dumb, girl?" Advancing a step, the dark-skinned girl never lost her sneer.

"I, I, was just riding," Lisa managed to choke out. "Exercise." Somehow, she had thought once the two met, they magically would start talking and immediately become friends.

The girl snorted derisively. "Your kind don't ride here. Your high and mighty strawberry-cake behind had best run off before I bust this ball in your ugly face!"

Blood rushed into Lisa's face. She was not one to be intimidated for long. Shock wearing off, she started getting angry. "You wouldn't do that!" she cried.

"Try me!" dared the girl. "With your looks, it'll be an improvement! Your mama might even thank me!"

"She'd sue you! She'd get you thrown in jail!"

The girl nearly did throw the ball in Lisa's face then. Holding back at the last second, she suddenly laughed. "Just because you're rich and ugly, you think you run the world. You probably sue the dirt that gets on your shoes."

Before Lisa could think up a reply, the door of the house banged open to reveal a hulking boy several years older than the girls. Stepping out on a sagging stoop, he glared at them. Lisa couldn't stifle a gasp. Though he was only slightly taller than Lisa, the boy's bulk extended horizontally. A bulging chest pushed against the dirty, sleeveless T-shirt, covered in stains. While his stomach pushed out, his calves were muscular, and massive thighs kept his baggy jeans from falling to the ground. A large overbite made him resemble an oversized beaver. However, his two beady eyes bulging from his wide face gave him the appearance of a very nasty individual. Lisa wasn't about to be seen calling him a beaver in front of his face.

"What's this, sis?" He spoke in a deep voice with a lazy accent he probably borrowed from a gangster television show. At seeing Lisa, his glare curved into a cruel smile. "Whatcha got here?"

"She's been a following me, man," the girl said, as if the words gave a sour taste. "She's from *Camelot*."

"That right? I didn't know redheaded stepchildren were allowed to live there." Cackling at his words, the large boy advanced at a steady pace toward Lisa.

Lisa visibly flinched and unconsciously fingered a strand of her scarlet hair. The insult hurt more than he knew.

Standing still with her bike beneath her, she knew she should ride away right now. But her flaming hair color also matched her temper. She could feel her freckled face taking on a similar hue.

"Best take a breath girl," the boy drawled. "Your face looks like it's about to burst on fire."

"I'm allowed to be here," Lisa said tightly, "and you two can't do anything about it."

The brother and sister made eye contact and then smirked at Lisa. "Oh, yeah?" asked the girl, her voice dripping with malice.

"Y-yeah …" Lisa answered with less assurance.

And that was how she lost her flashy pink bike … the same one a few weeks before she had vowed never to use, unless forced.

Before taking it, the boy laughed and the girl only shook her head, almost in pity. They demanded she get off the bike and said then she could stay there as long as she liked. Before Lisa could ride away, the girl dropped the basketball and quicker than spit took hold of Lisa's handlebars. Scared, Lisa slid off the seat and backed away. The look on the girl's face spoke of violence. Grinning, the girl pulled the bike to her yard and patted the seat. Lisa's protests of them stealing her bike only made the two thieving siblings exchange glances and smile without humor. The boy said, with great pleasure, that in this neighborhood tattletales and snitches were nothing but lowly snakes that got what was coming to them … Besides, Lisa was giving them the bike, right?

By this time, Lisa was backing away, not liking the look on the teenager's face one bit. His hand dropped lazily to his pocket. In a fit of terror, she turned and ran. She didn't stop until she reached her house. So much for finding a new friend … Lisa only made new enemies.

But she would get her bike back. That much was for certain.

That was why she was wide awake at now 5:37 on a cool May Saturday morning when she should still be fast asleep. She was plotting revenge.

Just the thought of what had happened made her face burn all over again. Now it was time for action.

Sliding from her bed, Lisa stared grimly into the large mirror extending over her dresser, across the room. She liked to imagine it opened to a different world—a world where the girl inside was really a princess in a great kingdom. In that world, when some trashy girl called her ugly, she and her ugly brother would be thrown into a dungeon and left to rot.

The girl in the mirror nodded approval and for a moment Lisa allowed herself to become that princess. Her fiery red hair matched the bright freckles dotting her cheeks and nose. Hanging to her shoulders, the hair was straight and as smooth as silk. Clear blue eyes stared without blinking; set firmly in the round face. Lisa knew her reflection wasn't gorgeous—she was too tall and skinny for that. Still, she was far from ugly. And she *wasn't* a redheaded stepchild. Thinking of that ugly boy calling her that name made her cheeks flush. All at once she became Lisa again.

"I may not throw anybody in a dungeon," she growled to her reflection, "but I will get my bike back!"

Immediately, reality sunk in as she thought about the large boy and girl who lived on Flamingo Street. Their cruelness and power were too much for her. A pasty white returned to her face. "I'm not afraid," she whispered.

The girl in the mirror blinked, not believing her. Lisa would need help.

Ten minutes later found Lisa closing the door to her room softly. Having used the bathroom and now fully dressed in jeans and a white blouse, she crept silently to her brothers' room. Her socks pressed into the thick carpet and made barely a sound. The last thing she needed was to wake her parents.

Just as the faint lines of daylight began brightening the edges of the windows hidden by shades, Lisa slipped through the open door and paused. All she could hear was the sound of snoring.

Boys, she thought, couldn't do anything quietly … not even sleep! Shaking her head, she boldly marched to the foot of the nearest bed. Then she crossed her arms and frowned with disapproval.

Her brother lay on his back and looked to be drowning beneath the single blanket. Only the mop of thick wavy hair and the smooth lean face were visible. Otherwise, the bed could have been empty.

Steven, at nine, was nearly two years younger than Lisa, but could be rather mature for his age, most of the time. He just wasn't very big. With a lithe, athletic body built by swimming and playing soccer, he didn't have an ounce of fat to spare. Of course, it didn't stop there. He also possessed a good-looking face that everyone seemed to immediately like. More than once, a tourist in Florida had stopped the family at the beach to ask for his picture, and birthday invitations from classmates were an almost daily occurrence.

While this could easily have warped the boy into a spoiled brat, Steven treated it with a shrug and one of his amused half smiles. Easygoing, well mannered, and sometimes shy around strangers, he attended birthday parties more out of politeness than anything else. This, of course, made him liked even more. Lisa couldn't understand it—she would have loved to receive even a quarter of the invitations he got … but Steven barely seemed to notice. Their parents said he was too intelligent to throw his life away to fame at such an early age. Lisa thought he was just too lazy. Steven would rather lie around and soak up the sun than stand in the limelight and soak up attention.

"You're not going to be lazy this morning," Lisa growled softly. "Today, you're going to help me … like you said."

The night before, after their parents had checked in all their bedrooms and made sure all the teeth were brushed and prayers said, Lisa had snuck in and given Steven the particulars—she'd lost her bike and needed to get it back. It had been a hastily whispered explanation short on details. Robbie, the youngest boy at seven, had been dropping off to sleep in the next bed and would have woken instantly if he'd suspected anything. Sporting golden curls and the fresh face of innocence, Robbie followed his older brother anywhere and everywhere. Every kid would—

Steven attracted followers like light attracted moths. Steven represented a goodness that everyone wanted to be near … and so far nobody had gotten burned.

Lisa had no such power or leadership, especially with her siblings. The youngest of the four children, five-year-old Margie, wouldn't follow her older sister anywhere without a bribe. If Margie knew anything about Lisa's plans that morning, she would demand a payment to keep quiet and then tell their parents anyway. Thankfully, the youngest slept in a room adjacent to their parents and could be counted on to sleep another two or three hours. So Lisa hoped.

That left Steven. Of her three siblings, only he could be trusted to help without blathering about it later. If he ever woke up.

Sighing, she leaned in and gave the mattress a gentle shake. The boy didn't even twitch. Snorting in annoyance, she pulled out the end of the sheet from under the mattress and fumbled her hand underneath, searching for her brother's bare feet. She'd forgotten how small he was and had to get on her knees before finding a foot. Giving a tug produced no results. Then a sharper tug only caused the boy to kick out his foot and catch her in the nose.

Backing hastily away with a sharp gasp, Lisa got to her feet with her eyes watering in pain. She was about to leap on his bed with an elbow extended when Steven lifted an eyelid and gave her something between a half grin and a half frown.

"What are you doing here?" he mumbled.

"Making sure my brother is sleeping well," she snarled, rubbing her nose. "What do you think?"

Yawning, Steven lifted himself to a sitting position and rubbed his eyes. "What time is it? Isn't it Saturday?"

"Time for your lazy bones to get up before I grab you by the hair and drag you out of bed." Lisa's nose still hurt.

Blinking rapidly, Steven rubbed his eyes and then peered at her as if seeing her for the first time. Even in the early morning, full of sleep, hair disheveled, Steven managed to keep his good looks. He and Lisa didn't look very much alike, and many found it hard to believe they were brother and sister. Thicker than Lisa's, his hair was a dark blond in the darkened room but would turn a rich auburn in light. Rumpled, with two tufts extending down his cheeks nearly to his chin like sideburns, his hair almost always appeared unruly unless fought down with a brush and lots of water. Mostly straight, it curled in the back where it reached his neck. With a wide mouth, deep brown eyes, and a thin pointed face, Steven had an appearance and demeanor that reminded Lisa of a young wolf cub.

Yawning again to display most of his perfectly straight, pearly teeth, he snapped his mouth shut. "Isn't it Saturday?" he asked again.

"Yes! And you need to get your bony backside out of bed before I kick it to Mars!" Lisa was more like a young fox with a knot tied in her tail.

"Ah, great," he groaned. "Lisa … maybe in a few more hours." Dropping back, Steven rolled to his side. "It's too early," he groaned.

Stifling a growl, Lisa breathed in deeply. Everyone thought she had the perfect brother. She knew better. He acted this way on purpose! Enough was enough.

Grabbing the sheet, she threw it aside, exposing Steven in dark-blue running shorts and a white T-shirt. Snatching a handful of T-shirt, she yanked it up and made to pound his back until it turned the color of her hair. "I told you last night," she seethed. "I need your help!"

"Hey, what's your problem!" Twisting away, Steven rolled free and rose to his knees at the edge of the mattress, away from Lisa. Too close to the edge as it turned out. Arms flailing for balance, he suddenly slid over and off the bed. A solid thump announced his landing … This was followed by a painful groan.

"Serves you right," Lisa muttered, kneeling on the bed. "I told you I would be up early."

"This isn't early," mumbled Steven's voice from the floor. "This is torture."

"Try being your sister!"

"Wh-what's happening?" Robbie sat up in his bed, his eyes struggling to open. "Lisa?"

Throwing up her hands, Lisa kicked a pillow off Steven's bed in the vicinity where his head should be. "Now look what you did!"

Steven scrambled to his feet and tossed the pillow back at Lisa, catching her in the face. "You started it," he reminded her.

"Started what?" Robbie wanted to know, still vainly fighting to be fully awake.

Lisa threw aside the pillow. "Steven is helping me with my schoolwork. Go back to sleep."

"You don't do your schoolwork …"

Lisa shot a look at Steven, who flopped back on his bed next to her. Twisting his body, his eyebrows rose as he regarded his sister. "Um, how serious is this?" he whispered.

"Serious," she hissed back.

Twisting his lips, Steven scooted to the other side of the bed and got wearily to his feet. Walking to Robbie's bed, he leaned over, his hands on his knees. "Shh, Robbie. Lisa and I are going to check something outside, that's all." He spoke almost gently. "We'll be back before you wake up."

Lisa marveled how the young nine-year-old could speak so softly to his siblings and get them to listen. She wanted to aim a swift kick at the back of his shorts but knew that would only upset things further.

Robbie slumped back on his pillow. "Okay," he muttered, "but you'd better not do anything important without me."

Steven grinned. "Sure, Robbie. Lisa never does anything important without Mom's credit card."

"Yeah … okay." Robbie drifted into sleep.

"It's like you put a spell on him," Lisa said with outright jealously.

Steven stood and lost his grin. "It's called being nice."

Lisa held back a nasty reply and stuck her tongue out instead.

Ignoring her, Steven started searching for clothes on the dresser and floor. His idea of putting clothes away was either taking them off and letting them drop or, more likely, letting his mom or sister put them away. He never knew where they could be. "Where did you leave your bike?" he asked as he shoved away a pile of polo shirts.

"I didn't leave it. Somebody stole it."

He frowned. "Shouldn't you tell Mom and Dad?"

"Why? I know where it is." They were talking in whispers, but Lisa paused and lowered her voice even more. "It's in the neighborhood behind the woods."

Steven stopped his search. Behind the woods meant the neighborhood their parents had specifically forbidden any of them from ever going. Turning from where he crouched in front of his dresser, he gave her cool look. "You're going to get in big trouble."

"Not if you hurry up! I put your clothes by the door … so you could *quietly* sneak out." As Steven moved in that direction, Lisa aimed a kick at him anyway. "And if you tell anybody—"

Dodging her foot neatly, Steven grinned back at her. "What? You'll kick me in the nose?"

Lisa's hands went to her aching nose. "You … you were awake, weren't you!"

"Shh! You'll wake Robbie!" Steven grabbed the jeans and long-sleeved shirt by the door and quickly slipped out.

Lisa could only glare after him. "Lazy, good-for-nothing brother," she huffed. She stalked out the door in time to see the bathroom door firmly shut. Her watch told her that 6:00 a.m. had just passed.

At the rate they were going, it would be nightfall before they got her bike back. Lisa never did do well with being patient for long.

Steven leaned lightly with his right shoulder, curving his ripstick to meet the downward slope of the road and pick up speed. Lisa had to run to catch up, but her brother didn't bother slowing down. A cool breeze ruffled his hair, now a rich auburn in the yawning sun that slowly stretched from behind the trees before them. Putting out his arms, he let the unbuttoned shirt he wore over his T-shirt flow behind him like a cape. It gave him the feeling of flying. Despite the early hour, he was enjoying himself. For a brief moment, he closed his eyes and imagined all these troubles away.

"Hey!" shouted his sister. "Watch where you're going!"

Eyes flashing open, Steven had just enough time to jump from his board and come to a running stop before plowing into the mailbox of their new neighbors.

The two were finally off to retrieve the bike ... and already running, almost literally, into problems.

"What were you trying to do, hug the mailbox?" Lisa called to him sarcastically. "I thought you only hugged trees."

Ignoring her, Steven raced back to where the ripstick lay on its side next to the nearly hugged mailbox. Crouching, he tugged the lock of hair hanging in front of his right ear while running his left hand over the ripstick, searching for scratches. Finding none, he relaxed in relief.

Lisa snorted and shook her head. "My brother the dope. You're an accident waiting to happen." Secretly, though, she was relieved nothing bad had happened.

Looking sheepish, Steven turned to give her a half smile. "I'll go slower," he mumbled.

"Hmmph. Just keep your eyes open for trees. They're like mailboxes and like to jump out on you. Come on, let's hurry up."

A ripstick can be described as the child of the marriage between a skateboard and a pair of roller blades. Two wheels support separate flexible platforms connected by a tube. Once mastered, a ripstick can provide better speed and maneuverability than an ordinary skateboard. Using the flexible platform and good balance made it easy to build speed without putting a foot on the ground.

Steven had gotten his ripstick for Christmas and had just gotten the hang of it. The best lesson he'd learned so far was to roll both legs of his jeans up to his calves to keep them from catching on the platforms. The worse lesson he had yet to learn—and hopefully would learn in the safest way possible—was the need of a helmet. Unless forced, he never wore a helmet or pads, saying they slowed him down. Of course. his parents would never let him in the street without the safety equipment, but Lisa didn't care. If her dumb brother wanted to plaster his good looks on the street, that was his business. Ordinarily she would yell at him for being so stupid, but on this morning she just felt happy to have him with her.

Even at a slow glide, Steven still easily pulled ahead. When she caught up with him at the end of the road, she nodded at Steven's ripstick. "You can't use it in the woods. You should leave it here."

Steven pursed his lips in his version of a frown and lifted the contraption into his arms. "I can carry it." Being a gift from their mom, he treated it as his most treasured possession.

"Suit yourself. But if this doesn't work out, it might end up where my bike is now."

Steven gave another half grin and shrugged. "Don't forget that you're the one who told me to bring this. You wanted a fast getaway, remember."

Lisa tossed back her hair in frustration. "Then come on, then!" She hated when her brother got the better of her.

The two siblings made it through the tall grass and into the trees. The thin stretch of trees extended miles in two directions. Peering into the deep woods on their left and right brought a feeling of uneasiness. No songbirds were out in the early morning, and the only squirrel they saw quickly vanished an instant later. It was as if nature sensed the coming danger.

"How far is this house?" Steven whispered.

"Off to the right, about eight houses down. Don't worry, we'll find it soon enough." She sounded grim and also whispered. Leaving Camelot Acres, the two felt as if they were trespassing and being watched.

As Steven followed his sister, he eyed her thoughtfully.

Lisa could be very quiet and nice one moment and extremely loud and violent the next. In between, she acted surly, especially when afraid. She liked to be in charge, and that suited Steven fine. He just hoped she knew what she was doing … not that it mattered. He would help her no matter what.

When very young, Steven had been very sensitive about his small size. On his first day of school he'd even tried to wear his mom's high heels to the bus stop. Instead of laughing at him, Lisa vowed to be his protector and meant it. Ever since, whenever a larger boy even looked to be picking on Steven, it was always she who'd rushed to his defense. One time, she'd even decked a classmate after he called Steven one of Santa's elves. That was at her birthday party five years before—the last time that she had invited classmates over to her house.

While the siblings often spoke harshly to each other, they each knew the other would be there when it truly mattered. Steven had gotten over his height issues, but he hadn't forgotten all that his sister had done for him. He'd promised to help her and so he would. But he secretly wondered if Lisa could help herself. Lisa had always complained about her bike and even once said that she wished it would be stolen ... Obviously there was more to this than just a lost bike. Still, Steven didn't worry too much. Lisa was in charge. He just had to follow her lead.

Chapter Two

Camelot Acres was a nearly brand-new development where the poorest house cost somewhere in the vicinity of a million dollars. It had been built just on the outskirts of a poor section of Dougarsville, but only after months of heated debate in the political world. The poor section of Dougarsville had its supporters who didn't want their land being taken away and turned into rich fancy resorts that drove up taxes and brought in upscale "yuppie stores." Of course, this section lacked money, and ultimately that was what mattered most.

Even with newspapers supporting the poor area, Camelot Acres was approved. As a compromise, though, the new Camelot Acres was constructed on the former site of swamps and thick forests. At one point, these swamps and forests had provided hunting grounds for the poor section. Now they had been filled in and destroyed to make way for humongous houses, each guarded by high-tech security systems and no-trespassing signs. A park was located in the center of this expensive layout, but only for the residents of Camelot Acres. Another compromise was to have the borders of the district redrawn so the poor section and rich section would be firmly divided. This was why the trees remained—they served as the border, as well as a small wildlife refuge.

Many residents of Camelot Acres joked it was not an environmental reason to keep the trees, but a scenic one. They didn't want to have to physically look down on poor houses not more than a stone's throw from their immaculate green yards and manicured hedges.

In protest of their backyard and rights being torn from the roots, the youth in the poor section—Dougar Circle, as it was officially called—regularly trespassed into Camelot Acres to use the park. Since most of the residents of Camelot Acres owned other houses and were frequently away, nobody complained. Even a homeless man roamed the richly furnished neighborhood and begged at corners. While causing some tongue wagging, he also gathered some hefty handouts that kept him in business. After all, even the rich felt guilty sometimes.

On this morning, as Lisa and Steven emerged on the other side of the tree line and entered Dougar Circle on Flamingo Street, it was as empty and silent as a school on a weekend. So quiet it was almost unnerving.

"It's like we're at a funeral," Lisa whispered, shuddering.

Steven grimaced. "Maybe it's ours," he mumbled. But his large brown eyes roamed the neighborhood with interest. Somewhere behind one of the battered doors lived his best friend from school. This was the closest he'd ever been to Geoffrey's house.

Scowling, Lisa threw an elbow back in her brother's chest. "Everyone is just asleep," she said loudly. Straightening her shoulders, she pulled her brother's arm after her. "Come on. We're nearly there." Walking with her head taller than she felt, she led the way down the familiar cracked street where she'd followed the girl the day before.

Perhaps she was right and everyone in the houses was asleep, but then so were the birds. Not a single chirp accompanied the rising sun. For a perfect sunny spring day in Florida, this felt very odd.

After moments of silent walking, Lisa suddenly grunted with triumph and reached back to grab Steven's arm.

"See!" she hissed. "I knew it would be there!"

"Okay, Lisa!" Steven said, squirming. "Ouch! Let go. I mean, why else are we here?"

Releasing him, Lisa put her hands on her hips and stared with satisfaction. Just as she'd imagined, behind the old twisted oak, leaning against the side of the old ramshackle house, her shiny pink bicycle glistened in the early sun.

"I knew they would leave it out," she said softly, her eyes shining. "They don't even have a garage … Why, I bet those two idiots don't even know how to ride a bike! This was the first one they'd ever seen."

"Great." Steven rubbed his arm and gave her a sideways look. "Are you going to get it, or just tell a story about it?"

Lisa gave him a dirty look back. "Just wait here."

It was a setup. They must have been waiting for this moment since the crack of dawn. Just as Lisa reached the middle of the dirt and gravel driveway, just ten feet from her bike, the teenage boy stepped from behind the house. Wearing ripped jeans sagging below his waist, he had on a cutoff tee that barely covered his middle, giving the world a good look at his red boxers. At the same time, the front door opened.

"Well, well, well," the boy purred, his teeth jutting from his mouth like a pair of diving boards pointing in different directions. "Not only are you ugly and stupid, you're also a thief!"

"See?" called the girl, shutting the door behind her as she stepped out. Dressed in gray sweats, she appeared as wide awake as her brother. "I told you she was stupid and would come back!" A nasty smirk covered her face as she flexed her arms and advanced toward Lisa. "Thought you could sneak up on us in the morning, did you? You are dumb, girl. We've been waiting for you!"

Lisa had stood frozen at their sudden appearance. Now she tried to work her mouth. It wasn't possible! Or fair!

Behind her, Steven fingered his ripstick and stared at the newcomers with his lips squeezed tightly—it was a common look he wore when uncomfortable. While he appeared almost thoughtful and in complete control, Lisa knew inside, his emotions were beginning to churn. This wasn't supposed to happen this way! Taking a deep breath, she stared at the girl with the fiercest look she could muster.

"I came for my bike." Her voice didn't even waver, but had the effect of spitting to stop a hurricane.

The boy scoffed. "At this time? Why didn't you come yesterday, or later? You come like a skunk. Probably stink like one too. Besides," he grinned. "It's not your bike no more, girl."

"It's mine," the girl said, not smiling.

Lisa shook her head and crossed her arms. "No, it's not, and you know it! I want it back."

The girl looked ready to hit her. Stopping three feet from Lisa, standing between her and the bike, the girl planted her arms on both sides of her narrow torso. Her face dared Lisa to just try to get past her. "I don't think you heard what I just said." Her head moved like a snake sizing up a rat as she spoke. "It's mine."

Lisa used the remainder of her bravery to keep from shrinking away. "I-I heard you. You're just wrong."

"Um, maybe we should come back later," Steven said nervously, moving to Lisa's side. It wasn't as much to give his sister support as it was to find security … even if it only brought him closer to danger.

"Who's this?" the bucktooth teen croaked, pouncing on the younger boy's presence. "Your pint-size boyfriend?" Now standing next to the girl, he eyed the ripstick greedily. "And what has he got there?"

"Leave my brother alone!" growled Lisa, her hands bunching into fists.

The girl actually snorted in disbelief. "That's your brother? Dang, girl. How can an ugly, strawberry-headed frog like you be related to *him*? Let me guess, your momma found you on the street and felt sorry for you. Probably got you outta the gutter."

Lisa's ears went pink and her face boiled with rage. Only Steven grabbing her arm kept her from jumping on the girl. Steven's eyes narrowed, and he took on the girl with a surprising fierceness.

"Yeah, well your mom thought you were so ugly she made Halloween your birthday to make you feel better!"

Both the boy and girl blinked, staring down at Steven in surprise. Lisa also stared down at her brother. Where did the little kid get that from?

"That's lame," the girl finally managed to say.

Steven took a breath. "Yeah, well, at least on your birthday you can wear a mask to hide your ugly face! That's the only way other kids would come to your party!"

Now the girl gaped. Lisa tried to pull Steven back by the shoulders, but he shook her off.

"Oooh, man," the bucktooth teen said. "Kid, you're really asking for it, ain't you?" There was a hint of admiration in his voice.

The girl looked almost confused at what to do next. Steven came up to her shoulders and looked as thin as a Popsicle stick. Clearly years younger, picking on him wasn't going to boost her image much.

"You can't let the small fry get away with that!" her bucktooth brother chided from behind her.

"Shut up!" spat the girl. "What you want me to do?"

"Well, you have the bike. I think the kid has something that's mine." He licked his lips and eyed the ripstick again. "Give it to me, kid, and then you and your ugly sister can go."

Lisa tried again to pull her brother away, but Steven smoothly stepped to the side. His skin was warm to the touch and his face appeared calm. Too calm.

"Do you even know what this is?" he asked, holding up the ripstick.

The teen smiled. "Yeah, it's mine."

"It's called a ripstick. Let me show you how to use it."

"Sure, dipstick. Then you and your redheaded loser can get off our property."

Lisa bent low and hissed in Steven's ear. "What are you doing, *idiot*?"

Steven pulled away, jerking his head toward Lisa's bike. "Your bike, *stupid*," he whispered back.

Lisa bit her lip and stood up. She had almost been able to hear her brother's heart thumping as wildly as hers.

"You know, kid, you're all right!" the teen said, thinking the brother had brushed off his sister. "Show me how your dipstick works."

The girl eyed Lisa with distaste, but then she turned to watch Steven. Her curiosity was also stirred. Obviously, neither one had seen a ripstick before. The dark-skinned boy and girl gathered in front of Steven, leaving Lisa alone for the moment.

Taking a deep breath, Lisa slowly edged away. If she started running now, she would easily make it to her bike, but then what? The girl would catch up to her before she even threw a leg over the seat. And her fat, ugly brother would have Steven. What was the little idiot's plan?

"Well," said Steven, as if instructing a private class, "first you have to check the wheels."

"Why?" asked the girl. She and her brother moved closer. Lisa started slowly for her bike, still not sure how it was going to work. She found out soon enough.

"Because," Steven explained, "sometimes they go crazy … like this!" All at once, he slammed the end of the ripstick into the middle of the bucktooth teen, driving a wheel deep into his stomach.

Taken completely by surprise, the teen's eyes popped wide and his mouth dropped open. No noise could come out. As he doubled over, his pants dropped. Trying to step back, he tripped over his pants and fell to the seat of his boxers. He desperately tried to find a breath while pulling at his pants bunched around his knees.

Growling, the girl grabbed Steven's arm.

Twisting away, the boy squatted low and broke free. Springing to his feet, he raced onto the road. His eyes widened in terror. All his bravado had gone. Once on the pavement, he put down his ripstick and quickly hopped on.

"Get him!" wheezed the teen, finally finding his voice. He struggled to rise. "He-He's getting … away."

"You're going to pay, brat!" screeched the girl. "I'm going to blast your scrawny rear and then rip your face!"

"First kiss the bike goodbye!" shouted Lisa, now mounted and already pedaling. "Thanks for keeping it for me!"

Whirling from her pursuit of Steven, the girl's eyes went wide with anger. Then with a strangled cry, she tore after Lisa.

Yelping, Lisa started pedaling with all her might, angling the bike to the right to cut through the next property, in order to reach the road before the girl caught up. The rough grass slowed the bike tires and the pedals felt stuck as if glued. Standing hunched over the handlebars, Lisa strained to make the pedals turn faster. Looking back with a stricken face, she saw the girl's wide nose flaring and her white teeth gleaming.

"I'm going to destroy you!" seethed the girl. And she might have done so … if she hadn't stumbled on the uneven ground hidden by long weeds in need of a good mower.

The girl's neighbors hadn't cut the grass since the last summer, and spring had been kind to the plants. Sprawled face-first, the girl received a mouthful of dandelions as Lisa sped away to finally get her bike on the road.

"Bye!" Lisa couldn't help but shout back in triumph. Her feeling of triumph lasted as long as her goodbye.

"I'm not done with you!" howled the girl. Bouncing to her feet as if yanked by invisible ropes, she tore after the pink bike.

"Get them, Macie!" wheezed her bucktoothed brother, joining the chase. Despite his bulky size, he proved to be a decent sprinter. Only the need to constantly pull up his pants slowed him.

"They're gaining!" shouted Lisa, ducking her head and pumping her feet.

At her side, Steven shifted his crouched body back and forth to generate speed on his ripstick. "I never did find out how fast this can go," he cried, his voice lost in the wind.

"We're going the wrong way!" Lisa suddenly yelled to him, horrified.

"Well, I'm not turning around!"

The way back to Camelot Acres receded farther and farther as they sped down the bumpy street full of potholes, heading deeper into Dougar Circle. Behind them, the girl and boy gave chase. Their knees and elbows pumped as furiously as their anger. They refused to give up.

Steven gritted his teeth in frustration.

With a head start, they were still leading by several yards, but every step brought the girl closer. Her larger brother had dropped back considerably. However, the girl curled her lips back and threw her body forward. She looked like an Olympic runner out for gold.

"Can't you go faster?" Lisa shouted at him.

"The road is too bumpy," Steven complained, shifting to avoid another pothole.

"Here, grab on to my seat. There's a hill coming up!" Standing on her pedals, she moved her bike so Steven could snatch a hold of her empty seat. Then she started pedaling harder than she ever had before.

The brown rabbit sniffed nervously into the wind that ruffled her soft fur. A little more than a year old, the small, furry mammal had long since learned the dangers of humans. Just after the sun rose, when all appeared quiet, she knew she could prowl safely through the green yards to eat with little fear. But on this morning, something felt odd … The rabbit pricked her ears. Something dangerous was coming.

From a few feet away, hidden in the bushes just outside his bedroom window, Geoffrey Brown poised to strike. His small body crouched low, resting on a knee as he stared hungrily at the rabbit—the same one he often watched from his window when waking for school. For months he'd dreamed of snatching the furry critter and giving it to Nana for a stew. In the afternoons he would practice in the backyard by racing after dragonflies and any other bug that decided to fly too low near the boy. Now he felt ready. Muscles tensed as he readied to leap out and give chase. Suddenly the rabbit froze.

What was it? Geoffrey hadn't dared breathe louder than a whisper and crouched downwind of the creature. Then from the road, up the hill from Flamingo Street, a very odd sight appeared.

A girl with hair so red it could have been on fire—especially the way she pedaled her bike—zoomed into view. Leaning in great concentration, she took the hill like the ski jumpers Geoffrey had watched during the last Winter Olympics. A girl riding a bike wasn't that odd—but a girl with skin lighter than white bread in this part of town, this early in the morning? Stranger still, a boy crouched on a skateboard held on to the bike's seat for dear life. Both screamed as the hill zoomed to meet them.

To make it even stranger, Macie White sprinted into view behind them just as they began the descent.

At the same time, the door swung open just to Geoffrey's right.

"Yo, Geoffrey, where are you?" His older brother Rosco blinked away sleep as he stood wearing only his bed shorts. Then his eyes widened like headlights when he saw the sight coming down the hill.

Of course, this proved too much for the rabbit. Hopping in a panic, the ball of fur dashed into the road, desperate to reach the other side. She vanished in the clump of bushes lining the street.

Geoffrey cringed. From the looks of it, it was not going to be a good morning.

"Rosco!" hollered Macie. "Get them! Stolen bike!"

Macie and Rosco knew each other well—Macie's brother was part of Rosco's crew. Not hesitating, Rosco leapt off the front step in his bare feet and ran for the road.

Lisa saw the rabbit dart into her path just as she reached the bottom of the incline. At the same time, she saw the hulking teen flash from the house on her right. Panicking, she pressed the brakes and swerved all at once.

At the same time, Steven let go of her seat and shot forward. Without realizing it, both were screaming like they were being murdered.

The hill was not terribly steep, and by loosening her brakes, Lisa managed to get a foot down in time to come to a jerking, sliding stop without harm. Steven wasn't so lucky. With no real brakes, he stopped the only way he knew how. He sat back.

The back of his jeans struck hard pavement at a great speed. Sliding several feet in such a fashion, he managed to hook a foot over the ripstick to keep it from escaping down the street while turning his body so it slid into the hedge of bushes on the left. He came to a jarring halt as his back crashed into the thick brush.

Suddenly it was quiet.

"Steven!" Lisa cried. Hopping off her bike, she ignored the stinging in her left calf where the bike chain had cut into it during her stop.

Lying on his side, Steven gingerly rolled to his stomach. It felt like the back of his pants were on fire. His left hand dripped blood from where it had touched the rough asphalt. Taking deep breaths, he managed to get on a knee. Warm liquid ran down the back of his legs … he wondered what color it was.

"What's this?" demanded the dark-skinned youth, crossing two bulky arms over his well-muscled chest. He sounded slightly shaken.

Not especially tall, Rosco had wide shoulders and the build of a linebacker. Flexing his arms, he glared not at Lisa but at Macie, who was huffing and puffing as she made it down the hill.

"Dat boy and girl …" she paused for a breath and wiped sweat from her face. "They took my bike!"

"Is *dat* right?" Rosco drawled. "Speak English, Macie."

Seeing Steven in one piece, Lisa immediately latched onto her bike and glared. "This is my bike," she said firmly.

"Two crackers like you two don't belong here, sunshine girl," Rosco said, frowning.

Lisa met his stare and held it. "It's a free country! We can go where we like! Come on, Steven."

Rosco spat. "You're ignorant. You're from Camelot Acres, ain't you?" He spoke as if calling them a dirty name.

Lisa tossed back her hair. "What if we are?"

"Why," Rosco said disdainfully, "nothing. Just that you ain't allowed here."

"You come to our neighborhood," Lisa shot back. "I've seen you. You go to our park!"

Macie glared at Lisa. "Your park? You think you own that, do you?"

"Well, then you don't own this street either!" Lisa said. No longer afraid, she held herself up high and let her anger do the talking. "So we can go to your neighborhood if we want!"

"Sorry, Sunshine," drawled Rosco without humor, "but that ain't how it works."

"Lisa, let's just go home." Steven rubbed his sore thigh carefully, nearly trembling from the pain. "Leave them alone."

"You tell her to leave us alone?" exploded Macie. "You two go home, but leave your bike and, and that dipstick thing here!"

Steven grinned, a bit painfully. "Do you want me to show you how to use it again?"

Macie made a face and stepped toward him. "Why, you—"

"Cool it, Macie," Rosco said. He nodded his head down the street. "Let the little punks go."

Macie protested. "But Rosco, that boy done took down Tay!"

"That little tadpole?" Rosco frowned. "No way!"

"No, he tricked him!" Macie said. "And we need payback!"

Rosco shrugged. "Relax, Macie. I think the little tadpole already got the beating he deserves. I bet he won't sit for a week!"

"But Rosco, that girl—" Macie began, but Rosco held up his hand.

"Take a look down the street, Macie," he said softly. "That homeless hobo is watching."

Macie suddenly shuddered. "Oh …"

Lisa saw the change go over the girl—suddenly she looked young and afraid. Lisa brushed a strand from her face and looked to where Rosco pointed. Suddenly she felt afraid too.

A tall, thin figure, huddled behind a long, brown jacket that covered him from chin to boots, indeed watched them. Standing in the middle of the street four houses down, his pale-blue eyes were slanted in a very thoughtful manner. Aimed at the small boy and girl at the foot of the hill, they briefly, ever so briefly, flashed a dark red—a red much darker than Lisa's hair. Then they were blue again. None of the kids noticed the brief change.

"Come inside," mumbled Rosco to Macie. "You can have breakfast with us."

"Yeah … thanks." Macie hurriedly followed him into the house.

Lisa and Steven were left to slowly trudge back up the hill. Behind them, Geoffrey shivered from behind the bush as the homeless figure continued to watch.

Nobody in the poor neighborhood knew when the homeless hobo had showed up, or where he slept at night. But they all knew he was somebody to keep far away from—something very peculiar surrounded that man. Perhaps it was the way he stood and watched everyone with his cold blue eyes—and the way he seemed to shift appearances almost daily. Some days he was clean-shaven, and some days he sported a trimmed beard or mustache. And on other days, he seemed to vanish in midair only to reappear just as suddenly. "Spooky" was the word to describe him. Let him go to Camelot Acres and beg for money there. His kind didn't belong in their world.

Lisa didn't look at Steven until they reached the end of the path leading back to their world, where the roads were smooth and the grass always cut short.

"Well," she said a tad too brightly. "I got my bike back."

"Yeah …" Steven winced. "Just like you said." He breathed in sharply as a gust of wind caught him in the back.

"So, uh, how is your—"

"Fine," he said through gritted teeth. "Look, Lisa." Steven stared at her seriously, the wind whipping his hair over his face. "You don't tell Mom and Dad what happened to me, and I won't tell them what happened to your bike. Okay?"

Lisa sighed. "Fine. Deal."

On the flat pavement, Steven resumed riding his ripstick, but at a very slow pace. Lisa smiled from her bike, pedaling slowly to match. "So," she said, "how's your b—"

Steven cut her off quickly. "It hurts, okay?"

"Like when Robbie put a match to light his—"

"Just don't talk about it!" Steven said through gritted teeth

"When we get home," Lisa said after a moment, "go take a shower … I'll give you ointment for—"

Steven kept his eyes on the road. "Okay, I got it!"

"If you need any help—"

"I'll be fine!"

They were passing the new neighbors' house, and a girl and boy around their ages were standing in the front yard, passing a soccer ball.

"Great," muttered Steven. "Does everyone have to get up early today?" He veered to the other side of the road and pretended not to see the girl waving in their direction.

Lisa went to wave back, but stopped herself at the last moment. Friends, she was quickly discovering, could be very overrated.

As they reached their driveway, Lisa gasped when Steven bent down to pick up the ripstick. "Oh my gosh, Steven!" she exclaimed. "Your pants! They're ripped and you're bleeding!"

Standing up stiffly, Steven groaned. "Great … Mom is going to find out."

Lisa then saw a familiar car parked up the hill on the driveway and sighed with relief. "No, I don't think so. Our housekeeper is here. She'll help us, I'm sure of it!" Steven looked at her doubtfully. "Trust me," she said with more confidence than she felt. "I'll get her to help—she likes us."

Frowning, Steven rubbed his sore area gingerly. "I don't know why …"

As it turned out, all went according to Lisa's plan, so she thought. Their housekeeper, a dark-haired immigrant from Eastern Europe, proved very delighted to help the children. After Steven's long shower … and time attending his wounds, she gathered his clothes and put them through the washer without a hitch. She even promised to mend Steven's jeans by Monday.

By the time their parents rose after ten that morning, Steven sat sleepily in relative comfort at the breakfast table with Robbie and Margie. Lisa stood at the counter flipping the last round of pancakes.

"What is this?" Mr. Winter asked in mock horror at seeing the children. "My sons and daughters not watching cartoons on a Saturday? And they're all dressed? And they made us pancakes?"

"Must be a magic day!" Mrs. Winter said brightly, going behind Lisa toward the coffeemaker. "Good morning, everyone!"

The scent of hot pancakes and melted butter filled the room. What started out grimly had turned into a wonderful, cheery Saturday morning.

"Magic day?" asked Mr. Winter in mock horror. "More like a day of horror! Obviously these are clones from another planet and they kidnapped our children."

"Hey! Let go of that pancake!" Lisa slapped a spatula at her father's hand as he reached for the hotcake fresh off the griddle. "It's not even buttered!"

"Dad!" Robbie protested from the closest chair. "I'm supposed to get the first one!"

"No," Margie immediately cried. "I get the first! Lisa promised!"

Steven grinned. "No, Dad gets the first."

"Sorry," Mr. Winter said gruffly, his mouth already full. "But I have to make sure one of you clones didn't poison the pancakes."

"Dear, leave the children alone—there's more of them than us, remember."

"Believe me. When I pay the bills I'm very aware of that."

"That's the only one you're getting," Lisa said gruffly.

Mr. Winter shook his head. "No, I have to make sure the other pancakes aren't poisoned too." He shrugged. "Sorry, but that's one of the roles of a good father."

"But, Dad!" Robbie complained. "You'll eat all our pancakes!"

Built more like an athlete than a father of four, Mr. Winter was a tall, broad-shouldered man who'd kept his boyish good looks. He had dark hair, a square jaw, and soft blue eyes that always seemed to be looking for trouble. His loose T-shirt swelled with upper-body strength, which he used to lift Robbie right out of his chair.

"Mister," he said gruffly, "I resent that comment. I only plan to eat *your* pancakes. And Steven's. And maybe Lisa's."

"What about mine?" Margie wanted to know.

He winked at his youngest. "Not yours, Margie. I need you on my side when your mother yells at me."

"Ah, put me down," Robbie said, trying hard not smile.

"Sure." Mr. Winter pretended to drop him before settling him gently in the chair, backward. He tousled his hair.

"Dad, you're such a five-year-old," Lisa said with disapproval.

"Nah, I'm thirty-five. I'm like seven five-year-olds." Moving around the table, he stopped to give Margie a kiss on her head and then reached Steven, who sat on the far end. "Move over, kid, let your old man sit. Later on we'll go swimming, right, guy?"

With his half smile, Steven stood carefully to give way to his father. "Sure, Dad."

"So what have you kids really been up to all morning, huh?" Dropping to the seat, Mr. Winter gave Steven a light tap on the seat of his fresh shorts. Immediately the boy's knees buckled and he fought to keep from wincing.

"Hey," his father said with concern. "What's wrong?"

"Uh, I just slept the wrong way last night. That's all." Gritting his teeth, Steven awkwardly made it to the next seat.

"Well, pancakes are done!" Lisa called loudly before their father could ask more questions. "Let me serve them. Everybody just sit right where you are."

"Wait until we say grace!" called Mrs. Winter from the other room. "Let's be thankful for what we have, because many aren't so lucky."

Steven and Lisa exchanged a look. Didn't they know that.

"Ah, come on," groaned Robbie. "I'm starving!"

"Yeah, I'm starving!" echoed Margie.

"Hey, none of that," Mr. Winter told them. "Your mother is right. There are many people out there who aren't as fortunate as we are."

"Yeah, and they would love to steal everything we have because of it," Lisa said unkindly, bringing a large stack of pancakes to the table.

Steven lifted his eyebrows and brushed hair from his forehead. He kept silent.

"Lisa, how can you say such a thing?" Mrs. Winter came from the kitchen carrying two cups of steaming coffee and a rather shocked look on her otherwise pretty face. A former swimmer and fashion model, she had golden curls that hung past her shoulders, framing a smooth oval face with sparkling blue eyes perched daintily over a delicate nose, and a wide mouth with full lips that rarely frowned. She carried her looks well but resisted adding any vanity. This morning she wore a bright, flower-printed dress of orange, yellow, and red. Lisa couldn't help but admire her, even when the look of disapproval was directed at her. "We shouldn't say stuff like that, sweetheart."

Lisa dropped her gaze but still muttered a response. "Well, some of them do. They're jealous of us."

Mrs. Winter turned her look to her husband. "Doug, I think we need to have a talk with our children."

Mr. Winter's eyebrows shot up. "You mean *that*? *Now*?"

"No, not *that,* but *now*!"

Steven looked between his parents and then at Robbie. The two brothers both shrugged their shoulders. Grown-up talk could be a different language.

Mr. Winter took one of the coffee mugs from his wife and smacked his lips. "Ah, first, let's eat the pancakes," he said. "*After* we say a blessing for all those who, er, may be jealous, and, ah, for all those who aren't thankful."

"I guess that'll do," sighed Mrs. Winter. "Lisa, you make wonderful pancakes. Maybe you can save a couple for the housekeeper—okay?"

As the blessing was said and the pancake breakfast began, nobody noticed the tall figure just outside their house. Standing very still while leaning against the side of the garage, he stuck both hands in the pockets of his long coat.

"Looks like Isabella may be right after all," he mumbled. A slow grin spread across his grizzled face. Then at the snap of his fingers, his cheeks turned as smooth as the skin of a baby. "Our hunt is nearly over. And then, oh, boy, it really begins."

Chapter Three

Later that morning, when the breakfast dishes were drying and only the scent of coffee and syrup remained, Lisa found her father reading the paper at the kitchen table with his coffee mug close at hand. Mrs. Winter had left to take Margie to ballet class.

"Dad, can I sit down?"

"I would hope so," murmured Mr. Winter without looking up. "Don't tell me you 'slept the wrong way' too." Now he looked up with a cocked eyebrow. "Are you going to tell me what really happened?"

Blushing slightly, Lisa took the seat across from her father and started inspecting her nails—freshly painted pink. "What do you mean?" she asked carefully.

"The way Steven's been moving all morning—it's like he has pin cushions stuck in his pants." He narrowed his eyes at Lisa. "You didn't beat up your brother, did you?"

"Dad!" Turning, Lisa looked out the glass doors lining the back wall of the kitchen. Through it, she could see Steven sitting on the back stoop with Robbie and Susie Perkins, the nine-year-old from a few blocks away who visited as often as she could … just as long as Steven was around. The three were slouched in relaxation and using binoculars to search for birds—a fruitless task, since, for some reason, no birds had been around for the last couple of days … Maybe they all went up north for the upcoming summer?

"Well?" asked Mr. Winter.

"Uh, Steven may have had an accident on his ripstick this morning—but I was wondering, what's it like on the other side of the trees?"

"Whoa—hold on, Lisa. Steven had an accident?"

"Maybe he fell, okay? He's fine. I promise."

"Well, okay … but what's this about the other side of the trees?"

"You know, the neighborhood behind the trees—near the new neighbors."

"Oh … why do you want to know? Does this pertain to, uh, Steven's accident?"

Lisa looked away. "Dad, I just want to know. Are they poor?"

Sighing heavily, Mr. Winters dropped his paper on the table and fingered his coffee cup thoughtfully. "You mean poor in money? Yeah, I would say some of them lack money. And, yes, some might even act jealous that we don't." He smiled sadly at Lisa. "But can you blame them? Living can be hard. We are very fortunate to have what we have."

"But what if they hate you because you're rich?"

"Well, for one, you stay away from them." Mr. Winter shifted a tad uncomfortably in his chair. "But you don't hate them back." He put a finger to the side of his mouth thoughtfully. "I can understand why some of those families aren't happy with our neighborhood … but that doesn't mean we should be unhappy about their neighborhood."

"Why not? If they started it—"

"Lisa—nobody is born rich and nobody is born poor. Just because we have money at the moment doesn't mean we're better than anybody else—we're all just people."

"I know that! But it's not my fault we're rich!"

"And it's not their fault they're poor. The point is, nobody deserves to suffer—nobody. If we see somebody suffering, then we must do what we can to stop it. The same would be true for any person anywhere."

Lisa banged the table, tossing back her head in frustration. "Oh, so we should just give them my bike then."

"What? Lisa—"

"Dad, if I try to be nice and they're not, then I don't care if they're suffering!"

"Look, Lisa, what's this about?"

"Oh, uh, nothing … I just think some people hate us for being rich."

Mr. Winter ran his hand up through his dark hair. "Unfortunately, a lot of people hate what they don't understand. That goes both ways. But take a look at your brother Steven. Robbie follows him everywhere he goes …" He smiled with a twinkle in his eye. "And so would Susie Perkins and just about every other girl on the block his age. And he gets along with all his classmates, no matter where they're from. You never hear him speak meanly about people, do you?"

Lisa snorted. "Just me."

"Well, ah, that's different. The point is, Steven goes out of his way to understand others."

Lisa grunted. Steven also knew a few mama jokes that might surprise her father, but she kept this to herself. "So?"

"Do you know why he gets along so well with everyone?" Lisa shrugged, going back to looking at her nails. "Because he doesn't judge or try to act better than any of them … and we know what he's been through."

Lisa bit her lip in thought. "I'm not Steven," she said after a long moment.

"No, you're Lisa. My daughter that I love. My daughter who is extremely beautiful, gifted, and intelligent."

Lisa sighed. "Sure, Dad."

"My daughter who has a secret about what happened this morning." Lisa immediately went red. "I'm confident you'll be fine, Lisa." Draining his coffee, he slammed it on the table, smacking his lips. "In the meantime, your job is to make sure your brother avoids any more 'accidents.' Try to understand other people before doing anything rash—take me for example. At the moment, I'm going to be very understanding and not demand to know what happened this morning in regard to Steven's accident and you wanting to know about the other neighborhood. Fair enough?"

"Uh, yeah. Thanks, Dad."

Lisa had two of the most beautiful parents … warm, kind, and always there for her. She couldn't imagine life without them …

even if they did look nothing like her and Steven. To her, they were everything. Then everything changed.

That night, a family meeting was called shortly after dinner.

"I thought only corny TV shows had family meetings," Lisa grumbled, flopping onto the couch.

"Here, Steven, you sit with your old man," her father called as Steven entered with Robbie in tow. "You don't want to get too close to Lisa when she's in one of her moods—she's liable to bite."

Steven grinned as he crossed the room to carefully squeeze next to his father in the great armchair by the mantel.

Robbie promptly climbed on Mr. Winter's lap. "I don't want to get bitten either," he said half-seriously.

Lisa stuck her tongue out at all of them. At least Margie didn't join the boys. She lay drowsing on the floor by Lisa's feet. Dancing was the only thing that seemed to wear the kid out.

"Are we all here?" Mrs. Winter asked, coming from the kitchen with a plate of cookies and balancing a tray with several glasses of milk.

"Present and accounted for." Putting his arm around Steven's shoulders, Mr. Winter flicked his hair in the back. "You know, Steven, if you're going to take swimming seriously, you'll have to get a haircut."

"I don't take swimming seriously," Steven said with a small grin.

Mr. Winter chuckled. "Yeah, you're just the best swimmer on the team." He tousled the boy's hair. "Just keep from sleeping the wrong way in the future, hey?"

Crossing his arms, Steven lifted his eyebrows as he turned his neck to look up at his father. "Sure, Dad."

"Doug, the meeting?" Putting down the food, Mrs. Winter waved Robbie back from grabbing a cookie. "Before we eat the fat and sugar, your father and I have something serious to say. We found out today about something very important."

Immediately, Steven lost his smile and stared at Lisa, not daring to breathe.

Lisa visibly jumped and met his stare with one of her own. Had their parents found out about that morning? Maybe somebody called and complained?

It turned out to be much worse.

Clearing his throat, Mr. Winter nodded. "You know how Margie loves to dance, right? Well, we confirmed something we've known about for some time … Margie has been accepted to a special ballet school in Colorado this summer. Your mother and I will be going with her for about a month … maybe longer."

At the sound of her name, Margie's eyes jerked open. "I'm going to ballet school?"

"Yes, dear. Robbie, you're coming with us."

Lisa's mouth was open wider than a canyon. Colorado was where she and Steven were born. And where … well, she didn't have to ask, but she did anyway. "What about us? Me and Steven?"

"Steven and me," corrected Mrs. Winter with a smile. She knew how Lisa hated being corrected for anything. "You two will be staying here—we're actually leaving during the last weeks of school."

"You mean, we'll be staying here *alone*?"

"What, you think your parents are that crazy?" Mr. Winter put an arm around Steven's neck and pulled him close. "I would hate to have any more 'sleeping the wrong way' incidents."

Lisa shot to her feet. "This is serious!"

"That's what we said, sweetheart." Mrs. Winter moved and put her arm around her red-haired daughter. "We won't leave you two alone without proper supervision."

"But who?"

"Well, your father and I still have to find a babysitter. A good one we can trust."

"Where are you going to find a babysitter who's going to stay here for a month?"

"We'll have to pay her well," Mr. Winter joked.

"Dad!" Lisa stamped her foot.

"Extremely well."

"You raise a good question, Lisa." Mrs. Winter suddenly smiled. "Remember all my stories I like to tell about my best friend in high school?"

Lisa groaned. "No more of those stories! Don't tell me she's coming!"

"Well, I haven't spoken to her in years, but I hope to find somebody like her ..."

"Where would you find somebody like that?" Lisa nearly exploded. "To you, she walks on water—there's nobody that perfect in a million miles!"

Outside the house, the tall figure in the long coat slipped around the side. While he didn't hear what was going on inside, he knew something big was happening. Something so big, he wanted to be ready ... ready for all the patient searching and planning to finally pay off. The last view of him came from an owl. Perched on the top of a giant oak just behind the Winters' property, the feathered beast had settled itself on a branch to prepare for another long night of hunting. No insects or birds filled the night with their music ... only snakes were out.

The strange figure now approached the pool. Muttering, the figure extended a hand over the still water. A dark red glow emitted from the figure's eyes.

Blinking, the great owl suddenly saw nothing. The figure had utterly and completely vanished. The water remained still as ice.

The shadowman visited Steven's dream soon after ...

When the sun rose the next morning, the air was again alive with birds and their songs. The threat had passed ... for the moment.

On that same morning, Mrs. Winter began her search for a babysitter ... but where would she ever find the one she needed? Whom could she trust with two of her most precious possessions for such a long period of time? Whom indeed? It would have to be somebody very special.

Chapter Four

Some days later, in another state …

Always start with what you know …

Well, let's see. I know nobody likes me in gym class … In English I don't even think the teacher knows my name … ditto for history …

Rachel Pugsley sighed. She knew too much, but only of the wrong things.

People say the high school years are the best years of life. If that was true, she might as well jump off the nearest bridge.

Don't say that—don't even think it! Rachel furiously scribbled in her notebook.

In a few short weeks she would be finished with high school forever … Four years of pain, humiliation, and sitting alone in all her classes, even when surrounded by classmates, would become only bad memories. But before this happened she wanted to write something important—something to give meaning to her high school years and something for her high school to remember her by. Otherwise she would be a forgotten loser who might never have existed. Besides, if she could write something big, then it would be worth it.

Rachel Pugsley had a miserable time in school, but that was okay with her. She wanted to be a writer one day, and all the best writers had miserable lives growing up.

"So I should be great at writing," she mumbled to herself.

She sighed again. The only difference was that the great writers knew how to express their misery in words. All Rachel had written so far was:

PANTERROR!

"High school is like eating cafeteria chili dogs. At first, it looks like it might be good, but very quickly it becomes a sour feeling in your stomach, and then it all ends in a big heaping pile of"—and that's where she stopped.

"I should just give up now," she mumbled, crossing out her poetic lines that were only fit for the toilet. "I can't write … I can never do anything important."

All around the school, excitement bubbled from her fellow seniors. They were already planning graduation parties, completing job applications, and taking last college visits. If she were to get up and go to the cafeteria now … well, first, nobody would notice her, and second, she would find everyone stuffing down food while talking about great summer plans. Third, she would have nowhere to sit. She had no friends, no job, no college, no summer plans … and no lunch. What she did have was severe writer's block and a headache.

It only got worse.

Head down and pencil trying to create some wonderful first sentence, she never noticed the shadow fall over her until it was too late.

"Hey," said a voice next to her. "Rache—whatcha doing?"

Startled, Rachel jerked her head back, nearly jerking herself out of her chair. Whirling with a gasp, she managed to grab the table with both hands and keep her balance. But she lost her pencil. In a terribly beautiful arc, it spun across the table before bouncing off the back of the head of the girl sitting at the computer several feet away.

"Ouch!" yelped the girl.

Ducking her head, Rachel became extremely interested in her notebook. "Uh, oh, hi …" Her voice quickly ran out of steam, collapsing before the finish line, with her face red from embarrassment.

Sarah, the girl who'd startled Rachel, barely noticed. With her nose stuck in the air while trying to brush lint off the shoulder of her tight black T-shirt, featuring a screaming skeleton playing a guitar, she looked like a preening monkey.

Meanwhile, the girl at the computer rubbed her head. Turning, she aimed a scowl at the back table. "Jerk," she muttered, loud enough for the whole library to hear.

Luckily, besides the three students, only Ms. Stauten, the ancient librarian, made up the rest of the library. Short, squat, and maligned with hairy moles on both sides of her face, she resembled a short, squat prune with spots. A well-known complainer about students, it was only a matter of time before she completely banned students from the school library. Now, however, this late in the year, the librarian barely looked up from her laptop and gave a brief grimace.

Rachel wanted to crawl in the table and hide.

Only seniors were allowed in the library during lunch—if they were quiet. This meant that only losers and those needing to finish up schoolwork, such as the girl at the computer, took advantage of the privilege. Rachel, of course, made up the loser part.

"Um, Rache, you there? I was talking to you!" Sarah's whiny voice bounced sharply in Rachel's ear.

"Oh, uh, okay, uh …" Rachel tried to say Sarah's name, but failed as usual. Ever since she could remember, saying another person's name felt as awkward as giving them a hug—it felt too intimate, like they were friends on equal footing. Not that she would ever admit it, but Rachel's most intimate moments came when she talked to her stuffed animals. They at least listened and allowed her to express her true feelings without interruption. Nowhere else did that happen.

"I was just saying," said Sarah, clicking her tongue, "how do you stand being surrounded by all these books …" She gave a distasteful look around her. "My gosh, I feel nauseous just looking at them! I mean, if I was put in charge, the first thing I would do is take them all out and remodel this dump!"

"It is a library," muttered Rachel so softly that it sounded more like she'd just cleared her throat. Biting her lip, she cast her eyes back at the wall of books behind her. How could she admit it out loud, but inside those dust collectors were the best friends she'd ever had. Never would she get rid of books. Within their spines were stories of countless lives, all better than hers—and more exciting than hers. Thinking they would one day be squashed and zapped into tablets and other silly gadgets frightened her. Reading was about escape … and right at the moment, Rachel really desired escape. She looked back at the girl in front of her.

Sarah Watkins had arrived at Brookline High School in Waterville, Virginia, earlier that year. On her first day, she entered the school wearing a skirt left over from her sixth-grade birthday party—a gaudy yellow thing barely long enough to cover her thick, meaty thighs. With her navel hanging out of a cutoff T-shirt with large holes on either side, Sarah spent her first day in school sitting in the nurse's office, being lectured about the dress code. It didn't help that her middle was more round than flat. In any case, for the rest of the week, the big talk in school centered on the new, fat, ugly girl who wore her little sister's clothes. Sarah had spent the remainder of the week slouching low as idiot boys continuously asked her when her baby was due.

One fateful day, Rachel, in a moment of pity, had made the mistake of lending Sarah her English homework before class.

"What's this?" Sarah snarled.

"Uh … um," Rachel faltered. It was the first time she ever tried to initiate a conversation the entire year. "I, uh, heard you didn't get your homework finished. It's going to count as a quiz grade."

"Yeah?" Sarah never said thanks. Hunched over her desk, way in the back corner of first-period homeroom, she just snatched Rachel's homework, and that was that … until the following week when Sarah all of a sudden started talking to Rachel.

If Rachel had any grand thoughts of finally finding a friend, she was quickly corrected. Sarah certainly spoke to Rachel, but that was it. Rachel rarely had an opportunity to speak back, and when she did, Sarah never bothered to listen. Rachel soon became Sarah's self-esteem boost. She was the one senior in the school that Sarah could feel superior over, without trying. Even after a while, when Sarah started making friends with a group of girls who enjoyed thick makeup, black fingernails, and short haircuts, she would still randomly stop to converse with Rachel, much like a weed would randomly appear in a garden. Nothing Rachel did could get rid of the girl.

Now, stuck with Sarah once again, Rachel inwardly sighed. She knew this was Sarah's way of making sure she was still better than somebody. That was Rachel's service to the world—she was

Sarah's self-esteem boost. And "better" to Sarah meant more popular.

"Hey, Rache—come back to the world!"

Blinking, Rachel looked up, suddenly aware she had been asked a question. "What?"

Heaving a sigh like Rachel was interrupting her, Sarah admired her nails in the fluorescent light. "I asked what you were doing this summer. Can you believe we're graduating? Like, it's crazy. I still have to get a tan for my new bathing suit . . ." She trailed off and gave a look down at Rachel, biting her lower lip in some sort of seductive smile that made her appear constipated. "Do you know why?"

"Why we're graduating?"

"No," Sarah said, making a sour face. "Why I need a tan—why I have my new bathing suit." She smiled almost pityingly at Rachel now. "I guess you don't know. Beach week is coming."

Beach week was traditionally held the week after graduation and was when all the seniors—the popular ones—drove a few hours south to North Carolina and rented houses on the beach. Partying and swimming were the main order for the week. Rachel had no intention of even thinking of going.

"I know—"

"And Trent Long is probably going to invite me."

Rachel lifted her eyebrows. Back in middle school, she'd actually had a crush on Trent. She even wrote him love letters and hid them in her room. But four years of watching his arrogant growth of popularity and total lack of compassion had cured her of any lovesick feelings.

A tall, golden-haired jock with a Grecian profile and loaded parents, Trent Long ran the senior class. Wherever he went, a gaggle of stooges followed—and so did the eyes of almost every female in the school. Teachers bent over backward for him, and girls spoke of him in awe.

Brett Bufford was a stocky, sandy-haired shadow to Trent and acted as his liaison with the lower forms in the school. Almost without fail, every Wednesday, Brett would make the rounds with individual invitations for Trent's next party on Friday night. His parties were something of legend, and everybody who had hopes for success in life had to attend. It got to the point where if you hadn't received at least one invitation, then you might as well change your name and move to a new state. You were nothing.

Sarah was obsessed with being popular and wanted more than anything to get an invitation from Brett to one of Trent's special parties … So far this hadn't happened for her. So to get invited to his precious beach week—an event he'd talked about since the beginning of the school year—that would be like winning the lottery.

Rachel couldn't have cared less. Back when she was a pathetic sophomore, she used to dream of an invitation … until she heard Brett making cow noises when she walked by and Trent laughing.

I'm trapped in a cruel world where people of my kind are persecuted for who they are—ugly and dumpy. No, that wouldn't start a good story either.

"Rachel? Hello? You there? Good grief, it's like you're from a different world!"

Head jerking up, Rachel nodded. Sarah was only warming up. Sniffing loudly from her nose while clicking with her tongue, the girl did her best impression of a diva giving her time to an undeserving fan. It was like she expected Rachel to fall at her feet and beg for an autograph.

"I was just saying, I saw Brett and Trent watching me in the cafeteria. I'm not kidding. And they were writing invitations to beach week! You do know about beach week with Trent Long, right?"

Rachel resisted snorting. In her mind, she pictured Sarah, in her tight jeans and black shirt stretched over her flabby torso, carrying a loaded chili dog in front of Brett and Trent, who were sitting like judges of a reality TV show. "And here's a good contestant for beach week," the imaginary Brett crowed. "You mean beached-whale week!" the imaginary Trent howled.

Stop it! Don't stoop to their level! Shaking such thoughts from her mind, Rachel drew invisible lines on her notebook with her finger. She wished she had her pencil … The girl at the computer had stopped typing and seemed to be listening. Rachel's face burned even more.

"You know, they say beach week is one of the greatest weeks in a teenager's life. Everyone is going, you know. Trent already rented three houses at Nags Head. No parents, adults, or anything! It's, like, going to be awesome! And Jennifer, like, you know, Trent's girlfriend, told Samantha that Trent is inviting almost the whole class! Everyone worth knowing is going!" Sarah spoke down at Rachel as if shoving a mud pie in her face, twisting it until it hurt. "And of course, you know, Samantha is Jennifer's best friend!"

Tossing her hair back, Sarah lifted her chin to strike a pose. Her belly nearly bopped Rachel in the nose.

Feeling a surge of anger flash through her veins, Rachel blurted the first thing that popped into her mind. "I'm going to Florida."

Immediately she cringed.

The belly backed off her. "Huh? What did you say?" Sarah stared down at Rachel like she'd just stolen something of hers. "For beach week? Who's taking *you* to Florida?"

Rachel swallowed and wished she could disappear. "Oh, uh, nobody …"

Sarah scoffed. "Oh, right. That's what I thought."

"I'm flying there."

"What? You're going there by *yourself*?" Crossing her arms, Sarah snorted in disbelief. She sounded like a cross between a horse and a pig.

Gritting her teeth, Rachel tried to speak with more confidence. "Uh, yeah … I'm, uh, meeting … some people." She refused to meet Sarah's eyes. Sweaty palms gripped her notebook.

"Yeah, right. I don't believe you."

Rachel didn't believe herself either. In fact, before Sarah had arrived and started bragging, Rachel absolutely knew she wouldn't be going to Florida … but now, without pausing to think, she opened her fat mouth and said, "I am going. I'm going to be a babysitter."

For a moment Sarah said nothing. Then she barked out a laugh that carried across the entire library. The girl at the computer threw a glare back at her, before resuming typing. Ms. Stauten cleared her throat at her desk, but left her eyes on her laptop. Much to Rachel's embarrassment, Sarah did not quiet her voice.

"A babysitter? Really, Rache? You're *babysitting* for the summer? In Florida?"

Feeling miserable, Rachel shrugged. "Well, uh …"

"You don't even like going to the mall without your mom! I mean, you're eighteen years old and barely have a driver's license and no car! I would think *you* would need a babysitter if you ever went to Florida!"

Rachel Pugsley's face turned a bright shade of pink. "I can babysit," she mumbled. As a prerequisite for getting her driver's license, her mom had made her receive a certificate in babysitting, soon after her sixteenth birthday. Her mom's voice came back to her …

"You can't spend your entire teenage years locked up in your room with your homework and books, Rachel," her mother had told her over and over. "At least as a babysitter you can make some money and get out of the house. I did it at your age and met some wonderful friends in the process."

"Like who?" Rachel had growled one miserable morning before school while staring at her soggy cornflakes through half-closed eyes. "Five-year-olds and infants who threw up all over you?"

"No, Rachel, other babysitters, silly! That's where I first met Lizzy Michaels!" Rachel's mom had stopped buttering toast and leaned against the counter with one of her wistful smiles that always happened when she thought of her glorious past with Lizzy Michaels.

Rachel had groaned and nearly planted her face in her soggy cornflakes. Lizzy Michaels had been Rachel's mom's best friend in high school and then through college. From her mom's stories, which were repeated constantly, Rachel imagined Lizzy to be a swimsuit model, a saint, and a caped crusader all rolled in one. "Blond curls, golden skin; she was the most attractive girl in our town. Every boy wanted to date her and every girl wanted to be her friend" was one of her mother's more mild descriptions.

Yet, somehow she chose to be best friends with Rachel's mom. Right. Rachel didn't believe it. She had stopped listening to these stories a long time before. Just looking at her mom, her plump legs bulging with veins supporting her bulky body with its sagging skin, made Rachel doubt their truth very much. Lank brown hair pulled back from her round face of puffy, rose-colored cheeks, full lips, and large nose, Rachel's mom resembled the Pillsbury Doughboy's mother … and minus the few wrinkles around her eyes and bulging veins, she also was the very image of Rachel. And what attractive person wanted to hang out with Rachel?

"Is your mom going with you to babysit?" Sarah asked rather nastily, snapping Rachel back to reality. "Or is this one of your dumb stories you're always trying to write?"

Rachel gripped the notebook so tightly it started bending inward at the sides. She was aware of her flabby arms quivering. The girl at the computer had stopped typing again and the librarian had cocked an ear while pretending to be very interested in her laptop.

"I'm going to Florida alone," she managed to say. "I'm flying down right after graduation."

Sarah would not let it go. "What kook would hire some babysitter from Virginia? Did you meet this creep on the Internet? I'm guessing you didn't send a real picture, but still, I wouldn't meet him. Once he sees you, he's going to run."

Rachel actually felt tears forming in her eyes. When she'd first gone to Sarah, she had managed to trick herself into thinking she could actually make a real friend. Maybe Sarah would be a Lizzy Michaels, she had actually thought.

Perhaps, one day she would … one day when Rachel was old and even fatter, she would tell her children about her great, wonderful friend Sarah Watkins, the most popular girl in school who always was so nice and treated Rachel as an equal … Her mom's Lizzy Michaels was probably no better—some frumpy jerk who grew "nicer" with age and memory loss.

Then the door to the library flew open. "Sarah, there you are!"

A small, skinny girl in a tight black shirt with matching lipstick and hair color burst into the library like a cyclone escaped from the prairie. "Sarah, what are you doing? Oh, sorry, Ms. Stauten."

"This is a library," huffed the warped librarian with a halfhearted glare. At the beginning of the year, she would have made a big scene of tossing everybody out who spoke above a whisper. Now, she cocked an ear to hear more of Rachel's dignity being ripped to shreds.

"Hi, Samantha," Sarah said sweetly, stepping back a bit from Rachel. "Come back here and hear Rachel's plans for the summer."

Samantha, actually a pretty girl under all her attitude and makeup, frowned and walked briskly to the back corner and Rachel's table. "Rachel who? Oh, her. Hey." Rachel did her best to sink into her chair and hide under the table. Samantha turned to Sarah. "Sarah, you need to come back to the cafeteria to hear about *our* summer plans."

"Hold on," Sarah said snidely. "Rachel says she's going to Florida for the summer."

Samantha blinked. "Oh," she said. "Well, that's cool."

"No, but she's going to be a babysitter in Florida!"

"Really?" Samantha looked again at Rachel, this time with halfway interest. "That's cool. You're going to make money while we're probably going to make idiots of ourselves. Speaking of which, Sarah, we're going to be idiots if we don't get to the cafeteria double quick. Brett and Jennifer want to talk to us!"

Both girls screeched at the same time and looked ready to hug each other.

"Really!" Sarah cried. "Why didn't you say so?"

"Just come on!" Samantha said. "This is it!"

Sitting like a lump, Rachel didn't have to look up to know both girls were beaming. At least they were leaving.

Samantha stopped at the computers. "Oh, hey, Karen. Do you want to come too?"

"No, thanks," the girl at the computer replied sweetly. "I got my invitation from Trent last week."

"Well, okay. See ya!"

In a burst of giggles, the two girls practically flew across the library, leaving Rachel and her misery in their wake.

At least they forgot about me quick enough, she thought. She thought wrong.

"Hey, Rache!" Sarah called from the door. "When you go babysit those brats, don't bring any pencils! You don't want to poke their eyes out, or brain any of them!"

Karen grunted from the computer. Then there was silence.

The best years of life … Rachel buried her face in her arms on top of her notebook. *I'll never be anything … not a writer … not a friend … not a babysitter* … But if she didn't go to Florida now, then what would happen? Sarah would find out and it'd be all over the Internet the next day. Not that it mattered—*I can hardly be a bigger loser than I already am.* At the same time … *I hate this place! Everybody here is as bad as each other, or worse! After I graduate I don't want to spend another minute longer than I have to here.*

But how could she leave? Rachel hadn't any college plans. Too poor to afford a large university, her parents had suggested enrolling at the community college. That was her biggest dream possible …

From above her, something tapped her lightly on her neck, this followed by a rough clearing of the throat, sounding like an engine trying to start.

"I believe you dropped this." Ms. Stauten, her creviced face looking grim, placed Rachel's pencil firmly on the tear-streaked notebook.

"Uh … uh, thanks," she managed to mumble.

The librarian didn't leave. "Rachel, you are one of the few seniors in this school who treat this place as a real library. You actually come here because of the books and not to socialize, or skip class … you even read the books here. That shows you have a good head on your shoulders." Surprised, Rachel couldn't help but stare. Never before had the librarian sounded so gentle and sincere. "I know you have plans on becoming a writer. Your trip to Florida sounds like a fabulous start to a great story. Take your pencil and notebook with you when you go. Use both as often as you can."

"I, uh," stammered Rachel, ducking her head. "I actually might not go."

"You're going, Rachel," Ms. Stauten said firmly. "I've been doing this job for over twenty-five years. I've seen some really nice boys and girls and some not so nice boys and girls. Go to Florida. Have a blast and teach those brats how to treat people kindly when they get older. I think you know some people who need that lesson very much."

When Rachel looked up again, she was alone.

When the bell rang soon after, Rachel left the library in a slight daze. Before exiting, she looked back at where Ms. Stauten sat behind her desk typing furiously on her laptop, her face sour as ever. Then, feeling Rachel's gaze, the old librarian looked up and actually winked.

Karen held the door open for her to exit. "Don't worry about those girls," she told Rachel softly as she went past. "I'm not going to that stupid beach week either. I think you'll have more fun in Florida." Then she was gone, lost in the sea of high school youth flooding the hall.

As Rachel entered the sea herself, she felt a warm smile prick at the corners of her mouth. Perhaps not everyone here was so bad … As Rachel followed the tide to her next class, Sarah Watkins came from the other direction walking with a crowd of girls, all holding white envelopes like they contained million-dollar checks. Rachel gave her the brightest smile she could muster. Sarah never glanced in her direction.

Chapter Five

The Florida trip was never Rachel's idea or plan. It had all come about the previous day while Rachel was still stuck in school.

Coming home that day, Rachel had found her mother waiting for her in the kitchen … standing over a batch of fresh chocolate-chip cookies while humming merrily and pretending not to see Rachel.

Immediately Rachel knew something was up. Her mother never baked during the week except on special occasions—and she *never* hummed. Her father was an overworked lawnmower salesman and off on another business trip—maybe he finally found a new job?

"Rachel, is that you?" her mother practically sang when Rachel entered the kitchen.

Who else would it be? Then her mother giggled. Her mother never giggled.

Growing increasingly nervous, Rachel grunted as she dropped her heavy backpack by the table. "Uh, hi, Mom."

"Oh, Rachel, I'm sooo glad you're home!"

By this time Rachel was on full alert. This could not be good. Swallowing, she moved into the kitchen, trying hard to ignore the smell of freshly baked cookies. What did her mother want?

"What're the cookies for?" she asked as nonchalantly as possible.

"Cookies? What cookies? Rachel, I have some great news for you!"

Rachel all at once groaned. Her mom must have called somebody at church to arrange a prom date—it was something she'd been threatening to do for weeks. Rachel shuddered at the thought of being forced to go to the prom with pimply, bucktoothed Ben Freenie, a sophomore who still played with action figures.

"What are you doing after graduation, sweetie?" her mom asked innocently.

Now Rachel went still. Her hand inches from a warm cookie, she glanced carefully at her mother. Whatever her mom had done, it had to be much worse than arranging a date for the prom. The last time she'd had this conversation with her parents, they ended up arguing. Her parents wanted her out working and not staying home all summer like she had the year before and the year before that.

"Mom, what did you do?"

"Rachel, you'd never guess who called this morning." Rachel waited, but her mother was in no hurry. "Do you remember all those stories about Lizzy Michaels? Well, guess what! She called me!"

Rachel all at once relaxed. "Oh … that's great, Mom." False alarm …

Suddenly her mother turned on her and beamed. "Oh, Rachel. We hadn't spoken for ages!" Her mother then laughed, causing her cheeks and throat to shake. "Can you believe it? She found me on Facebook and got a hold of my number! She's Lizzy Winter now. She's married and has four kids, can you believe it?" The beaming smile on her mother's face caused Rachel to roll her eyes.

"Yeah, Mom," she said without enthusiasm. "That's great."

"She's now living down in Florida. Two boys and two girls. Her husband owns two car dealerships—can you believe that? Two!"

"Uh-huh." Rachel mentally prepared to receive a lecture on applying herself so one day she too could be married to a guy with two car dealerships. Sighing, she took a large bite of warm, delicious chocolate-chip cookie …

"So," her mother said as if telling her about the weather, "I of course told her you'd love to go down for the summer."

Cookie shrapnel fired across the kitchen. Coughing hard, Rachel dropped the rest of the cookie onto the floor. "Wh-what?" she choked out.

Mrs. Pugsley busily turned to the sink and hastily started washing a clean plate. "We had a long talk—we spoke of everything, and, well, her youngest daughter is going to a ballet school in Colorado."

Still gagging, Rachel stumbled to the fridge for milk. "So what?"

"And," continued her mother, "I told her all about you graduating from high school and not having a job lined up."

"MOM! You didn't!" Rachel pushed away the cartons of yogurt and grabbed the milk container.

"Of course I did!" her mother said defensively. "Your father and I are so proud of you graduating from high school."

She slammed the milk on the counter and grabbed a glass from the cabinet. Her mother could not be serious.

"Anyway, they're taking her and their youngest son with them."

"Huh? Who?" Rachel poured the milk.

"Lizzy and her husband, silly! They're taking their two youngest children to Colorado in the summer! Isn't that wonderful? Can you imagine us doing something like that?" Rachel didn't even bother to shake her head. They never went anywhere except shopping. Vacation to her meant a trip to the mall to buy new shoes. "Well, in any case," continued her mother, "she was so happy to hear all about you and your babysitting work. Remember how I told you about Lizzy and I and our babysitting adventures? She thought it was wonderful that my daughter was following in our footsteps! She hopes hers will do the same!"

Slamming the milk on the counter, Rachel blew out from her bottom lip, sending her dark brown bangs into the air. She hated when her mom talked about her to other people—she always bragged about things Rachel didn't even know she'd done. "Oh, that's great," she said sarcastically, moving to grab a clean glass by the sink and put it away before her mother started washing it again. "Babysitting is the most pathetic job on the planet, Mom, especially for a high school senior!"

"Oh, Rachel, you do such a fantastic job as a babysitter."

"Moomm, I only babysit two kids for the Dashers, and that's like once a month." Rachel couldn't look at her mother.

"Well, that's a hard job and you do great at it," her mother said defensively.

Rachel snorted. "They have two kids, Mom. One is a baby who sleeps all the time, and the other is eleven and doesn't even need a babysitter."

Her mom ignored her in the rush to finish. "And that leaves their two oldest children home alone."

"Lucky them," Rachel growled. She picked up her glass of milk.

"They go to private schools that don't end until the end of June—and well, I didn't even ask, but Lizzy did … She wants you to fly down and take care of her kids." Whirling from the sink, Rachel's mother clasped both hands below a beaming smile. "Isn't that great!"

Rachel had just taken a sip. "Wha-erupa!" Milk blasted from her mouth; some ended up in her nose. The little that made it to her throat stayed there and tried to choke her.

"Rachel! I just knew you would be excited, but not that excited!"

Standing by the counter with milk dripping from her nose, Rachel could only stare in disbelief while struggling for a breath as her mother grabbed a towel to clean up the milk.

"You'll have such a good time! They live in a gorgeous house and the children sound wonderful! There's Lisa—she's eleven and the oldest—and Steven. He just turned nine."

"*Mom*!" Rachel finally shouted. "Are you crazy! I'm not going! No way! I'd rather spend the summer in the library!"

"But, Rachel, I already told her you would be thrilled! She's going to pay you—"

"She's not going to pay me, because I'm not going! How can you do this to me? I'm nearly eighteen! I can run my own life and don't need you trying to do it for me!"

Scooting back from her livid daughter, Mrs. Pugsley suddenly looked deflated—like a punctured beach ball. "I'm so sorry, Rachel—I thought, I thought you would jump at the opportunity. She said she would fly you down first class! I know I would—"

"I'm not you, and I'm not going to Florida!" Turning from her mother, Rachel tried to rush to her room. Never graceful or quick on her feet, she slipped in a puddle of milk and flew backward.

"Rachel!" shrieked her mother.

With a resounding thud, Rachel landed on the hard kitchen floor with her soft posterior right in the remains of spewed cookie.

And that was how the cookie crumbled. Rachel cried over spilt milk.

And now, after the most unfortunate meeting with Sarah Watkins, Rachel's mind was in a quandary. The rest of the school day passed in a blur as she internally debated on whether or not she was going to Florida. By the time she got off the bus for home, she was finally set. She would be going to Florida. She would do it. She was positive. As she went up the driveway, every step brought self-doubt, and her strong will started cracking.

Was she crazy? There was no way she could be a babysitter for two kids of her mother's best friend. *I'll be in another state!* her mind screamed. *I hate traveling!* The last time she'd slept under another roof was back in sixth grade at summer camp. She'd gotten sick the second night and had to be driven home before morning by her mother. There. It was settled. She would most definitely *NOT* be going to Florida.

Then her mind cruelly reminded her of Sarah's gloating face.

All the more reason to not go. I'll just meet more people like her. It wasn't worth it.

But what if she did go? Then what could Sarah say? Maybe she would go … As Rachel approached her front door, she had it. She would do it. Why not? Then she could write about her experiences and shove it all in Sarah's face.

But wait! Her step faltered. That would mean meeting Lizzy Michaels.

To be honest, Rachel had almost believed that her mom had made Lizzy Michaels up and she was just some imaginary friend. Now that she was real, Rachel was terrified to imagine meeting her. She would probably be a grown-up version of Sarah Watkins, looking for a cheap babysitter for her two brats. Why not find somebody closer to babysit? Really, finding a babysitter *in Virginia* when you lived in Florida?

I'm definitely not going. Besides, she reasoned, her mom had probably already called Lizzy Michaels and explained that her daughter couldn't make it after all.

Sighing with relief at coming up with her own decision that made sense, Rachel opened the door and jubilantly entered her house.

Her mother sat waiting for her at the kitchen table. Her eyes were red, like she'd been crying.

Rachel dropped her backpack and swallowed. In all her years, the only best friend she'd ever really had was her mother. Her father was traveling around the country so often that he barely knew her. Only her mother had stuck by her side during all the hard times and was there to celebrate the good. Sure, they sometimes disagreed and even argued, but in the end, they always made up and grew even closer. The biggest reason Rachel hadn't buckled down and pushed for a college scholarship was that she couldn't bear the thought of living far away from her mother. Seeing her sitting all alone at the table, fighting back tears, was too much.

"Mom, uh, Mom, are you okay?"

"Oh, hi, Rachel …" Sniff. "I'm so glad you're home." Mrs. Pugsley gave a sad smile and wiped a puffy cheek. "I've been waiting all day for you …"

Nodding uncomfortably, Rachel moved to sit by her mom. That morning had been a silent affair with Rachel gobbling down her cereal without even glancing at her mother.

"Mom," she started, "I—"

"Oh, Rachel, I thought a lot about yesterday … I did a pretty rotten thing, didn't I? I'm so sorry, I sort of acted without thinking … I never, never should have gotten Lizzy's hopes—"

"Mom, it's okay. I'll go. I'll do it."

Her mother blinked rapidly. "What did you say?"

"I think, I mean, I'll go to Florida." Rachel gritted her teeth. "I'll do it."

"Oh, Rachel! I knew you would change your mind!" Shooting off the chair like a much younger woman with much less weight,

Mrs. Pugsley threw her mighty arms around Rachel and squeezed tightly. "I'm so proud of you!"

Moving to stand, Rachel struggled to return the hug without sending either of them crashing down. "Okay, Mom … You don't have to choke me." Rachel managed to disentangle herself from the bear hug. Her mother was crying again.

"Oh, Lizzy is so excited! She called here early this morning right after you left! She's so anxious to meet you! Oh, we talked for hours about you, and we both know you'll be great!"

Rachel's mouth dropped. "Mom! You didn't even know—I mean, I wasn't—"

"She wants you to call her as soon as possible. Here, right by the phone is her number. I wrote it down twice just in case I forgot."

Rachel threw up her hands with a sigh. One day she planned to make an independent decision. Instead, Rachel Pugsley, soon-to-be high school graduate, was going to Florida.

Chapter Six

As Rachel stepped onto the plane that would fly her to Atlanta for a short stop before flying to her doom in Florida, she thought of Sarah Watkins. She smiled grimly. It was the day after her high school graduation and just two days after Brett Bufford was caught drinking while driving home from one of Trent's parties. Beach week, if it happened, would be postponed until after his grounding, which would be after his court date, which meant it would be sometime in July, maybe.

Her smile was short lived.

"This way, dear," said a smiling flight attendant in her navy-blue suit as she took a look up and down Rachel's frame. "We'll find you more comfortable seating near the front where there're larger seats."

"Uh, thanks …" *I think.* She never got used to the looks people gave her because of her weight. Well, she'd better. Taking one more glance back toward the airport where her parents were probably still waving from one of the windows, she sighed. Now she was really alone. Her mother, she knew, would be crying. Her own tears threatened to spring from her eyes and had to be tightly controlled.

"Say hello to Lizzy for me and give her one of my hugs," she had told Rachel over and over. "I so wish I was going with you!"

A single tear managed to escape the corner of Rachel's left eye. Following the stewardess, she didn't bother to brush it away.

"No need for tears, miss," the cheerful stewardess said over her shoulder. "This is the safest plane still flying. Why, we haven't crashed once since I started working here, and that was two weeks ago!" She laughed. "Just some in-flight humor, dear." The girl had to be only a few years older than Rachel.

Following her down the aisle, Rachel hastily wiped her eye. Her stomach started going queasy, like it was screaming at her to get off. A tumult of emotions churned inside.

I can't believe I'm doing this. I'm going to Florida for the summer to babysit two kids I haven't met, for my mother's best friend, somebody else I haven't met in person … and I really need to go to the bathroom.

They had spoken over the phone, but that was it. Over the last few weeks, Mrs. Winter and her husband had called separately to interview and thank Rachel profusely. Mrs. Winter—Rachel had long since dropped the "Lizzy Michaels" stuff—sounded very friendly and so did Mr. Winter. Not having a Facebook account of her own, she had yet to see any pictures.

"I want it to be a surprise," she'd told her mom over and over.

"But, Rachel, you have to see their kids!" her mother had begged. "And Lizzy is so gorgeous—she and Doug make a perfect couple."

Now Rachel rolled her eyes just thinking about it. *They're probably all overweight rich kids with overweight parents.* These overweight parents, as Rachel imagined them to be, were offering her $4,000 for the summer. And the use of a car. And the weekends off to enjoy Florida. *They must be desperate for a babysitter because they have no friends in Florida to look after their brats!*

"Here we are, dear. You're the first one here, so you get your choice of the window or aisle. Which would you prefer?"

Arriving at a spacious seat near the cockpit, Rachel threw her small bag, which was loaded with mostly books and chocolate, overhead. The only thing she kept out was her notebook and pencil. Turning to the stewardess, she blew hair from her face. "Uh, actually, uh, the restroom?"

Flying for the first time proved to be an experience for Rachel. Her nerves were so jumpy from just thinking about her summer, she barely registered her first takeoff—not until looking out the window and seeing the ground rapidly vanishing below her did she realize she was airborne and on her way to Florida. Looking down at all the suddenly tiny houses and cars, her stomach did a flip. *Too late to turn back now.* Her first great adventure … and she already felt like throwing up.

Soon, after deep breaths, Rachel's stomach settled and she tried to enjoy the experience. She couldn't take her eyes off the miniature world below her—like a model train set her father took out every Christmas. *I wonder if I'm that small to everyone at school. Well, no longer!* she vowed. *From now on I'll be known as the babysitter for Lizzy Winter!* A smile played across her lips and she gripped her notebook tightly. In Florida she'd have a new start without people prejudging her. And then, she vowed, she would have a story to write!

Just then, before her smile fully settled, her seatmate, a beefy businessman with iron-gray hair and a red face, nudged her in the arm. Indicating Rachel's stomach, he grinned to reveal rows of yellowing teeth.

"So, young lady, when's the baby due?"

Four rows back, a tall gentleman sat ramrod straight and stared intently at the back of Rachel's head. His sharp blue eyes, hidden by dark sunglasses, were trained on Rachel's dull brown hair as if he expected it to catch fire or something. A puzzled look swept across his creased face. One hand went up to his carefully trimmed mustache, the color of fresh snow that matched his swept-back hair, and stroked it gently.

"So … this is nothing to be fearful of," he murmured. He almost sounded disappointed. His other hand strayed into his right pocket and tightly gripped a small, handheld mirror … that suddenly shifted colors from dull red to a vibrant green.

"What was that?" the woman on his left asked politely. "Is this your first trip in the air?"

"In an airplane, yes," the man sniffed without turning his head.

"Oh …" The woman waited for the man to explain, but was disappointed. Then she gasped. "Um, sir, your pocket is glowing—"

"And you're sleeping." Turning with a precise jerk, the man moved his hand up from his mustache to his glasses. Lifting them, he stared directly at the woman. At the same time, his hand over the mirror squeezed hard.

A sort of mist spat from the suddenly fiery red eyes, blasting into the surprised woman's face. Before she could raise a shout of alarm, her head fell back against the window and her eyes slid shut. Slumping against the glass, the woman stirred no more until hours later. It happened so suddenly that nobody else noticed.

Lowering his dark glasses over his now blue eyes, the man turned back to Rachel. He no longer stared with fierce intensity, and a small smile played across his lips. "The whole warning was nothing but a hoax," he scoffed. "She's just a … babysitter." He pretended to smile. "Isabella is right for once."

Next to him, the woman snored.

Rachel's first impression of Florida was pretty tame. It reminded her of Virginia, only different. At least the airport seemed mostly the same—just much bigger and full of potted palm trees and tons of people. Large windows, lots of seats, and crowds of people greeted Rachel as she exited the plane from Atlanta. And among those people were the Winter family. Rachel felt a touch of fear pull her forward.

The flight from Atlanta had been quiet and lulled her into feeling relaxed. But now reality was settling in. Feeling her pulse quicken, she followed the gaggle of travelers through the busy Palm Beach airport using the baggage claim signs as a guide. Each step brought a new feeling of trepidation and self-doubt. Busily, her eyes scanned the small crowd of people waiting for the new arrivals at the end of the flight terminal.

Maybe it was all some horrible joke—nobody was coming. A sick joke to laugh at the Pugsley family.

Mothers hugged children, husbands kissed wives, families greeted grandparents, and businessmen dressed in suits shook hands. Nobody even glanced at Rachel. It was like she was invisible, which seemed to be no small feat. If Lizzy Winter asked her when the baby was due … Only there was no Lizzy Winter. The plan was to meet before going to the baggage claim.

Great, Rachel thought ruefully. *I'll be abandoned in Florida and will be forced to live my life in an airport … on salted peanuts.*

"She said she'd be here," Rachel muttered to herself, shaking off her overactive imagination. "She'll be here." It sounded like a hope. Hefting her bag to a better position, she hugged her notebook like a security blanket and walked on.

She never noticed the tall, distinguished gentleman several yards behind her, following her every move. Eyes still hidden behind dark glasses, his hair was now a dark brown and hung loosely over his forehead.

Nearing the bag terminal, Rachel stopped with a jerk. Standing in front of an airport bookstore, separate from the crowd, was a haggard-looking, middle-aged woman with a beefy boy pulling on her sleeve. He had to be about nine. On her other side, a hefty girl, slightly older than the boy, looked bored as she busily typed away on her phone. All were blond and had very pale skin.

Rich people, thought Rachel. This had to be them. *Ha! If Mom only saw her precious Lizzy now. Overweight, pasty, and wearing a sour face like she just drank pickle juice.* A feeling of relief washed over Rachel. This, she knew, was a family she could deal with. They were like her. Putting on a pleasant face, she started for the family.

Distracted by her son's tugs, the woman kept searching the new arrivals—it was like she was desperately searching for somebody.

That's me, Rachel thought, smiling a little. *Rachel; meet your family for the summer in Florida. Winter family; meet your babysitter.*

In truth, Rachel was vaguely disappointed and more than a little relieved. She wanted the Winter family to be as perfect as her mother said, but knew that if they were, she wouldn't know what to do except run and hide. These kids looked like typical spoiled American brats. She could manage.

Knowing that first impressions were important, Rachel kept her shoulders firm and arched her back straight. Hastily, she smoothed out her loose-fitting blouse. She and her mother had spent the past week shopping for this trip. Against her mother's wishes, Rachel made sure to get only loose-fitting clothes that weren't too tight or too baggy—both of which made her look even fatter. For arrival, she'd chosen a dull white shirt with a pink flower on one side and jeans with sneakers. *Something simple and neat and—*

A brown smear formed across the side of her stomach where she pressed down.

She'd forgotten to wipe her hands after eating the last piece of melted chocolate during landing. Groaning, Rachel looked down at the stain. Quickly she turned to find the nearest bathroom. Too late! The boy had seen her and was now openly staring. He stopped tugging on his mom's sleeve as his fat lips gaped open.

Quickly Rachel shifted her notebook to cover the stain. Swallowing, she resolutely started again for the family. A nervous smile spread across her face.

Soon the mother and both children were looking her way. Almost as one, their faces lit up.

Rachel's smile grew broader. "Hi—"

"Daddy!" squealed the girl, stuffing her phone in her purse.

"Oh, Hank!" gasped the mother. "You're finally home! You made it!"

Rachel froze with her smile still plastered on her face … only now it looked sick with fear. The mother and children rushed by her, nearly knocking her down in the process.

"Weirdo," she distinctly heard the boy mumble as he went past.

Turning, she watched a tall man in jeans and a polo shirt catch the woman in a tight embrace. The kids joined in, leaving Rachel very much alone.

"Rachel!" called a cheerful voice. "Rachel! We're over here!"

A gorgeous model stepped from a magazine cover and parted the sea of people, heading straight for her. Rachel's eyes popped open and her stomach did a double flip. The beautiful woman was waving at her while giving her a dazzling bright smile. This was Lizzy Winter.

Vibrant golden curls poured from her finely shaped head like shining rays of sun. Her smooth, flawless face radiated a sparkling smile, highlighted by ivory-white teeth and soft-blue eyes shaded under long lashes. A shapeless pink and white dress buttoned high at the collar could do nothing to hide her beauty. Many heads turned as she passed, but she never noticed. Her eyes were only on Rachel. A purse hung from her shoulder, and two young boys followed in her wake, holding hands with another woman.

Rachel could only stare at Lizzy. The woman in front of her was exactly how her mother had described Lizzy Michaels—now

Lizzy Winter. Everything her mom had said was true … she was beyond gorgeous.

Just to confirm it, the woman smiled even wider, showing off dimples. "You look just like your mother! I can't believe you're here! I'm Elizabeth Winter! It's so good to finally meet you in person, Rachel!"

Before Rachel knew it was happening, the woman was hugging her and asking about the flight.

"Uh, it was, uh, fine," she said dully, not quite understanding what was happening. "In Atlanta there was a woman who wouldn't wake up on the plane, but that's it."

"Oh, that must have been a scene! Well, welcome to Florida! I hope you haven't been waiting long?" Mrs. Winter stood back and peered almost anxiously at Rachel.

Embarrassed by the attention, Rachel scuffed the polished floor with a shoe and shook her head. "Uh, I, uh, just got here."

The memory of noticing a pimple forming on her forehead that morning didn't help with her comfort level. Mrs. Winter, no surprise, had an unblemished face. It practically glowed as she quickly stepped aside.

"Good! Come meet my boys—oh, and my good friend Vikki Rosa. Vikki, this is Rachel!"

The woman looked to be about the same age as Mrs. Winter, but even with the figure of an hourglass, lacked the stunning beauty. Makeup and mascara couldn't hide the wrinkles forming around her eyes and mouth. Still, she held her head high and walked with a stiff upper back. Nodding coolly at Rachel, she gripped the hand of the younger of the boys tightly. Raven-black hair was mostly hidden by a wide-brimmed hat shading a pair of cool gray eyes surrounded with makeup that studied Rachel closely. With a clinging, silky, red dress hanging just past her knees, Vikki looked expensive. And her thickly painted eyes said Rachel looked cheap.

That was the biggest difference between Vikki and Mrs. Winter that struck Rachel. Mrs. Winter's kind smile and friendly personality enhanced her beauty and made her shine. Ms. Rosa's smile was cold and distant. Vikki Rosa looked like a million dollars, but Mrs. Winter made others feel like a million dollars.

"So this is the one you've been talking my ear off about," Vikki Rosa purred with a thin smile hidden under thick ruby lipstick. "I'm charmed." She sounded amused. Again, she nodded, as if she expected Rachel to bow to her or something.

"I, uh, I'm Rachel," stammered the young girl, feeling very put out. It felt as if Vikki was inspecting her as a scientist would inspect a specimen under a microscope.

Vikki Rosa smirked. "Yes, I know, dear."

Mrs. Winter smiled sweetly at Rachel. "Vikki lives just a few houses down and promises to give all the help you need."

"Yes," said the expensive woman, still smirking. "I would offer to take her children in with me—you see, I live alone—but I'm afraid I often travel." Vikki laughed lightly. "I may fly to New York or Paris, who knows where?"

"Whatever help you can provide, I'm grateful," Mrs. Winter said, giving Rachel a sideways look. "Now it's time to meet my boys—Oh, Robbie, don't pick your nose!"

Vikki's hand immediately dropped from the smaller of the boys and she stepped back almost in horror.

"I was just wiping it," the smaller of the boys said indignantly. But mischievous blue eyes sparkled, and he gave a rueful grin as he shook out both hands, wiping one on his tan slacks.

"My youngest boy," Mrs. Winter said ruefully. "He's seven and is still growing into manners."

With light curls swept back to just above his shoulders, Robbie had angelic features that probably allowed him to escape good manners. He wore a navy-blue dress shirt and red tie and looked ready for a big date. His sharp chin, wide mouth, and dimples very much resembled his mother's, and so, as Rachel would learn, did his personality.

Grinning, Robbie offered the same hand he'd just wiped.

"Hi," he said boldly, looking Rachel in the eye.

Rachel shook it limply and grunted a greeting. She could feel Vikki watching her with amusement. Never before had she felt so small … yet so fat at the same time.

"Robbie will be going to Colorado with us, unfortunately," Mrs. Winter told Rachel. She ruffled his hair. "But you'd rather stay here instead, right?"

The boy shook his head. "No, not really." Almost unconsciously, he moved closer to his mom and grabbed the edge of her dress.

"Ah, that's what you think." Mrs. Winter turned to Rachel and smiled. "And standing behind Vikki is Steven. The quiet one."

The other boy smiled shyly at Rachel. Then he moved to the other side of his mom and leaned against her side before looking up at her. "Are we still stopping for soda on the way back?" he asked.

Vikki clicked her lips and coughed. "Oh, sorry, Liz, I promised your boys I'd buy them sodas if they didn't both—if they behaved."

Putting an arm around both her sons' shoulders, Mrs. Winter sighed. "I'm not even gone and already somebody is getting spoiled. Go shake Rachel's hand first, Steven, and then you'll have your soda. But only one—a small one." She gave him a light but firm push in the back, propelling him forward. "Go on, now."

"Hi," Steven said. He barely made eye contact as he allowed a slight smile while offering a small, lean, brown hand. Rachel could tell he was a little embarrassed. His voice and manner were friendly but cautious.

Rachel almost couldn't breathe in response. Almost tentatively, she reached down and grasped the boy's hand. His grip was firm but unsure. Almost instantly she let go. In a moment of panic she wanted to turn around and run for the airplane. No way could she do this—she didn't belong here! She felt like a fat, ugly toad next to him.

Steven Winter was nothing like she'd expected at all. Slightly built, he was rail thin and a tad short for his age but possessed devastatingly good looks. He stood inches below Rachel's shoulder and had an unruly mane of thick blondish, brownish hair that curled slightly in the back and was brushed haphazardly to the side. Two long strands ran down either side of his smooth cheeks like sideburns. These framed a narrow, well-formed face with a pointed chin, wide mouth, and the softest brown eyes Rachel had ever seen. They were the shape of teardrops, each dripping inward toward his small, narrow nose. His smooth, sleek skin had been browned by the sun and seemed to glow under the airport lights. Rachel also noted, of course, that he had perfectly straight teeth the color of ivory. Carrying no visible fat, he looked especially trim in a bright white dinner suit—white pants, buttoned shirt, and beige vest with large gray buttons.

In fact, all the Winters and Vikki Rosa made Rachel appear like the toad who didn't belong. Swallowing a terribly large lump in her throat, she resisted the urge to hop away.

Perhaps Mrs. Winter noticed her distress, because she hastily pushed the boys to Vikki. "Go ahead," she said, "and we'll meet you for drinks at Mr. Coffee. I'll take Rachel to get her luggage. We'll meet you there."

"Of course, Liz," Vikki said, raising her eyebrows and giving Mrs. Winter a look. "Rachel looks as if she needs a walk. Come on, boys, let's find us a drink!"

"No cola!" called Mrs. Winter after them. Smiling at Rachel, she took her hand and gently led her through the airport. "Come, Rachel. Let's get acquainted."

Chapter Seven

Rachel swallowed a lump in her throat and allowed herself to be guided toward her luggage. She would be staying. What choice did she have?

People bustled in either direction past them, and on either side were food shops, luggage stores, and gift shops. But Mrs. Winter only paid attention to Rachel Pugsley.

"They can be a handful, my boys," she said almost apologetically. "But they are very good looking. Almost too good looking." She gave a dry laugh. "In a few years, Steven's going to have his hands full, I promise you that!" She smiled warmly at Rachel. "It's so good that you're here."

Rachel couldn't help but nod. In her chest, her heart was hammering hard—trying to get out of this situation. Didn't Mrs. Winter see it? Her boys were the popular crowd—the Trent Longs of their class! They didn't want or need a Rachel Pugsley in their lives—especially Steven. Vikki Rosa certainly understood—why didn't Mrs. Winter?

Oblivious to Rachel's distress, Mrs. Winter kept talking. "I'm sorry the girls couldn't make it. They're with their father, preparing dinner for us, so I hope you're hungry!"

"Yeah … that, uh, sounds good, Mrs. … uh …" Fumbling, Rachel threw a quick glance back at the departure gate.

Mrs. Winter squeezed Rachel's hand. "Call me Elizabeth." She couldn't stop smiling, and her voice threatened to break into musical laughter at any moment. "It's hard to believe you're Margaret's daughter and you're actually here! You have no idea how happy I feel! I know you'll look after Steven and Lisa just like your mom would, and that's what I need, Rachel."

Rachel actually blinked. "Uh, well, I'll try."

"Oh, you'll do great." Still squeezing Rachel's hand, she led the way to the baggage area, oblivious to all the stares directed her way. "I'm sure you've already noticed, Steven is a special boy."

Rachel's face flushed. How could she not notice? The kid looked like the perfect child every mom dreamed of having.

"He's quite the charmer without really even trying. Poor guy doesn't even realize it half the time." Mrs. Winter laughed breezily. "We're actually just coming from a birthday party for one of his classmates. That's why we're dressed up. That little guy seems to be invited to at least one birthday party a week." Pride was evident in her voice but also a trace of sadness that Rachel didn't understand.

Rachel nodded with a dazed expression. That explained the fancy clothes. The Winter family dressed better for birthday parties than her family ever did for church. She hadn't been invited to a birthday party since ... Well, she couldn't remember it ever happening.

A throng of Rachel's fellow plane passengers had gathered at the baggage claim and were waiting for the luggage. Rachel felt very self-conscious standing in her drab clothes next to the beautiful Mrs. Winter. If the feeling was mutual, Mrs. Winter never let it show. Asking about Rachel's parents and school without prying, she managed to put Rachel at ease. When the luggage started flowing onto the automated track and Rachel went to track down her three bulky suitcases, Mrs. Winter left for a minute, returning with a young airport employee who had a beaming smile.

"Rachel, this is Jimmy. He's going to take your suitcases to the front and wait for us there."

"Yes, ma'am," Jimmy said, never losing his smile. "Miss, you just go ahead and leave your things with me. I'll take good care of them."

"But I—" Rachel began, but Mrs. Winter's hand guided her away.

"Come, Rachel. Let's meet the others and have a cold drink. I'm sure you can use a little time to relax. Jimmy, we're in parking lot D."

"Yes, ma'am. I'll wait there." Jimmy gave a cheerful wave and started collecting Rachel's luggage.

Rachel looked back once and saw Jimmy wink at her. It must be nice being rich.

Looking like a tropical fish leaping out of water, Vikki Rosa lurched to her feet when Rachel and Mrs. Winter entered Mr. Coffee—certainly the woman in the red dress appeared as a fish out of water in the casual food shop. She sat alone in the front booth just inside the entrance. Steven and Robbie, both with Cokes, stood next to a large map of the airport just inside the coffee shop and seemed to be in a serious discussion. When Rachel neared them, it sounded like they were talking about how to get lost the quickest way and how they would survive.

"There you are," Vikki said loudly, meeting Mrs. Winter just inside the entrance. She practically ignored Rachel. "I just got a call from Richard—he's going to pick me up for a night on the town, so I must be off! Oh, and …" now she threw a quick glance at Rachel, "call me tomorrow about, you know."

Mrs. Winter accepted the hug and small peck on the cheek. "Vikki, we'll be busy tomorrow with Rachel. Remember, we're leaving in the evening."

"Yes, but I thought—"

"I'll be sure to see you before I leave. Did the boys treat you well?"

"I, well, of course they did."

Mrs. Winter waved her hand. "Thank you for coming and have a good drive back."

Vikki left with a slight frown and without a goodbye or hug to Rachel or the boys. She did give Mrs. Winter a funny look before disappearing in the crowd. Rachel didn't mind, and neither, it seemed, did the boys.

"Come, Rachel," said Mrs. Winter with a sigh as she slid easily into the open booth. "Take a seat."

Very aware of many eyes watching them, Rachel awkwardly managed to sit opposite of her. How many times did a beautiful lady sit with a slug of a teenager?

"So, overwhelmed yet?"

Surprised, Rachel looked up to see a touch of concern in Mrs. Winter's smile.

"I, uh, no," she stammered. "I think I'm just new here."

"Yes, well, you'll get used to Florida and all the wonderful people here." Mrs. Winter overplayed "wonderful" and laughed. Reaching across the table, she clutched Rachel's hands. "Oh, this reminds me of the time when I first met your mother. You know, Steven reminds me a lot of her—they both have something about them that everyone seems to naturally like. Sort of like you, I bet."

Rachel coughed and looked hastily away.

Mrs. Winter released Rachel's hands and slapped the table. "Oh, I'm sorry, I forgot! Drinks!"

Steven and Robbie, seeing their mother with Rachel, had left the map and come over to the booth.

"Hi, Mom," Robbie said. "I bet you that me and Steven could get lost in two minutes."

"And I bet you that would not be a good idea—I specifically told you rascals to not get colas! And it's 'Steven and I.' Come here, you rascals." Mrs. Winter wrapped her arms around her sons' waists and then gave each a small tap on their thighs. "And where's Rachel's drink? And mine, for that matter? Do I have two hooligans for sons or two gentlemen?"

Steven grinned slyly and shrugged. "You can have mine." He offered the can of Coke he'd been carrying that had yet to be opened.

"Ms. Rosa got them for us without asking us," Robbie explained. "So we're sharing a can. That way you can only be halfway mad."

Mrs. Winter chuckled. "I don't think it's possible to mad at you two—not even halfway." Pulling them closer, she planted a kiss on each of their foreheads. "Now go get two more drinks. I don't think Rachel wants a Coke from a boy with sweaty hands. You can share the second Coke on the way home just as long as your sisters and father never find out. Rachel, what would you like?"

"Uh, water … please."

"That's why I hired you as a babysitter," Mrs. Winter said, reaching in her purse for money. "You have manners and good sense." She produced a twenty and gave it to Steven. "Two waters, boys." She shooed them off. "Now what was I saying before? Oh, yes … do you know the story of how your mother and I first met?"

Rachel started to nod—she'd heard almost every story about Lizzy and her mom—but then she stopped herself.

"Actually, no … I don't think my mom ever told me that one."

Somehow this made Mrs. Winter's eyes twinkle and she laughed. "In that case, I could be getting into hot water. Your mom probably doesn't want you to know this, but she has a wicked sense of humor when she needs it."

Rachel smiled—she couldn't help it. Mrs. Winter was treating her like a long-lost sister. "I doubt that," she mumbled.

"Well, listen to the story, and you'll change your mind! We were babysitters, your mother and I—I'm sure your mom told you that much." Rachel nodded. "Well, I was new in Virginia and didn't know a soul. Gosh, we had to have been only thirteen. It was summertime, and the only job I could find was to babysit for the Johnsons—they had a seven-year-old girl, Mabel.

"Well, one Friday night I was going over there and your mother was walking on the other side of the street with little Danny Owens. I remember Danny, because he was missing his front teeth and always whistled when he spoke. They were eating ice cream cones on the way back to Danny's house, which was just around the corner. It was the first time I ever saw your mother and a most fortunate occurrence!

"You see, a group of boys came straight my way from around a house. Let's see, there were Darrel Long, Charlie Bufford, and a few more of their friends."

Rachel's eyes widened. Trent's and Brett's fathers knew her mother and Mrs. Winter?

"They had just finished playing football and were on their way home. Your mother swears they set it all up—that they saw me going to Mabel's house the week before and were just waiting for this chance." Mrs. Winter chuckled. "She's probably right. Darrel came straight up to me and blocked my path, not letting me move around him. I, being new, didn't know what to do, so I just stood there. I was frozen! He said he wouldn't move until I gave him a kiss—can you believe that? All his friends egged him on … you know." She rolled her eyes. "Boys trying to be cool and grown up. But Rachel, I promise, at the time I was never so scared in all my life!"

"So what happened?" Rachel asked, totally into the story. Her mother never mentioned anything like this before.

"Well," Mrs. Winter smiled mischievously. "Your mother came to the rescue."

Before she could continue, Robbie and Steven arrived with the water. Steven set both bottles on the table as Robbie hopped onto his mother's lap with a newly opened can of Coke. "Are we going now?"

"Oof, Robbie! Let's scoot some to let Steven sit. We just got our water and I've been talking to Rachel." Winking, she slid a bottle to Rachel and took the other. "It's girl talk."

"Is this a makeup talk?" Steven asked, his eyebrows lifting and a faint smile tugging at the corners of his mouth.

"They take hours!" Robbie groaned.

"No, boys. I promise, I'll never have you sit through a makeup sale again." She smiled up at Rachel. "Vikki has a small makeup company and likes to meet for sampling and sales."

"They're boring," Robbie said with feeling, visibly shuddering.

"Well, let's just keep quiet about that. This time I'm telling a story you both like. It's how I met Rachel's mother."

Steven grinned, slid into the open seat next to his mother, and leaned his head against her arm. "What part are you on?"

"Just about the good part. Now shush and listen." Picking up where she left off, Elizabeth continued the story. Robbie forgot about the Coke, and Steven made himself more comfortable against his mother's side.

Rachel again felt way out of her league, watching the family before her. Public affection was not something she was used to—her family rarely displayed any. Under the lights of the restaurant, she noticed that Steven's hair actually had a reddish tint, more of an auburn color. *Must be from his father's side.*

Then the boy's eyes found hers, and for a second their gazes locked. Rachel hastily glanced away. It was unthinkable, but the boy's deep brown eyes actually held sadness.

She directed her attention back to the story—where her mother saved Mrs. Winter.

"You should have seen the look on Darrel's face! She went right behind him without anybody noticing and stuffed her ice cream cone straight down the back of his pants. By the time his friends saw her, it was too late!"

Rachel's mouth hung open and Robbie laughed so hard that Coke threatened to spray over the table.

My mother did that? The same mother who wouldn't even let Rachel walk the half-mile to the library alone? She forgot her water.

"It gets better. Then she kicked the back of his pants right where the ice cream cone was! Chocolate splattered up his shirt, down his legs, and everywhere else!" Elizabeth had to wipe tears from her eyes and hold tightly to Robbie to keep him from rolling onto the floor.

Rachel was very aware of many stares being directed at their table, but she didn't care. Her mom had really done that?

"What happened next?" she asked.

"Before the boys could do anything, Rachel, your mom grabbed my hand with one arm and still held Danny by the other. Running, she got us into Mabel's house so fast Darrel didn't even have time to close his mouth. We ended up spending the rest of the night there until Mabel's parents came back."

"Weren't the boys mad?" Robbie asked.

"Oh, were they ever! Oh, my goodness, I'll never forget that day! They went to the windows and everything … at least until Rachel's mom went upstairs and started dropping cup bombs on their heads." She glanced down at Robbie and Steven. "And let's just say the water wasn't the cleanest."

"My mom?" Rachel asked, her eyes wide with disbelief.

"Your mom, Rachel." Mrs. Winter smiled across the table. "Ever since that day, we were best friends. She was always there for me when I needed her … just like now."

That's when Robbie spilled the Coke.

"There is no problem with the plan," breathed the man sitting at the next booth. Facing the entrance where he could see Rachel and the Winters easily, he bent his long torso low and angled his head so it appeared as if he spoke into his pocket. "All is as you said."

"Florida—it brings all types," muttered an older woman wearing bright red shorts and a hideous pink top that were both too small and too tight for her girth. Passing by with a disgusted look, she took a wide arc around the front booth where two well-dressed little boys and their young mother clamored to clean up a river of Coke that was pouring on a dumpy teenager in front of them. "Rich and poor, they're all freaks," she sniveled.

She never noticed the man rise, and fall in step just behind her. Tall, and moving with grace, the man wiped his mouth and suddenly his mustache was gone. The only thing that remained was the cold, uncaring stare hidden behind his dark glasses. By the time the woman finally noticed him, she was out of the airport and at her car, about to climb in. Then, quite suddenly, she vanished.

Lisa Winter smoldered inside. Standing at the kitchen sink, she slashed and stabbed at the lettuce, wielding the sharp knife like a warrior doing battle. Shreds of green fell in heaps into the colander below.

"Uh, honey, I think it's already dead," her father said critically from where he had paused by the kitchen table. On the way to the pool, he wore his swim trunks and carried a towel draped over his wide shoulders.

Lisa dropped the knife on the grim remains of the chopped lettuce and directed a nasty glare at him.

"Is that how you want the babysitter to see you?" she demanded.

Her father grinned. "Well, I'd rather her see me like this than see me murdering a head of lettuce, missy. And turn that glare down, before you boil my eyes." Squinting, he pretended to stumble into a chair.

Lisa stuck out her lip and snarled from the back of her throat.

"Come on, Lisa, lighten up! She won't be that bad."

"Dad, why can't we take care of ourselves?" she wailed.

Mr. Winter stared up at the ceiling. "Lisa, we've been through this already. It's illegal and," now he grinned at her, "after watching you with a knife, extremely dangerous."

"Dad!"

"Lisa, calm down … your face is turning the color of your hair again. Look, we just want somebody looking after you and your brother. We don't want you two alone if he—well, if something happens."

"But, already you have our housekeeper spending the weekends with us when you're gone! Why can't she check on us during the week when she cleans?"

"Our housekeeper, Ms. Lovington, poor woman, has graciously agreed to spend the weekends in order to give Rachel a break during that time. She'll be too busy during the week to take care of you and the cleaning."

"I can clean just fine!"

"Uh, sweetheart, I've just gone past your room. There's a swarm of beads all over the floor—only they're hidden by the pile of clothes your mother told you to hang up this morning."

"I was making Mom a necklace! And then I had to get dinner ready for that stupid babysitter!"

Mr. Winter frowned. "Enough of that, Lisa. Give her a chance. Your mother and I have to go on this trip; you know that. We want you to be safe while we're gone." He relaxed. "Now, if you want, I can have Ms. Vikki Rosa come over more often …"

Lisa nearly threw the colander of chopped lettuce at her father. "I wouldn't trust that lady with a pet rock!"

"Exactly. That's why we're getting a babysitter."

Any further attempt by Lisa to argue was thwarted by the appearance of young Margie. "How do I look, Daddy?" she asked before waltzing into the kitchen, wearing a white, two-piece suit that still managed to cover most of her short, squat body. At only five and already having been accepted into an out-of-state ballet school, she suffered from an ego much larger than her stature.

Lisa rolled her eyes. Mr. Winter grunted.

"Like a little marshmallow," he said, suddenly lunging at her. "And I'm the hungry bear who loves to eat marshmallows!"

Shrieking, Margie abandoned her walk and ran for the back door. Roaring, Mr. Winter gave chase.

Lisa watched through the window as the two ended up in the deep end of the pool with a mighty splash.

Then she heard the garage door opening. Immediately her glare returned and she went back to chopping the lettuce. The babysitter had arrived.

I want to go home, thought Rachel for the millionth time since landing. If she had red slippers she'd be clicking them three times. Instead, she stared out the passenger window of the minivan. Her suitcases were in the back behind the boys, and sporting a brand-new, hot-pink, "I LOVE FLORIDA" T-shirt, she was on her way to be a babysitter.

The Winter family lived a good thirty minutes from the airport, and Rachel felt every minute like an hour. After the Coke spill, the boys remained mostly quiet. Sitting in the back, they were now occupied with games on identical cell phones.

Staring out the window at the shops, stores, and restaurants going by, Rachel was surprised at how similar the area seemed compared to her home in Virginia—the same steamy hot weather, similar clothing and food stores, and the same heavy traffic.

Up where she lived, tourists visited the colonial and Civil War sites. In this part of Florida, old people lived in retirement and tourists came for the beaches. This meant a slightly different dress code—she was a little dismayed at the number of people walking around in outfits that would have sent them to the principal's office at her old school. At the same time, many senior citizens dressed in outfits fit for church.

This made her very self-conscious of her own looks. Right then she decided to not even try to unpack her bathing suit.

"So what do you think?" Mrs. Winter asked cheerfully. "Little bit different than home?" For most of the trip Mrs. Winter had remained quiet and allowed Rachel to soak in her new surroundings. The radio played soft classical that did nothing to fit the scenery.

"Uh, well, we don't have all the palm trees," Rachel said, knowing she sounded like an idiot. The palm trees were everywhere, dotting the medians and lining the sides of the road.

"Yes, we do have nice palm trees here. I think you'll find Florida a nice place. I really do hope you enjoy your stay here."

I just want to go home.

The boys still played their games, which suited Rachel just fine. Even with Robbie apologizing three times for spilling the Coke on her, she couldn't shake the feeling that both boys really just wanted to laugh at her … If this were her high school, she would have thought the boy had done it on purpose. Steven had at least looked chagrined at the incident, as he sat staring with pained eyes, but this only embarrassed Rachel further. His selection of the pink T-shirt to replace her ruined one did little to comfort her … it was an XL for men.

Mrs. Winter, never one to ignore a guest or let silence pass for too long, switched off the music and started telling more stories about Rachel's mom. Some Rachel had heard, but others were quite eye opening—like the one where Rachel's mom let the air out of the tires of Darrel Long's car during high school prom so he couldn't take Lizzy home.

Then the minivan turned off from a long stretch of road, with nothing but acres of flat land covered in rich, green swamp grass, and onto a rising lane dominated by large trees with towering branches. It was like entering a new world.

"Almost home," Mrs. Winter sang out.

Dougarsville, where the Winters lived, was a small town just outside of West Palm Beach where, Rachel quickly found out, millionaires liked to live. Past the first wave of trees came towering mansions and estates fit for royalty. Immaculately trimmed lawns, some decorated with flowers and carved bushes, others resembling golf-course greens, were on either side of the road. Rachel felt like they were going down the Valley of the Kings.

"This is the old part of town," Elizabeth told her. "We have a new house up a little ways."

"Oh …"

Up a little ways meant going up a twisty hill and moving into wide-open land stretching for miles. Dotted with hills and palm trees, the land was marred by large sprawling houses that almost resembled fortresses. Many had long driveways leading up to high walls of stone or tall hedges—defense against the outside, poorer world.

They passed a sprawling park with playgrounds, brand-new basketball courts, tennis courts, a baseball field, and a soccer field on the left. A sign at the entrance proclaimed that all facilities were open only to residents of Camelot Acres. A small crowd of roughly dressed teens loitered by this sign and glared at the van. Only Rachel seemed to notice, and she hastily averted her eyes.

This was getting worse and worse. Now she had to worry about gangs in the neighborhood.

Then Robbie suddenly sprang from his seat and shouted in her ear, "There's our house!"

Wincing, she looked out her window and swallowed. *That's a house?*

Rising above the van just ahead on the right, mostly hidden by a wall of immaculately trimmed bushes, a long, flat, gleaming white structure peeked down. It was like the house was so elaborate that it was ashamed to be seen in public. Rachel guessed this was the one Robbie meant. The only other house on the right was about a half mile farther up on another hill. Just behind this last house, it was like the open land finally grew too exhausted to continue. A thick gaggle of trees served as a sudden border for the upscale neighborhood. The trees extended as far as the eye could travel on either side of the neighborhood, but at the dead end, they clumped particularly close together—like these trees were curiosity seekers trying to get a view of what had replaced their wooden neighbors.

More likely the trees were left there to form a wall to keep the common people out, Rachel thought. If that was the case, though, it wasn't working.

Just before reaching the house, they passed a tall homeless man shuffling on the side of the road.

Elizabeth sighed. "That poor man is still here after all … I hadn't seen him for a while and hoped he'd moved on." She shook her head. "Some people just don't want to be helped."

She was speaking more to herself, and Rachel decided not to be nosy. Instead, she stared at the man.

Dressed in a large overcoat, which actually looked to be a woman's coat, he wore a stocking cap that left only a weathered face visible. A scruffy white beard and mustache mostly hid that. As the van passed, he stepped back and openly stared. For a second his eyes locked with Rachel's.

Blinking, Rachel shuddered. *Why is he wearing a coat?* It was well over eighty degrees out … Then she realized why. The poor man was probably wearing everything he owned. Rachel could only imagine what he thought of the towering wealth around him.

But then the minivan was pulling up the driveway.

"We're home!" announced Robbie.

Rachel forgot about the man as the house behind the hedge came into full view. *This is definitely not home!*

On top of the hill, the driveway opened into a wide space flanked by tall hedges on two sides and a long garage door. If she didn't know any better, Rachel would have thought they had arrived at a four-star hotel. Connected to the garage, the Winter family's house stretched before Rachel like it went forever. It was like five of Rachel's homes put together. It was mostly a single story, but a second floor rose in the middle like a minifortress. On one side of the double story was a flat roof hanging over the edge. A long balcony covered by an awning supported by white pillars loomed above the garage. Rachel's breath was taken away. Gleaming box windows almost as tall as she was lined the front of the house. She saw at least three doors in the front. Which was the main door?

"Oh, I almost forgot," Mrs. Winter said, pushing a button that smoothly opened the garage door. "You brought your swimsuit, right? We promised Margie one last family swim before dinner."

"Sw-swim? Where?" Rachel asked, dazed. She didn't remember seeing a pool back at the park.

"In the backyard," Robbie said, pulling open the door. He laughed when seeing Rachel's face. "Everyone has a pool here!"

Steven smirked, putting down his phone. "Last one changed has to take the garbage out tonight!"

"Hold on, boys! Let's help unload Rachel's suitcases first!"

It was too late. Steven and Robbie were out of the van like a shot and scrambling for the front door—the middle door, Rachel noted.

Mrs. Winter grinned at Rachel. "Well, welcome to our home."

"Thanks … Don't worry, I'll, uh, I'll get my suitcases."

"We'll just put them in the garage and Doug will carry them to your room. First, I want you to come in and meet everyone else." Reaching out, she suddenly touched Rachel's sleeve. "Thank you for coming. Really."

Blushing, Rachel ducked her head. "I, I think, uh, Steven is … nice."

"Oh, don't worry about him. He hasn't spoken to you, but that's his way. He's just feeling you out." She sighed. "The one you have to worry about is Lisa. I'm afraid she hasn't quite accepted the fact that we're leaving."

Rachel gave a sickly smile. "Oh, I'm sure it'll be fine."

Chapter Eight

Lisa gripped the knife tightly before slowly placing it on the counter next to the sink.

Better not tempt myself, she thought, smiling grimly.

Moving to the front of the house, she tried to breathe deeply while wiping her hands on her shirt.

It'll be a nice, wonderful babysitter—somebody straight out of The Baby-Sitters Club, she thought. Then she snorted. *I bet she's bright, perky, and full of cheesy jokes.*

And I'd like to cram every one down her throat! She hated *The Baby-Sitters Club.* Striking a bored pose, she leaned against the stair railing and watched the front door with false disinterest.

A thump announced their arrival, and it flew open so suddenly that Lisa was caught off guard.

Startled, Lisa leaned back and lost her balance. Falling to the hard floor with a thump, she watched Robbie and Steven tear toward her, each kicking off his shoes and laughing like maniacs. They were doing their best to get in each other's way.

"Hey!" she protested sharply. "What are you idiots doing?"

"What are you doing?" Robbie shot back, racing to the stairs. "Falling?"

"Stop!" Lisa shouted.

Steven caught up to Robbie and neatly wrapped an arm around his waist. At the same time, he twisted on his heel and took a quick seat on the bottom step, abruptly thumping his brother down next to him.

"Time out!"

"Ouch!"

Lisa pushed herself up from the floor. "You two are such idiots."

Steven put an arm around Robbie's shoulder. Both boys were breathing hard. "You're the one sitting on the floor," Steven pointed out, giving her his half smile.

"Yeah, you're the one sitting on the floor," parroted Robbie, stifling a giggle.

Lisa frowned. The two of them always ganged up on her, without fail. "Only because you knocked me there with your stench! Where's Mom?"

"Still talking to the babysitter," Steven said.

"No kidding," huffed Lisa. "I thought she might be flying to Pluto. What's she like?"

"Mom?" asked Steven with a grin.

"The babysitter, stupid!"

Robbie shrugged. "Fat. And she didn't know we had a pool."

Steven jabbed him in the ribs. "Not everyone has a pool."

Lisa sniffed. "And everyone is fat compared to you two. What does she act like?"

"Well, she didn't get mad at me for spilling Coke on her."

"Not yet," grinned Steven. "Mom will do that later."

"Come on, guys. This is serious!"

Steven suddenly shot to his feet. "Not right now—we're racing for the pool. Time in!"

"No fair!"

Laughing, the boys fought their way up the stairs, leaving Lisa to grit her teeth and wish she had only sisters.

From outside the door, left wide open by the boys, she heard her mother's voice coming closer. Gasping, Lisa ran for the stairs after Steven and Robbie.

At the top of the stairs, she found her brothers in various states of dress, in front of the bathroom.

"Hey!" shouted Steven when seeing her. "You're supposed to be downstairs!" In his boxers with his dress shirt and vest still buttoned, he looked like a young rooster about to crow. His thin chicken legs were very apparent.

Lisa eyed his legs and made a face. She was about to say something sharp when she heard a strange voice mixed with her mom's. "Shh!" she said quickly. "The babysitter is coming!"

Robbie yanked off his dress shirt, dropping it to the floor. "What are you going to do?"

"Just watch. Now hush!" She knelt at the top of the stairs and peered down, hiding behind the banister.

Their mom laughed at something said by the stranger. Lisa frowned. The babysitter had a dull monotone voice, which sounded quite boring.

Robbie crouched beside Lisa, and Steven stood above, leaning over to peer down.

"Don't breathe on me," Lisa growled to Robbie. "Your breath stinks."

"Shh," Steven shushed. "They're here!"

Lisa licked her lips and watched the bottom of the stairs intently.

First, their mom came in, and then came an overweight, pasty teenage girl with lank brown hair that hadn't seen a good brushing for a long time. She clutched a notebook tightly to her chest like it was a security blanket.

Lisa's heart sank. This was even worse than she imagined! Robbie was right; the babysitter was fat! And ugly! And boring looking … she could go on. Every horror she imagined the babysitter to be was standing just below her.

"Where is everybody?" their mom said, closing the door. "It's never this quiet here."

"Should I take off my shoes?" The babysitter was eyeing Steven's and Robbie's loafers littering the front room.

"Oh, that would be great—just make yourself at home."

"I, uh, like the plants."

"Yes, they're quite something, aren't they? Lisa takes good care of them."

Lisa's face burned. Two potted trees were on either side of the door—prizes she'd won back in the third grade when they were shrubs. Now their slender trunks rose almost to the ceiling.

"She may have hair redder than cherries, but her thumb is definitely green."

Robbie nudged Lisa and grinned. "Mom just said you pick your nose with your thumb," he whispered.

Steven stifled a laugh.

"Shut it," hissed Lisa.

Thankfully, their mom was taking the babysitter toward the back of the house and didn't hear.

"I can't imagine where the kids went—Lisa was going to make dinner."

Steven nudged Robbie in the back with his knee. Unseen by Lisa, the boys made brief eye contact.

"Lisa's up here!" they suddenly called out loudly. Then it was a sprint for their room.

Horrified, Lisa couldn't even manage a good whack at either of them before she was left alone at the top of the steps with her mother calling her.

"Lisa, come down and meet Rachel! She's been dying to meet you! Hurry up before she thinks we only have boys here!"

"It's my brothers who will be dying," Lisa muttered to herself. Getting to her feet, she marched with as much dignity as she could muster down the stairs to where her mother and the babysitter—*Rachel*—stood waiting for her.

"Rachel, this is our oldest. Lisa, Rachel has been waiting to meet you for over a month."

Well, thought Lisa, *she certainly doesn't look too excited to see me now!* Rachel's face looked almost fearful, and the girl held out her hand awkwardly. Ignoring it, Lisa gave a slight smile.

Rachel grunted and choked out a greeting.

"Do you want to help Rachel get some of her luggage upstairs, Lisa," said her mom, like it wasn't really a question. "She needs to find her bathing suit."

"No, thanks," Lisa said stiffly. "I have to get dinner ready." With that, she marched toward the kitchen, passing Rachel without another glance.

"Well," laughed her mom, a little forcedly. "Let me show you your room then."

"Be careful," warned Lisa from the kitchen, almost regretting it. "Steven and Robbie are getting changed up there."

Rachel couldn't get the fearful feeling out of her stomach—it sat like a lead balloon that constantly expanded. It was only a matter of time before it exploded. Nothing was like Rachel had imagined and everything was like she feared. One thing was certain, the kids, especially Lisa, would never like her. Following Mrs. Winter to the stairs, she felt like the houseguest nobody wanted.

"Okay, boys!" hollered up Mrs. Winter, looking back at Rachel to roll her eyes. "The women are coming up, so you better be in your room or decent!"

"I can't find my bathing suit!" yelled Robbie's voice.

"Just put on shorts, but hurry up and clear the way!" A scramble of feet pattered on the ceiling and then a door slammed. "Don't worry," Mrs. Winter told Rachel. "It's not always like this. Sometimes it's worse."

Swallowing, Rachel only nodded.

Keeping a bright smile, Mrs. Winter led the way up to a spacious floor divided into two hallways—one straight ahead and one to the left. The hall to the left was strewn with Steven's and Robbie's clothes. A loud thump came from one of the rooms near the end.

"I'll deal with that later. Your room is straight ahead on the right, next to ours. It should have everything ready for you. We had it especially designed for a long-term guest."

"That, uh, that sounds great," Rachel grunted.

"If you like, we can go back down now and find the suitcase with your bathing suit at least. You have your own bathroom and can change."

"Oh, no," Rachel said hastily. "Actually, I would, uh, really like to take a walk around your neighborhood for a bit."

"Are you sure?" asked Mrs. Winter doubtfully. "A swim will feel good after a long flight."

"Uh, yes." Rachel gulped. She wanted to take a long flight right now and go back home. Instead, she mustered up her courage. "After sitting so long, uh, I think it would be good to walk. Also, it'll be a chance to look around the neighborhood."

"Well, would you like company?"

"That's okay," Rachel quickly replied. "It'd be good to be alone … I could get a feel for this place and, uh, make it feel more like home."

Mrs. Winter smiled widely. "I think that's a great idea! We have a pretty safe neighborhood, but bring your phone just in case. The plan is to have supper at six, so you have an hour to relax and get comfortable before then. Let me show you your room, and then I'll go hunt down my husband so you can meet him. We'll let him bring up your luggage. I have a feeling he's already in the pool. But first, to your room!"

In Virginia, Rachel lived in a small, three-bedroom, brick house plopped on a shrunken patch of grass and squeezed tightly between other houses just as small. Her room was just big enough to fit her bed, bookcase, dresser, and computer without being too cluttered to move around in. In other words, her room in Virginia was about the size of the closet in her room in Florida.

A queen-size bed took the back corner next to a large window that took up most of the wall. To the right was a full bathroom with a tub the size of a small pool. With the closet on the left, there was a dresser, a metal-framed bookcase—mostly empty except for a stack of magazines—and a small desk with a lamp.

At least I have space to write, Rachel thought as she walked in with dazzled eyes. She hadn't let go of her notebook since saving it from Robbie's Coke spill. Now she gently placed it on her desk—*her own desk.*

Mrs. Winter excused herself to check on the boys and told her to come down whenever she was ready.

Rachel didn't think she'd ever be ready. *I can't be a mole and hide,* she thought. *Let's get this over with.* Taking a deep breath, she left her room and started for the stairs. Reaching the hallway junction, she heard a shout and a slam.

Robbie flew out of the bathroom dressed in a red bathing suit and socks. From down the hall, Steven raced from a room in a dark-blue bathing suit and light-blue T-shirt. Racing for the stairs, the boys saw Rachel at the last moment.

"Look out!" Robbie threw out his arms for balance and slid on the hard, gray floor to keep from plowing into her. Steven crashed into his back and the boys tumbled to Rachel's feet.

Rachel jumped back and was at a loss for words. "Oh my, uh, are you okay?"

"I think we tied," groaned Robbie, staring at Rachel's feet.

"Nice going," Steven muttered, getting to his feet. Pulling up his brother, he smiled sheepishly at Rachel. "Sorry … We're not supposed to run in the house, but don't tell our mom … please."

"I, uh, okay …" She choked out a return smile and moved aside. Following the boys at a more sedate pace down the stairs, she wondered if she should have been more forceful or concerned. She chose neither. Then she met their father.

"Hi, there!" Tousling his dark hair with a towel, Mr. Winter greeted Rachel in the open room in front of the kitchen. Stepping around a sofa, he extended his muscular arm and grinned. "I'm Doug."

"Oh, nice to meet you, Mr.—"

"Doug." He crushed Rachel's hand in a firm grip and pumped vigorously.

"And call me Elizabeth," Mrs. Winter called from the kitchen. "Now that you're eighteen and finished high school, you're a true adult, remember."

Lisa audibly snorted, but Rachel didn't notice. She couldn't help but stare at Mr. Winter—er, Doug. Wrapping the towel around his neck, he breathed in deeply. "So how was the flight down here?"

"Great," she murmured, staring at his well-muscled chest. "Uh, I mean, okay."

"Good. Well, how about a tour of the house?"

"Doug, actually I thought you would give her a hand with her suitcases. They're in the garage."

"Of course! Here's the first one!" Moving past Rachel, Doug swooped down and grabbed Robbie before the boy could react. Easily lifting him, he threw the boy over his shoulder, bouncing him up once so he could grab his legs. "Now, ladies and gentlemen, let us embark on the tour of the Winter home—where it's always summer!"

Lisa groaned from the kitchen.

"Dad!" protested Robbie. "You're soaking wet!"

"Hush! You're the tour guide. Steven, you lead the way."

Watching with lifted eyebrows, Steven shrugged with his half grin. "No, thanks. I think I'll watch."

"I'll do it! I'll lead the way!" A tiny girl about five burst from the kitchen and skidded to a halt. Dripping wet in a bathing suit, her blond hair plastered to her skin, she beamed up at Rachel. "I'm Margie and I'm five years old."

Rachel grinned and nodded. "I'm Rachel."

"Fine, Margie-and-I'm-five-years-old," Mr. Winter said. "You're hired. Lead the way! We'll give Rachel the grand tour and then carry up her luggage."

"Doug, don't take too long," Elizabeth Winter called. "Let's give Rachel time to relax—and don't drip water everywhere!"

"He's just dripping on the floor, Mom!" Robbie called. This earned a slap on the rump.

"Start talking, tour guide," ordered Mr. Winter. "I want the accent like the guy we had in France. It'll make our home even grander."

Robbie giggled. "Ah, Dad!"

"Now!" growled his father.

"The TV room first!" cried Margie.

"Okaze," Robbie managed to say through trying not to laugh. "Thiz way!"

Rachel had no choice. She got the grand tour of the Winter home, complete with a terrible accent.

While the outside of the Winters' house resembled a fancy motel, the inside was more like an upscale resort with the comforts of home. Everything was gleaming white or a soft gray. Potted trees and plants were in every room, and the furniture was modern and sleek. Hard gray floor led to pure white carpet. What amazed Rachel the most was the lack of dust, dirt, and stains. There had to be a team of maids that cleaned daily to keep such a large house so clean. Going through room after room, Rachel was quickly lost.

"Andz now we iz backs to the el kitchenz!" Robbie said in a horrible accent. Bouncing from his dad's shoulder, hanging mostly upside down, he flourished a hand.

"Not yet, Robbie," his father said. "We're in the sitting room."

"Well," Robbie protested, "I can't see where we're going!"

"Just keep talking," Mr. Winter said. "You still with us, Rachel?"

Rachel swallowed. She'd rather not be with them. "Uh, yes … thank you."

Steven looked up from the sofa with a lopsided grin. "I bet she wishes she wasn't," he said, crossing his arms. It was the first time he'd spoken about Rachel. She wondered if the boy knew how right he was when saying it. Why had she ever agreed to come to Florida?

Mr. Winter shook a fist at him. "Okay, Steven, we'll deal with you later." And the tour moved on.

"Now," proclaimed Robbie, "we iz in the kitchenz!"

Sure enough, Rachel somehow found herself almost where they had started.

Lisa glared from behind a counter made of solid marble. "Mom is waiting at the pool. She wants you to hurry up."

Robbie ignored her. "Thiz iz where we dooz the cookingsz!"

"And where Lisa steams too," joked Mr. Winter.

Lisa didn't even smile.

Rachel grimaced. Behind Lisa were gray walls, spotless cabinets, a stove, and an oven. While clean and neat, it appeared very cold—much like Lisa.

Whirling toward the stairs, Robbie flung an arm, pointing through the kitchen to where more rooms were. "Behindz thee kitchenz iz the garagez and another sittingz roomz."

"Behind? Did you just say 'behind'?" Mr. Winter tossed Robbie up higher on his shoulder and smacked him lightly. "There. There is the behind!"

"Dad!" Robbie smacked his dad's shoulder.

"What?" asked his father. "You asked for it."

Robbie kneed him in the chest before continuing. "Andz herez iz the bestz partz," Robbie said, flinging an arm to the left. "Itz the place wherez Dad spendz the mostz timez—the bathz roomz."

"Oookaayy, I think the tour is over." Doug slid Robbie to the floor and ruffled his hair. "Nice job, tour guide."

Robbie stuck up an open palm. "Now give me my tip!"

Mr. Winter slapped the hand. "Sure, never order burritos on your first date. You kids go ahead to the pool, and I'll get the suitcases with Rachel."

"I want to go too," Margie said, latching herself to Rachel's leg.

"Good idea," said Mr. Winter. "You can continue leading the way. Robbie, go get wet. And Steven? Go soak yourself too."

When Doug finished bringing the last suitcase to Rachel's room, he leaned against the wall and groaned. "Oh, boy, I forgot teenage girls liked to collect rocks."

Rachel grunted from where she was helping Margie unpack her shoes. "Thank you for carrying them up … I don't think I could have done it."

"Oh, sure. Not a problem. I always could do with more weightlifting. We're just happy you're here … I know it can't be easy for you yet." He rubbed the back of his head and grinned ruefully. "Lisa … can be a tad difficult, you might have noticed."

"Oh, uh, well, she's fine," Rachel said lamely.

"Well, she will be. She's nearly a teenager and is trying to grow up a little too fast. Just keep being calm and she'll come around." He nodded at the window and the brilliant blue sky. "Lisa is sort of like the weather here. It can be nice and sunny, but have no doubt, it'll storm while you're here." He gave Rachel a dazzling grin. "Lisa will calm down and become sunny again. You'll see."

Rachel nodded and did her best to meet Doug's eyes. "I'm sure it's hard for her."

"Yeah, oh, hey, Margie! Don't go near the bed with your wet suit! Come on. Let's go to the pool before the boys dirty the water too much." He looked at Rachel. "Will you be coming to the pool?"

"Oh, uh, I told, er, Mrs. … Elizabeth, that I, uh, I would take a walk instead … to stretch out." Her face was burning and turning a shade that resembled Lisa's hair.

"Oh. Well, have fun. Come on, Margie."

"Just a second, Daddy!" Before following her father, Margie bit her lower lip and then looked up at Rachel with calculating eyes. "Rachel, what rocks did you bring? Can I have one?"

Smiling, Rachel leaned down to the girl. "Well, actually, I'll tell you a secret. I didn't bring any rocks. They're really books."

"Oh." Margie nodded seriously. "I like books. Can I have one? Please?"

"Uh, we'll see."

Margie then dashed from the room. "Guess what?" she yelled excitedly. "The babysitter is going to give me one of her books!"

Sighing, Rachel flopped backward on her oversized bed, sinking into the cushions. *This is going to be a nightmare …*

Mr. and Mrs. Winter, or Doug and Elizabeth—she was going to have to practice saying their names—were the perfect couple. Good looking and rich. And their kids were just like them. So how could she, dumpy Rachel who'd never had a friend, ever expect to give orders and run this household?

Suddenly she felt as if she was drowning and she struggled to sit upright.

If only Lisa and Steven were leaving and Robbie and Margie were staying … they seem much nicer. She knew Lisa already hated her. And Steven … well, he just didn't care about her. *They're like the kids at home … no way do they want to associate with me—I'm too low for them.* She groaned. *What am I going to do?*

She ended up calling home and having a long talk with her mom. It took only a minute before tears started falling.

"So," Lisa said carefully, running water over the very finely chopped lettuce. "What do you think of her? You know, *really* think of her."

Shrugging, Steven slouched on a stool by the counter and fingered a glass of iced lemonade. He didn't look at his sister. "What do you mean?"

"Well, you know … did you feel anything?"

His eyes tightened. "Huh?"

Sighing, Lisa shut off the water. "Look, Steven. I just want to make sure Mom and Dad made the right decision getting this girl from *Virginia.*" She made Virginia sound like a bad name. "Okay? Because I don't think we need a babysitter!"

"Well … I think I'm going to the pool now."

"Steven, if you're not with me on this, then … then you're an idiot!"

Steven twisted his lips and gave his sister an annoyed look. "What do you want me to do?"

"I don't know, try to understand her by—" She stopped as Steven gave her a cool, measured look. Going any further would be dangerous. "I-I guess you're right … let me handle it."

Steven relaxed and gave a hint of a smile. "Does that mean you're putting something gross in her food? That'll make our day."

Lisa's face brightened. "Now you're talking! Do you think you can find some ants outside? Gosh, Mom would go bananas!"

"Don't you mean antsy?"

Lisa snorted. "Yeah, it is a nice thought …" Then she sighed. "But I guess it would be wrong to mess up Mom and Dad's last night. Well, go ahead to the pool."

Steven put down his glass and hopped off the stool. "Aren't you coming?"

"No, I'll finish dinner and think about what to do about Rachel."

"Just don't put worms in my spaghetti," Steven said.

Lisa watched him walk to the glass door leading out to the pool. He was so small and innocent … but the nightmares had come back. That meant his beast was stirring …

Could it be because of Rachel's coming? If so, then Lisa would definitely do something. She would do anything to protect her little brother. Especially from some rotten babysitter.

Rachel turned off her cell phone and wiped the remaining tears from her eyes. Not even an hour in Florida and already she was crying.

"You have to make the best of it, Rachel," her mom had said after listening to her blubber like a baby. "You're a great person, and I think Lisa just needs a friend. To make a friend, you have to be a friend. Just keep being yourself and have patience. Lizzy told me about Lisa—she's growing up fast and she's scared. You'll be a good role model for her. Rachel, do you hear me? Rachel?"

Role model for Lisa? *More like I'll be a good target for her,* Rachel thought. The sound of high-pitched squealing from outside interrupted her thoughts. Moving to the window overlooking the backyard, she looked out and saw the pool.

"Wow …" was all she could say. Their backyard was impressive, just like the rest of the house.

A large, gleaming, white paved surface ran the length of the house and extended out several feet before ending in a drop-off. From there, stairs led to a beautiful flower garden bordered by tall hedges that ran around the property like a fence. To the left of the stairs and built into the pavement was a full-sized swimming pool. There, the entire Winter family, minus Lisa, was enjoying the sunshine. Doug and Elizabeth swam laps near where Robbie was doing cannonballs off the side. Steven lay on his stomach at the end of the pool closest to the house, facing Margie, who was in a similar position. It almost looked as if they were pint-sized sweethearts saying their goodbyes.

Rachel breathed out deeply. How would Steven ever accept her as a babysitter? She eyed his lean, brown back and dark auburn hair glinting in the falling sun. No good-looking, athletic, nine-year-old boy was going to like her. And Lisa … the girl was probably downstairs sharpening a knife or something.

Rachel shuddered. *I can't think such thoughts!* She had to get out of there. Fast.

Stuffing her cell phone into her pocket, she stopped. Looking down at her touristy shirt, she grimaced. Finding a new shirt from her bag—a nice button-down blouse—she quickly changed and grabbed her notebook and a pencil. It was time for that solitary walk.

Before she left, though, she couldn't help but take another peek at the perfect family by the pool. Something was puzzling her …

She was relieved to find the kitchen empty of people. A bowl of salad was on the counter and pot of finished spaghetti sat on the stone. Lisa was not to be seen. Taking a breath, Rachel moved through and into the sitting room Robbie had mentioned on the tour. Like most of the rooms, the walls bordering the outside were almost all windows. Feeling a little guilty for spying, Rachel took a closer look at the family.

Steven still faced Margie, his back half almost completely lost in his baggy swimsuit that went well past his knees. His torso was long and lean—and bent at an extreme angle without causing any discomfort. The boy lay with his stomach flat on the pavement, but still leaned on his elbows.

It's like he has a rubber spine.

On the other hand, Margie, a star ballerina and younger, was not nearly as flexible. She had to bend at the waist and could barely arch her back as she rested on her elbows.

The two were nothing alike in looks. Margie definitely resembled her mother—her light blond hair, very straight, and soft facial features were just like a younger version of Elizabeth's. The same was true with Robbie, but with Doug's chin and nose. Steven, on the other hand, had unruly auburn hair and sleek features that bore no resemblance to any family member … And Lisa's fire-red hair and round face, where did that come from?

"He's adopted, like me," said a voice from behind, causing her to jump nearly out of her skin.

Nearly shrieking, Rachel caught herself just in time. Grasping at her heart, she took several deep breaths. "Oh, my—you scared me!"

Lisa stood just inside the room with her arms crossed while she glared at Rachel. "What are you doing? You're wondering about Steven, aren't you?"

Rachel blushed. "Oh, uh, I was, uh, just going for a walk …" She trailed off.

"The front door is on the other side of the house." Hostility filled Lisa's tone like lead in a balloon.

Trying hard not to panic, Rachel nodded. "I know … I just wanted to look at your family … they're, uh, really nice."

"I saw you looking at Steven and my parents," accused Lisa. "I know what you were thinking. Steven and I aren't really part of the family, okay? I was adopted when I was a baby. Steven came when he was four."

Rachel swallowed uncomfortably. Could she believe Lisa? Elizabeth had never mentioned any of this. Still … she peeked quickly out the window again. It would make sense.

"I don't," she stammered. "I, uh, I know your parents think you're a part of the family."

"What do you know?" Lisa sneered. Wearing jeans and a bright pink shirt, she stood tall and skinny like a flower next to an ugly shrub. Even though she was inches shorter than Rachel, she still managed to stare down on her. "Doug and Elizabeth are kind to everybody." *Even fat babysitters,* she didn't say, but clearly meant.

Feeling awkward in her blouse and baggy jeans, Rachel knew she was no match for the young girl. Self-consciously covering her girth, she swallowed. "I, I do know they'll miss you …"

"Ha!" Lisa snorted derisively. "They're leaving me with you, aren't they? You don't know us, so don't even try." She took a quick breath. "But don't worry. Our housekeeper is coming during the week to check on us. So you don't really have to do a thing. We'll take care of you. Now, I'm going back to finish making dinner. Enjoy your walk."

To make a friend, be a friend. Rachel gritted her teeth and managed to look up with some form of a smile. "Oh … maybe I can help," she practically mumbled and instantly regretted her words.

Lisa sniffed and actually looked Rachel up and down. "I don't think your type of cooking is good for us. I'll see you at supper." It sounded like a challenge and a dismissal all in one. It felt like a slap in the face.

Stunned, Rachel was left alone as Lisa whirled and returned to the kitchen. Taking rapid breaths, she saw that her hands were shaking. And she had to pass through the kitchen to reach the front door …

Somehow Rachel reached the front door. In her wake, Lisa whistled a jaunty tune.

Chapter Nine

As Rachel stumbled to a form of temporary freedom, back in the pool it looked as if things were getting serious. Steven's and Margie's hands were almost touching, and they were looking deeply into each other's eyes.

Their dad, sitting across the pool with their mom and Robbie, cupped his hands to his mouth.

"Steven, Margie, what are you doing? Marriage proposals between brother and sister are not allowed in this state! Besides, you're both too young!"

"Doug!" admonished Mrs. Winter, trying hard not to laugh.

Embarrassed, the children looked over at their parents. Steven wore a sheepish expression while Margie just frowned.

"Dad, don't be stupid!" she said. "I made Steven promise to watch my room and all my books with all his heart while I'm gone. Rachel promised to give me a new one. We were doing the finger promise."

"Leave your poor brother alone, dear," Elizabeth called. "I have to stop reading you fairy tales at night."

"Well," breathed Margie indignantly. "I'm going to miss Steven!"

"C'mon over here, you two," Doug said, waving them over. "No, better yet, we'll come to you. We need one last family hug before supper." To the side, he muttered, "Maybe Lisa will see us and actually join us for a change."

"Give her time, Doug. She'll come around."

"Right."

Soon the family, except for Lisa, sat together at the edge of the pool with their feet dangling in the water. Enjoying the peaceful evening, they each became lost in their own thoughts … until Robbie grew bored and dove face-first in the water.

"Careful!" cried Elizabeth, raising a hand to ward off the splashing.

"I'll get a towel," Steven said quickly, rising to his feet.

Doug chuckled, wiping water from his face. "Asking Robbie to sit still is like asking the government to stop spending."

"Mom?" asked Margie, scooting close to her mother. "Does Steven have to stay here?"

"I'm sorry, dear, but Steven and Lisa still have school, sweetie … in fact, Steven has two weeks left, poor guy."

"It's not fair!" Margie kicked the water angrily.

"Margie, what's wrong?" Elizabeth looked down at her daughter, who had suddenly burst into tears.

Returning with a towel, Steven dropped it and leaned between his parents, putting arms on each of their shoulders. He stared at his younger sister with concern. "Don't worry, Margie, you'll have fun."

"But I want you to come too!"

"Margie," Doug said. "Steven will miss us too, but he has to stay here for his school and swim-team practice. You should be happy, because he's going to have a lot of fun. Right, guy?"

Now kneeling between his parents, Steven grinned. "Yeah, you should just feel sorry for the babysitter."

Doug chuckled and patted Steven's back. "Yes, she does have her work cut out for her, doesn't she?"

"Why do you say that?" Elizabeth retained a smile but narrowed her eyes as she turned from Margie to her husband.

"Well," Doug began, "for one, she and Lisa don't quite get along."

"Nobody gets along with Lisa right now. I know Rachel's mom, and if she's anything like her, I think you're underestimating her."

Doug snorted. "I hope so … I would hate to find out in Colorado our babysitter quit on us and needs a flight home to Virginia."

"Don't say that! She's going to be fine. You'll see."

Doug poked Steven in the ribs playfully. "I think you better be on your best behavior to make sure that's true."

Grinning, Steven said, "Sure, Dad."

"I mean it, guy." Doug held up a hand in front of him, holding it horizontal in the air. "You see my hand? That's Rachel right now. She's wavering." He started shaking his hand back and forth. "Lisa sort of rocked her world, and guess what happens if you decide to jump on her now?"

Steven eyed the hand seriously. "She falls?"

"No, guy, you fall!" Doug jabbed the hand in Steven's middle and started tickling him. Steven cried out and retreated by leaning on his mom.

"Oh, that's great," Elizabeth laughed. "Wonderful speech."

Doug relented his tickling and slapped Steven's thigh. "Ah, I'm sure you're right. Rachel will be fine. Now say a nice goodbye to your mother, guy. I'm going to teach Robbie it isn't nice to splash people." Ducking his head, he also went headfirst into the water, sending a great splash behind him.

"Oh, if I wasn't married to him!" groaned Elizabeth, wiping her eyes.

Steven moved behind her and wrapped both arms around her shoulders, giving a hug from behind. "You wouldn't have me, right?" He planted a kiss on her cheek.

Laughing, Elizabeth grabbed his wrists and squeezed tightly. "Oh, Steven, I'm so going to miss you. You always will be my little guy."

Boy and mother stayed there for a while, neither wanting to let go. They shared a special bond that few children and mothers had—it was a bond of infinite love that could never be broken.

"Hey," shouted Doug from the other end of the pool where he was wrestling with Robbie. "I'm still married to your mother, guy!"

"Ignore him," Elizabeth said loudly. "You're a much better kisser."

It didn't take long for a splashing war to break out.

In the meantime, Rachel was dealing with her own splashes. Fat tears dropped steadily as she reached the end of the driveway.

This is too much—I'm a babysitter, I can't cry!

The number one rule of babysitting was to never take anything personally. Babysitters didn't deal with brats. Instead, their charges were responsibilities—something precious. A brat could be ignored or treated with disdain. But if Rachel ever hurt Steven or Lisa in any way, it would mean she had failed in her job. If Lisa wanted to be mean, then Rachel just had to roll with it. She had to take Lisa's punches and move on. Lisa's barbs stung now, but Rachel would return … unfortunately for her.

I can't quit yet.

Wiping her eyes with the back of her hand, she sniffed. With her notebook under her other arm, she at least had an outlet. Once her father had told her, half in jest, that if she ever wanted to be a great writer, all she had to do was go out in the world and hit rock bottom—do everything wrong, fail, become miserable, and then write a book about recovering. The public loved such stories.

Thinking about it now, Rachel actually smiled. Just maybe the time had come for her great story of recovery—*The Fall and Rise of the Fat Babysitter* by Rachel Pugsley.

Feeling better, she started walking toward the park with the sun bouncing on her hair. The street was empty and she felt small walking between the enormous houses that were staring down on her from both sides of the street.

As she walked, she thought of everything that had happened that day—it was hard to believe she hadn't even been in Florida for a single day yet and already she felt she'd experienced so much. Suddenly, she felt the urge to write.

Mind running in circles, she reached the park. Hearing voices, she looked around and saw a family of kids on the soccer field. Not wanting to bother them—or rather, not wanting to be bothered by them—she sat on the curb next to the park's sign.

Opening her notebook to a blank page, she smoothed the paper. A thrill ran down her spine and soon an avalanche of thought tumbled from her head and onto the paper. All that she struggled to say came out so easily in words …

You won't beat me, Lisa … you'll see. The pen is always mightier …

She'd been writing for some time when she became aware of the shadow. Evening was approaching, but the sky remained clear and a warm summer breeze felt more soothing than bothersome. Yet inside the shadow, Rachel suddenly felt cold. Putting her pencil down on the notebook, she slowly looked up.

At first she only saw a dark shadow standing almost on top of her.

"Well, well," purred the shadow tauntingly. "I guess she has a brain after all. I was starting to think you was dead, girl."

Suddenly scared, Rachel made the shadow out to be a tall boy a few years younger than she, with sharp, handsome, but cruel looks. His skin was a rich chocolate brown and his entire head was shaved to black stubble. This highlighted his lean cheekbones and broad nose. Wearing a ragged, white tank top pressed tightly against a flat stomach, his bare arms glistened with sweat and were packed with muscle. Wide jeans hung loose low on his hips, and Rachel got a good look at faded red boxers. Her gaze fell to his large high-top sneakers. Her face burned. The scariest part of the boy was his eyes. Bright green, they glinted with cruelty and bore into her without mercy. He stared down at her like she was a piece of dirt needing to be kicked.

Snide chuckles came from behind the boy. Her mouth shaking, Rachel forced herself to look up. Three more rough youths stood in a sloppy row behind their leader, to serve as an audience. Rachel was surprised to see a young girl about Lisa's age in the mix. Standing just to the right of the tall boy, the girl crossed her arms and sneered at Rachel.

Rachel quickly averted her gaze.

To the girl's immediate right, a heavyset teen with buckteeth grinned crookedly. On the opposite side of the leader stood a rail-thin teen with a long, scrawny neck and blond hair cut so badly it looked as if it had been bushwhacked in the dark. He was inches taller than the leader, but too goofy looking to appear tougher. With skin so pale that it appeared almost bleached, he resembled a corncob with part of the husk still on his head. The girl and the hefty teen had dark skin and identical eyes so they looked like brother and sister … especially the way they wore identical scornful looks.

The message was clear. Rachel had no friends here.

Swallowing, Rachel fought hard not to panic. In Virginia, bullying was something that mostly left her alone. By ignoring the stares and odd comments, she had blended into the background and escaped most of the harassment that sometimes plagued high schools. Bullies only had fun when they got a reaction. Here in Florida, she hoped the local toughs played by the same rules.

"What's the matter, girl?" barked the heavy, bucktoothed teen in a deep voice. "Can't you talk?"

"Relax, Toothy," grinned the leader, revealing slightly crooked white teeth. "Don't you know? Only good-looking chicks talk to Rosco Brown. The fat, ugly ones keep their mouths shut. Ain't that right, girl?"

This caused more chuckles from the audience.

"Yep, she's keeping her mouth shut," cackled the corncob teen.

"You tell that pig, Rosco!" the girl chirped.

Rachel's face turned a deep red. Her hands were shaking. Taking deep breaths, she slowly rose to her feet while trying to control her thumping heart.

"Watch it, Rock," warned Toothy, pretending to be scared.

"Yeah," added the tall one. "She might have rabies or something."

"Worse, don't you know who she is?" Toothy garnered all the attention now.

"Who?" asked the girl.

Rachel's heart only thudded louder and faster. Did they know she was the babysitter of the Winter family? How?

"Why she's … she's the Incredible Bulk!"

This caused the group to erupt in raucous laughter.

Rachel could only stand there and feel deep, dark humiliation flow through her.

"She's going to sit on us," howled the girl.

"Hey! Hey now, Macie!" Rosco, as the leader, couldn't let Toothy steal his attention. "Quiet now, everybody!" Turning slowly to his audience, he raised his hands for silence and then spoke in a gentle voice full of mock concern. "Can't you see, y'all? You got to be nice to the poor girl. Can't you see she's scared?"

"Of us?" Toothy asked. "How's that? Why, her looking in the mirror every day is scarier than seeing us!"

Rachel's heart continued to beat wildly. Hugging her notebook close to her chest, she stared at the asphalt in front of the leader's big sneakers and fought hard not to cry.

"I don't want trouble," she managed to whisper without whimpering.

"What was that?" Rosco cupped an ear. "Did you just bark? Or did you moo?" He stood and gave her a derisive look. "Dang, girl! I can't tell if you're a dog or a cow."

"Maybe she's both," suggested Toothy. "She's a dow."

The girl hooted and gave Toothy a high five.

The tall, pale boy laughed. His voice was in the process of breaking and came out squeaky like a wheel rolling over rocky ground, needing oil. "Do you bark and give milk?"

Ha, ha. That was so funny. Rachel slowly felt anger overcoming her fear. This was ridiculous! These kids were years younger than her. Still, she kept from reacting. Stories of gangs and drugs in Florida were nothing new … what did this bunch want? And what were they willing to do to get it? She hoped they just wanted their laughs and would soon leave.

Then Rosco bit his lip and eyed her carefully … calculating. "Hey, now, let's not make the girl cry."

"What do you want?" Rachel asked bluntly through clenched teeth, still not looking up at him.

"What do we want?" Rosco stepped forward, thrusting his face so close to Rachel's she could smell his squalid breath. *Maybe he wanted a breath mint …*

"Easy, Rosco," warned Toothy, suddenly sounding serious.

"I am being easy," seethed Rosco. "What I want is your notebook, girl. We just want to know what a rich girl like you been writing down, 'cause you know us poor folk hardly know what writing is and all. Right?"

His audience nodded in approval.

"Good idea, Rock," the tall kid said. "We want to see her writing."

"Man, Shoes, you can't even read yourself!" the dark-skinned girl said.

"So what? Reading is for rich fatties like this girl."

Rachel shuddered and shrank back. Not her notebook!

"Just give us the notebook," Toothy said. "Then you can go cry to your mommy and she'll buy you ten more."

Taking gulps of air, Rachel backed away, clutching her notebook tightly. Running would be a waste of time, but she wasn't going to give in.

"What you gonna do, girl?" Rosco asked, grinning evilly. "Bite me?"

"Careful," warned Shoes. "She might eat you. I know rich people like her. They eat everything and then want more. Last month one ate my dad's job."

"Just give up your notebook," growled Rosco. "I want to see what rich fatsos write about us!" He looked as if he was about to lunge at Rachel.

Just then a young, shrill voice full of venom cried out.

"Hey! Leave her alone!"

A small boy, no more than seven or eight, streaked from the park and arrived at Rachel's side like a youthful missile. Standing firmly in place, he glared up at the bullies with flashing blue eyes while he raised two tiny fists as if to fight.

On seeing him, Rosco's eyebrows shot to his forehead. At first he took a step back, but then he did a double take. Pretending to wipe his eyes clear of something, he looked again. "Who said that?"

"I did, you idiot!" The boy didn't look impressed or scared. Carrying a soccer ball under his arm, he wore white soccer shorts and a thin red soccer jersey. A pair of tiny cleats covered his feet.

"Where did you come from, munchkin?" Toothy asked, grinning. "Oz?"

Rachel didn't know what to make of the turn of events. The boy at her side barely came up to her waist. Straight, light-brown hair hung loosely just above his eyes and over his ears before ending up in almost a rattail in the back. Sharply handsome with narrow cheeks and a pointed chin, his young face held no fear. Scrunching his small nose, he bared his teeth and narrowed his large eyes. Rachel could only think of a puppy dog trying to stare down a pack of wild wolves.

"Call me a munchkin and I'll break your nose!" the boy hissed at Toothy.

Rosco laughed loudly. "Dang, girl. Looks like you got a real hero standing up for you!"

Now Rachel glared as her anger was getting the best of her. Deep inside, a line had been drawn. They could mess with her and make fun of her, but they couldn't touch her notebook and they *most definitely* couldn't hurt this boy. His arms and legs were like matchsticks and he couldn't weigh more than sixty pounds. There was no way she was going to let the pack of wolves touch him.

"What's your problem?" she demanded, stepping in front of the boy. "Can't you people find something better to do?"

Rosco eyed her coolly as if seeing her for the first time. "Well, well. You got some spirit after all."

Rachel bit her lower lip. In reality, she was nearly scared stiff. "Just leave us alone."

"Yo, munchkin," Toothy said to the kid, ignoring Rachel. "This your girlfriend?"

The gawky tall boy also got into the act. "How do you two kiss, man? Doesn't she squash you?"

The boy's eyes narrowed even tighter, which only gave him a cuter appearance. "Just wait until my brother comes!"

Rosco laughed. "Your brother is coming to beat us up, huh?"

Toothy grinned so his teeth jutted out like a row of capsizing boats. "I hope he's bigger than you, munchkin."

"Tell you what," Rosco said. "I like your spirit. You give us your soccer ball and we'll let you both go. We'll even let your girlfriend keep her notebook."

Rachel shook her head. "I'll tell *you* what, buster. You all leave, and I won't call the police!" From her pocket, she whipped out her cell phone. "I mean it!"

"Call the cops for what?" Rosco said nastily. "This may be your rich neighborhood, girl, but we live just through the trees on the end. Last time I checked, this is a free country and we're allowed to walk here."

"Then do it! Walk!"

Rosco glared and looked like he wanted to punch her, but suddenly he relaxed. Crossing his arms, he grinned. "Actually, I think we want to stand right here." He smiled in Rachel's face.

"Go ahead and call the cops. See what happens. What are you going tell them?"

"She'll tell them four bozo brains are polluting the street," the boy said.

"Polluting?" Rosco turned on the boy, his mouth twitching. "Whatcha mean polluting? How are we polluting?"

"With your ugly faces!"

Toothy took a step in his direction. "You better watch your mouth, munchkin. I'll take that soccer ball and kick it up your tiny—"

"And I'll call the police for assault!" Rachel cried shrilly.

"Ooo, I'm so scared!" snarled Toothy.

The young girl had remained silent for a while and was starting to look nervous. She started backing away. Clearly this was getting out of hand.

Then the boy's brother arrived.

"What's this!" hollered a deep voice. Jogging through the palm trees in the park, a tall teen about Rachel's age hurried to the scene. "If anybody touches my brother, I'll pound them into last week!" Curly black hair bounced over his square face, which was tense with anger. Fierce, blue eyes took in the bullies in a single glance. Moving to stand in front of the boy and next to Rachel, the newcomer opened his arms as if daring an attack. Like the boy, he was dressed for soccer in shorts and a jersey. Unlike the boy, he was well built and sturdy. "Well?"

"Ah, we were just messing around," Rosco said, laughingly, quickly changing tack. Like many bullies, he was tough as long as he had total control. "No harm, man."

"Go mess around somewhere else. If you touch my brother, I will hurt you."

"You and who else?" Toothy challenged before being shushed by Rosco's glare.

"I don't need anybody else for you, *kid*."

"We didn't come to fight," Rosco said evenly. "We're just going home. Come on, Toothy. Let the rich people have their stupid park and their *street*."

"Toothy? Nice name."

Rosco put a hand on Toothy's shoulder and glared at the dark-haired teen. "We call him that because when we first saw him, he was ripping out the throat of the last rich punk who made fun of him."

Smiling, the older brother shrugged. "I thought you all were going home."

"We are. For now. See you, fat chick."

With a show of lazy contempt, the gang started down the street in the direction of the Winter house and toward the trees.

Rachel watched them go. All of a sudden, her knees went weak and she nearly fell … what else could happen on this day?

"Don't you ever run off like that again," the dark-haired teen growled, taking the young boy by the arm and not looking at Rachel. "What were you thinking?"

Frowning back, the boy kept his fierce look. "I heard those jerks being jerks. And," he grinned. "I knew you were coming."

"Yeah? Well, maybe next time I'll decide having a young brother like you isn't worth it." Ruffling the boy's head, the teenager turned to Rachel.

Having managed to get her balance, Rachel averted her eyes from the teen's good looks. "Uh, thanks for, uh, helping," she stammered.

"Thank my little brother," he said dryly. "I would have come too late if he hadn't run off." Suddenly, as if remembering his manners, he thrust out a hand and then pulled it back. "Oh, I'm Jason Richardson. This is my little brother Jakey."

Surprised, Rachel nearly dropped her notebook as she took the offered hand. "Rachel … just Rachel." She tried to grin, but her nerves only allowed a slight move of her mouth in that direction. She nodded awkwardly at both boys.

Jason eyed here curiously. "Are you new here? I haven't seen you before."

"Well, kind of."

"Jakey, go run and get Alison and Courtney. Tell them to hurry up." He smiled at Rachel. "They're our sisters," he explained as Jakey jogged back into the park.

Rachel tried a tight smile. "Didn't you just tell him to never run off alone?" It was meant to be a joke, but came out like a rebuke.

"Huh?" Jason frowned at her. "Oh, he'll be fine. I just don't want him to run off in the street where strangers are—"

"Oh, I, uh, was just, uh, kidding."

"Oh … Do you live around here? Alison is graduating high school next week and you might know her. Courtney is only eleven."

Rachel blinked furiously. If Jason knew that she was just some babysitter from Virginia, what would he think? The only reason why he was talking to her was because he thought she was rich like him. So if he knew the truth, would he treat her like the gang of toughs? Like an animal needing to be run off? She took a deep breath. Telling a lie could be much worse—how many stories had she read about a character telling a lie only to regret it by the end?

"I'm, uh, actually staying with the Winters right now. I just came from Virginia. Today, actually. I graduated high school a few days ago … I'm, uh, their babysitter for the summer." She held her breath. *Why can't I just stop talking?*

Jason's eyes widened and he seemed excited at the last part. "Really? No kidding? I mean, really?"

Rachel nodded.

"Why, that's great!"

Rachel's breath returned. Suddenly keenly aware that she was alone with an attractive male around her age, she smiled shyly and nodded. "Their parents are going out of town with their two youngest for a month."

"That's really cool." Jason sounded as if he meant it. "Wow."

All at once, a warm feeling flooded Rachel's insides. *I'm alone with a cool guy and he's being nice!*

Little did Rachel know, but they were not totally alone. Hidden among thick bushes and in a copse of palm trees at the edge of the park, just past where Rachel and Jason stood, a pair of red eyes watched everything with great interest.

And that was how Rachel met the neighbors.

Not surprisingly, Alison proved to be a beautiful teen with soft features and a slim figure. Sleek, straight hair the same color as Jakey's bounced softly on her shoulders. Her face was rounder than her younger brother's and she had fuller lips and thicker cheeks. Courtney was nearly a perfect copy of Alison, only years younger and with dark hair similar to Jason's.

Rachel bit her lip when seeing them come back with Jakey. *Did every rich person have to be so attractive and skinny?*

At least the Richardson siblings proved to be as nice as they were good looking. Both girls greeted Rachel kindly and looked horrified when hearing what happened. Although Jakey's description of giant monster jerks with booger faces probably didn't help …

"We'll walk you home," said Alison, immediately after Jason and Jakey had finished explaining.

"No, no," protested Rachel, going red in the face all over again. "I'll be fine, really."

Courtney grinned. "It's okay, Rachel," she said. "We're actually neighbors. Our house is the last house on the right."

"Oh."

Jakey was juggling the soccer ball on his thighs while impatiently waiting for the talking to end. "Hurry up, guys! Dad said we can watch soccer tonight if we're back before sunset."

Jason rolled his eyes. "Jakey is a soccer fanatic."

"So are you!"

"No. I'm a soccer fantastic."

"Lame, Jason," Alison said with a groan. "Rachel, you'll have to excuse our brother."

"Which one?" snorted Courtney. "Here, Jakey, stop showing off and pass me the ball!"

Rachel smiled, feeling much better. "Okay, then. Thank you."

While Courtney and Jakey ran ahead dribbling the soccer ball between them, the three teens followed at a more leisurely pace.

Rachel could scarcely believe it. One moment she was crying because of Lisa, and the next moment she was being bullied by thugs. And now she was walking with an attractive boy and his gorgeous sister—and they were treating her as a good friend they'd known for years. Only in rich Florida, she thought, could this happen.

For a while the teens fell into an awkward silence.

"Aren't you worried about cars here?" Rachel finally had to ask as she watched Jakey run full tilt after the ball in the middle of the street.

Jason shrugged with his hands in his pockets. "Have you seen any lately?"

Rachel looked around and shook her head.

"Look closely and you'll see a lot of windows boarded up," Alison said from Rachel's right. She pointed to a house on the left. "See that one? We never saw anybody use it. Ever."

Squinting up a long driveway and past a row of palm trees, Rachel saw a large, blue-sided house with every window firmly blocked with dark, painted boards. It made the house look like it had multiple black eyes.

"Most families only visit for the winter or spend a week or two here for vacation." Jason spoke as if this was normal behavior.

Rachel swallowed as she took this in. "That's a shame," she finally said.

"Tell us about it," Alison said with sudden feeling. "We moved here in the fall and still haven't made any friends in this dump of a neighborhood."

Jason laughed without feeling. "Yeah, the only people we ever see on this street are a homeless guy and those jerks you just ran into."

"Who were they?" Rachel asked, still feeling a little fear at seeing Rosco and Toothy. In the future, she would have to be careful when walking alone.

"Just some bums who come from the woods." Jason sighed, removing a hand from his pocket to rake back curls from his forehead. "You'll soon find out that Dougarsville is not exactly a paradise. This is called Camelot Acres, which sounds really nice, but it ends at our house. If they built a road through those trees, it'd lead to a dump where those jerks live. They don't exactly like us."

Rachel raised an eyebrow but kept silent.

Alison sighed. "It's pretty dumb. There used to be some poor houses here too and a lot more trees, but they were all taken out. The county tried to buy the houses behind the woods too, but it got in the papers and created a huge stink. Nobody there would sell. There was a court battle and everything."

"So," continued Jason, "now the poor people hate our guts, and we can't build a stupid road through the trees. We have to drive around the long way to get anywhere."

Rachel couldn't tell if he was being sarcastic or serious.

"It really is the pits," Alison said after a moment. "I can't wait to leave."

Jason laughed. "Yeah, lucky you."

"Where, uh, are you going?" Rachel asked.

Alison grinned and her eyes immediately brightened. "Two days after graduation I'm flying to England with my parents. I'll be attending university over there, and we're going to look for a place for me to stay."

"Yeah, which means I get to be left with Courtney and Jakey for a week and a half. Or longer, if our mom and dad have too much fun." Jason smiled ruefully at Rachel. "So I guess we'll be babysitting neighbors for a while. Maybe we can get together and sort of join forces. I think the Winter kids are close in age to Courtney and Jakey, right?"

Rachel's heart nearly leapt from her chest. It was just what she wanted to hear, but never thought possible. Hastily swallowing, she nodded, trying to play it cool. "Uh, yeah. Yeah, that would be cool. I mean great. Just great."

Chapter Ten

Rachel's emotions were a topsy-turvy wreck when she returned to the house. And the roller-coaster ride was not over.

Mrs. Winter stood just inside the front door as if waiting for her. She had a towel around her slim waist, as she still wore her white, one-piece bathing suit. She looked more like a swimsuit model than a mother of four.

"There you are," she said in way of greeting. "How was the walk?"

Immediately Rachel was back to being tongue-tied. "Um, it was, uh, great," she stuttered. "I met some of the neighbors—the, uh, the Richardson kids."

"Oh, that's nice. I confess, we haven't actually gotten around to meeting their parents, but they seem like a really nice family. They have kids around Steven's and Lisa's age, right?"

Rachel nodded. "Uh, yes, uh, they actually, uh, wondered if, uh, they might come over some time."

Mrs. Winter bit her lip. "Actually, I want to talk to you about that. Do you mind coming with me to my office?"

It wasn't really a question, and Rachel felt a terrible weight press against her chest. Immediately, blood rushed to her head and her heart thudded heavily.

In her entire school career, Rachel had never been sent to the principal's office before. She imagined it probably felt similar to this. "Uh … yes, uh, okay," she stammered.

With great trepidation, she followed Mrs. Winter through the expensive house to the east wing, an area where her earlier "tour" never went.

A few muffled thumps were heard from the upstairs.

"Doug is having the kids shower before dinner," Mrs. Winter said over her shoulder. She moved with a purpose and with obvious tension.

Rachel couldn't help but feel like she was in trouble.

Did Lisa tell her that I was spying on them in the pool? Or is it that she also realizes that I'm just not good enough for her children?

This is where she would be sent home … It would be for the best. Her mom would be crushed, but Rachel actually felt a sense of relief. Who cared if the Richardson family seemed nice? Rachel didn't belong here.

Mrs. Winter opened a door on the left and ushered Rachel in. "This is my office—where I spend my quiet time, if I ever find any." She said it like a joke, but forgot to laugh or even crack a smile.

Mrs. Winter's office was a soft-blue-carpeted room with a desk with a computer, three cushy chairs, and a large couch. In the corner was a large, blue bouncy ball and hand weights next to a mat and a treadmill. Pictures of the family lined the walls, and potted plants sat on either side of the desk.

Mrs. Winter directed Rachel to a swivel chair next to the desk. She took the massive cushy chair behind the desk. Sitting at the edge, she immediately faced Rachel with a no-nonsense look. Her fingers tapped lightly on the desk as if she were nervous.

Rachel found it hard to look at her. She was going to be fired before even starting.

"So, Rachel," Mrs. Winter began slowly. "What do you think so far?"

Rachel took a deep breath. *Might as well make it easy.* "Uh, Mrs. Win—"

"Please, Rachel, call me Elizabeth. You make me feel so old."

"Oh, uh, sorry."

Mrs. Winter smiled at her. "Your mom had just turned eighteen when she married your father. I went off to college, and she fell in love with the guy we met while bowling. You know the story, right?"

Rachel nodded thickly. Mrs. Winter told it anyway.

"I'll never forget that night … Your mom had just bowled three straight gutter balls and your father claimed that the sound of the gutter balls was ruining his game."

Rachel grinned. She heard this story so many times—both from her father and mother. "And he gave my mom free lessons."

"Right," laughed Mrs. Winter. "And then she proceeded to roll five more gutter balls!"

"My dad said she was the worst bowler he ever met and that he married her to stop her from bowling ever again."

Mrs. Winter chuckled. "I guess even with the gutter balls, your mom still got a strike, huh?" Then she sighed. "I lost my best friend that night, but I was still happy. I knew Margaret had found a good man."

"You, you didn't see her again?"

"Oh, of course we saw each other, but it was never the same. And soon I was off to college, and your mother … well, she had you. We lost touch … until now." Rachel blushed as Mrs. Winter reached over and patted her arm. "Never in my wildest dreams did I ever think I would have Margaret Meech's daughter in my house as a babysitter. It's really good that you're here. Lisa and Steven don't know what they're getting."

Rachel swallowed. Neither did she … then it slowly dawned on her that she wasn't being fired. She didn't know if this made things better, or worse. *Why was she here?*

"They, um, seem really nice … the kids."

"They are, but they need somebody special to look after them." Her hands started drumming on the desk again and the tension returned to her face.

The sick feeling crept back. *Maybe this is her way of saying I'm not good enough, or that they need somebody better qualified—in looks and behavior.* Her hands grew clammy.

"What do you think of Lisa? Have you talked to her?"

"Uh, a little," Rachel confessed and immediately shifted uncomfortably. "She, she's very helpful."

"Yes, she is that," Mrs. Winter said dryly. "You probably noticed. She wants to be twenty-one, not eleven. You're going to have to give her time to get used to you." She smiled. "Do you have any questions about her, or Steven yet?"

Rachel took a breath. Before she could stop herself, she asked. "Are Lisa and Steven … are they adopted?"

Mrs. Winter gave her a sharp look. "Why do you ask that?"

Her cheeks burning, Rachel shifted in her seat again. "Uh, Lisa told me," she mumbled. "I-I talked a little with her before going for a walk."

A moment passed. Looking to the ceiling, Mrs. Winter sat back in her chair and sighed. "And she called me Elizabeth and my husband, Doug, right?"

Rachel nodded.

"She says that when she's angry … it makes her feel less wanted, the poor thing." Leaning forward, Mrs. Winter stared at Rachel in the eye. "What I'm going to tell you is confidential. I'm telling you this because I trust you." Rachel nodded, her mouth going dry.

"Doug and I didn't have children for a long time. He worked hard and I worked hard, and one day we both woke up to a large, empty house with not a whole lot to work for. Sure, we had money and we had a house, but what we really wanted was children. Well, we came across this opportunity to adopt a baby girl … this was Lisa." Mrs. Winter smiled warmly. "Bringing her into our lives was the best thing we ever did, I promise you. And some years later, we found Steven in foster care." Now her mouth formed a grim line.

"I was volunteering at a preschool when I met Steven … he was a little beat up." Her voice tight, Mrs. Winter continued speaking while Rachel struggled to take it all in.

"Apparently, his father had a mental problem that he dealt with by developing a drinking problem." She sighed heavily. "Well, Steven's mother was used as an outlet for his frustrations. I'm afraid Steven witnessed his mother being beaten badly. Several times, probably."

Rachel barely dared to breathe and was at a loss for words.

"It gets worse, I'm afraid." Scrunching her lips, Mrs. Winter clasped her hands on the desk and squeezed them tightly together. Rachel could see pain in her eyes. "Finally, after a beating that nearly killed her, Steven's mom was sent away and his dad was locked up. This forced Steven into foster care … the poor boy lost everything. His home and parents were ripped away. As you can imagine, he didn't cope well. He started getting very angry and very aggressive. Well, a lot of people saw this beautiful boy and immediately took him into their home. Then he started throwing wild tantrums. The good families sent him back. But more than a few tried to 'teach' him discipline. When I first saw him, he was just four years old and already being called emotionally disturbed. He had a black eye and bruises all over his body. I didn't care. I was so angry. I took that boy home that very day and called social services." She smiled. "Having money has its benefits. Doug was able to pull some strings, and the next day I was given custody. And then, oh, boy, did we have a time here. Doug, myself, and little Lisa worked with Steven for a long time. We adopted him within the year, and well, he's gotten better. He's a very, very bright boy. Once he realized we were his family and weren't going to hurt him or leave him, he warmed up to us. Now he's the sweetest boy in the world … and off any medication."

Rachel was horrified. Never in a gazillion years would she have guessed this perfect family would have such a story. Her mother's words came back to her—something she often told Rachel. "There's only been one perfect person in the world—and we killed him. Everybody has pain behind their smiles, Rachel. To believe otherwise is fooling yourself."

Mrs. Winter brushed hair from her face. "Steven attends a private school. He goes there because he had trouble with the public school. Steven can be very clingy, especially to me. I promise you, it's not because he's a mama's boy… Quite the opposite. He's very protective and doesn't want to lose anybody he loves. It's gotten much better over the years, but when he was younger, whenever somebody tried to hurt somebody he liked, he would react quite violently. He swims, now. Before that he played soccer and was very good at it. Then, during one game, a player from the other team hurt his best friend—kicked him in the back of the leg. Well … Steven jumped on this player, brought him to the ground, and started beating him with his fists. No matter that the player was over twice Steven's size, Steven was kicked off the team."

Rachel swallowed hard. "Uh, he seems fine now … He's very calm."

Mrs. Winter grimaced slightly. "He is, but have you noticed how he's always in control? He never laughs out loud or acts with abandon like a lot of other boys his age. Ever since that soccer game, which was two years ago, we haven't seen him completely lose it. He's fighting it … He's learned to be very relaxed and carefree, but he still battles himself. Sometimes he has dreams … terrible nightmares. He's very guarded, Rachel. You being here will be a big step for him. He seems perfectly okay with it, but I do worry." Biting her lower lip, she reached down to grab her purse. From inside, she fumbled around before pulling out two blue tubes and holding them toward Rachel. "You took First Aid, right?"

Staring at the tubes nervously, Rachel nodded.

"Did they go over how to use an EpiPen?

Rachel again nodded, definitely not liking where this was going. "They, uh, showed us how."

"Well, this works the same way." Mrs. Winter suddenly smiled kindly. "I know I'm scaring the wits out of you … I promise, Steven has been fine for years and we've never had to use this. However, just in case, inside is an injection that will calm him down in seconds … It'll actually knock him out for a few hours. One of our doctor friends helped us get it. Use it only in an extreme emergency, and I mean extreme emergency. Then you call his doctor straightaway. His number is on the tube. I have two, just in case one doesn't work."

"Uh, how do I know if it's an emergency?" Rachel asked thickly.

"When or if Steven loses control, you'll know. Trust me." She didn't smile now. "He'll be on the floor, screaming, and probably trying to fight anybody or anything near him. He's a small kid, but can be quite powerful. If that happens, just sit on him, or something, and shoot a dose in his thigh … He can hurt somebody, or more likely hurt himself, very badly. But I'll say it again. We've never had to use these. This is in case of an extreme emergency."

Rachel took the tubes cautiously. They felt heavy in her hand.

"Keep them with you always. Put them in your purse whenever you leave and always have them available. It's … it's a precaution, Rachel. Steven is off medication. But if he has another of his episodes, there's a good chance the state will take him away from me. Do you understand?"

"Uh, I understand."

"I knew you would. I don't want to scare you, but there was a big push to have Steven sent away to a special school … I can't have that happen. I hope you understand …" Mrs. Winter's eyes were almost pleading.

Nodding, Rachel gave a faint smile. "I'll make sure he's okay. Really."

"Oh, Rachel, I know you will … just keep a special eye on him. It's fine having people over, like the Richardson kids, but be careful."

"I will."

"Just like your mom … Oh, and this office is yours when we're gone. Use it as often as you like."

Rachel wanted to use it right then and lock herself away. Now she really did wish she was fired. The tubes she possessed were a heavy burden … a heavy burden of responsibility that she didn't want.

Leaving the office with Mrs. Winter, Rachel felt like the woman who knew too much in a mystery novel. She also felt like a grown-up—Mrs. Winter, no, *Elizabeth*, had confided in her. She trusted Rachel not only as a babysitter but as a family friend. And just a few weeks before, she had been sitting in the school library listening to Sarah Watkins brag about being grown up for going to a beach party with Trent Long.

If she only knew.

At the supper table that night, Rachel made sure to ignore Lisa's coldness and did her best to sit back and keep out of the way. It was not to be. Robbie and Margie entertained the table by peppering Rachel with questions about Virginia. Steven watched with mild amusement and even asked a few questions himself. Even Lisa's icy glare thawed into a small smile when Rachel told about her neighbors owning a goat that always got in trouble. One Fourth of July, her neighbors had tried to make coffee ice cream outside but had left it unattended for a few minutes. The goat drank the entire mixture before they got back and spent the entire night trying to bark like a dog.

As they spoke, they ate. The food was good—Lisa had made excellent garlic bread to go along with piles of pasta and homemade tomato and mushroom sauce. Rachel tried to be careful and take only small portions, but still managed to spill sauce on her shirt and have three helpings. She would have had more salad, but it was cut so fine, it resembled a green stew and made her stomach queasy just looking at it.

Lisa insisted on doing the dishes when it was over. The other children went out back to play with binoculars. Elizabeth and Doug kept Rachel at the table and went over phone numbers, schedules, and rules one last time. After the meeting with Elizabeth, Rachel somehow felt calm and actually confident. Having someone voice belief in her ability helped a lot … and she needed it, because at the sink Lisa kept throwing frowns her way.

Later, after pudding for dessert, the family gathered in the sitting room for one last family time. Rachel sat on a couch by herself, feeling like an intruder … a feeling ably helped by Lisa's frequent glares.

The redhead sat in a chair next to the sofa pretending to read a book. Across the room, Doug relaxed in an easy chair reading *Pollyanna* to Margie and Robbie, who were both crowding his lap. In the middle, Steven lay on the floor with Elizabeth close to his side. Schoolbooks and papers were scattered in front of them.

"Steven's teacher has no mercy and no kids of her own," Elizabeth said to Rachel, looking up with a rueful smile. "Ordinarily I don't help with homework, but this woman is different."

"Moomm, are you helping or not?"

"Well, I'm trying!"

Rachel grunted and watched as mother and son worked together. Leaning close to Steven, Elizabeth whispered encouragement while providing nudges and back rubs when necessary. Both were armed with pencils, and Rachel had to stifle a grin when they both started writing an answer at the same time.

"If you only knew how much homework this woman assigns," Elizabeth laughed when Steven hastily erased their twin answer. "The hard part is to match my writing with his."

Steven smiled at her. "You mean the hard part is for you to get the answer right."

"Oh, you!" Elizabeth hugged him around the shoulders and kissed his cheek. "I love you, Steven, but sometimes you need a good whack on your pants! Your mom is trying hard!"

"But, Mom, the preposition—"

"Oh, who cares about prepositions besides Ms. Fathomb? Just get this done and move on to math. Learn prepositions in school tomorrow!"

Steven only grinned wider. "Do you have a calculator?"

"Why, you!" This earned a light whack on the pants. "Can you believe this boy? I can do math well enough! The question is, can you? Just wait, tomorrow night I'll be gone and you'll be stuck doing this alone. Because Rachel won't put up with your attitude!"

Steven only grinned. "Sure, Mom."

The two started nudging each other like school friends.

Rachel relaxed and for a moment imagined what it would be like to have younger siblings of her own …

Then Lisa nudged her leg with her foot. "You really need a shower," she whispered. "I can't concentrate with you smelling so badly so close by."

In another house, across the line of trees, away from the rich, happy families, Geoffrey Brown lay on his stomach with his chin propped on small hands, wearing a serious look. He was doing his own homework without any help. Lines creased his young forehead and his nose wrinkled in concentration.

Below him was the dreaded math homework, doing its best to kill him. Not a quick death by any means, but a slow, painful, mind-numbing, snot-dripping, and overall boring death.

"Soon my mind will melt into my toes," he groaned to himself. "Ms. Fatbottom, why do you hate me?"

His bright green eyes flicked toward the front room, where his older brother Oliver lay on the couch watching television like he did every night. Geoffrey considered a retreat to join his brother, but that would mean a full surrender and consequences the next day.

"Not that it really matters," he grumbled.

The math homework had already won—there was no way he could defeat it. Even if he did, Ms. Fathomb, or Fatbottom, as most of her students called her, would just give more the next night. Geoffrey was under the impression that teachers hated kids and spent gleeful hours at night planning new ways to ruin the next day for their students.

But Geoffrey set his jaw and picked up his pencil and went back to work. He would not give up.

Before he could make another squiggle, the front door burst open and slammed shut. "Yo, Oliver!" crowed Rosco, who was actually years younger than Oliver, but acted as if he was the older brother. "You still here watching that junk, man? Why don't you get off your duff and do something outside for a change?"

"I'm not on my duff. I'm on my side," Oliver's bored voice answered. "Besides, there's nothing to do outside but get in trouble."

"True that, man." Rosco's footsteps could be heard sauntering through the room. "True that."

Immediately Geoffrey blew the mental bugle, sounding the recall. It was time to get busy and fight back against the homework! "This math won't beat me," he growled softly. In a sudden burst of new energy and using the tactical genius of a calculator, Geoffrey quickly cornered the first problem and brought it down. "The answer is forty-two. Eight down, and only three to go," he grunted in satisfaction.

"Eight down and what?" Rosco had entered the room without Geoffrey noticing. The small boy's face crashed down. Uh-oh. It was time to get real quiet and hope the enemy's reinforcements would move past without taking action.

Rosco snorted. "Little bro, are you still trying to do rich-boy work? Don't you know it's not for people like us?" He grinned mockingly. "Oh, yeah. But I done forgot. Little boy Geoffrey Brown has got himself a scholarship to rich-boy snot school. Too bad it's only for white boys."

"It's not a white-boy school. It's First Seminole Academy, named after some of the best warriors who ever lived. And if you were smart enough, you'd be there too!"

So much for being real quiet. Geoffrey bit the inside of his mouth. It was always that part of him that got him in trouble.

"What did you say, little boy?" Rosco lost his smile and took a menacing step toward Geoffrey.

"Leave him alone!" called Oliver from the couch. "Let the kid do something with his life."

Rosco made a rude gesture toward the front room. "I'm leaving the boy alone," he hollered back. "I'm just going to my room." Walking across the floor, he suddenly shot a sneaker-covered foot out and snagged the corner of Geoffrey's homework. Crouching low, he breathed foul breath of old hot dog and onions all over Geoffrey's face.

"Listen, Geoffrey," Rosco hissed. "You'll never be like the rich white boys. I just ran into a few outside a minute ago." He reached a hand and patted Geoffrey's short black hair. "Your poor brown head ain't meant for them. They have no respect for our type. To them, we're nothing but garbage. Like this."

Dragging his foot back, Rosco pulled Geoffrey's nearly completed homework away. His brother grabbed it up with a hand and crumpled it into a ball. Then he opened his mouth and let a huge wad of spit fall onto the crumpled remains. This was then dropped in front of Geoffrey's face.

The battle was over. Ambushed and beaten. Geoffrey's heart sank.

As Rosco strolled away, his hands deep in his pocket, Geoffrey kept looking at the disgusting leftovers of his hard work. He started breathing hard. The battle was over, but not the war. Geoffrey would keep fighting. He would defeat his math, English, history, and science, even if it did kill him. Because giving up would make him like Rosco. Biting back tears, he rose to his knees and slammed his math book shut.

"You're the garbage, Rosco!" he shouted. "At least I have a real friend in my school and not the jerks that follow you around like flies on a garbage truck!"

Stopping just at his room, Rosco whirled around. "You have yourself a mouth, little boy. Your so-called friend at your stupid school ain't your friend. He's a white cream puff who uses you as his little token black friend. He don't care about you, man. He's just the trash and you're just the fly. One day you'll be swatted too. You'll see." Then he went inside his room, slamming the door.

Geoffrey stayed in his room for supper. Nana came home from her job late as usual. Not even her kind words and homemade baked chicken with fried potatoes got Geoffrey to the table.

"What's wrong with Geoffrey?" Geoffrey heard her demand from the kitchen. Their house was so small and thin that you could hear everything that happened in any room from any other room.

"Probably realized his black skin don't come off," Rosco grunted, talking with his mouth full. "No matter how hard he scrubs, he's still a little black boy stuck in a white school."

"Nonsense, Richard," Nana barked. "Don't you dare speak that way in this house!" Only Nana dared call Rosco by his real name.

"Fine by me. I was just on my way out."

"Where are you going, Richard? You better finish your peas!"

"Whatever you say, Nana. I'll be back before bedtime." Geoffrey heard the front door slam.

"Now what was that about?" Nana demanded.

"Rosco gave him more grief about his schoolwork and his friends," muttered Oliver's voice.

There was a pause and then Nana's voice seemed to deflate. "Oh, boy … I do feel tiredly old sometimes."

"You're pushing seventy, Nana."

"And you're pushing my buttons, mister. Finish your supper and I'll get the apple pie in the oven. Maybe the smell will tempt little Geoffrey from his bed. Hear that, Geoffrey?" she hollered.

Geoffrey ducked under his covers. Since he was three, he had been raised by his grandmother. His real mom was out somewhere in California being stoned, or something. This confused Geoffrey. In the Bible the saints were always being stoned and stuff … yet this was good and it meant they died and went to Heaven. When his mommy was stoned, it meant she was a bad mother who deserved to die and go to … the other place. He'd rather his mom not be stoned and go home to him.

He must have fallen asleep, because one moment he was watching a dusty street full of bearded men acting funny while tossing stones at his mom, when all of a sudden his eyes shot open and he saw his grandmother kneeling at his side.

"Hush, little boy, don't you worry. Nana is here." Taking her gnarled hands that had raised two families, buried two sons and a daughter, worked two separate jobs, and still had time to grow a garden and cook the best-tasting food in town, she gripped Geoffrey's face tightly. "You listen here, young man. Never let your brother dictate what you can and cannot do. He's had a hard life, Geoffrey. But that's no excuse for his hard head. You go and make whatever friend you so choose. And never, and I mean never, let the color of your skin dictate who you are, or what you do. Never let it determine the people you associate with, Geoffrey, either. You hear me?" Her right hand dropped from his cheek and found his heart. Pressing gently, she said, "Instead, use this. It will never lead you wrong unless you fill it up with a whole lot of junk like hating and fighting. When that happens, my little boy, then life is truly a hardship."

"Yes, Nana," Geoffrey said, swallowing his last sniffles. "I'll remember."

"Sure you will, my little boy. Go out and do wonders in this world. Maybe then your brothers will see what's possible and stop lookin' at what's not. But not now. Oh, no. Instead, get your little behind outta your bed and get to the table and eat your supper! I didn't cook it for nothing!"

Rachel lay back on her pillow and breathed in deeply. Ready or not, when she woke up the next day, she would be the babysitter. For the next several weeks, her job would be to take care of Lisa and Steven … their parents would be flying out in the afternoon.

I can do this … I can really do this … Feeling confident, she closed her eyes and smiled.

Down the hall, a boy tossed and turned. The moonlight flooded the windows, filling the room with a soft, eerie light. A moan rose from the depths below, calling out for help. Then came a shriek—

Steven's eyes flew open and he gasped for air. Just another dream … he'd been on a mountain. Below him, thousands of people were calling for help as a giant wave was coming from the distance.

Now all was quiet and he was safely in his room. Across the way, Robbie lay snoring.

His pulse still racing, Steven swung his bare legs over the bed and shivered. A rumble then stirred in his stomach. The monster was trying to waken.

Gulping, he rubbed his eyes. As he did so, a breeze suddenly struck him head on. Coldness enveloped his body and ruffled his hair. Startled, he hugged his arms tight across his narrow chest and shivered. His T-shirt was plastered to his skin from sweat—before it had been stifling. Where had the breeze come from? The windows were all shut. Feeling very afraid, Steven forced himself to his feet. Peeling off his T-shirt, he dropped it to the floor. Then, taking a breath, he treaded softly to the window facing the front.

The small boy, his skin glistening and glowing in the moonlight streaming through the glass, peered out at the darkened world below. Something was out there … He froze.

Standing below, just inside the driveway, a tall, shadowy figure stared up at him. The shadowman was watching him … Red eyes flared like burning coals.

Leaping back, Steven raced back to his bed and dove onto the mattress. Tearing at the sheets, he covered his entire body and hugged his pillow tight. Curled in a fetal position, he did his best to keep calm. Several moments went by and nothing happened.

Slowly he relaxed and peeked above the covers. All was still. The cold breeze had gone, and once again the room was stifling hot.

It had to have been a dream … just his imagination. A deep tiredness suddenly washed over him. *Tomorrow can't come soon enough*, he thought to himself. He rolled to his side and curled into a ball. Closing his eyes, he surrendered to the darkness.

The monster purred from within.

Chapter Eleven

Morning, as it had the habit of doing, came much too early for Rachel. One second she was lying down in darkness and drifting, off and then …

"Rachel?" asked a soft voice. "Honey, are you awake? Rachel?"

Rachel groaned. She cracked an eye and only saw pure white. *Did it snow overnight?* Blinking, she saw it was only the wall of her bedroom … her bedroom in Florida.

Eyes snapped wide open as she turned with a jerk.

Elizabeth smiled from the doorway. Fully dressed in pressed tan slacks and a thin cotton blouse, her hair beautifully brushed, she looked ready to pose for a fashion magazine.

"I know it's early," she said apologetically, "but since Doug and I are leaving this afternoon, I thought you might want to see how our mornings usually run."

"Oh, uh, great." It sounded more like a groan. "I mean, it really sounds great." Rachel sat up groggily and fought to keep her eyes open. The bed was so soft and warm …

"Excellent! The coffee is ready downstairs. Lisa is in the shower, but Steven is still asleep."

Instantly Rachel snapped awake. This was her job! Mentally, she searched her memory for the daily schedule. Yesterday was Sunday, so today was Monday—school day! Lisa had a bus to catch for the public school, which lasted for another week before being out for the summer. Steven got a ride to his private school, which had two more weeks before its summer vacation. Lisa could get off by herself, but Steven needed help and might sometimes need a ride.

"Uh, what time does Steven have to be ready?"

"Well, his ride usually comes at 7:30 each morning." Elizabeth winked. "Since it'll be your job starting tomorrow to see him off, I thought you can get some practice today. He's all yours."

"Oh, sure," Rachel did her best to smile and exhibit as much energy as she could. Getting herself up was going to be a problem … hopefully Steven was a light sleeper.

"Great. His room is just past the bathroom on the right. Robbie sleeps like a rock, so don't worry about him. Just give Steven a good shake to get him moving. He's pretty self-sufficient after that."

"Right," Rachel said, fighting a yawn.

"Oh, and Rachel, I was thinking. Steven usually gets a ride with his friend Tommy, but you could take him today, if you'd like. That way you'll know where to go in the future when you have to give him a ride."

"Uh, sure. That would be fine."

"Thanks, Rachel. I'll call his mom straight away."

"What time is it now?"

"Just past six. I'll see you in a little bit!"

Rachel nodded and immediately flopped back into her warm soft pillows just as soon as Elizabeth left.

I can't do this. But she had to. Groaning, she used all her will to roll out of bed.

After splashing her face with water and hastily dressing, Rachel dragged herself from the bathroom, past her warm, inviting bed, and into the hall. Stumbling to Steven's room, she passed the bathroom and heard Lisa's high voice singing a love song. Thankfully, most of her song was drowned out by blasting water.

Steven and Robbie slept at the end of the hall on the left toward the front of the house. Knocking softly on their door, she gently pushed it open.

Pale sunlight and gentle snoring greeted her.

"I feel evil doing this," she mumbled.

Like the rest of the house, the room was immaculate. A bookcase, desk, and dresser separated two beds. Posters of sports stars, mostly swimmers, decorated the wall. Steven had swim practice after school, Monday through Thursday. Once summer began, then the times changed to the morning and included Saturdays. She couldn't wait.

Steven lay on top of the nearest bed, huddled on top of his sheets facing the wall. Rachel frowned. The boy's tanned back looked wet, and a discarded T-shirt lay on the floor next to him. Across the room, Robbie was curled under a blanket for warmth. The air-conditioning had been on all night and made the house almost cold.

I wonder why he's so warm …

Rachel gently shook his shoulder, but he didn't stir.

"Steven, wake up," she whispered.

His eyes flashed open. Facing her, he looked like a frightened wolf cub. Dark circles surrounded both eyes.

Taken aback by his sudden awakening, Rachel cleared her throat.

"Uh, it's, um, me … your mom is downstairs waiting in the kitchen. It's time for school." She tried to grin.

"Thanks …" murmured Steven. Then he pressed his face into his pillow and covered his ears. "Why can't Lisa learn not to sing," he groaned.

Lisa had reached the finale of the song and was giving it all she had.

Rachel coughed. "Uh, does she do this every day?"

"Mostly …" Steven squirmed. "And I have to go to the bathroom."

"Well, you can use the one in my room."

Steven twisted to look at her. His hair disheveled, he gave her a look that she couldn't read. She was sure, though, that the boy was reading her.

Inwardly she cringed. Rule number five of babysitting had just been broken—NEVER invade the privacy of the kids you're babysitting. Offering the use of her room was unthinkable for any reason. Quickly she corrected herself. "Uh, I mean, you can use the one downstairs."

"Okay …" Then he ducked back into the pillow as Lisa cranked out a new song with long notes.

After a quick breakfast of toast, eggs, juice, and coffee, both Doug and Elizabeth accompanied Rachel to the real reason they wanted her to drive Steven to school.

A brand-new, sparkling red Toyota Corolla sat in the driveway.

"We know you need a car for the summer, and this is one that should suit you," Elizabeth said, smiling at Rachel's shocked face.

"I had this dropped off last night while I was, uh, 'packing,'" Doug said, stifling a yawn. Still, he was clearly pleased with Rachel's reaction. "It doesn't have all the latest gadgets, but it'll get you where you need to go in one piece."

"It's-It's amazing," Rachel gushed after she got over her surprise. "Are, are you sure you want me to drive it?"

"That's why we got it," Doug said. "Please, don't let the kids drive it. The key is on the driver's seat. Go ahead and fire her up. We'll send Steven right out … Now, I don't have to tell you drag racing is off limits, right?"

"Oh, no," Rachel said, visibly blanching at the thought. "I never speed."

Elizabeth laughed. "Don't worry, Rachel. We covered this with your mom. You have a perfect driving record, I'm told. The tank is full and there's a gas card in the glove compartment." Her eyes twinkled. "We trust you'll use it wisely."

"Yeah," grunted Doug. "No visits to Virginia."

"I promise." Rachel could not believe it. Her own car for the summer, and it was brand new.

By the time Steven came out in his school uniform, Rachel had already driven up and down the driveway three times.

First Seminole Academy sat just outside of downtown Dougarsville and between a large church resembling a warehouse and a long strip mall with an assortment of shops. Here was where you could get your religion, your education, and your shopping done all in one convenient location. Enclosed by a low brick wall, the school was accessed by an iron gate with palm trees on either side.

Driving to the school, Rachel looked in the mirror to where Steven continued to sit in silence. During the entire ride neither spoke. The boy had stared out the window the entire time. Now Rachel cleared her throat.

"Where should I drop you off?" Rachel asked, looking in the rearview mirror.

Blinking almost as if just waking up, Steven looked at her. "In the front is good."

Come on, you have to say something better than that! Build a relationship with the kid! "Uh, you can call me Rachel. Okay?"

"Sure." Steven didn't sound too convinced and neither had Rachel.

Sighing, she pulled to the curb in front of the large brick building. Built in an old style, it looked quite awkward. Shaped like a giant house with a slanted roof, it boasted three stories and two wings of rooms. However, it had modern rectangular windows, and concrete stairs led to a pair of white institutional-looking doors. Old and new styles met but did not like each other.

Steven gathered his backpack and opened his door.

In the driver's seat, Rachel swallowed. This was her first opportunity to bond with the kid. She couldn't blow it. Taking a deep breath, she took off her seat belt, opened her door, and stepped out in the bright Florida sun.

"You don't have to come in," Steven said, eyeing her with caution. "I'm okay here, really."

"I, um, just want to see how you get in the school," she said lamely. "So I know where to go if I ever have to pick you up."

First Seminole Academy served grades K–12, and at that moment two well-dressed boys around her age walked by on their way to the front door.

"Whale watching!" one muttered to the other. "I spotted it first!"

Stifling laughter, the other coughed loudly in his hand. "A whale that shops at the thrift store!"

Swallowing, Rachel ducked her head. Like the upperclassmen, Steven wore a navy-blue blazer with the school patch prominently displayed on the front pocket. This he wore over a pin-striped dress shirt with an open collar. Black jeans clung to his skinny legs, and dark blue converse sneakers covered his feet. His auburn hair neatly combed, he looked in sharp contrast to her faded blue jeans, oversized long-sleeved shirt, and floppy sandals. Her wardrobe did little to enhance her figure.

She became very aware of other students piling out of cars and vans. Many eyed her openly. The boys had matching blazers, collared shirts, and anything but blue jeans. The girls wore the same, but wore skirts instead of pants.

"On second thought," she muttered, "I'll just watch from the car."

"'Bye," Steven said, shrugging on his backpack. He practically ran from the car. However, at the top of the steps, he turned.

Watching him the whole way, Rachel returned the half smile with one of her own. *Amazing what a smile and a wave could to do lift the spirits.* She swallowed a lump in her throat. His backpack was about the size of his torso, and his legs were like pins sticking from his blazer. Then she noticed the front of his shirt was already no longer tucked in. Sometimes he looked like a little grown-up ready to lead the world, and other times he looked very much like a very little boy stuck in a world much too big for him.

A sharp beep on her left jolted Rachel's attention. Turning, she saw a blue minivan had pulled next to her. The window rolled down and a woman with blond hair cut in the shape of a crashing wave glared at her. Cut short above the neck, the front of her hair curled up just over her brow.

"Are you Rachel?" the woman demanded when Rachel had quickly rolled down her window.

"Uh, yeah. Yes." Confused, Rachel could only stare at the strange woman.

"I'm Mrs. Hunt. Tommy's mom. I'll be picking Steven up after school. Do you understand?" Her voice was curt and her eyes not friendly. She never smiled once.

"Uh, yes …"

"And," continued the woman, "I'll be providing him the rides to school and from school and swim practice from now on."

"I, I know," Rachel said. "Elizabe—I mean, Mrs. Winter—told me."

"Good. Don't you forget it!" Then the minivan shot forward, nearly running over a small, dark-skinned boy who was crossing to the school from the parking lot.

Horn beeping, Mrs. Hunt kept going without slowing.

Shaken, Rachel forgot about Steven.

What is with these people? Either they were super nice, or just plain mean for no reason! Driving home, she made sure to stay under the speed limit. No reason to risk the chance of having another stranger yell at her. She was so shaken that she failed to notice the small green car following her until she reached the turnoff to Camelot Acres. As she turned, the car suddenly sped up and zoomed by.

"Hey, Steven! Wait up, man!"

Steven obediently stopped and let a crowd of upperclassmen pass by. He ducked as several girls patted his hair.

"Hi, Stevie!" one cried back to him. "You're the cutest boy in the school!"

"Hi, Teresa," Steven mumbled back, embarrassed.

"Man, you better watch yourself," Geoffrey said as he caught up to him. "Those senior guys are going to pound you if you don't stop messing with their girlfriends!"

"Hey, Geoff," Steven muttered.

Geoffrey glared at Steven. "That's all you got, man? Dude, you gave Teresa more than that and you never saw her before!" He mimicked Steve's wave. "Hiii, Tereesa," he purred, fluttering his eyes.

"She's on the swim team," Steven said.

"And I'm your best friend."

Steven grimaced. "What do you want me to say?"

"Well, how 'bout, 'Hey, did you do Ms. Fatbottom's homework over the weekend?' Dude, speaking of fat bottoms, who was that girl who dropped you off?"

"My babysitter." Steven plunged ahead before Geoffrey could comment. "You didn't do your math homework, did you?"

"Your babysitter? Man, I'm sorry. I thought you'd have some beauty queen—"

"Did you do your math or not?"

"Well, uh, funny thing … I tried, I really did. But Ms. Fatbottom is too much for me! She did a sneak attack and blew me apart. I mean, what could I do? She has two bottoms—one on either end. One makes all this noise and the other makes all the smell. Man, I tell you. Between the two, I feel like a kid trapped in a nuclear explosion that won't stop! Every time I do my homework, I think of her and pass out. I mean, her momma never knew which end to change when she was a baby."

Steven grinned. "Stop being gross."

"Have to be, in this school. Don't you see what they serve as lunch? I'm more afraid it'll eat me than of me eating it. So, uh, can you help me out?"

Sighing, Steven retrieved his math notebook from his backpack. "Just give it back to me before math—and don't let anybody see you," he told his friend. This was nothing new. The two had been best pals since the first day of school—they were an unlikely pair, but a pair that never split, no matter the differences or the attempts by certain teachers.

Geoffrey slapped Steven on the back. "Don't worry, dude. I'll coordinate my attack of this homework so nobody will know what hit until it's too late. Thanks, man. I owe you." Beneath his joking manner, relief flooded Geoffrey's face.

Shrugging, Steven nudged Geoffrey's shoulder. "Just pick me for your team next time we play basketball."

Geoffrey laughed. "That I can do!"

Though fast and quick in most sports, Steven's one weakness was his lack of height, something very apparent when playing basketball. His feet were big, so he would grow, but for the time being, he stood inches shorter than most of his classmates. This kept him off the "good teams" and forced him to play in the side games, where there were mostly girls. They just wanted to be near Steven instead of actually playing a game. Geoffrey, on the other hand, as one of the best players in the grade, was always a team captain.

Walking shoulder to shoulder, the two friends were suddenly split when a third boy wedged himself between them.

"Hey, there you are!" said the newcomer. "Gosh, Steven, I needed you this morning!"

Tommy Hunt pretended to glare down at Steven. A head taller, he was a large, sturdy boy with a small, tight mouth and a chin as square as a box. His blond hair, short on the sides, long on top, was always plastered with hairspray and parted neatly in the middle. One of the best freestyle swimmers on the swim team, the joke was that his hair never got wet and acted as a secret weapon—it cut through the water like the bow of a ship. The other members, Steven excluded, called him Tommy the Boat, or just Boat.

"Hi, Tommy." Steven winced as Tommy planted a friendly elbow in his ribs.

"The Boat has pulled in," Geoffrey muttered.

Tommy ignored Geoffrey, as he often did. "Why didn't you ride with me today, man?" Another elbow jabbed Steven's ribs. "I couldn't do Ms. Fatbottom's homework—I got stuck doing yard work and then had to help my mom with church stuff." Besides the freestyle, Tommy was also good at making excuses. "You were supposed to help me on the way here!" His whiny voice made it sound like it was all Steven's fault the work hadn't been done.

Steven brushed back hair from his eyes. "Today is when my mom and dad are leaving, so my, uh, babysitter brought me."

Tommy lifted his eyebrows. "Your babysitter brought you to school?"

Steven pursed his lips and nodded. "I don't think it will be every day."

"It had better not!" Tommy said hotly. "Well, can I borrow your homework, man? Just to see how it's done—"

Steven shook his head. "Sorry, but Geoffrey asked first."

Tommy made a face and for the first time turned to Geoffrey. It was no secret that Tommy and Geoffrey never really got along. The only thing they had in common was their friendship with Steven. Truth be told, neither one would miss the other if he ever moved away.

"Come on, Geoffrey," Tommy said. His voice deepened and tone grew firmer. "Let me use it first. I'll be real quick."

Geoffrey shook his head. "Sorry, dude. But see me after gym."

"After gym is math class!" Tommy said.

Geoffrey grunted. "Well, come find me in the locker room at the end of gym. We can both copy—I mean, research Steven's homework."

"Whatever." Tommy abruptly turned away and angrily stalked to his locker.

Geoffrey put an arm around Steven's shoulder. "Come on, friend dude. Let's get to class."

"Hello, Steven," a girl said going the opposite direction. "That was a fun party yesterday!"

Another stepped in front of him, forcing both Geoffrey and him to stop. "Hi, Steven," she said, batting her eyes. "Here's an invitation to my party for this Saturday. I hope you can make it!"

Steven took the offered envelope. "Uh, thanks, Emily."

"Sure, Steven. It'll be great to see you there."

Geoffrey stared at the girl and then yanked Steven away from her. "He might be busy Saturday, unless you invite his best friend," he said.

"I already invited Tommy," the girl said to him rather snottily.

Geoffrey coughed. "Ahem. What about me?"

Making a face, the girl whirled away. "Come to my house at one, Steven!"

Steven shoved the invitation in his pocket. "We better hurry so we're not late," he mumbled.

"I don't got to hurry nowhere," grumbled Geoffrey. "I wasn't invited. I'm never invited."

As Rachel rolled slowly up the driveway, Lisa stomped in the opposite direction toward the red car. Dressed in a pretty pink and white top and khaki shorts, the girl's face did not match her outfit. Twisted in an angry glare, she made it a point not to notice Rachel's car.

Slowing to a stop, Rachel lowered the passenger window. "Bye, Lisa!" she called, trying to sound cheerful.

Turning sharply, Lisa stuck her head through the open window. Her glare only deepened. "Listen, Rachel. My parents are leaving today. You might think you're in charge, but you're not. I don't want you here, and we don't need you to be our babysitter. Okay? The housekeeper is coming today, and that's all we need. Got it?"

Then she was back to stomping down the driveway.

Mouth stuck open, Rachel didn't know what to do. She ended up sitting in the car for a long time—until a shiny, blue Ford Mustang pulled behind her.

The housekeeper had arrived. A tall, skinny, young woman with tight jeans and a bright blue top climbed out of the car and made a point of stretching her long legs in front of Rachel.

Great, that's all I need, Rachel thought.

"Finished!" Geoffrey proclaimed, sticking his tongue out as he copied the last answer. "I'm proud to say, the battle is over and we are victorious!"

Steven grinned from the next bench. "It's about time."

The two boys were among the stragglers of their class. Both still wore their blue gym shorts and white T-shirts. Most everyone else was just finishing putting school uniforms back on.

Geoffrey looked up with a frown. "Where's Tommy? He's supposed to be here for your homework, right? You don't think he's mad because I got him out in dodgeball, do you?"

Shrugging, Steven lifted his right sneaker to the bench and started playing with its laces. "Maybe he got the work from somebody else."

"Or he did it himself," snorted Geoffrey. "Yeah, right. That dude lives off you, dude."

"I do what?" demanded a hard voice. Tommy had just entered the locker room from the front. Shoving his way to the back where Geoffrey and Steven sat, he jammed both hands to his sides. Also still in his gym clothes, he had a line of sweat dripping down his forehead and it looked as if he just finished running. He directed a hard glare at Geoffrey.

Immediately the jostling and laughter in the room ceased as all eyes turned to the scene.

Geoffrey stood from where he'd been kneeling and using a bench as a table. "Tommy," he said coolly. "What's up?"

"Where were you?" Steven asked uneasily. "It's almost time for the bell."

Tommy ignored Steven. Glaring at Geoffrey, he crossed his arms. "You're up, mister."

"Okay, all boys freeze!" Two upperclassmen dressed in school uniform rushed in from the front of the locker room.

The locker rooms were built much later than the original school and were in a long, flat building in the back near the athletic fields. One side was only for boys, and only girls were allowed on the other. Separated from the rest of the school, it served as the designated area for shady dealings. The rooms were rarely monitored and what happened at the gym lockers had the habit of staying at the gym lockers.

One of the upperclassmen asked roughly, "Is that the kid, Tommy?" He gestured at Geoffrey. Tall, his face spotted with pimples, he had a thick mane of light brown hair and resembled a giraffe with measles. His companion was a head shorter but sported a solid build. He already sported a decent mustache.

"That's him," Tommy said grimly.

"You had to ask?" Geoffrey demanded. "Let me guess, he said it was the black kid, right?"

"Shut your mouth," the giraffe boy growled. He slowly made his way through the maze of nervous students. "You're in a lot of trouble, buddy."

"What did I do?" demanded Geoffrey.

"Well, mister smart mouth," purred Mustache, following close behind and clearly enjoying his role. Having an audience made him puff up. "We're members of the honor council. Seems to me like you were cheating off another student's paper. That right, chocolate boy?"

"Chocolate boy?" Blood rushed to Geoffrey's face. He stared angrily at Tommy. "You seriously ratted me out to these clowns, dude?"

"He didn't rat anybody out," Giraffe boy snapped. "We can sniff out a cheat, right, Corey?"

"Right, Bo," responded Corey.

"I bet," Geoffrey snorted. "That's because you sniff each other's—"

Giraffe boy, also known as Bo, leapt the last yard and grabbed Geoffrey by his shirt and shoved him into the lockers. "Watch your lip, Chocolate," he snarled.

Steven rose to his feet. His eyes became narrow slits and his mouth a grim line. Otherwise he appeared totally calm. "We were just looking at our answers," he said tightly.

Corey waved him off. "Stay out of this, Steven." It seemed like everyone knew his name. "This guy needs to learn a lesson. If he thinks he can cheat his way through life, then he has a terrible future ahead of him. It's best he learns now."

"Ooo, lookee here!" Bo held up Steven's completed homework in his free hand. His other still held Geoffrey against the locker. "Steven Winter … is that you, boy?" He shoved the paper in Geoffrey's face. "You're no winter, not unless you're dirty snow!"

Corey and Bo both laughed.

Many of the boys watching were too afraid to speak, or move. However, a few cracked smiles and seemed to be enjoying the show.

Geoffrey glared balefully at Corey. "Let go of me."

"First let's look at the other paper," Bo said. "Corey, if you please."

Steven folded his arms across his chest. "I said we were only checking answers."

"Shut it, Steven," Bo snapped. "Well, Corey?"

"At least he got his name right," drawled the teen, taking Steven's paper from Corey and holding it up next to Geoffrey's. "But everything else looks to be copied directly from Steven's. He even has the same problems." He laughed at his joke.

"Let me go, I said!" Geoffrey said louder.

Corey chuckled. "No can do, chocolate boy."

Steven closed his eyes. He could feel his knees trembling—not from fear, but from a deep anger. From deep inside his chest, the monster stirred. He swallowed hard and fought for control. Ever since he could remember, he'd had the knack of reading people's intentions. By reading body language he could usually tell when somebody really meant harm and when somebody was only bluffing. And when somebody meant harm, Steven reacted by unleashing his monster. That was when he went crazy. Years ago he promised to never allow the monster loose again. But now his promise was slipping. The monster slid upward toward his throat.

His eyes flashed open and he stared intently first at Corey and then at Bo. They were juniors and members of his swim team. Corey's mother also served as the school's vice principal and as a head mom on the swim team. Bo was Corey's best friend and bragged that he would join the Marines after graduating. Both were showoffs who liked to be in power, but neither ever acted truly evil.

His hands dug into his shorts and his nails stabbed into his thighs. Sitting abruptly back down on the bench, he stared at the cracked green floor and did all he could to keep his monster locked inside.

Then it was over.

"Next time, we're taking you in," breathed Bo in Geoffrey's face.

"Let this be a warning," Corey added. "Now get dressed while we wash our hands."

Steven's shoulders slumped and he felt sweat dripping from his hair. His heart beating wildly as the monster eased back down and went back to sleep. After Corey and Bo left, the other boys quickly followed. Soon Geoffrey and Steven were all that remained.

Geoffrey sat on the floor huddled against the locker where Corey had shoved him. In front of him were the crumpled remains of his homework. Steven's homework sat unharmed on the bench.

Wiping his eyes, Geoffrey looked up at his … friend.

"Are you okay?" Steven asked softly, rising from the bench.

"Okay?" Geoffrey actually spat. "Okay, you ask? What do you care! You just sat there!"

"They didn't mean—"

"Don't touch me! Some friend you are!"

Steven kept his hand extended. "Just get up. You can copy it again."

Geoffrey's eyes widened and then narrowed. "You mean the homework? Right. After what those stupid jerkwads did, all I care about is homework!"

Steven made a face. "Just forget them. They didn't mean anything."

Ignoring the hand, Geoffrey pushed himself to his feet. "How about I just get up and forget you!"

"Hey—"

"I said don't touch me!" Drawing back his fist, Geoffrey swung wildly and connected with Steven's mouth.

Head snapping back, Steven tripped over the bench and went crashing backward into the lockers. Stars flashed and suddenly he sat on the floor with a split lip, too stunned to move.

Grabbing his bag, Geoffrey forgot about changing as he ran from the locker room.

The next class of boys found Steven still sitting where he had fallen, with his head bowed against his knees. A trickle of blood ran down his left leg.

"Steven!" cried a fourth grader in horror. "Who did that to you?"

Hastily wiping his eyes, he gave a wan grin. "Nobody. I fell and bit my lip."

Chapter Twelve

"Thanks, Jane," Elizabeth said warmly after the housekeeper wished them a lovely trip. "And you'll be staying here on the weekends to give Rachel a break, right?"

The lovely housekeeper nodded, flicking a strand of her long, shimmering, dark hair behind her. "The downstairs guest room, yes?"

"That would be great."

Then with a nod, Jane Lovington disappeared upstairs to start her routine cleaning.

Rachel squeezed out a smile as Elizabeth turned to her. They stood just inside the front door, where luggage was beginning to pile up.

"Jane is a nice woman," Elizabeth said kindly. "Once you get to know her."

"That's one way to put it," Doug said coming into the living room with both hands full of luggage. "She's a little creepy, if you ask me."

"Doug, she'll hear you!" admonished Elizabeth. To Rachel, she said, "She came highly recommended by Vikki and so far has been great. It's been nearly a year, and as you can see, she's keeping this house in good condition … even with our kids around."

"We pay her enough." Doug wiped his brow. "Honey, are you almost ready to go? Our flight leaves in a few hours, and we have to get through security."

"Oh, yes." To Rachel, Elizabeth said, "Rachel, now is everything okay? You have everything under control?"

"I have everything," Rachel said, almost in a whisper. She smiled meekly. "I'll be fine." Her stomach tightened. She wished she could say it and mean it.

"Well, do be careful—it was in the paper this morning that a woman just vanished," Elizabeth said. "Her car was found just a few miles from here. Keep the doors locked tight at night."

"I will," Rachel promised.

Elizabeth smiled sweetly. "My kids are in good hands—your mother has to be very proud of you, Rachel. Thank you for doing this."

"Come on, Lizzy," Doug said, gathering two massive suitcases. "Rachel, it was great meeting you—let us know of any problems."

Elizabeth turned to her husband. "Doug, where are Robbie and Margie?"

"Out back murdering your flowers, I think. They want to surprise you with a bouquet."

Elizabeth squeezed her eyes shut making a face of horror. "Not my flowers! Are you sure?"

"Yep—pretty sure. I'm the one who told them to do it." He planted a quick kiss on his wife's forehead. "I'll go gather them. You still have to go up and get your last item."

"My last item?" Elizabeth asked, still trying to decide to laugh or be angry about the flowers.

Doug grinned at her. "On your bed. You won't miss it."

As Rachel said her tenth goodbye to Robbie and Margie at the front door, secretly wishing they were the ones staying and the other two were going, Elizabeth Winter came behind her with her last item.

A gleaming white beaded necklace with a sparkling silver wolf in the middle hung around her slender neck.

"It's beautiful," Rachel said without thinking. She was surprised when Elizabeth wiped away a tear.

"It is, isn't it?" she said softly. "Lisa made it … She makes a necklace for her favorite person whenever she feels sorry about something." Suddenly she grabbed Rachel's shoulders and gave her hug. "Oh, Rachel, you take good care of them, okay? And when we get back I'll see a necklace on you too."

Rachel returned the hug awkwardly. She so desperately wanted to be home.

Yeah, right. The only thing Lisa would put around my neck is a noose—much too tight.

As Doug and Elizabeth drove away to the airport with Robbie and Margie waving vigorously in the back, it really hit Rachel. She was now alone in Florida as a babysitter for one girl who hated her guts and a boy with angelic looks but also with a troubled past who might or might not care for her.

At least I have a nice car to drive …

Rachel barely had time to gather her thoughts when the house phone rang, startling her. *I'm no longer a guest.* Now she was the woman of the house. She swallowed her nerves as she picked up the phone. "Hello? Uh, um, Winter's, um, residence …"

It was Steven's school. He'd hit his head and needed to go home. As she hung up the phone, she wanted to hit her own head. What a way to begin her babysitting.

"You mean to tell me, Steven," said the vice principal in a stern voice, almost dripping with sarcasm, "you, one of the most athletic and coordinated boys in your class, tripped and fell in the locker room?"

"And bit your own lip so hard it left a bruise around it?" growled Mr. Haas, the gruff gym teacher.

Steven awkwardly nodded from where he sat on the bed in the nurse's room. He held one ice pack to his mouth and another to the back of his head where it'd struck the lockers.

The sea of faces gathered around him did not look very happy. The principal, vice principal, gym teacher, and school counselor were all present, trying to get Steven to say what *really* happened.

In the center of the crowd, Corey's mom, the vice principal, threw up her hands and stepped back in a huff. "That's just great," she wailed dramatically. "Now his parents will probably sue us for negligence. I knew we needed a monitor in the locker room!"

Mr. Haas's face turned red. "I'm the only gym teacher you hired, Mrs. Lee. I can't be in two places at once. One of the girls had her locker stuck, and I had to wait for everyone to clear out before I could help her."

"Everyone calm down," ordered the principal. Built like a bowling ball, the principal, with the unfortunate name of Mrs. Duff, put up two flabby arms as if they alone could squash the situation into nothing. "Now, Steven, you're not really hurt, are you?"

The small boy shook his head. His face, mostly hidden by ice packs, was impossible to read.

"Nurse, did you call the parents?" Mrs. Duff asked.

The nurse sighed, clearly not liking this. She said, "This is Steven Winter, remember? His parents just left for their vacation. I got in touch with the babysitter and she's on her way."

"Oh, even better," Mrs. Lee said sarcastically. "A twerp of a babysitter will probably panic and call an ambulance. Then we'll really be up the creek."

"Maybe Steven can wait outside for the sitter," the nurse said quietly, eying Mrs. Lee with distaste. "I don't think he needs to hear this."

"Excellent idea," said Mrs. Duff. "Mr. Haas, go call the new janitor and have him take Steven to the front and wait there for his ride. What's that man's name again?"

Mr. Haas grunted. "Mr. Red," he said.

"Yes, that's right. Just have him stay with Steven until his ride comes." Sidling over to Steven, she gave a soupy grin. "You don't mind doing that, do you, sweetie?" She tousled Steven's hair.

"Careful with his head!" cried the nurse. "He banged it, remember?"

"Another lawsuit," groaned Mrs. Lee.

The new janitor was a tall, thin man with a stiff back and heavily lined face. Mr. Red, despite his name, actually had a full head of snowy white hair with a matching mustache hiding his upper lip. He wore the dull brown uniform of the school janitor and walked stiffly. Dark sunglasses were added just before he opened the door for Steven to exit outside.

"Always got to watch out for Mr. Sun," he said. "You're feeling okay, sonny?" He spoke in a surprisingly high-pitched voice as he followed the boy out.

Steven nodded and removed the ice pack from his mouth to show the janitor his lip.

Peering intently, the janitor audibly swallowed. His hands shook slightly when they raised his glasses. Two brilliant blue eyes sparked as they stared down at the boy.

Steven frowned. Something about this man seemed familiar.

"No swelling, that's good," said Mr. Red. Then the janitor's eyes flickered and a red glint started to appear in the blue. "Now, boy, just go to sl—"

A loud beeping startled the janitor as he was just leaning down. His eyes immediately twitched to blue, and he barely kept from toppling on top of the boy.

"Uh, that's my ride," Steven said, shoving both ice packs at the janitor. It'd happened so fast that Steven never noticed the danger. But he did have an uncomfortable feeling about the janitor and just wanted to get away. His monster swished restlessly around his belly.

Mr. Red jumped when the cold packs touched his skin. Stuffing the items in his pocket, he hastily followed the boy down the steps. "I, uh, yes … boy, you, er—" He sounded too amazed to form coherent words. And this was the truth.

Mr. Red, as he currently called himself, was not only amazed—he was ecstatic. Isabella was right. This had to be the boy! It must be! And this was a golden opportunity to snatch him. But then the boy reached the car.

Mr. Red quickly sprang into action. Moving much faster than his appearance would suggest being possible, he caught up before the boy could grab the handle to the car door.

"Boy, sonny, are you sure you feel okay? Uh, here, maybe you still need this." Reaching into his pocket, the janitor yanked out an ice pack and pressed it on Steven's reddish-brown hair. His other arm grabbed the boy's shoulder and slid down to bare skin.

Still in his gym clothes, the boy's thin arm of muscle and bone could easily be enveloped by the janitor's large hand. Yet when Mr. Red tried to squeeze and send a burst of energy into the boy, it felt like grabbing a handful of live wires.

Yelping, the janitor immediately let go and jumped back. His hand twitched in pain.

Rachel frowned from the driver's seat as the man stumbled back. Her eyes were on Steven, and she thought the man had tripped. The poor boy … Dressed only in an oversized T-shirt and shorts, he looked so small and thin next to the tall janitor. As she took in his disheveled hair and blank face, she knew something bad had happened. There was no half smile, and his brown eyes were lost in deep thought. A purple bruise marred the left corner of his mouth.

He just wants to go home. Thinking to help him, she twisted in her seat and reached back to open the door for him.

After shocking the janitor without realizing it, Steven stepped back and glanced back at the school. He had to blink away tears as he pressed his lips tightly together. Geoffrey and Tommy were still inside somewhere.

"Ah, excuse me, miss," said the janitor's voice from outside the window. "You're Rachel, correct?"

"Um, yes …" She had to look ridiculous—her head was tilted back as her body stretched awkwardly in the backseat for the door handle. *Almost got it …*

"Good." Smiling, Mr. Red raised his sunglasses. Again his eyes began molting into a dark fiery red. They bore down on Rachel. He started to chant, "Go to—"

"Here, Steven, get in!" Rachel managed to catch the handle and push the door open. Swinging wildly, it nailed the janitor in the shins.

"Ouch!" His red eyes suddenly brimming with tears, Mr. Red stumbled back. Fiery pain raced up and down both legs.

"Oh, uh, sorry," Rachel mumbled, pushing herself to an upright seated position. "I didn't see you."

Steven retrieved the icepack that had fallen and silently handed it to the janitor.

Muttering, the janitor took the ice and limped back from the car as Steven climbed in.

Before Rachel could completely pull away, the front door of the school burst open and two young girls rushed out, one carrying Steven's backpack and the other holding school clothes.

"Wait, Steven!" they cried in unison.

Rachel pulled the car back to the curb, several feet away from the janitor, who still stood like a statue. "Uh, do you want to see them?" she asked.

She lowered Steven's window when the boy shrugged.

"Here's your stuff," said one of the girls, smiling sweetly as she handed over Steven's backpack while preening her blond hair at the same time.

"We're from Steven's class," the other explained to Rachel. Then she smiled at Steven, flicking back brunette curls. "Ms. Fatbottom actually sent us."

Steven blinked, puzzled. "Really?"

"Yes," said the blond. "The boys told her everything."

Steven visibly slumped in his seat. "Everything?"

"Well," began the blond. "Tommy explained it all. He said that he thought Geoffrey stole your homework and was cheating."

"But," cut in the other girl, "really he was just checking answers."

Steven felt dazed—more from what he'd heard than from banging his head. The way the girls explained it, Tommy, with the other boys' support, had come up with the story that it'd all been a misunderstanding. In the end, two upperclassmen bullies, both unidentified, had crumpled up Geoffrey's homework.

"Don't worry," the blond girl said. "Ms. Fatbottom is going to count Geoffrey's homework and says there won't be any tonight."

"Really?" Steven asked.

"Yep," said the girl. "Well, except for you." She made a face. "She put all the makeup work in your bag already. If you want, I can come by later to help you."

"Me too!" chimed the other girl.

"Um, that's okay," said Steven. "What about Geoffrey?"

Both girls shrugged.

The blond said, "Oh … he came to class late. He won't talk to anybody."

"Oh." Steven found his half smile. "Thanks, Callie. Thanks, Susie. I'll see you tomorrow."

The girls giggled and waved. "He's so cute!" they said in unison as the car rolled away.

Rachel closed Steven's window and pressed harder on the gas. *So, that's what it's like to be popular in school,* she thought. The whole class, including the teacher, comes to your aid. Looking in the rearview mirror at Steven, she smiled. "Those girls were, uh, pretty, uh, pretty nice, Steven."

Twisting his mouth, Steven grimaced. "Did my mom and dad leave yet?" he asked, sounding tired.

"Uh, yeah. Sorry. They just left a little before your school called. Don't worry. I already sent a text to your mom. She said to have you take it easy …"

Steven crossed his arms and stared out the window.

Feeling lost and over her head, Rachel put her eyes on the road. At home, she always talked with her mom when they were driving … but that was because they were friends.

The rest of the ride home was as silent as the ride to school that morning had been. This gave Rachel time to think. And as she was thinking, she glanced once in the rearview mirror and saw a familiar green car pull behind her. Once again, it followed her to Camelot Acres before speeding off.

Rachel's heart pounded the rest of the way to Steven's house.

As soon as the red Corolla left the school, Mr. Red tore off his sunglasses. His blue eyes sparked as they blinked rapidly.

"He's the one," he said hoarsely. "Blast that babysitter! I nearly had him!"

Then he moaned and rubbed his shin. If it wasn't for that stupid babysitter, he would already be gone with the boy. Isabella's fool plan would take days before it could ever work. By that time, the others might act first. And his powers seemed to have little effect on the boy … There had to be another way. Suddenly he relaxed and smiled.

After he'd listened to the two blathering girls, a plan was quickly forming. Nobody believed that Steven simply fell … oh no, somebody had punched him. And Mr. Red knew who.

Limping away, he started tearing off his janitor's uniform to reveal new clothes underneath.

Rachel did her best not to slam the phone as she hung up. Rubbing her eyes, she took deep breaths and thought happy thoughts. Ms. Lee, Steven's vice principal, had just tried to talk her ear off and finally had run out of breath. She'd gone on for almost a full hour about how wonderful Steven was and how terribly sorry the school felt about his "accident." Of course it was nobody's fault and blah, blah, blah …

I really need to learn how to hang up on people. She sighed. *This is not as I envisioned my first day … What am I even doing here? These people have nothing in common with me. I can't stand being part of their lives!* Sarah had been right—going to Florida to be a babysitter was a mistake. And her first day had only begun.

Looking at the clock, Rachel saw that Lisa would be home soon. *Great.*

Steven lay on the floor in the living room, working on his homework. Jane Lovington, the housekeeper, still floated around somewhere doing the cleaning. Rachel hadn't seen her in some time, but her car was still parked outside, so she had to be somewhere.

And I, of course, am alone … This wasn't how it was supposed to be. Rachel took a deep breath. A great babysitter would be making cookies for the kids or *helping Steven with his work!* If she could get him on her side, then maybe Lisa would come around! *I just need to connect with him, let him know I'm there for him …*

Walking nonchalantly into the living room, she looked where Steven lay, still dressed in his gym clothes. His bare legs sprawled in a V-shape, he had his head bent over his book and appeared hard at work. Then, moving closer, she noticed he was actually staring at the floor and not writing a thing.

Stuck on a problem … Here goes nothing … Rachel cleared her throat. "Are, uh, are you going to swim practice today?"

"No." The boy didn't even look up.

"Okay." There went nothing. Standing like a lame politician having her handshake rebuffed, she watched him for a few seconds before quietly leaving for her room. It just didn't work.

Popular kids had no use for people like her—no matter their age. It was a thought that she just couldn't drop.

Rachel had just come downstairs a little while later when the front door swung open, giving way for Lisa to stomp through. She barely glanced at Rachel. The door slammed behind her.

"Where's Ms. Lovington?" the young girl demanded. "I need to talk to her."

"Hi, uh, uh, what do you need to talk to her about?"

"Never mind. I'll find her on my own." Dumping her backpack by Rachel's feet, the redhead disappeared upstairs.

Her face burning, Rachel retreated outside to the pool area. Outside brought little relief. The hot Florida sun burned down without mercy and the humidity was sweltering. Nobody and nothing liked her here. Stepping to the edge of the pool, she looked down at the clear blue water. It seemed to be begging her to jump in. *No chance.*

Staring down at her flab, Rachel gritted her teeth, remembering the whale comment from that morning. The sounds of happy children carried over from the next house. Looking up, she heard a faint splash and knew the Richardson kids were having a blast in their own pool. From across the way and behind their fence, came shrieks and roars. Laughter and splashing carried her way like songbirds telling her of a better place.

Then the door behind Rachel opened, and she was no longer alone.

Rosco palmed the fist-sized rock, admiring its size and shape. Then with a flick of the wrist, he sent it skipping across the pavement until it bounced into the finely cut grass of some dumb millionaire's lawn. The monstrous house stared back at the boy with uncaring windows. People like him didn't matter to the rich. Searching for another rock, he thought maybe he would put out one of the windows—then maybe the rich would care about him.

"You know, you're only hurting the poor landscaping crew."

Startled, Rosco whirled with catlike quickness, snatching up a rock and looking for the voice. On the other side of the street, the homeless bum stared at him through his dark glasses.

Rosco swallowed and stood to his full height. Sneering, he deliberately wiped his mouth in contempt. Still, he kept hold of the rock and warily watched the man.

"What's you talkin' about?"

"You really think millionaires do their own work? I've watched you throw four rocks onto that lawn. Some poor kid like you will be mowing that lawn. The millionaires, they have their heads stuck so far up their money holes they don't have the time or inclination. So you're just hurting people like yourself."

Turning, Rosco chucked the rock into the grass. "So what?"

The man grinned, revealing startlingly white teeth. "Rosco, you don't like rich people very much, do you?"

Rosco glared. "Maybe I don't like you either, man."

"Maybe not. What about your brother? Do you like him?"

Raising a fist, Rosco took a step at the old bum. "What's you got to do about my brother?" he snarled. "I don't care who you are, but I'll hurt you if you mess with him!"

"Calm down, Rosco. It's not me you're mad at. I know some people at your brother's school, that's all." The bum had a smile and he spoke easily. Only now, he frowned. "I was told he had a rough time from his so-called friends today."

Rosco glared. "That white-bread school is nuthin' but trouble. Why you telling me this?"

The bum shrugged. "I've been walking this street, being looked down on by all these fancy houses for too long. I know how these rich, pompous oafs treat poor people. They only show respect if we stand up to them. Throwing rocks won't do anything. But I know some things … Your brother was disrespected today." He lifted his sunglasses and stared straight at Rosco. "If he or you want to do something about it, meet me tonight."

As if mesmerized, Rosco stared at two of the brightest blue eyes he'd ever seen. They seemed to be glowing, even in the afternoon sun. "Where at?" he heard himself ask.

"In the woods, at the old shack where you like to sneak smokes. Bring your friends." The bum gestured down the street toward the trees. Toothy, Macie, and Shoes sauntered toward them.

"And who are you?"

Lowering his glasses to cover his eyes, the bum smiled. "Just call me Red."

Jakey Richardson hugged his father's leg tightly and stared into the pool. Above him, his father was in deep discussion on his cell phone but made it a point to nudge Jakey's chin with his knee. Leaning against the knee, Jakey squeezed, pressing his cheek against his father's warm skin. He never wanted to let go. In a short while, both his parents and Alison would be flying to England for two weeks. It sounded like an eternity to the young boy. Just thinking about it made his heart drop.

Inside the Richardson house, Courtney grabbed Jason and pointed out the back window to the forlorn sight. Jakey's bronzed back soaked in the sun as he clung to their father. "Look at him. You'd think spending two weeks with us was worse than school."

Jason chuckled. "Poor Dad may not be able to detach himself when it's time to go."

"Think we should cheer him up?"

"Sure … just wait until Dad is off the phone. You don't mind getting wet again, do you?" The siblings had just completed one water war in the pool and were mostly dry.

Courtney grinned. "The last one wasn't with Dad or Mom."

"Go tell Mom to put on her bathing suit. I'll watch."

At the pool, Mr. Richardson clicked off his phone and glanced down at the full head of hair belonging to his youngest son. "Jakey, my friend, you'll have a good time when we're gone. You'll see." Reaching down, he ruffled his hair. "Isn't there a boy about your age next door?"

The boy grunted. "Yeah, but he doesn't play soccer."

"Is that right? Maybe you should ask him … but first, I was thinking of a swim."

Jakey looked up, squinting in the sun. "You don't even have your suit on."

"So? I wasn't thinking about me." Reaching down, he pulled Jakey to his feet and smoothed his hair. "You'll have a rattail growing, mister, if you're not careful."

"So? I like it."

The house door slid quietly open and Jason silently crept out. Father and elder son exchanged looks.

"You like it, huh? Well, do you know what we do with rats?"

"What?"

"We drown them!" Mr. Richardson snatched Jakey's arms and Jason rushed to grab his legs.

Jakey's gloom dissipated as he was soon flying through the air. His bright orange and yellow bathing suit flashed brilliantly in the sun before striking the water with a loud splash. Moments later, the entire Richardson family took to the pool, each leaving their troubles behind. Little did they know, some of their troubles were only beginning.

Chapter Thirteen

As the shouts and squeals resumed, Rachel shaded her eyes to look toward the Richardson pool again. Over there was fun … over here, well, she wasn't quite winning the most fun babysitter in the world award.

Behind her, Steven skated in circles on his skateboard, which was the strangest one Rachel had ever seen. Two wheels supported flexible platforms connected by a tube.

Gathering her courage, Rachel turned to the boy. "You're pretty good. What's that thing called?"

Steven turned sharply to face her. Wearing jeans rolled up on his calves and a button-down shirt rolled to his elbows, he looked in much better spirits. His bruised mouth was barely visible, and he even gave her one of his half grins. "It's a ripstick. Want to try?"

Rachel swallowed. "Uh, I don't think so. Are you sure your mom lets you use it without a helmet? And without shoes?" These weren't listed on the rules from Elizabeth, but it couldn't be very safe.

"I do it all the time. I don't fall anymore." He grinned slightly. "Much, anyway."

"I bet … just don't fall while I'm here, okay? That's a new rule."

"Sure … Rachel?" He said her name shyly—it was the first time he'd ever used it.

Her heart quickening, Rachel gave him her full attention. "Uh, yes?"

"Could you give me a ride to swim practice today? I think I want to go now. And to school tomorrow?"

Taken aback, Rachel stared down at the small boy. His brown eyes were serious, and his mouth was tightened in a firm line. Despite his relaxed shoulders, it was almost a pleading look. "Ah, sure, but what about, uh, Mrs. Hunt?" She hadn't forgotten Mrs. Hunt's animosity from that morning.

He shrugged and looked around nonchalantly. "I just want you to do it."

How could she refuse? "Go get changed for swimming."

Another yell of joy from the Richardson pool—Jason, she was sure of it—made Rachel get a wild thought.

"Oh, and …" Steven stopped at the door and looked back at her. "Tell your, um, sister that I'll get dinner for tonight. I have a plan." She smiled and was relieved to see Steven return it. Half of it.

"Everything okay?" Rachel asked Steven. She looked at him in the rearview mirror and couldn't help notice the sad look covering the boy's handsome face.

They were in the car and on the way to swim practice. Since they had started off, there had been silence. Rachel didn't understand what was wrong, but something definitely was bothering Steven.

For a moment she thought he was ignoring her or hadn't heard her. Then he coughed. "Sometimes … I feel alone."

Rachel gulped and nearly swerved off the road. Steven Winter feeling lonely? It was like saying the Hamburger Helper was feeling vegetarian. At the same time, it was the first time one of the kids confided in her … this was a big opportunity to gain much-needed trust and even an ally.

Taking a deep breath, Rachel pulled her eyes to the road and resisted looking back in the mirror. Her hands clenched the wheel so tightly her knuckles were white.

"Why do you say that?" she said carefully, knowing she was treading deep water. "Do you miss your parents?"

She heard Steven give a slight sigh. "It's not that … It's different at home with Mom and everyone. Even with her gone, I'm fine. But at school … it just feels different."

"But don't you have friends at school?" Rachel couldn't help but sound incredulous. Just the other day, two invitations had arrived for Steven in the mail—one smelled faintly of perfume.

"I just don't know if they're really my friends." The kid was almost pleading with her. "You know what I mean?"

No. Rachel did not know. Friends were one topic Rachel was completely clueless about. Might as well ask the spare tire for friendship advice before asking her. Like the tire, she was there but nobody ever noticed unless there was an emergency and she was needed. Then it was just to borrow her homework to copy or something.

"Yeah, uh, well," Rachel said, sounding lame, "friends can be complicated, heh."

The two fell silent until they reached the pool. Rachel risked a glance in the mirror and saw Steven staring out the window with one of his forlorn puppy-eyed expressions. How could such a cute little kid have so many problems that it caused a face like that? And he was asking her for help, and what had she given him so far?

It wasn't fair! She knew nothing about friends. If anything, he should be giving her advice! But he needed *something* from her. She found herself going back to what her mother had told her.

"Uh, oh, Steven … about friends … you have to, uh, be a friend to get a friend." *No, that was stupid! He didn't need to hear that!*

Steven leaned forward in his seat. "But how do I know somebody is really my friend?"

"Well, uh, that can be, uh, tough." She slowed the car and slid to a stop in front of the YMCA where swim practice was held. "Well, this is it. Bye, Steven."

"Yeah, bye."

"Wait!"

Steven stopped halfway from climbing out of the car.

Rachel twisted in her seat and immediately got her seatbelt tangled in her face.

"Oh, shoot! Hold on …" Snapping the belt off, she focused all her attention on the boy in front of her.

His brown eyes were wide and innocent as they locked onto hers and he waited patiently. *This,* she thought, *would be a good friend.* "A friend, Steven, is somebody who is always there for you when you need them. They never leave you when trouble comes … even if they get you in trouble, they'll always stay with you to get you back out. Okay?"

It was all advice she'd gleaned from reading the hundreds of novels she'd read growing up. And it sounded true—just the qualities she wanted in the friends she never had.

"You know," she continued, "it's like your mom and my mom. Remember the stories. They were always there for each other."

Steven nodded thoughtfully. Then he gave a slight grin. "And that's why you're here."

Rachel couldn't contain a grin of her own. "You know what? I think you're right. I—"

Just then the loud horn honked behind them, startling Rachel so that she switched the windshield wipers on. It ruined the moment, but not the trust that had just been built. Just maybe it wouldn't be such a terrible summer after all. Maybe.

After swim practice, Steven left the local YMCA with a scowl. Tommy hadn't shown up, and all the other kids had kept asking him what had happened. Dragging his swim bag to the bench near the flower garden, he slumped into a sitting position.

"Hey, Steve!" hollered Mr. Bob, one of the coaches, who was heading to his car. "Great practice, kid!"

"Um, thanks, Coach." He threw a wave.

Shaking his head, the coach turned to one of the other parents. "That boy, the way he can bend his back and kick with those flipper feet, he's about to take off out of the water with his butterfly."

Corey and Bo came out of the YMCA next. Looking slightly nervous, the two cautiously approached Steven. During practice, they had kept looking his way, but were pointedly ignored.

"Hey, Steven," stammered Corey. "We, uh, just want to say sorry about school today."

"Yeah," Bo added, kicking a stone on the path into the flower bed. "We didn't mean for anyone to get hurt. We heard about what happened afterwards."

Staring up at them, Steven said nothing.

Corey ran a hand through his still-wet hair. "Listen, Tommy came running down the hall … it looked like he'd been crying. We asked what was wrong and he wouldn't tell us."

"Yeah, uh, we sort of pressed him. You know, swim team members got to stand up for each other. Anyway, he let out that some kid had been picking on him in dodgeball, and, well, that he was also copying your homework." Bo ducked his head. "We sort of overreacted."

"Yeah," Corey added. "Things got carried away. We're sorry, man. Things okay between us?"

After a moment of hesitation, Steven slowly nodded. The question was, were things okay between him and Tommy and Geoffrey?

"Cool," said Bo, sounding relieved.

Corey grinned. "Thanks, man."

The two teens each slapped Steven's hand and quickly ran to the van where Mrs. Lee impatiently waited. Then she saw it was Steven on the bench. Getting out of the van, she went over to check his head for any lumps.

"I knew you were okay. It was nothing, right?" she kept saying, fussing over him.

By the time Rachel pulled in, Steven was not in a good mood. Climbing in after his swim bag, he crossed his arms in the backseat and refused to say a word.

"So, how was swim practice?" she asked.

Steven mumbled something unintelligible.

Not knowing what to say next, Rachel turned on some Florida rock station and tried to swallow her nerves. "The good news is," she finally said minutes later, "I picked up supper on the way home from dropping you off. It's in the oven."

"Pizza?" The look of disgust visible on Lisa's face was enough to cause Rachel to physically stumble. It was like Rachel had just committed the ultimate sin and bragged about it.

"Yes, pizza," Rachel said. "I got two mediums." She started to stammer and then talk too fast as Lisa gave her a look of horror. "One is cheese and the other is pepperoni. I got it fresh, for you, for supper. It's good …" Rachel blanched. She thought she'd been giving them a special treat, but the way Lisa stared at her made her want to crawl in a hole and die.

Steven looked at Lisa and then at Rachel. He wore a helpless expression—one that said he wanted no part of this.

They were gathered around the table with the two boxes open before them. Instead of a supper, they looked to be gathered for a funeral … maybe Rachel's.

"What did you do that for?" Lisa seethed, gripping the back of her chair like she wanted to use it to pummel Rachel. "Are you crazy?"

"Wha—um, didn't you make one of your salads? Your mother said you always made a salad …"

"*You* said *you* were getting dinner tonight! You obviously didn't need my help!"

"But—" Looking helpless, Rachel gestured at the steaming pizza. The smell was overpowering and wonderful to her. "I brought you … pizza."

"We don't eat pizza, Rachel!" snapped Lisa. "It's full of grease and fat! We're not like you!"

The last part hurt the most. Eyes watering, Rachel did stumble back, striking the glass window behind her. "I thought every kid liked pizza," she mumbled.

"Only the fat ones!" Spinning around so fast that her fiery red hair whipped behind her, Lisa stomped out toward the stairs.

"I'm not that hungry anyway," Steven mumbled, walking after his sister.

Left terribly alone, Rachel sat down in front of her pizza. Putting down her head, she cried. She couldn't help it. The pizza was supposed to be the ice-breaker that led to a fun first night. Instead …

"I just want to go home …" But she couldn't.

Elizabeth and Doug had originally planned to have Rachel stay with them for a few days to get her and the kids used to each other. Rachel's graduation and Mr. and Mrs. Winter's last-minute plans in Colorado didn't for allow this. So Rachel was stuck …

Wiping her eyes, she stared at the two boxes. "Come on, Rachel," she told herself. "Play the happy game—now I get all the pizza to myself."

It's full of grease and fat! We're not like you! Lisa's words burned within her like an iron to her heart.

"Arrggh!" Pushing back her chair, she grabbed the pizzas and ran for the door. "Enough is enough!" she growled to nobody.

Ignoring the succulent smell of hot cheese and pepperoni, she dashed down the driveway not even knowing where she was going. She just wanted to get rid of the pizzas and get out of the awful house where she ruined everything. Then at the bottom of the driveway, she spotted the homeless man coming up the street.

Taking a deep breath, she marched to him with pizzas in front of her. Seeing her approach, the man stopped, stroked his thick snowy beard, and looked nervous, almost scared.

"Here," muttered Rachel, not looking at his face. She pressed the pizza boxes into his arms and turned back.

"I, er, …" Surprised, the man took the pizzas and stared after her.

Something was very familiar about him, but Rachel was too upset to stop and think about it.

Reaching the house, Rachel couldn't go in. Hurt, anger, and fear weighed too heavily on her. The last thing she needed was to face the kids. Pacing the driveway, she finally went to her car and retrieved her notebook. The setting sun still provided enough light, so sitting on the front stoop, Rachel pulled out a pen and started writing. As she wrote, more tears flowed. When it got too dark, she stopped long enough to reach inside to flip on the front light. Then she wrote some more.

From the front window, Lisa watched for a long time. Then she left to go make salad for supper. Steven was out back on his ripstick, with a tube of bubbles … the boy skated in a circle of bubbles … Sometimes, that was life.

When the tears were gone and her wrist ached from writing, Rachel sighed and put down her pen. Looking up, she was startled to see Jane Lovington standing before her. She'd forgotten the housekeeper was still there—her blue Mustang sat next to Rachel's Corolla.

The housekeeper smiled at her sadly. "Do not worry, miss. We all have bad days on the first day. I return tomorrow and make supper, yes? And soon, you will see, I stay the weekend. And you will be free. Things will get different, yes? You will see. Things will get different."

Rachel couldn't resist smiling back. Just maybe she could find a friend here after all …

Geoffrey heard Nana's door shut for the night. Oliver still lay on the couch watching television and would not move for hours, probably. The house went still. Outside his window the dark had overtaken the day and would keep it hostage for hours to come.

Shivering slightly, Geoffrey pulled his covers to his chin. Maybe it was all a joke … Rosco liked jokes. The floorboard creaked outside his door.

Nervous, he willed his head to turn toward the sound.

The doorknob of his room started to turn. Mouth dry, Geoffrey tried to swallow, but couldn't. Slowly, he watched the shadowy shape of his door swing open.

Then the dark shape of Rosco stepped through the threshold. "Ready, little bro?" he hissed. "We're going out your window so nobody sees us."

Perched on the edge of her bed, Rachel took her cell phone and called the only person who could possibly understand.

"Hi, Mom," she said into the phone, with false cheeriness.

"Rachel! I'm so glad you called! How was your first day?"

"It, it …" It was no use. The tears she thought were gone returned. Rachel related everything that happened, ending with the pizza fiasco.

There was silence on the other end for a while. *"Oh, honey, I'm so sorry … you tried your best, didn't you?"*

"I tried everything, Mom! She hates me!"

"That's not true, Rachel. Don't ever think that! She doesn't even know you."

"She knows I'm poor, ugly, and fat, and that's enough for people like her."

"Rachel! Don't ever think that! Listen. Tonight you tried to please Lisa with pizza, right? But, honey, you got her what you *wanted. You like pizza, not her. You have to go out of your way to find out what Lisa likes and give her that."*

"But Mom, she's going to hate anything and everything I give her! What she really needs is … is a better babysitter."

There was a long silence on the other end. Then her mom's voice came softly.

"Rachel, did you ever hear the story of how I became friends with Lizzy?"

"She actually told me yesterday."

"Yes, yes. No doubt she embellished it. But the fact is, I took the chance and went out of my way to help her when she needed it the most. Do you know why I took that chance? Because one day, my mother, your grandmother, ordered me out of the house. She told me she would no longer talk to me until I found another friend." Over the phone, her mother sighed. *"I was like you. I spent all my time at home using my mom as a lifeline. As long as I had her, I never strayed far from shore and never took risks."*

"Mom, I know what you mean—"

"You already helped Lizzy by agreeing to babysit. Now you have to find a way to help Lisa. On your own."

"Mom, what are you saying?"

"Honey, I love you, but as long as you can call me and talk to me, you're avoiding talking to Lisa. Talk to her and work things out. Love you." Her mom hung up.

Rachel fell back on her bed with a resounding thump. Her cell phone plopped next to her. Even her mom was abandoning her. It was not going to be a good night. And the second day would be coming all too soon.

Despite the warm breeze, Geoffrey shivered. His legs burned from scratches as brambles and other unseen obstacles blocked his path. Before him, there was only deep, empty darkness. Of course, he went first. Rosco, Toothy, and the others followed him. Only Rosco's steady arm on his shoulder kept him moving forward.

Every so often, Toothy would cackle about something or, more often, curse when meeting a nasty prickle.

"Shh!" finally ordered Rosco. "We don't want anybody to hear us!"

"Like who?" snorted Toothy. "We're the only lamebrains out in the woods this late."

"This is spooky," whispered Macie. "We be dumb coming out here."

"Well, there better be one other lamebrain out here," snarled Rosco. "And he better have a good reason for it!"

Geoffrey swallowed. Why did he ever agree to this? Then he remembered the locker room—the pain and humiliation as the boys laughed at him, watched as he was ridiculed. And Steven was one of them. He had no friends now. He was the only survivor of a terrible battle … and now he wanted revenge. He walked on.

"Man," mumbled Shoes. "Why didn't we bring a flashlight?"

"So we could be stealthy!" Rosco shot back.

A deep laugh from the darkness caused them all to freeze and tremble in their tracks.

"Stealthy? Kids, I heard you wheeze and waddle your way this far for a good five minutes!"

"Red?" called Rosco hoarsely. "Is that you?"

"Yes, it's me." A light snapped on, revealing a shadowed face with a rather nasty grin. Then the light turned to outline a rundown shack, left over from the days when the area was a working farm. "Come on in, boys. There's pizza waiting."

That got them going. "Pizza?" wondered Toothy. "Where did this dude get pizza?"

"Who cares?" Shoes, the tall boy said. "I just want to eat it!"

"Pizza now," Red said mildly. "Planning later." The light suddenly whirled and caught Geoffrey's face. "It is good to meet you, young Geoffrey. Our planning has a lot to do with you. Now come."

Suddenly wishing he were asleep in bed, Geoffrey complied.

Groaning, Rachel rolled over in bed and rubbed her swollen eyes. Sunlight was shining through her open window, accompanied by a warm breeze. Both seemed to be telling her something … something important …

Nonsense, I'm in Florida … I—Rachel shot straight up in bed as if stuck with a needle in a very bad spot. "Steven!" she gasped. She was supposed to be driving him to school! After the fiasco with the pizza, Rachel had forgotten all about it.

Leaping out of bed, still in her nightgown, she rushed from her room. "Steven!" she cried. "Steven, get up!"

Lisa poked her head out of the bathroom, having just finished dressing. "I thought you already left! Steven's school starts in like ten minutes!"

Rachel's hands went to her hair and she nearly pulled clumps out. It took tremendous effort not to screech in frustration. Checking the clock on the wall, Rachel groaned. She should already be driving at this time.

"What time is it?" Rubbing his eyes, Steven stumbled from his room. His hair was a tangle and he still wore his shorts and T-shirt.

Lisa rolled her eyes. "I can't believe this! Steven, you're supposed to be dressed and downstairs by now! Your ride is probably already here!"

Blinking, Steven looked at Rachel. "Rachel is taking me. I sent a text to Mrs. Hunt yesterday."

"Oh, that figures! You're stupid, now you're late!"

Rachel wasn't sure if Lisa meant Steven or her. A hard look entered her eyes.

"Not yet!" Rachel ran to her room. "Get your clothes and bring them in the car! You can change there while we drive!"

"Are you crazy?" cried Lisa.

"Just about! Now where is the key?"

"What about his breakfast?"

"Oh, I don't know! I don't know! Oh, I need the bathroom!" She rushed back to her room.

Brother and sister stared at each other with wide eyes.

"I'll make your breakfast, Steven," Lisa finally said. "You better listen to her. She might cause an earthquake with all her stomping."

Two minutes later, Rachel pressed down the gas as the red Corolla shot backward down the driveway. In the backseat, Steven struggled to pull on his dress shirt while keeping a hunk of whole grain bread from falling from his mouth. All his other school clothes were strewn around him.

"I am so sorry," Rachel kept repeating, jerking the car into drive after they pulled into the street. Thankfully, no other cars were on the street. Especially police cars. "Don't worry, I'll take all the blame."

The car sped forward, only to come to a screeching halt at the stop sign at the end of the street.

A bicyclist gave a dirty look as he pedaled past. Rachel banged her head on the steering wheel. Immediately the horn went off, causing the bicyclist to swerve and throw back a rude finger toward the car.

"What am I doing?" Rachel moaned. "I can't be doing this! I'm so, so sorry …" Fighting tears, Rachel turned and did a slow arc around the bicyclist, who quickly ran off the road and promptly jumped in a ditch, probably fearing retaliation. "I can't speed, sorry. I promised your parents …" and she promised Steven to drive him to school on time … and promised supper the night before … "I'm such a failure," she mumbled. "You okay back there?"

Lying on his back, Steven was pulling his pants over his bed shorts. "I think so …" He grimaced and kicked his legs. "I just can't button my pants like this!"

"Well, hang on … we're almost there!"

It seemed as if they hit every red light possible. Gripping the wheel until her knuckles were white, Rachel chewed on her lower lip as they stopped just before the street to the school. Her stomach growled, reminding her that she hadn't eaten supper the night before, or breakfast that morning.

"Blast, blast, blast!" she cried, striking the wheel, away from the horn. Beside her, a man in a Porsche gave her a funny look before hastily looking away. Rachel didn't care. The light switched to green and the red Corolla zoomed forward, leaving the Porsche in its wake.

Finally, lurching to a stop in front of the school, Rachel hastily jammed the car into park and shut off the engine. "Ready?"

Steven took another bite of the bread and nodded. "Uh, I think so."

"Come, let's get out and make sure you didn't miss anything." Climbing stiffly out of the car, Rachel knelt to view her young charge.

Steven stepped out, wearing untied sneakers with white socks. His black jeans were a wrinkled mess, which was okay. They matched his shirt. Rachel sucked in a breath. It was the same outfit as the day before. At least his blazer looked okay, besides the crumbs on the collar. And his hair was a disheveled mess. And yet, despite it all, he still managed to look good.

"Looks great," she muttered, wishing she could say the same about herself.

Reaching for his backpack, Steven gave a small grimace before dashing for the school. At the door, though, he stopped. Once again, he offered a half smile and a small wave back to Rachel.

Confused as to why he would bother, Rachel returned the wave. The poor kid was probably embarrassed out of his mind. Then she noticed other students still walking from the parking lot to the school. A small smile formed. Despite everything, Steven was not totally late. She did it!

Mrs. Hunt's minivan rolled to a stop beside Rachel's car. "Was that Steven looking like—" Mrs. Hunt jaw dropped when seeing Rachel. "What in the—"

Gathering what dignity she never had, Rachel threw her chin up and quickly climbed back in her car. Only after the minivan drove off did she dare look in the mirror. She groaned. It was like staring at a monster from a horror movie. Red, swollen, puffy eyes stared back. Overnight acne medicine still stuck to areas of her face like green scales. And her hair—the tangles resembled a trampled bird's nest. And she was still wearing her nightgown.

Closing her eyes, Rachel breathed out slowly.

At least Mrs. Hunt will be happy to give Steven rides again. Sighing, she started the car and drove off. This time the green car stayed so far back, she almost missed it. When turning into Camelot Acres, she saw it in the rearview mirror.

Three times now … Her heart was beating by the time she reached the house.

Steven didn't see Geoffrey when entering school and didn't have much time to look. Almost immediately he was corralled by two girls.

"Steven, OMG. What happened to you?" screeched one when seeing him.

"Poor you!" said the other.

Steven gulped. Callie Edwards and Susie Perkins blocked his way. Both stared at him with horrified faces.

"Um, trying a new style?" he tried.

Susie rolled her eyes. "You can't go around like that!"

"Your poor hair!" Callie nearly wailed.

Steven frowned. "What's wrong with it?" he asked.

Smiling, Susie took his shoulder. "Steven, it looks like you have lopsided wings on your head. And your clothes look like you jumped on them before putting them on and then got pecked by a hundred birds."

"Oh."

"Speaking of which, are you trying to be a human birdfeeder?" Susie brushed off some of the crumbs.

"Oh, Steven … poor you." Callie looked ready to cry.

"Come on, Steven," Susie said firmly, taking his arm. "We're taking you in."

"Uh, where are you taking me?" Steven asked nervously.

"The girls' secret headquarters," Susie told him. "When I tell you to, close your eyes. Come on, Callie, we have major repair work to do."

"Susie, listen—" Steven tried.

It was no use. Shielding him as best they could, the two girls dragged Steven to the girls' secret headquarters. It turned out to be an old closet, converted into a bathroom no longer in service for students. Way at the end of the music hall, it looked like a closet door. After making sure nobody was watching, Susie and Callie dragged Steven inside. All that remained inside was a cracked sink and large mirror.

Flipping on the light, Susie shut the door. "This is where girls go to get their hair fixed. Now it's time to fix you up."

"Uh, I'd rather you didn't," Steven said nervously.

"Oh, but we want to." Callie grinned. "I'll comb your hair." Already she had produced three combs and a bottle of hairspray.

"No way," Steven protested. "I'll smell like a flower!"

Susie wriggled her eyebrows. "And look like one!"

"But I have to get to class!"

Susie sighed. "Steven, there are some things more important than class. And looks are one of them. Now hold still and we'll make this go fast. Are you wearing shorts under those pants?"

Sinking against the back wall, Steven groaned. "I'll never wake up late again."

"That's what I thought. Take them off and I'll start smoothing them out."

"This is a nightmare."

"Not yet it isn't." Callie went to Steven and leaned forward. Before he could pull away, she planted a quick kiss on his cheek. "There, now it's a nightmare."

"Just hurry up so I can wake up."

Five minutes later, Steven slunk into class.

"Mr. Winter," Mrs. Fathomb rumbled, "it is nice of you to join us."

Giving a slightly sick smile, Steven nodded. His hair was matted down so his long locks on the sides acted as sideburns and his jeans were smooth and still damp from all the hot water Callie had rubbed in them. Scanning the room, he saw Tommy in his usual spot in the front. Geoffrey sat way in the back and had his head ducked low. Usually he sat behind Steven in the middle. In this seat now, Callie beamed widely at him.

"Love the hair," she mouthed.

"Callie has informed me that you *might* have had to visit the nurse about your fall yesterday, is that correct?"

Susie scooted in from the hall and stood by Steven's side. She had sent Callie ahead before the bell so they all didn't have to get in trouble.

"We're sorry, Ms. Fathomb," she said smoothly. "Steven just needed a little help getting checked out. I was with him."

"And I saw them," Tommy said quickly, his face growing red. He didn't meet Steven's gaze.

Steven sure hoped he was fibbing … otherwise he would die from shame. He eyed Susie and gulped.

In the back, Geoffrey coughed what sounded like, "Liar."

"Very well," Mrs. Fathomb said dryly. "Let us remember to raise our hands when we wish to speak and cover our mouths when we cough." A tall teacher with graying black curls, she did in fact carry an unfortunately wide load behind her. Still, there was a glint of sharp intelligence in her eyes. Standing before the children, she put her hands on her hips. "I know Mrs. Lee likes her tardies marked, but today I'll be lenient." The entire class let out a sigh of relief as Steven and Callie quickly went to their seats.

"Thanks, Ms. Fathomb," they mumbled.

"Just don't let it happen again." She suddenly sniffed and wrinkled her nose. "Steven, you smell … different."

"Oh, um, new deodorant—it's what football players wear."

She gave him a strange look and turned back to her desk.

Sighing with relief, Steven sat back and promised to never use the term Ms. Fatbottom again. At least she had a heart.

Something pricked his neck and Callie whispered near his ear. "From Geoffrey." A note was stuffed in the back of his collar. Pretending to stretch, he took the note and glanced at it quickly.

Meet me outside in the front after class. Don't tell anyone! We need to talk. G.

Chapter Fourteen

Rachel stumbled into the house and was about to collapse back in bed when she saw the note lying on the kitchen counter. It was from Lisa.

YOU FORGOT STEVEN'S GYM CLOTHES THAT HE TOOK HOME YESTERDAY!

The articles of clothing, though smelling a little ripe, were neatly folded next to the note.

Rachel covered her face and groaned. "First I'll at least get changed and wash my face … and maybe find a new job …"

At the bell, Ms. Fathomb called Steven up to her desk. As the boys and girls filed out to go to art, Callie gave him a sympathetic look. Geoffrey met his eyes and nodded toward the front of the building. Returning the nod, Steven hurried to see what the teacher wanted.

"Mr. Winter, is everything okay?"

"Um, yes, Ms. Fathomb."

"Good. Steven … I know you have a lot of friends—more than probably any other student in this school… I also know it isn't always easy for you."

Steven glanced toward the clock. Art was taught by Mr. Daniels, a former hippie who still had a ponytail and often wore a far-off look. It would be the perfect class to be late to. Even when Mr. Daniels remembered to take attendance, he often forgot who was and who was not there. Still, Steven wanted to meet Geoffrey as soon as possible.

"Steven," continued his teacher, "just make sure you know who your real friends are and who just likes you because you're popular. A real friend will stand up for you when you need it most. The others only stand by you when you're on top. Understand?"

"Um, sure. Thank you, Ms. Fathomb." He edged to the door.

Suddenly the teacher's face grew almost scared as she leaned forward. "Steven …" Her voice went husky. "There are dangers out there … you may not know this, but—" She stopped to lick her lips. "Just be on your guard and stick by your *real* friends. Understand?"

"Yeah, okay …" A little puzzled by his teacher's behavior, Steven gave a nod.

Sitting back, Ms. Fathomb relaxed and waved a hand. "That's all, Steven. Hurry along, now."

No longer in a rush, Steven slowly left the room with a puzzled look. What was Ms. Fathomb talking about?

In the hall, students were still in the midst of switching classes and they clogged the way. Ducking his way through, Steven avoided several pats to his head and soon forgot about Ms. Fathomb. Students smiled and waved, but he barely acknowledged them. Geoffrey was probably waiting for him.

Finally he neared the front of the school. Suddenly a student popped out in front of him and he nearly ran into her.

"Steven, where are you going?" Susie asked, folding her arms in front of her. "Art is the other way."

Jerking to a stop, Steven sighed impatiently. "I'm just checking something."

"We saw the note Geoffrey gave you. What did it say?"

Shrugging, Steven nodded toward the door behind Susie. "He wants to talk outside, that's all." He gave her a funny look. "And what are you doing here? Aren't you supposed to be in art too?"

"I knew what the note said. Callie read it and told me. I was just seeing if you were telling the truth."

Steven frowned. "Why?"

"Because, despite your looks, you're not always the sharpest knife in the drawer, Steven. You trust people too much."

"How do you know?"

"Well," she grinned, "you trusted Callie and me to fix you up. I want to make sure you don't get hurt."

"Susie, Geoffrey is my friend."

"And so am I, right?"

"Um, sure."

"Hmmph. You don't sound so convinced. Well, I think I'm your friend. I'll wait here for you and make sure nothing happens. And if Mrs. Lee comes, I can think of a good story for why two students are outside during school hours. How does that sound?"

Steven thought for a second and then shrugged off his backpack. "Okay, then you can also hold this for me."

"Oh. Sure."

As Susie reached for the backpack, Steven stepped in close. "And you can have this too." Puckering his lips, he kissed her cheek.

Susie rolled her eyes. "Now I'm the one dreaming."

"Not a nightmare, I hope. Thanks, Susie!" Slipping out the door, he ran down the steps.

Susie sighed behind him, shaking her head.

Geoffrey stood waiting at the bottom with his hands in his pockets. "Took you long enough," he mumbled. He didn't look too happy to see Steven.

"Yeah, well, Ms. Fathomb talked for a while."

"Fatbottom," muttered Geoffrey, staring toward the school gate.

Steven shrugged. "So … what's up? What do you want?"

Geoffrey looked around nervously. "Let's go for a walk. I just want to get away from school for a minute."

"Uh, okay …"

Leaving school grounds was nothing new—many students had done it before. Mostly upperclassmen would walk out during lunch to eat at a burger place at the strip mall. Still, it was Steven's first time. Taking a look back toward the school, he hesitantly followed his friend through the gate.

"Are you sure about this?" he asked.

"What, you scared?" Geoffrey sneered.

"No …"

"Then come on, dude." Geoffrey didn't sound right. A nervousness clung to the usually laid-back boy like an invisible jacket.

Heading out the gate, he led the way to the right, turning the corner to follow the school's boundary. Across the road was the large church, looking like a giant block. A sign out front proclaimed Youth Day to be on Sunday and open to children of all ages. At the moment, though, it looked as if no children of any age should be there. Past the church were a few old buildings and little else. No cars were on the street, and the boys appeared very much alone. A silence filled with tension was their only company.

Steven finally stopped and leaned against the brick wall. "Geoffrey, are you going to talk or what?"

His friend stopped walking, but wouldn't face him. Taking a deep breath, he looked up the street past the church and school. "Listen, dude," he said loudly, practically shouting. "Ah, about yesterday …" Then he trailed off.

At the sound of his voice, three figures had turned the corner from the back of the school. They were headed straight for them. Tough-looking teenagers, they wore baggy jeans slipping down to their thighs and tight T-shirts showing off thick chests and muscular arms. Two had dark skin and one had light skin. All wore pleasant faces. The dark-skinned teen in front had an uncanny resemblance to Geoffrey. This was the leader, and he headed straight for Steven.

"Look at this," he said, throwing out his chest. "Two First Seminole tadpoles have escaped the pond!"

"Looks like they're trying to grow legs and hop away," snarled a round teen with buck teeth behind him.

"Yo, what's up, homies?" The tall, light-skinned teen raised an arm in the air flashing two fingers in a sideways peace sign. There was nothing peaceful about their appearance.

Steven could feel the animosity radiating from them like a strong odor. Stepping in front of Geoffrey, he whispered. "We need to run."

"I don't think so," muttered Geoffrey. He grabbed the back of Steven's shirt and held on tight.

"Geoff, what are you doing? Let go of me!"

"Now you know what it feels like …" Geoffrey started to mumble, but couldn't continue. Only his grip remained tight.

Twisting his body while arching his back, Steven managed to jerk free, but by that time the teenagers had arrived. Leering down at him, they neatly blocked his escape.

"What's up, little shrimp?" taunted the toothy teen. His front teeth, grayish yellow, looked like two crooked tombstones. "Trying to go somewhere?" He moved to Steven's left and nudged the smaller boy's shoulder.

"Maybe go in his pants," laughed the tall teen, moving behind Steven. "Scared, punk?"

Steven did his best to control his breathing. Inside he could feel the monster awakening.

The leader kept Steven in front of him. Suddenly he shoved him in the chest, knocking him back into the tall teen. Geoffrey had slipped back and huddled against the wall. He looked miserable.

"Well, rich guy, whatcha gonna do?" barked the leader. "You think you're better than us because you wear that stupid jacket and your mommy and daddy make a whole lot of money? Huh? Well, looks like Mommy and Daddy ain't here."

The toothy teen sniggered. "You tell him, Rock!"

Rock shoved Steven again. His face twisted into a snarl. "You think you can mess with poor people and get away with it, huh?" Spittle flew from his mouth and his eyes were cold, but wild. "How do you like the reverse?"

Steven could feel the anger welling up inside the teen. His own monster was struggling to meet it head on. Keeping his head low, he tried to control his breathing.

"Give me your jacket, boy," growled the leader. "Give it to me and we'll show you what we think of you and your pathetic school."

The teen behind Steven reached for the blue blazer, but with a snarl, Steven threw back his elbows in rapid succession, knocking him off.

"Ooo, a feisty one!" the teen said.

"Let me at him," grinned the toothy teen. "I'll teach him to respect his betters."

A squeal of tires screeched from the street. An old, beat-up pickup swung around the corner of the back of the church and jerked to a stop by the boys.

"Get the kid!" shouted the driver. "Now! Bring him here!"

Geoffrey stared up, almost in hope, as the pickup shot into view. *Maybe somebody was coming to the rescue!* Then he saw the driver and his dark face nearly turned white.

"Red!" cried his older brother in confusion. "What are you doing?"

Only Toothy seemed not to be surprised. Moving with speed, he swooped in on Steven and grabbed him around the arms.

Caught staring at the truck and trying to place the driver, Steven didn't see the attack until too late. Lifted off the ground, he started thrashing and trying to break free.

"Toothy," Rosco cried in alarm. "What's going on?"

"Part two of the plan, my man!" Squeezing tightly, Toothy kept Steven in a firm grip as he lumbered to the pickup.

"Take him around the passenger side. Hurry, boy!" yelled Red hoarsely.

"Geoffrey!" screamed Steven. "Help! Get off me!"

Huddled against the wall, Geoffrey barely looked up and did not move. Now he knew what it felt like to see a friend in trouble and then do nothing … Tears streamed down his cheeks.

"No," growled Rosco, finally moving. "This ain't right. Toothy, put the kid down!"

"Sure thing, Rock." Toothy made it to the passenger side and shoved Steven's head through the open window. Immediately the boy's thrashing feet caught him in the face. "Oof! He's not easy to deal with, with all his kicking."

"Let me go!" Steven screamed.

Red put the pickup in drive but kept his foot on the brake. The boy's kicking and thrashing managed to get his belt caught on the door lock. His back half stuck out from the window and would not go in. Reaching with a gloved hand, Red grabbed Steven's arm and pulled tight.

Suddenly Steven looked up and recognized the driver as the school janitor from the day before. Shocked, his struggles slackened.

The driver hastily glanced away, but kept hold of his arm.

"Get him in!" he roared.

Steven felt a hand shoving on his waist, and instantly he resumed his kicking. His monster rumbled inside of him and rose to the surface.

Rachel once again pulled up in front of the school. Sighing, she wiped her tired eyes and grabbed Steven's gym clothes. Before she could exit, though, the school door burst open and one of the girls from the other day raced toward her. "Steven is in trouble!" she screamed.

"What?" she asked.

"Quick," gasped the girl, stopping at the passenger window. "Drive around the road toward the church. He went that way but hasn't come back yet!"

"He what?" Rachel glanced at the boxlike church in puzzlement.

Then Steven's screaming was heard from the street.

The girl covered her mouth with both hands. "Oh, no."

Face white, Rachel jerked the key to start the car. "Go get help. Hurry!"

With only one thought in mind—get to Steven as fast as possible—Rachel spun the car, squealing the tires. Mind numb, heart pounding, she sped out of the school, turning hard right without slowing. When she turned right again, her eyes nearly popped at the scene before her.

An old rusty pickup drove toward her. From the passenger window, the back half of a boy in black jeans stuck out. The skinny legs in the jeans were kicking wildly and keeping two teens at bay, who were giving chase. Another teen gawked at the side of the road, next to where another boy sat huddled against the school wall. She immediately recognized the teens as the ones who had accosted her near the park on her walk.

Forgetting her fear, she reacted without thinking. Spinning her wheel left, she threw her car sideways to block the pickup. At first it looked as if the driver wanted to move around her, but by this time it was too close and there wasn't room. Almost like a sigh, it slowed to a stop and shut off.

Flying out of the car, Rachel charged the teens chasing the pickup.

"You get out of here!" she screamed. "Now!"

Seeing her, the two teens quickly beat a retreat. Cursing, they ran the other way like their pants were on fire. The one on the sidewalk joined their flight and soon the three disappeared around the corner. Rachel didn't care. She sprinted to the boy hanging from the pickup.

"Steven! Steven!" Reaching him, she launched herself at the door and threw her arms over the struggling boy. "It's okay, Steven! I'm here!" Looking up, she stared balefully at the driver. Then her eyes widened when she recognized the janitor. "Oh, it's you … what—what is going on?" Something about him seemed terribly familiar, like she knew him from somewhere else and not just as the janitor.

Seeing Rachel, the man immediately let go of Steven's arm and went to his sunglasses. "I, ah—"

Just then a host of teachers, led by Mrs. Lee, raced around the corner of the school.

Dropping his hand to his lap, the man smiled, revealing gleaming teeth. "Why, it's Rachel—you came just in the nick of time, miss. I was driving by and saw this boy being bullied by some unruly teenagers. I did what I could to rescue him, but it seems you did a better job. You okay, boy?" He patted Steven's head.

Rachel struggled to control her breathing. "Oh, my goodness, I thought, I thought …"

"I was just taking him back to the school," the man said carefully. "You help him out and I'll go see about the other student." His mouth curved into a smile as he opened the driver's door. Behind the dark glasses, his burning red eyes did not smile. "It's a good thing you showed up when you did."

Rachel ignored him as she grabbed Steven around the chest and pulled him loose of the door. The boy was trembling like a leaf. "It's okay, Steven. It's okay. That man was only helping."

Once free, he slid from the cab and immediately turned, throwing his arms around Rachel. Giving a fierce hug, he refused to let go.

"Oh—" Awkwardly, Rachel returned the hug and then started to rock the boy like she remembered her mom doing to her when she was small and scared. "It's okay," she repeated. "It was all just a mistake."

"What is all this?" hollered Mrs. Lee, stomping into the middle of the street. "You, there!" she pointed to the man. "Aren't you the new janitor? Where did you go yesterday and why weren't you at school this morning?"

Standing up straight, the man turned from Geoffrey. "Why, I am so sorry, Mrs. Lee," he said, hanging his head meekly. "I got the hours mixed up and thought I only worked a half day yesterday. Then this morning I had troubles with my truck." He gestured helplessly at the old pickup. "I wanted to call, but my phone wasn't working. In any case, I was just on my way here when I found these two boys being accosted by some teenagers up to no good, by the looks of them. Now, I didn't get any close looks at faces, but I didn't want to take any chances. One of the boys," he gestured at where Steven and Rachel sat, "seemed in worse trouble, so I called to him to jump in my truck. One of the teens must have wanted to help, because he picked up the boy and brought him to me while the others tried to stop him. Unfortunately, there was a miscommunication and stuff. Boys, with their imaginations, I fear he thought he was being kidnapped. In reality, he was being saved. Ain't that right, Geoffrey?"

Swallowing, and wiping away tears, Geoffrey looked miserable as he nodded.

"Oh, great!" Mrs. Lee threw up her hands. "This could mean another lawsuit! What were you boys doing outside of school? Don't you know we have these walls for a reason? We've had troubles with the locals in the past … Oh, never mind. I suppose you learned your lesson! It's a good thing our janitor showed up when he did. Mr. Red, I need you in the office to write a statement. And then you need to go to the boy's bathroom in the upper hall. There's another clog causing an overflow. First, though, you better find a better parking spot. Hurry up before this thing gets blown way out of proportion and we have people actually thinking a kidnapping almost took place!"

Mr. Red's mouth twitched. "Uh, yes, Mrs. Lee."

"Okay, everybody!" cried Mrs. Lee. "Back to school! Nurse, you may take Geoffrey and make sure he's ready to return to class. I'll speak to him later." Clapping her hands, she acted as if she was a mother hen putting the barnyard back in order. Then she turned to Rachel and Steven. "Oh, Rachel, right?" She smiled sweetly. "We spoke on the phone—you better find a better parking spot too. Take your time, though. Steven can stay with me and then we'll talk together, okay?"

Rachel could still feel the wild heartbeat of Steven. She managed to get to her knees as she continued to hold the boy. "I, uh, think Steven will come with me. I'll go park and then we'll come find you inside."

Clearly not liking it, Mrs. Lee put on a big smile. "Well, if you think that's best …"

"We'll be there in just a minute." To Steven, Rachel whispered in his ear. "I won't leave you." The boy went limp and rested his head on her shoulder. His heart slowed. Rachel swallowed. The boy appeared exhausted and still frightened. Mrs. Lee watched them and so did Mr. Red. Rachel's own heart kept beating a mile a minute. Never before had she been so scared or acted so rashly. Babysitting training never included the part about posttraumatic stress. "Well, Steven, I have to move the car now. Do you, uh, want to come?"

Finally releasing Rachel, the boy stood and nodded. He looked at the sweat stains now covering Rachel's shirt from his hair. "Sorry," he said, managing to give a sheepish grin.

Breathing a sigh of relief, Rachel got unsteadily to her feet and awkwardly patted the boy's shoulder. "That's okay. I don't sweat too often, so I can always borrow some. Ready?"

Taking her hand, the boy nodded. They went to the car together.

Mrs. Lee watched them go with her lips squeezed tight. "Bullies are the scum of the earth, Mr. Red."

Staring at her, the janitor rubbed his clean-shaven chin. "I'm glad I was there in time, Mrs. Lee. Who knows what would've happened."

The assistant principal sighed. "And who knows what will happen next?"

In the driver's seat, Rachel fought hard to control her nerves and stop her hands from shaking. Managing to get the car started, she slowly relaxed. *It's all over … Nothing happened. Just a big misunderstanding.* She looked in the rearview mirror at Steven.

"I really thought you were in big trouble for a minute," she said tentatively.

Steven shuddered. "Me too." Then his face turned questioning. "How come you're here?"

Rachel gave a wry grin. "Well, in our rush to get here this morning, we forgot your gym clothes, so I was bringing them to you. When I pulled up, a girl ran out and said you were in some trouble …"

"But I don't have gym today."

"Really?" Rachel suddenly laughed. Nothing could be worse than losing a child to kidnapping while babysitting. Now that it didn't happen—or even come close to *really* happening, she felt great. "Well, I guess mistakes sometimes can be good!"

Before taking Steven back into the school, Rachel checked him over for injuries. Lifting up his shirt, she saw an ugly red line across his stomach, but otherwise he appeared fine … except for a strange, red burn high on his arm—almost like a handprint.

"Where did that come from?" Rachel asked.

"It started yesterday," the boy said, shrugging.

"Odd … Well, you seem okay, though." Flicking his hair, she suddenly gave him a funny look. "Steven, are you wearing perfume?"

"Um … just wake me up early tomorrow." He rubbed his smelly hair ruefully and frowned. "Some girls … um, helped this morning."

Rachel snorted. "You're having quite a day. Come on, let's see what happens next."

"What are you going to tell my mom and dad?"

"About today?" Going up the steps to the school, Rachel paused and looked at him seriously. "How about I tell them how I went to your school and found you with your bottom sticking out the window of a strange pickup?" She grinned. "Sound good?"

Steven gave her a light shove. "Then I'll tell them how you parked illegally in the middle of the street and ran like a screaming chicken, scaring away everyone in sight."

Without thinking, Rachel grabbed him by the back of the neck and pretended to squeeze. "A chicken? I ran like a chicken?"

"A chicken that runs like a duck!"

After the horrible scare, humor proved a big relief. Both were trying hard not to giggle when the front door of the school suddenly opened and the school nurse popped her head out.

"What is going on out here?" she demanded.

Rachel quickly let go of Steven and smoothed out her shirt. "Oh, uh, nothing," she said. "We, uh, are coming."

"Chickens go first," Steven whispered, moving aside to let her pass.

"What?" whispered Rachel back. "Not boys that smell like flowers?"

Rachel couldn't lift her eyes as the nurse grunted with disapproval when the two went past.

Mrs. Lee sat at her desk, shuffling papers, as Mr. Red worked on his written statement across from her.

"Where is that girl?" she muttered crossly. "Mrs. Duff can't get off her duff and leaves me to deal with this mess …"

The nurse popped in her head. "I just sent Steven and Rachel home," she said, trying to smile.

"What! But I was waiting to talk to them!"

"Sorry, Mrs. Duff's orders. But I recommended that they leave. The poor boy is utterly exhausted and has a nasty scratch from Mr. Red's pickup. Besides that, he managed to sunburn his arm. Sorry, but he needs rest and quiet."

Mr. Red looked up and narrowed his bright blue eyes. "You say he has a sunburn?"

"It does happen," the nurse replied. "Although, this one is a bit strange."

"On his right shoulder?"

"Yes." The nurse looked at the janitor with surprise. "How did you know that?"

"Uh, well, I thought—"

"Never mind that!" snapped Mrs. Lee. "Steven Winter is one of the top students at this school! This is the second day in a row he's had to leave early due to trauma of some sort. Ever since his babysitter arrived, this has been happening …" She gripped the papers in her hand so hard they wrinkled. "Just who is this Rachel Pugsley?"

"A good question," Mr. Red muttered. "A very good question."

Chapter Fifteen

Lisa arrived home to find Rachel sitting on the sofa, nursing a full cup of coffee.

"Where's Steven?" she demanded. "What happened to him?"

Jumping to her feet, Rachel barely managed to keep the coffee from spilling. "Nothing really happened. He's upstairs in his room resting."

"You don't understand!" Lisa dropped her backpack and went for the stairs.

Putting down the coffee, Rachel hurried after her. "What do you mean I don't understand? How do you even know something happened?"

"Somebody from his school texted one of my friends and she texted me in English class. They said some jerks tried to hurt Steven at school!"

"Yes, but it's okay, I—we, uh, got there in time."

At the top of the stairs, Lisa whirled to face Rachel. Her face matched the color of her hair. "You don't know if it's okay or not! You don't know us!"

"Well," she stammered. "Go check on him then."

Lisa had already turned around again. Rachel couldn't be sure, but she thought she saw tears in the girl's eyes. Rachel went quietly back to the living room.

Lisa found Steven lying on his stomach facing the wall. Awake, he rolled to face her and sat up.

"Steven, what happened?"

Wearing only shorts, he had a bandage around his stomach and another around his right shoulder. "Nothing really …" He sounded embarrassed. "The school is being extra careful."

Lisa knelt next to his bed. "Did, did, your … did your monster get loose?"

A few years back, Steven had described to Lisa his struggles with the monster. Once loose, it took control of his body and did things he couldn't stop. At first Lisa found it hard to believe, but over time, she knew it to be true.

His eyes narrowing, Steven stared at the carpet. "Almost," he finally said.

"Can you tell me what happened?"

Steven shook his head. "I don't really know what happened," he said slowly. "But I think Rachel stopped the monster. When I saw her coming, I knew it would be okay."

"Rachel *came*? She rescued you?"

Steven nodded as if it was expected. "Yeah … I'm kind of tired now …"

Lisa didn't say anything or leave his room until he was sound asleep. Even then, she remained at his side for a long while.

From down below, the doorbell rang.

Before going to the door, Rachel peeked out the front window to see who it was—rule number ten of babysitting. She swallowed and nearly retreated when seeing Mrs. Hunt standing on the front step.

Could she be here for Steven's swim practice? Or perhaps to give me a stinging lecture? Whatever it was, she had brought reinforcements. Another woman stood next to Mrs. Hunt. Both looked resolute for whatever mission they had planned.

Steeling herself, Rachel opened the door. Rule number nine of babysitting: No matter what, be courteous to all adults; especially when they are rude and are guests. She put on her best smile.

"Hi—" She was surprised when both women beamed right back.

"Rachel!" cried Hunt, as if greeting her best friend. "How are you?"

Rachel's smile drooped a little. "Uh, fine …"

"Excellent! We met at school, if you remember …" She at least had the courtesy to blush a little. "I'm afraid I wasn't in the best of moods at the time—both times, in fact." She laughed a little too pleasantly. In her arms she carried a pot, which she offered to Rachel. "Do you mind if we come in? I brought over some chili for you and the children. Oh, and this is Ms. Proom, Susan Proom."

Taken aback, Rachel opened the door wider. "Oh, uh, yes, uh, come in … uh, please."

Susan Proom was a smiley middle-aged woman with tight curly hair cut in a boyish style close to her scalp. Wearing a tad too much makeup and clothing that hung too loose, she had the appearance of someone who spent hours carefully trying to look like someone much younger than her years.

"Rachel," she said gaily, stepping inside, "I've heard so much about you! All good, don't worry!" She laughed pleasantly. In her hands was a plate of cookies.

"Are-are you here for Steven's swimming?"

"Swimming?" Ms. Proom blinked and looked at Mrs. Hunt with owl eyes.

"Oh, no, we're not here for swimming!" Mrs. Hunt laughed too loudly until Ms. Proom gave her a small grimace. "Oh, well. Should we put the food in the kitchen?" She had already started in that direction.

"Oh, um, yes. Uh, thank you." Good to her word, Jane Lovington had mysteriously come and gone sometime during the day and left a delicious-smelling pot of grilled chicken, vegetables, and rice.

"Elizabeth and Doug have us over quite often, so I know where to go!" Mrs. Hunt called. "I made my special chili recipe, so I hope you enjoy—" She must have noticed Jane Lovington's pot on the stove, because her voice fell. "Er, enjoy it tomorrow."

"And here are my freshly baked homemade cookies that I just made from scratch!" Ms. Proom beamed like a child giving a teacher an apple as she handed the plate to Rachel.

Still confused about what was going on, Rachel nodded hesitantly, taking them. "Thank you … the kids will be, uh, happy."

"Oh, we didn't do it for the kids … not entirely." Mrs. Hunt came back from the kitchen and joined Ms. Proom in beaming at Rachel. "We did it for you. We realize how busy you must be. Oh, may we sit and talk?"

"Uh, I, sure …"

"I know the way. Oh, it's so great to finally really meet you, Rachel!"

"Um, yeah." Rachel scratched her head and meekly followed her guest. Mrs. Hunt had already met her in the school parking lot. Twice.

Finding seats in the living room, Mrs. Hunt chose a large armchair, and Ms. Proom took a smaller chair across from her. Rachel was forced to sit on the couch between the two. Realizing she still held the cookies, she put the plate on her lap, not knowing what else to do.

Biting her lower lip nervously, she waited to see where this was going.

At first it was small talk. Mrs. Hunt had heard what happened to Steven and felt dreadful. She just simply had to do something, so she called Ms. Proom. Together, the ladies decided to take some food over and provide comfort.

"Really," said Ms. Proom, nodding after every word, "what you're doing here is truly remarkable. Coming all the way from Virginia to look after two children you haven't even met is something, Rachel."

"Well, uh, my mom knew their mom," Rachel mumbled, feeling her face growing hot.

"And," Mrs. Hunt laughed, a bit forcedly, "to top it off, now Steven doesn't want to ride with me! His best friend—my son Tommy—misses those rides, you know."

"Uh, well, I think Steven might be happy to get those rides again." After this morning, Rachel was willing to bet half her salary on it. Blushing, she scratched at a stain on her jeans—for lunch she had made tomato soup with cheese sandwiches for her and Steven … and managed to keep souvenirs of both. Carefully, she slid the cookie plate over the stain.

"Good, good. He's a good boy, isn't he?" Mrs. Hunt said.

"Uh, yeah. I mean, yes. He is." Rachel couldn't stop blushing.

"Well, I'm sorry for not visiting sooner, but I do want to help you more."

Ms. Proom nodded. "What we're trying to say is," she said, leaning forward on her seat, "are you taking care of yourself?"

Rachel nearly lost the cookie plate as she looked up, startled. "What?" she croaked.

"You're spending a lot of time with the children, Rachel. What about you? Is there time for you? You know women, we need our 'me time'!"

Rachel stared at the two women blankly.

Mrs. Hunt smiled kindly. "That's what we thought. I'm a mother. I understand. It's so easy to forget about yourself. Tell us, Rachel. Forgive me for prying, but are you, you know, saved?"

"Saved?"

"What I mean is, do you go to church?"

"Wh-what?" Rachel was a semiregular Baptist, which meant she sometimes attended services. But it wasn't anybody's business.

Ms. Proom smiled. "You see, we're both members of the Lord's Faith Church of Finding Grace. It's right next to the school—Steven's school."

"And we'd love to see you and the children attend this Sunday."

Nodding vigorously, the two women never lost their smiles.

"We're having a special children's blessing," Ms. Proom said. "Oh, did I mention? I'm the youth pastor. Pastor Smith and I hope to bless as many children as possible Sunday. Pastor Smith is a lovely man. He'd just *love* to meet you and the children. You'd love him!"

Her mouth opening and closing, Rachel had to take a minute to process what had just happened. The Winters were Protestants, but before leaving, Elizabeth had confided to Rachel that if Rachel could get her children to any church on a Sunday it would be a miracle, and be perfectly okay.

"Uh, the church—I think that's where I found Steven today being attacked …" It was the only thought that came to her head.

"Oh, my, that's truly remarkable!" Mrs. Hunt raised her eyes to the ceiling and murmured something like a prayer.

Beaming, Ms. Proom kept nodding. "In the shadows of our own church, the child was saved! Surely you must come, Rachel. Bring the children! While they have their special service, we're providing fellowship for young people like yourself. There are a lot of young people you could meet—who would, dare I say, benefit from your example."

"My-my example?"

"Why, Rachel, you're like a living saint! You treat those children so kindly."

"And," added Ms. Proom, "our Pastor Smith would love to meet you. He's from up your way, you know. From Virginia."

"Really?"

"Yes, Rachel. He arrived last year—secretly we think he's sent directly from heaven, though."

"Well, uh, that sounds … nice."

Mrs. Hunt jumped to her feet and nearly flew across to Rachel, extending both hands. "Then you'll come Sunday! And bring the children!"

"I'll, uh, ask … I think, I guess it sounds good."

Ms. Proom's eyes lit up. "Divine grace has sent you, Rachel. The services start at 8:00 a.m. sharp. Be there and be ready to have your life changed!"

"Uh, actually, I'll go, but I still need to ask Lisa and Steven if they want to."

Ms. Proom's face fell just as fast. "But you must bring them. The service is for the children! Bring them, Rachel!"

"I'll try," she said with uncertainty. Personally, she thought a little church could benefit them all—but she could only imagine Lisa's reaction. The redhead would probably spit in her eye.

"You do that." Ms. Proom patted her arm. She then stooped down and grabbed a cookie. Rachel did her best not to flinch.

Mrs. Hunt gave a friendly smile. "Well, we'll be off and look forward to seeing you on Sunday!"

"With the children!" Ms. Proom added. She bit into the cookie and smiled as she followed Mrs. Hunt. "Excellent!"

Shaking her head, Rachel hastily ran the plate back to the kitchen before following the women to the door. She had no desire to try any of Proom's cookies.

No sooner had the two ladies left the house and driven off when another car pulled in. A shiny, silver BMW parked, and out stepped Vikki Rosa.

Maybe she saw Rachel through the window, because the dark-haired lady didn't bother knocking. Opening the front door, she glided into the home with a look of distaste—as if she expected the door to open for her.

"Rachel, what are you doing gawking? You remember me from the airport, don't you?"

Rachel managed to close her mouth. She'd been watching through the front window and had been about to answer the door. Swallowing, she moved to take the lady's hat.

"Don't worry about my hat, dear. I won't stay for long."

"Oh, uh, well, I, won't, uh, you come in?"

"I'm already in. Ask me to sit down." She spoke as if Rachel was an idiot.

"Oh, uh, of course. Sit down, uh, Vi—uh—"

"Call me Ms. Rosa. I thought I would drop by and make sure you were still in one piece. Babysitting must be a terrible strain."

"No, uh, it's okay." Rachel followed Vikki Rosa into the room just vacated by Mrs. Hunt and Ms. Proom. She waited for her guest to sit before taking the couch again. The seat was still warm.

Vikki Rosa watched her with amusement bordering on disgust. Dressed in a silky black dress belted at the waist, she had blue high heels and a large fancy purse. The purse itself cost more than the entire outfit Rachel was wearing.

"I will tell you, Rachel," she said, not unkindly, "I was against Lizzy ever hiring you. But, the dear girl, perhaps she knew what she was doing. The fact that you're still here says something."

Not sure if she'd been complimented or insulted, Rachel merely squirmed. Very much she wanted this woman to leave. "What, uh, could I do for you?"

"Today, Rachel, I'm actually here for your sake. I heard there was a minor mishap at school today. One involving young Steven."

"Oh." Surprised, Rachel frowned slightly. "How did you know?"

"Rachel, in this community, there are no secrets. In any case, I want to make sure you are handling it properly."

"Oh, well, uh, I actually …" Rachel's face suddenly burned. She'd never reported that she recognized the teenagers! "Well, I haven't yet, but I'll report to the school, er, police, that I recognized the bullies and—"

"Rachel!" Vikki Rosa said severely, frowning. "That's just why I'm here! You will do no such thing! Just the thought of it!"

"Wh-what?"

Vikki Rosa sighed. "I understand this is a new world for you, dear. But really, you must try to understand. Such matters involving people such as myself and the Winters simply can't happen."

"What do you mean?'

"I will speak clearly. You must forget the whole matter today. Pretend it never happened. Otherwise, you'll only bring unwanted attention and shame to the family. Now, I'll talk to Elizabeth and explain everything."

"But I know who did it!"

"Did what? Rachel, nothing happened. Steven is fine. You are fine. Pressing charges or reporting foolish boys will only stir up trouble. We in this community do not like trouble. Now, you are an outsider, and I don't expect you to appreciate our way of life. Nevertheless, it is not for you to decide. You are a babysitter, and that is your only job. As I said, I'll speak to Elizabeth. Do you understand? If she decides, which she won't, to press charges, I'll take care of it."

Rachel took a deep breath. "I'll also speak to … to Steven's mom."

"I imagine you will, Rachel. You are her employee, after all." Vikki Rosa frowned at Rachel. "You do not like me very much, do you? That's perfectly okay; I expect it. You are probably like the many other fools out there who think it's easy having money. I promise you, Rachel, it is not that simple. When you're at the top, there are certain rules you have to follow. You'll have to trust me, of course, because you'll never know."

Trying hard not to be angry, Rachel averted her eyes, fixing them on the carpet. "Is that why you came, then?" she asked.

"No, that's not all. I was going to stop by later, but I saw you had some visitors earlier." She made an unpleasant face. "That *Mrs. Hunt* and her scary friend. No doubt they wanted you to join their church for buffoons."

Rachel had to grit her teeth from saying something she would regret. She was saved when Lisa came into the room.

"Hello, Ms. Rosa," Lisa said sweetly. "I heard you come in."

"Please, dear, call me Vikki. Come, take a seat. You may listen to our *friendly* grown-up conversation."

"Thank you."

Vikki Rosa frowned slightly when Lisa chose the space next to Rachel. Rachel herself was surprised and it probably showed on her face.

Lisa only shrugged. "I just came in because I overheard Rachel talking about going to church on Sunday." She turned pointedly to Rachel. "I was wondering if Steven and I could come with you. We've always wanted to go."

Rachel nearly fell off the couch. "Uh, well, uh, yes. Yes, that would be great."

Vikki Rosa positively glared at both of them, but then she sniffed. "You know nothing about that church and those women. Mrs. Hunt has been trying to pull herself up by grabbing onto Elizabeth's feet for years. She thinks she can use young Steven to gain a foothold in our society with her foppish son. And if that won't work, she'll try to drag Elizabeth's children to her silly church. I guess she finally found a way to succeed."

Her face burning, Rachel used all her courage to stare up at Vikki Rosa. "I think we can be the judge of that."

"I hope so, dear." Vikki Rosa smiled wickedly. "Go to that church if you wish. You may perform the act of a fool, but I have confidence that you have some sense. Otherwise Elizabeth would never have let you near this job. You'll see that I'm right."

Rachel breathed a sigh of relief when the silver BMW backed out of the driveway and vanished from sight. Turning from the window, she nodded at where Lisa still sat on the sofa. "Do you really want to go on Sunday?"

"Of course," the girl said, flipping through a magazine. "I said I did, didn't I?"

"Yes, yes, uh, you did …" Rachel gave a faint smile. "I kind of thought you said it just to, uh, annoy Ms. Rosa."

"You mean Vikki?" she said icily. "Yes, I did that too." She put down the magazine. "Well, should we have supper? I'm hungry."

Rachel approached supper cautiously, careful not to upset Lisa … That girl, she decided, was hard to read. For the rest of the night, Rachel planned to stay in the background and keep her mouth shut.

It was as if the night before had never happened.

Steven came down bleary eyed but hungry. Together, he and Lisa prepared a salad full of the greenest leaves and reddest tomatoes Rachel had ever seen. Homemade dressing in a crystal glass bottle was set on the table. This, when added to Jane Lovington's chicken and vegetable stew with rice, made a hearty and, Rachel had to admit, delicious supper. It also made her doubly embarrassed about trying to bring pizza in the house.

Picking at her plate, Rachel listened as the kids talked.

"I miss Mom and Dad," Lisa said after a while. "I hope Margie and Robbie are having fun." Steven, standing up to put more salad on his plate, grinned. "Remember when Dad picked through the salad and left all the tomatoes and carrots?"

"Oh, yeah. He said the tomatoes were eyeballs of zombies and the carrots were teeth from giants who never heard of toothpaste." Lisa suddenly turned to Rachel, startling her.

"What about you? Do you miss your parents?"

"Why, uh … I guess." Rachel gave a wry smile. "My dad is always traveling, so I never see him that much … but I do miss my mom." *Who won't be talking to me for some time … not until I get through to Lisa—but how?*

"Oh." Lisa turned away and started telling a story from school about boys who stuck a ketchup packet under a chair. When a kid sat down on it, the packet exploded and sent ketchup flying across the cafeteria—right onto the skirt of the assistant principal, who happened to be wearing white.

Rachel swallowed a bite of potato and wiped her mouth with a napkin. "I, uh, have a food story … if you like."

"What is it?" Steven said before Lisa could glare at him.

"Go ahead," Lisa said after a moment, almost reluctantly.

"Well, you know how school food is always a mystery? This past year my school served chili dogs …" She went on to describe how half the school ended up needing to use the bathroom almost at the same time—the principal and several teachers included. Even Lisa stifled a laugh when she got to the part about the teacher walking quickly and awkwardly down the hall to his car.

Rachel stared at the children when finished. "And now," she said ruefully, "we have a pot of chili from Mrs. Hunt to deal with."

Lisa swallowed her mouthful of rice and shook her head. "Maybe we can use mom's rule for that stuff. And the cookies." She made a face. "I'm almost positive they're from frozen cookie dough."

Rachel looked at her. "Oh. What's, uh, your mom's rule?"

"Any time I get extra food from school, I give it to Steven to take with him to his school and he gives it away at lunch. And the same thing happens when he gets extra food. That way," explained Lisa, "the food isn't wasted, students are fed, and we don't have to eat everything people give us."

"Well, uh, that sounds sensible."

"Our mom is sensible," Lisa said.

"Yeah," grinned Steven. "She hired Rachel."

Could it be true? Did Lisa actually give a slight nod of the head? *No way,* Rachel thought.

"Okay!" Lisa suddenly announced. "Time to clean up! I'll do the dishes. Steven, you can do your homework."

"I didn't get any … I left before it was handed out."

"Great—now you'll have double tomorrow. Fine, go to the fridge and get the brownies Jane made." She looked at Rachel and kept a straight face. "She makes them low fat … if you wanted to know."

"Uh, right." Rachel couldn't tell if she was making progress or running into a red brick wall that was not going to budge.

That night, just before bed, Rachel tried to call Elizabeth, but her phone was busy … immediately she thought of Vikki Rosa.

Well, at least I think Steven is coming around …

Outside, as the last light of the Winter house blinked out, an eerie darkness began to stir. Insects and frogs increased their output, providing dinner music for the wild animals just beginning to stir. When all seemed peaceful and still, a life was ending not a few yards away. Over in the next house, the Richardson family had also settled down for bed. They too were oblivious to this strange, different world outside. A full moon lit up the sky. Somewhere below it, a rabbit quavered in fear as an owl swooped downward with talons poised.

Back in the dark woods, outside the decrepit shack, a man violently yanked off his hat. His eyes sparking a dull red, he kicked open the rotting door and stomped into the shed.

"This is it!" he seethed, tossing the hat to the floor. "I can't handle this anymore!"

"You can handle it," snapped a voice in the darkness. "And you will. You utter fool."

Red jumped to attention. The figure of a woman stepped slowly from the back corner and entered the faded gloom created by the moon casting light through the dilapidated shed. Violet eyes lit up the dark like fireflies of another race.

The man quaked at her sight. "Is-Isabella, I-I did not know y-you were here."

"You do not know many things, Rudolph Pendleton. But I know … I know *everything.*"

"No, Isabella, you don't understand."

"I understand *purrfectly* well." The woman's shape sauntered farther into the room, her glowing eyes casting eerie shadows on the decaying walls. "I understand you went behind my back and tried to snatch the boy for yourself."

"That's not it!" Red, or Rudolph Pendleton, raised his hands in almost prayerlike fashion. "I did it for you!" he almost pleaded.

"Keep your voice down, Rudolph," said the woman lightly. "We don't want to raise attention from the locals. Besides, I'm not here to destroy you. Not yet."

"Isabella, you must believe me, I am totally at your service."

"Yes. You are. So then why did you *NEARLY RUIN EVERYTHING?*" Her voice rose to a furious pitch and roared like thunder. The walls shook and dust fell.

"But I—the locals—"

"I have plans, Rudolph! For years I've been hunting in this wretched swamp of a land and dealing with these pinheads. I've been hunting for the child, and after so much suffering, I find it! I have found the child. I am close. So very close." The woman's jaw opened. Sharp, jagged teeth, the color of glowing blood, flashed in the night. "And I will have him. You and the other wizards will not stand in my way. Do you understand?"

Falling to his knees, Red bowed his head. "Isabella, whatever you command, I shall obey."

As fast as her fury had appeared, the woman calmed. "For your sake I hope so. You will stay in your janitor position."

"What? No! You don't understand. These kids poop and blow snot all over the place. They barf, they—"

"Enough! Let that be a lesson to you. Stay away from this place with your foolish beard and disgusting clothes of a common peasant. We don't want anybody here to put two and two together. As the janitor, you can at least keep an eye on the boy while he's at school. I fear the other wizard is trying to close in on him. But, Rudolph, if you go near him, or try to take him again, I will have your head. For breakfast."

"What of Rachel the wretched babysitter? It is *she* who is messing everything up! Everywhere I go, she is there!"

"Yes, I admit Rachel is more of a problem than I imagined. But do not worry." Even in the dark, he knew the woman was smiling. "I have already sprung the trap for her. Starting today, the boy is as good as mine. In fact, I mean to take both children. His sister will make a good dessert … Don't you think?"

"Isabella … I thought you promised her to me."

"That was before you stepped in my way. Be thankful I don't include you on the menu, Rudolph Pendleton. When you gave your service to me, you gave me your life!"

There was a sharp bang and the woman vanished.

Shaken, the man mumbled to himself and moaned softly. "I never want to clean another bathroom …"

Chapter Sixteen

During the same night, other tears were being shed. Beyond the woods, just down the street from the old shack, Geoffrey sat up in his bed, his face buried in his hands. He was dead. Next to his bed his math book lay open on the floor with a blank piece of paper on top. Going to war with his homework problems had fizzled into total withdrawal. Never again did he want to fight anything or even do anything. What he did that day … it made him sick to his stomach. He was a traitor. Worse than Benedict Arnold. Worse than … worse than anything. And Steven had almost been taken, because of him. Geoffrey shuddered in the darkness.

Red, or Mr. Red, whoever he was, scared the daylights out of him. Something about that man creeped him out.

What type of janitor dressed up like a homeless man and then organized bullies to pretend to kidnap a kid? And when he came to Geoffrey in the aftermath … the boy shivered when reliving that memory.

"You open your mouth to a soul about what just happened, and I will *kill* you," he had hissed at Geoffrey earlier that day. "And I'll kill your Nana." Then he'd lifted up his sunglasses to reveal two horrible red eyes. Unable to look away, Geoffrey had nodded.

The man was no man, he decided. He was something evil—a spirit.

A tap on his door nearly sent him leaping to the roof.

"Yo, Geoffrey, you there?"

He relaxed slightly, recognizing Rosco's voice. "Yeah …" he whispered.

The door opened and Rosco slunk inside. Ever since the incident, Rosco had changed. No longer did he walk with his arrogant strut and act as if he owned the world. Instead, he was furtive and flinched at almost every shadow. Any distant siren sent him into a cold sweat. "You okay, bro?"

Geoffrey shrugged.

"Look, man. What we did today … it was my fault. I did it, man." He sighed. "The police will probably arrest me tomorrow." Geoffrey jerked his eyes to his brother. "Don't worry, little boy. I won't turn you in." He tried to grin, but it wouldn't come. Tears came instead. "I thought, I thought we were doing something good … like we were fighting back … but we were used, man. Used royally."

"Wh-what do I do?" Geoffrey asked.

Rosco sighed and ran a hand through his short bristles. "Same as me, I guess. Go to school and hope the cops aren't there. Don't worry about it, little bro. They won't be there for you. Just act as if nothing happened. Avoid that Steven kid and it'll blow over. You'll see."

That was just what Geoffrey did not want to do. But he had to do it and so that was exactly what he did.

Rachel woke up the next day with a full stomach and terrible morning breath. Fumbling for her phone, she saw it was just before seven in the morning.

At least Steven has a ride today, she thought. Then she remembered the number seven rule of babysitting. Never assume or take something for granted. How could she fall back asleep and let Lisa and Steven get up and off to school by themselves? Doing so would just prove Lisa right—that Rachel wasn't needed.

Groaning, she swung her feet over the bed and forced herself upright. Immediately she felt her stomach heave. Jane Lovington's food was good, but not anymore. Before she could do anything about it, a faint tap sounded at her door. Opening it, she blinked.

Standing fully dressed in pressed khakis, a white button-down shirt under his blue blazer, Steven grinned up at her.

"Are you ready to drive?" he asked shyly. "Lisa is just finishing making breakfast."

"B-but I thought you had a ride with, uh, Mrs. Hunt."

The boy twisted his face and shrugged. "Nah. Not anymore. I'll be downstairs waiting."

Rule number seven … "I'm, ugh … getting my keys."

Later, after warm toast and orange juice, Rachel pulled out of the driveway just as Mrs. Hunt's minivan drove up the street. Giving a quick wave as she went by, Rachel made sure not to make eye contact with the van's driver. The rest of the way she was very conscious of the minivan following them … a little too closely at times. This made it even more difficult to keep her stomach from doing funny things. After Jane Lovington's food, the bread for breakfast felt like a rock that wanted to come out.

"Stupid chili dog story," she mumbled. Finally they made it to the school.

As Steven ran for the school, waving back to Rachel before entering, Mrs. Hunt briskly approached. She had left her van running for this meeting.

Groaning, Rachel rolled down her window and squirmed. Still in her nightgown, she also had the terrible sense of needing to release gas. *This was not going to be good.*

"Rachel," started Mrs. Hunt rather crossly, "I—"

A loud, steady rip shot from the car. "Uh, sorry—I have to go. Uh, car trouble. We'll see you at church on Sunday!" *Maybe that would cheer her up.*

Mrs. Hunt was left choking on gas as the red Corolla sped away. Rachel saw no sign of the green car following that day.

For the rest of the week Rachel remained Steven's driver without Mrs. Hunt interfering.

The days went quickly as a routine started to take shape. Rachel provided the rides when needed, ferrying Steven to and from school and swim practice, but she otherwise stayed out of the way. Since it was Lisa's last week of school, she stayed busy making beaded gifts for friends and teachers. Still, she managed all the suppers and set up breakfast in the mornings. Jane Lovington arrived sometimes and left sometimes, but always managed to leave a healthy, tasteful supper. During the day, with the kids at school and Jane somewhere, Rachel started spending a lot of time in Elizabeth's office—walking on the treadmill, working out on the mat, and lifting weights. She tried the ball, but ended up on her seat with the ball rolling the opposite direction too many times. Also she went exploring. Besides the rooms previously seen, she found two more living rooms, a TV room, with a flat-screen television nearly the size of the wall, and her favorite, a library. The library had bookshelves on every side, each one crammed with books of all types and subjects. As soon as the weekend arrived, she meant to temporarily move in and find refuge in her best friend—books. Currently, they were her only friends. Friendly conversations never made it as part of the routine.

While Steven now spoke to her and even came to her with questions on homework (math proved easy, but English grammar was a different language), he was only nine and hesitant around her. A lot of his time was spent outdoors on his ripstick and indoors playing on the computer in Doug's office. Lisa, of course, completely kept her distance from Rachel. While she no longer outwardly displayed defiance, she often acted evasive and, besides meals, rarely spent time in the same room as her babysitter. Vikki Rosa hadn't come back, but when Rachel did reach Elizabeth on the phone, she seemed to agree about the bullies picking on Steven. *"I don't want to do anything to make Steven upset—as long as he's okay right now, let's keep it that way. Thanks, Rachel. You're doing great!"*

If only she could believe it …

Suddenly it was Friday and Rachel had her first time off. Jane Lovington showed up just as Lisa returned from school. The two, seeing Rachel sitting reading on the couch, quickly disappeared upstairs like two peas in a pod.

I wonder what they're up to. Rachel put down the novel and picked up her notebook. She hadn't written anything since the pizza night … now, thoughtfully, she added another entry. *Pizza is not a food for rich people …*

Minutes later, that was where Lisa found her.

"Rachel," she asked innocently, "what are you doing tonight? You know, on your night off?"

Rachel looked up from writing. *Could this be the moment where she and Lisa connected?* "Uh, well, I thought I would stay here and read … I want to explore your library …" she trailed off as Lisa made a face that resembled a sour pickle meeting horseradish.

"Don't you go out?" asked the girl, sounding incredulous.

"Oh, uh, well, I'd just rather take it easy. I actually like reading better." No point in telling Lisa that she *never* went out on weekends. How, to her, a boyfriend was just a character in one of her novels. Immediately, though, the picture of Jason Richardson flashed in her mind. This was the night *he* became a babysitter. Earlier that day his parents and Alison had left for Europe, leaving him with his siblings. He was just like her now. A babysitter. A slight smile started forming on Rachel's lips, but she quickly tossed it away. *Only in books, Rachel.* "I am kind of tired," she confessed.

The redhead smirked. "Too tired for a date?"

"Hmm?"

Lisa took a deep breath. "I, um, found this guy …"

"Really?" Rachel put down her notebook and did her best to be interested. This was the most Lisa had ever talked with her in a friendly manner. "That's nice … is he from your school?"

"Huh? What? No, not for me!" She sounded horrified at the thought. "I mean, I found this guy for you!"

Rachel froze. "What?"

Lisa rushed on. "His name is Billy. He graduated from high school last year and works in a food market. He's nearly six feet and has dark wavy hair. And he's coming to pick you up at seven." Then she turned and ran for the stairs.

Rachel sat stunned for a moment. Then she threw down her notebook. "Wait—what are you talking about? Stop! Come back here!"

Only at the top of the stairs did Lisa stop and explain. "Jane and I thought you were bored … and like, lonely, so we worked out a way to find a guy for you."

"Wh-what?"

Somewhere above, Lisa's door slammed.

Face red, Rachel ran up the stairs faster than she had ever moved before. Banging on Lisa's locked door, Rachel worked hard to control her temper. "Why did you do this? Are you crazy?"

"You need to go out!" Lisa shouted through the door. "All you do is sit around like a lump and write in your stupid notebook! You have no life! I'm only helping!"

"I have a job! It's to take care of you—"

"You don't do a very good job! Besides, Jane is here. She even approved this guy."

"You're joking."

"No. He likes to eat, so you should go out with him for dinner. We're having gross vegetable soup and bread here."

Rachel squeezed her eyes shut and tried her best to keep her temper. Oh, now it was clear … Lisa wanted some twerp to come in and take all of Rachel's attention—basically she wanted Rachel out of the house and out of her life as much as possible.

"You-you … I'm not going anywhere!" Stamping her foot, Rachel turned away.

Jane Lovington stood at the end of the hall near the master bedroom, watching with apologetic eyes. Vacuum in hand, she shrugged and quickly looked down at the floor. Breathing hard, Rachel managed to walk down to the living room without jumping on the housekeeper and throttling her with the vacuum.

Steven, the smart kid, was outside on his ripstick. Clearly he knew something was up.

A minute past seven found Rachel sitting nervously on the couch, fingering her notebook. *It's all just a joke … no guy would be stupid enough to let an eleven-year-old girl set up a blind date with her babysitter.*

Another minute went by and Rachel took a deep breath to relax. Then the doorbell rang.

Butterflies in her stomach, Rachel got slowly to her feet. Shaking from either fear or anger, probably both, she nearly forgot to check out the window. The doorbell rang a second time.

Peeking out the window, her worst fears were confirmed. There was a guy that stupid … and he was standing in front of the door with no sign of leaving.

"See, he's not that bad," Lisa said, coming from the kitchen. She looked ready to run. "He's really nice. Really."

Rachel didn't even turn. "Go away," she growled, not even trying to hide her feelings.

The guy at the door came up to Rachel's nose. His hair made up the rest of his height. Dark strands combed back and glued down with grease gave an additional five inches. With sideburns, he resembled a stunted Elvis with the face of a ferret.

Opening the door a crack, Rachel coughed. "Uh, yes?"

Breath smelling of sharp mint mixed with heavy fumes of expensive body spray blasted her in the face.

"Yo, Rachel?" the guy asked. "Is that you?"

Sighing, Rachel opened the door wider. The guy's eyes grew like eggs just cracked in a pan.

"They told me you were pretty fa—I mean …" He blinked and leaned against the doorframe, raising his arm in a loose manner. "You're not pretty! You're gorgeous!" Smiling, he showed off well-groomed teeth. "I'm Billy, your date."

A fresh cloud of body spray fumigated his upper body and threatened to choke her. Blood rushed to her face, and she knew it was turning a different shade. Besides the greasy hair, the guy had pimples and dressed like he belonged to a circus. Tight black jeans showing off thick thighs kept tight hold of his bright yellow shirt that had ruffles around the center.

"Uh, well, uh …"

"Billy," purred the guy. "Just call me Billy." About her age, he had fuzz on his upper lip that he kept licking. Red dots decorated his forehead like tiny volcanoes.

Rachel wanted to slam the door so badly. She could feel Lisa's eyes on her back. *HOW DID THIS HAPPEN TO ME?* her mind screamed.

"Look, uh," she stammered. "I don't—"

"You ready to go?" His voice turned slightly aggressive and he gave her a wink. "I got a flower for you, but I, uh, left it in the car … you'll have to come with me to get it."

"Uh, there, uh, has been a mistake."

Billy flashed his teeth. "You're Rachel, aren't you? There's no mistake. Tonight I'm taking you for a whirl, girl!"

"Maybe, I, uh, don't feel good …"

"You'll feel better with me. Trust me. I have a Mexican joint all picked out. Hot food for a hot lady."

The guy didn't look ready to leave and couldn't take a hint if it hit him over the head. Rachel resisted the action. "Uh, hold on … just a minute."

"Sure, I'll be right here waiting, sweetheart." He winked again.

Rachel shut the door and turned to lean against it. Breathing heavily, she tried to remain calm. Lisa had wisely vanished.

Well, the guy couldn't stay here forever, could he? She hurried into the kitchen and ducked behind a potted tree.

The doorbell rang again.

The back door opened and Steven came in. Seeing Rachel, he gave her a sideways look. "Are you hiding or something?"

Seeing him, she beckoned him over. "I need a huge favor, fast!"

Curious, he went to her. "What's wrong?"

Kneeling to his level, Rachel put both hands on his shoulders. "Look, there's a guy out there … uh, a date that I need to get rid of. I need your help." Again the doorbell rang. "I'll give you ten dollars and let you stay up as late as you want tonight. Just help me get rid of him! Please!"

Steven blinked and bit his lip. "I get the money tonight?"

"Just do it!" Her voice cracked with desperation.

"Yo, Rachel?" called the guy through the door. "You coming? Come on!"

She pushed Steven away. "Quick, think of something. I'll go to the door, but come quickly. Please, Steven."

Pulling open the door again, Rachel managed a strangled smile. "Uh, are you still here?"

"Come on, you ready?" Fidgeting on the stoop, Billy smoothed back his hair and wiped his hand on his pants. "Look, if you want I can come in and we can talk some … get to know each other before going out."

"Uh, that won't be good, uh, the kids I'm babysitting …"

"In that case just come with me. We'll talk over dinner."

"But the kids—"

"They got this babe doing babysitting tonight, don't they? Let's go—"

Suddenly there was a clatter and a thud near the garage.

"What was that?" Rachel leaned out the door, poking out an arm to back the guy off.

"You got a pet here or something?"

"No—" Then Rachel screeched.

Steven stumbled toward them, coming from the driveway. Dark red streaked his arms and legs and covered his face. His hair, cheeks, and forehead looked to have been ripped to shreds. "I … f-fell …" he croaked. A dark substance leaked from his mouth.

"Oh, my—" Billy froze at the sight and his eyes went like fried eggs again.

"What happened?" Rachel cried, flying out of the house, her mind going numb.

"Sl-slipped …" As he reached Rachel, Steven gurgled and nodded toward Billy.

About to comfort the boy and stop the bleeding, Rachel suddenly jerked to a stop. Mouth dropping open in horror, she watched as the boy stumbled past before collapsing at Billy's feet. Then he promptly threw up. Thick, greenish, lumpy matter mixed with red spewed right on Billy's shoes—a pair of long, flat, brown loafers. They would never be the same.

Standing frozen with arms in the air as if surrendering, Billy didn't move until too late. Leaping back, he jumped from the boy. "Hey, man!" he cried.

"Sorry," groaned Steven, "but I need the hospital …" The boy looked up at Billy. "Can we use your car?" He lurched to his feet and spit up another mess.

"Oh my, oh my …" Billy stumbled back. "Look, Rachel, we got—" Suddenly his nose wrinkled and he gave Steven another look. Rachel swallowed. The strong smell of ketchup radiated from Steven like Billy's body spray.

Staring down at his shoes, Billy's face turned colors. "I don't believe it," he hissed. Suddenly he looked ready to kick the boy.

Rachel quickly moved between them. "Oh my, uh, sorry about your shoes … He likes to play emergency, you know … kid stuff."

"Oh, that's just great! Just great!" Billy turned on Rachel and jabbed a finger in her face. "Look, you, I went to a lot of trouble for this! They told me you were fat, but not ugly! You know what? You're the one who blew it, not me! I'm the only date you would have had, if you'd had it, but I've had it! Too bad for you! Nobody else will ever take you out! Ever!" Whirling, he stomped for his car. Then he stopped and turned on Rachel again. "It's a good thing they paid me for this, but it's still not enough! Besides, none of my acting classes are good enough to make me act like I like you!"

Suddenly his thick greasy hair exploded in mush.

"Get lost!" shouted Steven. "Get off our property!" Steven had another handful of his fake throw up that he'd scooped from the walk ready to toss.

"Why, you—" Billy ducked as the next handful flew over his shoulder. Spinning for his car, he ran the rest of the way in a panic. Honking madly, he drove out of the driveway. His car slid to a stop at the bottom of the driveway and the window rolled down. "I won't forget this!" he shouted, shaking a fist. Then he was gone.

Shaking, Rachel tried to keep the tears away. Steven was breathing hard at her side. Wiping his nose with the back of his wrist, he looked up at Rachel. "Well, how did your date go?" he asked.

Blinking away tears, Rachel smiled down at him. "Fast." Then she forced a laugh. "I doubt we'll ever see Billy the Hair again."

"Yeah. He's a real jerk, isn't he?"

Rachel sighed. "Yes … he's a jerk and a creep." *And probably spoke the truth.* Then she gasped. "And what about you? When I saw you coming from the garage, I thought you crashed your ripstick and were dying. You nearly gave me a heart attack!"

Steven shrugged and answered, "I used all the ketchup in the fridge." Then he grinned self-consciously. "Plus I put applesauce, guacamole, and ketchup in my mouth for the throw-up."

"That was pretty gross." She rubbed the top of his head—about the only part of him not covered in ketchup. "Now you better go up and use all the soap. If Vikki Rosa comes by and sees you like this she'll think I'm skinning you alive—either that, or trying to eat you like a hot dog." Then she sighed. "And I better clean the front step."

Just as the two looked that way, the front door burst open and Lisa jumped out, her face horrified. "Steven! What happened to you! You're bleeding all over the place!" Running to him in a panic, tears were in her eyes.

"Wait!" Rachel moved to intercept her, but Lisa batted away her arms. Steven retreated from his sister.

"What did you do to my brother!"

"Nothing!" Rachel shouted at her. "It's ketchup! He's fine!"

Lisa whirled on her. "He's blee—Huh? What did you say?" Turning on Steven, her horrified panic switched to anger in a flash. "What did you do, Steven! Are you serious?"

"It was a joke," Rachel said hurriedly.

"A joke?" Now Lisa turned her wrath on Rachel. "You think that's *funny*? It's sick and horrible!"

A few days before, Rachel would have broken down and run away in tears. Now she crossed her arms and stared at the angry redhead. "You mean sort of like setting me up for a date with a gremlin? I think we've had enough funny business for tonight. Come inside, both of you."

Lisa ran to the steps. Seeing the remains of Steven's fake throw-up, she stopped and faced Rachel. "This was my last day of school, and it's a Friday. It's supposed to be fun, but you made it the worst day ever!"

Rachel's shoulders dropped. "Mine too," she whispered.

Steven meekly followed after his sister. But before going inside, he glanced impishly back at Rachel. "Do I still get my ten dollars?"

He disappeared inside before Rachel could answer.

After washing down the steps with a bucket of water, Rachel shut the front door and locked it. Jane had wisely kept out of sight, and Lisa had long before shut herself in her room. Steven was busy in the bath scrubbing off the ketchup. Feeling tired, angry, remorseful, and amused all at once, Rachel found a seat on the couch and looked for her notebook.

And then the doorbell rang.

Anger rose from all the other emotions. *Billy!* The creep just didn't know when to quit.

Rule number twenty of babysitting was to never let your emotions control your actions. Breaking this rule made her forget rule number ten. Stomping to the door, she didn't even bother to check out the window.

She had never yelled at somebody in public in her life, but Billy deserved it. "Go away, Bil—" Throwing open the door, she came face to face with Jason Richardson.

Taller than she remembered, he wore a burnt-red polo shirt, open at the collar, and dark blue jeans. Hair neatly brushed and smelling of aftershave, he took Rachel's breath away. Raising his eyebrows, he backed away.

"Is … this a bad time?" Jason asked sheepishly.

Mortified, Rachel's hands flew to her hair and then to smooth out her shirt. Shapeless and old, the shirt went with her old jeans to create a most unflattering wardrobe—she'd chosen these clothes for Billy. And now she smelled faintly of ketchup to go along with it.

"No, uh, I'm sorry …" Rachel gulped. "I, uh, thought you were … uh … somebody else." She didn't dare meet his liquid blue eyes—she might drown. Already she was flailing. Just the thought of it made her blush. *I read too many bad romance novels!*

"Oh, okay. You remember me? I'm Jason Richardson from next door."

"Of course … uh, yes," she stammered. *Oh, I'm acting like an idiot!*

"Yeah, uh, I don't want to bother you …"

"Not at all, do you want to come in?" Rachel moved back too quickly and her backside bumped into the door with a thump.

Jason's eyes darted side to side and he licked his lips. "That's okay, I, um, actually have a favor to ask you. A really big one."

Nodding, Rachel swallowed hard. "A favor?" Now she did dare to meet his eyes.

After brief contact, it was Jason who quickly looked away. He appeared slightly embarrassed, perhaps nervous. "Well, uh, are you free tonight? You see," he said quickly, "Alison's school is having their summer bash party—she's on her way to Europe, remember? Well, uh, I graduated from there last year and, uh, still know a lot of people. Well, I've been trying to go and …" He suddenly sighed. "I'm just going to ask you flat out."

Rachel's heart skipped and thudded to a complete stop. Not daring to breath, she barely nodded. Her hands trembled. Was this seriously happening to her? A gorgeous guy wanted to ask her out on a date?

Wiping his mouth, Jason said, "Courtney and Jakey would be home all alone and I can't let that happen."

Rachel nodded again without comprehending what he'd just said. Her heart restarted and beat like a drum leading a parade. Of all the luck—this was about to be her best Friday ever!

"So I was wondering, would it be okay if they came over here tonight? You know, Courtney and Jakey? Could you, um, watch them?"

Her heart skipped a beat and the parade crashed to a terrible halt. "Uh, what?"

Jason rushed on. "I know you're babysitting, and well, you see, my girlfriend has been getting ready for this dance all week. I had a babysitter lined up, but some guy just asked her to the same dance yesterday … so, you see, I'm kind of stuck."

"No, yes, no, I, uh, understand." Rachel's mouth opened and closed like a flickering flame going out. Tears threatened to burst from her eyes.

Jason stared at her worriedly. "Um … so do you mind?"

"So you want your brother and sister over here?" she tried to force a smile, but only ended up looking sick.

"Would that be, er, okay … ? I'll pay, of course—"

"No. No, I mean, yes." Rachel closed her eyes and took a long breath. "No, don't pay me. Yes, bring the kids over. I don't mind … It'll be … fun."

"Oh, man, really? Rachel, that's great!" Jason launched himself at Rachel and before she could move, he gave her a giant hug. Then he jumped back. "Thank you so much. I'll walk them over in about twenty minutes!"

"Okay …" Rachel watched Jason leave, pumping a fist as he went.

"Thanks again!" he called back when reaching the street.

Lifting her head back, she slammed the door, not realizing her big toe was in the way.

"OUCH!" she cried.

Sucking in her breath, Rachel let the tears come. They fell like rain on a lonely night. Hobbling to the couch, she collapsed in a fit of pain. It really had to be the worst night of her life. Ever.

Chapter Seventeen

Twenty-five minutes later, when the doorbell rang again, Rachel rushed to answer, again ignoring rule number ten of babysitting. Now she wore a forest-green sweater and tan slacks that weren't too tight or baggy. Her hair was brushed back and slight blush was applied to her cheeks. Throwing the door open, she gave a full smile.

Courtney and Jakey stood awkwardly at the door. Jason was already climbing in his car where the silhouette of a slim girl could be seen in the passenger seat.

Raising a hand to wave, Rachel caught herself in time and instead ushered in the children. Jakey carried a soccer ball and Courtney had a backpack. Both unsure of themselves, like they were searching for the fun but not finding it.

Nor will they, thought Rachel. *What did I just do? These kids are going to have a miserable night, and Jason will never talk to me again!*

Putting on a fake smile, Rachel clapped her hands. It was time to be what she was paid to be—a babysitter. "Well, I'm, uh, glad you're here. We just finished having supper, but if you haven't eaten yet—"

"It's okay," Courtney said quickly. "We ate already. But thank you."

Rachel breathed a sigh of relief. Her supper had consisted of a hunk of artisan bread left over from breakfast and two glasses of water.

Lisa remained in her room, and Steven, freshly scrubbed, sat in the kitchen with a bowl of macaroni salad left over from

Rachel's lunch. Jane Lovington had quietly left when Rachel mentioned the Richardson children were coming over.

"I'm here to give you a night off," she had simply said. "Not babysit more children. You stay? Then I go. I be back Monday." Apparently, she, like Lisa, was not happy their handpicked date hadn't worked out. *Too bad!* Rachel was not sorry to see her go.

"Well," said Rachel much too brightly. "Let's go in the kitchen anyway. Come on, don't worry. It'll be fun!" Rachel hoped her voice didn't betray her thoughts. Babysitting rule number eight said to fake it until you make it.

Steven looked up from his half-eaten bowl and gave Courtney and Jakey a timid smile.

"Uh," Rachel stammered, "This is Steven … Steven, this is Courtney and Jakey from next door."

Courtney smiled and waved and Jakey just stared, narrowing his eyes.

Great start. "Well, what do you think?" she asked. "What should we do?"

"Do you play soccer?" Jakey asked hopefully. Dressed in shorts and a T-shirt, he held the ball out with a hopeful expression.

Steven pushed away his bowl. "A little," he admitted. He looked up at Rachel. "Is it okay if we play out back?"

"Oh, uh, sure … Just don't break a window, or get hurt." She gave Steven a look. "No more ketchup. And no real stuff either."

Courtney could only scratch her head in confusion as Steven grinned wider. "Sure," he said.

"Let's go!" Jakey quickly moved toward the doors and Steven got up to turn on the back lights.

"I can show you my ripstick if you want," Steven said as they went out.

This left Rachel and Courtney alone. Lisa had never responded when Rachel had told her about the company coming over.

"So, um, thanks for having us," Courtney said politely, putting down her bag. "I'm glad you invited us."

"Invited you?" Rachel asked dumbly.

Courtney's smile faltered. "Jason told us you met him on the street and asked if we could come over. Otherwise—" she made a face. "We'd probably be stuck at home with Jason and Shawna."

"Shawna?"

"That's Jason's girlfriend. She's something else … It's like Jason's her robot sometimes. I mean, he does everything she says. And they're always kiss—"

"Yeah, um," Rachel quickly cut in. "Lisa isn't feeling well, so she's upstairs … So, uh, should we join the boys?"

"Oh, sure! That'll be great."

Amazingly, against all of Rachel's expectations, it turned out to be just that. Great.

In bare feet, which broke babysitting rule number fourteen—no bare feet on concrete, the children and Rachel soon were playing a wild game of keep-away that turned into boys versus girls.

Jakey and Steven quickly turned into a dynamic duo and both proved to be adept at soccer—at least against Rachel and Courtney. On the other hand, the girls had less skill than potted plants when it came to the sport. Potted plants could at least sometimes get in the way. Still, the girls made up for their lack of skill with their undying enthusiasm. Any time Courtney touched the ball, or came close to touching the ball, she screeched in delight, or in surprise. Rachel started doing the same and joined the game with gusto. After the boys went up 5–0, the teams switched to Steven and Rachel against Courtney and Jakey.

Playing on the top tier away from the pool, with shoes to mark the goals, this game went on until Rachel tried to clear the ball from Jakey. Giving it a good kick, her first all evening, she sent it flying into the glass window of the kitchen. Thankfully, it bounced harmlessly off the glass.

"Watch it!" hollered Lisa from her bedroom window. "You're going to break something!"

Wheezing and sighing with relief at the same time, Rachel took a seat on the concrete. She knew Lisa probably had been watching the whole time.

"Come take my place!" she called up. The window slammed as an answer.

"Sorry," Courtney said, gathering up the ball. "Maybe we should stop."

"Yeah," agreed Rachel, wiping her sweaty forehead. "I'm afraid … I'm … going to die if I keep running."

Jakey sighed. "Ah, man! And we were just starting!"

Rachel gasped for a breath. "You got to be kidding," she wheezed. "Why doesn't Steven show you the ripstick?"

Bad idea. She was breaking babysitting rule number thirteen: Never encourage dangerous play.

Sure enough, after watching Steven's demonstration, it didn't take long for Jakey to want a turn. Shortly after, he ran into the hedges.

Courtney burst out laughing. "Jakey, you have to turn, you know!"

"You try it!" sputtered the boy, picking out leaves from his hair. Thankfully, he had no injuries.

"Okay," said his sister. "Sure!"

"On second thought, maybe we should do something else," Rachel said hastily. Mentally she reminded herself to buy Steven a helmet.

Courtney looked at her with gleaming eyes. "What about a night swim?"

By now the stars were out and the night's humidity felt suffocating after the soccer. Still sweating, Rachel looked at the cool water and bit her lip.

"Well, I don't know …" she started.

Courtney squeezed her hands in anticipation. "Jakey and I brought our bathing suits—they're in the bag."

Jakey looked at her, his eyes growing extra big on his thin face. "Please?"

"Yes, but …" She glanced at Steven. "What about a movie? We can make popcorn and have leftover brownies."

"We can do that after," Steven said, suddenly giving her a mischievous grin. "Remember, you have to let me stay up late tonight."

Rachel coughed. "Uh, yeah … but, uh, you'll owe me ten dollars if you swim."

"Deal," said the boy.

"But—" Rachel could only stare as the children yelled in delight. Later she would find out Steven's weekly allowance—30 bucks.

Courtney already headed for the door. "It'll be perfect! Night swims are the best!"

Throwing up her hands in surrender, Rachel sighed. "Fine," she said. "Steven, show, uh, them where to change and … I'll go get my bathing suit. Does anybody need sunscreen? Steven, your mom gave me some to put in my purse—" she stopped as the three kids just stared at her. "Oh, right," she muttered. "Night swim …"

When Rachel emerged from her room wrapped in a towel, she made sure nobody was watching. This would be her first time wearing a bathing suit in public since the sixth grade. Cautiously stepping out, she crept to the stairs. After making sure Lisa's door remained shut, she hurried down and went out back.

Of course the children were already waiting for her.

"Hurry up, Rachel!" Courtney called. "We want to have a diving contest!"

"Um, maybe I'll just watch from up here!" she nearly begged.

"But you promised!" Courtney said in a hurt tone. "Hurry up!"

Gathering her courage, Rachel dropped the towel and walked to the edge of the pool, not daring to look up. Her suit was new and felt awkward. Yet there was no laughter or rude comments.

When Rachel finally did look, nobody was staring at her. Instead, the three children leaped into the water. Swallowing, she watched the children as they began a race across the pool. They were like sleek fish, their slim brown bodies easily cutting through the water. She sighed and looked down at her bloated body and pasty white arms.

I feel like the Pillsbury whale.

"Come on, Rachel!" Courtney screamed, having abandoned the race that Steven easily led. "We need you!"

Oh, what the heck? "Okay …" Pinching her nose, Rachel went off in the deep end. For the first time in years, Rachel went swimming.

Much later, when the kids started a game of monkey-in-the-middle with the soccer ball in the shallow area, Rachel sat on the other end with her feet dangling in the water. Water dripped from her and puddled around her to serve as proof of her swim. She'd really gone swimming.

What a strange night … she thought. It was horrible and wonderful all at once … *The worst night of my life is turning into the best night of my babysitting.*

She heard the door open and turned to see Lisa glaring at her. *And it wasn't over yet.*

"What are you doing?" hissed the redhead, not hiding her venom when she came to stand over Rachel. "Where's Jane?"

"She went home." Rachel hunched forward, feeling embarrassed to be seen by Lisa this way.

"This is ridiculous!" Turning in a huff, the girl stormed back inside.

Rachel stood searching for her towel. The pool didn't feel so wonderful anymore.

Courtney left the boys and paddled over to her. "Is she okay?" she asked. "Lisa?"

"Uh, yes …" Rachel answered. "She's, uh, just not feeling well." Having wrapped herself in a towel, Rachel tried to smile at Courtney.

"Maybe I can go talk to her," Courtney said, staring thoughtfully up at the house. "She's probably lonely."

Rachel's eyes widened. Lisa, lonely? At first it seemed impossible, but thinking about it … She spent most of her days in her room and rarely talked to any friends. Her dance class had ended for the summer, and the only time she went anywhere was with Jane for shopping.

"Maybe I can go talk to her during the movie," Courtney said brightly.

Rachel nodded slowly. "Oh, uh, yeah … speaking of which, it's getting late and I'm cold."

After toweling off, the children went to change back into their clothes and Rachel went to the kitchen to make hot cocoa and popcorn. She didn't know what time Jason planned on coming back but decided she didn't care. Despite its ominous beginning, this was a night she couldn't help but enjoy.

As Jakey and Steven gathered in front of the giant television with the cocoa, popcorn, and cookies that Rachel had managed to find, Courtney asked if she could see Lisa upstairs.

"Oh, uh, sure ..." Rachel told her. "Her room is down to the left and then the right—the one with the picture of a cat on the door."

Lisa was reading on her bed when a tentative tapping sounded on the door. Slightly ajar, it swung open.

"Can I come in?" Courtney asked.

As if jolted with lightning, Lisa shoved a notebook under her pillow. "What do you want?" she asked quickly.

"Just to see how you're doing. What were you reading?"

Her face turned the color of her hair. "None of your business."

"Oh. Well, I'm Courtney. You know, from the next house."

"I know." Lisa stared at her with narrowed eyes. Slowly she relaxed. "I'm sorry," she mumbled. "I'm just having a rotten day."

Courtney smiled and walked into the room. "I know what you mean. My idiot brother, Jason, was supposed to get us pizza today and have a party, but instead ran off with his stupid girlfriend. I thought this was going to be the worst night ever! Thanks to Rachel, it's one of the best, though. You're lucky to have her."

Lisa blinked. "Did Rachel send you up here?"

"No. I just thought you might be bored." She rolled her eyes. "Besides, they're watching the second *Shrek* movie. I think I can do without that." She sat on a beanbag chair near Lisa's desk. "I really like your room. The pink walls and sunroof are cool."

"Oh, thanks. Do you like beads? You know, like making necklaces and bracelets?"

Courtney's eyes lit up. "Are you kidding me? With my sister gone, I'm stuck with two brothers. All we do is watch sports and play soccer!"

The doorbell rang well after midnight, startling Rachel awake. Sitting up with a jolt, she blinked rapidly. Slumped in an easy chair, she faced the mega television that was playing another Shrek movie—the second of the night. On mute, the screen showed villagers being repulsed by the green ogre.

"That's me," she snorted groggily. Then the doorbell rang again. It hadn't been a dream.

Groaning in protest, she forced herself to her feet. She barely missed stepping on Steven, who was on the floor to her left. He had curled under a blanket. Jakey lay above him on the couch. Both boys were out cold. Empty cups of cocoa, loose popcorn kernels, and cookie crumbs littered the area around them.

And the doorbell rang yet again.

"Coming," she muttered to the door, scratching her hair. Having not showered after swimming, she knew her hair was a mess. She wore a dumpy pair of sweatpants and a super large gray sweater sporting old food stains. Too tired to care, she opened the door … just in time to catch Jason in the midst of a passionate embrace with a skinny blond in a slinky bright-blue dress.

"Ugh," she said without thinking.

"Oh, er, excuse me …" Jason hastily wiped his mouth and quickly disentangled himself. "I'm here for Courtney and Jakey. And, er, this is Shawna. Shawna, this is Rachel, the babysitter." He gestured awkwardly between the girls.

The girl eyed Courtney with ill-disguised disgust. Her dress clung to her thin shape and sparkled in the porch light. Soft blond curls hung loosely to her shoulders. A thick layer of makeup covered an otherwise pretty face. Batting her eyes at Jason, she purred, "Hurry, so I can say goodbye … I need to leave soon before Daddy starts to worry." She licked her lips and threw Rachel a sideways look.

Jason swallowed. "Yeah, sure, I—"

Rachel's face flushed and suddenly she was wide-awake. "I'll, uh, go get them." Turning quickly, she stopped. "Uh, actually," she said, twisting back around. For some reason her hands couldn't stop moving and she stared more at the floor than at Jason. "You've been gone so long that Jakey fell asleep. I don't know if you want to wake him—"

"Oh, er, I can carry him. Sorry, we've been, um, delayed."

Rachel couldn't help but look up.

"Yes," Shawna said, looking at Jason like he was a pastry that needed eating. "We were … delayed."

"We actually went to a diner with some friends and ended up in a Ping-Pong tournament," Jason confessed. "One of the guys' uncles owned the place."

"Right." Rachel managed to breathe a little better. "Uh, I'll go show you where he is."

"And I'll go too," Shawna said immediately, clicking her tongue and grabbing Jason's arm.

Rachel gritted her teeth. "Go right and look for the room with the bright lights … I'll go up and get Courtney."

Racing up the stairs as fast as she could, Rachel worked hard to control her emotions. Shawna reminded her of the popular version of Sarah Watkins. The way she glanced at Rachel, as if she were some fat toad ready to be made into roadkill … Rachel's face burned at the memory. She hoped to never see Jason again.

At the top of the stairs she heard girlish laughter from Lisa's room. Her blood grew hot. She'd forgotten about Courtney and Lisa being together all this time …

I bet Lisa is telling stories about me … probably telling Courtney all about Billy.

"Courtney!" she yelled louder than she intended. Almost instantly the laughter stopped, which served only to confirm her suspicions. "Your brother is here to take you home!"

Lisa's voice shouted back. "We'll be down in a second!"

"Hurry up! It's late!" Going back down the stairs, she heard footsteps race across the hall to the bathroom. She assumed Courtney had gone to collect the wet bathing suits. Feeling so very tired and more than a little hurt, she took a seat on the bottom step as Jason, cradling Jakey, returned with Shawna close to his side.

At the front door, Jason stopped to give a goodnight kiss to Shawna, shifting Jakey to his shoulder to keep him out of the way. Jakey laid his head against his brother and didn't stir. Shawna put her head on the opposite shoulder. "Love you, baby," she said, looking past Jason and straight at Rachel. "Call me when you get home, okay?"

"Er, yes, of course. Thanks for tonight, Shawna. It was really fun."

"Yes, it was." She didn't acknowledge Rachel as she reached up a finger and slid it down Jason's cheek. Then she sauntered out the door, swishing her dress behind her.

Rachel resisted throwing up the cookies, popcorn, and cocoa.

"We took her car," Jason said in a way of explanation to Rachel, awkwardly shifting his brother to a better position. "She, er, said that mine smelled, so—

Outside there was a dull splash and a high-pitched scream. From upstairs, several loud thumps followed.

"What in the—" Jason rushed to the door and yanked it open, startling Jakey awake. "Shawna!"

"What!" came the answering roar, no longer sounding lovey-dovey. "I'm going to kill her!"

"Huh?" Jason started out the door, but quickly backed up with his mouth hanging wide open.

Stomping back into the house, Shawna pushed Jason aside and glared straight at Rachel.

Rachel covered her mouth with her hand.

The blond curls were smashed, mangled, and dripping wet. Water smeared with makeup and eyeliner ran down her face in ugly green streaks. Sticking in her hair was a ripped plastic bag. She'd just been water-bombed.

Courtney ran down the stairs behind Rachel, but stopped at the sight. Lisa came down at a much slower pace.

There was a shocked silence. Then Jakey rubbed his eyes. "What happened?" he said sleepily. "She looks like Shrek."

With the face Shawna wore, she did resemble an ogre. "You!" she hissed hoarsely, pointing a long finger ending in a long, red nail. "You did this!"

Rachel's hand fell away. "What?"

"You told them to do this!" Shaking her head violently and pointing to her hair, Shawna sprayed droplets of water all over Jason.

His mouth open, Jason looked at Rachel and then at Shawna. "B-b-but—"

"Is that all you have to say?" Shawna screeched, turning on him. "Don't bother calling me tonight!" Fists clenched, she stormed back out.

"Shawna, I—" Jason made to follow, but stopped. Burdened with Jakey, he didn't know what to do. He looked helplessly back at Rachel, who was too shocked to move.

The sound of a car starting broke the silence and then came the screech of tires as Shawna rocketed out of the driveway.

"I hope that doesn't leave a mark," murmured Lisa. "The tires, I mean."

Rachel rose unsteadily to her feet. "I'm sorry, but I—"

Jason held up his free hand. "It's fine … it's probably been a long night. I'm sorry I asked you to look after Courtney and Jakey."

"I—"

"Let's go, Courtney. We have to walk home."

Steven appeared and wordlessly handed the soccer ball to Courtney. Looking apologetic, Courtney gave him a quick smile and then exchanged looks with Lisa.

"Bye, Rachel," she said meekly before hurrying after her brothers.

Clinging to his brother, Jakey gave a small wave. Jason never looked back.

"Oh, uh …" Rachel nearly sank to the floor as Steven closed the door behind them. Lisa had run back upstairs. Rubbing his eyes, Steven slowly trailed up the stairs after her. Rachel, as was often the case, was left quite alone.

Returning to the messy television room, she collapsed onto the couch and closed her eyes. She woke the next morning still on the couch. And still very much alone.

It was around noon that day when Rachel realized her notebook had gone missing. Having just dropped Steven off at swim practice for his first Saturday practice of the summer, she'd returned home with the strong urge to write. After the previous night, she had a *lot* of material to get down … and a lot of stress to blow off.

But where did I put it? Just thinking about the previous day gave her a headache … so much had happened. *I was sitting on the couch when Lisa told me about Billy and I …* A terrible feeling struck her. *LISA!*

Rachel pounded up the stairs. Babysitting rule eighteen—never be angry—and twelve—never accuse without proof, were far forgotten. Bursting into Lisa's room, not bothering to knock (violation of babysitting rule twenty), Rachel nearly leapt on the redhead.

"Where's my notebook!" she demanded. "Give it to me now!"

Lisa looked up from where she sat on the floor stringing beads into a necklace. At first she appeared startled, but then she snorted. "What on earth are you talking about?"

"I'm talking about my notebook!" Rachel tried hard to keep her temper reined in. Her notebook—it was her life—all her secrets, all her dreams were written in it! "How can you be so cruel? I know I don't have much of a life, but that's my notebook and it's private, okay? I need it back!" Tears were actually in her eyes.

Lisa didn't look up as she kept stringing the beads. "I don't have your stupid notebook. Besides, you spend too much time with that thing."

Rachel kicked the box of beads in front of Lisa, sending it flying into the bedpost where it snapped into pieces. Beads flew everywhere.

"I need it back!" Her face was scarlet and her chest was heaving. "I know you took it, so give it!"

Frightened, Lisa dropped her unfinished necklace and scooted back. "What's wrong with you?" she screamed. "You're crazy!"

"What's wrong with you? You stole my notebook!"

"So what if I did?" screamed back the girl, all of a sudden furious. "All you care about is Steven and that stupid book! Well, what about me? I live here too, you know! You do nothing for me! *Nothing!*"

Shocked, Rachel took a step back. Her fury instantly abated as genuine puzzlement took over. "What-what are you talking about? You don't want me to care about you!" she spluttered.

"Since when! How do you know? You never talk to me! You never do anything with me! You invite people over and spend time with them, but you leave me alone!"

"But, but you don't even like me!"

"You get up to see Steven off to school. You drive him everywhere. You help *him* with homework. What do you do for me?" Tears were running down Lisa's cheeks now. Taking the unfinished beaded necklace, she flung it against the wall, causing another explosion of beads.

Completely, utterly shocked, Rachel could only shake her head. "But, but, I thought you didn't want me here—"

"That shows how much you know! You're stupid! Get out of here!"

"Lisa, I—"

"Here." Lisa got up and ran to her bed. "You want your notebook? Then here it is!" Reaching under her pillow, she pulled out the familiar notebook. "Take it!"

"Lisa—"

"GO AWAY!" She flung the book on the bed and turned to face the wall, sobbing. "You're right, I stole it! You're right about *everything!* I don't need you! Go back to your stupid home in Virginia and leave us alone!"

Rachel stood frozen. Finally, quietly, she gathered up her notebook and left, closing the door softly behind her. Lisa never stopped sobbing.

When safe in her room, Rachel collapsed on her bed and rolled on her back. Now her mind was a complete mess. How could this have happened? No matter what she did, how hard she tried, everything ended up in disaster. Poor Lisa … Rachel shifted her head to look at the notebook beside her. Was it worth it? That stupid book full of nothing but words—was it more important than a small eleven-year-old trying so desperately to grow up but stuck in the throes of childhood?

Groaning, she grabbed the book and flipped through the pages. How was she going to get out of this one? The only solution she could think of was to purchase a ticket home. Let Jane Lovington take over. Suddenly her heart went to her throat. The last page of writing was not by her. Her stomach spun like a washing machine as she stared at the neat, girlish penmanship covering the entire page. Rachel never wrote in red ink. And she never dotted her *i*'s with hearts.

Rachel, you write good stories … I want to be a writer when I grow up too … I was so sure when I took this notebook that I would find how much you hated me. I thought you would write that I was this ugly, redheaded monster who needed a spanking. That's what Vikki said about me once. Instead, you only wrote nice things about me. WHY ARE YOU SO NICE? Even Steven trusts you now and he only trusts Mom and Dad. And sometimes me.

I guess I really messed up. I didn't want you here because … Mom always talked about your mother and how great she was. She made your mom sound like the greatest friend in the world. I don't have too many friends … not real ones. Imagine. My temper usually scares them away. Maybe I am jealous. I don't know … I wish I could be older and understand things! Really, though, I think it is good that you came.

I'm sorry about Billy … that was pretty stupid of me, wasn't it? He actually claimed to be an actor working at Foodmart … but I guess he wasn't that good. I wasn't that good either.

Then on the next page was the newest entry that had probably come that morning.

About last night … the water bombs were my idea … I told Courtney the story of how your mom met my mom and how they threw water bombs on the boys … I don't think we were thinking right, because we decided to … you know. I'm really, really, really sorry. Really.

It was signed hastily *Lisa.* Swallowing, Rachel could not stop the flow of tears. *I'm crying way too much for this job.* But what else could she do?

Wiping her eyes, Rachel sighed. She knew there could only be one answer. Finding her pen, Rachel turned to a new page and started writing. An hour later, when Lisa slipped down to make the salad for supper, and as Rachel readied to pick up Steven, the notebook ended up on Lisa's bed.

Chapter Eighteen

Jason rubbed the top of his head and grimaced. A dull pain had moved in that morning and had yet to settle or decide to move on. Holding his cell phone in his other hand, he stared at the screen and sighed. From upstairs the grand finale of Beethoven's Ninth blasted from Courtney's room. Outside, Jakey kicked the soccer ball against the back fence. Both were activities his younger siblings did when they were mad. All because of the previous night and the stupid babysitter …

That morning at breakfast—what should have been a joyous occasion of donuts and cartoons, Courtney demanded that he apologize to Rachel. She claimed the water bombs were all her idea. Shawna needed a cold bath of reality was how she phrased it. Besides, she had said, now at least Jason didn't have to spend all day talking to Shawna on the phone like he usually did. Now he could actually have fun for a change.

This, of course, caused Jason to blow up and scare his siblings away. Now, sitting at the head of the kitchen table staring at the uneaten donuts, he bit his lip.

Fun … yeah, this is real fun for a change, he thought.

Shawna still hadn't called. And all he could think about was Rachel's shocked expression of hurt and dismay when he'd left. The poor girl—it wasn't her fault he had a moron for a little sister.

"I don't even have her number," he muttered aloud, slapping his phone against his thigh.

"I do." Courtney emerged from the hall and held up a slip of paper. "I just looked up the Winters' number in the phone book."

Jason tried to glare at his sister, but he couldn't help but smile. "Somehow I'm not surprised. You know, it really is a nice day today, though. Why don't we join Jakey for a soccer match?" He wiggled his eyebrows. "I have a feeling it may end in the pool."

Shaking her head, Courtney held out the paper. "Only if you promise to call Rachel."

"I said I would, okay? Come on, hurry up before Shawna calls. And turn your music off! I mean, rock I can stand. But *classical*?"

Geoffrey sat between his brothers on the couch, watching a basketball game on TV through half-opened eyes. During the past few days, the brothers had spent more time together than ever before. No police had come for Rosco, and he no longer jumped when hearing sirens. Still, Geoffrey's older brother had changed. Now he wore a belt and stopped prowling outside during the night. And he absolutely avoided the woods and Camelot Acres.

Oliver understood that something had happened, but never pried. When the brothers first came to watch television with him, he simply moved aside and passed the remote to Rosco. They started watching a lot of sports after that. Oliver was seventeen, but no longer attended school. He'd stopped the day he was expelled for participating in a gang fight. Ever since then, he took to staying indoors and watching a lot of television.

Geoffrey sighed. He guessed it was better than going to jail, or worse … *like betraying a friend.* The last few days of school had been torture for him. He'd taken to avoiding Steven, which wasn't that hard. Steven had started hanging around some other boys in the class. Tommy also stayed away. Any time one of the three passed each other in the hall, they would immediately look the other way and pretend not to notice. Now only a week remained of school—and it would consist of taking finals and cleaning out lockers. It was pretty much over … school and his friendship.

Oliver suddenly jumped to his feet and hit the power button on the controller. "Man, I think we need to go outside and toss the football around, hey?"

Surprised, Rosco looked at him. "You serious?"

"Yeah …" Oliver stretched. "I haven't thrown a football since I was quarterback in the eighth grade. You boys down for a little game of pass?"

"Uh, yeah. Geoffrey?"

"Sure …"

"That's all I get?" Oliver shook his head. He suddenly grabbed Geoffrey and threw him over his shoulder in a fireman's carry. "Man, come on, Rosco, Richard, whatever your name is! I don't think Geoffrey knows what it's like to play football with the Brown boys!"

Football with the Brown brothers involved trash talk and random tackling without warning. Geoffrey laughed for the first time in days, even though he got a busted lip by the end. It felt great to be outdoors and running.

When their Nana arrived home from work, she saw the three boys playing in the front yard and nearly broke down in tears. All of them together and smiling … not since Christmas had she seen such a sight.

"The Lord works in some mysterious ways," she muttered, wiping her eyes. Then she beeped the horn.

"Get your good-for-nothing selves over here and help an old woman with groceries. My goodness, it's like I raised a gang of hooligans!"

"Not no more," Rosco panted. "No, ma'am!"

That afternoon when Rachel arrived home from picking up Steven, she found Lisa waiting at the front door.

"About time you two showed up!" greeted the redhead sourly.

Just exiting the car, Steven's swim bag slipped off his shoulder. Looking over the car at Rachel, he lifted an eyebrow.

Taking her time to shut her door, Rachel licked her lips. "Uh, what's wrong?"

"Nothing." Lisa stood and grabbed a hanger that had been lying behind her. It held Steven's white dinner suit—the same one he'd worn the week before when picking Rachel up at the airport.

Had it only been a week? It felt like forever ago.

"Steven, this is for dinner. Tonight we're having a party."

"Huh?" Steven frowned at his sister.

"One of your girlfriends called to remind you of her party that you just missed."

"Oh, I forgot …"

"That's okay. I knew you'd be disappointed, so I decided to have a party here. Go and shower. You reek of chlorine. Rachel and I will prepare dinner."

"We will?" Rachel asked doubtfully. "Are you okay, Lisa?"

"Yes to both questions. We'll have chicken tacos and Spanish rice. Hurry up, you two. Oh, and, um, Rachel, something of yours, well, it's on your bed!" Turning, the girl fled into the house with the suit flapping behind her.

Rachel broke into a broad smile. Could it be possible? Had she finally broken through with Lisa?

Steven stared at her like she just lost her mind.

She mussed up Steven's hair and laughed. "You heard your sister! Go shower!"

Lisa waited by the stairs fumbling with her hair. The suit lay next to her.

"Uh, Lisa," Rachel began, praying this wouldn't blow up, "I was, uh, thinking. You're done with school … Why not after supper we all go to a bookstore and pick out some books—for you when Steven is still in school. We, uh, can also get you a good journal—they're much better for writing than notebooks."

Lisa swallowed and ducked her head. "Oh, um, really?"

"Sure, why not? I have a car and your mom left plenty of money. Don't worry, Steven, we'll get you a soccer book, or something."

"Maybe a book that explains girls," he muttered, heading for the stairs. "Do I really have to dress up?"

Lisa glared at him. "Yes! It's like when Mom's here and we have parties. Besides, think of it as a dress rehearsal for church tomorrow."

Rachel had nearly forgotten. The next day was Sunday, and she'd promised to be at the Lord's Faith Church of Finding Grace. "Well," she said brightly, "it'll all be fun!"

"Forgiveness is the heart of life! We are the brains of life! We think, therefore we live. However, if we do not use our hearts, our lives become meaningless! Therefore, we must forgive!"

Shouts and clapping greeted Pastor Smith's words with great enthusiasm.

Rachel squinted and shook her head as she tried to grasp the meaning.

The Lord's Faith Church of Finding Grace advertised as being nondenominational, and based on the crowd gathered that Sunday, it was the truth. It also was maybe nonsensical …

Inside, the outer walls resembled an auditorium, only with pews instead of seats. At the front loomed a large stage in the shape of a half-circle with a giant pulpit in the middle. Behind the pulpit was a rock band of mostly teenagers, accompanied by a choir of mainly middle-aged men and women. After a few songs about Mother Earth and loving everything, the preaching started.

Pastor Smith took the podium like he was born for the moment. Standing confidently, he stared across the pews and started his message like he was talking to each individual personally.

Almost every seat was taken. Old and young, male and female, all dressed in various fashions, listened to the pastor with open ears. There were some in flip-flops and shorts. Others wore suits and ties. No form of dress seemed wrong in this setting. Only their rapt attention to the preaching gave them something in common. Many calls of "Amen" echoed the preacher's points, whatever they might be.

In the third row, feeling slightly out of place, Rachel sat wedged between Lisa and Steven. The children were easily the best dressed in the entire church—Steven, in his white suit, looked incredibly handsome, and Lisa was beautiful in her soft, lime-green dress topped with a light blue sweater. Rachel paled in comparison with her tan skirt and white blouse—the nicest clothes she had.

When they had arrived, just minutes before the service started, there had been several gasps among the congregation. Ms. Proom had run from the stage and greeted the children with high fives and had given Rachel a quick hug. "We're so blessed that you made it! Please, sit near the front! Oh, this is truly a special day! I must tell Pastor Smith. He's going to be so pleased!" Then she'd gone back onto the stage, leaving Rachel and the kids slightly dazed.

Mrs. Hunt and Tommy sat in the pew on their right. Mrs. Hunt kept smiling down at Rachel. Tommy snuck several glances at Steven, but they were never returned.

"I, my brothers and sisters," now continued the pastor, raising his hands as if appeasing the crowd, "forgive. And I need forgiveness! From you, I do!"

Many gasps were heard.

Lisa leaned across to Steven and audibly whispered, "Probably for using too much hairspray and polluting the environment."

The sandy brown hair of the pastor did stand in all different directions but never seemed to move, no matter how hard he shook his head. Shining under the lights, it appeared more plastic than natural.

"Quiet!" shushed Rachel. After last night, an uneasy truce had developed between Rachel and Lisa. The two were communicating, but mostly through the notebook. When talking to each other, they stayed polite and neutral.

The pastor cleared his throat. Not a tall man, he still had an imposing presence in his dark-blue suit and red tie. He had a round face with a large nose, and a stocky build, which produced a powerful, deep voice. Clear and without an accent, it didn't require the microphone to reach across the large church.

"We all need forgiveness, my friends. It's not what we *did* that needs forgiving … it is what we *will* do! We need to forgive our future transgressions against one another!" His voice growing in volume, he raised his hand in triumph and nearly got a standing ovation for the effort.

"What is he talking about?" Steven whispered.

"Uh, we'll see," Rachel whispered back. "Maybe," she added under her breath.

Pastor Smith's voice dropped a few decibels and he smoothed his tie, appearing to calm. "Now, before we continue today, we have some very special people here with us." As he spoke, his eyes seemed to find Rachel and then moved on before locking on Steven. He licked his lips. "With us today, is the future of our great Lord's church. With us is the one who will lead us to the promised land!" The pastor's voice rose again and his hands lifted with it. "We have a great guest with us! We have the future with us!" Twitching uncomfortably, Steven scooted closer to Rachel. Finally the pastor's eyes moved on to sweep across the crowd. "My friends, youth day has arrived!" He waited for the applause and shouting to die down.

Rachel used this moment to look around and she saw several other children also fidgeting. Many, though, had a bright look in their eye.

Breaking into a smile, the pastor continued. "Forgive me for getting carried away … I get so excited and blessed when days like this arrive. For today is a blessing. And now we want to share this blessing—share it with our guests!" He extended both his arms out and broadened his smile. "Will all children six years to twelve years come up to receive their blessing? Come up, children, and be blessed! Then you will go with our lovely youth pastor, Ms. Proom, for a special children's service. Again, all children six years to twelve years! Don't be shy!"

Backing up, the pastor gave way to Ms. Proom, who was all smiles as she took the podium and microphone.

"Thank you, Pastor Smith! And thank you, children, for coming! This is indeed a great day! Pastor Smith spoke about forgiveness—this is done to purify ourselves for the glory to come. We want each child to come up here for blessed purification. And all of us adults will witness the power of a child! Now, don't worry, children. Pastor Smith and I will assist you. Once you have been blessed, come to the back of the stage and I'll meet you there. Now this is only for the children … so all you bigger folks, sorry!" She giggled and drew spatters of laughter.

Rachel didn't laugh. Lisa was pinching her in the arm. "I don't want to go up there," she hissed.

Steven pressed against her. "Me neither. I don't understand either of them."

Rachel nodded nervously. "I'm sure it'll be okay—you won't have to go." She didn't blame the kids. By now she was thinking it would have been best to have avoided this church altogether. Mrs. Hunt turned and smiled widely at her and then the children. No smiles were returned.

Pastor Smith joined Proom at the podium. "All children, come on up!" he boomed over the microphone. "Let's go, let's go! Don't be afraid of a blessing! Be afraid of your sins! If you don't come up, you're wallowing in darkness! Come to the light!"

Hesitantly, children started wandering toward the front. Parents and grandparents gave a few nudges and prods.

Mrs. Hunt patted Tommy's back and pushed him ahead of everyone else. With round eyes and the frightened look of a rabbit caught on a highway, he was the first to make it on stage.

"What is your name, son?" Pastor Smith asked in the microphone. "Don't be shy about a blessing of forgiveness!" Tommy mumbled something. "Say it louder, with pride, son!"

"Tom—Tom Hunt." His voice did not sound very proud.

Suddenly Pastor Smith's eyes seemed to spark. "Tommy Hunt!" He raised a hand over the boy's head and it started to tremble. "Tommy, I command you, by the power inside of me—fall on your knees! There is a darkness inside of you that wants to come out, but you won't let it!"

Stumbling back as if socked in the stomach, Tommy looked stricken. "Wh-what?"

Immediately the pastor's eyes closed. His trembling hand descended toward Tommy's head. "I feel it … You hurt a friend … You hurt a friend badly—didn't you?"

"I-I …" Tears suddenly sprang from the boy's eyes and he fell to his knees. Gasps and shouts erupted from the seats.

"Tell it, boy!" commanded the pastor.

"Let go of the darkness!" cried Ms. Proom, lifting her head to the ceiling. Her eyes also closed.

"That's right!" cried Pastor Smith. "Pray for this boy! Pray that he finds forgiveness! Now, Tommy, renounce your old life of sin and rise to receive a new one. Go ahead, boy! Renounce and receive my blessing!"

Ms. Proom now moved to kneel beside Tommy. Whispering, she gripped his arm and then smiled out in the crowd, opening her eyes. Tommy ducked his head.

"I-I renounce my bad life." Then the boy looked up with tears running down his cheeks. "I renounce my bad life!"

Opening his eyes, the pastor threw up his hands. "You are blessed, Tommy!" A bright light seemed to flash from his hand and the crowd gasped. Eyes going wide, Tommy slowly rose to his feet with an amazed look on his face. He was greeted by a thunderous ovation.

"Now, who shall we have next?" the pastor shouted, sweat dripping from his forehead.

Parents called out for their children to be next, but the pastor shook his head. "Why don't we call some guests up here? Let us have a very special guest get a blessing. Steven Winter! Steven?" He looked to the third pew, but it was empty. Confusion wrinkled his brow.

At the back of the worship area Rachel rapidly led Lisa and Steven toward the exit. Ducking her head, she ignored the stares and calls for her to stop.

Immediately, Ms. Proom rushed from the stage and gave chase.

"Rachel," she puffed, finally catching up with them in the front hall outside the worship area. "Where are you going?" She reached out and grabbed Steven's sleeve, stopping the escape just at the door. "You can't leave now!"

Rachel turned to the youth pastor, who wore a smile on her sweaty face.

"Sorry," she said, "but we have to go … I'm, uh, not feeling well."

"Good," Ms. Proom said, still grinning like a crazed maniac. "Then Mrs. Hunt can take the children home. See? It's no problem."

Lisa moved closer to Rachel and frowned at Ms. Proom. "We want to go too."

Proom looked momentarily angry, but she quickly recovered. "But the children's service! It'll be great! I'm in charge—"

"They're coming with me," Rachel said flatly.

Ms. Proom ignored her. Bending to Steven's level, her smile seemed to widen further. Her mouth stretched like a rubber band being yanked separate ways. "You want to stay, don't you, Steven? My, you look handsome in that suit—like a real angel." She still had hold of his arm and did not seem to want to let go. "Tommy would be *so* happy if you stayed. We're having a pizza service!"

Rachel had heard enough. "I'm sorry, but we have to leave now." She pushed her way between the youth pastor and the boy. Ms. Proom had to let go of the boy or force a scene.

Grabbing Rachel's shoulder, she stared almost desperately at the babysitter. "You can't leave. We must go through with this! Talk to Pastor Smith, he'll explain! You have to stay!"

"Uh, bye." Turning, she pulled away from Ms. Proom and herded Lisa and Steven out the door.

Ms. Proom must have been related to Billy. She refused to take a hint or leave Rachel alone. Following her outside, she rushed to keep pace as they crossed into the parking lot. "Don't you understand? A child should lead them! Yes, a child! This child is the one!" She tried to reach around Rachel and grab Steven's shoulder, but Rachel moved her body to block her. Being big had its uses. "You don't know what you're doing, girl!"

Rachel stopped and whirled to face Ms. Proom. Her voice started to shake. "Wh-whose car is that?" She pointed to a small, green car.

"Oh, that car!" Ms. Proom's face lit up. "That's Pastor Smith's car—"

Rachel's voice hardened as she glared. "Tell your pastor that if he ever follows me again, I'm calling the police on him!"

Turning, she hustled the kids to her car, leaving a stunned Ms. Proom with her jaw dropped. As they left the church, Ms. Proom had yet to move from her spot.

Rachel didn't look back and tried hard to settle her shaking nerves. Once on the main road, she glanced in the rear mirror. "Uh, that was, uh, a mistake."

Lisa grunted. "I guess Vikki Rosa was right."

"I hope Tommy is okay," Steven muttered, shuddering.

Rachel nodded in agreement. Watching the boy go through that made her want to stop the car and march back in and shake Mrs. Hunt.

Lisa sighed. "Are all churches like that?"

"No, not all," Rachel said with feeling. "I think Ms. Proom and Pastor Smith probably invented this church on their own."

"Well, if I ever made up my own church, I would do better than that!" Lisa said with feeling. Then she grew thoughtful. "Then again, what would be the point of going?"

"What do you mean?" Rachel asked.

"I mean, no matter what, in the end I'll know it's all just a bunch of baloney. The whole thing would be stupid."

"Hmmph," agreed Rachel. "You're right. Church should be truthful, I guess."

They drove in silence.

Then Lisa had to say it. "Ms. Proom flies a broom ..."

Steven looked at her. "Zoom," he finally said.

Lisa laughed. "Then boom—Rachel, look out!" she shrieked.

As they turned into Camelot Acres, they nearly ran into a black sedan heading the other way.

"Drive on your side," Rachel mumbled, slamming the brakes and spinning the wheel to avoid the oncoming car. Still, the black car honked and slowed. "What's his problem?" she growled.

"Rachel, stop the car!" cried Lisa from the back. "I see Courtney!"

Rachel nearly slammed on the gas, but instead jerked to a stop. If Courtney was in the passenger seat, that meant—

The black car rolled back and Jason Richardson grinned awkwardly from the driver's seat.

Gulping, Rachel lowered her window.

"Hi!" exclaimed Courtney brightly, sitting next to Jason. "Jason meant to call you later, but this works better!"

"Uh, oh, yeah." Jason looked sheepish. "I think I, er, should apologize for the other night. My, uh, sister explained everything ... You know, the water on Shawna."

"Oh, it's fine," Rachel said quickly, gripping the steering wheel tightly. "I, uh, didn't mind at all—uh, I mean, I didn't mind, well, I'm sorry for, uh ..."

Jason was gracious enough to wave it off. "I think we were just tired. Besides, Shawna is okay." He chuckled. "You know, it was a little funny thinking about it."

"It was a lot funny,' Courtney amended. "Although," she added very quickly, "I'm very sorry I did it and I won't ever do it again."

"Yeah, right!" Jakey said from the back.

"Sit down, shrimp!" Jason said to him. Then he eyed Rachel. "Are you all just coming back from church already? We were just heading out."

"Uh, oh, well …" she stammered. Jason wore a white dress shirt with a blue tie matching his eyes. That was all her mind could comprehend.

Then Lisa leaned over the passenger seat. "Actually, we sort of missed church. We, um, went to the wrong one."

Jason's eyebrows went up. "Oh?"

Lisa plunged ahead. "Yeah, and we sort of need to find one to go to now."

Courtney's eyes lit up. "Really? You could come with us!"

"No, Courtney," Jason said quickly. "They have other plans."

"But they missed church!" cried Jakey. "Maybe we can play soccer after!"

"And there's always good food after too," added Courtney.

"Jakey, Courtney—they aren't, you know …" Jason looked at Rachel for help.

"We should go with them," Lisa said quickly in Rachel's ear. "Right, Steven?"

Steven suddenly jumped as if bitten. He'd actually received a sharp kick in the shin from his sister. "Ow—I mean, sure."

Rachel offered a weak smile toward Jason. "I did promise to go to church today …"

"But—" Surrendering, Jason threw up his hands and forced a grin. "Just turn around and you can just follow us."

Rachel felt her heart start pounding as she complied … Life sure had its twists and turns …

After church, a pleasant service *very* different from Pastor Smith's, Jason and Rachel somehow agreed to stop at a pancake house on the way home.

"But what about your mom?" Rachel whispered to Lisa, bending down as the redhead climbed in the backseat. It was Lisa who'd suggested eating at a restaurant. "I thought she didn't want you eating unhealthy!"

Lisa looked over Rachel's head and shrugged. "I just said that … We do eat out sometimes. Besides, Steven is too skinny. He needs the calories for swimming." She quickly slammed the car door in Rachel's face before the word "pizza" could be said.

Not believing this could be happening, Rachel rubbed her forehead. Jason honked as he pulled out behind her. Courtney waved.

"All this because of water bombs," Rachel mumbled.

At the restaurant Rachel ordered whole-wheat pancakes and eggs and then sat back as the boys started talking about sports and Lisa and Courtney discussed summer plans. Jason had barely spoken to her at church and now seemed very comfortable not speaking to her at the restaurant.

Then, as they were just about to leave, Rachel found herself agreeing to have Jason come over with the kids and go swimming. Again, Lisa led the way by inviting Courtney … which led to Jason and Jakey being invited.

"Uh, sure," stammered Rachel. "Why not?"

So, after changing from church clothes to swim clothes, the afternoon turned into Jason wrestling with the boys in the shallow end and Lisa and Courtney practicing dives in the deep end. Claiming her bathing suit was in the washer, Rachel watched glumly from the side.

I don't know if this is my lucky day, or unlucky day … Lisa found a friend and no longer hates me, Steven is happy, and a really good-looking guy is here, while I sit like lump on a log … And the good-looking guy is coming my way.

She gulped as Jason pulled himself out of the pool and walked over to sit on the pool chair next to her.

"Not a swimmer, huh?" He grinned to show he didn't care. Water dripped from his curls and down his tanned shoulders.

Rachel hastily stared down at the concrete. "Uh, no … So, uh, so you finished high school last year?"

"Yeah …" Grunting, he wiped his face and stretched out his legs. "I did a year at the university, but I don't know … I'm undecided on a major right now and don't really know what I want to do. I've been thinking about school for a while." Rachel looked at him in surprise. She had to keep her eyes on his face and not his muscled torso. He sighed when confronted with her gaze. "Shawna wants me to go to work for her dad. He manages a cruise line, and she thinks it'll be fun to travel for a year."

Rachel tried hard not to react when hearing that information. "Oh … Uh, I guess that sounds … interesting."

"Yeah … my parents don't think so, but I don't know … I just don't see the point of three more years of school. I mean, there's really nothing I want to work for. I think I had enough schooling in high school." He looked at Rachel. "What about you?"

"Oh, uh, I'm not sure …" She blew out her breath. What did it matter if she told her plans or not? It wasn't like he really cared. "I'm thinking of community college and then maybe transferring to a university, or something."

Jason shrugged. "Cool." Standing, he stretched out his arms. "Well, I think I'll go jump in and teach those kids the art of surfing on a kickboard. My poor brother is failing miserably."

"Yeah … I better start supper—Uh, do you, uh, do you all want to stay? I'm making spaghetti and can make extra."

"Thanks, but I'm supposed to meet Shawna later. She called on the way back from the restaurant. Oh, but Courtney and Jakey, um, if you don't mind—"

"Oh, of course. No problem." Without looking at him, she got to her feet. "We'll, uh, leave out the water bombs this time."

That night she nearly burned the spaghetti, as all she could think about was Jason … and his girlfriend. By the time she'd remembered the pot full of boiling noodles, the water was nearly gone and the noodles were a congealed mess sticking to the sides. Falling in love in books, she decided, was so much easier … and less sticky.

Chapter Nineteen

After Courtney and Jakey left, Rachel tried her best to clean up the place before Jane Lovington returned. Now that Lisa seemed nicer, Rachel didn't want to risk getting on the housekeeper's bad side.

Just as she finished vacuuming the television room, she heard a loud cough from the living room.

"Excuse me?" she heard Vikki Rosa's voice croon. "Rachel, dear, what are you doing?"

Hastily putting down the vacuum, Rachel smoothed out her shirt and kept herself from going out the back way to the kitchen. Taking a deep breath, she went to the living room.

"Oh, uh, hi, Ms. Rosa."

"I asked what you were doing, dear. Surely don't tell me you were vacuuming." Again dressed like she was on her way to a cocktail party, Vikki Rosa eyed her like an unwanted insect that needed crushing.

"Oh, uh, well, we had a movie night, and, uh, I was just getting rid of … crumbs."

"Where are the children?"

"They're out in the back, uh, reading."

"Rachel, dear. You're a babysitter. Your job is to mind the children. Jane's job is to clean the house. Let us not forget our places, okay?" Turning from her, Vikki Rosa went and took a seat uninvited.

Biting her lip, Rachel eyed the woman but then sighed. Suddenly, the woman's presence no longer scared her. Bothered her, yes. But over the last week, especially the weekend, Rachel had started to realize it didn't matter what other people thought of her. What mattered was what she thought of herself. Calmly, she sat on the sofa. She tried her best to keep her voice level and somewhere around pleasant. "So, uh, what do you want?"

"How did you like the church today?"

"Oh, uh, it was great …" Rachel's face suddenly burned and she ducked her head. "We, uh, ended up not making it through Ms. Proom's service and, uh, found another one. A really nice one."

Vikki Rosa smiled. "Yes, so you see that I was right."

Rachel nodded, and met Vikki Rosa's eyes. No longer would she be cowed by this woman. "It … it was pretty awful there," she admitted.

"Well, I'm known to be right sometimes. But that's not why I'm here. I spoke to Elizabeth today." Rachel's heart jumped. What did Vikki Rosa say about her, she wondered. Fear tingled inside her. "Oh, don't worry, you're doing fine." Vikki Rosa waved a hand as if shooing a fly. "But apparently they'll be staying in the mountains for a week where there's bad phone service. You may contact them through, eh, the computer, but in case of emergency she wants you to call me. So I'm leaving my number and my promise. If you need anything, just give me a ring and I'll be there. Okay? Don't worry—despite my manner, I do have the children's best interest at heart."

Rachel's mouth tightened, but she nodded. *Remember, it's all about how I feel about myself—not how Vikki Rosa feels about me!*

"Oh, cheer up, Rachel! Elizabeth and I both think you're doing fantastic! Just keep your eye on the kids, and everything will turn out grand. Jane will return tomorrow, so leave the cleaning until then. Remember, I'm just a phone call away."

With Vikki's assurances, Rachel hoped everything went well for the week. At first, it appeared she would get her wish.

The only uncomfortable incident on Monday came when dropping Steven off for his last week of school. Mrs. Hunt stopped her minivan by Rachel's car and rolled down the window while gesturing for Rachel to do the same. Not looking at her, the woman's face was a cold mask of disdain. "I won't be able to offer rides to Steven anymore," she said sharply. "Not for school or for swimming. Tommy is off the swim team as of today. You'll have to do it all yourself!"

Rachel fought hard to control herself. Swallowing hard, she turned to the bitter woman. "I understand … but I don't think any child should have to go through what your son did yesterday." Not waiting for a reaction, she pressed the gas and drove off. Pulling out of the school, she gasped for air. That was the first time in her life she had ever told off somebody in public—and it was a grown-up. No green car tailed her home.

With Steven at school and now Lisa home all day, Rachel's day quickly changed. While still finding time to exercise in Elizabeth's office—in just under a week she'd already dropped five pounds and an inch around her waist—she now spent a good amount of time with a redheaded girl who never seemed to tire. On Monday they baked chocolate-chip cookies. Then on Tuesday they went to the library for more books. One of the ones Lisa got from the bookstore had a sequel.

Only Courtney saved Rachel from doing countless other activities. With the same school schedule as Lisa, she had Lisa over in the afternoons and sometimes long into the night. Steven was too busy with studying for his finals and going to swim practice to join the fun. Jane Lovington continued bringing pots of stew for supper and then going about her cleaning, always managing to stay out of the way.

By Wednesday morning, Rachel felt everything coming together. Waking up refreshed, she lay back in bed and allowed a truly satisfied smile. *You know what? I can do this job!* Not only that, but she was enjoying it. Lisa and she had continued passing back and forth the notebook and were actually bonding as friends. Steven now talked during the car rides and genuinely looked forward to seeing her. While Jason never came around, she didn't mind … that much. For her and him to ever—well, Rachel was just happy he didn't make fun of her to her face.

That afternoon, after Rachel brought Steven back from school, she went up to take a nap. Jane Lovington was vacuuming the front hall when Lisa sauntered into the living room wearing shorts and her bathing suit. Steven lay on his stomach in his usual spot, studying for his math final the next day.

Humming softly, Lisa wandered over and stared down at her brother. Still in his school pants and dress shirt, Steven had yet to change for swimming and seemed distracted. His pencil hadn't moved for a good thirty seconds.

"How's school?" she asked loudly, to be heard over the vacuum.

Steven didn't look up, but shrugged.

School was like a bowl of party mix without the party. His classes were going fine, but that was it. Tommy now only hung around kids from his church. Since that Sunday, he had changed. No longer caring about swimming, he only spoke of doing great things in the "Lord's Army." He totally ignored Steven. This was bad enough, but Geoffrey would give Steven furtive looks and then deliberately avoid talking to him. And everywhere he went in the hall, Steven kept running into the janitor. Mr. Red would smile at him, but Steven never returned it. Something about the "rescue" from the bullies never added up, but like most of his problems, Steven kept quiet about it. Mostly he kept with a group of kids that included Susie and Callie. This was fine, but … the summer started in just two days … and he'd already lost two of his best friends … and didn't have a clue why. He felt plain mixed up.

Suddenly he jerked when Lisa kicked him in the thigh, interrupting his thoughts. "You there, Steven?" Then she planted a foot squarely on his backside. "Stop studying and listen."

Twisting his head, Steven glared. "Hey, get off!"

"Oh, you're so boney, you hurt me more than I hurt you. Listen, we should have a party." She removed her foot and squatted next to her brother.

He rolled to face her. "Another party?"

"Courtney and I have been talking. Rachel has been here almost two weeks. We think she's been, you know, pretty nice. So on Saturday we want to celebrate. Besides, you'll be done with school then."

The vacuum shut off and Jane Lovington stuck her head into the room. "Party for Rachel?" she asked, excitement catching in her voice. "Did I hear right, yes?"

Steven and Lisa exchanged glances. Their housekeeper had been ignoring them all day. And how did she hear them over the vacuum?

Lisa shrugged. "We're thinking of one …"

Clapping her hands together, the housekeeper simply beamed at them. "I help! But, children, we must have Rachel out of the house when we set it up, yes?"

Lisa's eyes lit up. "Great idea, Jane! A surprise party would be perfect!"

Steven looked doubtful. "I have swim practice in the morning. She'll drive me there."

"Not long enough," Jane said quickly. "We want her out of the house longer time. How about if we say Richardson boy is in the park after you come home and wants to speak with her? That work, yes?"

Lisa leaned closer to Steven and whispered, "Rachel likes Jason—that'll definitely work!"

"What you say?" Jane asked, cocking an ear.

Lisa grinned. "Only that your plan is perfect!"

"I feel sorry for Rachel," Steven muttered.

Lisa smacked the back of his pants and shot to her feet to avoid retaliation. "Get back to studying! You have school tomorrow. Me, I'm going to the pool for a nice summer swim."

The next day, as Steven worked on his math final, Rachel sat on the couch with her notebook. Jane was somewhere cleaning and Lisa had gone over to Courtney's house. Relaxing, she was about to reply to one of Lisa's notes when the doorbell rang.

Once again forgetting rule ten of babysitting, she opened the door without checking. Pastor Smith stood just on the other side with Ms. Proom.

Her good mood evaporated in a flash.

"Good morning, Rachel," grinned the pastor. "May we come in?"

"Uh, I actually don't think that's a good idea. What is it that you want?" Her voice wavered slightly, but she didn't back up. Inwardly she kicked herself hard in the rear. Never again would she forget to check the window.

"We just want to apologize," Proom said smoothly, smiling under layers of makeup, which couldn't hide the wrinkles around her mouth. "The way you left on Sunday, we don't think you understood our church."

"Uh, well, too bad. I mean, uh, I can't let you in … it's not really my house."

"Please," Pastor Smith said with his eyes reflecting sincerity, "allow me to explain everything. We really don't want any hard feelings between us … some in the congregation might get the wrong idea."

Breathing deeply to control her feelings, Rachel shook her head. "Just, uh, explain right here … I don't think you should come in—the housekeeper is cleaning," she finished lamely. How she wished Jane Lovington would appear just now! The way the pastor's eyes stared at her—it felt like they were staring right into her soul and seeing way too much.

Proom started to say something, but the pastor held up his hand. "Perfectly sensible of you, Rachel. I understand perfectly well. You do a fabulous job of looking after those two dear children."

Rachel's eyes burned at him and for a moment she lost all her fear. "You would know. You follow me in your car enough."

"Ah, oh, about that, I'm afraid it's another misunderstanding."

"Rachel," Ms. Proom added, "we're just concerned about the children. That's all."

"Yes," Pastor Smith said. "Steven is a special boy—surely you see that."

Rachel narrowed her eyes. "What do you mean?"

Sighing, Pastor Smith scratched his head and then stared hard at Rachel. His eyes seemed to spark as they grew suddenly flinty. "Do you recall hearing about a woman vanishing not too far from here? A woman who flew into the same airport the same day you arrived?"

Rachel flinched under his gaze and then suddenly grew cold. Elizabeth had mentioned the story—the woman's car had been found not too far from there. Her steely resolve wavered. "Uh, yes …"

"People do vanish sometimes, Rachel. I would certainly hate to see that happen to Steven." *Was that a threat?* His eyes softened. "Believe me, Rachel. I want to protect the boy. That is why I am here. There are others who wish—"

Anger burned in Rachel and the resolve returned, but double. "You have to leave now. Both of you."

"Rachel, you have to believe me."

"Think of the children," murmured Ms. Proom.

"I am." But she couldn't close the door. The pastor's eyes remained locked with hers and seemed to be changing color—a strange blurry mist was forming before her. "I-I think you really have to go …" Dots were flashing in her vision, but she couldn't pull herself away from the pastor's stare.

"Rachel, no. I didn't want to do—"

Suddenly the dots disappeared and the pastor jumped. Blinking, he looked as if he'd just seen a ghost. Visibly shaking, he stepped back into Ms. Proom. "I think you're right. We do have to go."

"Go?" Proom sounded angry as she tried to push past the pastor. "But we can't go. Not without—"

"Ms. Proom, you forget. We have that meeting …" Face pale, the pastor grabbed Ms. Proom's arm and dragged her away, ignoring her protests.

Rachel rubbed her eyes and tried to clear the buzz from her head. "I hope to never see those two creeps again."

From behind her, Jane Lovington sniffed. "I think I clean the front steps next."

The rest of the day passed without incident, and Rachel decided to forget the odd encounter with Pastor Smith and Ms. Proom. *If they ever show up again, then I'll call Vikki Rosa.* Otherwise, she would rather forget the whole thing happened. After all, that would be exactly what Vikki Rosa would tell her to do.

On Steven's final day of school, a major scandal broke loose. Walking into his class he saw not Ms. Fathomb sitting behind her desk, but a lady substitute teacher who looked to have rolled straight from bed and into the classroom. She kept rubbing her eyes and staring sourly at the classroom while fingering a hairy chin.

"I think Ms. Fathomb is playing a joke and is just pretending to have a sub," Susie whispered as Steven went to his desk.

Steven nodded. On his desk he found a note. Unfolding it, he read a familiar scrawl and immediately glanced back at Geoffrey.

Geoffrey quickly ducked his head and didn't look up.

"Beware of Mr. Red. He's lying."

Steven crumpled the note and stuffed it in his pocket. After the first note from Geoffrey, he had no use for the second.

Just as he settled down to read from the swimmer book Rachel had bought him, two shadows fell across his desk.

He didn't have to look up. "Hi, Susie. Hi, Callie."

Returning his greeting with bright smiles, the girls both leaned over him. "Do you want to see a movie with us tonight? Everyone is going to celebrate the summer."

"Everyone?" Steven took a quick look back at Geoffrey.

Susie made a face. "Well, almost everyone." She nodded to where Tommy sat in the back talking furtively with a few other kids. "The 'Lord's Army' have their own party."

"Really it's just our swim team," Callie confessed. In the last week both girls had joined and were proving to be loyal if not capable swimmers.

"Yeah … okay."

"Great!" Susie smiled wickedly. "We can stop by your house and fix you up."

Callie giggled when Steven made a face. "Now that we have practice …"

"Um, no thanks."

"Okay, but I'll pick you up around six." Susie grinned. "Don't worry. My mom is picking up Eric too. You won't be alone with girls."

Before Steven could react, the sub cleared her throat loudly and called the class to attention.

Immediately Susie and Callie looked at Steven in horror. It could not be possible … Ms. Fathomb had never missed a day all year and had promised a party on the last day.

Instead of a party, the pinch-faced sub quickly proved to have no sense of humor and had the students work on word puzzles most of the day. Mrs. Lee came in near the middle and frowned at seeing the substitute. She disappeared, mumbling about teachers quitting early without warning … "This time," she muttered, "I should file a lawsuit."

Rachel had planned a small celebration for Steven's official start of summer, but this quickly fizzled. Lisa, surprisingly, displayed little interest and said she was going out shopping with Jane Lovington. Then Steven brought home the news that he would be going to the movies with friends.

"Well, it is my night off," Rachel mumbled and found herself heading to her room as Steven's ride pulled out. A little disappointed, she resigned herself to a night of reading quietly.

Then, just before leaving, Lisa banged on her door with a message.

Jason had called and invited her to meet him at the park the next morning at eleven.

Her heart jumped. Rachel actually rolled off the bed and crashed to the floor.

"Bye, Rachel!" called Lisa, hastily retreating.

By the time Rachel got to her feet and rushed out for more information, Lisa had run down the stairs and out the door. Jane's car zoomed out the driveway and left Rachel standing in the doorway.

Alone with the news, Rachel couldn't do much reading the rest of the night … or eating. Despite being hungry, her waist continued to shrink. A new diet of lean, healthy food, combined with exercise and perpetual stress seemed to be working wonders.

Saturday morning crept in with overcast clouds and the chance for severe thunderstorms later in the afternoon. Jane Lovington made fresh cinnamon buns for breakfast and said she would spend all day making supper, so she needed the kitchen. She didn't really care … her entire breakfast was a glass of orange juice and half a bagel. Much of the time she kept checking the window and thinking about Jason and the meeting. The clouds persisted and maybe the rain would come early …

However, as Rachel returned with Steven from swim practice, the clouds suddenly parted to allow the brilliant hot sun to pour through. Rachel sighed with relief and groaned with despair all at once. One part of her wanted it to rain to wash out Jason's meeting, but the other part couldn't help but be excited.

What does Jason want? And why didn't he speak to me personally? Maybe this is just something about the kids … nothing to do with me … he'll offer me another babysitting job.

Speaking of the kids, they were acting very peculiar, even for them. Lisa went out of her way to be nice at breakfast and never once teased her for her behavior. "It's your day off!" Lisa kept reminding her. "Remember, Jane is in charge today." In the car ride to and from the pool, Steven kept too quiet and wore an expression a little too innocent, even for him. He only gave her his half smile and a slight shrug whenever she asked him what was going on.

As Rachel parked in the driveway, Steven immediately hopped out and grabbed his bag. Then Lisa stuck her head out the front door of the house.

"Rachel!" she cried as Rachel opened the car door. "You have to hurry up! Jason called again to remind you to meet him in ten minutes!"

"Ten minutes!" Rachel tumbled out of the car and beat Steven to the house. "Did he say what the meeting was about?"

Lisa's nose twitched and she shook her head, dropping her gaze. "I, uh, think it's a surprise."

Steven brushed by Rachel and his sister and announced he would be at the pool.

"Oh, uh, wait, Steven," Rachel called to him. "You need sunscreen. Let me get you some."

"I got it!" Lisa said quickly, pushing Rachel toward the stairs. "You just hurry and get ready!"

"Well, uh … okay. Here, there's some in my purse—just put it back when you're done." Rachel couldn't think straight. Jason really wanted to meet her privately? *Now?* She somehow made it up the stairs with Lisa urging her on. Fumbling inside her purse, she couldn't seem to find that blasted sunscreen.

"Eight minutes, Rachel," Lisa reminded her.

"Oh, here, just take the whole purse. Take it and leave it by the front door."

"Okay, I got it!" Lisa took the purse and shoved Rachel toward her room. "Now hurry up and don't be late!"

"Uh, no, uh, of course not. Are you sure you don't want me to help with the sunscreen?"

"Rachel! Stop being so nervous. Here, show me what you're wearing."

Embarrassed, Rachel went to her bed and held up a modest green summer dress that her mom had picked out—something Rachel had adamantly told her mom she would never, ever wear. Ever.

"Oh, that's really cute, Rachel."

"You think so?"

"Yes! Now hurry up and put it on and go!" Lisa grabbed her purse and shut the door behind her.

Sighing, Rachel held the dress in front of her. Then she smiled. "Hi, Jason," she purred, trying to sound like Shawna. "And how do you do? Oh, this thing? What, does it make me look fat?"

Grunting, Rachel quickly turned from the mirror.

Taking out the pump bottle of sunscreen from Rachel's purse, Lisa shook it vigorously. "Steven, where are you?"

"Over here," he answered from the kitchen. "Where did Jane go?"

Dumping the purse by the door, Lisa ran to him. "Probably getting the sign ready; now stay away from the food! Not until the party!" She knew what caught Steven's attention.

Sure enough, he knelt on a chair at the table eyeing a plate of hot brownies. Jane Lovington had said they were made extra special, using a secret recipe from her home.

Steven looked at her. "Can't I test one?"

"You do, and I'll pump this in your eyes!" Lisa held up the sunscreen like a weapon. The type their mom bought stung the eyes worse than soap.

Steven quickly slid off the chair. "I'm only joking."

Lisa smiled. "Good, then get away from the table and turn your back so I can put this gunk on you."

Rolling his eyes, Steven pulled off his shirt and complied. "Lisa, do you think Mom and Dad will call tonight?"

Frowning, Lisa lowered the sunscreen. "Rachel said they're in a place where phones don't work very well, so I don't know … is there anything wrong?"

Steven shrugged. "No. I think I'll ride my ripstick before the pool."

Looking a little concerned, Lisa squirted a stream of gunk onto her brother's back. The ripstick served as therapy for whenever Steven grew overstressed.

"Just don't forget to shower and change before the party," she said carefully.

"Okay." Steven turned his head back and grinned. "I don't want to miss being there when Rachel finds out Jason never called her."

This earned an extra hard slap to his back.

"Ow!"

"So sorry," Lisa said pleasantly. "Don't worry, the party will be an extra big surprise for her. Especially when Jason shows up, so there!" Spraying a liberal amount of lotion on her hand, she reached around him and slapped his flat stomach. "You finish the rest. I have to put the sunscreen back in Rachel's purse."

"Thanks, Lisa." Steven wiped a gob of sunscreen from his stomach and rubbed it on his lips. Turning quickly, he planted a swift kiss on her cheek and dashed for the back door.

Lisa returned it with a swift kick to the back of his departing suit. "Don't fall off and break your head open! This is Rachel's party, and I want everything perfect."

"Oh, it'll be perfect!" sang a new voice as Jane Lovington swept into the kitchen. She'd come from the back room, where she'd been hiding the party supplies. She beamed at Lisa. "You children, and Rachel, will have a day none will ever forget! Now go shoo that Rachel out of the house so we can begin setting up."

The housekeeper's smile only grew brighter as Lisa left the room. It would truly be a day to remember. First, work had to be done.

Chapter Twenty

Rachel entered the sunny park with a fair amount of apprehension. Scanning the athletic fields, she saw nobody and heard nothing. Nervously, she kicked a stone in front of her. The sun still peeked through the clouds, but the humidity was thick. Beads of sweat were popping on Rachel's arms. Bordering the athletic fields was a path for joggers and walkers. Far into the park to the left was a playground that was mostly hidden by a row of palm trees. Going that way, the only other person she spotted was a young boy with dark skin. He walked toward her whacking his leg with a stick and never gave her a glance when he passed.

Where's Jason? Isn't it the girl's job to be late? Stop, Rachel! This is not a date!

Sighing in frustration mixed with nervousness, she eventually found a shaded bench between the soccer field and baseball field where she got a good view of the park entrance. Putting down her purse, she folded her hands on her lap and waited.

Minutes passed. Suddenly a shadow fell over her from behind. At the same time, dark clouds appeared in the west and the sun chose to take cover.

Heart jumping into her mouth, Rachel whirled on the shadow.

"Excuse me, mind if I sit?" asked a deep, hard voice. It was not Jason.

"Oh, uh, um … no." Clutching a hand to her heaving chest, she took deep breaths. "You, uh, scared me." Her fear never entirely evaporated as she moved her purse out of the way and scooted closer to the edge of the bench. A quick look toward the entrance failed to spot Jason. What had started as nerves was switching over to fear. Something felt terribly wrong.

"Expecting someone else?" the newcomer asked.

"Actually, yes." Rachel eyed the tall, distinguished-looking man as he took a seat on her right. His blue eyes sparkled and his snowy white hair glinted in the sun. Sunglasses were perched on his head—very familiar-looking sunglasses. "You're, you're the janitor, aren't you?" she said slowly. "Mr. Red, right?"

A dark look crossed his face, but it could have been a trick of the light as it quickly vanished. "I was the janitor at First Seminole Academy, yes. The year ended, though."

Rachel nodded and then stared at him hard. "Wait … aren't you … uh, do you have …" She swallowed. Without his janitor's uniform he looked so very different. And without the beard, he also looked so very different for another reason. Dressed in a blue suit with a black tie, he still managed to resemble the homeless man. It was his eyes—they were definitely the same. "You-you—who are you?"

"Ah, Rachel," the man purred, "you are quite the quick one, aren't you? Yes, I did wear a beard sometimes … and I did prowl these streets."

Suddenly a bolt of fear struck her like lightning. Looking away, she was very conscious of the man sliding closer to her side.

"I knew you would figure it out eventually, Rachel. Despite what the others think, you are quite quick with your mind. But not so quick … tell me, Rachel, where are the children?"

"Who—who are you?"

"I've been watching you for some time, Rachel. In fact, I sat on the plane with you from Virginia. You see, we've been planning for this moment for a long time."

"Wh-what?" Heart pounding, Rachel scanned the park for help. Not another soul was seen. Thunder rumbled in the distance.

"Oh, are you looking for Jason Richardson?" The man laughed mockingly. "Do you think a boy like him would really invite a girl like you to the park alone? My, my, but perhaps you are a fool after all."

Rachel froze. Even her heart seemed to go still. How had she been so stupid? Of course Jason wouldn't invite her to the park! She trembled with fear. How did this man know so much and what was he talking about? Then a terrible thought hit her. She had left Lisa and Steven alone—but, no. Jane Lovington was there. So what was going on? Was this all some sadistic joke?

"Wh-what are you, you doing h-here?"

"Keeping you occupied."

Rachel squeezed her eyes shut. "No," she gasped. "No …" Lisa and Steven were in trouble—big trouble.

"Yes, Rachel. And now I think I'll kill you." The man spoke calmly and seemed to be enjoying this. "Open your eyes and look at me, Rachel. Do not worry. You won't feel pain. Actually, what I'm going to do will be a relief in the end. In fact, it's a *blessing*. Ah, yes, Pastor Smith is part of this too … unfortunately for him, he's not here. So allow me the honors."

Rachel shook. Her left hand slowly slid onto her purse and slipped inside. Feeling for a weapon, all she grabbed was the sunscreen bottle. She'd hoped to find one of Steven's emergency shots, but even if she did pull one out, how could she pull off the cap and stick the man without being overpowered first? Though he appeared old, the man seemed quite strong.

"Rachel, it is useless for you to resist. Look at me." This voice demanded obedience. "Look at me now!"

As the storm clouds rolled in, the sun defiantly came out from behind a cloud. For a brief moment, brilliant rays were cast down on the park. More thunder rumbled, but the sun didn't give way so easily. Neither would Rachel.

"Did you put on your sunscreen today?" she asked, avoiding his gaze.

"What?" Sounding irritated, the man grabbed Rachel's right shoulder. "I said look at me!" he snarled.

Twisting, Rachel jerked out the sunscreen and aimed it straight at the man's face. She shrieked when saw his eyes had turned a flaming red.

"Die—" Rudolph's shout of triumph turned into wails of pain.

Rachel furiously pressed the pump and sent streams of sunscreen into the glaring eyes until they were completely covered with white gobs. Now they really burned.

Screeching, Rudolph let go of Rachel to cover his eyes. Tumbling from the bench, he rolled in agony.

Jamming the bottle back into her purse, Rachel shot from the bench and sprinted away without looking back.

"It's too late for you!" shouted the man. "You are doomed!" His shouts turned to whimpers of pain as he stumbled blindly to his feet and tried to go after her. "Doomed!"

WHY? screamed Rachel to herself. *Why were they trying to get the children? And who were "they"?* Pastor Smith, Ms. Proom, Red, the homeless janitor, and who else? It didn't seem possible or make sense.

Maybe it was all some mistake. Jane Lovington would be vacuuming or baking more brownies. Lisa and Steven would be playing in the pool …

She picked up her pace, barely slowing when she lost a shoe. Kicking off the other, she kept going, ignoring the hot pavement.

Lightning streaked in front of her. Thunder crackled overhead. The sun had gone for good this time.

Wrapping her purse around her arm and lifting the bottom of her dress with both hands, she ran even harder. When the pavement grew too hard on her feet, she hopped into the grass. Sweat poured off her brow and her breathing became labored. Still, she refused to allow herself to stop.

Finally reaching the driveway of the Winter home, she found a fresh burst of energy. Bursting into the house, she finally collapsed to her knees. Taking deep gulps of air, she put a hand over her beating heart.

Silence greeted her. Looking up, she saw a huge banner. *SURPRISE, RACHEL!*

Confused, she staggered to her feet. The smell of brownies and other baked sweets filled the house. Still, the silence loomed large.

"Lisa!" she gasped. "Hello?"

Nobody answered.

Entering the kitchen, she saw through the glass windows an empty backyard. Steven's ripstick lay near the pool.

Where was everybody?

A thump sounded from the back of the house. Then a muffled scream.

"Lisa! Steven!" Rachel stumbled in that direction. "Jane?" Entering the living room, she came to a dead stop.

"Surprise, Rachel." Jane Lovington stood in the center of the room. Only, it wasn't Jane Lovington. Usually the housekeeper wore jeans and a loose top. The woman before Rachel wore a long black robe, open in the front, to reveal a tight, shiny leather uniform that covered her from neck to knee. True, her facial features were the same as Jane Lovington's, but now her dark brown hair was pinched back in a tight bun. Her large eyes, once gorgeous, had turned dark and scary. They held a deep, furious hatred. Much worse, she had the children.

Draped over her left shoulder, wearing his white dress clothes, Steven hung like a limp blanket with his back half facing Rachel. Jane Lovington's right arm tightly covered Lisa's mouth, squeezing it so the young girl's face turned red. She pressed the girl tightly to her side.

An overturned chair, scattered cushions, and a broken lamp told of a struggle. In the midst of it, a half-eaten brownie lay crumbled. Another brownie was gripped in the left hand of the woman who called herself Jane Lovington.

"Wh-what are you doing?" Rachel asked stupidly.

"Taking what is mine!" snarled the suddenly fearsome woman. Then her face twisted in pain. "Ouch!"

Lisa had bitten her hand and shook loose. "Rachel!" she shrieked. "She poisoned the brownies!"

With a roar, the woman let Steven's limp body fall to the floor in front of her. She grabbed Lisa's hair and yanked the girl back.

Lisa screamed in pain but couldn't break free.

The woman tried to shove the brownie into Lisa's mouth, but the young girl managed to turn her head at the last second. Brown crumbs smeared her face.

"Leave her alone!" shouted Rachel, horrified. Her mind numb, she moved with only the thought of freeing Lisa from the wicked beast. She prayed Steven was only unconscious and nothing worse. The boy lay on his back and seemed dead to the world.

"*You*!" the woman roared, pulling Lisa back as she faced Rachel. The voice had also changed. Gone was the accent. Gone was the coyness. Only fury and shock surrounded the deep, terrifying voice. "Stop there or I will destroy this girl!" Her left forearm moved across Lisa's neck and tightened. Her right hand took the mashed brownie from the left.

Rachel froze. "Get back from her!" She could scarcely believe what she was seeing. "Why are you doing this?"

The woman smoldered at Rachel. "Why are you here?" Her voice seethed and sounded deadly. "Why must you ruin everything?"

"What are you talking about?" Rachel took a cautious step toward Lisa while keeping a close eye on the woman once called Jane Lovington. Jane Lovington, who had practically done all the cooking for the past two weeks, who had always lurked in the background, who had slowly gained Rachel's trust to watch the children … There was nothing loving about her now. Eyes flashing and her face the picture of fury, she raised her hand with the brownie at Rachel.

"Don't cross me," she spat. "You know me as a housekeeper. Now know the truth! I am Isabella, the greatest Wizard of Panterra! I'll destroy you right here if you don't stop!"

"Wh-what?" Her heart thumping wildly, Rachel found it hard to breathe. Tears pricked her eyes. How could she be so stupid as to let this happen? And what on earth was happening? Fear gripped her insides and squeezed tight.

"For years I planned this moment, and your stupidity won't ruin it!" the great wizard Isabella screeched as she suddenly hurled the brownie at Rachel's head.

Rachel ducked and felt it brush by her hair before splattering on the wall behind her with great force. "Let go of her," Rachel cried with more certainty than she felt.

The woman snarled, pulling Lisa back another step. The redhead gasped for a breath. Tears running down her face, she stared pleadingly at Rachel. Wearing her lime-green dress, she looked like a flower being crushed in the hands of a spoiled child.

"You ruin everything, Rachel!" wailed the wizard. "It is as if the spirits of evil have sent you here themselves!"

"Th-that's what I was thinking about you." Rachel swallowed to keep her fear from bursting through. Her face drained of blood. Never before had she felt such a sense of fear and the presence of evil. She looked at Lisa and nodded, as if everything would be okay. At the same time, she slowly unwrapped the only weapon at her disposal—her purse.

Isabella cruelly pulled Lisa off her feet. The young girl choked and tried to resist, but the woman proved too strong. "Hush, before I squeeze your head off! Stay back, Rachel, and don't try anything foolish. I planned your death, but instead I'll let you live. You will live with the sight of these children leaving you. Now stand aside!"

"No!" Rachel freed her purse and rushed the woman.

Snarling, the woman swung a fist, connecting a glancing blow to Rachel's head. It felt as if a sledgehammer struck her.

Rachel's body flew into the side of an easy chair. Knocking it over, she rolled to a painful stop next to a standing lamp. It was the same chair and lamp Doug Winter had used when reading *Pollyanna* on Rachel's first night. That seemed like a very long time ago. Head ringing, Rachel was aware of Lisa screaming and the woman, Isabella, laughing manically.

"I still have it!" cried the woman. "My power lasts despite you being here!"

"Leave her alone," Rachel hoarsely groaned, pulling herself up with the help of the overturned chair. Her purse had wrapped around her wrist and served as her only weapon.

Isabella sneered down at her. "Go to wherever your kind comes from." Pointing her right index finger at Rachel, she grinned nastily. Then a green flashing bolt exploded from the tip of her finger and zapped toward Rachel.

Instinctively, Rachel flung herself behind the chair. The bolt struck just in front of her, causing a tremendous explosion. Pieces of chair and sparks flew in all directions. Picked up like clutter in the wind, Rachel's body flew back, hit by a tremendous force. She crashed into the wall before falling in a heap.

"Rachel! Rachel!" Lisa tried to run to her, but Isabella easily pulled her back by her hair, twisting it cruelly.

"I gave you a chance at life, you fool," the wizard spat at Rachel's sagging body. "Now you'll a be mess for the next housekeeper to clean up." Jerking Lisa, she turned to Steven. "Come, we'll collect your brother and be gone from this wretched world. Never again will I wash dirty laundry or scrub a bathroom floor!"

"Rachel!" screamed Lisa.

"Hush, girl. She's dead!"

I'm dead? Dazed and with visions of stars bursting in her head, Rachel struggled to rise, but couldn't. For some reason, her body wouldn't cooperate. It just wanted to sit there. *But I'm not dead … I am sleepy. Yes. Sleep.* Sleep sounded good. She could close her eyes and it would all just be a bad dream.

"Rachel!" wailed Lisa. "Help!"

Sleep … it's so much easier.

"No," Rachel whispered, beginning to stir. Blinking away her mental fog, she gave a tremendous effort and managed to move her legs. Thousands of invisible pins pricked her all over. Grinding her teeth at the pain, she next moved her arm. Blackness threatened to overcome her. With a roar, she pushed through to consciousness and managed to propel herself to her feet.

Isabella had just lifted Steven by the collar. Yanking him up like a piece of luggage, she carried him under her arm. His arms and legs drooped toward the floor. Isabella's other arm pressed firmly against Lisa's throat. She headed for the kitchen without pausing.

"No," croaked Rachel. "No!" she cried louder as she staggered forward.

Turning, Isabella's eyes went wide when seeing Rachel upright. "Not possible," she murmured. "You should be dead."

"Help!" screamed Lisa. "She's taking us away!"

"Hush, girl!" Isabella hurried for the back door, jerking Lisa with her.

Rachel, still weakened, struggled to catch up. She could barely walk.

Isabella reached the sliding door to the back. Slamming Lisa against the glass, she ordered her to open the door.

"No!" shouted the girl.

"I will kill you, your brother, and then Rachel!"

"Why?" cried Lisa. "I thought you liked us!"

Isabella growled in frustration. She jerked Lisa roughly to the side. Then muttering a command in a strange language, she kicked the glass with her foot. Immediately, the entire door flew apart, bursting into pieces. Shards of glass and metal rained on the concrete. "Any more questions?" she snarled.

Lisa only whimpered. "My parents trusted you," she whispered.

"Your parents are fools," Isabella sneered, dragging her outside. Their feet crunched on the remains of the door. "They should never trust another person with their children. Nobody really cares about children of others."

"Rachel does!"

Wind whipped about their heads and lightning flashed overhead.

"Rachel is not normal!" screamed the wizard. Snarling and snorting, she dragged Lisa and carried Steven toward the calm waters of the pool.

Rachel reached the broken door and stumbled out to give chase. Nothing mattered to her except saving the kids.

At the same time Rachel stepped on the shards of glass with her bare feet, the front door burst open.

Thunder boomed from overhead and the storm unleashed its powers on the world below.

In the moments before, the Richardson family had been preparing for the party.

Jason ran a hand through Jakey's hair with gel, making it stick up in front. "There, now that's perfect!"

"No it's not!" Frowning, the boy quickly smoothed his hair back down.

"Come on, Jakey, the way you care about your hair, you're beginning to remind me of Shawna—"

"Jason!" screamed Courtney, banging on the front door. "Come quick!"

Rising from where he knelt in the foyer, Jason mussed up his brother's hair and pulled open the door. "What is it? Is there a fire or something?"

"I heard screaming from their house! I think it was Lisa." The girl's face was pale and Jason lost his smile. Jason didn't have to ask which house. They were just about to head to Rachel's surprise party.

"Stay inside!" he snapped. "Both of you!"

"But what is it, do you think?" Courtney asked.

"Probably something from the storm, I'll go check it out. Wait until I get back before coming over!"

Courtney watched her older brother sprint to the street with a fearful look.

Moving beside her, Jakey nudged her shoulder. "What should we do?"

"Follow and see what's happening. Come on!" Mouth in a grim line, Courtney grabbed Jakey's hand and together they hurried after their brother.

The sky had darkened to a deep, blackened gray. Angry gusts of wind began tossing grit and leaves with great force. A torrent of rain started to fall.

Holding a hand in front of her, Rachel moved out into the storm. Broken glass bit into her bare feet, but she barely noticed. Isabella had Lisa and Steven and now stood at the edge of the pool.

Terror filling her heart, Rachel hobbled toward them. Blood trailed from her feet. Yet with each step she felt stronger. But what would she do once she caught up? Whatever and whoever she was, the woman, even burdened with the kids, seemed much too strong. Rachel's only weapon remained her purse.

"Rachel!" screamed Lisa, seeing her coming.

"No!" roared Isabella. "I'm nearly finished!"

The roar of rain mixed with the howling wind and drowned out their voices. Gritting her teeth, Rachel bent down to scoop up Steven's ripstick. Never before had she been in a fight. Still, she meant to take down the woman. Ducking her head, she wiped soaked hair out of her eyes with a forearm and broke into a hobbling run. Isabella had her back to her and didn't turn.

At the pool's edge, the wizard started mumbling in a strange tongue. Rain pelted the pool's surface with miniexplosions. Then, the water flattened. Despite the heavy rain, the water became flat and still. "Yes," Isabella breathed. "My powers have not failed me yet." Then Lisa bit her hand.

Roaring in pain, Isabella grabbed hold of Lisa's shirt and leapt into the pool, dragging the girl with her. Steven, under her arm, followed headfirst.

"*No!*" screamed Rachel. Reaching the pool an instant too late, she leapt without thinking. The ripstick vanished below her as she reached out her arms and just managed to grab the back of Steven's shirt, yanking it hard. Twisting to the side, she pried the boy from Isabella just before striking the surface and … vanishing.

Without a splash, all signs of life were gone. In seconds, as the rain suddenly ended as fast as it started, the pool went smooth, silent, and very empty.

By the time Jason reached the back of the house and saw the broken door, the bodies were just crashing into the pool. Crying out, he charged outside. Rain struck him from all directions and then stopped. Jason didn't stop. Not until he dove with his arms extended into the pool did it hit him. There had been no splashes … and there was nobody in the water below him. Then he too vanished.

Courtney and Jakey staggered to a stop just outside the open door. They stared at each other with wide eyes. Water dripped off their hair and their soaked clothes clung to their skin. But now the storm had ended … and so had the screams. From inside the house came only a deep silence.

"Should we go in?" whispered Jakey, shivering.

Her face pale, Courtney wiped water off her face and dug into her wet shorts to pull out her cell phone. "I'll get ready to dial 911 just in case … stay behind me." Tentatively, she knocked on the open door. "Hello?" she called out. "Jason? Lisa? Anybody home?"

They had definitely seen their brother go in, hadn't they? The rain had been so hard and fierce and Jason had run so fast, it was hard to tell if he went inside or not. But the door was open …

Tentatively, Courtney stepped in with Jakey a step behind.

The sign Lisa and Courtney had made for Rachel greeted them, but that was it. Only the sound of dripping water could be heard.

"I don't like this," Courtney whispered. "Where is everyone?"

"I feel wind," Jakey said. "From the back."

"We're coming in!" Courtney called loudly. Stepping to the kitchen, the children saw a cake and a plate of brownies on the counter. And then saw the broken glass door.

A slight cough behind them caused both children to nearly leave their skin.

"Excuse me," hastily said a man, stepping into the kitchen. "I heard a commotion—are you kids okay?" The man loomed over them and his head looked like a mountain covered in snow. He wore a neatly pressed blue suit and a friendly smile. Yet his bright blue eyes seemed to shine unnaturally as they viewed the children intensely. Surrounded by raw, red skin, they sparkled as if he'd just won the jackpot.

Courtney bravely held up her cell phone like a weapon. "Who are you?"

"You can call me Red. I'm a neighbor passing by." The man stepped closer, but held up his hands as if to show them he was harmless. His clean-shaven lips twitched into a kind of smile. "I thought you two were in trouble. What's going on here?" He *sounded* concerned. But that didn't mean anything.

Courtney could feel Jakey's hand trembling slightly on her shirt. Taking a step back, she waved the cell phone. "I already called the police!"

"No you didn't—but maybe you should." The man ran a hand through his hair. "Look, I'm trying to help."

Jakey suddenly glared at him, stepping in front of his sister. "If you were walking by, how come you're not wet?"

The man's eyes hardened. "Clever boy …" Suddenly he chopped his hand in the air.

Courtney's cell phone flew from her hand and smashed into the counter. Her wrist went numb.

Screaming, she grabbed her brother with her other hand and pulled him toward the nearest escape—the broken back door.

Their flight was short lived. Displaying great speed, the man lunged forward and grabbed the back of Jakey's shorts before he reached the outside. Jerking back, he lifted the boy up before dropping him to the floor. Landing with a thud, the boy gasped for a breath, stunned.

Courtney turned with a scream and struck the man with her fist.

"Leave us alone!" she shouted.

Laughing, the man grabbed her arm and shook her. "Quit struggling, girl. I mean you no harm."

"What are you doing to us!"

"Why, bringing you closer to your brother, I imagine. Didn't he run through here a short time ago?" Still gripping her arm, the man reached down and plucked Jakey up by the shorts and shirt, carrying him like a suitcase. Ignoring the children's struggles and cries, he calmly brought them to the pool.

"If Isabella can take her prizes, I shall take mine," he muttered.

"What are you saying?" wailed Courtney, tears running down her face. "Let us go!"

"Oh, very well." The man flung Jakey and Courtney over the pool and watched in satisfaction as the portal sucked them into his world.

When all went quiet, Rudolph kicked off his shoes and started pulling off his suit, revealing a brown tunic and linen trousers underneath. Whistling, he calmly walked into the surface of the pool. Almost majestically, his body sank into a whole different world. Just as Rudolph faded back into his old life, his mouth formed a wide smile.

Tommy Hunt clicked off the TV and went to find his mom in the kitchen. Stirring a pot of soup that was to be for church the next day, his mom seemed lost in thought. She didn't look at him until he cleared his throat a couple of times.

"Oh, Tommy. There you are." She didn't smile at him. "Did you finish your Lord's homework?"

"Mom," he said softly. "I don't want to be in the Lord's Army anymore."

His mom stopped stirring and looked at him. "What did you say?"

"I … I miss swimming … and I'd rather hang out with Steven than some of those kids at church …" Lifting his head, Tommy stared at his mom. "Sometimes they scare me."

"But-but, you can't!" she sputtered. "Ms. Proom needs you, she said so herself!"

"No she doesn't need me! She just wanted Steven in her class—she said that herself!"

"That boy rejected the Lord's church—he's confused about it because of his babysitter. Just give him time. Ms. Proom said he'll come around, and I believe her."

"But, Mom—"

"We'll talk to Ms. Proom tomorrow, she'll explain it better."

Tears welled up in Tommy's eyes. "If Dad was still here, he wouldn't let Ms. Proom boss you around!"

"Tommy!"

"Ms. Proom flies a broom!" he shouted, running from the kitchen.

"Tommy, get back here! Tommy, where are you going?"

"To see Steven!" yelled her son. The front door slammed shut.

Grabbing his bike from the garage, Tommy pedaled furiously and didn't stop until nearly to Steven's house. Then he slammed the brakes and skidded to a stop. Sitting on the curb, looking very down, was Geoffrey Brown.

Rejecting the urge to turn around, Tommy took a deep breath. "Hey," he said cautiously.

Geoffrey looked up and barely seemed to look at him. "Hey."

"What are you doing here?" Tommy asked.

"I dunno …" Geoffrey hung his head.

"I'm going to talk to Steven … do you want to come?"

Geoffrey shook his head.

"Well, okay, then. I'll say I saw you."

Again Geoffrey shook his head.

Tommy took a huge breath. "Look, man. I'm sorry about what I did … I was stupid, okay? Come on, let's just drop everything."

Geoffrey looked up and Tommy was surprised to see the boy was crying. "Don't you get it? Steven isn't here! The janitor took him!"

Back at Tommy's house the phone rang. Mrs. Hunt picked it up and soon dropped it. Her hands were shaking too badly. One of the parishioners of the Lord's Faith Church of Finding Grace was calling with terrible news. Pastor Smith had mysteriously vanished and so had the entire bank account of the Lord's Faith Church of Finding Grace. Over a half million dollars had left with the pastor. Oh, and services were canceled for Sunday.

Sometimes children knew more than parents. This was something Mrs. Hunt thought as she slid to the floor in shock. And she'd just bought a new dress …

PART II—*The Babysitter Is Lost*

Chapter Twenty-One

A blue sky greeted Rachel when she opened her eyes. Yet she heard raindrops pattering on the leaves next to her head.

Trying to move, she gasped in pain. Burning pain tortured her feet and a terrible ache attacked her head. It felt as if her old high school band was trying to perform Sousa's greatest hits in her brain while roasting marshmallows on her feet. Moaning pitifully, she managed to shift her head.

What am I doing here? And where is here?

She lay in damp soil at the bottom of a small slope. From the slope came a thin, steady stream of liquid heading toward her nose. A sour smell filled her nostrils. Following the stream with her eyes … she sat up with a jerk, momentarily forgetting her pain.

Immediately a wave of dizziness assaulted her and she collapsed back, but at least farther from the crawling stream.

The source of the stream was a young, dirty boy with chestnut brown hair. His back to her, he was in the process of relieving himself. That explained the raindrops …

Finished, the boy tied his trousers and turned to her. He flashed a bright smile when seeing her awake. Rachel blinked. Who was this kid? He didn't look familiar at all. Built like a stick, he possessed rounded cheeks that narrowed into a sharp chin. A small, narrow nose and two slanted, large, almond-shaped eyes gave him a distinctly elfish look. Dirt lined his lips, and when they smiled, white teeth sparkled at Rachel. She guessed him to be no more than nine or ten. Nine … who else did she know that age?

Thinking just made her head ache more.

"Who are you?" she groaned, trying to clear her muddled head. "What happened to me?"

Ignoring her, the boy knelt low and proceeded to stick his hands into the freshly soiled soil. Gasping in horror, Rachel watched as his small slender fingers squished and kneaded mud into two long, flat cakes.

"I think you'd better stop," Rachel wheezed. "This is getting gross. Your mother would not approve, and you better wash your hands before eating!" Wincing, she struggled to sit up but still found it too difficult. Pain and nausea wracked her body. Dropping her head back, she tried to understand what had happened to her.

Far above, she made out the tops of trees swaying gently in a cool breeze. Against the brilliant blue sky, a large gray and white bird flew across her vision. All she could hear was the boy continuing to smack his mud pies into shape.

What am I doing lying in a clearing, surrounded by woods, with some savage kid making urine mud pies? Lifting her head, she stared at the boy again.

A sleeveless brown tunic made from animal skin covered his torso, secured about his slender waist with a leather cord. Heavy trousers covered his thin legs, and he wore moccasins on his feet. A bag that used to be the coat of a raccoon hung from his waist.

"Where am I?" she whispered.

Clicking his tongue, the boy held up a completed pie and smiled. Already flies were buzzing around it. Pie in hand, he approached on his knees, to Rachel's feet.

"N-no … what are you doing?" Trying to twist away, she threw out a hand and struck another body. Turning, she saw another young boy asleep next to her. In a mental explosion, it all came crashing back to her.

In the park meeting Jason Richardson—but he wasn't coming! Instead the horrible man with red eyes tried to do something to her—and her children were in danger! The agonizing race back to the house. Jane Lovington becoming a mad wizard blasting bolts and carrying away the children—her children! She was a babysitter! She jumped into the pool to save—

Shooting up to a sitting position, she stared down at the sleeping boy. "Steven!"

The boy lay on his stomach, his face tilted toward Rachel. Rolling him gently toward her onto his back, Rachel breathed a sigh of relief as she looked for and found a pulse. His thin face remained relaxed in deep sleep, and his narrow chest rose and fell evenly under his white dress suit.

"But where's Lisa?" Rachel searched in all directions but did not see any other body … except for the filthy boy with the filthy pie still kneeling by her feet while eyeing her curiously. "Where are we?" she asked him to no effect.

A small pool of water the size of a giant puddle was nestled in the rocks a foot above where she lay. Otherwise, they were surrounded by at least a few acres of thick verdant grass. Heavy woods enclosed the clearing. While she could now hear birds singing in the distance, there were no signs of other people.

Then her eyes fell on Steven's ripstick and her purse. They lay in the grass to her left.

How in the world did this happen? We fell in the pool, right?

Groaning, she rubbed her forehead with both hands. The burning in her feet intensified and caused almost as much agony as not knowing what had happened.

Then the first mud pie splattered on her right foot.

"What the—" Jerking, she tried to kick it away, but suddenly sighed in relief. Instantly the burning pain on that foot soothed. Lying back, she rested her head on the soft earth. Another slap on her other foot again brought instant relief. Reaching out her right arm, she touched Steven's chin. "It's going to be okay," she whispered. Her eyes slid shut. "I don't know how, but it'll be okay …"

When Rachel woke up again, the sun had moved behind the trees in front of her. Steven stirred in his sleep and shifted to his side. She could hear birds chirping in the distance. The aroma of sweet grass and fresh dirt filled the air. Feeling refreshed, she lifted up her feet and saw two dry clumps of dirt still attached. Wincing, she put them back down.

It hadn't been a dream. What was going on? Where did the boy go?

As an answer, a harsh voice carried from the trees to her left. Instantly Rachel lay back down and feigned unconsciousness. That was what had woken her. Keeping her face pointed toward the voice, she cracked open her eyes.

Soon the dirty little boy came back into focus. Next to him walked a stunning young woman about Rachel's age, but that was where the similarities ended. Wearing tight leather armor over a brown skirt, she carried a long, unsheathed sword. Long, flaxen hair hung past her shoulders, and she had the tight figure of an athlete. An ugly sneer marred her otherwise pretty face.

Snarling, she slapped the back of the boy's pants with the flat part of her blade.

"Where is this mighty wizard with the boy?" she demanded harshly. "If you are having a go with me, I'll use this blade on your hide much harder so you shan't sit for a moon cycle!"

The boy seemed oblivious to her attitude. Pointing to where Rachel and Steven lay, he skipped lightly ahead.

"Keep by my side, fool." Rushing to catch up, the woman grabbed his shoulder and pulled him back. "Wolves roam these woods!"

Rachel closed her eyes. Both figures were slim and good looking. *They must be rich.* They wouldn't be much interested in a poor, overweight babysitter. *Probably a family of weirdos playing dress up … but where are we?*

"THAT CONFOUNDED BABYSITTER!" bellowed Isabella, sparks literally shooting from her blood-red eyes. Stomping around the small stone chamber deep under the Fortress of Belford, she waved her arms in extreme anger. "She will be the ruin of me! I will tear out her eyes and rip off her lips!"

Isabella paused in her pacing and leaned against the damp stone wall, trying to control her anger. A grand wizard shouldn't throw tantrums in front of her followers. A small circular pool of water lay at her back. Lined with heavy stone, the pool served as her portal to Earth and had been where she had emerged with Lisa. Only Lisa, not Steven … The boy—the one she wanted—the key to her absolute power—had been snatched from her grasp by that hideous Rachel and ended up who knew where. By the pool, Lisa lay unconscious after the harsh, unexpected journey. Two guards stood across from the pool by the door, eyeing each other uneasily.

"Most high wizard," spoke the taller of the two carefully. "If you wish it, I will return with you and find this wretched babysitter."

"That won't be necessary," Isabella growled. "They at least made the journey into our land. Besides, I won't have to go back to that cursed land and grovel as a *housekeeper* any longer!" She looked at the guard who had spoken. "Bodin, I trust in my absence that you have been busy. Are the coffers full?"

"Yes, mighty one. And as you requested, I have established your personal guard—hand selected by myself. Your guard has over three hundred men; all yours to command."

"And what of Sir Rudolph?" asked the other guard, suddenly sounding a little nervous. "Has he not returned?"

Isabella waved her hand dismissively in this guard's direction. "I will need my guard to act swiftly. We haven't much time."

The taller guard glanced down at Lisa. The only light came from a torch above his head, casting his bearded face in shadow. Wearing armor covered with a purple tunic, he carried a long spear and had a sword belted at his waist. "What should we do with the girl? I can use one like her for a serving wench."

"Leave her!" snapped Isabella. "Take that hungry look off your wolfish face. I have need of this girl." Her mouth twisted in an evil grin. "If I know the fool, Rachel, she will come looking for her. And the boy will be at her side. She won't let him away from her again … not until I kill her." She slammed a palm against the wall. "And I do want her dead!"

Bodin grunted. "Is that all then?"

"No, Bodin, it is not all. Put down your foolish spear, bring the girl to my chambers, and put her in my bed. Better yet, I shall take her." She stood over Lisa. "When Rachel makes it here—*if* Rachel makes it here—she will have a nasty surprise awaiting her. Bodin, meet my new apprentice."

Grunting, Bodin bowed stiffly. His dark eyebrows lifted slightly but registered nothing. His duty was to serve the wizard, not to ask questions. Questions got you in trouble.

The other guard shifted uncomfortably. Dressed similarly to Bodin, he wore a red tunic and carried a much more nervous look. "Does ... does this mean Rudolph is no longer your apprentice?"

"I know this must distress you, Tendl, but you may consider him dead." It was the first time Isabella spoke to this guard, and she never once looked at him. While her voice went soft, it held a taste of false pity.

Tendl swallowed. Bodin smirked at him. Yes, questions only led to trouble. He had never liked Isabella's uppity apprentice, or his personal protector, Tendl.

"The red-eyed fool has tried to betray me," Isabella said bitterly. "We'll find him as we search for Rachel and the boy. I want you to gather our men, Bodin. Send them out. Go to every surrounding village, town, and farm. Spread the news that I seek Rudolph and a babysitter—a fat woman ..." Isabella proceeded to describe Rachel as a horribly ugly woman with hair like moldy string, a belly like a kettle pot, and the arms and feet of bloated trees. "I'd rather her alive, but she can be dead ... but the boy *must* live. Find every wanderer and cutthroat you can and add them to my guard. Offer a reward large enough for the weakest of hearts to join us."

Bodin grunted. "And of Rudolph? When we find him, what should we do?"

"I want him dead. Kill him on sight."

"As you command." Giving a mock bow to his comrade, Bodin opened the door and waited for the wizard to gather Lisa in her arms.

"We cannot fail in this, Bodin," she said before leaving with her limp burden. "I trust you'll do the right thing." She nodded meaningfully at the other guard.

Bodin bowed. "Of course, mighty one."

"Good. I will meet you for the evening meal. That shall allow time for news of my arrival to spread. Those who thought me gone for good will no doubt tremble."

"No doubt, mighty one." Bodin leered at the other guard, whose knees had indeed begun to tremble.

Isabella carried the girl up the stairs. Bodin waited until they were nearly to the top. Then he turned to Tendl.

"You were close to Rudolph, were you not?"

"No—nay, Bodin. I merely did as I was told—"

Bodin stepped to him and swung his spear in an arc, smashing the top of the shaft in the guard's face.

Crashing into the wall, the guard groaned, slid into a heap, and went still.

"You'll wake in the dungeons. That is your last order. Now do what you're told!" Cackling, he marched up the stairs with his spear at his side. He would send guards down to fetch Tendl. In his mind he already counted the reward he would collect for finding that babysitter, Rachel … and then he wondered. What exactly was a babysitter?

"Keep back, Jak," warned the girl. "If she wakes she'll make you a toad sure as the sky is blue."

The boy snorted and crossed his eyes. Getting on his haunches, he began to hop and stick out his tongue as if he was catching flies.

"Mock me if you wish, boy! Fat wizards such as this are known to eat little boys in a stew. And this one looks like she's always eating something …"

Rachel worked hard not to frown. The strange girl now practically stepped on her. Suddenly her sword poked Rachel's stomach. "I should run you through right now, ugly wench," the girl growled. "Then the village will proclaim me as Suzella, the warrior and slayer of wizards!"

Rachel's eyes snapped open and she knocked the blade away as she sprang to a sitting position. "Watch it!" she cried. "Are you crazy? That hurts!"

Leaping back, the warrior girl waved her sword defensively. Fear showed in her eyes. The boy, Jak, went still.

"I only jest, most great wizard," the girl said hastily, quickly lowering her sword. To Rachel's amazement, she fell to a knee and bowed to her, pressing her forehead to the ground. "I dared to doubt your powers and remain greatly sorry for it! I come to assist you, wizard! I vow this is the truth!"

Staring at her like she'd lost her mind, Rachel shook her head to clear her mental fog. The extra sleep had done her body well. That and the mud cakes … her feet actually felt good. Stretching her neck, she tested all parts and found they functioned. Then she turned to the strange girl. "Uh, who are you? And where are we?"

Next to her, Steven coughed and sat up groggily. "Rachel?" he asked sleepily. He looked around. His lips trembled. "Wh-where's Lisa? Wh-what happened?"

"Hush, Steven. I'm not sure what is going on, but I'm going to find out." Rubbing his back, she brushed off the dirt before turning to the girl. Taking a deep breath, she forced her fear and confusion from her voice. "Well?"

The girl glanced up, looking between the two, and seemed to make a decision. Rising to her feet, she sheathed her sword and bowed again. "I am the humble servant, Suzella, warrior of Durnwirk. My village lies just through those woods. I-I know why you come, o great one. We have a great many ray berries."

Rachel stared at her and then looked at Steven.

Steven only blinked and rubbed his head.

"Right," muttered Rachel after a moment. She reached and gathered Steven by the shoulders, lifting him gently to his feet. "Steven, I don't know what you remember, but we seem to be in some trouble … I think we might be lost." Gritting her teeth, she flicked a glance at the woman. "Can you bring us to, uh, your village?"

"Of course, wizard. You shall use our village this very night for your work. We will help you!"

"Okay …" Getting stiffly to her feet, she grunted with pleasure. The mud cakes remained spongy and cushioned her feet like a pair of slippers. "Wow, I would kill to have my feet feel this good all the time," she mumbled.

Suzella's eyes widened and glanced at the boy. "You like Jak's work, do you?" She indicated Rachel's feet.

"Uh," Rachel coughed uncomfortably. "I don't exactly like how they're made, but they do work." She grinned a bit sickly at the brown-haired boy. "But, uh, thank you."

The boy grinned and shot to his feet to give her a low bow, mocking the one given by Suzella.

Suzella eyed the boy with distaste. Then she looked at Rachel. "That is good, great wizard, that you like this boy."

"Uh, what? Uh, I'm not a wizard … I'm, uh, uh, a babysitter."

Suzella's eyes went wide. "So I was right … You are one of those." She bit her bottom lip and again eyed Jak.

Rachel grunted. "Uh, yeah. Huh? I'm, uh, one of those." She patted Steven's back. "This is, uh, Steven. He's the one that I, uh, babysit."

"And so you shall," Suzella said suddenly with feeling. "Not only shall you babysit that boy, but you must also take Jak!" She grabbed the brown boy and thrust him at Rachel.

"Huh? What?"

Jak's eyes widened in surprise and he leaned back.

"He is a gift from our village." She bowed low, shoving Jak forward.

The boy stumbled and then shrugged. Standing his straightest, he struck a pose with his hands on his hips.

"Believe me, Babysitter," continued Suzella, "our village will want this. Having a babysitter come so far north to us is a great honor. Take the boy as our gift … he may not look like much, but there is more than what you see."

"Oh, uh, I'm sure …" Rachel eyed the boy.

His pose faltered and his large eyes measured her carefully back. He frowned slightly and offered a filthy hand to her to shake.

"Okay … I'll look out for, uh, Jak for now …" Avoiding the hand, she patted him on the head instead. "He, uh, needs it." Grease and filth encrusted his hair, but she at least knew where it *didn't* come from. "Oh, er, my name is Rachel."

Suzella immediately dropped to her knees and pressed her head on the earth again. Right where Jak had earlier made his mud cakes. "It is an honor to have your name spoken to me."

Stifling a groan, Rachel looked down at Steven. "You know, I don't think we're in Kansas anymore … or Florida … or even reality."

Shuddering, Steven pressed close to her. He wrinkled his nose at the stench of Jak. "We're not in heaven either," he mumbled.

Rachel managed a small grin. "Well, let's get your ripstick and my purse. Wherever we are, we'd better keep what we have close by. Hopefully somebody in their, uh, village will know something." She definitely hoped so. Especially when taking her phone from her purse and finding it with no service.

The image of the horrible housekeeper taking the children and dragging them to the pool came back to her, and she forced down her feeling of horrified panic. She had to stay in control and find out where they were and where Lisa ended up. The pool … she started to fear the worse. The pool had brought them here. Jane was not Jane the housekeeper, but a terrible wizard from a magical land … no, no, impossible! But then, what else could she believe? *I just have to keep cool … keep cool and find Lisa and get home. I can do it … one step at a time. Then I'll panic.* Rachel gulped. Overhead, the sun blazed down heat through the trees. She refused to wilt.

Jak led the way as Rachel and Steven remained close together. Suzella followed in the rear—to guard from wolves, she explained. As they traveled, Rachel started asking questions and only grew more frustrated with the answers.

"Are we still in Florida?"

"Flor-i-da?" the girl asked, saying the word slowly as if trying to taste it. "Is that where you come from? I have never heard of such a place, but I know so little." She stared wistfully into the woods. "I grew up in Durnwirk and have rarely ventured from its woods." Her voice turned bitter. "My task is always to watch Jak and pick ray berries. That is all I do! I am ready to fight! I seek to become a huntress and serve a lord, or a prince, or … or a wizard!"

"Oh, uh, that's nice." Rachel guessed Suzella to be at least a year younger than her and in some serious need of growing up. She was glad she was responsible for Jak now and not this wild girl. "Does, uh, Jak talk?"

"No. He's a halfwit mute." When Rachel gasped and turned to look at her, Suzella quickly corrected herself. "Perhaps not a halfwit. Just silent. He is very able with medicine—even our medicine man is astounded at his healing powers. His father, before he vanished, was known throughout the land as The Healer. You are greatly honored to have him with, er … your Steven."

"His father is missing then?"

"Aye, and his mother. They left during the plague years and have yet to return." She made a face. "He has a sister who sits in the village doing little. She should be glad to have him unburdened from her. I'm sure of it." It sounded as if she was trying to convince herself.

Before Rachel could inquire what that meant, Jak turned on the narrow dirt path and pointed to a hill before them.

"Ah," announced Suzella. "Our village is just over the hill. You will be most welcome, Rachel the Babysitter."

Maybe … but Rachel had her doubts she would welcome the village …

When they broke from the trees on the other side of the hill, Rachel and Steven were amazed to see a cluster of crude log houses with slant-slatted roofs below them. They were perched above an incline with a large field of swaying grass lying between them and the buildings. Almost all the buildings were single story except for one. In the center of the village rose a massive structure at least three stories high and shaped like a warehouse. Smoke wafted from several chimneys, but Rachel spotted no people. All she saw were animals walking the streets as if they owned them—cows, horses, chickens, ducks, and a few she couldn't identify.

"What the …" Rachel's mouth fell open.

"Welcome to Durnwirk," grunted Suzella, moving to stand beside Rachel. "It is rather squalid, especially for a babysitter, but you will find the people willing to assist you. One thing they fear most is outsiders." She smiled grimly. "Especially the wizard kind."

"Uh …" Rachel could barely get her mouth to work. She could not believe what she was seeing. "Okay …"

She estimated there to be about fifty to seventy structures. She also made out fields growing what looked to be wheat. Enclosed by wooden rail fences, these and other crops were visible on the far side of the village. In front of these fields was an enclosed area where several horses grazed. It was an old-fashioned village that shouldn't exist unless it was a museum, or a movie set. Rachel had her doubts. She found Steven's hand and gripped it tightly. *Where are we?*

Encircling the village and fields, separated at most only by a hundred feet of tall grass, were thick, dark woods. All the houses were built close to each other as if huddling together. No houses strayed too far from the center, and they were connected by narrow roads … A single dirt road ran to the town from the woods to the right of where Rachel stood with her mouth still not working properly. The path they were on faded into a grassy field below the hill, meaning the road was the only way in and out of the village unless you went through thick woods. Staring at the far woods across from where she stood, Rachel shivered. For the first time, the warning of wolves scared her.

Thinking Rachel was admiring the view, Suzella grunted. "We spent many hard winters clearing the land around the village. Before that, wolves would come and attack us and our animals most every night. Now we live in relative peace … especially with warriors like me around."

"Where is this place?" Rachel whispered, pulling Steven close and gripping his shoulders tightly.

"Don't you know, Babysitter? You are in the north lands of Munolia. Few wizards travel so far north—not since the wizard wars have we seen your kind here."

Speechless, Rachel followed Jak down into the village. Steven firmly latched on to her hand and refused to loosen his grip. Rachel felt the same way.

The rutted and scarred earthen streets were empty, except for chickens and ducks wandering freely about. All the large animals—horses and cows—had mysteriously vanished as they had approached. Rachel eyed the buildings fearfully as only silence greeted their arrival.

Suzella seemed unconcerned. Moving to take the lead, she boldly led them toward the center, where the large structure stood. Dark smoke rose from this area. Walking beside Rachel, Steven covered his nose with his sleeve. It smelled of unwashed bodies, animal manure, and smoke.

News of their coming must have spread. The reason the streets were empty of people was because they were all waiting at the center. A crowd of men and women stood silently in a tight bunch watching their arrival. None of them looked very happy.

Dropping her gaze, Rachel pulled Steven behind her and struggled hard to breathe normally. Fear caught her tongue and refused to let go.

"They look mad," Steven whispered, gripping the back of her dress.

Dressed in rough clothes similar to Jak's, they all seemed to be looking at Rachel. Contempt and disgust clearly lined their faces. That and fear. Many of the men carried crude clubs. Some had spears. While a few dogs barked at the newcomers, Rachel noticed that no children were in sight. Except for Jak … The boy had moved next to Steven and now crouched in the mud, watching the proceedings with interest.

"Lay aside your fears," Suzella said almost cheerfully. "They will not harm you."

At first Rachel thought the flaxen-haired warrior spoke to her, but then Suzella spread out her arms and repeated it louder to the crowd. "Lay aside your fears, I say! We are honored with the presence of the great babysitter, Rachel!"

Many in the crowd gasped and murmured. If anything, they grew more afraid.

Suzella motioned to them for silence. Then she started speaking in a strange tongue to the crowd. At first they seemed furious and fearful at Suzella's words. Then they grew curious before finally relaxing. Some men even broke into smiles and women put hands over their hearts as if relieved. The whole time she spoke, Suzella kept gesturing back at Jak and at Rachel. Finally, in almost a huge sigh, the crowd raised their fists toward Rachel and shouted a greeting.

Flinching, Rachel looked up and nodded in return. Jak looked up at her with his wide eyes and kept silent.

Suzella stepped back and grinned at Rachel. "Our village will assist you, Rachel, just as I promised!"

"Th-that's wonderful," she replied weakly.

A man with a thick gray beard stepped from the crowd and bowed.

"We are deeply honored for you to select our humble village for your sacred ritual, great babysitter. I am Urslaf, chief of this village."

"Er, uh, okay …" Rachel blushed furiously and did not know what to say. "Is, uh, there a gas station nearby?" she finally stammered.

Urslaf looked puzzled and turned to Suzella. The girl spoke rapidly in the strange language and the chief nodded wisely. "We shall build you one, Wizard," he said loudly. "Then we shall have a feast in your honor while you use this … gas station. It will be a night Durnwirk will never forget! Long will our future generations tell the story of the gas station and the night of the babysitter!"

Open mouthed, Rachel stared helplessly down at Steven. "What just happened?" she whispered.

Steven shrugged then looked pained. "I don't know, but I hope it has a bathroom … Rachel, I need to go."

"Oh, uh, so do I!"

Suddenly a woman shouted from the crowd. "You take young Jak from us! Shame!"

Immediately the men and women around her shushed her.

"Pay no heed," Urslaf said hastily, moving in front of Rachel to block her view of the scene. "It is always a true blessing when one of our own serves you. Jak will do you well."

Rachel gulped and suddenly looked sick. "Uh, great, listen, uh, sir, is there, uh, a bathroom nearby?"

"A what?" asked the man, bending closer to her.

Beside her, Steven squirmed uncomfortably, started doing the universal symbol for needing to go badly. Somehow, in this universe, nobody got it.

"She causes the boy to convulse!" cried Suzella. "Quick, we must erect the gas station!"

"No, we just—" Rachel gritted her teeth. The crowd started talking all at once and splitting up. She felt ready to explode.

Jak saved them from further embarrassment. Getting lightly to his feet, he pulled Steven's arm and pointed toward the trees. Finally, somebody understood.

Nodding in relief, Steven hurried to follow.

Relieved that at least somebody in the village understood, Rachel hurried after the mute boy. Muttering about how much she hated the outdoors, she found a clump of bushes away from the boys and tried hard not to cry.

Back at the village, many of the men glared at where she disappeared.

"Wizards and their kind," growled Urslaf, wiping sweat from his brow. "They should all rot and shrivel away."

Many mumbles agreed with him.

"Hush, fools!" Suzella snapped. "The wizard can read thoughts in the air as we read words on paper! She nearly turned me into stone when I thought such things! Now hurry and prepare for her ritual!"

"Who made you in charge of us, Suzella?" cried a dark bearded man in the back. "You're the fool who gave up our healer!"

"Jak is a mere boy with little worth!" Suzella shouted angrily back. "Would you rather I give her your son, Jun Torga?"

Swallowing, the man ducked his head. "Jak is worth more than you," he mumbled.

"Jun Torga," seethed Suzella dangerously. "Do not forget it was I who found the wizard! If not for me she would have walked in here and taken all our children! Instead I managed to have her beholden to me and take only one. And," her eyes flashed, "if any dares to go against me, I shall remember it! The wizard follows my counsel! You may not fear for your own life, but think of your children!"

Gasps were heard from the crowd and many melted away.

Jun spat. "Just wait until Marcal returns—then we'll see if your high and mighty tone keeps!"

"Now, now," Urslaf said quickly. "Let us not lose our heads."

"Just our children," Jun Torga snarled.

"None of that!" Urslaf's voice rang with iron. "We are a poor people who survive only because we stick together!" Glaring, he surveyed the faces before him, stopping lastly on Suzella. "What is done is done. We must do what is necessary to have the wizard leave us without further harm. If all goes well, and Suzella is right, she may become our protector. A wizard who protects our village is nothing to be angry about."

"But what if she returns for more children?" wailed a mother.

"That won't happen!" The chief did not look as sure as he sounded.

"Get to work and I'll make sure it won't happen," Suzella said boldly. "You will see, the wizard listens to me … and so should all of you."

Chapter Twenty-Two

Lisa's eyes fluttered open. Groaning, she shook off the cool hand wiping her head.

"M-Mom?" She coughed. "R-Rachel?"

"No, young one. It is I."

Her vision clearing, Lisa blinked and saw Jane Lovington sitting on the edge of her bed, smiling. Only it wasn't Jane Lovington. It was Isabella—the wicked lady who'd drugged the brownies for the party—Steven had collapsed after only a few bites. Then she had tried to cram another brownie down Lisa's throat, but Lisa had managed to fight her off until Rachel came—

"Rachel!" cried Lisa, squirming away from Isabella. Then she went still. This wasn't her bed. And she wasn't in her room. Candles were everywhere and cast an eerie light on walls of stone. Her eyes darted and saw a large wooden door in the shape of a spade behind Isabella. Next to it was a long shelf of books perched over a thick wooden table. Four cushioned chairs and a large standing chest completed the furniture. Rugs looking more like dead animals covered the stone floor. On the other side of the room, a small fire crackled in the fireplace where a pot hung. Her eyes turned to her bed. Heavy blankets covered the mattress but were like nothing she had seen before.

"What's happening? Where am I?"

"Hush and relax," soothed Isabella, still smiling. "You are in my home, dear."

Trembling, Lisa shrank from the dark eyes. The candle, the fire, and the thick blankets caused the air to be thick with suffocating heat. Lisa fought off the dizzying need to close her eyes and fall back into darkness.

"Oh, do relax, Lisa. I am not going to hurt you—if I were, you would have not woken in such comfort."

Swallowing, Lisa stared up at her. "What happened? How did I get here?"

"Do you not remember? I tried to take you and your brother, but that fat babysitter got in the way!"

Lisa closed her eyes and shuddered as she remembered the storm and the pool … how Isabella had pulled her in and … pain and blackness.

Opening her eyes, she glared. "I don't trust you! You're a liar!"

"Lisa, I would be careful how you talk to me now. I am many things, but mainly I am a great wizard." She smiled down her nose. "And I want you to feel comfortable here."

"Well, I don't!" Lisa scooted farther back from Isabella. Looking under the blankets, she was relieved to see she still had on her clothes. Flicking a glance at the door, she wondered if she could jump up and escape. But then what? Besides, she remembered Isabella shooting the bolt at Rachel … poor Rachel. She shuddered. While she was not sure how, it seemed true … Isabella was a wizard. "Where're my brother and Rachel?"

"Now, that's a good question." Isabella stood from the bed, walked to the table, and picked up a tray. "Have a cinnamon bun. I know they're your favorite." She offered the tray to her.

Lisa refused to acknowledge the steaming pastries. "I asked you a question. Besides, your brownies didn't turn out so well."

Isabella laughed and withdrew the tray. "You are a clever girl, Lisa. But I disagree. I think my brownies were fabulous. Your brother nearly died for them."

"Where is he?" Lisa shouted. "And where's Rachel?"

Isabella lost her smile and tossed the tray on the bed next to Lisa. "I would like to know the answer, dear, but I don't, thanks to that fat babysitter."

"What do you mean?"

"I wished to bring you and your brother with me, Lisa." She sighed heavily. "Instead, your Rachel snatched Steven from me at the last moment … they're out there now in this cruel world. Yes, Lisa, I'm sure you realize it. We're in a new world. A world full of danger and death. While I brought you here to safety, Rachel's dull mind took her and Steven to some other horrid place." A flash of real anger spread across her face. "If she harmed the boy in any way … I will be very angry." She relaxed and smiled at Lisa. "But they are in this world, and I will find them, make no mistake about that!"

"Wh-what world? Who are you really? What are you talking about?"

"One question at a time." Standing in front of Lisa, Isabella raised her head majestically. "For now I am known as Isabella, the Wizard of the Western Kingdom. Very soon, however, I shall be called Queen Isabella, Wizard and Ruler of Panterra!"

Fighting back her rising fear, Lisa took time to stare up at the lady. "I only know you as the lady who cleans my bathroom."

Laughing without humor, Isabella shook her head in pity and again sat on the edge of the bed. "I have turned lesser men into insects for such insolence. Lisa, I brought you here to be at my side. On one side will be you and on the other will be Steven … In time you will understand."

Lisa folded her arms. The longer she sat there, the angrier she got. When Lisa grew angry, she found it very hard to control her mouth. She had to be careful. Whatever had happened, it was real. Very real. This certainly wasn't home, and Isabella had certainly showed she had some sort of power. Lisa needed to find out more information without panicking or throwing a fit.

"I, I think I just want to go home. Where is it?"

"It is too late for that. I worked very hard to bring you and your brother here."

"What do you mean?"

"You're a broken record, child." Isabella sighed and said bitterly, "For years, I traveled your world searching for a special child. And when I finally found him, I spent even more years planning how to get him in my grasp and take him to my world. And when the time finally came … I decided to take his sister as well." Isabella's eyes smoldered. "Unfortunately, a fat babysitter interfered and ruined it! But no matter, what's done is done. I shall find your brother and all will be well. You will see."

Lisa shook her head as if trying to loosen a chunk of understanding. "You mean … you became our housekeeper just to kidnap us?"

"In a manner of speaking, yes." Isabella shuddered. "Never again will I clean or return to your world in such a manner."

For a long moment, Lisa sat there stunned. Then she frowned.

"Wait, how come you just didn't take us before? You spent nearly a year as our housekeeper! Why wait until now?"

Isabella stood again. "I will not lie to you, child. I am a dark wizard who possesses only dark powers. The only weakness to my powers is the presence of strong … what you would call unconditional love. I call it foolishness." She sighed. "Quite simply, my power does not work in the presence of strong, unwavering, unconditional love … quite a nuisance, I assure you. In your world, my power is already weakened since I am so far from its source. In the presence of your parents, I had no power to match the love of your mother and father … they protected you without even knowing it." She smiled smugly. "Unfortunately for them, they went on a long trip without you and your brother."

"You're-you're really a dark wizard?" Lisa's lips trembled slightly.

"Do not look at me like that! Darkness is as natural as light! It is the other half of day!"

"But you said love defeats it."

"Yes, cursed love! What a waste of time and energy!"

Lisa grabbed a bun from the plate that had been set next to her on the bed. "So if I really loved this bun, I could beat you?"

"Don't be a fool. That isn't love—that's desire. Desire only strengthens me." She smiled and sat back down. "Why else did I offer the buns?" Lisa hastily dropped the bun back on the plate, pulling back her hand as if burned. "Love is different—it creates a bond that is impossible to break with dark magic. My magic cannot exist with love. The only way to have power over you and Steven was to have you turn to me against your parents, or to have your parents go far away where the bonds were stretched too thin."

Lisa thought for a moment. Then her voice went small. "So why wait for so long after our parents left? Couldn't you have taken us right after they left?"

It was like she'd pushed an anger button on the wizard.

Shooting to her feet, Isabella threw up her hands. "No, because of that stupid fat Rachel! She wouldn't let me! That's why!"

"You mean …" Lisa shook her head in confusion. "Her … love … ?"

"Stop talking such nonsense!" Isabella turned from Lisa, but then waved a hand in disgust. "Oh, perhaps you're right. I still don't understand how, but my powers remained drained with her around. It took careful planning to distract her enough to regain power to take you and Steven away … and Rachel still returned, almost in time! My power was draining when we went through the portal. That is why Rachel managed to escape with your brother."

"So … she saved Steven."

Isabella whirled on her. "YES! She did." She struggled to control her temper. "It is your brother, the one I needed, the one …"

"Not me," Lisa whispered.

The dark wizard suddenly relaxed and smiled cruelly. "Right. Not you. I guess we at least know which one of you brats she really loved, don't we?"

Lisa sat very still. Then she kicked out her foot and knocked the tray of buns onto the floor. "I don't care what you say!" Her face burned with anger. "You think you have me, but you don't! Rachel is coming for me, I know it!"

"She's not! She's not coming!"

"I can tell by your face! She is coming and you're afraid of her!"

"Nonsense!" roared the wizard. "She's a fat nothing!"

"For your information, she's not that fat anymore. You're the fat idiot!"

"Guards, come take this child away before I throw her to the dogs! I told you the truth, child! I expect respect for at least that! I may be a dark wizard, but I tell you the truth!"

"Why tell me anything? Why not just send me back home?"

"I told you so you would know your future! You'll learn to appreciate the dark arts, you'll see! You're my apprentice, Lisa!" If she expected a positive reaction, Isabella was sorely disappointed.

"No way! Never! You're a crazy toilet cleaner!"

"Don't you dare call me that again! You are a wretch and possess more of the dark power than you realize!"

"That's a lie, you stupid cow!"

"Guards, where are you? Take her to the dungeons until she appreciates my kindness!"

The door swung open as two burly men dressed in armor entered. Laying aside their spears, they marched toward the bed with menace. Lisa could only scream before being dragged away.

As Rachel leaned against the soft fur laid over the barrel, she felt something sharp prick her neck.

"I've been training a mere three years and already I can sneak up on a wizard," hissed a low voice.

Feeling a chill down her spine, Rachel sat up with a gasp. "Wh-what?"

Suzella stood and sauntered before her, grinning smugly. Shoving a short blade into its sheath at her side, she sat next to Rachel. "If you ever need such services, I need only to hear your request. Even babysitters need bodyguards."

"Uh, okay," stammered Rachel, rubbing the back of her neck.

They were behind the large wood structure, which Rachel learned served as the community warehouse for surplus food and also where the public events took place. At the moment, the front of the building had become a busy construction site. Hammering, sawing, and voices rang and barked as Rachel's "gas station" was rapidly taking shape.

After having returned from the bushes, Rachel had gotten Suzella's promise that it would be completed by nightfall and then the ritual would commence. Totally confused, bewildered, and frightened, Rachel had quietly nodded. Inside, panic had started to build. Directed to the back, Suzella told her to wait until it was time … and then what? What did these people think a gas station was, and what was this about a ritual?

Rachel eyed Suzella nervously and didn't know what to say. The girl made her scared. Back at home girls like Suzella would only make fun of Rachel—not help her. And they didn't carry sharp swords and sneak up on people. Across a mud patch and in front of a small house covered in animal fur, Steven sat with Jak and was unsuccessfully explaining the use of his ripstick. The two boys had at least bonded. Every few seconds Steven looked at Rachel, though, as if to make sure she still remained.

"No, it's not a weapon … um, put it down. I'll show you … You stand like this—"

Rachel nearly grinned as the ripstick sank in the soft road, causing Steven to fall on the seat of his pants. Only the presence of children caused her to keep her wits from totally leaving. She had to be strong for Steven … and Jak.

"So, wizard, what is the ritual to be?"

Jerking her gaze from Steven, Rachel stared at Suzella. "Uh, I'm a, uh, babysitter, okay?"

Suzella pulled out her blade and scratched at the dirt between her feet without looking at Rachel. "You are very loose with that word … I would be careful. And," she bowed, "that is why you require the services of my blade."

"Huh?" Rachel swallowed.

Glancing around suspiciously, Suzella leaned in close to Rachel. She stared intently into her eyes. "There are those in this village who fear babysitters, and for good reason. And many here will kill what they fear."

Rachel stared at her with incredulous horror. "Wh-what are you talking about?"

"We will talk later," Suzella mumbled. "Just do your ritual and proclaim yourself satisfied. And remember, you have a friend in me." The girl shot to her feet with little effort and slipped around to the front of the building.

"I don't have a good feeling about this," Rachel groaned. "Where in the world are we and what are we doing?" The more she asked the questions the more she felt lost.

Steven now sat staring at the ripstick. Jak curled up next to him and looked to be napping.

Rachel shuddered when seeing Steven—his auburn hair glinted in the sun, but his face was in shadow. Arms on his slender knees, he looked lost in dark thoughts. What ran through his mind could not be happy.

Turning her gaze to Jak, she saw the boy open his eyes and stare with deep concentration at the ripstick, as if trying to unlock its mysteries with his gaze.

Why is he the only child in the village? There must be more … But so far the streets remained mostly empty. No sounds of children and no sight of children.

Suddenly from the house behind Steven, a face appeared in the window. A young girl peeked out. Seeing Rachel, she immediately vanished as if afraid.

Rachel gave a start. She watched the window, but the face did not reappear.

It soon became evident. The children were hiding … but why? What did these people think babysitters did? Who were they and what in the world were they doing building a "gas station" *here*? She doubted it would be anything like Exxon.

"Oh, boy," she groaned to herself. "Why can't this just be a bad dream?"

As the sun began to fall, darkness stretched out its hand and Steven and Jak moved next to Rachel.

"Rachel, what are we going to do?" Steven asked, hugging his knees close to him. He sat on a wood plank next to her. Jak had stretched out on his stomach in the dirt next to Rachel's feet and rested his chin on his hands.

Rachel sighed. "We're going to find Lisa and then go back home … don't ask me how, though." Reaching over, she mussed up his hair. "And you need a bath … your poor clothes will never be the same." She tried to wipe dirt from his knee, but only smeared it into the cloth.

Steven grinned. "You make a better babysitter than a mom."

"Good, because that's what I am." She poked him in the side, causing him to squirm. "I just wish I knew where we were and how we got here."

Then from the front of the building came the loud blast of a deep horn. It sounded like a foghorn from a tugboat, only more dire.

Steven immediately covered his ears.

Rachel flinched. She hadn't realized it, but the sound of hammering and construction had ceased for some time.

"All is ready for the great Babysitter Rachel!" called a loud voice. "Come, let us gather to honor her and witness her sacred ritual where she takes one of us to be a part of her!" The horn blasted again. "The Festival of the Great Rachel is to begin!"

Rachel struggled to her feet. Steven hugged his knees tighter, and Jak sat with a wary look in his eyes.

Up the street from them, an orange glow flared and soon a procession of villagers came into view. Carrying torches, the men and women walked slowly in rows of three across. Moving somberly, they appeared to be on their way to a funeral rather than a festival. Glowering eyes matched the flames of the torches.

"Uh, I don't like this …" Rachel found Steven's hand and squeezed it. Trembling, the boy now stood on her right. Jak moved to her left and gripped her other hand.

A low hum started from the procession and soon turned into a chant.

"Babysitter Rachel," called Suzella, hurrying from the side of the building. "Come, all is ready!" Her cheeks were flushed and a look of excitement covered her face.

Courtney rolled to a sitting position and tried to clear her head. Beside her, Jakey lay on his stomach, staring at her with wide, frightened eyes. There were voices nearby and neither sounded very friendly. Blinking, Courtney looked around and saw they were in the entrance to a large cave of orange rock. A narrow stream of water about a foot wide flowed to their left. Flowing from under the cave's wall, the stream ran out of the entrance and into a jumble of rock before falling over what looked to be a cliff.

Moving to the stream, Courtney splashed water on her face as Jakey just watched.

"You!" screeched an angry voice from deeper inside the cave. "It was you who sent me here! I'll sue you so bad you'll never recover! You'll see!"

"Quiet, woman!" roared the frightful voice of a man.

Courtney immediately retreated from the stream and lay down next to Jakey. Putting an arm around her brother's back, she whispered. "It'll be okay. We're together." Her voice shook.

The voices were approaching from the back of the cave. The tall man with white hair appeared from the murk. At his side was a small, old woman wearing a dirty, ragged skirt and blouse. Neither seemed happy with the other.

"I'll not be quiet! I have my rights!"

"Silence!" snapped the man. "I could have killed you, but I didn't. I sent you to my home instead, so be grateful, you hag!"

They paused in front of the children and faced each other with angry glares.

"Grateful? Listen, whoever, or whatever you are, I may be old and I may be alone, but I do know some good lawyers!"

The man laughed harshly. "I'm sure you noticed. This is not Earth, woman. I took you from your miserable life and brought you here to mine. Now you will either be my servant, or my wife. You decide."

"What!" The woman looked ready to slap him.

"Settle your fears, old hag. I want you as a servant or wife in public only. In my home you are nothing more than my slave. And as such, you are charged to take care of these children." Now he gestured to Courtney and Jakey. "Take them in and bathe them. I want them cleaned and dressed in new clothes before I return. You will find the clothes for the girl in the back room to the left. The boy … give him one of my shirts. And when I return, we will be traveling a long way." The old woman's eyes nearly popped out of her head as she listened. The man spoke as if used to having his orders obeyed and he allowed no time for questions. "On this journey you can either be my wife on a trip with our grandchildren, or you can be my servant watching my grandchildren. Again, I give you choice in the matter." Finished, he stared at her. "If you fail to choose or do not obey, you will regret it."

The woman was so upset she could hardly speak. "I-I hate children!" she finally croaked. "I detest their kind!"

"I'm sure the feeling will be mutual. Heed my words, woman. If I get back and the children are not ready as I commanded, I will end up killing you as I should have done before!" Reading her thoughts, the man smiled nastily. "Don't think of it. You lived here for two weeks, woman. You ate my food and took my lodgings. Surely by now you know escape is impossible. You are on a mountain with only one way off and only I know it! Wild animals and falls of great heights await you if you try fleeing." Turning to the children, he retained his nasty smile. "That goes for you two as well." Then he started toward them.

Courtney tried to get up and flee, but her legs wouldn't work properly. Jakey also struggled to rise.

The man grabbed Jakey by the back of his shirt and yanked him to a standing position, twisting the shirt until it bunched just under his arms. With Courtney, he took her by the arm and gently got her to her feet.

"Children, I want you dressed and ready for my return. Remember, I am to be your grandfather."

"You're a jerkface!" Jakey growled.

His mouth tightening, the man lifted the boy so his feet dangled from the ground. "Little boys are so useless," he hissed.

"Jakey, no!" cried Courtney. She grabbed the man's hand. "He's just confused, that's all. Let him calm down."

The man's face softened as he looked down at her. "We shall see." Lowering Jakey, he proceeded to walk the children to the woman. He threw Jakey at her feet before placing Courtney in front of him. His hands grabbed her shoulders and squeezed. "Do your duty well, woman," he said gruffly. "I take no pleasure in killing." The man's eyes, shaded by the confines of the cave, suddenly sparked and flashed a brilliant red. "Or do I?" Releasing Courtney, he turned away. He was still chuckling as he left the cave.

When he had gone, the woman barked out what sounded like a curse.

"Watch your language!" Courtney demanded, helping Jakey to his feet and smoothing out his shirt.

"Shut your mouth, girl!" snapped the woman. "You have no idea what I've gone through in the past weeks!"

Wiping his nose, Jakey stared at her. "Who are you?"

"None of your business!" snapped the woman. She threw up her hands. "Besides, the question should be, where am I? Because this is certainly not Florida!"

"Florida," gasped Courtney. "That's where we're from!"

"Well, you're not there now!" The woman wrung her hands bitterly. "Two weeks ago … I had just gotten back from an author's convention in Pittsburgh and was getting in my car at the airport, when bam!" She smacked her hands together. "I turned around and saw that … that wicked man … that's all I remember. Next thing I know, I wake up in this dump!"

"I know who you are!" cried Courtney. "You're the woman who vanished! Your car was found near our house. I saw your picture in the paper!"

The woman stared at her. "What do you know?" she said after a moment. "Somebody actually cared enough to write a story about my disappearance." A bright eagerness came to her face as she peered intently at Courtney. "Tell me, did they mention my book?"

"Book?"

"You know, the book I wrote!"

Courtney shook her head. "No, I-I don't think so."

Turning from Courtney in disgust, the woman banged both fists on her thighs. "I spent half my savings and years of my life writing … and for what? Not one agent gives me the time of day, and I finally find publishers on my own. What happens next?" She waved both hands in the air. "My publishers only give me access to some stupid convention that *I* had to pay for! That's all I got! And then nobody cared about my book, even when I'm gone!" She whirled back to the kids. "I'm the only person who ever bought my book, did you know that? My stupid publisher, all they want is my money. That's all anybody cares about!"

Courtney and Jakey exchanged looks. Clearly this woman was a little crazy.

"We're, um, sorry." Courtney tried lifting a hand to comfort the woman.

"Get away from me, girl!" The woman glared at her and then at Jakey. "You heard the man. I, who should be a celebrated author, have to bathe you two scrawny brats! Two scrawny brats with no manners!"

"We do have manners!" Courtney cried. "It's you who's being rude!"

"Did you read my book, girl?" demanded the woman. "Huh? You don't even know the title! Young people are all the same today. Rude know-it-alls who spend all their time playing stupid video games instead of reading." She jabbed a finger in Courtney's stomach. "That's you, isn't it, girl?"

Crying out, Courtney jumped back.

"Leave my sister alone!" Jakey stepped toward the woman and waved a fist at her.

"Tell your brother to get away before I take him over my knee and really teach him the meaning of manners."

Courtney grabbed Jakey and pulled him back. "We don't want to hurt you, really."

"As if you could," snorted the woman. "The public did that already by ignoring me! Years of my life—my soul written down on paper—and not one person cares." Her face fell. "Come, follow me. I'll show you where to wash."

The cave proved much deeper than it first appeared. At first it grew darker and then much lighter. The light was provided by strange glowing rocks tied to the ends of sticks that were stuck in the walls like lines of torches.

"Magic," snorted the woman when Courtney asked about them. Somehow Courtney didn't doubt her.

Leading the way down a long passage over eight feet high and four feet wide, the woman walked briskly and pointed to various openings on the sides.

"Eating room … bedroom … library … oh, some other room …"

These openings were dark so the children could not see inside to tell if the woman was making it all up or not.

Finally they stopped outside an opening on the right. Ducking her head into the room, the woman clapped her hands, and immediately light filled the space. Stepping back out, she nodded her head. "There it is."

Amazed, Courtney and Jakey stared past the woman. Steam wafted from a large pool of water lined with smooth stone and about the size and shape of their pool at home. Beyond this pool, near the back wall, a fast-moving stream gurgled noisily. Fresh towels were laid out on a rack next to the heated pool. Next to the towels sat a wooden bowl holding a hunk of Ivory soap.

More stones tied to sticks lined the wall and provided the eerie light. Reflecting off the water, the light sparkled off the cavern ceiling.

"Well?" sniffed the woman. "Let's get going!"

Courtney pushed Jakey in through the opening and then turned on the woman, blocking her way in. "We can bathe ourselves."

"Suit yourself. I have no wish to wash brats like you." She turned her back and started back up the corridor. "When you're done, I'll have the clothes waiting in the room across from you. If you need to use the bathroom, that's what the stream is for in the back. Now, if you have any questions, don't bother. I'll be down the hall on the left in the drinking room." She stopped and turned. For the first time since meeting her, the children saw the woman grin. "Our host enjoys Jack Daniels as much as he does Ivory soap."

Courtney called after her. "Wait—what is this place?"

Turning, the woman cackled. "I used to think this was Paradise and that I was dead. Now I think it is the opposite and we're all dead!" Still cackling, she went to find a much needed drink.

Chapter Twenty-Three

Walking across the crude stage of logs, set up just in front of the entrance to the village warehouse, Rachel nodded nervously at the crowd standing in front, below her. Nobody smiled or nodded back. Her gaze fell onto her feet, still in their mud slippers. At her side, Steven and Jak pressed close to her and eyed the proceedings anxiously. Her mouth tightened.

Now what am I supposed to do?

Everyone, especially Suzella, acted as if Rachel was in control and knew exactly what she was doing … Swallowing, she lifted her gaze.

A small table covered in fur sat in the middle of the stage. On top of the fur lay a long, sharp knife and two ceramic bowls. Off the stage and to her left, a giant pot full of water sat over a large bonfire. The pot was the size of three bathtubs and looked to be the type witches in the stories would stand over, making their brew. Torches from each corner of the stage bathed the area with heat and flickering light. The villagers below the stage kept hold of their torches and watched with brooding faces.

Why do I get the impression they're looking at me like I'm Dr. Frankenstein and about to create a monster? Sweat dripped from Rachel's face and the urge to flee had to be quelled. Doom seemed to rise with the smoke of the torches.

Glancing again at the crowd, she tried to swallow, but her throat had turned to sandpaper. Hostile faces stared back without wavering. Only the village chief and Suzella, both standing by the table on the stage, were grinning.

Urslaf boomed a greeting. "Welcome, Babysitter Rachel! We have done what you asked and now ask to bear witness to the ritual!" He stretched out his hands and backed away from the table. "Which would you consume first?'

Eyeing him, Rachel swallowed. *Consume? First? What?* Both bowls were empty.

Still smiling, Suzella sidled up to her. "How do you wish to perform the ritual?" she asked from the side of her mouth. Seeing Rachel's indecision, she quickly added, "If you wish, I could do the honors."

Rachel nodded dumbly. "Uh, sure. I, uh, guess you, uh, can, um, start."

"Very well …" Suzella bowed low to Rachel and then turned to the crowd. "The great Wizard Babysitter Rachel has deemed me worthy to perform the first cut for her!" A wild look came to the girl's eyes as many gasps of horror swept through the crowd.

"What?" sputtered Rachel.

Steven backed behind her, holding on to her tattered dress like a safety line. Suzella ignored him and instead grabbed Jak by the arm, yanking him roughly from Rachel. She dragged him to the table. "Jak will be the first sacrifice!" she shouted.

"No!" cried out some of the villagers. These were quickly hushed.

Rachel watched in confusion. "What are you doing? What sacrifice?" Her voice was no louder than a whisper.

"As you command!" Suzella threw the boy roughly against the table and grabbed the back of his neck, shoving his chest onto the flat board. The boy's eyes found Rachel. Wide with terror, they begged her to do something. His legs kicked wildly but without effect. Suzella had grabbed the knife and raised it for all to see. Her eyes flashed madly. "In order to be consumed by—"

All awkward fear and indecision left Rachel. "Are you completely mad!" she cried as she rushed at the girl. "Let go of him!"

"Oh, do you wish to make the cut?" Confused, Suzella held the knife out to Rachel and tried to bow. "I shall still hold him—"

"Careful with that, you idiot! You can hurt somebody!" Rachel grabbed the knife from Suzella and dropped it on the stage, where it fell with a clunk. "Now let go of him!"

"Wh-what?" Suzella stammered. She stared at her in bewilderment. "You're a wizard, a babysitter. You're supposed to cut the boy and drink his blood and eat his heart—so you gain his pow—"

Rachel slapped her across the face and wrenched her hand from Jak's neck. "What is wrong with you?" she screamed. "Are you completely crazy? Get away from him!"

Suzella stumbled back from her, shocked.

Urslaf, his face very worried, fell on his knees and crawled to Rachel. "What is it, great wizard? Do you wish to boil the boys alive before consuming them? Tell me your wish!"

"NO!" roared Rachel, her face burning red in the light of the fire. She turned to the crowd. "If one of you sickos tries to lay a hand on one of these boys, I will tear out your eyes! Do you hear me?" All fear turned into fury. She meant what she'd said.

Then a terrible thought struck her. *Is that why there are no children here? Did the village kill them all?* She glared at the shocked villagers. "Any person who harms a child is sick!"

Her face white, Suzella reached out to her. "But you're a babysitter … I thought you were the wizard who ate children for their power …"

Rachel whirled on her with a snarl. Crying out, the blond girl shrank back. "I said I'm a babysitter, don't you get it?" Rachel shouted at her. "My job is to *protect* children, not hurt them, you, you *idiot*! I would never hurt a child, understand me? Never!" She moved to stand beside Jak and Steven. "And neither will you!" She took a deep breath, oblivious to the sweat pouring off her. "When you said you were giving me Jak, I thought it was some mistake. But no more! He's mine to take care of now! You're not going near him and neither is anybody else!" Fists clenched and chest heaving, Rachel glared at Suzella and then out into the crowd.

At first there was shocked silence. Then all at once a woman cried out, "Hail the babysitter! She protects children from the wizards!"

Suddenly the entire crowd erupted in cheers. Women openly wept and men shouted her name.

"Never … never have I seen such a glorious sight," whispered Urslaf hoarsely, pressing his forehead to the stage in a bow to Rachel.

Her anger retreated to perplexity. "Uh, what … uh, what's going on now?"

Urslaf rose with a smile. "My dear babysitter, you are the answer to our prayers."

A semblance of order was brought when Urslaf raised both hands as he stood beside Rachel. "People of Durnwirk, listen to your chief! We are truly honored on this night! A great guest is in our midst! She is not a wizard—a terrible being who eats the young." He paused as boos and hisses rose from the crowd. "But," he continued, "much better, she is a babysitter!" Grabbing Rachel's wrist, he lifted it up as cheers ascended from the villagers like roars from happy lions. "Let us honor the one who dares to defy the wizards by protecting the children! Let us bring out a great feast! And bring the children! Let them see this wonder of wonders! Then they will tell their children of this night—the night the babysitter came to visit!"

Drained, exhausted, and with her heart still pumping like mad, Rachel sank to the edge of the stage in utter confusion. Around her, the men and women had abandoned their grim looks and readied for a celebration. The large pot had been moved by six strong men and the fire built up again. The torches once carried in procession now hung around the streets, making the village light up like a Christmas tree. Several women were bringing pots of food from their homes. Over the large fire, an entire cow was placed on a spit. Soon the smells of breads, meats, and pastries took over the smell of manure and sweat.

Rachel's stomach growled. She hadn't eaten anything since breakfast … back in Florida.

Suddenly there came laughter and the shouts of children. They came in all ages and sizes—some shyly and others with rambunctious abandon. Several ran up to the stage where Rachel sat and bowed. She soon saw mothers pushing them to do so. A young girl shyly offered a handful of flowers. Then Rachel's face grew red. Young men about her age had grouped together and were giving her furtive looks. Girls her age also eyed her curiously … some even jealously.

A group of men gathered on the stage behind Rachel and carried drums and a lute. Soon lively music added to the festivities.

Steven sat next to Rachel and laid his head on her lap. Frightened and confused, he watched her with wide eyes. But soon the excitement proved too catching. Jak suddenly appeared at the front of the stage and grabbed Steven's leg, pulling him down. Behind him a group of young boys and girls beckoned.

A smaller fire was set up in the space where the hostile crowd had recently stood. In a complete switch in atmosphere, a lively dance broke out around the fire. Laughter and gaiety filled the air.

"Wait—" Rachel began, as Steven started off with Jak. He stared shyly at the children. "Steven …" Then she sighed. *What the heck?* She had no energy left. "Be careful," she finished lamely as the children ran off to join the dancing. This consisted mostly of running and skipping in a circle while laughing.

Groaning, Rachel carefully swung off the stage. As she did so, she caught sight of Suzella. The young woman glared balefully at her before jumping from the side of the stage and disappearing into the darkness.

Biting her lip, Rachel turned to the celebration. But just as the feasting began, a loud rumbling rose from the dark, sounding like thunder.

"Now what?" Rachel muttered.

Men ran from the main road. "Marcal has returned!" shouted one of them.

Immediately, the music died and the children started to melt away in the shadows. Rachel soon saw why.

Three large horses charged into the firelight and pulled up sharply.

"What is this!" roared a man from his giant horse. The animal neighed shrilly as if asking the same question. Just in case nobody heard, the man roared again. "What is this!" His face was mostly hidden by shadow and his voice held iron.

"Marcal," muttered Urslaf, stepping nervously from where he'd begun basting the cow. "We are so happy to see you." He didn't sound very happy.

The man guided his mount to stand in front of the chief. The glow of flames caused his face to appear murderous. A small tight beard the color of coal stuck sharply from his chin. His thin mustache quivered as his blazing eyes burned across all the villagers still in sight. "Are you mad!" he bellowed. "You dare feast for a wizard who eats your children?"

"Marcal," cried the chief loudly, gathering courage. "Calm yourself. We don't have a wizard in our presence."

"What!" roared Marcal.

"We have a babysitter!" the mayor announced grandly.

Marcal's anger turned to confusion. "A what?" he asked.

The chief beamed. "A babysitter—a protector of children!" he said with a flourish. "Marcal, it is a miracle! She only tested us, but would tear out the throat of any who harmed children. Finally, someone to stand up to the wizards! Rachel the Babysitter, come! Come meet our village warrior, Marcal the Fierce!"

Rachel hesitantly moved to the chief's side but was too scared to meet the fiery gaze of the man on horseback. He appeared to be in his early thirties, but standing in front of him felt like standing in front of an angry principal. Jak and Steven appeared at her side, but hid behind her.

Seeing her and the boys, the man's fierce look softened slightly. Hopping off his horse, he clapped the chief on the shoulder. "Perhaps I judged you wrongly, Urslaf. My apologies."

"Your warrior's heart is always in the right place, Marcal. No apology is necessary."

"Perhaps … Now let me meet this … babysitter in private."

"You may have the use of my tent. We have it set up by the fields for the babysitter … We fear our houses are not worthy enough for a babysitter." He then clapped his hands, visibly relieved to have the trouble averted. "But first we eat! Go put your horse up and you may join us. Let us celebrate this night."

Marcal grunted. "I will do so. We caught a prisoner in the woods and will take care of him first."

Several villagers gasped at hearing the news.

"Is he dangerous?" the chief asked nervously.

"Not at all—just a lost fool. Lineus and Meri will put him in the cell." He looked down at Jak. "Boy, your sister has returned with darrow root. Go help her and she'll give you some. She will want to see that you remain in one piece."

Grinning, the boy ran past him into the dark.

Marcal held up his hand when Rachel made a grab for him.

"I heard you were a wizard here to consume that boy …" His voice grew sharp like a sword. "It is good that he lives and this is not true. Otherwise, I would cut out your throat." He bowed stiffly. "It's a pleasure to meet you, Rachel. I will see you in the tent before long." Turning, he swung himself back up onto the horse. Without glancing back, he moved into the dark shadows.

"Marcal is our best fighter, but a stranger to these parts, Rachel," Urslaf said, chuckling nervously. "You must not hold his tongue against him. He came from the south and has seen much darkness, no doubt. That is where the wizards rule."

Steven squeezed her hand and Rachel nodded. "I-I can't wait to talk to him," she managed to choke out.

With her stomach growling after she'd refused to eat the strange food pressed on her, Rachel stumbled to the large rectangular tent indicated as hers for the night. Set up behind the chief's house, the tent resembled something from a small circus and was roughly the size of Lisa and Steven's living room. Thinking about Lisa and the living room made Rachel's stomach lurch. It had hurt all night, which was one reason why she didn't eat the spicy stew pressed on her. Even though starving, her nerves were too shot to think about eating.

Good thing, or I might throw up on the chief's best tent. He seemed awfully proud of it when he spoke about her using it. Only guests of high honor were allowed inside.

Ducking her head, she entered a roomy area lit by a fat wax candle resting on a table that was placed in the center. Beds of furs piled high and covered with blankets were set up on the earthen floor on three sides around the table. The night air had cooled considerably and Rachel was glad to see the blankets. She was also pleased to see that her purse and Steven's ripstick were on the ground under the table. A rope hung from the top of one end of the tent to the other and held a fur blanket that could be pulled out to partition the tent into different rooms. This allowed her to have privacy for her bed.

Bed, that's what I need … But first she had to be a babysitter.

Moving aside, she allowed Steven to drag himself in. Grabbing the exhausted boy to keep him from falling, she patted his back. "Don't sleep yet. You still have to brush your teeth and wash your face."

Blinking through heavy-lidded eyes, the boy looked up at her in confusion. "Brush my teeth? Wash? With what?"

"Uh, maybe just say your prayers and ask for clean teeth."

Then Jak slipped inside behind Steven. In his hands were two wooden bowls. One held water and the other held three plastic toothbrushes and a large dollop of green toothpaste.

Rachel could only stare. "What the … ?" Too tired and confused to care where Jak had found the stuff, she waved at the boys to hurry and clean up. "Maybe this is only a dream …" Inside, though, she felt a surge of hope. The toothbrushes were definitely modern and looked so out of place in the otherwise primitive world. Perhaps it was just a dream …

His mouth smelling freshly of mint, Steven undressed and fell onto the nearest bed, in his boxer shorts. Rachel piled his dirty clothes in the corner and knelt at his side. She ignored the dirt smudged on his arms and face. "I'll see about getting clean clothes for you in the morning," she mumbled. "You have a good night and don't worry … I'll be here when you wake up."

"'Night, Rachel," the boy murmured back.

"Goodnight, Steven."

The night air had grown cold, and she made sure to tuck him under a thick blanket. Before she finished, the boy was fast asleep. In the next bed, Jak also snored. He had pulled off his shirt, but kept his pants on. Going to him, Rachel covered her nose from his dirty stench. She gasped. On his small back, covered in dirt, were very visible bruises spread over his shoulders and lower back … some were fresh. Laying a blanket over him, she tried hard to keep her anger at bay. Marcal would be coming soon and he'd better have some answers.

Taking a seat on the floor by the table, she waited … Her eyes struggled to stay open.

Rachel woke with a start.

"Hush, Rachel," soothed a voice just over her face. "The boys sleep."

Looking up, she saw Marcal's dark beard nearly touching her nose.

"We need to talk," the warrior said grimly. "Now."

"Wh-what time is it?"

Backing away, the warrior sat facing her. "Later than you think, probably. Tell me of your presence. Why are you here?" Marcal flicked his gaze to Steven's bed. "And who is he?" He eyed Rachel with more curiosity than hostility.

Sitting up, Rachel rubbed her eyes free of any tiredness. "Uh, where is here?"

"Not your home, I think. You're from Earth, aren't you?"

Now wide awake, Rachel gasped. "You mean, this isn't …" She couldn't finish.

"I'm beginning to understand," murmured Marcal, rubbing his beard. "I feared you were a wizard here to feast upon a boy. Now I think you are somebody protecting the boy from such a thing."

Rachel swallowed and stared at Marcal in undisguised horror. "Wh-who would ever do such a—"

Marcal cut her off. "Quick, just tell me how you ended up in this place. Leave nothing out."

Taking a deep breath, Rachel left a lot out. Mostly she told of Jane Lovington slowly gaining their trust and then revealing herself to be some wizard, Isabella. Telling of how Isabella took the children and brought them to the pool, Rachel ended by saying how she had jumped in after the wizard and must have managed to pull Steven away. "But Lisa … Isabella kept hold of her … I have to find her."

Marcal listened to everything intently. His eyes only widened considerably when hearing the name Isabella. Now the warrior's eyes narrowed. "Tell me. Was it the boy Isabella wanted more, or the girl?"

"I don't know … I …" Rachel swallowed. "Uh, actually, it could have been Steven. She, she wasn't the only one trying to take him, I think." Quickly she told about Pastor Smith and Ms. Proom and about Red the janitor who posed as a bum.

As if hearing bad news he had already known, Marcal dropped his head. "Bring in the prisoner!" he called loudly.

The flap opened and the cheerful face of a young man around Rachel's age ducked in. "Are you sure? He's whining about needing a 'bathroom'—like we have a room for baths here!"

"Bring him!" growled Marcal.

The face disappeared. Moments later, Jason Richardson was shoved into the tent. He wore jeans, a polo shirt, and an angry look.

"Rachel!" he cried in shock when seeing her. He stumbled toward her and fell to his knees. Both his arms were bound behind him and dirt smudged his face. "What's going on?" he demanded angrily.

She could only stare back in amazement. "Jason?" she finally said.

Jason glared at her. "Yes, it's me! What happened? Where are we and who are these crazy people?"

"So you do know each other," Marcal said coolly. He gave a small grin. "We found this fool wandering the woods shouting your name like he wished to be eaten by the Wolves of Nyanhelm. Good thing for him we found him before the wolves and kept him alive. Lineus, cut him free."

The young man went behind Jason and pulled a knife from his belt. With a swift jerk, he slashed the rope binding Jason's hands. Then he brushed back a strand of foppish hair that hung over his forehead. He grinned.

"We haven't properly met," he said cheerfully. "I'm Lineus." He bowed to Rachel.

"Jerk," muttered Jason, wincing as blood started flowing into his hands.

Lineus winked at Rachel. "Tell me that he's of no significance to you, and you shall make me a happy man." He grinned rakishly. "Otherwise, I may bind him up again and toss him to the wolves."

Blushing, Rachel ducked her head.

"Just try it, buddy," growled Jason, rubbing his hands. "Just tell us what's going on!" He moved to sit by Rachel, throwing a glare at Lineus.

Unconcerned, Lineus sat by Marcal and yawned, stretching out his booted feet before him. Slightly built, he wore dark trousers, a faded white shirt, and a brown waistcoat. A knife was belted at his side. Despite his boldness, Rachel couldn't help but sneak another look at him. Thick hair the color of cinnamon hung loosely about his head. His square face was clean shaven. A small narrow nose and a dimple in his chin gave him a friendly appearance. Over his wide smile, his bright green eyes met hers. Catching Rachel's look, he winked again. Friendly and very good looking.

"Yes," sputtered Rachel, quickly ducking her head. "What is happening?"

"It would seem," Marcal said slowly, "that you are a babysitter protecting a boy from the dark wizards … This could only mean one thing." He sighed heavily and Rachel and Jason both looked at the man, dumbfounded. "As you probably guessed, you are in a different world. This is Panterra—a complex world full of dark magic and dark hearts. Here we are ruled by wizards and madmen." He grinned without humor. "And it would seem that you hold the key to it all." He nodded in the direction of Steven.

"I think you better explain," Jason said, losing his glare. "This isn't making sense."

"Sit back and listen," growled Marcal. "No more interruptions."

Chapter Twenty-Four

Lisa's cell door squeaked open. Wiping her eyes, the young girl sat up on the putrid bed of rotting hay. All around her was darkness, and only the smell of mold and urine had accompanied her for the last several hours. Now she blinked as the bright glare of a torch shone upon her.

"You are comfortable, dear?" Isabella's voice was mocking, but managed to hold a hint of kindness. "Forgive me for leaving you alone for so long. I've come to make peace and to tell you of your future."

"I want to go home." Lisa sat up straighter and masked all her fear and doubt. Her freckles seem to glow in the light.

"For now, dear, you are home. Your home is my fortress, soon to be the palace that rules Panterra!"

"You're crazy."

"Am I?" Isabella laughed. "Perhaps that is true, because I am offering you peace. I wish for you to be my apprentice and to stand at my side. That is why I tell you only the truth. Only fools lie to children and expect them to listen."

"What?"

"Save your breath, Lisa. Use your ears and listen first. Then make your judgment of what I really am."

Rudolph appeared at the cave's entrance and looked in. A dark frown crossed his face as only the loud snores of the old woman could be heard. The sharp smell of liquor permeated the air. "The children," he growled.

Moving swiftly down the corridor, he was relieved to hear Courtney's voice in the last room on the left … *her* room. For a moment, it was a different voice and a different girl. His eyes lighting up a shining blue, he rushed to the entrance.

Courtney sat on a bed next to Jakey. She had her arm around the boy's shoulder and was telling him a fairy tale. Both saw Rudolph at once and grew very still.

"Well," coughed the man, his blue eyes growing dull. "I see you are at least wearing the proper clothes."

Jakey shrugged uncomfortably in the shirt much too big for him that ended down past his calves. Only when Courtney let him wear his other clothes underneath had he agreed to put it on. Courtney, though, looked dainty in a long, soft, blue dress with a high neckline.

Holding her head high, she stared up at Rudolph. "What do you want with us?"

"Watch your tone," Rudolph said gruffly. "I may seem like the enemy, but in reality I am the only friend you have in this world."

"What do you mean 'this world'?"

"Hush and listen." Stepping into the room, Rudolph found a seat on a large easy chair like those usually found in living rooms of modern Earth. "Let me tell you both a bedtime story …"

Marcal began speaking in a low voice. "Long ago, when Earth was yet to be settled by mighty nations, it was a land of scattered tribes and wandering hunters. Among these tribes was a group of hunters who feared extinction above all else. Other tribes had attacked it and killed many of their men and stolen away their women and children."

"Only one solution remained for this tribe if they wanted to survive," Isabella said, a thrill catching in her voice. "They had to teach the surrounding tribes a lesson—one that none would dare forget!"

Rudolph sighed. "Only through fear could they be protected. So they came upon this village of strangers and, well … No males remained alive when the hunters were done with their work."

"That night, the hunters had a great feast on the remains of the village." Marcal's voice dropped to a hush. "From the ashes of the main lodge of the destroyed village, there rose a dark spirit."

Rachel shivered and unconsciously drew closer to Jason.

"This is just a story," mumbled Jason.

"Story or not, the spirit laughed at the hunters and thanked them for doing its job—it wanted to turn their hearts black and it succeeded. Their wickedness would be rewarded. The hunters were all to die and fall in the depths of eternal fire. Immediately, the hunters fell on their knees and pleaded for mercy."

The torch flared by Isabella's face. "That is when the ground split open and a pool of water formed in the midst of the hunters. They were given the choice—they could die as they stood, or they could enter the water into a new world and have one more chance at saving their cursed souls."

"Of course the hunters chose the new world," Rudolph said, wiping his cheek. He gave Courtney and Jakey a twisted smile. "Little did they know, it was a curse worse than death where they entered. You see, when the first hunter entered the water, he disappeared. Soon others followed until all were gone, dragging the remaining village females with them … and brought here to this world. To Panterra."

"In Panterra, the tribe was frightened and made sure to stick close together. Nothing terrible happened to them. This new world was full of animals to eat, and soon they found crops to plant. Centuries passed, and the tribe grew and spread out. New tribes formed. All the while, the dark spirit watched and meddled. Urged by the spirit, the new tribes developed the desire to dominate and to rule the others. Tribes began battling each other, and from these conflicts, kingdoms were formed. Soon kingdoms battled each other, each seeking to gain the dark spirit's favor and rule Panterra. War became constant, and to this day there is little peace in Panterra. Doubt it if you want, boy," growled Marcal when Jason audibly scoffed.

"What about the wizards?" Rachel asked. "Where did they come from?"

"The wizards … The wizards sprang up about the same time as the kings did." Marcal spat. "When tribes managed to conquer other tribes, men started proclaiming themselves as kings. Each was said to have been chosen by the dark spirit … of course, there can only be one king of Panterra, so the kings battled each other ferociously. Seeking advantage over their enemies, kingdoms were in constant search for new weapons. Riches were offered in return for new ways to kill. Longbows, catapults, and other tools of death were developed. Then one day, a poor man went so far as to dedicate his life to the dark spirit. He begged for power to show his king and gain riches … and the dark spirit listened. This man became the first wizard. At the time, there were many kingdoms, but this man joined his king and quickly brought destruction to the surrounding kingdoms. Terrible storms were conjured from blue skies. Fires blasted from his finger. This first wizard's name was Aerrius, and his name spread throughout the land. Quickly, other men and then women sought the same power and went on to devote their lives to the spirit. Some were also granted powers. Many, though, were deemed unworthy and died horrible deaths. Only the most dedicated to the dark spirit became true wizards. This started the Wizard Wars. Soon every king sought his own wizard armies. To make this tale short, wars and battles raged until only two kingdoms were left standing. The others were assimilated or destroyed. And the wizards … most of these also perished. Finally, when all settled, only those two kingdoms and only two great wizards remained. There are some others who call themselves wizards and possess magic, but they are nothing compared to the wizards Isabella and Borbu."

Rachel stirred. "Borbu? Who is that?"

"By your description," Marcal said to her, "I would say he's the man you called Pastor Smith. He resembles a fool, but be warned. He's wily as a fox and as cunning as a wolf. King Herman, ruler of the Eastern Kingdom, is said to rule through Borbu. And yet nobody is a match for Isabella … She is the mightiest of all wizards."

Jason snorted. "Who's really just a housekeeper?"

"More like a death-keeper," Marcal said softly. "Isabella worked for King Gretz the Sixth, of the West … until the king was poisoned and died in his own bed. Of course the East was blamed, but don't rule out Isabella. Her ambition is what drives her—that and the thirst for power."

Rachel shuddered. That woman had done her cooking and laundry for two weeks.

"I don't get it," Jason cut in. "How come you all speak English in this so-called new land?"

Marcal nodded at him. "Ah, now you are thinking, boy. The first wizard managed to lure the dark spirit into giving up the power of water travel—using water, he was able to bridge the gap between the two worlds and actually return to Earth. Nobody knows much of this Aerrius, but some say Earth is his native home and he was handpicked by the dark spirit to come to Panterra. No matter, other wizards picked up on this gift and used it. King Gretz the First used this travel the wisest. Knowing the wars of Panterra were not likely to end, he sent all his children and the children of his family to Earth to hide and live in peace. At the same time, he wanted at least one heir to return and rule a peaceful Panterra when the wars ended. For this to happen, he knew his subjects had to understand and relate to his children living on Earth. Sending advisors with the children, he started bringing back the language and customs of the Earth world he had found."

"Right …" Jason shook his head in disbelief.

That was when Lineus tossed him a thick book.

Catching it in the chest, Jason glared, but then gasped in shock. It was a battered copy of an English grammar book from the 1980s.

"I have many more like it," Lineus said with a grin.

Isabella grinned at Lisa's reaction. "That is right, dear. Panterra people have been infiltrating Earth—specifically America—for generations. They are called outliers. They lie outside of Panterra and are ready to help their world when needed. True, many forget their old lives and stay on Earth as fools. But there are outliers all over that we keep in contact with. King Gretz the First was very wise. By the time he passed on, his eldest son on Earth was ready to take over. In your world he taught English at a university. When he returned here, it was he who helped establish schools in all the villages to teach the new language."

"So, children, you see why I can speak your language and understand your customs." Rudolph sighed and leaned back in the comfortable chair. "I particularly enjoy the pleasures your world offers."

"Why not bring back other things from Earth?" Rachel wanted to know. "I mean, just English books, soap, and toothpaste sounds pretty dumb."

"The dark spirit will not allow it. Many wizards tried and died in the attempt. Most Earth technology will not work here—only small items do not immediately combust when they enter the world. You see, Panterra is still ruled by the dark spirit … and there is only one way to end its rule." Marcal flicked his eyes to where Steven lay sound asleep.

Rachel swallowed and had a terrible ominous feeling. "How?" she asked hoarsely.

Marcal told her. "Ten years ago, the dark spirit granted every wizard a prophecy—a prophecy that promises to free Panterra and rid it of its curse for good. The dark spirit proclaimed that whoever sacrifices the boy of innocent blood to it would then inherit all its powers and become the new ultimate ruler of Panterra. That, so the prophecy states, is when this world will find peace."

Rachel looked horrified. "That's-that's crazy!"

"Is it? You saw how this village acted when you first came. You can see that the murder of children is very possible here."

"How could that happen?" Rachel asked. "How?"

Rudolph scratched his leg and stared at the floor.

"Children are viewed differently here," he said gravely. "Shortly after the prophecy, a decree went out in both kingdoms. It was the first agreement the kingdoms had for years, and it even stopped the war." He laughed sardonically. "It is rather strange how men create what is right and what is wrong … Right reflects what they want to do at the time, and wrong becomes what is not so desirable. So, in this decree, nobody was a true person until the age of twelve. On that special day, there would be a naming day to celebrate the arrival to personhood. This means until a child lives to twelve, that child is not considered a human. He or she could be treated as an animal without a soul. So if a child died before their naming day … so be it. It is like a cow dying."

"Oh, don't look like that, my dear." Isabella smiled. "The rule has merit. Without proper medicine here, children die all the time. The rule made their passing more natural and less painful for the parents. In this land, on their true naming day, a child is well celebrated."

"They did this so wizards could start killing children in their search for the right boy," Marcal said flatly. "It was the darkest of dark times, and that darkness has yet to pass."

"That's, that's awful!" Rachel hugged her knees. "Horrible!"

"Is it?" Marcal asked, staring at her.

"Yes!" Rachel cried.

Marcal laughed harshly. "You say that as if you mean it. Look at your own world, Rachel. Earth, yes, I know of the place. I've been there many times. In your own land, Rachel, babies are snuffed out from the womb by their own mothers. Does this spark terror in your land? No, not at all! The only outrage comes when this right is questioned! Where you come from, people fight for the right to kill babies in the same manner, only at least here we give all children the chance at life."

Jason glared at Marcal. "Hey, back off! It's not all like that!"

Marcal glared back. "Then the same is true here. It is easy to judge what you do not understand as being wrong … Perhaps it would be best to judge your own beliefs and leave others' alone. Here, only wizards want to kill children, and even then very few follow this practice … but, as you saw today, some do embrace it. There is a belief that if a wizard eats the heart of a child, that wizard gains the child's strength. This is a fallacy held by the small wizards, curse them. Isabella and Borbu know better. They only have an appetite for one child …" He again flicked a look in Steven's direction. "In any case, the fear of wizards eating children has never slackened. Most of the people hide their children well when they believe a wizard is near."

Rachel put both hands to her head. "So, so they think Steven is the … one—the one who will grant them power?"

Marcal nodded gravely. "Borbu and Isabella will only go after the child they feel will lead them to power. You see, after the prophecy, an uneasy truce formed between the East and the West kingdoms. People here are tired of the wars and killing … the prophecy offers a way to find peace and a new ruler of Panterra with only one more death … the death of a single boy. Both kingdoms have left it to their wizards to find this child. After years of searching, Isabella and Borbu found nothing." He sighed. "Four years ago, they came together and begged the dark spirit for a sign of where to look. The dark spirit listened and told them the boy dwelled on Earth and possessed a great power only a wizard could understand. Isabella vanished from this land. Borbu left soon after. Both brought their apprentices with them. Since that time, the great wizards were no longer here and the smaller wizards started this child hunt. You see, many of the small wizards have never seen the dark spirit and have mangled the prophecy to mean they can gain power through eating any child sacrificed to the dark spirit. Many even believe Isabella and Borbu to be gone for good and wish to take their places as the most powerful in Panterra. But now, it would appear, the two great wizards have returned … and they will be hunting you, Rachel."

A chill went up Rachel's spine. "Is the man … Red, is he an apprentice?"

"He is Rudolph and the apprentice of Isabella."

"Then Ms. Proom is Borbu's apprentice."

Marcal frowned. "Ms. Proom? No, not by the sound of it. His apprentice is a woman, but a different woman."

"So, Lisa, it has come to this. It would appear my old apprentice, Rudolph, has betrayed me. He does not know it yet, but he's a very dead man. So sad, really. He was quite good at magic." Isabella held the torch up to her face and smiled. "But you can be much better."

It was then that Lisa realized the torch was actually a flame of fire coming from the palm of Isabella's hand. "Wh-what are you talking about?" she whispered.

The fire on Isabella's palm blinked out and was immediately replaced with two fiery eyes. Glowing like two burning coals, they lit the tiny cell with a malevolent gleam.

Lisa shrank from the sight.

"Lisa, inside of you is a great power. I can see it. Forget your old life. Come and accept something new and better!"

"No!"

"Listen, Lisa … you are adopted—I know you are. Have you ever wondered who your real parents were and what became of them? Elizabeth and Doug, oh, they act kind, but they have Robbie and Margie, don't they? After all, they left you to this fate, have they not?"

"They left me with Rachel and Steven!"

"Rachel! Rachel, your babysitter? Ha! That fat flesh abandoned you for your wonder-boy brother—your brother who isn't really your brother! Everybody liked Steven better than you, Lisa. Including Rachel. You know this to be true."

Lisa was reduced to terror and tears. "No! No!"

"Think it over," Isabella said more calmly. "With you by my side you will gain the power to find your *real* parents. Then you can do with them what you want. Imagine, finding the woman who hated you so much as to toss you out of her life … and having power in your hands. Tomorrow you will be given free rein in the fortress. Not only that, but I know how much you like to run things. You are now formally in charge of the kitchens of this fortress and will also be given a detachment of my troops to loyally serve you. They, Lisa, will do whatever you command them."

"Including fight you?"

"They will try if you ask … but then they would die." Smiling, Isabella's eyes lost their fire and the flame appeared again on her palm. "Pleasant dreams, dear."

"And that is the end of the story on this night." Rudolph rose to his feet.

Jakey rolled away from Courtney and squeezed the blanket hard. "That was a stupid story," he muttered.

"No, Jake," hissed Courtney, pulling him toward her.

Waving a hand dismissively, Rudolph shrugged. "Stupid boys think stupid things. I suggest you get your rest tonight. Tomorrow we start a long journey. Now do not bother me further. I have much to prepare."

Courtney didn't like the way his eyes flickered red when staring at her brother. She wrapped a protective arm around Jake and trembled. This was one horrible nightmare that would not end.

Rachel stared at the wall of the tent, watching flickering shadows, and she shivered. "So at the age of twelve, children are safe?"

Marcal nodded. "At that time they are people and cannot be murdered, yes."

"But, how does anybody know if they're twelve or not?"

"Each region is assigned an administrator who keeps track of all the births. Each year the village chief must send a copy to the administrator and the child must be presented there. Then when children reach their twelfth year, they are taken back to the administrator and given a special earring or tattoo, depending upon the region. People can hide births if they wish, but then they would find it very hard to prove their children are twelve if a wizard ever comes. Any other questions?"

"Uh, does Isabella rule the Western Kingdom?" Rachel asked.

"Only in her mind … After King Gretz the Sixth's death, next in succession is his eldest son. He hasn't reached his naming day, so he is still hidden on Earth somewhere. The rumor is that Isabella spent time on Earth also, to find and kill him. Until he is twelve, the king's cousin is acting as regent. This cousin is nothing but a scared fool who lets Isabella do as she pleases. Once the true king is officially gone, Isabella can easily proclaim herself as queen."

Rachel shivered. "And she has Lisa …"

"Do not fear. She wants the boy and will use the girl as bait. This I can almost promise you."

"How do you know?" Jason demanded. "You tell us all these stories, yet how would you know any of this?"

Marcal grinned without humor. "Before I came here, I served as Isabella's captain in her personal guard … but I did more than just serve under her … I also loved her." Ignoring the shocked stares, Marcal rose to his feet and bowed stiffly. "I now bid you goodnight. Jason, you will go with Lineus, and he will show you a room in the bachelor's house." He nodded at Rachel. "I noticed you did not eat the stew … that is good. A sleeping potion was added to your serving and to the boys' as well. Rag berries, I believe."

"Wh-what?" Rachel sputtered, her heart jumping again. "Why?"

"It would seem that somebody does not like you in this village, Rachel, and probably wishes to harm you during the night. Do not worry. The potion is harmless."

Rachel's face had paled. "But-but, who?"

"Likely," he said dryly, "the same person who has been listening outside this tent." His voice suddenly grew harsh and commanding. "Suzella! Come in here!"

Immediately the tent's flap was tossed open.

"How did you know?" the flaxen-haired warrior demanded, almost stomping inside. Her face held no shame, but only anger at getting caught.

"You smell of rag berries. Besides, I watched you slip some in the last bowls of stew being given to our guests." He rubbed his moustache. "Now that you heard everything, I suppose you wish to travel with us."

Everybody awake in the tent stopped and stared at Marcal.

"Are you going with me to find Lisa?" Rachel asked, hope rising to her face.

The warrior nodded slowly. "It would seem to be the case. Defeating Isabella is impossible … but at least with me you may find the young girl."

"Sounds wonderful," Lineus grinned. "Count me in too."

"You will need my blade," Suzella said grudgingly. "I will follow this … babysitter."

"What! But you just tried to drug her!" Jason cried, glaring at the girl.

"So what?" Suzella sniffed. "All I wanted to do was to cut off her hair—she humiliated me in front of my village! I just wanted to settle the score."

Rachel's hand went to her hair. She stared at the girl. "I don't care about my hair, but were you really going to cut Jak?"

"What if I was?"

"It's a good thing you didn't!" Marcal rumbled. "That boy is the finest healer in the area—many times he healed my wounds."

Suzella ignored him. "I did what I thought was best for the village," she said to Rachel hotly.

"Then you're … you're misguided!"

Marcal grabbed Lineus and Jason and headed for the flap. "This is where we let the females do their own battle," he muttered. "Men will be of no use here."

Suzella waited for the males to exit. Then she crossed her arms, glaring at Rachel. "You heard Marcal—wizards can find children and eat them. As a protector of this village I would give up Jak to save a child any and every time!"

"How can you say that?"

"How can I not?" challenged Suzella. "Jak lacks a voice and his life is useless. If somebody has to be sacrificed, it is better that it is somebody like him!"

"You're, you're heartless!"

"Heartless? What do you know about that? I lost three siblings before they reached five years. And I could not shed a tear for any one of them in public because they had yet to reach their naming day. My mom died giving birth to the last. Say what you will of me, but Jak is lower than my siblings. His life has no value to me."

"His life has value—all life has value!"

"Maybe in your world," snarled Suzella. She yanked out her sword and held it up for Rachel to see. "This is my concern now, and only this! I serve to protect the village! I would do everything in my power to defend our village from those who wish to hurt it! If Jak's life saved our village, then it is well spent. If not him, then which child should be taken?"

Rachel backed from the young woman's fury. "B-but, he's a healer! Didn't you hear?"

"When Jak grows into a man, what would be said of him? He healed old people. That is nothing!" She slid her sword back in the sheath. "But I will be known as a great warrior who protected all people! You don't understand!"

Rachel shook her head. "I-I always thought those who were stronger should protect the weaker. You can't end a life because you think it's defective—children aren't tools that can be tossed away if you think they're broken."

"Nothing is tossed away here." Suzella frowned. "If something is broken, it is used for something else. In Jak's case, his life would have been used to save the other children. His life would have been noble."

"Oh, you're killing my head! I can't argue with you … You're impossible and I'm too tired."

"Then go to sleep! You have Jak, be happy with that. He's yours to do with as you please. I must go and defend our village from wolves. They are the ones you should worry about. And if they do attack this night, I suggest throwing Jak out in front of you and running. They attack the weaker flesh first."

Never before had Rachel felt so angry. All the stress, tiredness, and fear of the day welled up. Before she could stop and think, she made a fist and meant to throw a punch. Suddenly the blade rested at her throat.

"Don't be a fool, Rachel," hissed Suzella. "I know you're not a wizard. You let me live my life, and I shall let you live yours as a babysitter. Whatever a babysitter really is!" Then she left the tent.

Rachel put a hand to her throat and gasped for a breath. Only the presence of the two sleeping boys kept her from completely going mad. That and knowing Lisa was out there needing her …

Chapter Twenty-Five

Lisa lay back against the filthy straw and tried hard not to sob … but why not cry? Nobody was here to see her … She felt awfully alone and stuck in a pitch-black jail … Alone and very, very frightened. Tears would be her only friend.

Something brushed her leg. Squealing, she kicked wildly.

Tiny feet scuttled off with a squeak.

"Hush, girl," spoke a deep voice in the darkness. The voice sounded ragged and grated like rusty metal being scraped. "They be only rats … They're the only companions we have down here."

Drawing a sharp breath, Lisa went still. "Wh-who's there?"

"My name is Tendl … I used to be soldier for Isabella. Now I'm a prisoner like you."

"Wh-why?"

The voice laughed bitterly. "Why, is a fool question, girl. The real question you must ask is what."

"What?"

"Aye. What are you going to do now? I heard what Isabella said … She's giving you freedom tomorrow, girl."

"I don't trust her," Lisa said hoarsely. Sitting still, she hugged her knees and did all she could to keep from screaming. Talking to the man began to settle her nerves, a little.

"Then trust me."

Lisa gulped. "Wh-what do you mean?"

"When you leave tomorrow, I will be forgotten. By everyone, but you … If you wish it, I can help you."

"H-how?"

"I know how to escape from here, girl. And I know where to go where it is safe from Isabella."

"B-but I need to find my brother and … a friend."

"Where I take you, girl, you can do that. It is where you can do anything you wish."

"I don't understand."

"You will … if you want to."

Lisa breathed in the dark. "How can I trust you?"

"You can't. You will have to decide. Isabella or me."

"I'll … I'll have to think about it."

"You do that, girl … and don't worry. I won't be going anywhere."

"You do realize that Isabella will be sending out hunters all over searching for this boy?" Marcal asked Rachel roughly. "This will include small wizards, cutthroats, and any other fool looking for reward."

It was morning time and already the village was bustling with activity. Standing outside the tent where Steven and Jak still slept off the rag berries, Marcal had just finished explaining the plan to Rachel. He had spoken to Urslaf earlier, and the chief had supported the journey wholeheartedly. All the supplies and horses would be provided, as well as ten men to add protection to the party. Marcal refused to allow more. He wanted a small, fast party that would not attract too much attention and would be able to move quickly. Everything had been going great until Rachel announced that Steven would also be going.

"The boy is a cub—too small and weak for a long journey," he told her. "We can't take him."

Rachel stood firm. "Urslaf came here before you and already promised a wagon."

"A wagon!" Marcal's face flushed with anger. "That will slow us down and be seen by many! Don't you know what that means?"

"I-I don't know," muttered Rachel, surprised she was not trembling and backing down from this man. "But he's still going."

"What—" Marcal struggled to control himself. "We can't be spotted, Rachel. Isabella must not know where we are until too late."

Rachel would not look up at Marcal. "I will not lose him. And I will find his sister."

The warrior looked up at the sky and sighed. "Babysitters are crazy," he mumbled. "I almost believe you. Very well, gather what you wish to bring and meet me here within the hour."

"Wait! Is it, uh, can the boys find a bath before we leave? Uh, Jak … he needs it."

Clenching his teeth, Marcal breathed out deeply, which caused his nostrils to flare. "There is a spring not far from the village," he finally said as if it pained him deeply. "Jak can show you the way … That is all I will say. Now I have more important work to do, like plan our journey to take down the most powerful wizard without getting us all killed and without allowing her to take over the world in the process!"

"Uh, thank you." Rachel took a breath. "Oh, and Jak is going with us too."

Marcal stood there staring at her. "Very well," he finally growled. "A healer is what we need on this trip, because I foresee somebody getting hurt really fast!" Turning on his heel, he marched away.

When Courtney emerged from the cave that morning, the old woman stared over the edge of the cliff overlooking a vast green land of forests and rivers. Joining her, Courtney gasped. They were on the side of a steep rocky mountain with no way down. This provided a breathtaking view, but gave little hope for escape.

Groaning when seeing the young girl, the woman held her head. "Too much drinking," she muttered. "And the brats are still here."

"Where would we go?" Courtney asked.

"Over the ledge, if you don't find some manners," snapped the woman, instantly groaning. "My poor head …"

"You don't have to be so mean." Courtney drew back from the edge.

"You don't want me to be mean? Then get me out of here! Go tell your precious guardian to send me home … and you may want to send your brother away too."

"What are you talking about?"

The woman turned to Courtney and for a moment she lost her hostile demeanor. "Put two and two together, girl. Red, or whatever he calls himself, has a room laid out with clothes for a young girl close to your age. Why? It is obvious he lost a daughter and hopes to replace her with you. The boy … he just wants to be rid of. Mark my words, girl. Your brother will be gone soon. I'd stake my life as a writer on it."

"What? No!" Courtney turned and raced back to the cave to where Jakey still slept.

Inside, she passed Red, just stirring from his room.

"Layla!" he called after, rubbing his eyes. "Layla—you're not Layla …" Groaning, he put a hand to his forehead. "Go bring your brother to the cave entrance. We have a long journey ahead of us."

When Courtney and Jakey went to the entrance, the boy's hand was tightly gripped by his sister's. Waiting for them was the woman, now wrapped in a thick cloak and looking miserable.

Red soon ducked in from the outside and nodded in approval. "Now we travel."

"Where?" asked Courtney. "How can we get down the mountain?"

"The same way you got up here." Red indicated the pool. "When I say so, step into the water. First, chew on this root—it will keep you from losing consciousness on the journey." He held a fistful of dark dried sticks resembling shriveled carrots. "Later I'll teach you a trick so you won't need the root." He looked only at Courtney and ignored Jakey and the woman. Courtney took the handful of root and gave some to Jakey and the woman. Trying it tentatively, she found it tasted of licorice and dirt. She chewed ravenously.

"Are-are you taking us back to our home … in Florida?"

"No. I'm taking you to the village at the base of this mountain. But first we must enter a spot on your Earth and jump from there." He eyed the three fiercely. "Do not get any ideas. I'm taking you to a dangerous area, and you must take hold of me as we make the transition. Once we reach the village, we will get a wagon and journey to visit an old friend of mine. Now, old hag," he said, turning to the woman. "Have you decided? Servant or wife?"

Flicking her eyes at Courtney, she bowed in thought. "I'll pretend to be your wife …" she finally said grudgingly. "But in public only!"

Red stared at the old woman disdainfully. "I wouldn't have it any other way. Let the journey begin!"

The journey did not start well for Rachel.

Terrible hunger plagued her and the hot sun beat on her brow like it was a frying pan. All she could think about was food and air-conditioning …

The morning had been too hectic to find food herself. Getting Jak to lead her to the spring had been easy, but convincing him to bathe was another matter. Finally she let the boys swim while she backtracked down to the village to find clean clothes for them to wear. Then she had to go all the way back up. Only by hearing Steven's shouts did she not get lost. Both boys were relatively clean—or at least wet—when she found them. Exhausted, starved, and feeling quite stressed, she dropped off the clothes and waited for them to change in the bushes. Then it was back down to the village …

She would have drunk from the spring, but knowing the boys just swam in it … her throat remained dry.

With sweat bathing her skin and clothes in grime, she next had to oversee the packing and make sure the boys were ready for the journey. The boys wore identical earth-brown pants and jackets of animal hide. Moccasins covered their feet. Jak had his own clothes, so they fit him fine, but Steven's were donated by a boy much older and larger than him. His clothes hung hopelessly too big on his small frame. Only a cord belt kept his pants up, and the sleeves of his jacket hung well past his hands. Not only that, but he complained everything was itchy and smelled rotten.

Rachel had to agree with him there. She wore a sleeveless short dress of animal hide that ended at her thighs. It had been given to her by a big-hearted woman who gushed proudly to have helped the babysitter, so Rachel dared not complain. She just quietly kept her undergarments. She also wore a thick pair of trousers that rubbed so it felt like a toothless mouth constantly gnawing on her legs. These came courtesy of Lineus, as did her boots. The only comfort she took was that both articles hung loose on her—her unwanted weight-loss program was working.

Sighing, she wiped sweat from her face. She leaned against the stage of the "gas station" and watched as the final preparations were made for the journey.

The sun stood high overhead and blasted sweltering heat on those foolish enough to stand in its way. The smell of mud, smoke, and manure filled the humid air.

"Noon," growled Marcal as he strode past carrying a heavy sack of provisions. "The worst time to start a long journey." Stopping, he turned on her with a scowl. "Now anything else we can do for you before we leave?" Sarcasm dripped from his voice like sour molasses.

"Uh, well, the boys could use another bath," she said truthfully. "But perhaps later—"

Making a strangled yell, Marcal had already twisted away.

In front of the stage, twelve horses stood in a line, waiting patiently for their riders. In the rear, two were attached to a small open cart that held the supplies and would later hold Jak and Steven. Currently the boys were off running with the other children—each slathered in sunscreen that Rachel got from her purse. She didn't bother with any for her—there wasn't much left and she wanted to save it for the boys. Jak had eyed the strange bottle and licked his arm after Rachel sprayed a gob of lotion on it. Making a face, he hastily wiped it off on his pants. Only after much haggling did she get any more on him.

What moms must go through … She felt so exhausted and they hadn't even started. Yet at the same time, Rachel couldn't help but feel a pulse of excitement. To think of it … one month before and she was in the library feeling like a total loser. Now she was about to embark on a heroic expedition to rescue Lisa and defeat an all-powerful wizard … Suddenly she had the urge to throw up. Lisa was her responsibility and so was Steven. She had no time for fantastic thoughts or anything that bordered on enjoying the moment. If she didn't get those kids home … She would be better off dead.

Meri, Jak's sister, stepped around the cart and joined her. She offered a bowl of stew with a spoon made of horn. "I hope you are ready for a rough day, Babysitter Rachel," she said with a smile.

"You mean it hasn't started yet?" Rachel asked without a trace of humor. She accepted the bowl and stared down at the pieces of meat floating in greasy liquid with chunks of vegetables. *Dead meat … I hope that's not my future.*

Meri had helped Rachel find clothes for the boys and also helped dry their old clothes. Her facial features were very similar to Jak's, only older and more feminine. Nodding at the stew, she said, "Be sure to eat much, Rachel. Marcal doesn't like to stop for rests."

Taking a bite, Rachel nodded. "Uh, thanks." It tasted a little better than school food, and she had to struggle to choke it down.

Meri put an arm on her shoulder. "When I first heard my brother was being taken by a wizard, I wanted to claw out your eyes. Then I learned how you saved him and became his guardian … Now I am very glad he goes with you."

Wiping her mouth, Rachel looked at the girl. She was beautiful, easily the most beautiful girl Rachel had ever spoken to. Yet she spoke with sincerity and with kindness. People like Meri were very uncommon. Beauty and compassion were rare partners in Rachel's experience. Swallowing more stew, she cleared her throat.

"Are you sure you want Jak to go?" she asked.

Meri pulled herself up to sit on the stage. "You saw how the villagers treated him," she said with a sad smile. "To them, he's a broken body with no future. But to you, I see the way you look at your boy and at him. There is no difference to you. You will protect both of them, Rachel … I know in my heart Jak is better off going."

"What about you?" Rachel blurted. Suddenly the need for a kind friend pulled at her. Lineus had been very friendly and helpful in gathering her supplies for the journey, but the way he looked at her made her feel awkward and confused. Meri would be more like having a sister of her own … "Would you, uh, come too?"

Meri smiled sadly. "I must stay here. Our parents may come back any day, and one of us should be here if that happens."

Rachel nodded miserably. "I understand …"

"You are kind to ask me to go—it is a great honor to be personally asked by a babysitter." Meri smiled, but then grew serious. "I know you are a good person. Go with caution but with courage. That is what will defeat Isabella. Now let me have the bowl and mount up. I see Marcal with smoke coming from his ears."

Quickly the call to mount was made. Marcal pulled himself on his horse and trotted down the line.

"On your mounts! Let's go!" he barked. "We must be far from here before the sun falls for the night!"

Rachel swallowed. After making sure the boys were on the cart, she trudged to the horse, chosen especially for her and saddled by Lineus. Horses were something she only knew about from books and movies. This was the closest she had ever been to such an animal. It scared her.

"Nice horse," she whispered hoarsely.

The horse, a giant gray gelding with black spots on his flanks, turned his head to stare back at her as if waiting.

"Here goes …" she whispered. Grabbing the saddle horn—she at least knew what that was—she put a foot in a stirrup. Counting to three, she yanked herself up.

The entire village had gathered to see them off. Men, women, and children, mostly dressed in the ragged clothes of peasants and farmers, watched with great hope as the famous babysitter, the one who would challenge the great wizards, stood facing the horse's backside. Rachel had put the wrong foot in the stirrups and would have to mount backwards if she continued.

She froze in embarrassment.

Lineus, astride the horse in front of her, turned and tittered in amusement. "Rachel, it helps to see where you're going when riding a horse."

"Perhaps," called a voice, "she has magic powers that allow her to see behind her head!"

Urslaf stood on the stage overlooking the proceedings. Seeing Rachel freeze, he hastily cleared his throat. "See how the babysitter checks out her saddle before mounting?" he bellowed.

"We should all strive to be careful like her! Check for dangers before doing our deeds!"

"Er, yes …" Blushing a bright red, Rachel lowered from the horse and quickly switched feet.

A small brown horse moved from near the back and clopped over to her.

"You've never been on a horse before, have you?" Jason Richardson asked without a hint of amusement. The dark-haired teen had spent most of the morning away from Rachel. This was his first time speaking to her since the previous night.

"Isn't it obvious?" Rachel muttered, not looking up.

"Hey, relax," Jason said. "Always mount with your left foot on the left side."

"Got that part down."

"Good. Once you're in the saddle, you use the reins as sort of a steering wheel. Pull left or right to change directions. To stop, pull back."

"Uh, how do I make it go?"

"Him go," Jason corrected with a crooked smile. "Horses are like people. They have feelings and show it. Tap the sides of the horse with your feet lightly to get him started. Come on, Rachel. It'll be okay. I'll move in front of you and you can just follow me. Let's show these people a babysitter is nothing to laugh at."

"Okay … thanks." She looked up and flashed a quick grin.

Jason nodded. "No problem. Us earthlings have to stick together."

"Hey, back there!" shouted Marcal. "Mount up and let's go!"

And so the band set out. In the lead, Marcal muttered furiously, and Rachel followed closely behind Jason near the back. In the cart the boys lay against sacks of grain and stared up at the clouds. All the villagers accompanying them, including Lineus, carried long swords and short bows and quivers of arrows. Suzella had left ahead some time ago, to scout. This suited Rachel just fine.

Urslaf sighed from the stage as the cart rolled out of the village. "I fear our future rests with them," he mumbled. "We are likely doomed."

After hours of travel, Rachel only had horrible thoughts left in her tired, broken body.

Her large gray, which Lineus told her had the name Bolder, was old and quite gentle. Rachel no longer panicked at every step and had begun to enjoy the choppy ride. Then Marcal turned his horse and galloped to her side. His face was furious.

"Rachel," he nearly snarled, "if we go much slower we shall be crawling on our hands and knees! We must pick up the pace!"

"But-but, what do you mean? I'm going as fast as the horse in front of me."

"Yes, and that is because you obviously would fall if I put the pace any quicker!"

Rachel frowned. "I can go faster."

"We shall see. Suzella is to meet us at our campsite for the night, but at the rate we're traveling, we won't see her until next week!" Turning his horse, Marcal galloped back to the lead. He never slowed. Suddenly Jason's horse was galloping.

"Jab your horse again!" he shouted back to Rachel. "Just follow and don't fall!"

Great advice, Rachel thought. *Thanks.*

Rachel didn't have time to follow it. Bolder had apparently lost faith in his rider giving him orders. Seeing the horse in front speed up, he started doing the same. Rachel barely managed to hang on at the first sudden lurch.

"Hey!" Screeching, Rachel hunched in the saddle and squeezed her legs tightly to the horse. This made Bolder go even faster. As she bounced all over the saddle, the rest of the day became a raging terror for Rachel.

With the sun setting before them, the procession finally slowed. All day they had been following the road, which narrowed and stayed within the woods. Now they came to a grassy clearing by a narrow stream.

"We camp here tonight!" cried Marcal, raising his hand for them to stop.

Lineus trotted his horse from the line and stared at the clearing. "Suzella, where are you?"

The flaxen-haired teen stepped out from behind a clump of bushes by the water, lowering a notched arrow. "I could have picked any one of you off easily," she said with a smirk.

"Make sure it's me first," growled Marcal. "Put me out of my misery from leading this folly." Hopping off his horse, he started loosening the saddle. "Do us a favor and go help Rachel with her mount. I fear she is rather clueless with animals." He snorted. "I suppose she's only good with babies."

"Of course." Suzella nodded behind her. "The grass is greener farther down the stream. That's where you'll find my horse."

Lineus beat Suzella to Rachel.

Grinning, the handsome youth gathered Bolder's reins. "So, how was your first ride? A little bumpy?"

Groaning with real pain, Rachel only looked down at him from the saddle with tortured eyes. "I-I can hardly move …"

"Here," Lineus said gently, "let me help you …"

Nearby, pulling the saddle off his horse, Jason glared at Lineus. "Shouldn't you be taking care of your own horse first?" he asked.

"I still plan to use mine a little while longer. But first, I wish to assist a beauty in her moment of need."

Jason rolled his eyes and hastily pulled a brush from one of the bags on his saddle. He turned his back and started brushing his horse vigorously. "Poser," he muttered.

Suzella crossed her arms and sauntered next to Lineus. "It would seem our babysitter is saddle sore."

"Please, just help …" Rachel nearly toppled from the saddle. Lineus quickly placed a hand on her waist and managed to guide her to the ground.

"Careful, there," he said lightly. "I would hate to be responsible for bruising your beauty."

"What's bruised right now is my …" Rachel suddenly looked stricken. Since they'd had a late start, Marcal had refused to stop for lunch. The greasy stew had bounced in her stomach all day and now it wanted out. Now. "Oh … no … I need to go … I'll be right back …" Walking awkwardly, her legs spread wide, she scurried for the trees to hide in shameful misery.

Lineus and Suzella shared a laugh behind her, and no doubt many of the men also watched in amusement.

Chapter Twenty-Six

Several minutes later, feeling a little better, but still extremely sore, Rachel waddled back to camp. The cart, unhitched, sat by the stream and the horses were picketed farther down where the grass stood like a vibrant green carpet. A small fire burned brightly by the wagon and pot of … Rachel sniffed and nearly choked. More stew for dinner. Her stomach nearly sent her running back to the woods. Taking a deep breath, she continued onward.

Some of the men were laying out bedding while others were preparing a guard. Marcal stood with Suzella, discussing something by the wagon. He didn't look happy.

Surprise, surprise. That man is never happy. Rachel stifled a groan. She wasn't happy either—and wouldn't be, not until she found an air-conditioned car and a packet of Tums. And a pillow to sit on.

Jason shared in the displeasure, but for another reason. Sitting with his back to the fire, he stared daggers at where Lineus had Jak up in the saddle of his black mount. The smiling youth gripped the reins firmly as he had the boy proudly walk the horse in a slow circle.

"That's a boy, Jak, just relax …" His voice drifted to Rachel and sounded pleasant to her ears.

At least somebody is enjoying the day.

Beside Jason, Steven sat with his knees tucked to his chin, watching the riding lessons with narrowed brown eyes. His young face held a frown.

Each step bringing fresh agony to her thighs, Rachel awkwardly went to join the dour boys. Steven softened his gaze when seeing her, but Jason never looked her way. Slowly, ever so slowly, she eased on the other side of Jason.

"Ooohh … this feels so bad …"

"Tell me about it," muttered Jason, still not glancing at her.

"Er …" Rachel fell silent. Despite the clear sky overhead and the cool breeze wafting from the trees, it felt rather stormy where she sat.

Lineus called out when seeing her. "There you are, Rachel!" He twisted to face her. Keeping a hand on the reins, he kept Jak and his mount traveling in a loose circle around him.

Giving a weak smile, Rachel nodded at him.

"I wanted to give young Steven a riding lesson, but your, uh, friend didn't seem too pleased with the idea." He smiled and flicked a lock of cinnamon hair in the direction of Jason.

Jason glared back. "I just said it might not be a good idea," he growled through gritted teeth.

"But you let Jak ride," Rachel said, frowning.

Jason shrugged. "Yeah, well, this is his world."

"So?" Rachel asked angrily. "He's my responsibility. If it isn't safe for Steven, then it isn't safe for Jak!"

"Then tell that to Lineus!" Jason shot back.

Rachel couldn't hide her anger. "Steven rides his ripstick without a helmet. A horse can't be any more dangerous! Besides, Lineus seems to be doing a great job!"

Jason made to say something but then only shrugged his shoulders. "Yeah, a great job at showing off," he mumbled.

Ignoring him, Rachel turned back to the lesson feeling slightly shaken over how angry she felt … and how easily she'd expressed it. Not a few days ago, just thinking about talking to Jason might have caused her a mental breakdown.

Lineus gave Jak control of the reins. "You ride like a true knight, boy," Lineus complimented him. "Now try without my help. Don't worry. I'll be right beside you with a hand on the bridle. Sit up straight in the saddle—that's a lad!"

Jason rolled his eyes. "He treats him like a little child!"

"He is a child," Rachel said. She waved when Jak rode by.

"He's a natural!" Lineus called to Rachel. "His first time on the horse, and it's like he was born there!" The riding lesson moved away as Jak steered his mount toward the woods.

Jason snorted. "What a jerk."

Rachel glared at him, surprised at his venom. "He's giving Jak his first riding lesson while you just sit there saying nasty things!"

"Really?" Jason turned to Rachel with a sardonic look. "Jak is how old? Ten? Eleven? He grew up in a village his whole life with nice-guy Lineus, and this is now his first riding lesson?" He shook his head. "Whatever."

Rachel looked away, and before she could think of a reply, Jason jumped to his feet and stalked off.

Hearing a shout, she looked up to see Jak now hunched in the saddle, wordlessly urging the horse to a canter. Lineus ran beside him, calling out directions. Rachel didn't know what Jason's problem was, but when she sat back, she only saw pure joy on the boy's face. Eyes squinting, hair blowing behind him, Jak leaned in the saddle and seemed to become part of the horse.

"Nicely done, Jak!" called Lineus. "You put us men to shame!"

Several of the other men had paused in their work to watch. Some grinned, but others chose the attitude of Jason. They did not look pleased as they glared with undisguised contempt.

Jealousy. Rachel gingerly stretched her legs in front of her and lay back against her arms. *Plain jealousy.*

Next to her, Steven scooted closer and copied her position.

"Rachel?" he asked. "Do you think Lisa is okay?"

She grimaced. The babysitting rules popped into memory. Rule nineteen was to never tell a lie. "I don't know, Steven … but I do know we'll find her and then get back home. You'll see. I won't let anything else happen."

Then she shifted uneasily. Rule number six of the babysitting rules was to avoid speaking crossly in the presence of a child.

Thinking of the babysitting rules made Rachel think of her mom … and made her think how much Steven must be missing his mom and dad.

Glancing at the boy, she saw his smooth face watching Jak through narrowed eyes. His hair flashed reddish brown in the gathering twilight and his lips slowly formed a slight grimace. Even a foot away, he managed to look miles away.

He's probably upset that he's not riding the horse …

"I hope so," he said quietly.

"What was that?" she asked.

"I hope we find Lisa soon."

The two settled in silence.

Then Lineus called out. "Your turn is next!"

Struggling to a sitting position, Rachel shook her head, protesting. "Uh, no—I can hardly move. My … uh, well, I'm too sore to even think about it!"

Lineus and his black had pulled up a few yards in front of where she and Steven lay. Pulling the brown boy from the saddle, Lineus tousled his hair and clapped him on the back. Then he turned to Rachel and gave a mischievous wink. "I was talking to Steven."

Sitting up, Steven smiled slightly but shook his head.

"Come on, lad!" Lineus urged. "Now's your chance to ride like a champion!"

The boy didn't budge. "No, I'd rather sit here for a while."

Blushing, Rachel looked apologetically at Lineus.

The young man refused to back down. "I promise. Blackie rarely bites."

Steven again shook his head.

Grinning, Lineus looked at Rachel, his eyes twinkling. "Very well, Rachel, then I guess it's your turn. Are you ready to ride, Rachel? Only joking. I'm guessing you'll be saddle sore for a number of days."

"What?" Rachel's head jerked up. Then she groaned. "That long?" Then she frowned. "Where did Jak go?"

Lineus jerked his head and shrugged. "Ran off in the woods back there. Don't worry, he's a funny kid. He'll be back."

"Still," Rachel said worriedly, "maybe I should go check."

"Relax, Rachel. You had a hard day." Lineus walked his black and sat across from Rachel. She shifted a little uncomfortably, aware of his gaze never leaving her face. However, when she looked up, Lineus was watching Steven. "Are you sure you don't want to at least pet Blackie?" he asked the boy. "He's a friendly horse."

Giving him a half grin, Steven shook his head.

Lineus sighed dramatically. "Very well, then. I shall go let Blackie have his rest with the others. Tomorrow, huh, Steven? Every boy should know how to ride." With a wave and whistling a merry tune, Lineus got up and led Blackie toward the other horses.

Suzella wandered from the fire to stand behind Rachel.

"What he sees in you," she said meanly, "I will never know."

Frowning, Rachel tilted her head back to stare up at the girl warrior. "What do you mean by that?"

"Lineus is trying to gain your favor," she said rather bluntly. "But why gain the favor of a soft-bellied babysitter who never used a saddle before?"

Rachel felt heat rush into her face. Looking at Steven, she saw the boy with his knees huddled to his chest and supporting his chin. His eyes were somewhere else again and he probably wasn't hearing a thing. Rachel wished she could tune people out like that.

"Lineus only wished to teach the boys to ride," she said to Suzella carefully. "Jak had a wonderful time—he should have learned earlier at the village."

Suzella barked out a laugh. "Teaching Jak to ride is like teaching a chicken to swim. Even if it works, it's still a waste of time."

Rachel gritted her teeth. "Jak has nothing wrong with him."

"Says only you!" sneered the other girl.

"Lineus thinks the same as I!"

Suzella put her hands on her hips and leaned back with a mock look of surprise. "What did you say?"

Rachel's face reddened. "I only said Lineus agrees with me."

"Is that the truth?" Suzella moved in front of Rachel and sneered down at her. "Then why does he wait until now to teach him? Only when a babysitter watches?"

The same question Jason had asked … Rachel fought for an answer but could find none.

Just then Jak appeared from the woods with his hands full of a dripping dark sludge.

Seeing him, Suzella snorted. "Perhaps you are right, Babysitter. Jak does have a use after all. Here he comes with soothing for your—soreness."

"What?" Rachel asked.

Having heard the raised voices, Marcal had joined them and grunted to make his presence known. "The lad made a paste for your—er, for your discomfort."

Suzella smiled snidely. "Do you desire help applying it?"

Lisa raised her foot for another step and stopped dead.

A door opened above her and the voices of two men echoed down to where she stood.

"What do you make of this charade?" asked a hoarse voice. "Being placed under a young brat—a girl, even!"

"We do our duty … that is all we can do."

She stopped breathing. Caught in the middle of the stairwell leading down to the back kitchens, there was nowhere to hide. Her saving grace was that the stairs were circular and she stood around the first turn.

"I'd rather have her over my knee than obey her orders," growled the first voice. "She is just days past the naming day, if that!"

"Hush! The wizard may have your head for such talk! You heard her speech yesterday—we are to obey the girl as she is our leader."

"A fine world we live in! I'm almost ready to join Borbu!"

"That's treason talk!"

"You'd rather obey a whelp of a girl? Skinny as a stick, she is. Probably just as smart as one too!"

"You're just talk, Bevin. I know you are—otherwise I'd turn you in myself."

"Not until there's a reward for it," snorted the first voice. "Speaking of such, I'd rather join Bodin's men hunting. Five hundred in gold for finding this babysitter? I'll never have to carry a spear again!"

"Yes, but you do have to carry a spear—now. Come, now. Hurry before some small cook comes up these stairs and finds us."

"Relax, nobody uses these stairs anymore. The first step is missing."

"Just the same, we're due to stand guard—remember that Isabella has returned."

The first voice suddenly muttered a sharp curse, and hastily the door opened again. "I forgot our days of bliss are over."

"The brat may have given us a day off, but we were already scheduled to guard for the wizard."

"Don't worry," chuckled the first voice. "If we're questioned, we'll just say the girl told us to first guard the vegetables."

"You mean our superiors?" his companion's voice said with a snort.

The first voice sighed. "Not long ago I wished for a hero to come into this land and make it a good place to live … Instead we get sent a pint-sized brat. Truly our land is forsaken."

Lisa's breath slowly returned as the door slammed, leaving her with only the torch light. She sat back on the step and tried hard to control her tears. Since that morning after Isabella had freed her from the cell, everything was just happening too fast. She wiped her eyes and remembered the horrible morning.

Just after the sun peeked over the dark horizon the wizard had shown up, banging on the bars and startling Lisa awake. "Come up and get dressed as a proper apprentice. We have much to do."

Lisa had left her jail in such a hurry she barely had time to glance at the other cells. All she caught in the dawn's dim light was the huddled figure of a man wrapped in a dark cloak in the neighboring cell. Then she was whisked back to Isabella's chamber, where a purple and gold dress had been thrust upon her. Not until she changed was she allowed out. Then it was off to the dining hall. After a breakfast of cold meat, bread, and cheese, Isabella had brought her to a courtyard in the center of the fortress. A small troop of soldiers had stood at attention, awaiting them. Wearing red tunics with the head of a lion emblazoned on the front, each man carried a tall spear and wore a long sword on his side.

"These are your men, Lisa," Isabella had said. "Do not fear them …" She had spoken with a lowered voice. "I told them you were twelve and thus a human. I gave them explicit orders that they must follow you … So, my dear, what is your first order?"

Not knowing what else to do, Lisa had nodded at the men, who merely stared straight ahead. Trembling, in a squeaky voice, she then gave them the day off.

"Interesting use of my men, Lisa," murmured Isabella. "I hope your next task is chosen with, let's say, a little more thought?"

Lisa's next task had been to take charge of the kitchens and plan the courses for that night's supper in the dining hall, where, Isabella had informed her, all the surrounding officers and nobles in the fortress would be dining.

And so, this was what she was doing … or trying to do. After asking a servant to show her all the ways to reach the kitchens, she chose to use the back stairs that, the servant promised, were never used … except, it seemed, by foot soldiers looking to take unscheduled breaks.

A tear ran down her nose. "I can't do this," she whispered. "I'm just a little girl …" Loneliness crashed upon her small shoulders like a boulder and refused to let her up. The soldiers already hated her … and now she had to meet the kitchen staff.

From the bottom of the stairs she heard a clatter, immediately followed by a shout of anger.

"You oaf!" roared a man's deep voice, so loud that it reverberated off the walls of the stairwell. "The wizard's apprentice is coming and you drop beans across my floor?" There came the distinct sound of flesh striking flesh. "Out with you!"

Lisa shot to her feet, fury crossing her face. "Put me in charge of the kitchens, did you? Well, then, so I will take charge!" Pushing aside all previous thoughts of loneliness, she marched the rest of the way down the stairs—taking special care to step over the first step, which indeed seemed to be missing. This only served to infuriate her temper further.

"I will bake you in a pie, I will!" roared the angry voice. Another slap resounded. "I'll bake your bones into broth! I'll bake your eyeballs in a sauce."

Lisa reached the door and grabbed the latch, pushing it. It didn't budge. So unused, the door had warped and refused to open.

A third slap was followed by a scared voice crying. It sounded like a kid.

Crying out in anger, she slammed her body against the door. In a crash it flew open, banging against rickety shelves holding sacks of flour.

The entire kitchen went silent as all eyes went to the back where Lisa stood. A cloud of white swirled before her. Cheeks burning, she marched through the cloud to the center space.

Fires were lit throughout the space before her. Several cooking pots, some the size of small cars, were in use over hot coals. Many others sat idle on the unwashed stone floor. Among the pots and fires were long preparation tables and shelves holding dry food.

Lisa's attention went to the other side of the flour shelves, where a large, beefy man, the size of one of the larger pots, stood next to a table covered in chopped vegetables. Wearing a brimless white hat, his bulging face, resembling an overstuffed pig, quivered and shook as if his cheeks were made of strawberry jelly. Bright red, they stood out against his cold gray eyes and otherwise pasty complexion.

At the feet of this man huddled a boy about Lisa's age. Pudgy and with fear plainly visible in his round face, he dripped tears and blood. Besides a busted lip, he sported a nasty red mark surrounding his left eye. Scattered in front of the boy were white beans and a broken straw basket.

Several cooks stood in awe at Lisa's presence and all the work ceased. Then the large man bowed to her.

All Lisa could hear was the sound of bubbling pots and the whimpers of the boy.

"Welcome, mighty apprentice … we heard of your coming, but assumed you would—"

"Who's in charge here?" Lisa demanded, putting her hands on her hips and imitating one of Isabella's glares. She ignored the beefy cook and glared at the others. This was a tip taught to her by her father. If you want to intimidate a bigger force than you, ignore them completely—look right through them as if they didn't exist.

The large cook bowed again. "We offer our deepest congratulations," he boomed. "I am—"

"I said," snarled Lisa, "who's in charge!"

The cook rose to his full height; easily over six and a half feet. A cruel look came over his face as he now sneered down at her. "Perhaps the apprentice needs to improve her hearing and her sight. It is I, Dosco, who runs the kitchens. My hat was given to me by Isabella herself and marks me as top chef."

"Who's the boy?" Lisa's courage was quickly running low. Fighting to keep in control, she focused on the fallen boy.

He shrank back from her gaze.

"That—" sneered Dosco, "is a miscreant called Darvy. He is a new boy fresh from his naming, so he claims. I haven't seen his naming mark. I already plan to get rid of him." His eyes sparked. "If it pleases your worship, I can bake him into a pie for you."

Lisa swallowed down her disgust. The meaty cook sounded as if he meant it. Pointing a finger at Dosco, her anger nearly burned as bright as her hair. "It pleases me to elevate the miscreant Darvy to top chef. You, you will clean up those fallen beans. Now!"

Dosco stared at her in disbelief. "What!" he thundered.

"I will not repeat myself! Obey, or maybe you'll be baked into a pie!" Turning from the chef, she smiled and knelt in front of the frightened boy. "Darvy, come here. I want to show you how to make a salad—something I want served at every supper." The boy could only open and close his mouth without uttering a sound. He looked ready to faint. So did Dosco.

Groaning in pain, Rachel stood at the stream with Jak's bucket of salve by her feet. A little ways from camp, she was covered in mostly darkness as clouds rolled over the setting sun. Back behind her, the orange glow of the campfire provided the only light and cast large shadows of the men gathered around.

Eating stew … Rachel groaned again. Starving, the thought of stew only made her stomach turn. At least Steven and Jak seemed well off—Lineus had taken them under his wing and promised to look after them while she … found comfort for her soreness, as he delicately put it. Jason had scoffed when hearing this and stomped away. Now looking back at the camp, Rachel could see his dark shape leaning against the cart away from the others.

And once I wanted him to like me … too bad he's like all the other guys from home. Well, he now knew what it felt like to be an outsider …

Suddenly Lineus's smiling face came to mind and Rachel blushed.

Stop it, Rachel. He doesn't like you like that! Suzella thought so, though … *Impossible. Nobody would like her.* She remembered Billy and shuddered. Lineus wasn't like Billy … not at all. When Rachel had pulled him aside before going to the stream and asked discreetly why he hadn't ever taught Jak to ride, Lineus never once looked embarrassed or ashamed.

"Ah, the jealous minds never cease their dirty work, eh, Rachel?" He'd raised his eyebrows but had laughed when seeing her mortified expression. "Not you, Rachel, I know you are only doing your job as a babysitter. Let the others be jealous. In truth, I have always wanted to teach Jak the skill of horseback riding." Then he'd frowned. Rachel couldn't forget his frown. How his dimpled chin tightened and eyes narrowed … his cheeks flushed … he'd looked handsome. "The people of our village do not understand. They see Jak not only as not a human but as a broken animal. To them, treating him like a boy is wrong. It is like adopting an injured chicken as your child. This is an attitude I cannot change in the village." Then his face had slowly relaxed. "But now you're here and we're out here, he's free, Rachel. If I'd taught him to ride in the village, the men would have abused him for it. When I'm not around they'd have possibly hurt him." He'd sighed. "Such is their misunderstanding. I, on the other hand, know better. I've been places, Rachel. I know how this world really works." His eyes had gleamed in the campfire and had taken Rachel's breath away. "With you around, well, I think it'll be okay to teach Jak anything. The people won't dare cross you. You're a very special girl. I mean that." Rachel had nearly melted under his gaze and very nearly—

A stick snapped in the darkness near her and she jumped. "Wh-who's there?"

"Relax, Rachel," Marcal's voice said gently. "It is only I."

"Oh, uh …" Rachel needlessly adjusted her clothes and privately gave thanks she hadn't started with the salve. She doubted she could use it now—with Suzella and Marcal around, there was always somebody sneaking up on her.

Marcal chuckled dryly. "You are still sore, I gather."

"Yes … uh, how long does it last?"

"You don't want to know." A dark shape moved to stand by her. "Rachel, I want to talk to you. This journey we are taking—it will not be in secret for long."

"Uh, what are you talking about?" Rachel didn't like Marcal's tone.

"Isabella has her spies throughout the land. They are everywhere."

Rachel went still. The stream gurgled behind her. "What about the water? Could she come to us—you know, travel through the water?"

"Thankfully, no. Water portals only connect this world with Earth and take much power to use. She will use others to snatch the boy and bring him to her. Rachel, I tell you this as somebody who wants to see you succeed. Do not trust anybody. Even me. On this journey, there are few friends."

Rachel gulped. "Few friends?" she whispered hoarsely. "What does that imply?"

Marcal stood silently for a moment. "In this world there are few who would help another, especially a stranger. Only if the reward is great enough would help come … Here everyone lives for their own benefit. If a stranger helps you, be sure that it is for his or her sake, not yours."

"What about the men from the village?"

"They have hopes that you will defeat the wizards and bring peace to the village. To them, a babysitter is a warrior against wizards who will fight for them."

"What?" Rachel yelped. "That's ridiculous! A babysitter is only—"

"Hush, Rachel!" hissed Marcal, sounding quite serious. "Whatever you believe a babysitter to be, it is no more. In this land, a babysitter is what others believe it to be. And this is a good thing, because if anyone suspects you to be nothing but a scared, ignorant girl, your life will be in grave danger."

Rachel's knees started to shake. "I don't understand …"

Marcal sighed in the darkness. A shadowy hand gripped Rachel's shoulder and squeezed gently. "They are good people—many in this land are. However, their good is hidden down deep.

Fear has ruled over them too long. The men that accompany us, they go because they think you have power. They firmly believe you have the power that can destroy not just Isabella but all the wizards and all that they fear. You are a hero they have dreamed of for years."

"Th-that's crazy!" Rachel tried to step away, but the soreness only reduced her to tears … that and the realization of what Marcal was saying. "Why do they think that?"

"Mostly out of blind hope, but also because you dared to defy the wizards back at the village. You do not know this, but standing up for a child's life is considered an affront to all wizards. None were brave enough to make such a public claim until you came."

"Um, what would happen if, if the people knew I was … a scared, ignorant girl?"

Marcal's voice tightened. "You would probably be taken prisoner and sold as a slave. Your boys would be sent to a wizard for payment. The villagers would hope this act would afford them protection and make wizards their allies. And no good would come out of it."

"Oohh," moaned Rachel. Her knees started to shake. "I can't do this."

"You have no choice. Besides, to the people here, you are a babysitter. Remember, to them, this means you are brave, fierce, and can stand up to any wizard. You have great power that few dare to cross."

Rachel shook her head in disbelief. "I can't even ride a horse," she moaned.

"That adds to your reputation. Here only poor farmers or very powerful wizards do not know how to ride. With your strange clothes and manners, you are clearly not a poor farmer."

Rachel more felt than actually saw Marcal's shadow slide back. "W-wait," she said suddenly, desperately. "If, if what you say is true, then why are you helping me? What's in it for you?"

The shadow paused. "A fair question. I have a debt to pay." Before totally vanishing, Marcal called back. "If I were you, I would wait until under blankets to use the salve. Suzella has been listening again."

"Curse you, Marcal!" seethed Suzella's voice from the darkness. Water splashed. "How do you do that?"

This time, Rachel did tumble backward, falling with a startled splash. It was not a graceful landing.

Chapter Twenty-Seven

The next morning, Rachel woke up stiff and still very sore. Only the salve, which she did apply uncomfortably under her blankets, provided enough comfort for sleep. Groaning, she sat up. Her stomach rumbled to join in the misery. Not being able to face the stew, she'd only had water and a crust of bread the night before.

Around her, she quickly realized, the camp was nearly packed up. The horses were saddled and the wagon hitched, ready to go. A small fire still warmed a pot, but most of the men in the party seemed to be finishing up their meal. And the sun had barely peeked over the trees, having caused only a faint blush in the sky.

"Oh, no …" Her face joined the blush. She'd overslept.

Turning on her side, she awkwardly used her hands to push herself to a standing position. Gathering her blankets, she shuffled to find her horse, Bolder.

"Your face glows in the morning sun, Rachel." Lineus stepped in her path like he'd been waiting for her. Grinning, he bowed low and stood with a wink. "I rose before light and had my horse ready long ago, so I took the honor of readying your horse for you. I thought you would want a slow start this morning." Stepping back, he gestured to where Bolder stood near the back of the line chomping on a clump of grass.

Too tired to think properly, Rachel grunted her thanks, keenly aware of a foul case of morning breath. Dimly, she thought of where she'd put her toothbrush from the night before. She stumbled past Lineus and over to her horse. Ignoring the curious stares of the men already mounted, she started stuffing her blankets in the bag hanging from the saddle. Once they were relatively secured, she had to pull them all out again to find her toothpaste—the one link to Earth.

"Here," Lineus said kindly, coming from behind her. "You take care of … what you need to and I'll get your gear stowed."

"Er, uh, thanks … I mean, really, thank you. I, er, uh …" She sighed. The stiff walk to the bushes was not very fun. To make matters worse, she knew her hair had to resemble a bird's nest after a hurricane.

Lineus called after her that he would meet her at the fire for a quick breakfast.

Returning from the bushes, she took the time to stop by the stream to drink deeply, brush her teeth, and wash her face. Combing the tangles in her hair would have to wait. Even though the sun had still yet to rise above the trees, Marcal stood tall on his mount and impatiently waited to get started.

Suzella, she noticed, was nowhere to be seen. Everything that Marcal had said the previous night, the blond warrior had heard. In the cool morning, Rachel shivered.

Before going to find food, Rachel made sure to check on the boys. Sitting in the back of the cart, Jak and Steven each held long sticks between their legs. Jak was demonstrating how to make a sharp point using only a stone.

Before she could go warn Steven that his mother would probably not approve, Lineus hailed her. Jogging up to her, he led Bolder by the reins. "There you are! Let me give you a hand up. We're nearly off."

"Oh, no …" Ducking, she became very aware of Lineus smiling at her. "Uh, thanks." She looked toward the pot on the smoldering fire. Stew … she wouldn't miss it. Only her stomach would.

Gripping the saddle horn, she awkwardly threw the correct foot and managed to connect with the stirrup. With Lineus guiding, she very ungracefully pulled herself up and over Bolder's back. "Oh my goodness," she wheezed as she settled in the saddle. "I'll need more salve tonight."

"Er, yes." Lineus scratched his floppy hair. "My father used to say, the man who hurts his bum will later sulk in rum." He chuckled. "I still don't know what he meant." Rachel didn't crack a smile. "Don't worry," he said kindly, "the soreness shall pass. And then your feelings will improve. You'll start to enjoy this trip, this land, and perhaps my company." He winked.

Rachel couldn't help but smile now. Lineus certainly wasn't bashful. Even if he told lies, his words gave her comfort. *He's only kidding with you … but maybe in this world it is different … there is a nice guy who isn't quick to judge … Marcal is wrong. People could be good anywhere.*

"How far, uh, will we go today?" she asked, running a quick hand through her tangled hair, wishing she had a comb.

Laughing, Lineus gestured toward Marcal. "It depends. How long before he grows tired of yelling at us for being so slow?"

Rachel grunted. "Er, yeah … Um, what do you know about him? You know …" she nodded in the direction of Marcal.

"Not much," Lineus confessed. Scratching his head, he grinned. "Nobody does. The other night when you first met him in the tent was the most I ever heard him speak. He's a mystery, that man …" He leered at her playfully. "And I know girls tend to like mysterious men." Holding himself up, he tried for a secretive look. "I'll just have to start acting mysterious too."

Rachel actually laughed—the first time since waking up in this strange world. "I'm trying to be serious!"

"Oh, well …" Lineus grew thoughtful. "In truth, Marcal is obviously a great warrior with a past. He came to our village to get away from his former life … For a long time I wondered why, but now we know."

"We know what?" Rachel asked, frowning.

"Do you not remember? He loved Isabella … Love is a blind arrow that strikes any man at any time." Lineus lost his smile and sighed. "You know, what puzzles me is that Marcal does not seem to fear her. Isabella, the most feared wizard in the land, has good cause to wish him dead, but he goes toward her almost eagerly." He looked up at Rachel. "I wouldn't be surprised if some of his love still exists. But fear not," he added hastily. "Marcal is a true man. He won't steer you wrong. I know you can trust him, just as you can trust me."

Rachel ducked her head to hide her blush. "Yes … uh, thank you."

Bowing low, he looked up at her. "I am always at your service, Rachel. But if you wish to repay me, let young Steven ride with me today. I keep thinking the boy wished to be in the saddle yesterday but was prevented by, well …" He paused meaningfully, leaning his head toward the front where Jason was mounting. "I just think it would do him good."

"Oh, well …" Rachel looked ahead where Marcal was yelling at one of the men to pack his blankets more carefully. Remembering how she had started packing her own bag before Lineus came along, she swallowed. "I don't know," she started doubtfully.

"He reminds me very much of myself at his age," Lineus said wistfully.

"Really?" Rachel stared with interest at Lineus, trying to picture him as a little boy.

Now it was Lineus's turn to be uncomfortable. "Ahem, well, er, it would do the boy good to get out of that wagon. Do I have your permission? I will only act with your approval."

Rachel looked back at the wagon and swallowed. *Quick, what would Steven's mom say?* "Er, he doesn't have a helmet," she said to stall.

Suzella, having just trotted from the woods, heard her last comment. Her cheeks glowed brightly. Turning in her saddle, she gave Rachel a mocking look. "The only helmet you need is for your bottom."

Rachel was left speechless as the blond curls flounced toward the head of the line.

Lineus patted Rachel's leg. "Don't listen to her, Rachel. You're going to make a fine horseman. I can give you lessons if you—"

Jason then galloped his mount past Suzella and pulled up next to the pair. Ignoring Rachel, he looked down at Lineus. "Lineus, you better go get your horse."

"My horse is fine," Lineus said dismissively.

"Marcal doesn't think so."

Lineus glared up at Jason. "What do you mean? He's saddled and tethered to a bush."

Jason lifted his eyebrows. "Is that so? Then why is he now wandering in the stream unattended?"

Lineus swore. Sure enough, Blackie, saddled and his reins hanging loose, stood knee-deep in the water while taking a long drink.

"Did someone forget to water their horse before a long journey?" Jason asked innocently. Then he added, "Somebody so careless probably shouldn't be giving riding lessons." Jerking his reins, he trotted to the back, leaving Lineus to run after his horse.

Rachel suddenly felt furious. Jason hadn't even glanced at her. It felt like high school all over. Loud enough for Jason to hear, she stood in the stirrups and called after Lineus. "You can ask Steven if he wants to ride once we get started! And later you can give me lessons!" In doing so, she managed to squeeze the sides of Bolder, causing her horse to rear back and nearly toss her backward. "Oh!" she cried in alarm. "Whoa!"

So the day began …

Steven winced as the wheel under him struck another stone, sending him bouncing several inches into the air before landing with a resounding thump. On the first day the rollicking four-wheeled contraption had been fun—like a ride in an amusement park. Now each bump served as a reminder that he was lost in a strange world, far from home and without his family …

Another bump sent him soaring. This time he came down on his right knee and he felt a flash of pain, which turned to anger.

Gritting his teeth, he felt the monster stir from deep inside his belly. For a time he'd hoped the monster had moved on—staying close to Rachel and Lisa had calmed him. But ever since waking up in the strange world and hearing stories of wizards and fear, he'd felt the monster's presence growing stronger …

Staring up at where the trees extended their branches overhead, he wondered what lay beyond. What did this strange world hold and how would they escape it? During supper the night before, Lineus had told stories of strange animals that could read the minds of humans and of dark plants that stole the minds of people who stepped on their flowers. At the time, Steven had refrained from rolling his eyes, thinking Lineus told only tall tales. Now he wasn't so sure. The branches above him suddenly seemed to be several arms with jagged claws, reaching for him. Their green leaves appeared as rough scales. More than once it looked as if a branch bent low only to miss snatching him. Ducking his head, he cradled his body against further bumps.

Too much television, he thought. They were just trees. And he would be safely home soon. Rachel would see to that. First they had to find Lisa … his sister was somewhere out there, in the clutches of a mad wizard housekeeper. Again he shivered. In his short school career, nothing had prepared him for this moment.

His mom always told him, when bad things happened to just hold on to the good things and never let go. Then, once the bad passed on, the good would remain.

Reaching between sacks of beans and dried vegetables, he pulled out his ripstick and put it on his lap. Despite it being useless in this world, he refused to part with it. It was his only link to home and Mom … his one good thing he could hold on to.

Jak lay asleep curled against sacks of flour, seemingly oblivious to the jostling wagon.

The driver, a tall, skinny man with a scrawny neck, turned to Steven and smiled. "We are lucky that these roads are so well kept!" he shouted. "Just wait until we leave the forest and near the village Tabitha. They have no use for roads, and then it gets bumpy!"

Another hard bounce sent Steven bouncing hard on his rear. Putting back his ripstick, he swallowed any bitterness. That was what the monster fed upon.

"Looking comfy, Steven?" called out Lineus. The young man had slowed his horse so it was even with the wagon. "Would you care for a ride and get a rest from that wooden hunk of misery?"

"Call it what you wish, Lineus!" yelled the driver. "Just remember this wooden ark holds all your food, and without me you'd be eating your horse!"

"All the bouncing has loosed your brains, man!" Lineus winked at Steven. "In the stew this morning I had what I thought was a pea. Then I looked real closely and saw it was one of your brains jostled loose."

The driver laughed. "My pea brain is what lets me on this trip! If I had sense I would turn around!"

Lineus dismissed him with a wave. He motioned to Steven. "Come closer, boy. Don't be scared."

Steven moved tentatively to the wagon's edge. They reached a smooth stretch where the jostling was minimal. "Is your horse okay?" he asked shyly.

"Of course he is! Why do you ask?"

"Jason said it drank too much water and could get sick."

Lineus pulled a face. "Jason says a lot, but nothing at the same time—he doesn't know what he's talking about. How about you try Blackie out on your own?" He clapped his horse's neck and grinned at Steven. "Hop on!"

At that moment, wakened by the voices, Jak moved to Steven's side and wiped his eyes. Grinning, he then held a hand out to Blackie's nose.

The horse nickered and nuzzled the small hand.

"Careful!" warned Lineus, pulling his horse back. "He does bite!"

Jak shrugged and only stretched out his hand farther. Again Blackie moved to meet it with his nose.

Steven watched in amusement. "I don't think your horse will bite Jak."

"But I might," muttered the young man, again yanking the reins to move his horse from the moving wagon. "It took me weeks before he would even let me get near him!"

Jak clicked his tongue at the horse, ignoring the rider.

"So, Steven," Lineus said lightly, "about that ride. Are you ready?"

Steven shook his head and nudged Jak's shoulder. "Jak can ride. I'm kind of tired."

Lineus laughed. "But he rode yesterday. Don't you want to get out of that dust tub?"

Steven merely shrugged and looked away.

"Well, okay …" Lineus sighed. Jak was already perched on the side of the cart and looked ready to jump.

"Whoa!" yelled the driver, slowing the wagon. Lineus reached out his arms, took the small boy by the waist, and smoothly transferred him to his horse.

"Fortune smiles on you, Jak. You get a second ride in as many days." Lineus turned to Steven. "You'll get your chance, Steven. Don't worry."

The boy in the wagon settled against the sack of flour previously used by Jak and barely heard Lineus. The bouncing now actually felt calm … it began to lull the monster to sleep. Drowsily, he was aware that Lineus and Jak kept pace with the wagon. The young man kept watching him.

"You're a good kid," Lineus said suddenly. "I can see why Rachel looks after you so well."

"She's nice," Steven murmured, shifting uncomfortably, not quite sure if Lineus was talking to him or to Jak … Since Jak couldn't speak, he answered for both of them.

"Yes, indeed." After a moment of traveling, Lineus coughed. "Steven, I must confess. Rachel has, er, caught my eye. You must tell me about her. What is she like as a babysitter? I want to know everything about her."

In front of Lineus, Jak's ears perked up.

The driver of the wagon snickered, but this was lost in the clatter of wheels as the road turned rocky once more.

It was around midday when the party left the shady woods and entered the large open fields outlying Tabitha, the next village. The road faded into a rough path full of holes and stones.

Jason dropped back to a walk next to Rachel. "Marcal told me this used to be a great road, but the people of Durnwirk had it destroyed to discourage wizards from traveling to their village."

Rachel looked over at him, her face sickly. "Do … do you believe all the stuff about the wizards?"

Lifting his eyebrows, Jason gave an ironic smile. "We're here, aren't we?"

Rachel grimaced. "Yeah." The hours of riding had dulled Rachel's senses, and she barely knew what she was doing. Earlier that day, she'd vowed not to speak to Jason until he apologized for his rudeness.

"Well, wherever here is, I think it's a good idea to learn as much as we can. According to Marcal, there was a gold mine north of Durnwirk, but it collapsed and never reopened during the Wizard Wars. Everyone moved south, out of the region, or settled in Durnwirk. It's one of the few villages left this far north."

"Uh, really?" Rachel tried to look interested, but the swaying of the saddle made her look ready to hurl instead.

Jason nodded. "He said few have tried going farther north than Durnwirk but none ever return … something about the woods around the gold mine being haunted by killer wolves."

Rachel grunted. "Great."

"Yeah, I'm thinking they're just stories spread by those in Durnwirk to keep people away." Jason seemed to be trying awfully hard to be making conversation.

"I wonder what your brother and sister are doing right now." Rachel now looked at the teen. "Don't you?"

"Jakey and Courtney?" Jason actually looked startled. "I-I suppose they're wondering what happened …" Then he shrugged. "Either that, or having the time of their lives." He smiled again. "They love having parties with no supervision."

"It's not funny. We were just zapped from the face of the Earth."

Jason cleared his throat. "Courtney is pretty responsible. She'll look after Jakey okay—she's done it before."

Rachel bit her lip from a retort. *What about me? What about Lisa? We're not okay!* she wanted to scream. All at once she felt too tired and too hot to care.

The two fell into an awkward silence. Twice Jason looked back with a scowl and glanced toward Rachel. Then with a sigh, he kicked his mount and headed to be next to Marcal.

Left alone, Rachel tried to comprehend what had just happened. *He was trying to apologize for acting like a jerk the other day. Well, he should apologize to Lineus!*

Her stomach growled and her throat felt as if a rock was lodged in it. Every swallow brought a lump of pain. A thin sheen of sweat covered her body like an extra layer. The lack of breakfast wasn't the only thing haunting her … Without the cover of trees, the hot sun beat down without mercy. Her eyes closed.

Stop it! You're a babysitter! Do your job!

Snapping her eyes open, she tried to shake herself awake. It was just so stuffy … her eyes began to droop. She began to dream …

Steven was riding Blackie … the large stallion dwarfed the small boy. Dressed in his white suit, Steven's face was somehow blurred, but Rachel knew who it was immediately. Jason stood in the background waving his hands.

"No, don't let him ride, it's too dangerous! Courtney will look after him!"

Lineus laughed and tossed the reins of the horse to the boy. "Here, take him for a ride!" Then he slapped the horse's hindquarters.

In the midst of this, Rachel felt herself just standing there. Then Steven raced by her.

"No," she screamed. "Come back!"

"Don't worry," Marcal said, appearing at her side. "He's going to find Lisa and then take you back to Florida."

"And you can take me with you." Suzella jumped out of a bush that had just sprouted at Rachel's feet and drew her sword. "Every girl needs a warrior to protect her in your world." The sword gleamed against the flames of a fire … fire … everything was so hot—fire!

Rachel pushed past Marcal and Suzella and rushed after the horse and boy.

"Where are you going, beautiful?" called Lineus.

"To save Steven!" Rachel screamed back.

"Well, just don't burn your beautiful hair!"

"It's okay," Marcal yelled. "I'm watching!"

It wasn't okay. No matter how hard Rachel ran, she couldn't catch up with the horse. And flames rose before them all. A giant red and orange inferno lined the horizon. Still the horse didn't slow.

"I'm coming!" Rachel screamed.

Then from the towering flames walked a figure—a tall, terrible figure that became Isabella.

"Too late, fatso!" screamed the wizard. Carrying a dusting brush, she leveled it like a wand. "The boy is mine! He's my afternoon snack, and I'm not sharing with you!"

"No!"

Then all was white.

Extreme heat tortured the entire kitchen—besides the numerous cooking fires and clay ovens, torches hanging from the walls served as the main light sources. At the far end, sunlight came through only a single, round window next to a narrow door leading to the butchering area and animal pens. The building was built into a hill, and the door was the only access to fresh air from the kitchen. Lisa stood next to this door as if standing next to a fan. It wasn't enough.

Staring back at the crowded kitchen, Lisa did her best to keep from hyperventilating. Cooks were pulling out steaming breads from brick ovens. Others were kneading dough, chopping vegetables, cutting meat … and a million other things. At first glance, it seemed like utter chaos in a sweatbox filled with fire—a scene direct from Dante's *Inferno*, something Lisa had read sections of in her English class.

Feeling like a baked potato left too long in a microwave, she shifted her dress, now soaked with her sweat.

"Apprentice Lisa, what do you wish the … salid to be like?"

"Salad," she corrected, pushing herself from the back wall next to a four-foot-high mountain of carrots.

A group of cooks had gathered around a table covered in fresh lettuce and vegetables. Young Darvy, looking miserable, stood at the head but never raised his head to look at her. A tall, skinny cook with a thin mustache, who had asked the question, bowed when she approached. It was the first time somebody had spoken to her since the humiliation of Dosco.

"We have put the leaves in a pile as you said, but do not remember the next step."

"Just as I said … carrots and onions. Chop them up and put them on the leaves and mix them!"

"Mix them?"

"Yes! That's what salad means—a mixture!" Cooking at home was so much easier. Here, nobody had heard of a salad, and tomatoes and peppers were foreign substances.

"Y-yes, of course …" The cook bobbed his head. Ever since Dosco, the cooks had treated her with deep fear. Many mumbled about her appearing from thin air and bewitching the former head cook. To them, the doorway she'd come from was unusable. Speaking of Dosco, the large man snarled and pushed his way to the table, glaring at Lisa.

"I am ready to take command of my kitchens," he growled. At least he made the semblance of bowing. His eyes only held hate.

Looking up at him, Lisa refused to show fear or be cowed. "You picked up the beans? Every last one?"

"Yes! I picked up every last one." He spoke as if grinding each word with his yellow teeth.

Lisa narrowed her eyes. "Good. Clean the floor then."

"What!" roared the man.

"The floor, it's a mess."

"You're a half-wit! Nobody cleans the floor!" At the last moment he remembered to whom he spoke. "I mean, your mighty apprentice, the floors are not cleaned by us."

Frowning, Lisa surveyed the blackened, grease-encrusted floor littered with fallen vegetables, cuts of meat, fresh animal bones, and what looked to be rodent droppings. "Who cleans up the mess then?" she asked.

"Guttersnipes come at night and glean for scraps—that is the way it has always been!" Dosco answered belligerently. He looked ready to throttle her, but managed to bow.

Lisa frowned deeper. "Guttersnipes?"

"Children from the village, Your Worship," the thin cook said, moving tentatively from behind Dosco. He looked slightly nervous, but not because of the situation. "You see, the children, they take the fallen scraps home and … feed their families. The guards let them in at night."

Shocked, Lisa stifled a gasp. Thinking of little kids picking their way through this rat-infested trash heap made her want to be sick.

"It is how many families in the village survive," the cook continued. "Otherwise, many would starve."

Lisa swallowed. "Where is the village?"

"Bel-Belford. It's just outside the gates … where many of the castle's employees live. Many there are struggling. With the wizard gone, those that ruled in her place have not been the best to the people." He gulped. "Of course, with the wizard back and with you here, it will surely get better." He looked frightened and stepped back.

Lisa folded her arms and bit her lip. "Starting tonight, no guttersnipes, or any other child will be allowed in the kitchen."

A shocked murmur rose throughout the kitchen as the news quickly spread. The thin cook put a hand to his chin, but said nothing and hung his head.

Dosco glared. "You'll start an uprising … Your Worship." The last part was more a sneer than a show of respect.

Lisa ignored him. Looking at the thin cook, she realized the entire kitchen had stopped working and seemed to be grumbling. Many eyes were glaring at her.

"Instead, I want the food production doubled for tonight." She licked her lips. "The leftovers will be gathered and put out back. You," she said, staring at the thin cook, "will take charge in distributing the leftover food fairly to the children for their families. I want all leftovers to be given to the village."

"That is madness," spat Dosco, not bothering to bow any longer. "You will ruin this kitchen!" He used his girth to loom over the much smaller girl.

Her face bubbling like the stew behind her, Lisa glared up. "And your job is to clean the floor! The stones should shine before nightfall! Now, I will take a break. The new head cook will come with me. I leave …" she paused and looked again at the thin cook.

Breaking into a smile, the man bowed to her. "Hube. My name is Hube, Wizard Apprentice."

"I leave Hube in charge!" Not waiting for a reaction, she grabbed Darvy by his dirty sleeve and dragged him to the door leading outside. Stunned and frightened, the boy provided no resistance.

As the cool fresh air met their faces, a new wave of excited energy crashed behind them. Never before had the kitchen cooked so much food of the best quality in a single day.

Chapter Twenty-Eight

Darvy refused to meet Lisa's gaze. They were outside the kitchen where the air was cooler … almost too cold.

Feeling suddenly lonely and embarrassed, Lisa wiped her forehead. "I'm … I'm sorry for saying you were the head cook," she said. "I'll make sure Hube will take the job."

The boy gave no reaction. Standing in a dirt yard crowded with wandering chickens and smelling of manure and blood, he looked ready to cry.

"Are-are you from Belford?" she tried.

Ever so slightly, the boy nodded.

"Oh …" Lisa suddenly blinked, feeling dizzy. "I need to find shade and sit …" She started to fan her face. "I don't know how you work in that place—it's like an oven set on broil."

The boy looked up at her for the first time. "I-I know a place where we can go," he said. "Follow me."

Breathing easier as the air cleared, the boy led the way down a narrow path that passed through an arched gate and into a grassy field dotted with flowers. A clump of small, twisty trees grew near a pool of brown water. The water came from a metal grate at the base of the outer stone wall. Well over two stories, the wall stretched in both directions until hitting towers marking the back corners of the fortress.

"This is where the soldiers sometimes practice," Darvy explained shyly. "The water is from the moat, so don't get too close. There are some nasty fish swimming in it." Lisa viewed everything with large eyes and didn't say a word. She became the scared mute while the boy became more confident as he steered them to the trees. "This fortress has never been taken, which is important because behind that wall is the dark forest with the path leading to the mountain. It's the only road to the mountain that an army can use, so whoever owns this fortress owns the mountain."

"What mountain?" Lisa finally asked, finding her voice. If ever she forgot she didn't belong to this world, she now remembered. This was nothing like she had ever seen.

"Look up."

In the distance, rising above the wall, stretched a great gray mountain that looked like a giant tent. Staring at it, Lisa shivered. It seemed to be looking straight back at her … "What's so important about the mountain?"

The boy gave her a hard look. "Aren't you the wizard's apprentice? That's Mount Aerrius—that's where the first wizard was born. Many years ago, Aerrius was a poor man from Belford, so the legend says. He climbed to the top of the mountain and spent over forty days and nights there without eating or drinking. Everyone thought him dead. Then, one night, the entire mountain lit up as a great fire burst from its top. From this fire floated Aerrius …" The boy's eyes were wide with wonder as he gazed up at the mountain, reliving the moment. "With him was the power of wizardry."

"Wh-what happened?"

The boy shrugged. "Aerrius joined the king and used his power to destroy many enemies. Others wished for his power. Some tried to climb the mountain and seek the dark spirit, but few came down alive. Others were taught by Aerrius himself. Then, when wizards rose in all areas of the world, Aerrius left the king's side and went back up the mountain. By then he had great riches and he built a temple there—a temple for the spirit who rules Panterra. Devoting his life to serving in the temple, he was never seen again." Darvy licked his lips. "Someplace inside the temple is where the dark spirit lives … If the right sacrifices are made, then the dark spirit can grant anything you wish. Priests live there now and take care of the place and never leave it. King Gretz the First rose to power by building this fortress and granting it to his wizards to command. With control of the fortress, the mountain cannot be taken. Over time, though, fewer climbed the mountain and now almost nobody goes there. The Wizard Wars killed most of the wizards and the new ones don't care for the old ways. But …" the boy said and wiped his nose, "a few years ago, your master, Isabella, and King Herman of the East's wizard, Borbu, went up the mountain together … That is where they heard the prophecy."

Reaching the trees, Darvy sat under the bows of a shady elm and sighed.

Lisa took a seat next to him. "What prophecy?"

Darvy gave her another look. "Are you sure you're Isabella's apprentice?"

Her face turning red, Lisa ducked her head. "I'm actually new here."

"But you must know about the prophecy!" Amazed, Darvy told her about the boy needing to be sacrificed and eaten in order to give great power to the wizard that did the deed … Lisa's face paled considerably.

"That's why she wants Steven," she whispered fearfully. "She wants to eat him!"

Tears sprung from her eyes.

"Hey, now!" Darvy knelt and put an arm on her shoulder. "The girl who treated Dosco like a fool can't cry! Where did you come from?"

"Oh, you wouldn't know or understand …"

"Try me."

It's … it's a place called Florida."

For the first time, the pudgy boy grinned. "No kidding?" he said. "I grew up in North Carolina!"

Rachel's eyes flashed open. *A dream … only a dream.* Lineus laughed from behind her. Blinking rapidly, she found herself hunched over her mount and nearly falling. Her arms slowly reacting to her commands, Rachel pulled herself upright. Swallowing proved painfully impossible. Just as the dream began to fade, Lineus cried out.

"Yaw! Go, Blackie!"

Turning in her saddle, her heavy eyes saw her dream coming to life.

Lineus's black horse thundered by, with two figures perched on his back—a man holding a boy. Screaming in horror, Rachel made to give chase.

"Why does everybody here have to be so stupid?" the woman growled, brushing off her dress where the man had just placed his hand when returning the change to Red after he'd purchased the horses and carriage. As he'd reached over her, the buffoon had tripped and scattered the coins across her dress and feet. In the commotion, the man had even stuck a filthy hand in her shoe!

"To a stupid hag, everybody is stupid," Red muttered, flicking the reins to the newly acquired carriage. "The man recognized me … he knew I possess magic and that I could have easily turned him into a chicken and simply taken what I wanted. Instead I paid gold. Get use to such reactions."

"Hmmph," muttered the woman, wisely deciding to keep quiet.

The carriage was an old, rickety, four-wheeled contraption with an enclosed cabin for passengers. Right now the passengers were two young children curled on the floor and sound asleep. The licorice root kept their smaller bodies awake long enough for them to reach the carriage and that was all.

The woman fingered her portion, which was hidden in the folds of her dress. She suspected it really did the opposite of what Red said—she'd chewed none and managed the portals without a reaction. However, the children dropped off a little too conveniently.

Keeping her eyes deliberately away from her supposed husband, she took in the unique village with sudden curiosity. Travelers of all types walked the streets. Almost all were men, she noted … and the women she did see certainly didn't appear to be the motherly sort. Large, bulky, and loaded with weapons, they looked as friendly as mountain lions. One woman sported more hairs on her chin than her head and spat a black wad in the woman's direction. The woman quickly switched her gaze. Few children ran the streets. These were mostly small, scrawny, and furtive. And mostly up to no good.

The woman watched as a young boy and girl pushed their way into a crowd while being chased by a fat man in a robe, crying thief. Nobody paid attention to him. What struck the woman as strange was the lack of horses. Theirs was the only carriage visible, and many passersby glared at them with contempt. The woman shuddered and, despite her feelings, moved closer to Red. The children, she saw, escaped by climbing the side of a raised building like a pair of monkeys. The boy waved his back end down at the red-faced man before vanishing over the wall. Such was life at Dunbar …

Often called the floating village on the mountain by visitors, the village of Dunbar actually sat in the valley between two great mountains in the west of Panterra. Due to heavy snowdrifts in the winter and extreme flooding in the spring from melting snow, nearly all the structures were constructed on tall pillars of solid rock lined with thick plates of polished crystal. On a clear day, when the sun sparkled off the crystal and reflected a blue sky, it did indeed make the raised buildings appear to be floating on air. This led to rumors of magic and sorcery in its midst. The presence of Red, a frequent visitor, did not hurt these rumors.

In actuality, the only reason it existed without being overrun by bandits and invaders was its extreme location and distance from the next village. Surrounded by harsh desert on one side and thick forest on the other, the mountains provided great hideouts for any of those wayward of the law or any who wished for the solitary life. However, to survive the harsh weather, the bandits and others had to depend on provisions from the village. Each summer, a wagon train arrived with fresh supplies and news of the outside world. This was exchanged for sculpted stones of crystal that the village was so famous for—that and stolen merchandise. Knowing their survival rested on the wagon train, the bandits made Dunbar a place of refuge and relative peace. Miners, artists, and bandits lived side by side in rough, harsh, and uneasy harmony. This made it the perfect place to start a journey that you wished nobody to know about. Few ever left or arrived except when the yearly wagon train came around. Horses, like most animals, rarely lasted the long winter. They were eaten.

Courtney and Jakey knew none of this as they slept. They also knew none of Red's plans or where he was taking them. Neither did the woman. Huffing under her breath, she scratched at her right shoe. Did the buffoon leave a coin in there after all? Something certainly bit at her.

Rachel jabbed Bolder's flanks. "No!" she cried hoarsely. Out in front, behind a cloud of dust and rapidly receding horses and riders, she saw a bright, terrible light—the fire! Isabella was coming.

"No!" she cried again, this time more strongly. Then Bolder leapt forward. Finally, he was being told to run. Ears flattened, he took off as if shot from a catapult. Jerked backward and not ready for it, Rachel clutched for the reins and saddle horn but was way too slow in her reaction. Tumbling back, she flew heels over head. The next thing she knew, she lay flat on her back with a splitting headache and choking on dust.

"Rachel!" she heard Jason scream.

Dimly she was aware of Marcal's voice shouting for a halt.

The rider just behind Rachel reached her side first. He was a bear of a man with a thick reddish beard and mustache who smelled of smoke and rotting meat. Rachel couldn't think of his name. He never spoke much and had small shifty eyes. Now those eyes were looking down at Rachel in fear.

Murd was what the others called him, Rachel suddenly remembered. Murd …

"What's wrong with yer?" he barked, blasting sour breath in her face. His nose had been smashed years before and had never healed properly, and his teeth were crooked and yellow.

"I, I—uh …" Rachel tried sitting, but immediately felt as if her head was full of thick jelly being mixed in a blender.

"Ya stuck that poor horse with ya feet and tumbled backwards like a sack of potatoes tossed from a cart!" Murd growled. "Never seen such a thing."

"Oh …" Rachel said slowly as everything started to swim before her eyes.

The anxious face of Jason pushed next to Murd's, and a crowd of other men joined. "Rachel, are you all right?" asked the teen. He sounded concerned.

"I'm fine," Rachel snapped, blinking her eyes in an effort to clear her head. Slowly her breathing returned to normal, which was not a good thing. Surrounded by unwashed males in the hot sun, she did all she could not to choke. Then she remembered. "Steven! I need to save—"

She stopped. A much smaller and much better-looking face had pushed through the crowd.

"Careful, lad, not too close," warned Murd, laying a hand on Steven's shoulder. "She's a little addled."

Rachel blinked. Then who was on the horse? Gasping, she pushed herself to a sitting position, which took tremendous effort. "Where's Jak?"

"Take it easy, Rachel," Jason said. "We're trying to help you."

"Then let go of me and let me up!" she shouted in his face. *Why did I do that?* Thinking clearly proved very difficult at the moment.

The men scooted back so only Jason and Steven remained next to her. Grabbing her right arm, Jason pulled.

Gritting her teeth, Rachel rose to stand unsteadily. Spots danced before her eyes, but she blinked them away. Pushing herself free, she stared about wildly.

"Where's Jak?" she demanded. "I saw this in a dream, I …"

"Relax, Rachel," Jason muttered. "You're making a scene."

Ignoring him, she saw Marcal chasing down Bolder … and beyond him, Blackie still raced away! Just like in the dream, nobody cared! Rachel stifled a scream. Then her mouth fell open and everything started wavering …

"Oh, great …" she moaned. What she had thought to be giant flames was merely the sunlight reflecting off a hill covered in golden wheat. Lineus had control of the reins and was turning the horse back. It had only been her imagination.

Red turned down a narrow alley and steered the carriage to a different part of the village. Pulling on the reins, he pulled the carriage to a sharp stop in front of a large square building raised several feet in the air. The streets were full of manure and other filth. The building and those around it were covered in the same filth and appeared dark and foreboding. They were at the edge of the village now and few people were about.

The woman quavered when catching a glimpse of the few who were. Rough-looking men draped in tattered animal skins, each one carried a club or sword on his belt. More than one stared at the carriage in ways that could not be considered neighborly or friendly. The heavy scents of smoky, unwashed flesh mixed with soiled mud and cooked meat filled her nostrils.

Covering her nose, the woman made sure to keep her gaze low. She didn't have to be told to know they were in the dangerous area of a dangerous village.

They were stopped in a squalid square. All the stone supports here were cracked and scarred—years of freezing and thawing had severely weakened many. Somebody had filled the largest gaps with plaster in attempts at repair, but this only made the buildings look more decrepit and even less safe. Thatched roofs needed replacing, and the stone sidings were crumbling in many walls.

Hopping from the seat, Red gave the woman a look that bordered between amusement and disgust. This could have been directed at her, or the setting.

"I have to pick up supplies for our journey … stay here until I return."

The woman looked at him with frightened eyes, causing Red to chuckle without humor.

"I know what you are thinking, woman. This is not like your Florida—escape here only leads to death. Driving a carriage is not like driving a car. Besides, where would you go if you did try to escape? In this village, you'd be easily found … you notice that few travel by similar means as us?" The woman didn't nod, but it was true. Almost everyone in the village walked. Many had goats with them that carried their goods. Horses and wagons were scarce. "When winter comes, the wagons and carriages become firewood and the horses become meat. Either that, or they leave the village before first snow." He smiled. "Here, survival is the only thing that matters. If you wish to live, listen to me." He nodded to where a particularly nasty-faced man leaned against the pillar of the next building and watched them unabashedly. "He'll not be as kind to you as I, that I promise … In the winter months, when meat runs low, men like him don't lose weight. Think about why."

The woman shivered and didn't realize it when Red had left. By the time she looked for him, he was already halfway up the wooden stairs leading to the building's door. The reins were by her side and the horses pulling the carriage were left untied. Feeling very alone and very scared, she risked another look at the man against the pillar. She didn't look once at the loose reins.

The man continued staring at her. Powerfully built with arms like slabs of meat, his belly hung over a black leather belt that secured a thick club the size of a baseball bat. Bareheaded, he had greasy curls the hue of mud hanging about his swollen face. With wild curls hiding most of his face, only a bulbous red nose and dark beady eyes stood out. The eyes continued watching the woman as a hairy hand gently caressed the club at his waist.

Breathing hoarsely, the woman stared down at her feet. "Where's a drink when you need it?" she muttered. Then she stamped her right foot. It still itched like crazy. Reaching down to scratch it again, more to get her mind off the man than anything else, she suddenly paused. It was not a coin lodged in her shoe causing the discomfort … it was a note. Perhaps not everybody here was so stupid after all …

Back behind her, Courtney and Jakey began to stir. Waking from dreams, they were blissfully unaware of the danger fast approaching

"We have to get out of here," Lisa said, pulling at her hair and stalking around the shady spot by the standing water. She shot a look at the boy again. "How many others grew up in America around here?"

"Uh, just me," Darvy said. He remained seated under the tree—now looking slightly uneasy. He'd just finished telling Lisa about how his parents had family in North Carolina and that they had sent him there at the age of five. "People in this world have been traveling in your world for a long time. I had to return though, because of, uh, trouble. My parents died here and my relatives … had to send me back," he finished lamely. "Bad economy …"

Lisa scratched her cheek. "That sounds rough. I'm sorry. So how did you end up working here with that, that Dosco?"

The boy's face flushed. "I-I didn't have a choice … it was either that, or starve." Suddenly he looked scared. "And now your master—"

"I don't have a master!" Lisa exclaimed through clenched teeth. "I'm just a kid like you. I was kidnapped by that twisted lady, okay?"

"Isabella, then—she's back. She's an evil lady … She won't be happy about what you did in the kitchen."

Lisa grew silent. Her mind started working furiously.

"So, uh, now what?" the boy asked her nervously.

Lisa gave him a look. "I … I think it's time we leave."

The boy gulped. "You want to go back to the kitchens?" he asked.

Lisa shook her head. "No. I mean, it's time we leave this place. We get out of here."

"What?" The boy stared up at her with disbelief. "Where would we go? You know nothing of this world, and I … I've only heard stories about it."

Lisa shrugged. "Look, never mind that. You live in Belford, right?"

"Um, yes …"

"Are you able to gather food for a week and … I don't know, whatever we need for a trip?"

"You mean, like horses?" He grunted when Lisa nodded. "Um, maybe … I think so."

Excitement sparked in Lisa's eyes. After waking up in this horrible world, she was finally starting to feel a level of control. Meeting a boy who understood her world helped tremendously.

"Good. Get everything ready for us to pick up. Meet me back here in say, two hours."

"Okay, sure—not that I have a watch, though. What are you going to do?"

Lisa grinned. "I'm going to find help."

"Wait, Lisa … do you even know how to ride a horse?"

"Don't worry," she called over her shoulder. "I've had three years of riding lessons with my brother!"

Trust is a dangerous thing that can easily lead you to greatness but just as easily betray you to utter darkness and despair. And the worst part is, you almost never know where trust will lead until it is too late. Using it took a leap of faith. Lisa used that faith now.

Lisa took deep breaths to control her breathing. What she was about to do … was unthinkable. Stupid. Foolish. And perhaps deadly. And probably wouldn't work.

After a few wrong turns and with the help of a servant, Lisa found her way back to the entrance of the dungeon. On the other side of the kitchens, deep in the bowels of the fortress, a scarred wooden door stood before her. A single torch flickered above the door and outlined two guards holding spears. When seeing Lisa descend the stairs before them, they hastily snapped to attention.

Lisa did not know this, but word of her actions had spread like wildfire in a dry forest. Servants from the kitchens told of the magical apprentice who appeared from thin air in a flash of white and let no man dare stand up to her. Why, the powerful Dosco, whom the servants feared almost as much as Isabella, had been turned to a meek kitten by her magic. Many minds took the kitten part literally.

"G-guards," stammered Lisa, edging into the flickering light. "I, I left something in the chamber last night. I've come to collect it."

The two men eyed her.

Lisa resisted the urge to flee—the last night had been a horror to her.

Locked up in utter darkness in rancid straw, while surrounded by all manner of creepy crawlies and rodents … she shuddered just remembering. With no bathroom, she had to use the corner … with no food, she starved. But worse was the dark. Fear often comes from imagining what you cannot see. Her imagination had a lot to work with.

Only the man, Tendl—his deep voice in the darkness—kept her from completely losing it. Telling her to relax and think of better times, to think of her mother tucking her in for the night, the man had started to sing. With his deep, baritone voice, his songs were gentle and soothing … that was how Lisa had slept until morning. And now she had returned.

"You'll have to see the jailer," one of the guards said gruffly.

Lisa flinched. She recognized the voice. Swallowing her fear, she forced herself to stare at the guards. Sure enough, in the dull light, she made out their tunics as red and each bearing the symbol of a lion. They had to be the two soldiers she had overheard when going to the kitchens.

"Is the jailor through the door?"

"Yes, but none can enter without the Wizard's or Captain Bodin's orders."

"You two … you are both under me, right?" Her voice was smaller than she wanted and sounded frightened. Still, the men nodded, after the briefest of hesitations.

"Good. Um, I need you … I need you both to go to the kitchens and guard the vegetables. Before you leave, open the door."

The two guards visibly jerked and looked at each other. "Wh-what?" asked the first one.

"You heard me." Lisa took another breath. "We have too much food in the fortress. Tonight, the leftovers are being given to the villagers. You two have the job of making sure the vegetables are divided among the families as well."

"But, I—"

"Do not question me!" Lisa said sharply. "Isabella will not like it! Now go do your job. Make sure all the vegetables are given away … and the chickens. Give them away, too."

"Wh-what about the dungeons, Mighty One?" the second one asked nervously as he turned and unlocked the door.

"Um, I, I'll put a spell on it! And I'll, I'll put a spell on you if you don't hurry!"

The guards hurried past her, each mumbling under their breath. The door opened before her.

"What's the meaning of this?" groaned a deep voice. "Who sends the guards away?" A shape about the size of Dosco, only wider, filled the doorway.

"Don't be afraid, Lisa," Lisa whispered. "You're in charge." Clearing her throat, she said loudly, "Are you the jailer?"

"Aye."

"I am Isabella's apprentice. I come to retrieve something from the cells."

"You're the girl from last night! Odd that the wizard throws you in a dungeon at night and makes you apprentice by day." For a moment Lisa thought the game was up. But then the shape backed away. "What do I know? Come with me. Wizards have their ways …"

Frightened, she followed the jailer.

Grabbing a torch from the wall, the jailer moved past his quarters and turned a corner, then led Lisa into the familiar hall lined with foul-smelling cells. Covering her nose, Lisa kept her gaze away from the jailer and walked to the cell she wanted.

"Open this one," she said.

"But that is the wrong one!" protested the jailer. "That's the one with the prisoner."

"I know. That's what I forgot. Oh, and jailer …" Lisa swallowed. "I also need your clothes—your outer, um, garments. Give them to the prisoner and take his place."

The figure lying on the straw stood and peered out. The right side of his face was covered with a massive bruise, which gave him a wicked appearance. Rough yellow hair hung over his forehead and covered his cheeks and lower face.

"You better listen to the girl," he said gravely. "She is powerful in magic and will turn you into a toad if you delay."

The jailer stood with the torch trembling. "How do you know this?"

The prisoner grinned wickedly. "What do you think happened to the last apprentice?"

Chapter Twenty-Nine

The woman crumpled the note with her shaking hands. According to the note, Red had done this sort of thing before … if she valued her life and the lives of the children, the note told her to flee. Red was a known slave trader.

"Where are we?" muttered Courtney, poking out her head while blinking sleepily.

"Hush!" whispered the woman hoarsely.

"I'm starving," Jakey groaned from inside the cab.

"You'll be a lot more than that if you don't hush! I need to think!"

"All I can think about is food," Jakey's voice returned.

"The way things look you just might become food if you're not careful!"

Courtney opened the carriage door and climbed out.

"Where are we?" she asked in wonder. "What's wrong?"

"A lot of things! Get back inside—no, come up here."

The woman waited for Courtney to climb up beside her. As the young girl searched for footing, Jakey stuck his head out and immediately wanted to get out too. Grumbling under her breath, the woman ended up pulling both children to the seat next to her.

All the time, the man against the pillar watched while licking his cracked lips.

"Does either of you brats know how to handle this thing?" the woman asked half-seriously.

Courtney gave her a look. "We're little kids from Florida. What do you think?"

"That I need a drink and better company. Listen, I don't want to ruin your day, and that man may dote on you, but he's a slave dealer. He's probably in there right now selling your brother. I'll be next!"

Courtney stared at her, horrified. "What?"

"You heard me. We need to get this rig out of here pronto!"

"Excuse me, hag," a pleasant voice said by their feet, "but did you say you needed a driver?" A raggedy boy popped his head from under the carriage and stood below them.

Startled at his appearance, the woman nearly fell off the other side of the carriage. Courtney grabbed her arm and hung on tight.

"Where did you come from?" the woman spluttered as she regained her heartbeat and seat. "Does any child have manners around here?"

Courtney stared down at the boy curiously. About her age, he had dark, unkempt hair that hung like a mop around his thin, dirty face. With a malnourished appearance, he wore a long, ragged tunic down to his shins, belted at his waist. However, his eyes were keenly intelligent and sparkled with mischief.

"Um, do you know a driver?" Courtney asked hesitantly.

A wide mouth opened to display surprisingly white teeth with a small overbite. "Joe!" cried the boy shrilly.

"Is that your name or the driver you know?" the woman growled. "Get away, street punk. Whatever you're selling, we ain't buying."

The boy ignored her. "Joe, come on! I found a ride!"

Another child scurried from behind a barrel across the street and joined the boy. About the boy's age and size, this was a girl who wore a rough dress that had once been yellow. Tangled hair fell past her shoulders. With features similar to the boy's, her green eyes also glinted with mischief and intelligence.

"Are you sure about this, Jan?" She sounded doubtful. "These people don't look so friendly."

The woman's eyes went wide. She recognized the two now—they were the kids she'd seen climbing the building to escape the man who'd been chasing them.

"What are you two doing here?" she snapped harshly. "You're thieves!"

The boy grinned and scampered up the front wheel, then the door, before reaching the top of the carriage.

"Hey, get down from there!" shouted the woman.

"Looks good to me, Joe," Jan said cheerfully.

Suddenly, a man burst into the square from the alley—the same man who had been chasing the children before. "Hey!" he shouted when seeing them. "Get those kids!"

"Yep," the boy said, leaning over the top of the carriage. "Looks real good."

The woman, Courtney, and Jakey sat trapped in a scene that none knew the lines for. Not knowing what to do, they sat in disbelief as the girl suddenly leapt up and pushed next to Jakey.

"Pardon me," she said. "Jan says you need a driver."

"I never actually said that, Joe," the boy said, "but you read my mind!"

"W-we don't need a driver," the woman practically spat.

"In that case," the boy said, lying flat on the roof. "We're thieves and we're stealing your wagon."

"Stop right there!" the man shouted, racing their way.

The man from the pillar pushed himself up and also started toward them.

"I'm going to die," moaned the woman.

Then the girl grabbed up the reins. "Ya!" she shouted harshly, shaking them. "Get going!"

The boy knelt on top of the carriage roof and threw something at the horses. "Get going, you old nags!"

Neighing shrilly, the horses responded, jumping forward so fast the girl nearly fell forward.

"Stop!" wailed the woman, barely keeping her seat. "Stop!"

"Sorry!" shouted the girl. "Hold on! I've never done this before!"

Courtney grabbed Jakey and hugged him close. The woman hugged them both. Shouting, the boy hopped down in the midst of them and grabbed the reins with the girl.

"Pull right!" he shouted.

"I'm trying!" Joe wailed.

"I mean the other right!"

"That's left, you dumphock!"

"Right!"

Somehow, the two managed to turn the horses to face the alley exiting the square and they were leaving at a run.

"Get out of the way!" shouted the boy. "Watch out!"

The man who had been giving chase had to leap aside to avoid being run down.

Then they were onto the main street and headed out of the village.

Red stepped out of the building with two large sacks full of supplies. His face was full of disbelief as he stared at the empty space below him. Immediately his eyes turned bloodred and he threw down the sacks in rage. Only after he stomped away did others leave the shadows and quickly snatch up the fallen food.

Once the last building of the village disappeared from sight, the boy and girl pulled back on the reins and hollered for the horses to slow down. They were on a flat, narrow road between steep cliffs and sparse vegetation.

"I think we made it," sighed the girl, as the rough ride settled to a walk.

"I hope so, but that guy is pretty stubborn. I thought we lost him three times already."

Rattled, the woman pushed away from Courtney and Jakey, who were nearly on her lap to make room for the wild kids doing the driving.

"That man seemed pretty mad at you," she huffed.

"He should be," the boy said cheerfully. "We stole his money purse."

"And his knife," the girl said.

"Not to mention his belt," added the boy.

Courtney and Jakey just looked at each other and said nothing.

The woman nearly pulled out her hair. "Do you mean you two really are dirty thieves?"

"Well," said the boy, "we can give back your carriage."

"Which we're very grateful for," hastily added the girl. "Thank you."

"Why, I—" the woman ended in a fit of coughing.

"Is she your grandmother?" the girl asked, looking at Courtney for the first time. This made the woman cough in rage.

"No," Courtney said quickly, "she's not … Are you two really thieves?"

"Yep." The boy stood on the seat and held the reins proudly.

Sitting, the girl elbowed the boy's knee. "Not that we're proud of it."

Courtney frowned while Jakey, now crushing her lap, looked at the boy hopefully.

"I wish you stole some food," he said. "I'm starving."

"Jakey!" Courtney admonished. "Don't say that!"

"Ah, that's okay," the boy said cheerfully. "We'll be stopping now."

The girl and boy both pulled back on the reins, bringing the carriage to an abrupt halt and nearly sending the woman headfirst into a horse's rump.

"Why are we stopping here?" Courtney asked uneasily. Jakey didn't fight as she put her arm around him. On either side, the rocky cliffs loomed over them dangerously.

Glaring, the woman stood unsteadily and shook out her dress. "I'm going to take you two brats by the ears and shake your heads until sense finally comes into them!"

The boy stared at her curiously while the girl just shook her head.

"Temper is a bad thing," she said wisely. "It makes you less careful."

"I don't have to be careful with you two scrawny twigs!" The woman made to push by Courtney and Jakey when something whizzed over her head and thudded into the dirt below.

"Wha-ho, down there!" cried a man's voice. A figure stood from the rocks above with an arrow poised to fire from a bow. "Consider yourselves surrounded and being robbed!"

"See," admonished the boy. "You should always be careful. Especially in these parts. Thieves are everywhere."

Nearly fainting, the woman collapsed next to Courtney and found the girl's hand with her own. "I-I've nearly been shot with … an arrow …"

Her own breath lost, Courtney only stared with wide, frightened eyes.

Walking carefully down an unseen trail, the man hopped into the road and lowered his arrow.

"Hiya, Conwall," the boy greeted him. "We were hoping you would be here."

"Like always," sniffed the girl. "Really, you should change your spot every once and a while."

"Yeah, and you'd never have stopped us if we didn't stop first."

Frowning, the man looked at them. "I should have known it'd be you two rogues. I wasn't trying to ambush anybody. If you must know, I'm on my way to Carson's hideout."

"Ah," said the boy, "you thought you had yourself a steal!"

"Well, when I heard your noisy carriage, I did hope for something," admitted the man. He glanced up at the woman. "Don't tell me you two are now dealing old hags and children."

"No, Conwall," the girl said with a smile. "They're our passengers."

"We had to run sort of quick from the village," explained the boy. "They let us use their carriage. We were kind of hoping to go get a hot meal from you." His eyes widened in innocence.

"Ah, kids ..." Throwing his head back, the man sighed. Looking sourly at the woman, he waved her down. "You're lucky the waifs found me and not some cutthroat. That's a pretty fancy outfit you got. But come on down, you'll be safe ... I can't risk getting on the wrong side of Joe and Jan. The boss would kill me."

"We knew you'd be here, Conwall," the girl said dismissively. "You're always on this part of the road."

Grunting, the man reached up and caught her as she jumped into his arms. Setting her down gently, he turned for the boy. Giving a sour look, the boy leapt unassisted to the ground, landing lightly on his feet.

"I'm staying right here," the woman said flatly. "So are the girl and boy."

"Not if you want to eat," growled the man, grabbing the reins. He secured them around the trunk of a dead tree near the side of the road. Looking quite content, the two horses bent down and started munching on a little grass that grew in the middle of the road.

Sullenly, the woman climbed down. Sitting against the front wheel of the wagon, she ducked her head and sulked. Courtney and Jakey followed her with uncertainty.

"I'm Conwall of the Mountains," the man said, bowing low. In his early twenties at most, he wore thick trousers, boots, and a white shirt under a black waistcoat. Head shaved close to his scalp, he had the beginnings of a dark goatee. A belted sword hung from his waist and he carried a quiver of arrows on his back. Sharp cheekbones protruded from his face, and a small scar was visible over his left eye.

"I'm, I'm Courtney. This is, um, my brother, Jakey."

The man knelt and motioned for the boy and girl thief to stand with him. Clapping each on the back, he introduced them as "Jan the mouse" and "Joe the snake."

"Isn't the boy Joe and the girl Jan?" the woman asked disagreeably.

The boy frowned. "I'm Jan."

"And I'm Joe," said the girl.

"And together, they're the two greatest thieves in Dunbar," the man said with obvious pride. "Pickpockets, burglars, or spies, these two are the best." He slapped the boy in the arm. "And right now Jan is going up to fetch my supplies so we can start eating."

"I'll go gather wood, Conwall," the girl said happily. "Courtney, do you want to come?"

"She stays here!" the woman said. "What about the others?"

"What others?" the man asked, confused.

"Didn't you say we were surrounded?"

"Oh, he always says that," Joe scoffed. "Don't you, Conwall?"

"Yeah," added Jan. "Too bad he hasn't any friends to make it true!" He danced out of the way of a halfhearted swipe by Conwall.

"Get your dirty hides going," growled the bandit. "Soon the whole land will know my game and I'll be out of work!"

Laughing, Joe and Jan dashed into the rocks, both climbing the terrain like they were born doing it.

"I'll get the pack down before you find your first stick!" shouted Jan.

"Only in your empty head!" returned Joe.

Sighing, Conwall turned sheepishly to Courtney and Jakey. "I guess you know by now, I'm not the greatest bandit in the world."

The woman snorted. "You can say that again. Young punks like you are good for nothing and should rot in jail."

Ignoring her, Conwall motioned for Courtney and Jakey to join him. Crouching, he started gathering small bits of dry grass.

"Help gather stuff like this—the smaller and drier the better."

"Leave the punk alone if you know what's good for you," growled the woman. "His kind is nothing but trouble."

As the woman scowled, Courtney and Jakey tentatively started to help Conwall. Each held doubts about the turn of events, but at least they were together and not captives of the awful man Red.

On top of the piled dry grass, Conwall stuck a single piece of charred cloth and produced a shard of flint and a piece of steel from his belt. "This is how you build a fire," he explained. He showed Jakey and Courtney how to hold the steel at an angle and strike the flint, creating sparks. It took some doing, but he managed to catch a spark on the cloth. Blowing on the cloth caused it to glow red and soon a small flame danced on the dried grass.

"First try," Conwall said proudly, giving Jakey's head a playful cuff. "You bring good fortune, boy. Usually it takes me half the morning to make a fire."

The woman chuckled. "Usually it takes me three seconds." Reaching into her pocket, she held up a book of matches.

"What are those?" Conwall asked, frowning.

"Magic sticks," hooted the woman.

Before Conwall could investigate, hollering came from above. Jan and Joe popped into view almost at the same time, each at a dead run.

"You dropped a stick, Joe. You hafta go back!"

"That's for you, Jan! We're playing fetch now!"

Jan held a heavy pack in front of him while Joe carried a heavy load of wood. Laughing, they jostled each other until leaping down onto the road and collapsing in panting heaps.

"Careful, Jan!" cried Conwall. "That's my whole life in there!" Getting up, he quickly snatched the pack away from the boy.

"Ah, there's nothing good in there," panted the boy. "I've already checked."

"If I find one thing missing, boy, I'll put you over the fire and roast you good and proper."

"Not without wood, you won't." Joe started chucking the wood one piece at a time toward the fire.

"I should've stayed at the hideout," Conwall muttered. Reaching into his pack, he pulled out a frying pan.

"If you did that, you wouldn't get our loot," Jan said carelessly.

Conwall's head jerked up. "What did you two snatch this time?"

"After we eat," Joe said firmly. "We haven't eaten since yesterday morning."

Soon the smell of fried meat and potatoes filled the air. Even the woman licked her lips in anticipation and moved closer to the fire when Conwall removed a pan full of crisp pork from the fire. Jan and Joe had showed Courtney and Jakey how to bury potatoes in the coals and were taking them out with sticks. Conwall had only one metal plate, but this proved no problem as Jan ran to the road and picked up several flat stones about eight inches across. The woman grabbed the plate, but everyone else happily used fire-washed stoneware. While the children shared water from an animal bladder (Courtney and Jakey gave a pause before partaking, but ended up being too thirsty to refuse), Conwall and the woman shared a bottle of wine.

"Tastes like warm acid," the woman complained before taking another swig from the thick bottle of green glass.

"I guess that's good," mumbled Conwall, eyeing the disappearing liquid.

Everyone was starving and Conwall ended up cooking his remaining food supply.

"Kids have no stomachs, only holes," he muttered as Jan and Joe fought over the last piece of pork. He licked his own knife.

"Thank you for the food," Courtney said to him timidly. "It was really good."

"Yeah," Jakey said, wiping his mouth with the back of his hand. "Much better than our brother can cook."

"I've had better," grunted the woman. She pushed herself back against the wheel and started licking her fingers.

Joe and Jan looked disappointed when Conwall raised empty hands to indicate the lack of food.

"I'm just glad I at least got to try a bite," the young bandit said dryly.

"Ah, it'll be worth it for you once we show what we got," Jan said with a yawn.

Immediately Conwall perked up. He tossed the frying pan to the side. "Then shall we get started?"

Jan had curled next to the fire, resting his head on his arms. "In a moment," he mumbled just before dropping off to sleep.

"Sorry, Conwall," Joe said, moving to lie down with her head resting on her brother's lower half, "but we had quite a night … and quite a morning."

Sticking his knife in the dirt, Conwall groaned. "You two are something else."

"How do you know them?" Courtney asked, turning to face him. "They're awfully young to be thieves."

"They're just awful," the woman growled.

"That story will take some talking," the man said after a pause. He frowned at where the two children slept. "But I guess all we have now *is* some time …"

Jakey moved to sit by his sister. Together they listened as Conwall spoke.

"I actually started as a shepherd some years ago—I was about your age, Courtney, to tell the truth. Well, times grew hard. The kingdoms were fighting constantly, and food became scarce. Soldiers on both sides needed to eat and took what they could when they could. This of course made many villages suffer and face starvation. One day, a group of soldiers came to our village. When they couldn't find enough food, they accused the village of holding out. Then a neighbor told them about my parents—how they kept a flock of sheep in the hills … with me." Conwall bit his lip. "My parents were killed by the soldiers, right there, and then they went after the sheep. Led by the neighbor, they found the flock just before nightfall. I saw them coming and guessed at what they wanted. Sneaking away, I ran as fast as I could to the village. Once there, I found the bodies of my parents … still warm." Conwall swallowed hard and kicked at the dirt. Neither Courtney nor Jakey dared to say a word. Even the woman seemed subdued and bit her tongue. "So … so I went to my neighbor's house and found a horse hiding in his bedroom. Taking the horse and some food, I left … I wanted to wait for him under his bed with a knife, but I couldn't. I, I remembered my mother … and well, I just couldn't kill anyone." Conwall breathed out. "That was the first time I stole."

"Not the last," the woman mumbled, but looked instantly sorry when Courtney glared at her.

Conwall continued. "Well, after some days of wandering, I ran into a group of bandits led by Carson. They took me in, and ever since then I've lived in these hills. At first, when I was just a kid, everyone liked me fine." He grinned without humor. "As I got older, they started expecting me to pull my weight and, well, I'm no good at stealing." He glanced at Joe and Jan. "One day I was trying to, um, pickpocket at a market in Dunbar." Conwall gestured at the sleeping bodies. "Those kids found me and offered me a deal. They'd give me stolen items in exchange for food. Well, of course I accepted, and soon I was bringing in a good haul. Carson took me to the side and asked what I was really doing. He's a smart man, Carson. He knew I couldn't be the one breaking into people's houses and snatching purses from pockets. I told him about the kids, and he thought it was a good business. Soon he started hiring them through me, as spies and for special burglaries. You know, Dunbar doesn't have many street kids like them. Every year there's a sweep to gather all the beggars and sell them to the wagon train as slaves. Somehow Jan and Joe escape every time."

"What about their parents?" The woman glared when the three turned to her with surprise at her question. "Well?"

Conwall shrugged. "The word is that their father was a passing mercenary and their mother died giving birth. Of course, this is rumor. It's assumed they're twins, but who knows?"

"Hmmph." The woman turned away. "Figures …"

Courtney sighed. "That's a sad story."

"It's not a story. It's life. It's all about survival." His mouth twitched. "Here, watch this." Getting to his knees, he picked up a pebble. Putting a finger to his lips, he tossed the pebble, striking Jan in the leg.

Instantly Jan rolled to the side, waking Joe with a start. Shooting to a crouched position, Jan faced Conwall with a knife in hand. His face had a feral look until seeing Conwall. Then, blinking away sleep, he stabbed the knife in the dirt. The knife had a gold hilt and a sharp, six-inch blade.

"Idiot," he muttered.

"What happened, Conwall?" Joe asked with a yawn.

Conwall didn't answer. His eyes were glued to the knife. The way his face went white and mouth dropped open, it was like it had just plunged in his side. He stumbled to his feet.

"Th-the knife," he finally gasped. "Where did you get it?"

"That's part of the loot," Joe said with a frown. "You ready to deal?"

"Oh my …" Conwall struggled for a breath. "You fools … that's Robinson's knife—the Mine Lord."

"So?" Jan grinned and grabbed the knife, sheathing it under his tunic. "He's rich. You should see the money purse we took from him."

Conwall covered his eyes. Then he ran to the fire and started kicking it out. "Robinson not only controls the mines, he controls most of the underworld at Dunbar! Nobody crosses him and lives!"

Joe got to her feet and stretched. "He did chase us pretty good."

"We have to get out of here! Hag, where were you headed?"

"I'm not a hag, I—"

"Tell me!" Conwall displayed real fear and his face brooked no argument.

Flinching, the woman raised her hands in surrender. "I have no idea—I'm a … stranger to these parts."

Smacking the top of his bald head with both hands, Conwall groaned. Then all at once he stood and glared. "Quick, get in the carriage. You'll have to come with me."

The woman frowned but got to her feet. "I'm riding in back," she mumbled.

Soon Conwall shook the reins and started the carriage down the road away from Dunbar. Jan sat at his side, but the rest piled in the back. Behind them, smoke still drifted from the smoldering fire. Trying to hide their presence would have wasted precious time—there was only one road from Dunbar and it was used little. Their tracks could be plainly seen.

Sitting in the high grass on the side of the trail, Rachel ducked miserably as Marcal loomed over her while trying to contain his fury.

"Of all the boneheaded acts you could do," he hissed. "Do you realize how foolish you looked?" He took a deep breath and rubbed his jaw in an attempt to settle down. Still, his cheeks shone red. "These men are risking their lives for you out of a belief that you're all-powerful, and you act like an imbecile!"

Her head felt like stone and too heavy to lift. Not bothering to try, Rachel glanced at the road where the men of the party were gathered with the wagon and horses. Jason stood apart from them, wiping his hands nervously on his jeans. Steven had retreated back to the cart and sat hugging his knees.

It wasn't Rachel's imagination that many of the men in the party were giving her odd looks.

"They hate me," she mumbled. "Don't they?"

"Much worse, I fear." Marcal sounded grim. "They believe that you had a vision of our journey." He scowled. "Now they believe we're doomed for failure. Many want to abandon you here."

Rachel swallowed. "But it was just a bad dream."

"That you had before midday while on the back of a horse—Rachel, how could you be so—" Marcal gritted his teeth and slowly relaxed. "What happened has happened. We'll just have to push on."

"Wh-where's Lineus?"

"Still searching for the boy."

Rachel closed her eyes. On their return, when Jak had spotted Rachel, he'd immediately leapt from the saddle and then had scampered inexplicably into the woods. Lineus feared it was because the boy believed he'd caused Rachel's "accident."

"This is all my fault," she moaned.

Grunting, Marcal didn't contradict her.

Chapter Thirty

Lineus wiped a sweaty brow and leaned against the dead, twisted trunk. Large flies buzzed in his ears, but otherwise the forest sat silent. Birds should have been singing …

Slightly nervous, Lineus loosened his sword. "Jak, you'd better show yourself soon," he muttered. "And when you do, I might just bend my sword over your scrawny backside." He sighed. So much for his plans for giving the boys a ride—Rachel could not be happy with him. Staring into the thick vegetation before him, he cupped his hands to his mouth. "Jak! Come out now! Everything is fine! Rachel is okay!"

A noise to his right made him believe otherwise.

Dropping to a crouch, his hand fell to the hilt of his sword. Inside his chest, his heart started hammering.

On a small bluff, behind a thick oak, arose the definite sound of heavy breathing. This was followed by a low growl.

Wolf, Lineus thought, immediately going cold inside.

Slowly drawing his blade, he turned in a circle. Wolves hunted in packs and loved to ambush. Somewhere there had to be more. They were probably watching him.

"Jak," he whispered, "you better be worth it."

Lineus was young, but not a fool. Having hunted for years, he knew the dangers of nature. Vividly he remembered the day Marcal and he found a traveler's body after a wolf ambush. Torn to shreds, the man had a broadsword and dagger lying unused at his side. Marcal, always a teacher, had taken pains to show Lineus how the killing bite had come from behind. While one wolf distracted the prey, the others leapt unseen for the kill.

His throat dry, Lineus readied for an attack. Behind the oak was silent, but danger lurked everywhere. He couldn't shake the feeling of being watched … hunted.

From his right came a slight cough. "You're dead."

Whirling toward the voice while diving to his right, Lineus rose to a crouch and flailed wildly at an unseen attack. None came.

"Calm, Lineus. Calm," Suzella said, stepping from behind a tree not three feet from him. She couldn't resist smiling.

Lineus breathed a huge sigh of relief and lowered his sword. "Suzella, I nearly ran you through!"

"Not likely, hunter boy." Suzella laughed and fingered her dagger in her belt lightly. "I would have had this blade through your neck if you were an enemy." She snorted. "Instead you're a scared, lost lamb."

Frowning, Lineus gestured to the surrounding trees. "Say what you wish, but there are wolves about."

There had been a heavy rain only a few days before, and the thick carpet of leaves had yet to dry. This made sneaking up on a person much easier … which, Lineus decided, was how Suzella had managed to get so close without him noticing.

Suzella kept her grin and merely shrugged. "Let them come if they want to die." Standing at ease, she sauntered to Lineus and brushed a leaf out of his hair. "What are you doing out here alone? Did your 'father' throw you out here?"

Lineus kept a calm face but felt his anger rise. Suzella liked to tease him about spending so much time with Marcal. "If you must know, I'm searching for Jak."

"Oh. In that case your mission is done."

Lineus swallowed hard and the image of the boy mauled by wolves flashed in his mind. "What do you mean?"

"I found the fool out collecting some of his medicines just a stone's throw from here."

"Alive and well?"

"Alive. That boy is never well. He was picking willow bark off a tree. I'm assuming somebody has fallen ill and that is why the party stopped."

Lineus sighed with relief. "That is fortunate. I feared that the wolves had found him."

"You mean wolf." Suzella's smile had tightened into a frown.

Lineus narrowed his eyes. "What do you mean by that?"

"I've just come from Tabitha. In less time than it takes to milk a cow, I found that we have a traitor among us. A wolf among the sheep, so to speak."

Lineus's face went hard. "Who?"

"Good question. There are two men in Tabitha watching for a young, plump woman with two boys in her care—neither boy is related to her. They have the smell and the mark of Isabella's spies … and must have gotten word from another spy, who has to be very close by. Very close by." She indicated her head in the direction of camp.

Swallowing hard, Lineus gripped his sword tightly. "Marcal has to hear about this!"

"That is why I'm on my way to him … though," she paused and smiled without humor. "The reward for turning in this woman and the boys is quite large. A poor man, or woman, could become rich."

"It is nothing to jest about!" Lineus said, his eyes narrowing. "Rachel's mission is our mission!"

"Is it really?" Suzella sniffed. "Is that what you think? Or what you hope? I know more about her than you, Lineus. Being her lapdog won't bring you any favors in the end."

Lineus's ears burned. "I'm trying to be her friend. Something she needs. She is not used to our world."

"But, is she of use to you? And if so, how?" Suzella twisted a finger around her hair and smiled not very nicely.

"Suzella, think what you want, but I will always stand by her side!"

"Strange, I never guessed the hefty kind would be to your taste."

Now Lineus slammed his sword back in his sheath. "That is enough! You should watch your tongue, Suzella. It has a habit of turning something beautiful into something putrid." Turning on his heel, he started back to camp.

Suzella angrily called after him. "Draw your sword, Lineus. Remember, there are wolves about!"

That night, the commanders of the fortress had a most lavish meal laid out before them. Puzzled at first, they stared warily as trays carrying plates of leaves and cut roots were carried out.

"What is this?" Bodin roared when a plate was set before him.

"A salid," the servant said with a bow. "The great Apprentice Lisa has asked that every evening meal starts with it, Captain."

"She feeds the Wizard's Guard as if we were cattle?" Bodin stared savagely around him. "Where is this whelp?"

"Patience, Captain," the servant said nervously. "We'll bring out the meat immediately."

A captain next to Bodin belched. "Careful, Bodin. It is the wizard who ordered the 'whelp' to take charge of the kitchens … already my men talk of fantastic powers she possesses. They say her hair gives her magic."

"They're fools," muttered Bodin, picking at the lettuce in distaste.

Then the trays of meat appeared. Roasted birds, shanks of lamb, sides of beef, suckled pig, and more were all laid on the main table. With the meat came loaves of hot bread, bowls of freshly churned butter, and platters of roasted potatoes, carrots, and wild onions. Dishes filled with sauces and dressings of all flavors appeared. The other tables set for lower members of the fortress received similar treatment. And that was just the first course …

"A feast for the wizard's return!" crowed the captain next to Bodin.

"Not just for her return," marveled Bodin, "but a feast for the king! What great guest is she bringing for such a meal to be prepared?"

But there were no guests and no wizard. Isabella remained in her room, and soon the amazed soldiers were stuffed full with the tables still full of rich food … and dessert had yet to come.

Later, overflowing carts laden with the leftovers rolled from the fortress and toward the village of Belford. A host of children in mostly rags accompanied these carts with amazed faces. Following were more carts weighed down with vegetables and grain—all under the orders of the wizard's apprentice. In one of the last carts, a young girl dressed as a guttersnipe hid beneath a pile of carrots. Her hair nearly matched the cargo. The driver of the cart was a man hidden beneath a flowing cloak that was much too large. At his side sat a boy in the garb of a peasant. Back in the fortress, a brilliant purple dress sank beneath ugly brown water.

Bodin hammered on Isabella's door.

"The girl has escaped!" he roared.

The door was flung open and Isabella peered out. Dressed in garb for travel, she wore a wild smile. "Never mind her. Prepare my carriage! I found Rachel and the boy. The fools are coming this way and I would like to meet her!"

Bodin stumbled back with a puzzled look. "But how could you know this? I have only sent the word out this morning."

Isabella gave an icy grin. "I have learned, Bodin, not to put all my faith in my captain. For years I have been recruiting spies to help search for the boy … one such spy just happens to be with Rachel—he has sent word to me through magic. Do not look so hurt, Bodin. You will accompany me and shall always be the one at my side … You just won't be alone there." Her voice hardened. "Now go!"

"But, the girl—"

"Let her go to her death out there, I don't care! The boy is nearly mine, Bodin! I nearly lost him before because of his sister and Rachel. Not again! I want my guard assembled and mounted within the hour. Bring my fastest horses for my carriage. We leave tonight!"

Hours later, the captain of the fortress was visited by a nervous guard. Feeling fat and happy, the captain of the guard licked his lips remembering the delicious supper.

"What is it?" he groaned, feeling his eyes growing heavy after all the wine he drank.

"Captain," the guard said nervously, "we have no chickens left in the fortress."

"Good, man. It's nice to know the cowards have fled with the return of Isabella."

"Um, no, Captain. I mean, we literally have no chickens left—they've been given to the village … and so have most of our vegetable supplies and much of our meat."

"What!" bellowed the suddenly alert captain.

"The orders of the new apprentice, Captain …" The guard coughed. "The village has our food supply, I fear."

"Where is this apprentice?" hissed the captain.

"That's another problem, Captain … She's gone. Vanished with the prisoner from the dungeon—Tendl, the man the wizard wanted executed tomorrow at dawn."

"And Isabella, she has gone with Bodin and her guard?"

The guard nodded. "Yes, Captain."

"So—so there're no chickens left in the fortress, s-soldier?"

"That is correct."

Shaking, the captain was left trying to find a way to wash the egg from his face.

Tendl yanked on the reins and turned in the saddle with a glare. "Who packed these horses? An imbecile?"

"What's wrong?" Lisa asked, glancing sideways at Darvy.

After reaching the village, the three hurried away from the carts and found the horses hidden away by Darvy. With the entire village rushing to meet the carts of food, nobody noticed them leaving. Tendl had led the way. Entering thick woods, he followed a narrow animal trail until reaching an ill-tended road heading upward … toward the mountain above the fortress.

Darvy's face had paled and he'd asked where they were headed.

Looking at him for a long time, Tendl only grinned. Then they had stopped to eat. The food had been ill prepared, and there was not very much. After muttering about it, Tendl called them to restart the journey shortly after. Ever since then, Tendl had muttered angrily before he now finally exploded.

"We have nothing but rotten vegetables, moldy cheese, and old meat—enough for two days, maybe. The water skin is not even half full, and we have no bedding! A pig could have done a better job!"

"You could be back in that dungeon, so leave him alone!" Lisa said hotly. "We left in a hurry."

The man grinned nastily. "My apologies, your highness," he said to Darvy with a mock bow. "These supplies took great planning—clearly by a great leader."

Darvy's face turned beet red and he looked away.

"Just tell us where we're going," Lisa demanded.

"To death, probably. We have a week's journey ahead of us. Very soon Isabella will be on our tails, so we can't turn back. But don't worry; *if* we make it, all will be made right. Even our young Darvy will find happiness!"

Lisa glared at Tendl but kept silent. Darvy looked ready to cry, but he glared at her when she went to comfort him. "Let's go," he said crossly.

Tendl snorted. "Of course, your highness."

With a grim outlook, the three aimed high and hoped for the best.

Well after nightfall, Conwall pulled the carriage off the side of the road. The horses were exhausted and could barely move. Stumbling, Conwall unhitched them from the carriage and led them to a trickling stream on the other side of the road.

"Why are we stopping?" groaned the woman's voice.

"The horses will die if we continue," muttered Conwall. "How are the kids doing?"

"Sleeping like logs," growled the woman. "All over me."

"We'll start again in a couple of hours … I need to rub down the horses. Jan, where are you?"

"Trying to sleep," mumbled the boy from the dark. "You drive a carriage like Joe wrestles me."

"Keep an eye out for anything."

"What about food?" asked the woman.

"We're out. There's water here, but that's all we have."

They were still in the valley, and the high mountains hid much of the moonlight from the impromptu campsite. In the utter darkness, the woman climbed stiffly from the carriage, after lifting Jakey's head off her lap and gently moving her feet from under Joe's head. Courtney lay asleep on the bench across. Grumbling, the woman hobbled toward the stream. It had to be late at night. After constant traveling with only breaks for the bathroom, she felt hungry and exhausted.

"Can't even see the hand in front of my face," she muttered.

"Hopefully that means we're protected," Conwall said from her left. "Nobody will find us in this cursed dark."

Then from the rocks on the other side of the carriage there came an eerie orange glow.

Conwall grunted. "On second thought …"

Sensing danger, Jan had climbed quietly to the roof of the carriage and lay flat. In his hand, he gripped the knife. The air grew still and silent.

The attack came soon after.

A man carrying a flaming torch charged up the road from the direction of the village.

"Hey!" shouted Conwall, running from the horses, pulling at his sword. "Get back!"

Another lighted torch flew from the rocks above the carriage. It landed in the middle of the road. Glass shattered, and orange flame flared brightly against the dark.

Blinded, Conwall stumbled back.

This allowed the charging man to reach the wagon and throw his torch into the flames. Tied to the torch's grip was a glass bottle that exploded when it hit the hot fire. Giant flames now leapt into the air, giving bright light to the area.

Screaming a battle cry, the man turned on Conwall with a sword in hand.

More men cried from the hills and joined the attack. All that could be heard were voices. In the darkness beyond the fire, they were invisible until too late.

Courtney woke with a start. Hearing the screams, she peered out to see a giant fire burning in the road. Beyond the flames, Conwall desperately fended off a fierce sword attack from two men as he retreated toward the stream. The horses reared on their hind legs, screaming shrilly as other men were trying to grab them.

"This way!" Joe shouted, tugging Courtney away from the horrid scene.

Jakey huddled next to the door on the other side of the carriage. Courtney quickly moved next to him. "What do we do?"

"Get out of here and hide! Now quiet!" Joe pushed open the door and quietly slipped out.

It was a trap. Instantly a horribly bearded face jumped in front of her. "Yaw!" shouted the man. He stood in front of the steep rocks with both arms raised.

Courtney and Jakey screamed, but Joe never hesitated. Launching herself at the man, she took hold of his beard with both hands and dropped all her weight down.

Bellowing in pain, the man fell to his knees. Releasing the beard, Joe poked him in the eyes with her left hand and rammed a fist in his unprotected throat with her right.

"Come on!" she shouted as the man fell away in strangled moans.

"Got you!" roared a mountain of a man. Swooping from the front of the carriage, he grabbed Joe and lifted her bodily from the ground. Arms the size of tree trunks squeezed Joe's middle.

"Run!" screamed Joe, struggling uselessly to break loose. Then her face started changing colors and eyes started bulging.

Courtney pushed Jakey ahead of her. "Get up in the rocks!"

"What about you?"

"I'll be right behind you!" Whirling, she hopped down to help Joe. Fear and adrenaline filled her every pore, but leaving a friend in trouble was unthinkable. Before she could do anything, a piercing shriek came from above and a shadow launched from the roof, landing on the attacker's head.

"Courtney!" screamed Jakey. "Look out behind you!"

Turning, Courtney saw nothing until looking down. A fist reached for her ankles.

Shrieking, Courtney kicked a hand away, but then her foot was grabbed and she went down.

Coughing horribly, his eyes blinking wildly, a filthy face glared at her as the owner of the fist started pulling her toward him. Snarling between coughs, he sounded more animal than human.

"Leave my sister alone!" Jakey jumped from the rocks onto the man's back and pulled his hair.

Meanwhile, the woman crouched by the stream with her eyes covered. At the onset nobody took notice of her and she remained far enough from the fire to remain hidden in the shadows. Too afraid to move, she did her best to ignore the screams of the children mingling with the shouts of fury from the attackers. Clanging steel crashed from in front as Conwall continued to battle. Outnumbered and outmatched, he used quick retreats and desperate parries to remain standing. The horses were brought under control, and now three men battled the young bandit.

Another shriek of a child caused the woman to peek through her fingers.

She saw Jakey and Courtney crawl under the carriage, kicking at something on the other side that was trying to grab at them. Then the woman smothered a cry.

A large man jerked from the other side of the carriage, throwing his head back and letting loose a mighty roar. In the firelight, the woman recognized him as the man who'd been leaning on the pillar watching her just that morning …

Two small figures were attached on either side of him like strange growths. Wriggling and howling, the figures seemed to be in a desperate fight.

Then Joe suddenly fell from the man's arms and immediately collapsed, clutching at her ribs. Still perched on the man's back, his knees bunched high, Jan hung desperately as he tried to stab the man with a knife.

His greasy curls flinging back like oily snakes, the man reached back for the boy with his thick arms.

Yelping, Jan ducked under the hands and snatched the man's hair. Pulling himself up with one hand, he stabbed wildly down with the other, plunging the blade into the man's right shoulder.

With a tremendous roar, the man spun and ducked, throwing back both arms while whipping his head back and forth.

"No!" screamed Joe.

Jan lost his grip and flew over the man's head. Flipping, he somehow managed to land on his feet, but his right ankle immediate buckled just before his right side smashed into the carriage wheel and he dropped like a stone.

The man advanced on the fallen body with a snarl. Joe stumbled after him but still had difficulty breathing.

"No," the woman said. "No!" Reaching into her pocket, she charged from the darkness and into the light.

The attacker holding the horses saw her. "Get the hag!" he shouted. "She's got something!"

One of the men attacking Conwall turned to give chase.

"Get back!" Conwall shouted. With a murderous glint, he suddenly launched himself at the remaining men in ferocious attack.

The woman never wavered.

"Hey, you big bully!" she shouted. "Over here!"

The large man had just reached Jan and was about to kick him. Turning, he saw the woman. Grinning savagely, he spread out his arms. Blood ran down his shoulder from where the hilt of Jan's knife remained in place. Sweat dripped from the man's face. He rushed to meet the woman.

All at once the woman came to a stop. Fumbling with her matches, she ripped off three and desperately struck them all at once. A brief flame lit from her hands just as the man reached her.

"Here, hot lips," she muttered, thrusting the matches into his beard. Grease, spilt alcohol, and bits of fatty meat clung to the beard and met the flame.

Having slowed in confusion at seeing fire suddenly appear in the woman's hand, the large man didn't know what had happened until the whole front of his face suddenly burst into a ball of fire. Panicked, he stood in shock as fire engulfed his beard. Then screaming, he wheeled about and ran blindly—straight into the burning fire in the road. Falling in a heap of sparks, he rolled in terror as flames licked all around him.

The swordsman chasing the woman stopped dead. Dropping his sword, he backed away. "Wizard!" he cried. "She's a wizard!"

Ignoring the frightened cries, the woman hurried to Jan's side. The boy had his eyes squeezed shut tightly and cradled his right arm. "Can you get up, boy?"

"My foot," the boy whimpered. "It hurts." His voice sounded weak and squeezed with pain.

"Well, this will hurt too." Gathering the boy from under his shoulders and legs, she lifted him up in her arms. "We have to get you out of here."

"Wh-what did you do?" Joe asked, stumbling to her side. Her eyes were wide with respect. "Are you really a wizard?"

The woman snorted. "No, those were my magic sticks." She grinned at where Courtney pulled Jakey from under the carriage. "I told you I could make fire in seconds."

Thinking they were in the midst of magic, the attackers had fled, including the smoldering man with the charred beard.

Conwall sheathed his sword and walked weakly to them. "Woman," he wheezed, "I shall never call you a hag again."

"Don't go soft on me, bandit," the woman snarled. "Matches won't keep them away for long. This boy is hurt and we lost our horses. We have to move out before they come back."

"Too late," Conwall said tiredly. "Listen."

The sound of many horses came from the road. At the same time, the glow of torches lit up the rocks on either side. Escape seemed impossible. Soon a line of horsemen entered the flickering light from the dying fire. In front of the horsemen, the six attackers were being herded on foot. They looked fearfully at the woman and seemed more scared of her than of the horsemen behind them.

From the middle of the pack, a single horse stepped forward, stopping next to the large, still smoldering man. Reaching over, the rider grabbed the hilt of the knife from the man's shoulder and ripped it free. Whimpering, the man clutched at the wound with a burned hand.

"So," said the rider in a cool voice. "I find my knife. But this great oaf didn't steal it … who did?"

Conwall stepped from the woman. "Be warned! Take another step closer and you will regret it!" He whispered back. "Now's your time, woman. Use your magic."

The woman, with Jan in her arms, stared helplessly back at him. "I can't," she hissed.

Conwall ignored her. "You saw what happened to your man! Each of you will eat a fireball if you don't back away!"

The rider paused and the six men on foot visibly shuddered, nodding vigorously.

"I have over thirty men with me. I can get hundreds more if needed. You are trapped. Give up what is mine and those who took what is mine and I will leave you in peace … otherwise, you will, and I mean it, be left in *pieces*."

"I told you," Conwall said boldly. "Attack at your peril!"

"Listen, fool," the woman whispered, "I can't—"

"Give me Jan and get ready!" Conwall took the boy from the woman, who was too surprised to resist, and backed away.

Raising his voice, he called, "Watch the wizard at work! She will send a fireball at your feet!" In his arms, Jan fought through the pain to raise his head to watch.

A nervous murmur ran through the horsemen, and the large man whimpered. Then silence settled.

"Come on, wizard woman," hissed Conwall. "Do your magic!"

"I-I can't!" This she said loudly.

"You hear that?" the rider called back. "She can't!"

"Just the same, Robinson," growled a voice. "She could be bluffing."

"True. You cowards on foot—the first to strike down the old hag receives a sack of gold. In fact, kill them all. Teach these young fools and old hag what they will never learn. Stealing from me is folly! Go!"

"You stupid old hag," muttered Conwall, thrusting Jan back in her arms as the six men warily advanced. Wearily drawing his sword, he moved toward the attack.

"Come and taste death!" he cried. He didn't sound very confident and could have been talking to himself.

Joe found a rock and threw it, striking the large man in the hand. Courtney and Jakey quickly searched for stones of their own to throw. But the woman only stood trembling with an injured boy in her arms and a world of doubt in her heart.

Gaining confidence with each step, the six men suddenly charged, knocking aside flying stones as they ran.

"Run!" cried Joe.

But the woman remained frozen.

All but two of the men charged Conwall. Only the large burnt man and the man whose beard Joe had pulled went after the woman.

"Let me down, hag!" Jan said, pushing himself free from the woman's arms. Limping heavily and favoring his right arm, he kept his feet and stood to face the large man.

Joe, Courtney, and Jakey kept the other men back with a barrage of stones and dirt clods.

"I'll rip you to shreds!" rumbled the large man, his fear turning into extreme anger. Advancing on Jan and the woman, his face resembled death. Charred skin hung from his cheeks and he smelled of burnt flesh. Reaching to his belt, he withdrew a long knife.

Barely standing, Jan watched him warily, his right arm hanging limply at his side. The woman had yet to move, and she appeared to be in shock.

Suddenly, when just under six feet away, Jan dove face-first at the man's feet. Rolling to his left, he snagged the toe of the man's boot.

Taken completely by surprise, the man tripped and crashed heavily in front of the woman. The hard surface bit into his burnt flesh, causing terrible pain.

Jan rolled to a sitting position behind the man. He tried to launch himself at the man, but moved too slow.

Howling, the man kicked out, catching Jan in the chest. With a grunt, the boy flew back and into a heap.

Joe screamed. Dropping her stone, she charged, throwing herself on the man's back and shoving his head into the road.

The other man went to stop her, but a hunk of rock from Courtney nailed his right eye. Stumbling back, he went to his knees.

In the meantime, the large man rolled and knocked Joe free. Panting like a mad beast, he grabbed her by the throat with both hands. Before he could squeeze—

Thunder blasted in the sky. A bolt of green flame shot seemingly from nowhere before exploding in front of the horsemen. Another flame shot from the sky and struck the big man's ample rear end. Releasing Joe, he hopped away in fright. Shouts of terror filled the air as the green bolts kept coming with amazing accuracy.

When it finally calmed, the horsemen and attackers were long gone. Their shouts faded into the darkness and only the smell of charred wood and flesh remained of their presence.

Joe crawled to where Jan lay and found the boy gasping in pain but clutching the big man's purse to his injured chest.

"We're rich," the boy said, grinning.

Joe nearly slapped him.

Conwall jabbed his sword into the ground and knelt before the woman in wonder. "I-I do not know what to say, g-great wizard. For-forgive me."

Eyes wide and trembling uncontrollably, the woman looked down at him and shook her head wordlessly.

Jakey clutched Courtney and the two sat back with shocked faces.

They all jerked when a bright green light flared from the road. Behind this light, a man walked toward them.

"Stand back!" Conwall cried. "We have a great wizard here!"

"Yes, I know," Red said in disgust. "I'm that great wizard, you fool. Now stand aside before I turn you into a turtle and eat you in a soup." Surveying the scene before him, Red only relaxed when seeing Courtney. "You are unharmed?"

Courtney's voice shook. "Y-yes …"

The wizard nodded curtly. "Good. Let's resume our journey. Shall we?"

Chapter Thirty-One

The woman slumped next to the carriage wheel, exhausted. She'd just finished checking Jan's injuries and doing what she could, using his filthy tunic for bandages. Now he sat by the fire in his underclothes as Conwall finished wrapping his chest tightly with torn cloth. The boy's right arm appeared only heavily bruised but would require a sling to keep the fool from using it to climb a tree, or more likely, pick the nearest pocket. The worst injury was to his right ankle. It was bruised horribly, and the woman had wrapped it as tightly as she dared. By the time she'd finished, the boy's tunic had been reduced to almost nothing. Jakey had quickly torn off Red's shirt and tossed it at Jan's feet. He seemed happy to be wearing his normal clothes.

Jan winced as Conwall patted his shoulder.

"Jan, you're now half-mummy. Now, let's get that sling on before you go try climbing a tree."

"I'd rather you climbed a tree," retorted the boy. "I can't move now!"

"That's the goal. Believe me, Jan, tomorrow you won't want to move."

Joe stepped into the light carrying a load of wood. Seeing Jan, she burst out laughing.

"It's not funny," huffed the boy.

"That's enough, Joe." Conwall stood. "Uh, wizard, do you have something for the boy?"

Jerking, the woman nodded and pulled herself to her feet. Despite Red's presence, Conwall still believed the woman had something to do with the green fire. Hobbling over, she pulled out a handful of the root that should put the boy to sleep. Making sure he had swallowed a good portion, she nodded to Conwall.

"I think it's time to call it a night."

Beds were set up outside by the fire. Joe made sure to sit by Jan until the boy faded into sleep. Then she lay at his side.

Conwall tried to stay up as a guard, but totally worn out from the day and night, fell asleep across the fire from the children.

Swallowing, the woman walked slowly to the stream to the real wizard.

Red sat watch as Courtney and Jakey finished washing up. For some reason, he insisted on the children being clean. Seeing the woman, Red rose to his feet.

"Old hag," he said evenly. "You should be dead."

"I, uh, I …" The woman didn't know what to say. "I'm sorry," she finally muttered.

"Sorry?" Red raised an eyebrow. "On the contrary, it is I who am sorry. I nearly lost what I loved … again." True pain laced Red's voice. He gripped the woman's shoulder. "Somehow you and that lot," he gestured toward the fire at the sleeping bodies, "didn't let that happen." He grunted. "We're going on that journey, hag. Continue watching over the children, and I promise to let you live."

"The-the others—are they coming too?"

"If they wish, they will come. Why not? They may have their uses."

"But what of supplies? We have none."

"None? Old hag, you doubt me. Just in those bushes are four horses full of supplies. Their riders have decided to give them up." Turning, he called in the darkness.

"Come, children. We have a long journey ahead of us! Time to sleep and tomorrow we will eat and then get started!"

"Where are we going?" the woman asked.

"As I said before, to visit an old friend. He lives on a mountain quite far from here."

On the way to the fire, Courtney and Jakey stayed close to the woman.

"I'm scared," Courtney whispered. "What's going to happen?"

"We're going on a journey, girl. That's all I know. We're going on a journey."

The next morning, Conwall said his goodbyes, but Joe and Jan decided to stay—after the previous night, returning to the village didn't seem very wise.

Before leaving on a horse left over from the night's battle, the young bandit ate a last breakfast with his new friends. Finished, he stood and wiped his hands on his trousers.

"Joe, Jan, I think I leave you both in far more capable hands than mine."

"What about you, Conwall?" Joe asked, kneeling beside her brother. "Who will take care of you?"

Jan grinned weakly from where he remained lying in bed. True to Conwall's word, he felt too sore to move. "Check under the seat, Conwall. There's a money purse for you."

"My thanks, Joe and Jan. But for now, I think I shall leave my life as a bandit." He stared off in the distance and rubbed his heart. "There is a village with a home I'm thinking of visiting."

"Then take the money," Jan mumbled. "You have to pay your neighbor for taking the horse at least."

Sputtering, Conwall nearly kicked the boy. "You were awake the other day, listening, weren't you?" In the end, he took the money.

Before leaving, he gripped Jakey's arm, patted Courtney's shoulder, and stopped in front of the woman.

"Wizard," he said to her solemnly, "continue looking after the young ones. It's been a true honor fighting at your side."

"I'm not a wizard," she growled. "And I'm not a babysitter!"

"Don't worry," Courtney told her, grabbing her hand with her own. "We'll help you."

Red had vanished earlier that morning and didn't reappear until just before midday. Offering no explanation as to his whereabouts, he barely noticed Conwall's absence and quickly got the journey underway.

Rachel ... Rachel ... you must come to the mountain ... It is the only way ... A hooded figure in black stood before her. Head bowed, the figure raised both arms and beckoned. *The mountain, Rachel ... Come.*

The voice penetrated her thoughts loud and clear …

Her eyes snapped open.

"Do you want water?" asked somebody above her.

"Mountain …" she muttered. Blinking, she saw that it wasn't the figure before her, but Jason.

Kneeling next to her with a concerned face, he held a wooden cup of water to her lips. "Just a sip … I think you need it."

"Wh-where am I?" The water felt cool, but swallowing proved a painful struggle.

"Under the cart. I don't know if you remember, but you kind of fainted." He tried to grin, but worry turned it into a frown.

"Wh-what?"

"Hey, relax. Just sip the water. Apparently you're kind of sick."

"What about Jak and Steven?"

"They're fine. Jak is the one who knew what to do. He came tearing out of the trees with his hands full of tree bark and, um, other ingredients for your medicine. He and Steven are out by the fire making it right now."

Rachel tried more water, but then dropped her head. "Mountain," she groaned.

"Rachel, Rachel—"

All went black.

Steven leaned over Jak's shoulder, watching in horrified fascination as the boy knelt while grinding worms, flower petals, bark, and flour into a slimy paste.

"Is she going to eat that?" he asked.

His tongue sticking from the side of his mouth, Jak barely nodded.

"Aye, young master," spoke the deep voice of Murd. "And drink this brew." Murd looked up from where he knelt over a small fire a few yards from the boys. He stirred a small pot of boiling water mixed with vinegar and willow bark.

"I don't think I want to be sick here," Steven said, gulping. He doubted he would ever complain about cough syrup again—just as long as it didn't contain worm guts.

"Many die from the Tree Fever," Murd grunted.

Steven swallowed and crouched down next to Jak. The thought of losing Rachel … was unthinkable. From his belly the monster stirred.

Briefly Rachel's eyes fluttered open … everything appeared dark, and thick blankets lay on top of her. It felt as if the mountain had collapsed over her and now was smothering her.

"H-help …" she whispered.

A shape crouched beside her, but she couldn't tell who it was. Tilting her head, she saw her purse beside her.

"Aspirin … I need aspirin."

Ignoring her, the shape reached into her purse, but turned away. The next thing Rachel knew, voices came from outside.

"How is she?" Marcal asked.

"I don't really know," Jason replied worriedly. "My mom handles sickness in my family. I feel helpless."

"Unfortunately, Tree Fever makes many feel helpless. The poor girl, I don't think she has eaten a thing all day." Marcal sighed. "But we must move on."

"Can we find a doctor in the village?"

"We can't go to the village. Isabella already has spies waiting there. We'll have to move around Tabitha and make for Mozhoven. It's a city a week's journey from here."

"What about Rachel?" Jason now sounded a little angry. "She's sick!"

"I know that!" snapped Marcal. Then he sighed again. "But she can't stay here. I will tell you this because you're one of the few I trust not to be it. There's a spy nearby—that's the only way Isabella could have known we were going to Tabitha. Either the spy is following, or, more likely, the spy is with us now. We have to keep moving and stay off the predictable trails. This means the traveling will be rough … We have to hope young Jak can work wonders … Jason, I need you—"

Too weary to listen, Rachel drifted off.

"Marcal, we are being followed, but not by whom you think."

Rachel's eyes were closed, but she could hear the voices plainly—they were right over her. It could have been seconds later, hours later, or days. Everything was a blur.

A cool hand stroked her forehead. "What do you mean by that, Suzella?"

"Wolves, Marcal. The Wolves of Nyanhelm are trailing us."

The hand stopped and then vanished. "You can't be serious!"

"As serious as death. Three of them came out of the dark right up to me. Earlier, Lineus said he heard one in the forest when searching for Jak."

"I don't understand … Quickly, let's get Rachel up in the cart. We have to leave now!"

"What of the men? They will panic if they know."

"We tell them nothing. Come, Suzella, we have no time to spare."

Darkness and light flashed through Rachel's mind. Sometimes it felt as if she were falling—other times flying. Voices mocked her.

Sarah came to her and yanked her hair. "Fatso babysitter!" she berated. "You should be with Trent Long, but you're too fat!"

Later Elizabeth Winter's face floated above her. "How are my children doing, Rachel? Are Lisa and Steven safe?"

Desperately, she tried to push them all away, to get up and run … but she could not. Trapped in a terrible mountain that rumbled and shook, she was doomed to an eternity of torture.

At some moments, a terrible taste filled her mouth and she heard voices prodding her to eat and drink … saying it would help her. She knew better—it would only make her fat! Often she threw up during these times.

Finally, a long darkness floated upon her … she would never awaken … never wanted to open her eyes … Never was a long time.

Marcal's grim face peered down at her. "Rachel, are you awake? Are you there?" His voice sounded tense and wound up, like a slingshot about to snap.

Staring up in fear, Rachel struggled to scoot back, but she couldn't. A hard surface pressed against her back. What was wrong? Then she remembered—she was sick. Her throat felt rougher than sandpaper, and her entire body felt stretched out and depleted like a deflated balloon. Yet she was alive.

Behind Marcal's head was blue sky with fuzzy clouds of white. Turning her head, she saw she lay in a pile of blankets in the back of the cart. All of the supplies had been pushed to the sides to allow room. Blinking with uncertainty, Rachel wasn't sure if she was dreaming or not.

"Marcal?" she whispered hoarsely, slightly upset that her voice came out so weak.

"Rachel!" Marcal's face lit up. "Yes, what is it?"

"What … what are the Wolves of Nyanhelm?"

"What?" Marcal blinked. "Where did you hear of the Wolves of Nyanhelm?"

"Tell me about them … I heard you and Suzella say they were following …"

"But that was over—" Marcal suddenly smiled. "If it makes you feel better, then I shall tell you. Lie back and relax. The Wolves of Nyanhelm are wolves with special powers—they're descendants of wolves that followed the first hunters into Panterra from Earth. In doing so, they somehow received greater intelligence. Some say they even have magic. For a long time they actually lived in peace with men. Then one day a man shot one with an arrow—who knows why. This sparked a war. For centuries they have been the most dangerous animals besides humans. Roaming in packs, they extended across the land bringing havoc to farms and villages. Farmers used to sacrifice flocks of sheep to them; otherwise they would destroy all their livestock. Those who hunted them never came back. Entire armies were wiped out. Then during the Wizard Wars, the wizards and wolves fought terrible battles against each other. Many wolves died, and finally only a single pack survived. Fleeing north, they continue to live near Durnwirk. No longer do they hunt humans and livestock unless provoked. Legend has it that they are only lying dormant. They await their leader who is supposed to come and lead them back to their former glory." Marcal sighed. "Not just men, but even animals hope to rule the cursed land."

"Why …" Rachel murmured. "Why would they follow us?"

"I don't know if they are. I've only seen a single wolf back on our trail. Suzella believes they are the Wolves of Nyanhelm, but perhaps they're just common wolves looking for food. I do not know. If they are indeed the Wolves of Nyanhelm, though, we are in terrible danger. They have never left the north for many years."

"I'm so tired …"

"Go to sleep, Rachel. Suzella will be back soon."

Rachel's eyes fluttered open. "Suzella?" she asked weakly.

"She has barely left your side for two weeks. Lineus and Jason have been making regular appearances too, but they've been busy keeping Steven and Jak occupied. We're worried about you, Rachel."

Two weeks? *Didn't I just get sick?* "But, I must get up … we have to keep moving."

"We've been moving, Rachel. It's now midday and we're taking a rest. The cart is set away from camp so you wouldn't be disturbed." He smiled warmly. "This is the first time you've been coherent."

"Marcal, who are you speaking to?" Suzella's voice called.

"Rachel. She's awake."

Suzella screamed. Lineus joined in the celebration.

"Hush, you fools!" Marcal barked. "She's still sick!"

"I'll get broth, right away!" called Lineus.

"You are quite a girl, Rachel." Marcal's eyes twinkled. "You have a lot of people at your fingertips … Perhaps you really are powerful."

The next day, Rachel could sit up without help. Still weak, she sipped on warm broth and soaked up the sun. Lineus had rigged a roof of animal hide on the wagon to give shade during the hottest parts of the day and for when it rained. At the moment, Rachel welcomed the warm rays. It let her know she was alive again. The best part of the day came when Marcal pronounced her sickness gone and allowed the boys to visit after the midday meal.

Steven's eyes lit up when he scrambled up onto the cart, but he hung back shyly. Jak followed but boldly sat at her side, smiling widely.

"They've been quite the pair," Lineus told her from the back of Blackie as they started out. Walking beside the cart, the good-looking youth couldn't take his eyes off her. "Turns out that Steven has been holding out on us—he's an expert rider."

Rachel grinned and looked at where Steven sat. "Is that right? What else have you been up to?"

"They've been riding Bolder for you and doing a pretty good job. I fear," Lineus said ruefully, "my next riding lesson is only useful for you."

Steven shrugged and gave a small grin back. "I've also helped make your medicine. I even made the last batch with Jak only watching."

"Oh, really? No wonder I feel so much better," Rachel teased. "What did you make it out of?"

"Um, actually, you don't want to know."

Jak reached in his tunic and pulled out a squiggly worm encrusted in dirt.

Rachel stared. "Uh, are you serious? I'm going to be sick …"

Steven pursed his lips and gave a half smile. "Maybe …"

Rachel laughed nervously as Steven told her about her medicine while Jak mimed demonstrations. When she looked up some time later, Lineus had gone. Shrugging, she turned back to the boys. Steven had scooted to her side and appeared relaxed.

The previous night, Marcal had confided to her that the boy had stopped eating properly and appeared to retreat into a shell during the worst of Rachel's sickness. Only Jak kept him occupied, bringing him into the woods and teaching him about plants.

"I'm supposed to be your babysitter, but I guess it's been the other way around, huh?" She tousled Steven's hair. "I'm okay now, though."

If possible, the boy appeared thinner and with darker skin. His hair had grown more and needed a good brushing. This only served to increase his good looks. He reminded Rachel of a small, lithe wolf cub.

Jak hadn't changed and ruined the moment with a loud, long burp.

Rachel hoped it hadn't been the worm he'd eaten.

Later, Steven told Rachel some of the news she'd missed. Soon after she got sick, they had gone off the main road to avoid Isabella's searchers and were now following a hunters' path through the woods. This had lengthened the journey considerably, but now they were expected to reach a city in a few days. And Jason had started to train with the sword with some of the men.

"He's not that good yet," Steven confided. "But he's getting better. I think."

Jak mimed a sword fighter being stabbed in the heart.

Rachel blanched. "Oh. That's, uh, that's wonderful."

A day later found Rachel walking and eating small amounts of solid food. Slowly her strength increased. Able to join the camp, she was disappointed when Jason avoided her. Steven and Jak sat near her, but were clearly used to sitting with the men now. Eyeing her curiously, many of the men seemed wary of her presence. At lot had changed while her mind had gone away … Only Lineus and Suzella seemed to treat her as if nothing happened. The blond warrior grunted and muttered "about time" when seeing Rachel walking. Lineus kept asking her about riding lessons. Everyone else seemed to be on edge.

Before she went to bed in the cart, Marcal pulled Rachel aside. "Are you able to ride?"

"Uh, I don't know. I guess."

"Listen, Rachel. I know you haven't fully recovered, but you must know the truth. Suzella has been scouring the area trying to find out information. What she's bringing back isn't good. Isabella has men searching everywhere for you. The longer we crawl through these woods, the more time they have to set up in wait."

"Are-are you sure you can trust Suzella?" Instantly her cheeks burned and she regretted speaking.

Marcal stared at her hard. "Why do you say that?" He sounded more curious than angry.

Swallowing, Rachel looked around, half expecting the girl to jump up with sword raised. "I-I guess, I don't think she likes me."

"Rachel, who do you think has been caring for you these past two weeks? There are some things men can't do, and Suzella has been doing all of it. Every minute not scouting she spent near you."

"I'm, uh, sorry … I guess I'm not thinking right." She ducked her head in shame.

"You've had a bad sickness—get some rest. Tomorrow I'm going to pick up the pace. I want to reach Mozhoven in no more than two days. From there we have to figure out Isabella's whereabouts. Don't worry, Rachel. Now that you are better, the worst is over. We'll find the wizard and get the girl back."

The following morning, Jak rose just before the sun. Tugging at Steven's shoulder, he shook the boy awake, jerking his head toward the trees.

"Too early," Steven groaned. "You want to go exploring now? Jak, sometimes you remind me of my sister." Rolling out of his blankets, he quickly got dressed. Thinking of Lisa brought a sharp pang to his gut. Ever since he and Jak had begun their morning jaunts, Steven's beast had settled down. Even with Rachel's sickness and Lisa being missing, he'd found comfort by walking through nature and hunting for specific plants that he'd never known about until Jak showed him.

After a quick stop for morning relief, the boys hurried into the trees. The guard gave them a friendly wave, used to their morning adventures. The camp lay silent behind them. An early mist covered the ground and distorted their sight. Otherwise, they might have noticed the pair of eyes watching them. Not even the guard saw the owner of the eyes slip after the boys.

Quietly, the traitor followed at a leisurely pace.

Chapter Thirty-Two

Steven leaned against the thick trunk at his back and sighed with contentment. Standing next to him on a heavy branch, Jak reached to grab a higher branch. Over a half mile from camp, the boys were near the top of a tall oak tree near the edge of the woods. Jak pointed through a gap in the branches. In the distance, the woods gave way to long fields of green. Rising over the fields was the breathtaking sight of an endless yellow wall, marking the outskirts of a large city. They were almost out of the woods.

From below, the leaves shook and Steven looked down with little concern. He grinned at Jak. "This would be a great place to build a tree house. Then we could have more room for company."

Shrugging, Jak crouched and straddled the branch. Scooting near Steven, his hands peeled away loose bark and uncovered a nest of thin, transparent insects.

Watching the insects scurry toward him, Steven leaned closer for a better view. That's when the hand gripped his ankle and tugged.

Shaking his foot loose, he stepped up another branch to make room for the newcomer. While he grinned slightly, his eyes tightened at the intrusion. "Should we get down now?"

"Good idea." Reaching the branch just below Steven, the newcomer nodded and pointed at Jak. "Let's start with him." Without a warning, a hand shot out and grabbed Jak by the collar. Twisting, it sent the boy over the side before letting go.

Jak scrambled to grab a branch, but was taken by complete surprise. Only the sound of crashing branches accompanied his descent before there was a sickening thump.

Before Steven could react, another fist had smashed into his middle, slamming his body against the trunk. Doubling over, Steven lost his breath and tried desperately to scream. The fist then opened as it moved up his chest until finding his mouth. Clamping down hard, it prevented any screams. Then something pressed against his thigh. Almost instantly, sharp and intense pain, the worst he had ever felt, exploded into his thigh and shot through his entire body. Throwing back his head, he screeched terribly into the muffling hand as the beast burst loose. Darkness closed soon after, but the last thing he remembered before blacking out was the look of terror on Jak's face as he fell …

Waiting for the boy to go limp, the traitor's grip loosened on the boy's mouth, catching him around the waist as he sagged forward. It took a good yank to pull the long, sharp needle loose from the boy's thigh. Doing so caused the traitor to overbalance and fall back. A desperate grab for the branch next to the boy kept the traitor upright, but sent the needle plummeting down to the foliage below. No matter. The job was nearly complete. Breathing a sigh of relief, the traitor stood and wiped away sweat with a free hand.

Then, pulling the boy up, the traitor effortlessly dumped him over a shoulder. Almost as light as a feather, the boy provided little hindrance on the climb down. Reaching the bottom, the traitor carried the unconscious prize to where two men stepped out from the trees. Both were dressed in black capes that covered dark armor. They eyed the traitor carrying the boy with little emotion.

"Take the boy and wait for me there," the traitor commanded, dumping the boy into the nearest arms. "I will send the wizard a message to meet us there."

The guard grunted as he transferred the limp body to his shoulder. He nodded to where Jak had fallen and said, "What about that one?"

The traitor spat on the ground. "He saw my face and had to die. Leave him."

The other guard didn't like it, but shrugged. "Perhaps it's a blessing in the long run," he mumbled. "Dying young stops more suffering." To the traitor, he nodded and said, "We'll see you at the inn."

The traitor waited to turn until they were gone. Then the traitor moved to stand over Jak's still body and nudged it with a toe, to be certain the boy wouldn't rise. The body didn't stir. Dark blood seeped from the back of Jak's head, staining the leaves beneath. Satisfied, the traitor returned to camp. Everything was going as planned.

"Where are Steven and Jak?" Rachel asked, stretching out her sore arms and legs. *There is no way I want to get back on a horse.* At the same time, her saddle soreness had ended and she felt ready for some exercise.

Lineus grinned at her and held out the reins to Bolder. "Perhaps they're sulking because they're back in the wagon and you're back in the saddle."

Ducking her head, Rachel ran a quick hand through her hair. "I doubt it," she mumbled. She accepted the reins. As she did, Lineus's hand caught hers and didn't let go.

"Believe me when I say this. I am very happy to see you ride again, Rachel." Before her sickness there had been a playful nature to Lineus's flirting. Now he sounded serious.

The sun had just peeked from behind the trees and the rest of the camp had nearly packed up. The fire was stamped out, and the horses were forming the line for another long day's ride. Rachel stood by the cart with Lineus as the others finished the packing. For a moment, there was just the two of them. Their eyes met and Lineus moved closer.

Breathing hard, Rachel swallowed and ran her tongue over her teeth furiously. They still had a good supply of toothpaste, but she'd forgotten to use it.

"Breathe easy, Rachel," Lineus said, his voice going husky. "I just want to say—"

Jason suddenly trotted his mount from the front and pulled up next to them. "I don't want to interrupt anything," he said rudely.

Rachel pulled her hand free of Lineus and busily petted Bolder's mane.

Lineus glared. "What is it?" he asked unpleasantly. "Blackie is up by the front with Marcal and there're no streams nearby."

Jason ignored him. "Rachel, I think Jak and Steven are missing."

Rachel's head jerked up. "What?"

Lineus audibly scoffed. "Those two run off nearly every sunrise. They'll be back."

Again, Jason ignored him. "I spoke to the guard this morning. He said he saw them head into the woods at dawn. That was hours ago."

Rachel's face paled. A terrible feeling entered her heart and stuck like a jagged piece of glass. It'd been over two weeks since becoming trapped in this world. Lisa remained missing, and Rachel had no idea how to get back home. Her only line left to babysitting was Steven. If she lost him …

"We have to find them!"

Lineus quickly moved to her side. "We'll find them, don't worry. I'll mount Blackie and search immediately. My horse has the nose of a fox."

Jason rolled his eyes. "Whatever we do, we better hurry. Marcal is awfully anxious to get started this morning."

"Sh-should we tell him?" Rachel asked.

"Let your boyfriend do it. Yaw!" Kicking his horse, Jason headed for the trees.

He didn't get very far when Suzella burst from the trees, riding her mount at a dead run. Flying by Jason, she also ignored Marcal and rushed straight to where Rachel readied to mount for the first time since falling sick. Lineus removed his hand from her waist and stepped back.

"Babysitter, you'd better come with me," she said somberly.

Rachel immediately went cold. Never before had she seen the blond warrior so serious. Sitting straight in the saddle, the young woman's lips were pressed tightly and her eyes stared straight ahead as if seeing nothing and everything at the same time.

"Wh-what happened?" Rachel asked. A terrible dread filled her soul and she knew she didn't want to know the answer. "Tell me."

Suzella didn't look at her. "You said Jak's life had worth," she said in a cold monotone voice. "I disagreed. I'm afraid we'll never find out … He's dead."

Instead of collapsing into hysterics, a strange weight settled deep into the pit of Rachel's stomach. As her mind struggled to grasp what she just heard, her body refused to believe it.

"Where is he?" she heard herself ask.

"I found his body not far in the woods. There's no sign of Steven."

Jason had returned and heard the last statement. Shouting a curse, he whirled his mount and headed to tell Marcal the news.

Rachel turned abruptly to face her horse. She wanted so much to believe Suzella was playing a cruel joke, but the warrior's icy exterior had started to crack. Rachel saw the tears pricking Suzella's eyes.

"Show me," she said simply.

Lineus moved behind her. "Here, let me help—"

"No!" cried Rachel, much too loudly. "I can do this!" Stepping in the stirrup, she mounted. "Show me, I said!"

Jak appeared to be sleeping in the thick leaves as Suzella and Rachel drew up. The boy wore his usual brown clothes and with his tanned skin, he was almost invisible on the ground. His eyes were closed, and he lay on his back with his head tilted to the left. Both arms, lined with scratches, were splayed beside him, and legs were slightly open as if relaxed.

Leaping off the horse, Rachel still imagined everything to be okay. Then she saw the thick blood framing the boy's head like a gory halo. "No!"

Running, she threw herself at his side, shaking his shoulder. "Jak, are you okay? Jak?" Quickly she remembered her babysitting first-aid training. *Check for vital signs and breathing* … Putting a finger to the boy's neck, she found no pulse. *No, no, no!* And the boy wasn't breathing.

"I-I am really sorry," Suzella said, stepping behind her. "I saw buzzards circling this area … I grew curious …" The warrior knelt. "It's hopeless, Rachel. Life is uncaring and cruel—there's nothing you can do."

Rachel turned on the warrior. "Don't say that! It's never hopeless! I've lost everything I love right now! My world, my parents, and the kids I'm supposed to protect! I'm not giving up!" Hot tears flowed down Rachel's cheeks and she barely knew what she was saying. "Bad things happen, okay? But life is more important, so, so grow up! All you care about is sneaking around with your stupid things and killing things. Well, you're not going to kill Jak! You're not!"

As she spoke, she continued working over Jak. First she grabbed the front of his shirt and yanked with all her might. Resisting at first, the rawhide garment tore open before her. Tears fell onto the still skin. His bare chest appeared much too young to not contain life. Roaring at the unfairness of it all, Rachel put both hands where Jak's heart once beat life and pressed down.

"Breathe!" she shouted. "Breathe!"

Suzella got to her feet and stumbled back. Marcal, Lineus, and Jason had silently arrived and sat in their saddles watching in shock. Eight armed horsemen stopped behind them and were nervously stirring.

"He must have fallen from a tree," Marcal said quietly. "Hit his head on a root or stone …"

"I don't understand," muttered Lineus. "Jak lived most of his life in the outdoors and climbed better than most walked."

Jason swung from the saddle and quietly approached Rachel.

"Is there anything I can do?"

Rachel looked up at him with red eyes. "Make him live!"

The boy stood in the bright white light as if floating … Blinking, he tried to understand how he got to this place. All around, light dazzled his eyes. Rubbing his head, he frowned. He wore a gleaming white robe and no shoes.

"Wh-where am I?" he asked. Startled, he spoke again. "H-hello?" His eyes widened in wonder.

Just then a figure appeared right before him. Dressed in a long, black, hooded robe, the figure pointed a long, thin finger at his face.

"Why are you here?" hissed the figure. "Have you come to cross to the other side?" The boy blinked and made no answer. "Are you crossing?" demanded the figure.

Finally the boy stammered an answer. "I-I don't know." Something about the figure terrified him.

"You don't know?" The figure in black seemed to expand until it towered over the boy. "Then you will have to be judged! Come!"

Turning, the figure started walking at a brisk pace.

Nervous, the boy hurried to follow. "Where is this place?" he wondered aloud. It felt as if he walked on air and the surrounding bright lights never wavered. It was impossible to tell how fast they were walking and what direction they were walking in, or if they were even moving.

"Silence! You have not been judged yet!"

The figure drew to a halt without warning.

Feeling even more scared, the boy also stopped. He started to edge back from the figure. Desperately he wanted to see a tree, or a patch of dirt, or anything.

Then, lifting both hands, the figure started chanting. Low at first, the chanting slowly increased in volume until the boy had to clap hands to both ears.

A dark mist began to swirl before the figure. More and more mist flowed until slowly forming a large black pool at the figure's feet. From this pool, a great form surfaced. The color of midnight, flat and with two large, red eyes, the form surveyed the figure furiously. The chanting came to a stop. The boy froze as if enclosed by ice.

The form started to speak, but no mouth seemed visible. *"YOU HAVE SUMMONED ME … WHY?"*

The figure bowed low and answered. "This boy has come, master. I-I wanted to make sure he is ready for the crossing."

The boy shuddered as the dark form groaned. *"HE IS NOT READY YET … IF HE CROSSES NOW, HE WILL CAUSE GREAT HARM TO ALL THAT I AM! SEND HIM BACK!"*

"Yes, Master." Bowing, the figure made a sign in the air and the dark form and pool vanished. Turning to the boy, the figure waved a hand dismissively. "Be gone from here. You will not cross today."

Pressing down, shaking the small chest beneath her, Rachel closed her eyes. "This can't be happening!"

"Come on, Rachel," Jason said gently. "Let's—" He froze.

A tiny but audible sound started in Jak's throat. As if crawling tentatively to the surface, the sound grew larger before all at once turning into a breath. The boy's chest rose and fell. The movement was barely visible, and Jason thought his eyes and ears were playing tricks.

"We must be off to search for Steven," Marcal called. "He could be hiding anywhere—after seeing his friend fall, he may be in shock."

"Rachel," murmured Jason. "Whatever you are doing, keep doing it! Jak is starting to breathe!"

"Rachel!" Marcal called sharply. "Think of Steven!"

Her own breath barely coming, Rachel looked up. "H-He's alive!"

The pulse was weak and the breath shallow, but Jak had somehow returned to the land of the living … temporarily.

Marcal and Lineus ran from their horses to see for themselves. Both stared in amazement. The other men murmured amongst themselves and eyed Rachel with wariness. Never before had they seen a boy come back from the dead like this. Truly, this babysitter was a magnificent protector of children.

"We have to get him to camp," Marcal said, running a tongue over dry lips. "But, Rachel, the injury is serious. You must know he may never wake again … and if he does, he may never be the same."

Exhausted, her face drawn, Rachel barely nodded. Smoothing Jak's hair, she only had eyes for the steady rise and fall of his chest. "I should have been there," she suddenly murmured. "I failed as a babysitter."

It's your fault only, Rachel. They're your responsibility. Sick or not, you should have done a better job.

"Stop it, Rachel." Jason kicked the dirt. "You were sick. It was Lineus and I who let the boys run off alone every morning … We shouldn't have done that."

"It does not matter whose fault it is," Lineus said quietly. "We must come together to find Steven. The past is the past."

"I think it does matter whose fault it is," Suzella said, her voice chilly. The blond warrior stood beneath the large tree Jak had probably fallen from. "Tell me, does anyone know what this is for?" She held up a plastic tube with a long sharp needle exposed. "There's blood on it."

Rachel's face went white and she started to shake. Suzella held a wicked-looking needle attached to a familiar tube. "Steven's," she gulped. "That's Steven's … his shot … it knocks you out." Then she collapsed.

High above the Fortress of Belford, near the top of the mountain, the temple stood like a small city. Enclosed by a high stone wall and containing everything needed to subsist, this was where the priests of Aerrius lived and oversaw the home of Panterra's dark spirit. Conditions were often harsh to reach the temple, but once inside, it seemed almost like a paradise.

Tendl stumbled up a rocky pass and fell to his hands. Looking up, he saw the great wall of the temple and sighed with relief.

"We are almost there!" he shouted back hoarsely. "Come!"

Barely awake and feeling the effects of no food for two days, Lisa and Darvy rode double on the remaining horse. On the third night, Darvy's horse had broken loose and had run back down the mountain. A few days later, facing starvation, Tendl had killed his horse for meat. That had been over a week ago.

"I was beginning to think we were chasing a wild goose," Lisa muttered, trying hard to keep her head up.

"Don't speak of food," Darvy groaned. Then his face paled. "I, I want you to stay close by, Lisa … when we get there."

"Sure, I will," she replied thickly. "Where else would I go?"

"Just don't leave me …"

Thinking the boy was just feeling hunger and exhaustion like her, Lisa nodded absently. "Let's just get where it's warm and there's food, okay?" Shivering, she urged the horse on.

Darvy whimpered behind her.

Snow flurries had been falling intermittently for the last several hours, and her hands were frozen. Tendl had managed to find blankets from one of the last houses they had passed before heading up the mountain, but the nights were bitterly cold. Only by huddling close had they survived. Wood was scarce on the mountain road and fires were not always guaranteed at night. Yet somehow, with Tendl's guidance and despite Darvy's incompetence at packing and tying horses, they had made it.

Nearing the wall, the massive double doors marking the entrance swung open, and a group of robed priests ran out to meet them.

A thrill ran through Lisa. Tendl had repeatedly promised—this was where she would find a way back home …

Marcal cradled Jak in his arms and walked slowly back to camp with Suzella at his side. Lineus had left to find moss and herbs to make a poultice for the back of the injured boy's head. The other men conducted a quick sweep of the area, searching for any sign of Steven, but it was only for show. A traitor among them had taken the boy … and had tried to murder Jak in the process.

Walking slowly in the rear, Jason and Rachel led their horses and spoke little. Rachel seemed particularly crushed. "I failed," she suddenly said. "I'm no good. I thought, I thought I was helping Jak … I even promised his sister …"

"Stop it, Rachel," Jason said. "You did your best. You were sick. This is a different world—you couldn't have done anything. Don't beat yourself up. It won't help."

Rachel stubbornly shook her head. "I could have done more." In a halting voice, Rachel told Jason of the night when she saw somebody going through her purse. "Whoever it was took that shot … if only I didn't get sick!"

"Whoever it was would have found some other way, Rachel. If you're right, that was more than a week ago. That means the person planned for this moment for a long time …" Jason paused. "And it has to be somebody who's close to you. Only Marcal, Suzella, Lineus, and I visited your side when you were out. The others were too scared to go near."

"So what do we do?" whispered Rachel. "We can't trust anybody!"

"We can," Jason said fiercely. "Listen, whoever did this wanted to make sure Jak couldn't point them out—that means he … or she, is alone. Everyone else is on our side."

Swallowing miserably, Rachel shook her head. "I-I don't know what to do."

"We don't give up … and we make sure Jak's well guarded. We have to keep an eye out, because if Jak starts recovering, somebody is in *big* trouble."

Marcal had similar thoughts. Upon returning, he ordered a tent to be constructed apart from the rest of camp and a bed made for Jak inside. Two guards were placed at the entrance.

Rachel bathed the boy's head and then watched Marcal apply the thick wad of moss and herbs brought back by Lineus on the wound before bandaging it tight.

"The surface wound isn't the worst," he said. "It's the internal that worries me. We'll have to wait … we won't be moving until he wakes, or …" he didn't finish. "We'll know in a few days at most. Until then, we're stuck here." Jak's breathing remained shallow and showed no improvement. If anything, he seemed worse.

Suzella and Lineus stood solemnly at the entrance. Neither one looked at Rachel.

"We'll make sure he is properly cared for," mumbled Lineus, tugging at his hair.

"I'll give my sword to Jak," Suzella said vehemently. "Whoever did this shall taste my blade."

Rachel whirled on her. "You and your stupid sword! Is that all you care about? Life is more than a sharp pointy object used to kill! Why don't you do something useful for a change? Actually help somebody instead of yourself!"

Shrinking back, Suzella gaped. For a moment she looked about to draw her sword but then fled from the tent.

Swallowing, Lineus quietly followed her, nodding once at Rachel.

"I don't know if that helps," Marcal said after a long pause. "I know you feel—"

"You don't know how I feel! I'm sick of everyone telling me what to do and how to do it! I'm a babysitter and … and those kids are my responsibility! I …" Rachel wiped her eye. "I, I'm sorry … I just don't know what to do or who to trust …"

Marcal nodded. Laying Jak's head gently down, he touched Rachel's arm. "You are growing up, Rachel. It's not an easy thing to do. But do remember, Suzella helped you when you were sick. Her sword isn't a toy and her heart is not guided by it. She's doing her best, just like you."

"I just want to find Steven."

"And perhaps we shall. There's a good chance he's been brought to Mozhoven. I was thinking of leaving within the hour, if you'd like to come."

Not long after, Marcal, Suzella, Lineus, and Rachel thundered from the camp on their horses, each, except for Rachel, armed with swords and knives. Suzella refused to even look in Rachel's direction.

Jason remained to watch over Jak, promising not to leave his side. But Jak soon found a new bodyguard. When the boy had been brought back like a broken doll, Murd, the quiet giant, had cried like a baby. Almost single-handedly setting up the tent, the large man had next gathered the wood for the fire before standing by the entrance as a third guard.

Taking a look at him, Jason waved him inside to keep him company. Time passed. Murd never left the boy's side. He crouched over the boy and constantly put a wet cloth to his lips, trickling in water a little at a time. His eyes were tender, except when looking up at the tent's entrance—something he did frequently.

Sitting by him, Jason smiled grimly. He knew what the large man thought—if the murderer tried to return to finish the job, Murd would happily tear off some limbs. Jason felt the same way. Even if wizards, or anyone else, tried to say otherwise, violence against children was frowned upon in any world. Jason almost hoped the killer would try to enter. Then they'd at least know who committed the crime.

Chapter Thirty-Three

Rachel barely registered that they had reached the city until passing through the main gate. Soldiers in bronze armor stood guard at the gate, but only for show. War had decimated the region but had since moved on like a plague. In the uneasy peace, the city of Mozhoven welcomed any and all visitors as long as they were able-bodied and brought hope of wealth in some sort of fashion. Marcal and his companions only brought hard faces and cold steel. Nobody dared try stopping them.

"Within these walls anything can be obtained for a price," Marcal said. "If a boy is to be sold, it would be here."

"They sell children here?" Rachel asked, shaken by the sights and smells of the strange city.

"Not officially or legally, but the city officials turn a blind eye to anything that brings them a profit. Children are not considered human until the age of twelve, but they still are protected, with rights. Dealing with child slaves is not allowed anywhere in Panterra, but it does happen—especially in Mozhoven. Here, poverty and prosperity are brothers. They live side by side and tolerate each other."

Rachel gulped. Within the city, odors of rich foods, terrible filth, exotic spices, and putrid smoke blended together to form an overpowering stench. Countless sellers of wares lined the streets and immediately started thrusting merchandise at their feet.

"Gold chains, emblems of warriors, buy a dagger used in the Wizard War!" hollered a bearded man at Rachel's left.

A large man thrust steaming pastries toward her from the other side. "Meat pies, pickled meats, we have meat for you and meat for all!" he bellowed.

"Buy a ring for the pretty lady?" hollered another voice at Marcal.

The shouts and smells of sweat, cooking meat, and animal dung swirled about Rachel and caused her to feel lightheaded. Only by Marcal's confident and steady guide did she manage to stay in the saddle.

Finally, after turning corner after corner, Marcal stopped across from a stall set in front of a large tent in the midst of a plaza lined with sellers of an assortment of goods. Fancy carpets, fine clothing, and other expensive items were laid out for the crowds of buyers to walk and pick among.

"This is the plaza where stolen merchandise is sold," muttered Marcal, swinging down from his horse.

The others did the same, and immediately a boy leapt from the shadows and grabbed the reins. "I hold horse, two pecs each!" he shouted.

Marcal barely looked at him as he shoved a handful of coins at the boy. Suzella and Lineus gave the urchin looks of disgust as they brushed by.

Rachel tried hard to take her eyes off the boy. About Steven's age, he wore a long robe that fell to his feet and a red ragged hat on his head of black hair. Scratching at a rash on his cheek, he stared warily back at Rachel. "What you want?" he demanded.

"Oh, only to say, uh, thank you." She smiled and hurried to catch up with Marcal.

"Do not be concerned with the children of this city," Marcal grunted. "They are all the property of businessmen. Doing odd jobs such as holding horses is what keeps them alive. They give a cut to their masters."

"That's, that's horrible!"

Marcal nodded. "Perhaps, but it is the way of things here. Come, now we'll see if the boy is among these wares."

Suzella and Lineus hung back and nervously watched the crowded plaza. Neither of them had ever been in a large city before, and they fingered the hilts of their swords.

Rachel accompanied Marcal to the stall.

"Do not say a word," Marcal whispered to Rachel. "We must do this carefully—the city's officials are well paid and will not be on our side."

"What do you mean?" Rachel asked. "What are you doing?"

"Just hush!" Marcal commanded.

Rachel went quiet.

A thin, bearded man in a turban sat on a wood box in front of a table, cleaning his fingernails with a small knife. Beside him lay a carpet of trinkets. Nothing stood out particularly, and few buyers even glanced his way. But the man did not seem concerned. Looking up at Marcal, he smiled widely, displaying rows of rotting teeth.

"Ah, a true warrior has come to visit!" said the man in the turban. "This I can see. Tell me, have you come to buy a charm for your lady?"

Marcal grunted. "In a manner of speaking, yes. But I am in search of a … particular charm. Have you had any recent merchandise come in?"

The man grinned wolfishly and displayed rows of crooked, yellowing teeth. "Of what type, great warrior? I see many things and many things come my way."

Marcal leaned forward and lowered his voice. "Let us say of the young type."

Putting down the knife, the man pulled his long narrow beard. "Young type? I do not know what you mean." A glare had come across his face and he no longer smiled.

"I have coin," Marcal purred, putting a hand to his belt.

The man gripped the knife and pointed the blade toward Marcal. "I suggest you look elsewhere—I assure you, I have no idea what you mean."

"My apologies," murmured Marcal, drawing back. "I leave you with peace."

The man did not return the bow and eyed the departure with an ill look.

"What just happened?" Rachel asked as they turned away. "When are you going to ask about Steven?"

"I just did," Marcal said curtly. "You must take care in this city—there are rules you must follow."

"What are you talking about?" demanded Rachel. "Was that man selling children or not?"

Marcal nodded. "He was and still is—that tent behind him is full of the young being sold … It takes a certain level of trust to get back there. The man did not trust me … I'll have to try again."

Rachel stared at him in horror. "What? Why? If Steven is back there, can't we just go and look?" she asked.

"That is not how it works," the warrior said patiently. "We must tread lightly."

"You said it's illegal to sell children here," Rachel said. "Why can't we get the police or something?"

"Because," Marcal said tiredly, "this is a different world. It's illegal to sell children, but it is not illegal to own children. Over half the officials in this city have probably bought slaves here. Nobody will help us if we are not careful."

A terrible feeling settled on Rachel. "So the children are in the tent, but we can do nothing? They just sit there and suffer?"

"At the moment, yes." Marcal sighed tiredly. "We do nothing for now. Believe me, Rachel, let me handle this! Now keep it down before we cause trouble. I don't like the way the man is watching us. I can ask around and find out if any new children were brought today. Trust me."

Rachel bit her lip and stared back at the stall. The man sat watching with apparent amusement. He smiled wickedly at Rachel.

Rachel swallowed hard. *That's it … I've had enough of this! I'm sick of people telling me what to do and how to do it—that's how I got in this mess!* It was Rachel's turn now.

"Uh, is there a, uh, bathroom nearby?" she asked.

Marcal rubbed his grizzled chin. "This isn't your world, Rachel. There's a bath house down the street, but it's not what you think."

"I need to go," she said anxiously.

Nodding, Marcal waved to Suzella. "Go with Rachel and make sure she finds … a place for privacy."

Frowning, Suzella left Lineus and went to Rachel. She still refused to look at the girl. Together, they walked from Marcal in an uneasy silence.

Rachel took a breath. "You didn't … push Jak or take Steven, did you?"

Looking up with a glare, Suzella's hand went to her sword, but fell just as quickly to her side. "On my life, Babysitter, I never did."

Rachel nodded, not sure if she believed her. The girl had already said she would do anything to help her village. And she'd had the perfect opportunity to take the needle from Rachel's purse. It didn't matter at the moment. All Rachel cared about was finding Steven.

"What are you trying to pull, Babysitter?" the blond warrior hissed. "I watch you and know when you are planning something."

Rachel eyed her frostily. "Just stay out of my way."

Rachel marched up to the next stall set up in front of the tent.

A man in the shape of a melon stood with a handful of cloth. "Beautiful cloth for the beautiful lady?" he asked hopefully.

Rachel stumbled to a halt and dropped her gaze. "Uh, no thanks …" So much for being tough. "Uh, excuse me, but I need to get by."

"No, lady—you buy cloth here!" The man put a thick quivering arm in Rachel's path. His voice turned ugly. "None may go there."

"I'd like some cloth," Suzella said dangerously, going to the stall. Yanking out a knife, she jammed the blade into bright blue fabric draped over the side of the stall. "Just a piece, though."

Crying out, the man rushed at her. "No! Crazy lady, you're killing my business!"

Left alone, Rachel hurried behind the stall to the tent. Large blankets covered the front. Before she rethought her actions, she grabbed the nearest blanket and yanked hard. With the sound of tearing fabric, the dirty blanket pulled free. Hurrying down the side, she started yanking the other blankets free, exposing the inside of the tent for all to see.

"Wh-what are you doing!" cried a voice in anger.

Shouts of shock behind her only gave fuel to her efforts.

"Stop that!" The thin man with the turban rushed over and grabbed Rachel's hand just before reaching another blanket. His free hand held the knife and his face quivered with fury. "What are you doing, you stupid woman?"

Rachel looked into his eyes and suddenly matched the fury. "The question is, what are you doing?" Shaking out of his grip, she yanked the last blanket down. "You should be ashamed of yourself!"

Rachel turned from the man to face the street. A crowd had gathered and watched in horror. Two men, each dressed in fine robes, pushed to the front.

"What is the meaning of this?" demanded one, shaking out his sleeves and trying to stand tall.

"We demand to know who you are and what you are doing!" cried the other. "We are officials of the government and speak for Mozhoven, so choose your words carefully!"

Rachel glared at the two officials. "You speak for this city? You're a bunch of cowards!" Turning to the tent, she abruptly gasped in dismay.

The tent was a tent of horror. Close to fifty half-clothed, half-starved children stood behind wooden bars, locked in cages of putrid straw. Near the middle of the tent, a large cage had been reserved just for young women. Standing in front of this cage, his mouth open and cheeks flushed, a corpulent man dressed in a robe similar to the officials' blinked stupidly at the crowd on the street. Trembling, Rachel had to control herself from tearing at the bars herself.

Several guards in the tent held whips and nervously backed away.

"How can you take care of a city when you can't even take care of children?" Rachel yelled. She turned to the man with the knife.

The man looked sick as he trembled. He stared at Rachel with a mixture of hatred and fear … and awe. "Wh-who are you?" he sputtered. "What are you?"

"A babysitter," she growled. "Now get out of my face!"

One of the officials moved toward her. "You can't, you can't do this … um, what are you doing?"

"I'm taking these children away from you," she said. "Now let them go!"

Suzella moved to stand next to her, smiling grimly. Her blade swished the air hungrily. "You heard the babysitter," she said lightly. Then her voice grew savage. "Obey her or answer to me."

Nobody dared to contradict the angry babysitter and sword-wielding warrior. In moments a host of children stumbled free and soon paraded down the street with Rachel leading the way. The children huddled behind her, buzzing with excitement. Many were still cowed and bore bruises and cuts on their arms and faces. The freed young women wore dazed looks on their happy faces. These were the ones who helped keep the younger children from falling behind.

When the prisons had first opened, none had dared to exit. Several pairs of young eyes watched the whips nervously. Finally Rachel had ordered everyone from the tent and called the former prisoners to their freedom. Since then, they obeyed her every command.

Marcal rushed from the crowd, catching up to Rachel just as she left the plaza.

"Rachel, you are mad!" he cried. Seeing the children, he pulled at his beard furiously.

"Uh, no … I'm, uh, actually happy." Even though Rachel had failed to see Steven among the sea of young faces, she did see joy and elation. Keeping her chin pointed up, she didn't look at Marcal.

"Your methods, they don't work here, Rachel!"

"They worked fine."

"So you think. Think about it. You freed these children, but now what?" Marcal waved a hand wildly. "Are you going to babysit them too? We can't take them with us! They'll be left here and end up back in the cages—probably with stripes on their back!"

Rachel's step barely faltered.

"For now, I'll stay here then," she said.

"You are mad!"

Rachel looked at Marcal and scowled. "I'm not going to leave these kids to suffer in your stupid world! You said you had money, is that true? Go buy some food and drink for the kids."

Marcal looked ready to explode, but he ended up sighing. "Very well … where should I meet you?"

Immediately Rachel's face softened and she ducked her head. "Uh, actually, I was hoping you'd show me a place before you go."

Marcal bit down his anger and led the bunch to a grassy area by a fountain with a few trees in front. Located on the other side of the city, the shady area took a while to reach. Along the way, people turned out in droves to see the amazing sight. At first Rachel thought they were angry and she feared some might run out and start snatching the children. Instead, women started running out and pressing loaves of bread and chunks of meat and cheese into the children's arms. Soon a group of adults followed the children, carrying jugs of water and loaded with food. By the time they'd reached the park area, it wasn't necessary for Marcal to buy food—they had an overabundance.

"We're ashamed we allowed this to happen," explained a man, stuffing a long loaf of bread into Marcal's hand. "The babysitter has opened our eyes … who is she?"

"The one who will destroy our world," grumbled Marcal, accepting the loaf.

"Then it is for the best!" the man cried. "Praise the babysitter!"

The news of Rachel being the babysitter to stand up to all wizards spread like wildfire. When the question of what to do with all the children came, a solution had already arisen. The young women freed with the children came to where Rachel sat rocking a toddler girl. Sitting in the shade by the pond, Rachel was desperately trying to think of what to do next. Seeing the girls approaching, most her age or younger, she tried hard not to panic.

One of them, a pretty, olive-skinned girl with raven-black hair and about the same age as Rachel, acted as their spokesperson.

"We wish to follow you, great babysitter," she said, bowing. "May we become your followers?"

Surprised and more than embarrassed, Rachel coughed. "Uh, do you, uh, mean you want to be babysitters?"

A rush of excitement pulsated through the young women. Chattering, they nodded enthusiastically.

"How?" asked the pretty girl. "How could this be possible?"

"Uh, well, uh, you just go through the training …" Rachel said with uncertainty. "I mean, I could give you a list of rules you have to follow. Really, you just need to protect kids and make sure they're happy."

"We want this—we want to be babysitters!" the girl said seriously. "Teach us!"

Marcal and Lineus left the city of Mozhoven with amazed faces. Rachel followed, but her face radiated joy. Suzella had decided to stay.

Patting her sword at her side, the blond warrior announced that she would join the ranks of the newest babysitters. Within the hour, she rose to be their leader. Armed with Rachel's babysitting rules written in careful script on papyrus-like paper, she was last seen dividing the freed children into "families" and would next assign babysitters.

"I want to thank you, Babysitter," she'd muttered to Rachel when it came to depart. "You have shown me that a sword isn't enough to make somebody great. I … only dreamed of glory by leading my village … I now want to be like you and give my life and sword to helping and defending these children. What you have is better than all the glory, and I want the same. For that to happen I'll have to study your rules and devote my life to a new direction. That's where I think I can be useful …"

"I, Suzella … I don't know what to say."

"Say nothing, Babysitter. For days I have watched you and did my best to find a flaw. All I saw you do is care for your children. I hope young Jak does live … his life is worth something with you around. This isn't goodbye, Babysitter. For now this city feels guilty about the children, but soon, once we're organized, we'll move on. I'll catch up to you. After you find Steven."

The two girls embraced in tears. No amount of arguing by Marcal would change the blonde warrior's mind.

"Take care of the babysitter, Lineus."

Face ashen, Lineus nodded. "I will."

"Not only have we failed to find your boy, Rachel," Marcal said bitterly, as they exited the gate, "but we lost our best scout."

Rachel said nothing and didn't look his way. Her face also glowed for another reason. A young man had approached her while she copied down the babysitter rules and introduced himself as Marlin, a wandering minstrel. He had heard of the babysitter's fame and had even written songs about her that he wanted her to hear. But that wasn't why Rachel was so happy. Marlin had given her some information concerning a young kidnapped boy …

"Jason," Rachel said in a low voice. "I need you … you're the only one I can trust."

"What is it?" Jason asked, also dropping his voice.

Neither trusted that they were away from prying eyes. The thought of a traitor hung heavy in the air.

The two sat in the back of the tent near the fire where Jak remained in a coma. Murd knelt beside the boy and trickled more water into the slack mouth, paying no heed to the young teens.

Elsewhere, Marcal was busy organizing a guard rotation. Lineus had taken over Suzella's scouting and would be gone for hours. After what had happened in the city, there was no stopping the news of Rachel's presence from spreading. The traitor in the camp would not have to hide for long … Isabella would be coming.

Rachel spoke in an excited whisper. "Somebody in town told me he saw two men carrying an injured boy to an inn this morning just outside the city. He overheard that they would be staying the night there."

Jason lowered his head at hearing the news. Then he frowned. "Rachel," he said gently, "why would a stranger tell you that?"

"Well, he's, uh, a minstrel. He says he, uh, heard about me being a babysitter and going against the wizards …" Rachel blushed. "He even wrote songs about it. Not very good ones …" Her face continued to burn. It started sounding more and more ridiculous in the retelling. "He, uh, knew we were in the area, and the men with the boy looked like Isabella's spies. He, uh, offered to take me … he said to meet at the edge of the road—he'll sit there starting at sundown and will stay until sunup."

"How convenient," Jason said dryly. "Did the boy he saw just happen to have reddish brown hair?"

"Y-yes. He said he had gone outside to find inspiration for a new song about, about … uh, well, he said the men rode in without seeing him. He heard them talking in the stable."

"Right," Jason said dryly.

"You don't believe me, do you? You think I'm stupid!"

"No, I think you're hopeful …" Jason sighed. "Did you tell Marcal or Lineus?"

"No … I don't know if I can trust them."

Jason raised an eyebrow. "Not Lineus?"

Ducking, Rachel heaved a heavy sigh. "If you won't come, I'll wait for him to return … Jason, I was sick—it could have been anybody in camp, or even somebody following us. My purse sat by me for days and nights and was never guarded."

"Maybe, but whoever it was knew where to look, what to look for, and then how to use it."

Rachel gulped. "Only Marcal has been to our world."

"I thought of that … and he used to be with Isabella. The traitor must be talking to her too."

Stricken, Rachel stared at him. "But how?"

"I've been talking to the men … they said wizards are able to communicate through the use of crystal mirrors—sort of like our cell phones. Keep an eye out for one. Whoever has one is probably the traitor."

Rachel shuddered. "The only person with a mirror I've seen was Suzella."

"Me too. And she decided to devote her life to babysitting all of a sudden."

"You think I'm walking into a trap."

"You'd go anyway, wouldn't you?"

"Yes! You don't understand. I need to find him!"

"Oh, I understand. If it was Jakey and Courtney I would be the same way … but I also don't understand. You're just his babysitter, Rachel."

"That's enough! It's my job to look out for him."

"Okay, okay …" Jason grinned. "So when do we leave and how do we make sure Jak's safe?"

Murd turned to him and growled. "I will watch this boy. Leave just before first rotation of the guards. If any unwelcome guests come in when yer gone, yer'll find their innards in the morning."

Sleep didn't come for Rachel, and night stretched far too long before Jason nudged her foot.

"I have two horses saddled in the woods," he said softly. "You ready?"

Instantly Rachel sat up. "Yes!"

"That's what I was afraid of … Come on, the guards looked mostly asleep when I went by."

Rachel snorted. "That's not very reassuring."

She'd made her bed behind Jak's tent, to be closer to the boy, she had told Marcal. In reality it made slipping away that much easier.

Overhead, clouds continued to build and the smell of rain hung heavy in the air. This also helped them sneak away, but it didn't help when it came to finding Marlin, the minstrel.

Luckily, he found them.

"Babysitter, is that you I see?" his voice asked from the darkness.

Leading their horses as they traveled by foot, the teens had just fought their way through a patch of dark, thorny woods in reaching the road. Every noise they made had caused Rachel to jump. Now sweat soaked her clothes. Hearing the minstrel's voice, she nearly shrieked.

"Uh, is that you, uh, Marlin?" she hissed back.

"Who is it with you?" asked the voice. If annoyed by Jason's presence, the young minstrel hid it well. Stepping from the trees on the opposite side of the road, the minstrel resembled nothing but a blob of shadow. A horse snorted by his shoulder. "I shall learn his name and sing of his praises in the song I write of this night."

"Is this the minstrel?" Jason asked. "Is he for real? Good grief. No matter what happens it'll be a long night."

Too nervous and excited to feel fear, Rachel completed her first night ride in silence. With Jason close by her side, she followed Marlin through the gloom to a fork in the road, choosing a narrow path leading downhill and away from the city of Mozhoven. Several minutes passed before they came out onto a wider road lined sparsely with trees and brush.

Marlin pulled up his horse. "The inn is not far from this here spot … soon we must dismount. There is probably a guard outside."

Working hard to control her breathing, Rachel nodded.

The inn stood on a small rise and consisted of a large double-story stone house with a small barn and stable in the back. Flaming torches lit up the yard and the glow of candles flickered from the windows. A single figure stood by the front door. Wearing a long cloak and sucking on a pipe, he was clearly watching for somebody.

"What's the plan, minstrel boy?" Jason muttered. "It's like they're waiting for us." They crouched in thick brush several yards away from the side of the inn farthest away from the outbuildings and torchlight.

"I heartily confess," swallowed the young minstrel, "I have not thought so far in the future."

"Wh-what room did you see Steven—the boy—taken to?" Rachel asked, her voice trembling.

"Ah, I do believe it was the top room closest to us, Babysitter."

"You *believe*?" growled Jason.

"I would stake my life on it."

Sighing, Jason turned to sit. "What do you think, Rachel?"

"I don't know … if we could get a distraction …" She stared at a thick tree just outside the lighted window Marlin had indicated.

Jason sighed. "I guess that would be me," he grumbled.

Chapter Thirty-Four

Jason rode up to the inn as if he didn't have a care in the world. Whistling, he hopped down in front of the guard.

"Stranger, you travel late," growled the guard, eyeing him suspiciously. "Are you also alone?"

"Um, here, my, uh, good man, put up my horse and give her a good rubdown. She'll take a bundle of hay, but no oats." Not looking at him, Jason tossed him the reins. "I don't want to spoil her."

Sputtering, the man glared at him. "I'm no hired hand, *boy*!"

"Oh, my apologies. Then let me buy you a drink!"

"What about your horse?" asked the man.

"She gave up drinking, but if you're that desperate for a date, go ahead and ask her in."

The man dropped the reins and put his hand to his sword. "I don't like your tongue, boy."

Jason stared above the man and shrugged. "Okay, but I don't like your face."

"Who are you?" demanded the man.

Jason took a breath. "The Wizard Isabella sent me. I've come for the boy."

Immediately the man's eyes jerked open. "Isabella sent you?"

"The Wizard Isabella. Now, do you want that drink?"

Swallowing, the guard grunted and turned to the inn.

Grabbing the reins of his horse, Jason closed his eyes and took a final deep breath. He made ready to spring up and flee at any sign the guard reached for his sword.

"Come on," the guard said, licking his filthy lips. "Let's get that drink."

Relaxing, Jason patted his horse's neck and loosely wrapped the reins around a rundown post outside the inn. Then he muttered a hope that Rachel knew what she was doing and followed the guard.

Inside felt like a sweatbox. A large open room with stairs in the center and lanterns lit in the corners greeted the new arrivals. A fire roared in the back and a bar was set up on the left. Lit candles hung around the wall to provide light. Round tables were on the right; almost all were occupied. Everyone fell silent to watch the new arrivals. Few looked friendly.

Boots booming against the hardwood floor, the guard led Jason to the nearest table, where a man sat nursing a tankard of ale. The other tables were full of various travelers on the way to a market in Mozhoven.

Slowly the hum of conversation returned and eyes returned to their own tables.

Serving maids were busy bringing platters of food and refilling cups of ale. Loud talking and sounds of eating filled the space. Jason's stomach growled. Smells of hot bread and cooked meat filled his nostrils. The innkeeper watched from behind the bar and seemed nervous. Sweat poured off his brow and he kept mopping it with a dirty towel.

"We want music!" demanded one of the merchants suddenly. "Where's that confounded minstrel run off to?"

Several cries supported the call.

"He, he will be here soon!" the innkeeper said, a tad fearfully. "Have more ale and wait patiently!"

"We travel all day and look for evening music to give us comfort," grumbled the merchant. "We pay enough for it!" A fresh mug of ale poured by a pretty serving maid distracted him.

Ignoring the merchants, the guard grabbed Jason by the shoulder, pulling him almost on top of the table.

"He says that Isabella sent him for the boy," he hissed.

"Oh?" said the already seated man. "She's early, is she?" The seated man was dressed similarly to the guard, but taller and with a scarred face. Ugly grooves lined his chin and forehead. Both men wore dark clothes and carried long swords at their belts. "Sit and be patient." The scarred man indicated a chair at his left. "The boy will be down in a minute."

Jason shrugged free of the man behind him. Clearly they weren't buying it. He hoped Rachel had made it up the tree ... well, she wanted a distraction.

"Actually, I wanted to buy you both a drink," he said boldly.

The two men exchanged smug looks.

"Is that so?" asked the standing guard. "Are you going to use coin given to you by the wizard?"

"Actually, how about a hot meal to go with it too?" Jason turned to the next table behind him and grabbed a plate and tankard from in front of a surprised merchant. "Here, have it." He flung the contents of the tankard in the face of the standing guard and smashed the food-filled plate in the face of the man seated.

Meanwhile, outside the inn, Rachel stretched out on the branch, reaching for the window. Praying the window would be unlocked and that she didn't fall, she refused to look down or back down. *Don't think about Jak ... just imagine yourself climbing into that room and finding Steven.* Eyes closed, her fingers found the edge of the window and pulled. The window opened like two welcoming doors.

Sticking in both arms, she grabbed the ledge and pulled herself with all her might. All at once she tumbled into the window and landed hard on her knees. Immediately her eyes blinked as they adjusted to the dim candlelight.

Marlin started climbing noisily in behind her.

"Welcome, Rachel," purred a familiar voice as Rachel sought to get to her feet. She went still. Standing before her, a figure stared down as if waiting. "The wizard wants you almost as much as she wants the boy. I'm glad you came."

Gasping, she scrambled to her feet. Lineus watched her in amusement.

"Surprised to see me? You are, aren't you?"

"Wh-what are you doing here?" she sputtered. "How did you get here?"

"Rachel, Rachel, don't you know? I arranged this meeting."

"You ... you took Steven?" A terrible feeling filled Rachel.

Bowing mockingly, Lineus gestured to his feet where the boy lay on his back on a pile of blankets. Hands and feet free, he appeared asleep.

"You're the traitor …"

"Very good, Rachel." Lineus clapped mockingly. "If you must know, I've been with Isabella ever since Marcal the warrior appeared at our village. She contacted me when I was a young lad and asked me to keep an eye on her former captain." He grinned. "When I was little, I wished to one day become a minstrel and act for kings and queens … you see, I knew I had the talent. Yet, fate is a fickle thing, is it not? As I grew older, I knew my talent could be used for much more than entertaining the masses. Isabella has shown me how. She's been giving me coin for some time, knowing a chance like this might come."

"But … but why?"

Lineus's dimpled chin hardened. "For years our village has escaped the notice of wizards and kings. Durnwirk meant nothing to the rest of Panterra … until Marcal showed up. His warrior ways are not our ways. He would bring destruction on us all, Rachel. When Isabella contacted me, I knew it was my duty to obey her. If I didn't, she would have sent others who would. Really, Rachel, you don't think the most powerful wizard in the land would allow her former captain to run out on her so easily? She promised protection for our village and when the time came … great power for me. For a long time, I thought I was wasting my time. The wizard vanished and Marcal seemed content to just stay in our village. Then you arrived. Listening to Marcal speak in the tent that first night, I knew my day had come. The Wizard Isabella had returned and would be looking for you. On the first day of our journey, I made contact with the Wizard Isabella. I've been working closely with her ever since to set up this meeting." Lineus lifted his eyes and sighed with pleasure. "First I got closer to you and tried to get closer to the children. You trusted me and they trusted me. The wizard will be pleased with my efforts. When this is over, Rachel, the Wizard Isabella shall make me a knight. Durnwirk will hail me a hero."

"I, I don't understand …" Rachel's head felt heavy and her breath came in gasps.

"Of course you don't." Lineus dropped his gaze to her and continued to smile. Arms behind his back, he stepped over Steven's prone body. "You're an utter fool, Rachel. I played you like a minstrel plays a lute. In this world, we protect what we love in any way possible." He pulled a hand from behind his back and held a single needle, nearly invisible in the poorly lit room. "Don't fret, Rachel. This won't hurt as much as young Steven's shot. I must admit, I didn't know how that thing would work, or how painful it would be to the boy … the Wizard Isabella had to tell me how to do it three times before I finally understood. What a strange, terrible world you come from. Now hold your arm out. Close your eyes if you like. But whatever you do, don't try to run. It'll only be worse for you."

Rachel could only swallow in horror. "You threw Jak out of the tree?"

Lineus bit his lip and stopped his advancing. He had clearly seemed to be enjoying this moment, but now his face clouded. "I'd do whatever it takes to gain protection for Durnwirk, Rachel."

"But killing children?"

"The ends justify the means, right? That's how your world says it, so I read."

Rachel tried to back away, but Marlin grabbed her from behind. The minstrel had quietly snuck up behind her.

"I apologize," he muttered in her ear. "I had to do as they said, or I'd be turned into a poetless frog … they heard my songs about you and forced me to help."

Lineus chuckled. "Surely you didn't think you could just climb in here and grab the boy that easily? And what about your boyfriend?" Roars and clatters rose from below, shaking the floor. Lineus grinned wickedly. "I fear that's him being pummeled." Lineus sighed contentedly. "He had it coming."

"M-Marcal will find us."

"Oh, I don't think so. Isabella will be here in due time. She took a detour to visit your Marcal and young Jak. I hope you said your goodbyes before you left. Now get a nice rest; you will need it."

"No!" Rachel shook her body, kicking her heel back into Marlin's shin. The minstrel squealed in pain and jumped back, banging into the wall.

"Hold still!" roared Lineus, stepping forward.

At that moment, Steven's eyes opened. Bloodshot, they narrowed into slits when seeing the traitor. The boy had been feigning unconsciousness for the last several minutes. Now with a snarl, he leapt from the blankets and threw himself at Lineus's legs.

Caught by surprise, the traitor tripped and crashed to his knees. "You blasted fool!" he howled. Leaning on his left thigh, he drew back his right leg and kicked the boy, catching a glancing blow in the arm.

Shrieking, Rachel tried to launch herself at Lineus, but Marlin jumped on her back, wrapping his arms around her neck.

Growling, Lineus got back to his feet. He held the needle with his left hand, away from his body. He only had eyes for Rachel. This would be a terrible mistake.

Steven's eyes narrowed like a wolf going for a kill. Snarling softly, he rolled to his feet and charged again. This time, he threw his shoulder at the back of Lineus's knees while wrapping his arms around his shins. Once again, Lineus grunted as he went back to his knees. Before he could recover, Steven scrambled up his back. Grabbing Lineus by the hair, he slammed both of his knees into his kidneys. Then he yanked on an ear while pummeling the exposed neck with his fist.

With an agonized scream, Lineus's face banged into the wood floor. Steven stayed latched to his back like a wild animal. Lineus still gripped the drugged needle and tried to stab back at the boy. Snarling, Steven jammed a knee into Lineus left armpit. Grabbing the back of the cinnamon-colored hair, he started slamming Lineus's face into the hard planked floor. What he lacked in size, he made up for in aggressiveness. The needle rolled free as Lineus started sobbing and screaming, desperately searching for protection.

Marlin and Rachel were both momentarily stunned by the boy's vicious attack. Feeling the minstrel's grip slacken, Rachel threw back her elbow and caught Marlin in the soft gut. Collapsing to the floor, he groaned and grabbed his stomach.

"Don't move or I'll break your fingers," Rachel growled back.

Trying to breathe, Marlin nodded, fighting back tears.

Rachel had already forgotten him. "Steven! Steven, stop it!"

Rachel rushed to where the boy continued to pound Lineus without mercy. The traitor feebly waved an arm as blood dripped from his face. His toughness had been an act as well.

Still, the boy paid Rachel no attention. His boyish looks were set in stone. Lips curled in a snarl, he concentrated only on bashing Lineus into the floor.

Breathing hard, Rachel tried to keep from panicking. Never before had she seen the boy act like this. Then she spotted the needle lying by Lineus.

Picking it up, Rachel gritted her teeth. Moving behind Steven, she reached down and wrapped an arm around his chest, pulling him back. At the same time, she jammed the needle hard into Lineus's hindquarters.

Lineus jerked once. His screams dwindled to a single groan before he went still. Ignoring Rachel's arm, Steven continued pounding the unconscious man's back.

"That's enough," Rachel said in his ear, her voice quavering. She remembered Elizabeth's warning about Steven losing control. The last sleeping shot remained in her purse in the saddlebag on Bolder. She did not want to use it. Ever. Hugging him tight, she sat back, pulling the boy onto her lap. "It's over, Steven, it's over! Listen to me, Jak is alive. He'll be okay. You'll be okay, I'm here now."

Struggling against her, Steven started throwing back elbows.

"Stop it, you're hurting me!" Her voice came out a scream.

All at once, the boy stopped. Rachel could feel his heart beating wildly, and sweat ran down his skin. His entire body started trembling. Then he slowly relaxed and lay against Rachel's arms for a long minute.

"I want to go home," he whispered.

"Me too, Steven. Me too."

Marlin remained where he sat, watching them like a scared rabbit who wanted to hop away. Lineus snored softly between them.

Then feet pounded the floor in the hall outside. Muffled voices rose from outside the door.

Rachel breathed in sharply. "But first we have to get out of here! Quick, the window!" Pulling the boy up, she hustled him to the open window. Trying not to think about how the boy must feel about trees after what had happened with Jak, she climbed out first, latching onto the limb before turning. "Can you make it?"

The boy had already climbed to the sill, and he quickly scrambled beside her as the first crash resonated against the door.

"Open up, by the order of the Wizard Isabella!" bellowed a deep voice.

Stifling a shriek, Rachel managed to keep from falling. In a near panic, she crawled to the trunk before half-falling, half-climbing to the ground—jumping the last five feet. As her feet hit the earth, a tremendous crash came from the window. The door had shattered. Angry roars filled the room above.

"Just jump, Steven! I'll catch you!"

Not hesitating, the boy ducked under a branch and leapt into the arms of his babysitter.

Grunting, Rachel caught the boy and wrapped her arms around him, barely keeping her feet as she staggered back.

The door of the inn banged opened at her back. "Find the babysitter and boy!" cried a man's voice. "They escaped! They can't be far!"

Rachel set Steven down and grabbed his arm. "Into the woods. Hurry!"

"Spread out!" called a voice behind them. "Gather the torches, quickly!"

The horses were gone. Ducking through the brush, Rachel ran to where she thought they had left them, but found only darkness and empty trees.

Then a soft nicker came from the right.

"Bolder," she gasped. Pulling Steven behind her, she found the gentle gray standing patiently behind a clump of bushes. The reins had been cut, but the horse hadn't wandered far. Soon she had Steven perched on the saddle in front of her. Having no idea where to go and with the reins useless anyway, she gripped Steven tightly and let Bolder take the lead. "I won't let you go," she muttered to Steven. "It'll be okay."

He shivered and made no sound.

Shouts and torches filled the night behind them.

Soon after Jason and Rachel had slipped away to find the inn, the camp had a visitor. A boy stumbled past a sleeping guard and into the firelight. All around the boy lay snoring men wrapped in blankets.

"Who is awake?" cried the boy desperately.

Marcal sat up with a jerk, sword in hand. Seeing the boy, he rolled into a defensive position.

"I come with a warning!" the frightened boy cried, seeing firelight reflected from the steel.

Marcal recognized him as the horse holder from Mozhoven. "What is it?"

Brokenly, the boy told Marcal of overhearing a plot to attack the camp that night and to lay a trap for the babysitter. "Isabella is coming! The wizard!"

"Who talked of this?" Marcal demanded, nearly shaking the boy.

Marcal went cold when hearing the answer … the boy described a man very similar to Lineus. Going to Lineus's bed, he swore loudly, as he found only stuffed blankets. He'd returned from scouting and had turned in early, feigning exhaustion …

Kicking aside the blankets, he bellowed to wake the camp. Chaos soon ensued. The guards were not asleep—but unconscious. Lineus had done his work well. Just as the guards were pulled to the fire and the men started searching for weapons, the baying of wolves rose from the night.

A chill swept over the men in the camp.

"Marcal!" called a man. "The Babysitter Rachel and the lad Jason are also gone!"

"What is this?" hissed Marcal.

Then an endless roll of thunder rumbled from the direction of the road. An army of stars filled the sky above. Horses were coming.

Marcal ran for the horses. "Scatter!" he cried. "Everyone scatter!"

"Save yourself!" cried one of the men. "The wizard is here!"

In the rush to flee, almost everyone forgot about Jak. Murd sat up with a snort inside the darkened tent as panic reigned around him.

They'd been riding for what felt like hours. Steven's body remained tight and tense while Rachel's shook with fear. "I, I think we're lost …" Putting a hand on Steven's shoulder, she squeezed. "It'll be okay, though. At least we're together, right?"

Bolder snorted and ducked into the trees, moving off the path they'd been following.

"Hey," Rachel cried. "Where are you going?" Then her eyes widened. Up ahead, there came a glow. Soon a fire could be seen through the trees. "Hello?" she called tentatively when they neared.

"Rachel!" cried a voice. "It's you! Lower your weapons. It is the Babysitter!"

As Bolder walked into the glowing light, five men appeared from the shadows. All were armed, and they looked extremely nervous. Rachel recognized them from camp—but where were Marcal and the rest? Where was Jak? *And … where was Jason?*

Climbing stiffly down, she ignored a fresh wave of saddle soreness. Helping Steven down, she turned to the men. She had a terrible feeling.

"Wh-what happened?"

"The Wizard Isabella," one of the men said flatly. "She sent riders into our camp … we barely had any warning." The other men, looking tired and worn, did not speak … or even look at her. These were the men who had always kept their distance and watched her with distrust. Now they wore haggard, frightened faces. One had a bloody bandage on his arm.

She wanted to ask if he was okay, but instead said, "Wh-where's Marcal …?"

"He left to find you and Jason." The voice was not very friendly.

"The-the others?"

"Who knows? The Wizard has her men still searching for us. We're staying here."

"But w-won't the fire attract them?"

"Perhaps." The man spat. "But it will also keep the wolves at bay … I'd rather face the Wizard's riders than have a wolf at my throat." He turned and went back into the shadows.

The other men followed and watched her from the shadows without friendliness. They were a rough-looking bunch … Rachel realized that she didn't even know their names. On the trail they'd only followed Marcal. Being shy and afraid, she had never made the attempt to know them. She hoped Marcal would return soon …

Shivering, Rachel hurried to join Steven at the fire. Somewhere out in the darkness, Isabella was searching for her … Jak lay helpless … and Jason was lost, perhaps captured … or worse. A lone wolf howled nearby.

Steven sat silent and still—like a stone statue. Feet crossed, he rested his arms on his knees and stared deep into the fire. He had yet to utter a word since being rescued.

Rachel moved to stand next to him.

"What you did back there, you saved my life." She took a seat next to the boy and tried to smile. He never looked up. If only Steven would give one of his half smiles and relax … if only he once again became the careful, controlled boy she knew. Instead, he remained frozen in shock. Rachel had to get through to him. "Where did you learn to fight like that?"

At first she didn't think the boy even registered her presence. Then he looked at her with terrified eyes. His face remained like stone.

"My dad taught me," he whispered. "That's how he hit my mom."

Rachel felt like she'd been punched in the gut. "Oh, Steven …" She leaned closer and put her arm around him. "What you did saved me, though. You saved me from that monster. Your dad didn't teach you that." She reached with her other arm and touched his chest around the heart. "This is what taught you that. Do you understand? Elizabeth and Doug are your parents. Your real mom and dad taught you to be kind. You have a good heart, Steven, don't forget that."

Steven buried his face in her shoulder and started crying.

"Shh! It's okay." She rocked him gently. Soon his muffled sobs quieted and he moved to lie against Rachel's shoulder. After a while, he fell into a restless sleep. Very briefly, the monster retreated …

Gently, Rachel moved his head so it rested on her knee. She stroked his hair and watched the dying flames. It was all falling apart …

One of the men pulled dry wood from the dark and threw it on the fire, causing a host of sparks to shoot up. Every few minutes, another wolf howl came from the darkness. Each time it seemed closer.

Even in the heat, Rachel continued to shiver. The men, aside from adding to the fire, kept away from her. After a long, terrible silence, Rachel's eyes started to droop, and she allowed herself to lie back. Closing her eyes, she wished very hard for morning to come and for all her troubles to disappear. She would wake up to find Marcal and Jason back with Jak …

Rachel woke to screaming.

"What is it?" hollered a man.

"The boy," cried another. "He's gone mad! He'll kill us all!"

Sitting up with a start, Rachel peered around her in panic. The fire still burned brightly and darkness still covered the sky. A terrible shrieking hurt her ears. Her eyes flashed wide as she spotted the source.

Digging his nails into his pants, Steven knelt in a pile of ash from a previous fire and pointed his tortured face toward the sky. Veins were popping from his arms and neck. Eyes rolled back, he shrieked like a banshee, without stopping.

Just beyond the fire, the men were backing away, drawing swords.

"We have to slay the beast!" cried one of the men.

"Steven!" she shouted hoarsely. "No, it's okay! Stay back from him!"

Getting to her feet, Rachel stumbled to the boy's side. She tried hugging him, but he twisted away. Not once did he look at her, but his body reacted violently to her touch. It felt like wrestling an alligator.

"Somebody help!" Again she tried grabbing the boy, but this time received a hard elbow in her ear. "Steven, you're hurting me!"

He only howled louder. Rolling onto his back, he covered his ears and kicked his feet.

Never so scared in her life, Rachel again looked for help. By now the men had retreated into the trees.

"He's possessed!" cried one. "The Wizard has cast a spell on him!"

"He'll kill us all!"

"No!" cried Rachel. "I need my purse! Please, help me!"

It was no use. The men fled into the night, no longer caring about the danger of wolves or Isabella's men. They left Rachel very alone with a tortured boy who couldn't stop screaming.

Tears ran down her cheeks. "Mom, I need you! Anybody!" Nobody came. *I'm not going to leave you! I can do this!*

Screaming herself, Rachel managed to grab Steven's legs and pulled him away from the fire, ignoring his wild thrashing. Once satisfied he wouldn't roll into the fire, she dropped his feet and ran for Bolder. The horse remained saddled but tied to a tree. Eyes rolling back, the horse snorted and seemed very anxious to follow after the fleeing men.

"One moment, Bolder," Rachel mumbled. Fumbling blindly, she reached into the saddlebag and groped for her purse. Finding it, she searched for the remaining needle. *I can't do this! This is impossible!*

The boy's tormented screaming told her otherwise. At last she found it. At a stumbling run, she raced back to Steven while uncapping the needle.

"It'll be okay. It'll be okay." She knew she was talking to herself. The boy now lay on his stomach and seemed to be trying to bury himself in the ashes. With a deep breath, she jumped on his back, pinning him down. Kicking and twisting, Steven did all he could to knock her off. "Sorry, Steven … I never wanted to do this." Reaching back, she patted for Steven's thigh with her fist gripping the tube. Finding a spot, she plunged the tube against the pants. The boy continued bucking and struggling under her. Using all her strength, she pushed the boy down and squeezed her eyes shut as she pressed the button to release the needle.

A violent spasm shot through the boy and his shrieks went an octave higher. He arched his back while jerking his leg forward, throwing Rachel off in the process. Getting to his knees, he looked ready to launch himself into the flames. Suddenly he groaned and flopped down into the ashes.

Heart thudding, Rachel threw herself back over the boy until she was certain he was out and breathing evenly. Counting to three, she yanked out the needle and tossed it away in disgust. Rolling Steven over, she checked his pulse and breathed a deep sigh of relief when she found it strong and steady. The terrible screaming had faded away, and only the sound of the crackling fire remained.

Sweat and fear pouring from Rachel, she wiped ash from Steven's face. Now unconscious, his tortured face had relaxed into that of a normal, exhausted boy. But what about after he woke up? Rachel shuddered.

Bolder snorted behind her and abruptly shrieked.

"It's okay, Bolder," Rachel said shakily. "Don't you start. Steven will be fine."

That was when she looked up and saw the first wolf.

The bushes on her right started to shake, and out stepped the beast. About the size of a small pony, the wolf stepped into the light and watched her with cold, yellow eyes. It stood a mere three feet away, looking straight into her eyes.

A snort announced the presence of a second wolf on her left.

Rachel couldn't move.

Bolder went crazy. Shrieking wildly, the horse rose to his hind legs and jumped sideways. The reins were already frayed and now snapped. Freed, Bolder leapt into the night. The wolves never looked away from Rachel.

Crouching next to Steven, Rachel forced herself to breathe.

"I-I'm just a babysitter, nothing more …" Rachel could hear her own heartbeat nearly in her mouth as she reached down and slowly gathered Steven, pulling him into her arms. Shielding him the best she could, she glared at the lead wolf. "Leave us alone!" she shouted at the wolf. "Get out of here!"

The wolf, its gray and black fur bristled on end, merely blinked. She became aware of snuffling from behind her. Prowling wolves emerged from the shadows and into the firelight. Soon she was totally surrounded.

"No!" she snarled. "You can't have this boy! Get back!"

Almost as if understanding her, the lead wolf nodded its head and backed into the brush. Soon the sounds of wolves faded.

Confused, and scared nearly witless, Rachel gasped with relief. For several moments, she didn't move an inch. Once satisfied the wolves had gone, she did her best to calm her breathing. Lifting Steven's limp body into her arms, she rose unsteadily to her feet. Holding him tightly, she turned, only to discover why the wolves had left so readily.

A twig snapped and a soldier stepped into the flickering light. His drawn sword flickered in the firelight. He was a massive man with a cloak the color of blood. Under the cloak he wore dark armor and black trousers. His head bare, he looked positively evil in the firelight. Above his dark beard, his black eyes flashed nothing but malice. Long, wild hair flowed behind him like a shadowy cloud.

Behind him, the brush moved and several more soldiers appeared at his back. Each wore similar armor and carried a sword and round shield. These men wore rounded metal helmets with open faces. All stared balefully at Rachel.

"Could it be?" drawled the red-cloaked soldier, grinning cruelly. "Is this the great Babysitter Rachel offering us the boy?" Lowering his sword to his side, he bowed mockingly. "I am Bodin, Captain of the Wizard Isabella's Guard. Do you come peacefully, or do you wish to give me more pleasure on this night? I would like to plant this blade in your neck, girl. You caused much trouble."

"Take care, Bodin," mumbled one of the men at his back. "She has power … remember the screaming that drew us to this place."

Bodin snorted, but lifted his sword to point at Rachel. "For your sake," he snarled at her, "I hope the boy still lives. Drop him and stand aside before I bloody this blade in your throat!"

This night of terror just would not end. Shaking, Rachel turned to put herself between the men and Steven. The fire still burned brightly and cut off her retreat. Bodin and his men advanced to form a semicircle around her, preventing any chance for escape.

"I believe you to be a fool, Babysitter Rachel," Bodin spat. "You mean to protect the boy, so he must live. Too bad you won't. You have nowhere to go." He laughed harshly. "You see, there is a reward on you … dead or alive. Only the boy needs to live." He shifted his sword to aim the point at Rachel's throat. "This will be a pleasure." Stepping forward, he all at once stopped dead—almost literally. A look of pure disbelief covered his face as the sword moved into a defensive position.

Cringing, Rachel stared at him and then at the other soldiers. They had also jerked to a stop. Their disbelief turned to absolute horror, all directed toward Rachel.

"Not possible!" growled Bodin. Lifting his sword, he stepped forward and made to swing a deadly arc at Rachel's neck.

Burdened with Steven, Rachel could only duck and screech. Then a deep growl cut through the air. Bursting through the flames, a vicious shape leapt over her and plowed into the soldier.

Screaming, Bodin went down, dropping his useless sword. The giant leader of the wolves slashed at his face with sharp teeth.

"What wizardry is this?" gasped a soldier.

"Kill the wolf!" screamed Bodin, fighting for his life. "Attack!"

At that order, the other wolves attacked. Rising from the shadows behind, wolves leapt on the soldiers and dragged many down almost immediately. Shrieking in panic, the remaining soldiers fled into the woods, straight into the jaws of more wolves. Bodin's last view was of yellow eyes and sharp, very sharp, teeth.

As soon as the shrieks and snarls of the soldiers started, Rachel fled. Cradling Steven, she rushed around the fire and into the woods, away from the wolf massacre.

Ducking under branches, she ran blindly through thick brush as the dreadful screams of the men continued ringing in her ears. At first, she only thought to get as far away as possible. It took time for her eyesight to adjust to the dark woods, but this didn't slow her. Little moonlight guided her path, and only instinct saved her from dashing headlong into a tree. Ignoring the stings of brambles and the lashing of branches clawing at her, she ducked and twisted her way through the forest. After a while, her arms started to burn as Steven began to grow heavy. Yet when she started to slow, a wolf snarled at her heels.

Yelping, she found a new source of energy. Another wolf panted on her left and kept pace.

Tears filled her eyes. Escape was impossible. Yet she continued to run with Steven held firmly in her arms. After a while, her arms locked into position and refused to budge. Still, the wolves kept after her, snapping at her heels.

Breathing became difficult, and she reduced her pace to a steady, lethargic jog.

At first, Rachel knew she would be eaten and the wolves were only toying with her … but soon it became apparent … the wolves were actually guiding her. She barely even saw them. At times they would appear at her side and nudge her in a certain direction. At some point, Rachel managed to shift Steven to her shoulder and throw him over—she didn't remember how or when. Steven's limp arms flopped at her back, urging her onward. Her chest was screaming for her to stop, but the wolves kept her going … and going. She would run to daybreak and beyond if necessary.

Lisa sat at the great table and frowned at the empty spaces stretching before her. "How many people are eating tonight, a hundred?"

"Actually, closer to a hundred twenty," Tendl said, going to the seat on her right.

"Are they all priests of the temple?"

"Mostly," agreed Tendl. "There's apparently a celebration for you."

"I don't want a celebration! I want to go home! You told me, Tendl, that if I helped you escape you'd get me home with my brother and Rachel!"

"I said this place is capable of doing that, Lisa … just be patient a little longer. The man who can help will be coming soon."

"Great. I'll be patient, meanwhile Steven and Rachel are out there running from that stupid wizard while I sit here eating with a hundred twenty fat priests! Where's Darvy?"

"Oh, he's about here somewhere." Tendl stared at her sideways. "I believe the celebration has something do with him too."

"What did he do?" she mumbled. "Match his socks all by himself?" As soon as she said it, she regretted it. Poor Darvy couldn't do anything right, but Lisa didn't blame him. After all, he grew up in North Carolina—where they didn't teach survival skills in the wild while fleeing from crazy wizards. She was just frustrated and frightened. The priests at this place were overweight and overly nice. She didn't trust them any higher than she could lift one. They let her do anything she wanted, except find out how to help her brother and Rachel. They also wouldn't let her near the cave above the temple where the Spirit of Panterra supposedly lived. Only Tendl got to go there, and he refused to tell her why or what he saw there. Lisa had begun to seriously doubt Tendl's words of being an ally.

Tendl now smiled at her. "Oh, I think our boy managed to do something more than match his socks."

On cue, the main doors to the dining hall opened and the head priest marched in.

"All rise for his Royal Majesty King Gretz the Seventh, the leader of the Western Kingdom of Panterra!" cried one of the following priests.

"What?" sputtered Lisa.

"Hush, there's more," hissed Tendl.

The priest raised his voice and cried louder. "The king arrives for the banquet in honor of his engagement to the Maiden Lisa!"

"What!" Lisa's shouts were drowned out as a band of priests playing horns and drums marched in. They were followed by Darvy, wearing heavy purple robes and looking rather dazed.

"Are you out of your mind!" Lisa shouted, nearly punching the king in the nose.

Darvy flinched and ducked his head miserably. "You don't understand …" he muttered. "The priests recognized me immediately … And so did Tendl. The only way they would let me see you is if I would marry you … otherwise, you wouldn't be allowed to speak to a king."

"Well, I'm going to give you a good reason not to see me! I'm going to rip out your hair!"

Her red hair flared in the sun streaming from the window above them. Standing at the top of the highest tower, the two were having their first private meeting after their engagement dinner. They had snuck off after each giving the excuse of not feeling well. Neither one had lied. Alone in their rooms, they'd slipped out by running past surprised priests acting as guards. Darvy had led the way to the tower. Their overweight pursuit had long fallen behind.

Darvy now stared at her with imploring eyes. "Please, Lisa, I-I don't know what to do."

"You're the king, call it all off!"

"I can't! It's not that easy! Don't you understand? The priests here are just using me, okay? Isabella wants me dead. The Eastern Kingdom wants me dead. And my cousin Polis, who is acting as king, was the one who sold my whereabouts to Isabella in North Carolina. Everyone wants me dead, except for the priests … and they just want me because they want to rule the people through me." He dropped to a cushioned chair and hung his head. "With me marrying you, it'll prove I'm ready to be king … I'd be better off jumping out that window right now … ending it all."

Lisa frowned. "Don't be stupid. When I get out of this dump, you can come with me. Go back to our world."

"This is my world, Lisa. I was sent to North Carolina when I was little, but I always knew I'd return to be king."

"Oooh …" groaned Lisa, rubbing her head. "I wish Rachel was here … She's the only one who could possibly make a mess like this better."

Darvy's head perked up. "Do you mean the Babysitter Rachel?"

Lisa gave Darvy a startled look. "How do you know about her?"

"The whole kingdom speaks of her! That's all the priests talk about. They say minstrels are singing about her everywhere and women are even naming their children after her—she's supposed to be on a quest to take down the wizards." Darvy grinned. "That's why Isabella hasn't chased me—because she's busy with her."

Lisa thumped back against the wall and slid down. "I knew she wouldn't forget about me … I knew it. Wait—how did the priests hear about her when they're stuck on this mountain?"

Darvy got up and pointed toward the mountain and the cave. His voice grew solemn. "Inside there is where the Great Spirit lives. The Spirit knows everything."

Chapter Thirty-Five

Dawn had just started to break when Rachel staggered out of the woods. Totally exhausted, she felt ready to collapse and never rise again. Running had always been a bane for her … only in gym class for the mile, had she ever tried … until now. Barely recovered from her illness, she'd been running and then staggering like a zombie for the past few hours, all the while carrying Steven. Only his limp body kept her from falling a long time before … that and the wolves. Blinking, she found herself standing on a small bluff overlooking a road. Below, she saw a wooden carriage parked for the night next to a smoldering campfire. No other person was in sight. Falling to her knees, she allowed Steven to slide from her arms. Pain pulsed from her stiff elbows. Brambles and branches had clawed at her face and ripped her clothes. Streaks of dried blood covered her cheeks. Behind her, the two wolf companions snuffled her shoulders. One of the animals licked her face clean … she was too tired to pull away.

"*Go to the mountain …*" A voice whispered above her. "*It is the only hope.*"

Blinking away exhaustion, Rachel looked up and saw nothing. *Perhaps it was my imagination … all just my imagination.*

The smell of frying meat wafted from below.

Woofing quietly, the wolves nudged her once more and then silently returned to the forest.

This is our destination. Relief filled Rachel and she once again found a new source of energy she didn't think she had.

"Come on, Steven," she mumbled. "There's help below." Surely the wolves had led her to this place for a reason … they were helping her. Who cared why.

With great effort, she got to her feet and hefted Steven over her shoulder once again. Finding a narrow path, she stumbled down to the campsite.

As she reached the road, a young girl dressed in a ragged tunic moved from behind the carriage and crouched over the fire. She watched Rachel approach warily. Lifting her neck, she called back loudly. "We got some more! It's like a plague of the lost!"

A boy limped from behind the carriage and scratched his head. Dressed in an overgrown shirt hanging to his feet, he had one ankle bandaged in a dirty rag and favored his right arm. "Joe, I think maybe you better put another ham on," he said worriedly. "I don't think there will be enough food now, and I'm starving!"

The girl gave the boy a dirty look. "You're always starving and always thinking of yourself."

"Ex-cuse me, I, I …" Rachel pulled up short.

"Rachel! Jakey, look, Rachel is here! And she has Steven!"

Rachel's eyes went wide as the carriage door burst open and Courtney shot out like a bullet. Jakey jumped out and ran after his sister.

Rachel could only watch with disbelief. She sat down with a thump as the Richardson kids reached her. Steven was moved to her lap. "Wh-what are you doing here?" she stammered.

"We came looking for you!" Courtney slowed when seeing Steven's limp form not stirring. "Is he okay?"

"He's only sleeping … Oh, Courtney, I'm sorry," Rachel found it difficult to talk. "I-I don't know where Jason is, I—"

"He's still sleeping too," Jakey said, rubbing sleep from his own eyes. "He came in last night with the others." He grinned when seeing her amazed expression.

Speechless, Rachel could only follow the children. Then Red came from the woods carrying firewood. Seeing her, he grunted and nodded. His eyes widened for a second and even appeared to go red … but it may have been a trick of the early light. In any case, his eyes quickly blinked and showed no more reaction.

"I feel the end is nearing," he muttered. "Hag, come and meet our latest guests!" His voice seemed to catch with excitement … but that too was quickly controlled.

Too tired to even try to understand what was happening, Rachel allowed herself to be led behind the carriage to the sleeping area under the shade … where Murd snored heavily, his large belly rising and falling like a mountain in an earthquake. Next to him, Jak lay with his head still wrapped and breath still steady, but shallow. Jason sat up with a yawn until seeing Rachel.

Yelping, he struggled to his knees. "Rachel! You're here!"

"How—" Overcome, Rachel nearly dropped Steven. Jason rushed to take the unconscious boy and lay him down next to Jak. "How did you get here?" she managed to say.

"I, um, sort of started a food fight and managed to sneak out when some merchants started to get a little physical." He rubbed a bruise on his cheek. "I've never been in a brawl before. Anyway, my horse had disappeared, so I snuck in the stables and, well, borrowed a horse. But when I was leaving, some guys showed up on horseback and gave me quite a chase. I finally lost them in the woods and sort of ran into Murd carrying Jak. He said the camp was attacked by Isabella, so we traveled most of the night and ended up here … where," he scratched his curls in wonder, "my brother and sister are, er, were apparently looking for us."

Rachel shook her head in disbelief. "I don't believe this."

Jason reached over and patted her arm. "You look exhausted." He smiled. "But it's true, we found each other. What happened to you?"

Rachel shook her head, too tired to even think straight. "Lisa is somewhere out there still," she mumbled. Finding a spot across from the boys, she more collapsed then lay down.

"We'll find her, you'll see—" Jason stopped.

Rachel was fast asleep.

"How did you get so big?" Jan asked in wonder.

"I ate little boys who wouldn't leave me alone," growled Murd.

Sitting by the fire, he was busy boiling a broth for Jak while Jan and Joe sat in awe watching him. The boy and girl couldn't take their eyes off the large man. One of his arms was almost the thickness of their narrow waists.

The woman perched on the seat of the wagon and wiped her nose. "About time those brats found somebody else to pick on," she mumbled. In the past couple weeks, Jan and Joe had hounded her in every way possible. While Jan recovered from his injuries, he still found ways to torment the woman, who had foolishly agreed to act as his nurse. Frogs, slugs, and worms kept appearing in her pockets. Once, she woke up to find herself tied up in blankets. And anything she touched and put down would constantly vanish only to turn up later in the same place. Jakey was immensely entertained by the mischievous duo, but Courtney went out of her way to be kind to the woman … this was even more annoying.

"Can't a woman get any peace around here?" she often complained. "Just leave me alone!" And now all these strangers were showing up. It was enough to make her go mad. "Are we there yet?" she muttered to Red.

"Almost, I believe," the tall man muttered mysteriously. "I'll be in the woods for the rest of the day. Do not disturb me."

Sputtering, the woman half stood. "You'll leave me with, with all these, these kids?"

Red smiled at her, revealing his teeth. For a moment he looked like a fox in a chicken coop. "Only for a time."

"Hello, the camp!" called a loud voice.

Rachel blinked her heavy eyelids. *That voice* … She remembered it. It sounded so familiar … *Where had she heard it?* Memories of another place surfaced …

Rachel shoved her blankets away and hurried to her feet. Steven slept near Jak, but otherwise the beddings were empty. Rachel grinned. The boy's ripstick was at his side—surely put there by Murd.

The sun stood high overhead, marking the midday with warmth and humidity. It all came flooding back … Somehow, someway she had managed to connect with Jason, Murd, and Jak. And they'd found Courtney and Jakey in the process! Yet there was also Red—one person whom she did not trust a bit. The others, a girl and boy and an old lady, were strangers. And now this strange, familiar voice …

"I'm coming in."

Where had she heard him before? Then it clicked. *Pastor Smith! Or was it Wizard Borbu?*

The short, stocky man sat astride a massive bay horse on the road. He searched the campsite with his eyes, frowning at what he saw. At his side was a giant black mare carrying a bareheaded knight in silver armor. The knight kept silent and deferred to the wizard.

"Who are you?" the woman demanded suspiciously. "Where did you come from?"

"That's Pastor Smith, or the Wizard Borbu," Rachel said, stepping from around the carriage. "I don't know who's with him, but he's not a friend."

Borbu's eyes lit on Rachel and widened. "So you are here!" he boomed in his powerful voice. "Where's the boy? Where's Steven?"

"Not around," Rachel said, crossing her arms.

"Is that so?" Borbu laughed. "Then who's this youngster?"

Rachel flinched. Turning, she saw Steven blinking sleepily as he staggered to her side, gripping the ripstick to his chest. Grabbing him, she pulled him close. "He's not going with you, if that's why you're here."

"Is that right?"

"Yeah, that's right." Jason stepped from the carriage, closing the door behind where Courtney and Jakey peeked out.

Murd stood by the fire, pushing Joe behind him.

"You fools don't know what you're messing with," Borbu said. A hard look entered his eyes and he raised a hand menacingly. "In this one finger I have enough power to reduce all of you to ashes." Everyone facing him froze, and the wizard smiled confidently. "Yes, so I think we can start the negotiations now."

"Negotiations?" Rachel gulped.

"Yes, negotiations. I'm willing to send all of you, who belong, back to your world—except for Steven, of course. The others, I'll give gold and a promise of protection by the great Borbu. Give me what I want and you'll all go away happy."

"And if we don't?" Rachel said loudly. Her knees started to shake and it took all her concentration to keep her eyes on Borbu.

"With me is Sir Hulse, commander of the Western Riders. We have a small army just up the road. About four hundred knights, all looking for a fight. And …" he raised his finger. "I have my power. We will have the boy, Rachel. No longer are we in your world. Here, I call the shots."

Rachel held her breath.

Sneaking out of the woods behind the wizard, the young boy, Jan, had slid down the bluff and was creeping silently to Borbu's horse. Even with a limp, he proved as silent as a mouse. Bending low, he went into a crouch and started to slowly and carefully unbuckle the saddle. Flicking its tail, the horse gave no notice to the boy. Once he'd finished, Jan silently moved to the horse of Sir Hulse. So smooth were his actions, the horses never reacted. Finished unbuckling the second saddle, he looked up and grinned.

"Uh, I'm afraid you might fall short," Rachel said, still not daring to breathe.

"Oh, is that so?" He jerked his horse to face her. As the horse moved, his saddle slipped a little … and it kept sliding. "I—hey, er—!" Arms flailing, he slid sideways with the saddle and crashed to the dirt.

"Wha—" Sir Hulse grabbed for his sword and soon found himself sharing the same fate. In a crash of armor, he too landed in a painful heap.

Snorting, the horses stepped calmly away from their masters and started chomping on grass beside the road.

Jan had disappeared into the trees, leaving Borbu befuddled at what had just happened.

"Wh-what magic is this?" Horse dung covered the front of his shirt as he lifted himself up. Confusion and anger filled his face.

"The old hag is a wizard," Joe shouted triumphantly. "Try anything and she'll make you into horse manure!"

"Impossible!" spat Borbu … but doubt crept into his voice. Sir Hulse sniveled at his side and made no attempt to rise. He looked fearfully at the woman.

Gulping, the woman glared at Joe before trying to stand up straighter with an air of confidence. Her legs shook.

"I-I know magic," she muttered halfheartedly.

Rachel stared at the old woman and winced. There was no way anybody would believe her.

Borbu's eyes glowed brightly. "Do you think you can fool a wizard? I will destroy you, hag! I'll destroy all who mock my power!" Face twisted in ugly hatred, he reeled to his feet and waved a finger toward the woman.

"I … the girl talks nonsense! I know nothing!" the woman cried, stumbling back.

Energy crackled, and an orange flash leapt from Borbu's finger.

This flash promptly bounced off something invisible and returned to its source with a brilliant explosion. From all around, a tremendous voice boomed louder than thunder. A green light lit up the sky.

"YOU WILL DESTROY NOTHING, BORBU!"

Blown back by the force of his reflected magic, Borbu now sat in another pile of horse manure with his face blackened and smoking. A look of pure shock dropped his jaw wide open. His lips trembled as he stared upward.

"R-Rudolph?" he stammered, sounding very small. "No … it's impossible!"

But it was … the former apprentice had become a master and a full-fledged wizard. Lifting from the trees as if merely stretching, he floated in midair standing over the campsite. A green platform of light shimmered at his feet and bolts of green energy ran up and down his body. Wearing a brilliant red cloak, he looked like an angry Christmas tree ornament. Where his bright blue eyes had been, intense red flames burned.

"I AM THE MASTER, BORBU! YOU ARE NOTHING COMPARED TO ME!"

"H-how—you're just an apprentice!" protested Borbu.

"NO LONGER!" His voice lowered, and his mouth formed a sneer. "No longer am I a minion to the wizards. Instead, I have become your deity! The Spirit of Panterra has chosen me over all of you!"

Borbu struggled to his feet. "That's impossible! The boy is still here! Whoever gives him to the spirit gains the power!"

"You doubt your senses?" The red eyes glowered.

Swallowing, Borbu looked a little lost. Gathering his courage, he snarled. "Whatever power you have will soon run out! I will have the Western Riders come through here and smash you! Remember, Rudolph, their armor cannot be harmed by magic."

"My power comes from a greater source, Borbu … and I'm afraid I grow tired of this conversation. I believe it is time for me to leave—and visit the spirit!"

"*No*!" shouted Borbu. "You're stuck here! We have you trapped!"

Rudolph merely extended his hands. "Do not be so sure about that."

A green mist started flowing from Rudolph's feet and spread down, covering the campsite.

The horses of Borbu and Sir Hulse screamed shrilly. Each loosened a stream of dung while charging back up the road. The horses for the carriage also broke loose and fled.

Everyone else stood frozen—scared stiff.

Rachel, like the others, had stood in awe at Rudolph's appearance. Now she pulled Steven closer to her as the green light encircled their bodies.

"You're creating a water portal from nothing!" screamed Borbu in amazement. "How is that possible!"

Fear turned into hope. Rachel dared to believe that maybe they were being sent home—but then she thought of Lisa.

"We'll be leaving now, Borbu," Red said, his voice booming loudly. "Just remember this. I now have the power of the Panterra Spirit! All things are now possible for me. Spread the news to my former master!"

The green mist grew thicker.

Rachel tried to move, but found it impossible. The same was true with the others—the mist now acted as ropes, encircling their feet, and holding them fast to the ground. She could at least move her hands. These she used to pull Steven even tighter to her. Whatever was happening, they had no choice in the matter but to stick together.

"Hold on, Steven," Rachel managed to mumble, feeling the boy tremble. "I think we'll be okay!"

Borbu tried to rush in, but an invisible force pushed him back. "Curse you, Rudolph!"

"Jan!" suddenly screamed Joe. "Hurry!"

The boy hopped from the woods and leapt down, cushioning his fall by landing on top of Sir Hulse's head. With a grunt, the knight crashed back into the dirt.

Scrambling to his feet, Jan hopped and limped before diving into the green mist.

Borbu snatched for him, but grabbed only air. "No!" he cried again. Then a huge blast of force exploded before him, knocking him, this time into a fresh pile of horse dung. Everyone in front of him had vanished with the mist. The fire remained. The carriage remained. The bedding and all else remained … just not the people.

Sir Hulse groaned at his side before slapping a hand to his ear. "My gold earring, it's gone!" he cried.

Emerald radiance blasted in all directions, churning and flashing. It felt like being trapped under an ocean of light. A dull roar filled Rachel's ears. Then the light shook and dissipated in a blink.

Rachel hadn't moved her feet, but suddenly, instead of soft ground, she stood on hard stone. Steven sagged in front of her and nearly fell in astonishment.

"Um, what just happened?" Jason sounded as amazed as Rachel felt.

Courtney and Jakey, who had been sitting in the wagon, now sat next to Jason, wearing surprised looks of their own.

Where they had been, on a dusty road lined with trees and next to a carriage, had now turned into something completely different. Now they were in a great stone hall the size of an airplane hangar and supported with massive marble pillars. Mysterious light descended from clumps of glowing rocks that lined the ceiling. A large stone pool of blue water sparkled behind them. The water stretched from one side of the stone wall to the other. On the far side was a narrow ledge with a stone slab, but otherwise the hall appeared strangely empty. Two great wooden doors over nine feet tall were in front of them. Across the vast walls were carved scenes of horrible beasts staring down at them. Between the carvings were strange lights that lit up the chamber.

"If I wrote a book about this, nobody would believe me," the woman muttered as she surveyed her new surroundings with eyes filled with wonder.

During the transition, she had moved to grab Joe. Jan lay at their feet. Now, breathing hard, he sat up and gripped the woman's leg tightly. The woman didn't mind. She was hugging Joe just as tight.

Grunting, Murd moved first. He rushed to where Jak stretched unconscious beside the pool.

A cough and a flash of green light gave everyone a start. Then Rudolph stood before them in front of the great doors. Raising both his arms, he nodded and gestured for attention.

"Welcome to the temple of Panterra," he said calmly. "I expected us to take the long route, but unforeseen events have speeded up our journey considerably." His eyes briefly sparked red. "Unforeseen events and power surges." He flicked a quick look at Steven. "In a moment, the priests will arrive and take you to your chambers. You'll be staying here for a time … as my guests."

"Wh-why?" Rachel said, finding her voice. "What are we doing here? Why are you helping us?"

"Do not worry yourself, Babysitter. Save your questions. All will be known when the time comes." Rudolph smiled softly. "Do as I say, and I promise, Babysitter, you will return to your world soon. Very soon. That goes for all of you." As he said this, he only looked at Rachel. "But first, I must make sure we are safe from the other wizards. Remember, I'm the only one who has helped you. I'm the only one you can trust."

"What is this place?" Jason asked, staring around him in awe. "I mean, this building … where are we?"

Rudolph lifted his head and breathed in deeply as if inhaling fresh air and peace all at once. Rachel made a face. To her the air smelled of dank rot, and the room had the charm of a prison.

"This is the home of the Spirit of Panterra," Rudolph said grandly. "The pool behind you is where the spirit resides."

Everyone immediately looked at the still flat waters, but saw nothing. "Few have seen the spirit, but it is there, I assure you." He paused for a moment. "Its powers are great. Those who bathe in the waters lose all their fear and find themselves free … if they survive."

"Wh-what do you mean?" Jason asked, not a little awed. Something about that pool of water … It appeared perfectly natural and safe … and all the more menacing for it.

"Many a man lost a monster in these waters, but many more lost a life. You see, whatever you hold inside of you comes out in the water … your true inner being is set free." Rudolph lifted a brow ironically. "Often what we keep inside ourselves consumes us. Those who cannot control their thoughts and feelings end up eaten by them in the water. Only those with strong control can defeat their monster. So," he said mildly, "I encourage you to stay far away from the edge and away from the water. Just touching the surface wakens the spirit."

Murd, his body quivering, lifted Jak and backed from the suddenly sinister water.

The double doors creaked and slowly opened behind Rudolph, letting in dull light. From this light, a group of ten bald-headed men in black robes hurried in. Seeing Rudolph, they pulled up short and at once fell to their knees.

"Ah," said Rudolph. "The priests are finally here. Come, we go. These servants of Panterra will take you to your lodgings. Rise and lead, my friends," he called to the kneeling men.

Nervous and awed, the group followed Rudolph to where the priests rose and almost reverently backed out the mighty doors of the cavern.

As the home of the spirit emptied, a single figure stepped from behind a pillar. Covered in a dark robe with a hood hiding its head, the figure lifted two arms over the still water.

"I feel the presence of the one …" groaned its voice. "He is very near … Be ready, great one."

Huge bubbles disturbed the surface of the pool's center.

Rachel flopped on the soft bed and frowned. "This isn't right," she said. "We're prisoners in these rooms, aren't we?"

Jason leaned in the doorway and grinned. "Some prison. Our rooms are better than most hotels." He waved a hand at the well-furnished room, gleaming with ivory-white walls.

Across from Rachel's bed, a stone counter held a pitcher of water and plates of bread, cheese, and cold meat. Combs and a mirror rested next to the food. Otherwise, there was a round stone table with comfortably padded chairs and a large dresser and cabinet—each full of an assortment of clothes. There were clothes of various sizes for men and women. Many of them fit children. Soft carpets covered the cold stone floor.

Jason grinned. "All the rooms are like this. The only thing missing is a TV."

"Yes, but we're stuck here and can't leave!"

Shrugging, Jason looked unconcerned. "We just can't leave the floor. Where would we go anyway? Where are we?"

It was a good question. A great question.

From the temple, the priests had led a quiet procession down a great flight of stairs to the middle of a walled complex lined with smooth stone. Looking back, Rachel had been amazed to see the great hall was built inside a cave and into the side of a mountain. At the bottom of the stairs, they'd entered a giant stone plaza covered in a smooth stone pavement. To the right was a large stone structure with sloping, brilliant red roofs and tall towers at two ends. Over six stories, it strangely resembled a house from Camelot Acres. All glitz and glamour. Beyond this structure stretched a wall with more towers and a massive gate. On either side of the wall, impassable rock rose straight up before being lost in the clouds. The procession had led the newcomers to the left, to where they were now, a tall blockhouse with four stories and a flat red roof containing halls of rooms, very much how Jason described it—like a hotel.

"I checked all the windows, and we're definitely near the top of a mountain somewhere. That fancy building on the other side is where King Gretz the Seventh is staying. Apparently he's getting married tomorrow."

"Are we invited to the wedding?" Rachel asked dryly.

"Not quite. The priest I spoke to said if one of us even entered the king's house, it would mean death. We're not clean, or something."

"Oh, that's nice." Rachel had already decided that she did not like the priests.

The priests had all been formal and distant. Leading the new arrivals up the stairs of the blockhouse, they had started assigning rooms as if their arrival had been expected, or at least not a surprise. Even the food in each room appeared to be fresh. They, Rachel noticed, took great care in dividing them up.

Jakey and Steven were given the room closest to the stairs. Courtney got her own room across from them. They tried to put Joe with her, but the twins refused to be separated. Finally, the woman, muttering under her breath, volunteered to share her room with the twins. Murd and Jason got the next room with poor Jak. Rachel was placed by herself—all the way on the other end from the children.

A priest stood at each floor like a guard. Nobody was to leave the floor or even think about leaving the house. Rudolph had gone straight from the cave to the king's building.

"We'll just keep our eyes open … Rudolph seems to be on our side," Jason now said with uncertainty.

"I still don't like it," Rachel muttered. "I'm worried about Steven." She hadn't had any time to talk to him about the horrible night before or even to ask how he felt. The shot to his thigh had left a mark and given him a limp, but he seemed oblivious to what had happened to him.

"Don't worry about him. Jan and Joe are getting him to show off his ripstick thing." Jason grinned. "Those two kids are the ones we have to keep an eye on."

Rachel nodded absently. "That's good." Ever since leaving the cave, Steven had seemed distracted. She remembered how the ripstick supposedly calmed him down.

"If it makes you feel any better, Jak seems to be improving. Murd has been playing nurse and thinks he might be waking soon."

"Really?" Rachel hadn't realized how worried and scared she'd been for the small, injured boy. She'd been too focused on Steven to allow herself to think about him. Now, a feeling of great joy surged through her to think he might be getting better. Without thinking, she swung her feet to the floor. "Oh, that's fantastic news!" All at once she threw her arms around Jason and they were hugging.

"Gee, I sort of hoped you would react like this," Jason muttered, returning the hug. Then he swallowed and stepped back slightly. "Rachel … Rachel, I, er, know this isn't the time, but, uh, have, uh, I ever told you, uh …"

"What is it?" Rachel was frowning now. "Is something wrong?"

"No, uh, just have I told you, uh, how beautiful you are?" Jason's face turned a deep shade of red and he did all he could to look at Rachel's face and meet her eyes.

Rachel froze. "N-no, you haven't." Almost hurt, she looked up at Jason to see if he meant it. What she saw made her body go slack and mouth drop slightly open. Jason was now staring at her seriously … and with unfeigned admiration.

"Rachel, I—Rachel …" Their eyes closed and mouths moved forward—

"Hey!" screeched Courtney's voice from down the hall. "Lisa! I see Lisa!"

Rachel broke from Jason and launched herself into the hall.

Gasping, Jason followed. "My sister," he muttered. "Of course …"

Rachel ran into Courtney's room. "Where? Where is she?"

Courtney's eyes shone with excitement. "Down there," she pointed. "Look!"

Rachel rushed to where Jakey and Courtney knelt by the rounded open window. They were on the fourth floor, and far below, near the king's building, black-robed priests were marching in two groups. With about twelve in each group, the priests seemed to be escorting a pair of children who were walking shoulder to shoulder. Even in the distance, bright red hair flashed in the sun from the girl on the left.

"Lisa," mumbled Rachel. Tears pricked her eyes. She would recognize her anywhere.

"Don't call out any louder," Jason said, following Rachel into the room. "We don't want the priests to get suspicious."

Rachel bit her lip. She wanted to rush down the stairs and grab the redhead, not caring about the consequences. Jason's grim tone and white face stopped her from doing anything. "What's the matter?"

"I just asked the priest out in the hall what was going on down there. That's the king and his future queen going on their final walk before marriage."

Lisa held Darvy's hand tightly. "Darvy," she whispered. "I'm scared."

"Me too."

"Will they really marry us tomorrow?"

"I-I think so … I mean no. Maybe. I hope not."

The two were on their last walk before going to bed on the night before their wedding. At first Lisa thought it was some horrid joke—surely an eleven-year-old and a twelve-year-old could never be married … but everyone thought she was twelve, the legal age for an adult in this world.

"My parents will not be happy," Lisa muttered.

"My parents are dead."

"What are we going to do?"

"I-I have a plan … my parents, they taught me the secret of water portals when I was young. If, if we can get to a big pool of water, I might be able to get us to Earth."

The wedding had been moved up … The priests firmly believed that if the king found a queen, then there would be enough evidence that he was ready to rule and could take kingship from his cousin.

Lisa looked up and struggled to keep tears from falling. She had always wanted to be older and to be in charge. Now she so desperately wished to be just a child. "Where's Rachel?"

Chapter Thirty-Six

Rachel couldn't stop pacing. "I'm her babysitter! I can't let her get married! Think of her parents! They would kill me!"

"Relax," Jason said, sitting at the table in her room. His knees couldn't stay still and his hands were clammy. "We just have to let Rudolph know, that's all."

"I don't trust that guy! He's the one who helped get us sent to this stupid place! What is wrong with these people? They're letting kids marry!"

"I know, Rachel, but we have to think this through! These aren't normal priests, if you haven't noticed. Under their robes they have swords and it sounds like they have big plans for their king and queen."

"Big plans? Like what?" Rachel's lips trembled.

Sighing, Jason rapped the table with his knuckle. "I spoke with my buddy, the priest. Apparently there's a power shift in the land. The priests here think they've been forgotten and nobody respects their great spirit. They want the king and queen to set up their palace on this mountain and make all the people bow down to the spirit, or something. I don't know; they're crazy."

Rachel couldn't breathe. "Poor Lisa … we have to rescue her!"

The door opened. The woman entered with Courtney, Jan, and Joe right behind.

"The little brat told me of your problem," the woman said, scowling back at Jason's younger sister. "These other brats have an idea."

By the time the plan was set, most of the priests had left the blockhouse to go prepare for a banquet to honor the king and future queen. Only a single priest remained to guard the door. A young man with dark fuzz covering his round head, he appeared more nervous than intimidating. Jason reached the bottom of the stairs to find him leaning against the door with his arms crossed and downcast eyes. Joe and Jan followed just behind Jason.

Seeing them, the priest guard immediately straightened. "You're supposed to be in your rooms," he said rather crossly. "All the necessary food is there."

"What about, if you, you know …"

"There's a covered pan under each bed. Tomorrow a servant will come by to bring more food and …" the priest's face went red and looked quickly at Joe, "take care of the pans."

Jan's eyes lit up and he nudged Jason.

"Oh, um, okay." Jason gave the boy a look of confusion.

Wary, the guard casually dropped his hand to the side of his cloak. Unlike the other priests, he wore a plain brown cloak and appeared to be unarmed. "Now return to your rooms."

"Hold on, we are, um, curious. These kids are interested in joining your cult—I mean, um, group. They want to be priests."

"Only the boy can join," the guard said after a moment. "Girls can only become maiden servants." His cheeks reddened again. "I wouldn't suggest she go that path."

Jason's eyes narrowed. "Some priesthood you belong to."

Probably even a year younger than Jason, the priest reddened again. "We do a noble service here! We serve the spirit for the benefit of all."

"I bet."

Jan pushed by Jason and looked the priest up and down. Joe did the same on the other side.

"How come you have brown and not black?" Joe asked.

"I-I am not a full priest yet. I still stay at the catacombs."

Joe frowned. "Catacombs? What are those?"

The young face turned bitter. "The catacombs are really the temple village. It's past the stone square and is where the animals and gardens are kept. The boys live on one side and the girls on the other side … only full priests are allowed to visit the girls."

"Who are the servants here?" Jan asked casually.

"Mostly children—it's a great honor to send a child to serve the spirit. Only those who show promise can be elevated and can train to become priests. The rest remain servants and move to the catacombs. All who live in the catacombs are said to be dead until they rise to life by joining the priesthood. Only then do they move to the square."

He looked at Jan. "Is that your wish, boy?"

Jan shrugged. "Maybe." Stepping closer, he touched the edge of the brown garment. "What do the servants wear?"

"White robes of innocence. The color of the robes change the higher you are elevated." He stared at his robe proudly. "I'm a brown robe. Next I will be a red robe, and then finally I will wear the black robe."

"Do any servants stay here?" asked Joe.

Pursing his lips, the guard gave her a look. "Sometimes. They have quarters on the first floor down that hall. But on this night, all the servants will be in the royal priest house for the banquet ..." A look of true longing crept across his face. "One day I will be there too. In a black robe."

Jason was about to snort with disgust, but Jan chose that moment to stomp on his foot.

"What's this house called?" Joe asked hurriedly.

"This is the ... guesthouse. You are the first guests in a long time." He smiled without humor.

"What's that supposed to mean?" Jason glared and stepped forward aggressively, locking eyes with the guard. Something about the priest's tone was a little ugly.

"Only that I grow tired of these questions! Go to your rooms." He scowled. "There are three other brown robes watching outside and I just need to raise a voice to have them come running!"

"Fine," muttered Jason. "Let's go!"

"Wait!" cried Joe. "I lost my pet mouse! Saliva, come back here!"

Even Jason appeared startled as the girl suddenly ran toward the hall behind the stairs.

"Hey!" cried the guard. "Get back here!"

"Little mouse, come here! Come back!" Her calls were getting farther away.

Jan shoved Jason toward Joe. "Get her!" he cried. "She needs help finding her mouse!" The boy jerked his head toward the back.

"Um, uh, okay … Here, mouse!"

Hesitating, the guard watched Jason and Jan rush after Joe. Gritting his teeth, he gave chase. "You can't go back there! That's the hall for visiting priests and servants! Come back!"

The three guards outside peered lazily through the windows. Hearing the cries for the pet mouse, they laughed and made no move to help.

Jan slipped from behind the stairs and ran into the servants' quarters.

Moments later, Jan reappeared. Hidden under Rudolph's long shirt, he now wore a white servant's robe.

"I found the mouse!" he called. "It's over here!"

Panting, the guard staggered from the back hall. Jason moved next to Joe and Jan and gave the brown-robed guard a shrug. "Kids. You never know with them."

"Oh," Jan said innocently. "Are these yours? I found them on the floor by the door." He held up a set of keys.

"Oh, I must have dropped them …" The priest snatched the keys and stared suspiciously at the three visitors.

The pet mouse had mysteriously disappeared in Joe's pocket, never to be seen.

At dinner that night, Lisa sat stiffly across from Darvy and stared tight-lipped as priests filed in, rubbing their chubby fingers that were covered in jeweled rings and smacking their lips. In fancy robes and layered in chains of gold, the priests appeared to be anything but pious individuals. This was to be another banquet in honor of the wedding scheduled for the next day.

As the head servants entered and started directing the young servants who were carrying trays of food and wine, Lisa stared out the window over the heads of the priests across from her. The cave sat against the mountainside. It was said to contain a pool of water—more than large enough for Darvy to create his water portal … if he knew where to do it. But how would they ever get there?

"This is good soup, eh, Lisa?" Tendl sat in the next seat and jabbed her arm. "You couldn't do better yourself."

"Don't touch me," Lisa said, glaring at him.

Tendl ignored her. "You may be happy to know why the priests have speeded up your wedding. We just got the news that the Belford Fortress has fallen without even an attack. The food supply has run low and the soldiers simply abandoned it. Now the villagers are happy and this mountain is unprotected."

"You're nothing but a liar. I wish I'd left you to rot in that dungeon."

Tendl laughed. "On the contrary, you're getting exactly what you want. Doesn't every little girl dream of being a queen?"

"*If* I become queen, the first thing I will do is banish you back to the dungeons."

The man's eyes darkened. "I think not. Rudolph, my liege, has returned as he said he would." Tendl smiled nastily. "I joined his side a long time ago when he revealed a plot to overthrow all the wizards and obtain all the power. He has already given me the position of captain in the Queen's Guard."

Before Lisa could say something back, a young servant knocked into her back and shoved a slice of bread onto her plate.

Lisa's eyes widened when she saw the dirty little hand slip back from the plate. Then she saw the paper sticking from under the bread. Notebook paper.

"Stupid oaf," snorted Tendl. "As captain of your guard I would have throttled the boy. Instead I laugh at you."

Twisting in her seat, she searched for the servant. She finally spotted him across the table as he continued to pass out bread in a businesslike manner. Smaller than most, he seemed to be more robe than human. A giant hood covered his head, hiding his face. Watching intently, she tried to recognize the boy beneath it but could not. He moved with a slight limp and possessed quick, slender fingers … that seemed to brush very close to the priests he served.

Tendl turned to the man on the other side of him and started a conversation.

Swallowing hard, she grabbed the bread and pretended to take a bite while slipping the note onto her lap. Bowing her head, she pretended to cough. Well lit by candles, the room provided ample light to read the note. The trouble was the writing—it was in Rachel's handwriting.

Amazed tears blurred Lisa's eyesight.

Lisa, don't get married! I have Steven with me and we must find a way home—

Lisa crumpled the paper and jerked her head up, finding it difficult to breathe.

Darvy grinned sickly across the table. *It'll be okay,* he mouthed.

For the first time in a long time, Lisa believed it.

"I want more bread!" she cried loudly. Standing, she pointed to the young servant. "Another piece, boy! Quickly!"

Startled, the servant nearly dropped the tray in the lap of a corpulent priest with red quivering jowls.

"Watch it, boy," the priest slurred.

Amused, Tendl looked at her. "Practicing your commands, are we? You have bread already."

Lisa refused to look at him. Her heart hammered against her chest as only her eyes followed the boy. When he cautiously approached, she scooted her chair back. "I hope you know what you're doing," she muttered. Then she grabbed the tray and dumped it across the table, overturning cups of wine and a candleholder in the process.

Priests roared and leapt back.

Tendl grabbed for his cup, but the bread tray ended up slamming into his chest. Flailing back, he struck the priest next to him with the back of his hand, sending the priest crashing to the floor.

In the confusion, Lisa grabbed the front of the white robe and pulled the boy down. "Tell Rachel to meet me tomorrow in the cave, ready to go home," she hissed. "Now go!" Shoving the boy back, she kicked him in the rear, sending him tumbling into a crowd of white-robed servants rushing to help. "How dare you throw bread at me! Be gone, boy!"

Around her were shouts, grunts, and several more spills.

"He'd better get away," she whispered, squeezing her eyes closed.

"Why is there a servant on the table?" bellowed a voice.

"Stop that boy!" roared Tendl.

"Which one?" cried a priest drunkenly. "They all look the same!"

Tendl slammed a fist on the table. "The one climbing out the window!"

A priest lurched from the table and tried to grab at the white-robed boy struggling to climb out the window. Then his hand froze. He stared in horror. "Hey!" he roared. "My rings are missing!"

The white robe found a fresh burst of energy and scrambled up and out the window.

Jan dropped lightly from the window and rolled when striking the solid pavement. His tender right ankle jolted with pain, but he scrambled to his feet. Leaning against the side of the house in the shadows, he struggled out of the servant's robe.

Hands reached to help. "Stand still!" hissed Jason. "What happened?"

"Ask later!" Jan said impatiently. "Run!" The two sprinted into the shadows.

A head popped out the window. "I see him! He's lying smashed below, hurt!"

When the priests rushed out to find the injured body, they only found an empty robe.

"He's at the catacombs by now," moaned a priest.

"We'll find him and feed him to the spirit with the others!" hissed another priest. "My gold ring, by thunder! It's gone!"

"Perhaps," slurred a particularly red-faced priest, "he wasn't a boy, but a magic spirit sent to punish us."

"Bah, you drink too much!" spat the priest missing his rings. "Back inside! I need more drink."

Jason shoved Jan's legs up into the window at the back of the blockhouse. While "chasing" her mouse, Joe had picked out the spot as being low to the ground and hidden in the shadow of the mountains.

After making sure no priests were giving chase, Jason grabbed the window's edge and pulled himself up. The young guard remained snoring from where he lay sprawled in front of the door. Earlier, the woman had made a special drink that Joe had shared with the guard, to thank him for helping find her mouse. In the drink were the last of the root shavings the woman had kept from Rudolph.

Jan walked with a heavy limp, but Jason didn't feel much pity. Under the robe, the boy had worn a black belted tunic and black trousers. On his belt now was a bag heavy with gold rings and chains he'd taken from drunken priests. If he'd been caught …

That night, Rachel gathered the adults in her room to make a plan. The children had been exhausted and were already sleeping. In the morning, they would move everyone to the cave and wait for Lisa … this was how far their plan got. Everyone was getting really sleepy … Promising to meet to discuss it the next day, they all stumbled back to their beds and collapsed.

Rudolph, with his own plans, had the priests add root shavings to the water brought to the guests for the evening meal.

Chapter Thirty-Seven

Rachel woke up the next morning with a headache. And something buzzing in her ear.

"Mmmph," she muttered, smacking her lips.

"Rachel … Rachel, look in the mirror … Rachel?"

"Yeah, yeah …"

"Rachel!"

Snorting, Rachel rolled out of the warm covers and rubbed her eyes. Was she back in Florida?

Not even close.

"The mirror, Rachel!"

"Okay, Marcal …" Stumbling across the room, she found the counter where she'd seen the mirror the other night. She smiled slightly. This would be the first time she'd looked in a mirror since entering this crazy world …

She shrieked and threw the mirror back on the counter.

"Rachel! No, listen!"

Heart pounding, she picked up the mirror and peeked at it. Marcal's rough face peered back. "M-Marcal? Th-that is you!"

"Rachel, thank goodness. Listen to me. Are you and the boy safe?"

"Y-yes. Wh-where are you?"

"Don't worry about that for now—Rachel, you must listen to me. You have to destroy Rudolph. He's trying to take over Panterra and will grab all the power from the wizards."

"Huh?"

"Rudolph—Rachel, you must defeat him to save this world!"

Rachel squeezed her eyes shut. "I, I don't understand."

"There's little time. Somehow he went behind the backs of the wizards and made a deal with the dark spirit—he can assume all power if he's not stopped. Rachel, he will take over this world."

"S-so? I'm just a babysitter. I can't do anything about that!"

"No, you're much more than you think you are! Rachel, don't you get it? You're a hero! It has to be you!"

"Hero?" Rachel suddenly grew angry and wide awake. "I am not a hero!"

"Yes, a true hero!"

"I'm not even close! Look, I'm fat. I can't run. I get nervous in crowds. Excitement terrifies me unless it's in a book!" She was just getting started. "I have no special scar, no tattoo, and not even a birthmark! I can't do magic—I can't even cook! My parents are both alive and they love me and they aren't even poor! There's no weird uncle in my entire family. Don't you get it? I'm Rachel Pugsley. I'm a babysitter and that's all! I don't even belong to a stupid club!"

Marcal's face paled in the mirror. *"Calm down, Rachel! You're already a hero whether you like it or not. You're a babysitter, as you said."*

"If you want to stop some crazy wizard, you do it! You're the warrior."

"I can't! Rachel, you're at the mountain. Do you understand this? Where you are is the temple of the dark spirit … if Rudolph gets the boy and sacrifices him …"

Rachel slammed the mirror down.

"Rachel! Rach—"

The babysitter alarm had gone off. She suddenly remembered. She was at the mountain. The dark spirit was here … So was Steven.

Steven padded in bare feet down the steps and across the stone square. Cut into the mountain, the long, twisting staircase rose before him like a hypnotizing snake. Deep within his stomach, the monster groaned and burbled, clearly feeling very much alive. Up those steps was where he could be rid of the monster … he knew it!

"Many a man lost a monster in these waters, but many more lost a life."

Swallowing, Steven barely hesitated. Since hearing those words, all he could think about was his monster. Groaning and rumbling, the beast stirred, biding its time before it surfaced again. This could be the only way to finally be rid of it.

Climbing the cold stone stairs up the mountain, he ignored the cool wind whipping about his face. The sun had just begun to glimmer when he reached the top.

Growing tentative, he nervously approached the final stairs leading to the great hall holding the pool inside. Halfway up the steps, the doors swung open before him. A loud creak echoed within. Then a figure in a dark cloak stepped toward him and stretched out a hand to greet him.

Steven froze … the shadowman.

"We have been waiting for you, boy," said an elderly voice from inside the cloak. The voice was kind and soft. "Come."

Blinking, Steven still hesitated. The face in the cloak was fuzzy and too dark to make out.

"Believe me, boy. I won't hurt you … I want only what is best for you." The shadowman sounded calm and seemed genuine. "Come."

Cautiously, the boy resumed his journey up the steps. His brown eyes peered closely at the figure but could spot nothing amiss.

The figure merely waited. At the entrance, it reached a long white hand to grasp Steven's wrist firmly but not too tightly.

"You will meet your long-awaited destiny on this day … have no fear." Guiding Steven inside, the figure stood with him at the edge of the pool. The blue water grew flat and calm. "Do you know who I am, boy?"

Steven shook his head. The shadowman had always been a mystery to him—only appearing in dreams and always bearing ill will.

"My name is Aerrius. I first stepped in these waters many years ago when only a few years older than you. Do you know what happened? I lost all the pain and suffering I had ever known and became what I am today. Unchanging." The figure threw back its hood to reveal the face of a mature woman who had retained her beauty with age. Her silver hair was pulled back. Mature wrinkles lined her face, but bright eyes gleamed with intelligence. "Many believe me to be a man. Some call me a deity.

In truth, I am a little of both. All because I swam these waters, boy."

"I just want to get rid of the monster," Steven whispered truthfully.

"Indeed you do. We all wish to be rid of our monsters, don't we? Swim these waters—reach the other side and you will find your peace. Be strong, boy. I will leave you and wait for your return outside."

Steven shivered slightly when the great doors shut behind him with a bang. As the echo died down, his shivers ceased. Silence gripped the chamber as he stood alone facing the still, blue water. Not a wave marred the glassy surface. A shelf carved into the rock with a stone table on top waited on the other side. It reminded Steven of an altar, and he knew this table must be his target. That was where he would go to be rid of the monster …

After breathing in slowly, he pulled off his shirt, shuddering when a cool breeze blew seemingly from nowhere. He dropped the shirt behind him and then briefly paused to look around and make sure he remained alone. Then he slid off his pants and soon stood only in his undershorts with his clothes piled behind him. The mysterious cool breeze brushed back his hair, but he paid no attention. This was the moment.

Swallowing, he moved to the very edge of the pool and rolled his shoulders and shook out his arms, going through his normal routine before a swim. It was all about the focus … inwardly drawing in energy and outwardly appearing calm and cool. Taking a final breath, he stepped into the pool, relaxing as warm, vibrant water slid around his body and closed over his head. He never hit the bottom. The water seemed to go down forever. Looking down below his feet, he only saw darkness. Quickly he kicked upward. He gasped and relaxed as he broke the surface. As always, once he was in the water, the monster seemed to disappear. Treading water lightly, Steven looked again at the altar. It beckoned. He started swimming.

"Steven!" cried Rachel, bursting into the last room on the left. Jakey tossed in his sleep and rolled to his stomach. He blinked blearily at Rachel. The bed across from him, where Rachel had tucked Steven in the night before, was empty and cold.

Where did the boy go?

Rachel felt her heart pound like a hammer against her ribs as she ran from the room and flew down the stairs, nearly falling twice in the process. Over a long white shirt and her underclothes, she wore a loose tunic given to her by the priests. She had to take care not to trip over it. Finally, near the bottom of the steps, she yanked at the fabric until it tore. Legs free, she rushed to the door.

The young priest stood as a guard and looked at her with large eyes, as if dazed and lost for words. "G-guests m-must n-not leave," he finally gurgled, not dropping his gaze. "H-have to stay."

For a moment Rachel was caught by surprise. She'd never had a young man act like that around her. His eyes were enflamed and embarrassed at the same time. He couldn't stop looking at her.

"Good," she snarled, shaking free any self-consciousness. She had a boy to find. "Take my place." She grabbed his cloak, yanked him forward and shoved him against the wall. Before he could recover, Rachel escaped out the door.

With a single goal in mind, she raced for the stairs to the cave. *Please let me be wrong! Please let Steven just be using the bathroom or something!*

The young guard behind her slid to the floor, his eyes starry and mouth slack. "What just happened?" he muttered.

When reaching the middle of the pool, Steven felt a rush of water from beneath him. A force struck his stomach and pushed him upward. Not yet afraid, he broke out of his freestyle stroke and started treading water. Bubbles rose in the water in front of him. Then in a terrible rumble, a great black shape blasted from the water, sending droplets arcing high in the air and knocking the boy back with huge waves.

A hideous dark face about the size of a truck and the shape of a clam stared down at him. Bulbous eyes the color of blood glared out from the center of the creature. Tentacles shot from the water around the boy, and something scaly brushed his foot.

"DO YOU KNOW WHO I AM?" roared the monster. Rows of sharp teeth gleamed from a large slit mouth below the eyes.

Steven felt little as he nodded from where he continued treading water. He knew exactly what loomed over him. "You're the monster," he whispered.

"DO YOU NOT FEAR ME?"

A thick, rough tentacle encircled Steven's waist and all at once jerked him from the water so his legs dangled in the air. Another tentacle lifted from the water. At the end, a single, sharp claw curled toward the boy's throat.

Out of breath, Rachel reached the top of the stairs and promptly collapsed to her knees. Just inside the mouth of the cave, the great hall loomed over her—silently judging her as unworthy. The doors were shut and looked very unwelcoming.

Rachel gasped for air. She allowed herself a brief moment of rest. Then she pushed herself to her feet. A figure stood at the pinnacle by the doors of the temple and watched her. It was the same figure who'd visited her in the visions.

"No," she said hoarsely. Grimacing, she forced her legs to run to the steps leading to the great hall. "This is not real."

"Rachel," the figure spoke softly. "Rachel, Rachel." It descended the steps to meet her and they met in the middle. The figure stopped to stand squarely in her path. "I've been expecting you."

"Wh-who are you?"

"I am Aerrius." Throwing back its hood, the figure showed itself to be a young man, but with silver hair. "I am the first wizard of Panterra and Speaker of the Spirit. I called you to bring the boy to this mountain. You have obeyed. You shall get a great reward."

Rachel shook her head in confusion. "Where's Steven?"

"Don't you mean, where is Rachel? Your reward—"

"No," Rachel snarled at him, suddenly not caring who or what he was. "I mean, where's Steven!" She knew the boy had to be inside. She grabbed the figure by its cloak and threw it aside. So great was her anger, she ended up using more force than she realized.

The silver-haired man cried out as he tumbled down the steps past Rachel.

"You cannot go in there!" he shouted from the bottom of the steps where he landed. "It's too late! Accept your reward. It's the will of the spirit!"

Ignoring him, Rachel rushed up the remaining stairs and yanked open the doors. She entered the hall without looking back.

Once inside, she met a terrible sight.

"Steven!" she shouted in horror.

With a deafening roar, the monster turned its beady eyes on her. Steven's body fell with a splash, and the sharp tentacle slammed next to where he landed. *"YOU DARE INTERRUPT? WHO ARE YOU?"*

"Steven!" shrieked Rachel.

"I SAID WHO ARE YOU?" the beast roared. The entire chamber shook.

Rachel held out her arms to keep her balance. "I'm his babysitter! Let him alone!" Trembling, she forced herself toward the terrible scene. The creature, like a horrific octopus clam, watched her approach with baleful eyes.

"HE IS MINE, DEPART FROM HERE!"

A tentacle swept around where Steven had surfaced and started wrapping around the boy. The boy gasped for a breath.

"NO!" Charging the pool, Rachel launched herself without a thought of what she was doing. Not until underwater did she remember that she could barely swim. Pools had always been a place for attractive girls her age to show off. They weren't supposed to hold terrifying monsters trying to eat children. Surfacing, she kicked and flailed her arms with all her might. Choking on water, she refused to give up. Using instinct and pure will much more than any skill, she somehow advanced toward the monster.

Groaning, the monster all at once released Steven and disappeared under the surface.

A dark shape flowed from under Rachel and headed into the deep.

Left alone, Steven sputtered and kicked to keep his head above water. In front of him, the altar beckoned. Behind him, Rachel thrashed and splashed desperately.

"I—Ste—urg . . ."

"*STEVEN,*" spoke the monster's voice throughout the great hall. "*REACH THE OTHER SIDE AND BE RID OF ME FOREVER! YOU WILL BE GIVEN GREAT POWER OVER ALL YOUR FEARS ONCE YOU DO SO!*"

Treading water, Steven looked once more at the altar.

Behind him, Rachel choked and fought to keep afloat. Steven took a deep breath and threw himself toward Rachel. With deft strokes, he quickly swam to her side.

"Stop splashing!" he yelled. "Just be still!"

Rachel, panicking, didn't seem to hear as she continued splashing wildly.

Steven twisted his body and dove under the water. He kicked toward Rachel's legs. Avoiding her churning feet, he found her thigh and reached out a hand, giving her flesh a hard pinch with all his might. Above him, Rachel yelped, losing some of her panic.

Steven shot to the surface. His head broke the water a foot from Rachel.

"Don't splash so much!" he shouted. "Pretend you're a jellyfish and just float!"

Nodding jerkily, Rachel tried to comply. Immediately she felt a sinking feeling and immediately kicked out.

"It's okay, I've got you!" The small boy lunged and grabbed her arm, pulling it over his small shoulder. Kicking wildly to stay afloat, he used his free arm to desperately pull toward the pool's edge they had started from. Suddenly it seemed a very long distance.

The water bubbled and stirred behind them. The monster had returned and was not happy at the turn of events.

"Grab my legs!" Steven called with his face just above water. Jerking free of Rachel, he shoved his feet at her face.

Crying out, Rachel desperately grabbed his ankles and started kicking wildly.

Steven arched his back and threw his upper body out of the water with his arms extended. It was an awkward butterfly stroke, but using his springy back to full advantage, he pulled Rachel toward safety.

Bursting from the depths, the monster roared in fury, lashing out with all twelve tentacles. A huge momentum of water surged behind Rachel and Steven.

"Look out!" screamed Rachel.

Caught by the wave, Rachel flew forward and over the boy, who lost control in the water's force.

She crashed into the water. At once she twisted to the surface and searched for the boy. She was relieved when Steven surfaced next to her. Each gasped for air. At least they had moved considerably closer to the edge.

Roaring in fury, the monster rose and fell against the water to cause a second wave—this one even more powerful.

She grabbed Steven and pulled him down, shielding his body with her own just prior to the wave striking. It felt as if they'd been punched by a giant fist that never stopped punching. Pushed at tremendous speed, they headed straight for the wall. Rachel curled around Steven and closed her eyes. Her back crashed heavily into the underwater stone. Screaming bubbles, she kicked her feet to the surface, dragging Steven with her. An undertow dragged her back toward the middle of the pool, but pure fear kept her by the wall. Throwing out an arm, she managed to grab the pool's edge while kicking her feet as hard as she could. Her other arm had Steven around his back and under his right armpit. Clamping her jaw, she used all her remaining strength to force the boy upward. Drained by the swim and dazed after the wave, Steven struggled to get both arms out of the water. Rachel, still holding her breath, pushed the boy up and then went low to shove him up from below. Finally he managed to grab the edge and, with Rachel's help, crawl out.

As Steven's knee reached solid ground, he looked up to see a stranger standing next to him.

Rachel's head broke from the water behind him and she started coughing while sucking in much needed air.

The figure next to Steven started to shake. "This is not possible!" seethed Aerrius. His, or perhaps her, features contorted and started to change. Wrinkles appeared with fuller lips and tighter skin. Now the face was a cross between a young man and an older woman. The figure drew a long sword from under its robe and stood at the pool's edge. "You seek to stand up to the dark spirit?" it snarled. "I will rip out your throat and feed you to my master, you horrid girl!" The sharp point lowered to where Rachel barely gripped the stone ledge. She still struggled to catch her breath. The monster had gone silent behind her.

Steven lay coughing at its feet. Weakly, he tried to kick at the figure. The shadowman … One of his nightmares had suddenly come to life before him. His feeble kicks only enraged the figure.

Aerrius snarled, turning on the boy. It planted a foot in Steven's stomach and pushed the boy back. "You will be dealt with later!" it promised with a hideous hiss.

Croaking, Steven rolled to his side and clutched his middle.

"No you don't!" Rachel cried out. Seeing the figure go after Steven caused a fierce rush of energy to surge through her body. Pulling herself up, she thrust both hands at the back of the figure's robe, just catching the hem. Yanking with all her strength, she leaned back and allowed herself to sink below the water.

Giving a startled yell, Aerrius waved his arms wildly to no avail. The sword clattered on the stone as the figure fell backward, plunging into the pool. The sword bounced and then tumbled over the edge. On contact with water, the sword hissed and melted to nothing. The figure splashed loudly.

Aerrius floundered to the surface. "NO!" It screamed, sounding terrified.

Steven sat up in fear. He watched in horror as the monster cut through the water toward the floundering figure.

"YOUR FEAR SHOWS THROUGH, AERRIUS! I MADE YOU A DEITY AMONG MEN, BUT YOU BRING ME THE WRONG BOY. WHAT'S MORE, YOU STILL FEAR ME! YOUR CROSSING HAS COME!"

"Master, no, I served—NOO—erp …"

The monster lunged over the figure and dragged it down into the depths. Bubbles appeared where they once were, and then the water went still. The shadowman and the monster had both vanished with the bubbles. So had his babysitter.

"Rachel!" cried the boy, crawling to the edge.

Rachel struggled back toward the surface, but her legs felt like lead weights with burning fires inside. Her arms felt more like overcooked string beans. Feeling herself sinking, she looked up at the surface knowing that at least Steven had made it.

Then a pair of slender legs shot into the water, sinking rapidly toward her face. They desperately fished for her. With the last of her strength, Rachel grabbed the ankles and started pulling herself up.

Above her, Steven gripped the side of the pool with all his might and acted as a human ladder. Rachel slowly climbed back to the surface.

Dots were beginning to appear in front of her eyes when finally her head broke free. She grabbed the side of the pool and sucked air in wildly. Next to her, the boy put his head down and sighed with relief.

"Th-thanks, Steven," Rachel gasped.

Too exhausted to answer, Steven only nodded.

Babysitter and boy crawled side by side from the pool and collapsed.

"I," Rachel wheezed, "really, really need to learn how to swim."

Steven rolled to face her. Still too tired to talk, he only gave a smile that lit up his face. For the first time since he could remember, he couldn't feel the monster inside.

"You look like a happy drowned puppy," Rachel finally wheezed, reaching over to rumple his soaked hair.

"Rachel?" the boy suddenly said, a bit sheepishly.

"Yes?"

"I think I used the bathroom in the pool."

"Now you tell me …" She groaned. Then she grinned slightly. "Don't tell anybody, but so did I. We should go before the priests come … I'm guessing what we did isn't allowed in the pool."

Steven murmured an agreement but made no move.

"Come on, Steven … you're shivering." Rachel shuddered herself as she forced herself into a kneeling position. Her soaked clothes hung from her, dripping with cold water and chilling her skin.

The boy grunted and managed to sit up. He hugged his knees tightly to his chest and rested his chin. Immediately his teeth started to chatter.

Rachel's babysitting skills snapped into focus. "Steven!" she practically shouted. "We have to get dry and warm … Quick, um, go in that corner and get into your dry clothes … I'll go look for something … dry over here …"

Nodding in obedience, the boy grabbed his clothes and went to the corner by the great doors. Rachel stumbled in the opposite direction searching for a dry cloak, blanket, or anything.

Every movement was torture for her, and the only cloak she found was the cloak of exhaustion that wrapped around her head and grew heavier with every step. Stumbling at the edge of the wall, she slid to a sitting position and then a lying position.

"Just too tired … I'll get up in a few minutes and find Jason …" Her eyes closed. Curling up, she found much-needed rest.

Fully dressed, Steven soon joined her. When seeing her shivering, he lay next to her and scooted close—like he did with his mother when they napped on the beach. Sharing his warmth, the boy closed his eyes and fell into a peaceful sleep free of all monsters.

The priests were too busy that morning to worry about the temple. Many of them woke in a foul mood as they remembered their missing rings, chains, and, in some cases, money purses. The twisted servant would suffer, they vowed, once he was found. But first there had to be the royal wedding.

Tendl banged on Lisa's door.

"You coming out, or do we barge in and carry you out?" he asked harshly.

"Let me finish dressing!" Lisa yelled back. Her room was in the center of the floor without windows and only one door. It was locked at night with two solemn-faced and sober priests standing guard. Escape had been impossible.

When she finally opened the door, she wore a heavy purple dress much too big on her and a veil that covered her like a giant spiderweb.

"Beautiful," Tendl said, grinning. "If your groom can find you in that thing, we might have a wedding."

"I won't be married," Lisa told him. "You'll see."

"Sure, right after your wedding. Hurry, the procession is waiting."

Lisa bit down her panic. Somehow she needed to let Darvy know of the plan. After the fiasco with the servant, the priests had brought her and Darvy straight to their rooms and locked them in. When given the chance, they had to flee to the cave, where hopefully Rachel and Steven would be waiting. Just thinking about them being nearby seemed impossible. Hope was so close … but at the same time, complete horror was just as close. Tendl kept firmly at her side and appeared wary of an escape attempt.

Courtney opened her eyes to find herself in a totally different and strange room. Bright light poured through a glass window on her right. Pink blankets covered her queen-sized bed. Next to it, a large, cushioned rocking chair faced the door.

Gasping, she pulled aside the blankets. She wore the same white nightgown she'd found in the dresser in the blockhouse, but this was a new place—a place she'd never been before. "Where am I?" she asked aloud.

The chair turned and Rudolph smiled at her. "You're in the chambers of my family," he said gently. "I moved you here early this morning so you could have your rest in peace."

Pulling the covers back up, Courtney bit her lip. "What about Jakey and Jason? Where is everyone else?"

"They're fine …" Rudolph sighed. "I once believed I would leave them to their fate, but you have changed me, Courtney. Your kindness has touched even me." He smiled at her. "I plan to send them back to your world."

"What about me?"

Rudolph got to his feet. He moved to the window and peered out. He spoke with his back to Courtney.

"Just starting now is a wedding … Your friend Lisa is about to become queen."

"What?" shouted the girl. "No! You said you'd send us back home!"

Rudolph turned to face her. "Lisa is a born leader, Courtney. Have you ever thought about whether she wants to go home? Oh, sure the priests have their plans for the king and queen, but it is I who will hold the true power. I promise. Lisa will do quite well here. I will personally see to it. She just needs to finish the ceremony—the king and queen must share blood and offer a sacrifice to the spirit."

Courtney struggled to restrain her fear and anger. "What does that mean—share blood and offer a sacrifice?"

"You may have noticed that the customs here are strange to your world. When a man and a woman unite under the Spirit of Panterra, it is through giving the spirit a blood sacrifice that they are united—the purer the blood, the greater the blessing."

Courtney stared at him in horror. "Th-that's not a blessing … That's disgusting! That's like a curse!"

Rudolph shrugged. "Call it what you want. I was thinking they will offer the young fool from the banquet last night. Oh, yes, I know all about the foolish plans of Rachel—how she thinks everyone will escape and be happy back in your miserable world. You see, the spirit can see everything here and tells me things. Just little things, here and there. I don't have the full power yet. But I will, very soon …" His eyes gleamed with fire. "Do you remember the story I told you of the prophecy? How whoever consumed the child chosen by the spirit will rule Panterra? Well, there was another part of the prophecy I failed to mention. The child must willingly give himself up—he cannot be forced." Courtney covered her mouth with horror as the man's eyes burned red and mouth curved into a smile. "Young Steven will soon make me the most powerful being in two worlds. He will allow the spirit to kill him and then I will eat his flesh!"

"Why?" Courtney asked in shocked horror. "Why are you doing this?"

Rudolph's eyes returned to blue and he smiled. "A good heart such as yours can't fathom such evil actions … You are very much like somebody I used to know. A long time ago, I was not a wizard or even an apprentice. I owned a shop in a city and lived happily with a woman and child I loved dearly." Rudolph's face darkened. "Then the Wizard War came—it took everything from me! Everything! Since then I plotted my revenge while trying to get my life back. Today, I will finally do so. Today I get my little girl back."

Courtney shrank from him. "I-I'm not your little girl!"

Rudolph blinked and stared at her gently. "I know that, Courtney," he said almost tenderly. "But with you, I will have her back … The spirit promised me that if I found a pure-hearted girl like my daughter, it would take her in exchange for my girl. It would bring my girl back to the world of the living. You, Courtney, are just like my girl used to be … and will be again."

"No, no!" Courtney rolled away from the bed, desperately trying to escape.

Rudolph sighed. "By now, Steven should be with the spirit. You'll be the next in the pool, I think. Now sleep, my sweet girl. Sleep." A brief mist fired from his eyes and covered Courtney. In moments, her struggles ceased and she lay still. Rudolph's eyes turned blue and even appeared touched with remorse as he gently lifted her sleeping form into his arms.

Chapter Thirty-Eight

Jakey stared out the window and frowned. "I don't see Lisa down there, but I do see that boy."

The woman stopped her pacing and peered over his head. "It looks like a circus of baboons down there," she muttered.

Below them in the plaza, the priests had formed two rows facing each other. The rows started at the front door of the king's house and led to where a single priest dressed in a purple and gold robe stood next to the boy—King Gretz the VII.

Jason stuck in his head. "Have either of you seen Rachel or Steven anywhere?" he asked worriedly.

"No," growled the woman. "And the girl, your sister, is missing too!"

"What!" Jason banged his head with his fist. "What's going on?" he demanded.

"I don't know," replied the woman, "but if we're going to make it to that temple in time, we'd better hurry. The wedding is starting, and there's a group of priests coming this way."

Jakey frowned. "I think Rachel came in my room this morning … but then she ran out. It was really, really early."

"Just great," muttered Jason. "That girl can never do anything predictable. Jakey, find some clothes." To the woman he said, "We need to get ready to move fast—especially your troublemakers. They're in their room playing with Steven's ripstick."

"*My* troublemakers?" the woman spat, but Jason had already gone.

"Where are you going?" Jakey called after him.

"To find out where Rachel went!" answered his brother from the hall.

Rushing down the stairs, Jason found the young monk nervously guarding the door.

"You can't pass!" he said immediately, planting himself in the doorway.

Jason rolled his eyes. "Great, but did anyone else go by this morning? Some kids and a girl?"

The guard's face went red and he shook his head vigorously. "Oh, uh, no, of course not!"

Grunting, Jason held out a hand holding a handful of gold rings he'd borrowed from Jan the night before—a small part of his stash. "Are you sure?" he asked.

The guard's eyes widened. Licking his lips, he suddenly looked very scared and young. "Th-the Wizard R-Rudolph came early this morning … He kicked me awake … and he left with a young girl." The guard took a breath. "He said a young boy would come down and I was to let him by, but no others." Swallowing, he continued. "The-the young woman went a little while after, to chase after him." Jason was surprised when the guard suddenly grabbed his arms. "L-listen … I shouldn't tell you this, but, but the boy last night, the one who wanted to be a priest?"

"What about him?"

"Tell him … tell him to run. The other guards left this morning to prepare for the wedding. As they left I heard them talking … They said the little mouse boy would be the sacrifice."

Jason stared at him. He felt his blood go cold. "What sacrifice?" he asked.

"For the wedding, of course. A sacrifice must be made to seal a man and woman. This isn't really a guesthouse—this is where the sacrifices stay before being consumed by the spirit." He seemed surprised that Jason didn't already know this.

Jason threw back his head and groaned. Well, that would explain the high windows on the first floor and there only being one door to the whole building. And why there were so many different types and sizes of clothes in the rooms—they were leftovers from previous "guests."

"Hey!" shouted Jakey. "Lisa is down there, look!" He pointed at where the redhead was being forcibly walked between the rows of priests.

Shoved by a large man wearing a red cloak, Lisa kept looking around as if searching for hidden help. The priests in the rows started to chant. Lisa made her way down the path to marriage.

The young king stood nervously at the end of the path. He tried edging away, but was immediately prodded to stay put by the priest in purple in gold. This priest carried a long white staff that he now raised over his head.

"Commence the wedding!" he shouted.

"It's too late," moaned the old woman from where she stood next to Jakey. The two could only watch from above.

"We have to do something," Jakey said fiercely. Behind them, standing by the door with the ripstick between them, Joe and Jan exchanged looks.

Jason shoved past the twins, his face masked with fear. "We have to get out now!" he shouted. "I mean, now!"

"What about Lisa?" Jakey asked.

Jason made a face. "Just hope she has a plan and we meet her at the cave. Get downstairs and wait there." He turned to exit, but then suddenly stopped. "Hey! Where did the twins go?"

Jason rushed to Murd's room and shook the large man awake. Jak lay in the next bed—Murd had slept on the floor.

"We have trouble, Murd—we need to get back into the great hall and stop a wedding already under way."

Murd blinked at him and nodded without really understanding. "Aye, but what of young Jak?"

"How is he?"

"He's breathing better but still sleeps. Moving the lad cannot be good fer him. He—" Murd turned and gasped.

The brown boy lay on the next bed with both eyes open and looking at them with a dull, tired expression.

"Jason!" screamed Jakey from the other room. "I see Joe and Jan, they have the ripstick and they're outside!"

"Yer know what?" Murd said as Jason audibly groaned. "I think it's time we got Jak some exercise."

At the door of the blockhouse, the young guard sat on the floor with his eyes shut, muttering. The door was bolted shut behind him. A host of angry priests were banging and hollering for him to open up from the other side.

Joe and Jan reached the bottom step and swiftly went to the back hall. Jan still limped, so Joe held the ripstick. Fear and excitement shone from her face. Using the back window, the children scrambled outside. Nobody was in sight. Thumps and yells came from the front of the blockhouse, so they went the other way. Moving to the back corner of the building, they peeked out at where the wedding continued.

Jan suddenly grabbed Joe's shoulder and pointed. Across from them, Rudolph hurried toward the stairs leading to the cave, carrying Courtney in his arms. The girl appeared awake, but extremely dazed.

A loud crash from the front of the house announced that the door had shattered.

The sound of feverish chanting swelled from the wedding.

"It's now or never," Joe muttered, putting the ripstick down.

"Remember, Joe," Jan told her. "Just bend your knees and don't fall. It's easy."

"Okay, I got it!" Joe said. "Just follow the best you can." She got on the wheeled contraption and immediately put out her arms for balance. "Whoa, this is harder than riding a horse!"

"You got it!" Jan called excitedly.

"You just turn like this, and … I think I'm doing it, Jan!"

Jan cried out in alarm. "Watch where you're going! And not so fast! Joe, wait up!"

Lisa pressed backward but hit the solid form of Tendl.

"It's no use, Lisa," hissed the soldier. "Just get it over with! You'll be queen!"

The chanting of the monks on either side drove into her head like hammers attacking an anvil. With the black hoods they wore over their heads, Lisa could only think of grim reapers leading her to her death. The head priest waited at the end. He looked like an evil ogre about to have breakfast rather than a pious minister performing a wedding.

"As the sacrifice emerges," he called loudly, "the man and the woman shall meet and share their blood!" It wasn't a staff in his hand but a spear. The wicked point waved dangerously toward Darvy.

Darvy looked helpless as he peered at Lisa with the hopeless look of doom.

Then a crash echoed across the plaza, and shouting erupted from somewhere. The chanting quickly rose in volume and drowned out the noise.

Tendl bent low to Lisa's ear. "The spear will cut your hand and then cut the king's hand. By pressing your blood together, you become married. Later you will both give a sacrifice to the spirit. Then it will be finished."

Lisa couldn't take it any longer. She threw back her head. "Rachel!" she screamed. "Help! Rachel!"

The chanting faltered momentarily. The head priest glared at her, but hastily waved his spear for the proceedings to continue.

"Grab the sacrifice!" roared an angry voice.

"We want the sacrifice!" shouted another.

Storming over the shattered remains of the door, the priests wore feverish faces with their black robes as they rushed into the blockhouse. They carried clubs, and these they waved dangerously as they charged the stairs. There were six in total, and each one had the same goal in mind. This was a wedding. They would bring down the sacrifice and take down any who stood in their path.

The young guard in the brown robe ran in front of the small mob.

"They're coming!" he howled. "They're coming!"

"Traitor!" shouted the guard in the lead. "You will become a sacrifice for this!"

Wailing, the young priest reached the landing to the second floor and tripped. Screaming in terror, he looked up and saw a mountain of flesh. Murd stood over him. His great bearded face twisted in a snarl.

Murd stepped over the fallen priest in brown to stand at the edge of the landing. He filled the entire space between the railings. The attacking priests slowed for a moment when they saw the barrier of flesh. Before they could continue, Murd bellowed loudly and launched himself downward.

Rachel groaned as she turned her head painfully. It felt as if somebody had stretched out her body, filled it with sand and water, and threw it on rocks. She opened her eyes and found herself still lying on the stone floor in front of the pool. Steven lay beside her … just like the first time they'd come into this horrid world.

Muffled thumps came from behind the doors in front. Then the latch clunked and the doors began to move. Whoever was on the other side was having a hard time opening them, but would not be denied.

"Steven," she hissed, forcing her resisting body to an upright position. She shook the boy's shoulder. "Somebody is coming!"

Blinking, the boy arched his back as he rolled on his stomach to face the newcomer. His face held more curiosity than fear.

Rachel staggered toward the door. She hoped it would be Lisa leading the others.

Instead, when the doors finally opened, Rudolph entered. He dragged a bewildered Courtney behind him.

"What!" he shouted when seeing her. "What's this?" The white-haired wizard stared at Steven and Rachel in shock. "Wh-what are you doing?" he spluttered in genuine amazement.

"I, uh, we were just leaving," Rachel stammered.

"You!" the wizard fumed, turning his gaze solely to Rachel. "It's always you ruining everything! What are you?"

Rachel blinked. "I, I don't understand," she said.

"Every time I have control," Rudolph said balefully, "you're there to snatch it from me! What are you, I say!"

Rachel didn't like the looks of this. From behind Rudolph, Courtney stared at her with a mixture of hope and fear. She also appeared half-asleep. "Listen—" Rachel began, but was quickly cut off.

"You!" Rudolph turned to Steven. "You came here to give yourself up! You should be on the table, ready to be consumed!"

Steven moved to a sitting position and blinked. He looked up at Rachel, appearing just as confused as she was.

"I should have all the power now!" Rudolph cried. The brilliant blue of his eyes turned a blood red. "If you can't do it yourself, boy, then I shall help!" He flung down Courtney's arm and the girl stumbled back, falling on her side. The tall wizard took long strides toward Steven.

Rachel remembered Marcal in the mirror. She jumped to action.

"Get away from him!" she cried, trying get in front of him.

Rudolph was too quick. He brushed by her to reach Steven. Bending low, he grabbed him by his arms and easily lifted him up so the boy dangled in front of him. Steven was too surprised or too tired to resist. "By the power I have," he rumbled, "you are mine!" Nothing happened. "What?" Rudolph asked, confused.

Then Steven shoved a knee in Rudolph's open mouth and kicked viciously. Rudolph cried out in protest. An instant later, Rachel grabbed Steven's waist, yanking the boy free. She set him down and launched a side kick right into Rudolph's stomach.

Still gagging and stumbling from the boy's kicks, the wizard offered no defense to Rachel's kick. As if a bowling ball dropped from his neck, his entire upper body collapsed until he was on the stone floor, rolling in agony.

"M-my p-power," he wheezed. "N-not working." Trying to get to his feet, he screamed in pain as Rachel grabbed his right ear and pulled.

"I've had enough of you and your games!" she yelled at him. "If you lay a hand on another child in front of me, I'll knock your head into yet another world!" She let go and shoved him back down. All the previous pain had gone from her. Adrenaline pumped full force as Rachel, the babysitter, stood over the fallen wizard, ready to tear him apart.

"Great Spirit of Panterra, come to my aid!" cried the wizard in desperation. Throwing his arms toward the pool, he started weeping. "I brought the girl for my daughter! I brought the boy for my power! Where are you?"

Nothing happened. Not even a bubble rose to the surface.

"I need you!" wailed Rudolph.

"Let him go, Rachel," said a soft voice.

Still breathing hard, Rachel looked down to see Courtney at her side.

The girl stared up with sad eyes. "I used to be afraid of him… but now, I just feel sorry for him."

Rachel put an arm around the girl. "You don't have to be afraid of him anymore. Ever."

Courtney managed a smile and looked up at Rachel. "With you around, Rachel, I don't think I'm afraid of anything."

Rudolph continued to weep and beg for the dark spirit to help.

"Um, Rachel?" Steven said nervously. He stood staring out the open doors. "You'd better come, quick!"

Courtney gulped when she saw out the doors. "On second thought, I think I'm afraid."

"HEEELLLLP!!!" screamed a girl's voice. Not from Lisa, this voice came from the direction of the blockhouse.

The head priest's eyes went wide with shock. Moving toward him at an alarming rate of speed, a young girl appeared to be flying off the ground.

At first the chanting tried to quicken, as if it could finish before the girl arrived, but quickly panic took over.

Screaming, the priests began to scatter.

"What is this?" growled Tendl. His hand dropped to his sword as he turned.

Lisa promptly stepped squarely on top of his robe, causing him to stumble. She kicked him hard in the backside with her other foot. Immediately after she hopped back off the robe, and Tendl crashed to his knees.

"Come on, Darvy!" she yelled. "This is our chance!"

"To do what?" asked the startled king.

"Look out!" screamed a voice in terror.

"Huh?" So scared, Darvy hadn't seen the turn of events. He turned just in time to catch Joe full in the chest. The girl and boy fell in a tangle, and the ripstick clattered to a stop near Lisa.

"That's Steven's!" Lisa shouted in amazement. She snatched it up and then raced to help Darvy and Joe. However, when she reached them, she faltered.

The priests hadn't run far. Once Joe crashed, they turned back, and now they quickly encircled the three children.

"The wedding shall continue!" bellowed the head priest, flourishing his bright robe and brandishing the white spear with a flourish. "This foolish girl will be the sacrifice! Right here we end it!"

Joe snarled up at the priests but then could only stare, as the spear's tip pointed right at her neck.

"Not on your life, jester!" spat Jan, leaping into the fray. When his sister went out of control, he'd hurried after and then slipped to his belly when the crash occurred. Nobody had spotted him in the confusion. Once the priests had turned back to resume the wedding, he'd gotten to his feet and had silently hobbled the rest of the way. Then, hearing the threat to Joe, he launched himself onto the back of the head priest, just as he had done during the fight at the carriage.

The head priest staggered forward as the force of the boy's landing nearly sent him crashing on his face. Jan's hands clutched around the man's prominent nose and covered his eyes. They gripped tightly. Squealing in pain, the priest brought the spear down and used it as a crutch.

"Jan!" cried Joe. "Watch it! He nearly stabbed me!"

"Sorry," grunted the boy. He squeezed his knees tightly around the head priest's back and wrapped his forearms around the thick, quivering neck.

Caught completely by surprise, the other priests only stared at the proceedings.

"Kill the boy!" shouted Tendl as he ripped his sword free, lunging to his feet.

Before they could react, Joe, who had remained on the ground from the crash, grabbed the hilt of the spear and twisted it from the head priest. His grip had weakened from Jan's choking. In a quick flip, the spear's blade suddenly pricked the head priest's neck. Jan relaxed his arms and grinned. He still hung onto the back of the head priest. The older man's face turned from a scarlet red to a chalky white. Death from choking had turned to death from stabbing. Neither looked appealing.

"If anybody comes closer," Joe growled. "I jam your purple jester dead!"

The other priests stepped back in fear. Nobody threatened the high priest. Tendl lowered his sword. "What will you do then?" he sulked. "You're still surrounded."

"We'll leave this stupid place," Lisa said, pulling Darvy to his feet. "Where are Rachel and Steven?" she asked the girl.

"I don't know," the girl said, with a slight frown. "Everyone else should be coming soon, though."

Lisa looked dubious. "Everyone else?"

From the blockhouse's entrance a scream erupted, followed by a priest flying into the street. Crashing down, he rolled twice before he writhed in agony. Another priest ran out and dove headfirst onto the stone, screaming for mercy.

The largest man Lisa had ever seen in her life stomped out next and bared massive arms.

Twisting from his perch on the head priest's back, Jan smiled and nodded at the large man. "That's Murd."

An older woman followed Murd and shook her head at the fallen priests.

"And there's the old hag," Jan said cheerfully.

Then Jason Richardson stepped into the sun with Jakey and another boy pressed against his side.

"Jason? Jakey?" Lisa stared in amazement.

Jan's eyes widened. "You know them?" Then he cried out. "Hey, Jak is awake!" He was so excited, he squeezed his arms, and the head priest's face started to match his robe again.

"Calm down, Jan," Joe warned him, never allowing the spear to waver. "This jester is our way out! Don't kill him yet."

"Oh, sorry," the boy said, relaxing his arms.

The purple priest only gasped for a breath.

Tendl and the other priests glared and squirmed. They seemed helpless. But then a dull roar made of many feet mixed with voices rose. Jason looked back and immediately pushed the two boys ahead of him. Murd and the woman followed right after. They looked scared. The last to exit the building, a young priest in a brown robe, took one look toward the roar and immediately fled back inside.

"Um, what's coming?" Lisa asked worriedly.

"Th-that," wheezed the head priest, "will be the people to witness your wedding! Lower your spear, girl. If they see you harming their head priest, they'll not stop. They'll rip you all to shreds!"

"Listen to him," Tendl said tightly. "The riffraff of the catacombs will be like a mob. They'll crush you all—king or not, nobody will be spared." He smiled wickedly. "Harming the head priest is not tolerated. They're like wild dogs who need a leader, and the man that fool girl is jabbing is that leader!"

"Save your breath, ugly one," Joe said. "The spear will stick this man before a finger is laid anywhere near us."

Darvy trembled. Tendl was speaking only to him.

"Order the spear to be lowered, Your Majesty. They will have to obey the king!"

"I-I—" Darvy said miserably.

"No," Lisa cried. "If we lower the spear, they'll force the wedding and kill everyone else!"

Darvy wrung his hands.

"Do not worry," Joe said cheerfully. "This spear has no king. It isn't going anywhere."

Jason rushed toward them. "What have you two done now?" he cried to Joe and Jan. Then he saw Lisa and the spear. Groaning, he staggered to a stop.

Murd, the woman, Jak, and Jakey had started for the steps leading up to the cave but had also pulled up. They had company.

After the stone plaza ended just beyond the blockhouse, the terrain dropped off. The plaza was completely constructed of stone and contained no vegetation. Below it, tall brown grass grew on a sharp slope with an occasional tree. A beaten dirt path twisted through the grass and led to small fields of grain and gardens of vegetables that bordered the village known as the catacombs. This was where the people lived. Now they left their homes to go up to the plaza to see the wedding of their king. Coming up the incline and through the vegetation, hundreds of adults and children began to pour into the plaza.

Some wore brown robes, others had robes of white, and some had white tunics with brown pants. Nobody seemed to be in charge, and very little order was present. The wave of humanity swept around the blockhouse and crashed into the stone area, cutting off the way to the stairs leading to the cave. When seeing the priests and the others, those at the front of the crowd jerked to a halt. Cries of alarm swept through the horde.

Murd and the woman pulled Jakey and Jak toward Jason. The crowd of villagers started to slowly press forward. Cries asking what was happening swirled from the mob.

Darvy openly dripped sweat, and Lisa found she had no spit to swallow. Men and women were staring at them with unfriendly faces. All the children in the crowd were being hustled to the back.

Finally the mob stopped ten feet from where Joe continued to point the spear at the head priest's neck. None in the crowd looked friendly. They were only mildly curious at best. Silence descended as everyone waited.

Jan scrunched up on the head priest's back and shrank against the purple robes. Many of the eyes were directed in his direction.

An uneasy silence filled the plaza. About three hundred villagers and thirty priests faced off against the small band armed only with a spear—pointed at the neck of the head priest. Then the priests started to smile and rub their hands.

Tendl lifted his hands. "Followers of the Spirit!" he roared. "Your king is being threatened by assassins! They seek to steal away his kingship and they threaten our head priest!"

"That's not true!" Lisa cried. "Your head priest is nothing but a fat slob who murders children!"

"Careful," Jason warned her. He'd moved back to stand near her. "Let's not do anything to start a riot."

Gasps and mutters swept the crowd. Tension filled the air.

"Let the Spirit prevail!" a voice in the crowd cried.

"Darvy, do something," Lisa muttered. "You're their king."

"I-I can't ..." he said wretchedly.

The redhead squeezed her eyes shut in frustration. "Oh, great ... *where's* Rachel?"

Darvy's head shot up hopefully. "The Babysitter Rachel? She's here?"

Jason grimaced. "I hoped she was with you—she went to find Steven. Courtney had better be with them ... in a place a lot safer than here."

"Demand they cease this mockery of our spirit!" Tendl now cried. "Lift up your voices and show that our spirit is—"

"Dead!" cried a faint voice from over their heads.

"Rachel!" Lisa's eyes sprung open. "Rachel is here!" Then she squinted. "Rachel?"

All heads turned toward the voice. Even the head priest jerked around to look, causing Jan to shift his position and nearly tumble.

Rachel stood on the middle of the stairs leading down from the cave, staring down into the plaza.

"Who are you?" roared Tendl.

"It's Rachel the Babysitter!" Darvy cried. "The babysitter has come to save us from the wizards!"

The mob of villagers started to buzz. Men pointed and women clasped their faces in amazement.

Tendl threw up his arms. "You lie about our spirit!" he shouted. "The Spirit of Panterra lives! It is all-powerful! You will die for your wicked lie!"

Chapter Thirty-Nine

When in high school, which now seemed like another life, just the thought of speaking in front of strangers used to send Rachel into a state of panic that usually led to tears, stuttering, and weak knees. But now, with lives hanging in the balance, she refused to give in. A deep calmness settled over her and no fear got through. *I'm an adult … I can do this!* Lisa was down there—so were her other friends. Steven and Courtney stood behind her. In moments, they could be together and free … or crushed and dead. *I'm calm!*

"I don't lie! Listen to me!" Rachel cried down to the people below. With the temple complex built between two rock walls of a mountain, her voice echoed and boomed so all could hear her.

"Silence, woman!" demanded the man with the sword who had just predicted her death. He turned to the people. "The Spirit demands her death! Kill her!"

Horrified gasps answered this cry.

"Hush!" cried a woman from the crowd. "Let the Babysitter speak!"

"It's really her!" gushed a male's voice. "She has come to us!"

"Speak, Babysitter!" cried another voice from the crowd.

Rachel gulped. All eyes were now firmly locked on her. She licked her lips. "This had better be good," she whispered. Forcing herself to stare down, she saw a mass of people looking back with hope on their faces. She blinked. These people didn't want to fight. They wanted to be free. And next to them were the fat priests … threatening her friends and their freedom. She saw Lisa and instantly felt a surge of energy.

"Everyone, listen!" her voice boomed, surprising even her. "Uh, you are good people!" Amazingly, nobody even stirred. Emboldened, Rachel started speaking her first thoughts. "But that thing in the cave is evil! It's not any great spirit, it's a putrid one! All it does is control you through fear! The only power the priests have here is the power they made up for themselves! They have no right to force you to do anything unless you choose to do it!"

Down below, Tendl barked out a laugh. "You are a fool who desecrates our mountain!"

Joe, who had kept the spear's point on the head priest's neck, looked away long enough to glare.

Jason and the others were too nervous to move.

"No, we are the fools!" shouted a woman in the crowd. "The babysitter answered our prayers and has come to deliver us from the evil spirit! She has destroyed the priests' power!"

The entire mob of three hundred strong roared their approval.

"No more sacrifices!" screamed a man.

"We aren't slaves anymore!" another voice cried.

Shaken, Tendl shrank back. The priests were also looking very nervous.

The head priest made as if to say something, but Jan hissed in his ear. The purple-clothed man only gulped.

"No!" suddenly cried a voice from above Rachel. "No!" Everyone looked up to see Rudolph. He'd stumbled from the cave's entrance and paused at the top of the stairs, looming over Rachel. Wild-eyed, he pointed a finger down at Rachel. "You can't take my power! I will destroy you!" His voice cracked. "The Great Spirit will destroy you!"

The crowd cried out and many ducked in anticipation of great magic.

Nothing happened.

"*No*!" The wizard tried again to blast Rachel with a bolt of magic from his hands. His eyes remained a dull blue and brimmed with tears. Staggering back, he collapsed and started sobbing uncontrollably.

Over the mountain, the clouds cleared and the sun cast down brilliant rays. In her white tunic, Rachel seemed to glow.

"All hail Rachel!" called a voice in the crowd. "Hail the Babysitter!" Immediately the entire mob of villagers took up the chant.

Tendl threw down his sword and raised his right first, joining in. The priests and black robes edged away nervously.

"You can get off my back now," the head priest muttered to Jan. "And please lower the spear. Or shove it through. Either way, it's over."

Joe chose to drop the spear and run to meet Jan in a wild hug.

High above the mountain overlooking the temple complex, a lone eagle swooped toward its nest. Far below, it eyed the congregation of humans curiously. What a strange race of creatures …

A large flock of humans in multicolored robes surged forward and expelled a much smaller flock in black from the large stone nest. In the wake of the noisy expulsion, a single flash of red reflected from the head of a young girl running up the side of the mountain.

"Rachel!" Lisa screamed, taking the steps two at a time. Not just Rachel waited for her, but so did her brother. Steven grinned at Rachel's side. And next to him was Courtney. Lisa ran first to her babysitter with arms extended. The incandescent light in her eyes glittered brighter than her hair. "I knew you would come!"

Kneeling at the top of the landing, Rachel met the redhead with a fierce hug.

"I missed you too, Lisa," she said.

Lisa pulled back briefly and stared with wonder. "Oh my gosh, Rachel … oh my gosh … you're different." For a long moment, all they could do was stare at each other. Finally Lisa broke into a tentative smile. "Rachel, I missed you so much … you, you've changed."

"So have you, Lisa." Rachel smiled back at her. "I mean, you were almost a queen!"

"Oh, I'd rather be with you—trust me." Lisa threw her arms around her again and found herself sobbing into Rachel's shoulder.

"Not that I want to break up this moment," called Jason, looking nervously at where the mob was forcing the last of the priests from the gates, "but soon they'll be back—those people down there. Then what do we do?" He was coming up the stairs with Jakey and Jak. The woman and Murd followed. Beside the large man, Joe carried the ripstick proudly. Jan rode Murd's shoulders, awed at being so high on such a big man. Darvy came last. His eyes were large as he stared up at Rachel.

Lisa disentangled herself from the hug and looked down at Darvy. "It doesn't matter what they do. We'll be home by then. Right, Darvy?"

"Oh, um, yeah …" said the king with little conviction.

Darvy knelt at the pool and stretched out a trembling hand. Courtney and Rachel, who were still in bed-clothes, had quickly managed to find better clothing in the blockhouse.

"I don't think this will work," he muttered to Lisa, who stood at his side. "Rachel already said the spirit thing is dead, so where will the power come from?"

"It's all about belief," Lisa said, squeezing the boy's shoulder. "You're the king, right? Just believe in yourself and you can do it. I know you can, Darvy."

"R-right." He didn't sound convinced.

"Listen, Darvy," Lisa said. "That thing, whatever it was, never ruled this land. Its power came from other people's fear. That means there is other power left in this world. Power that's good."

"I hope you're right." Darvy at least sounded more confident.

Lisa sniffed. "Of course I'm right. Now get ready to send us home."

Behind them, Rachel, Jason, Jakey, Courtney, and Steven were saying their final goodbyes.

"Are you sure you won't come?" Courtney asked, giving the woman a hug.

"Girl, are you kidding me? Back there I'm nobody. Why, I've been missing over there and not a soul cared. All I am is a failed author in that world." She smiled widely. "But here, I'll be something great."

"Yes," Jan said seriously, limping to her side. "She's going to be a babysitter."

Joe came on her other side. "We can't wait."

"What!" The woman looked between the twins and went pale. "I'm not a babysitter—I'm a writer! There's a whole world out there waiting for my stories—dying to hear about what happened here. Why, why, I'm the person who's going to write about the Babysitter … and all her friends and their adventures." She smiled down at Courtney. "And the first one will be about a young girl whose kindness saved a life."

Jan and Joe glanced at each other. Both shook their heads.

"Nah," said Jan. "You'll be a babysitter."

The woman reached down and gave him a hard slap on the seat of his pants. "I'll never be a babysitter for you brats—you have no manners!"

"Leave the hag alone," growled Murd over his shoulder as he clapped Jason on the back.

"See," muttered the woman to Rachel, "they treat me so well here."

The twins had turned their attention to the large man and were now trying to climb his back.

"Murd, thanks for everything," Jason said, giving a tight handshake.

Rachel echoed the thanks and gave Murd a hug.

Embarrassed, Murd bobbed his head and nearly sent Joe crashing from his shoulders. Turning, he directed his discomfort at the twins. "Sit down yer selves!" he barked.

The twins immediately obeyed, seemingly in awe of the powerful man.

Jak and Steven sat next to each other and stared out into the pool. The brown boy seemed a little unfocused at times, but remarkably recovered from the fall. Neither boy looked happy to be saying goodbye.

"I'll miss you," Courtney said to the woman one last time. "Thank you for taking care of us. Do watch Joe and Jan, okay?"

Grumbling, the woman nodded. “As long as that human mountain sticks close I will, I guess. Watch them break their necks, probably.”

Darvy stood up, his voice slightly strained. “Okay, I, I think it’s complete.”

The water appeared smooth as glass.

“You can’t do it!” rasped Rudolph from where he sat just inside the great hall, a huddled heap of self-pity and tears. The failed wizard seemed like an empty bag of flesh. “The power is gone.”

“He can do it!” Lisa said hotly. “He’s king!”

Darvy blushed. “I don’t know if I have any magic.”

“You don’t need magic to be king!” Lisa said. “You just need belief in yourself and a good heart!”

Rudolph laughed scathingly. “You’re all fools,” he said hoarsely. “You will only sink in that pool! You need the spirit … the Great Spirit …” He moaned piteously.

Jak tossed a small pebble over the pool. It vanished without a ripple.

Darvy held Lisa’s hand and squeezed as they said their final goodbyes. “Thank you, Lisa, for everything,” he mumbled.

“Aren’t you coming?” Lisa asked.

Shaking his head, the boy bit his lower lip. “I’m going to be the king here … It’s time I start acting like it.” Looking up, his eyes shone at Rachel. “Watching your babysitter made me realize the people here are tired of being afraid all the time. It won’t be easy, but I think I’m ready to try being a leader now.”

“Are, are you sure you will be okay?” Rachel asked him.

“We’ll look after him,” the woman said. Murd rumbled an agreement.

Both Lisa and Darvy blushed as they realized everyone was watching them.

“Bye, Darvy,” Lisa said hastily, trying to act casual.

“Goodbye … Sweetheart.” Darvy grinned goofily. He suddenly gave Lisa a quick peck on the cheek.

With the twins whistling, Lisa rushed into the pool and vanished. The last to go was her red hair just above her red face.

Rudolph's eyes boggled and bulged as he watched the return to Earth. Rachel was the last to vanish under the surface. "H-how?" he whispered. "N-not possible."

The twins hanging from each shoulder, Murd led the woman out of the great hall. Darvy went ahead of them with his chin pointed up and his face glowing—he, Darvy Gretz, had just created a water portal with only his mind! Outside, the crowd had regathered below … Taking a deep breath, Darvy started his first public speech.

Only then did Murd notice that Jak was missing.

Alone in the hall, Rudolph crawled to the edge of the pool. Dipping his hand forward, he touched water.

"No!" Slapping the surface, he suddenly felt a tremor below. Before him, the water stirred and began to bubble.

He sneered as the dark spirit broke the surface and stared down at him.

"You!" Rudolph spat. "What happened? You promised me power!"

"*THEY WERE NOT WORTHY OF ME—THE BOY WAS NOT THE BOY I DESIRE.*" It may have been Rudolph's imagination, but the dark spirit seemed to be shaking, almost trembling like a giant leaf. "*THIS BOY'S HEART COULD NOT BE CHANGED … AND THE OTHER WITH HIM … THEY COULD HAVE DESTROYED ME.*"

"I, I don't understand! You are the most powerful—nothing can destroy you!"

"*ONLY THE GIRL … ONLY SHE COULD HAVE DESTROYED ME. THAT IS WHY I HID AND SENT THEM BACK.*"

"Y-you sent them back?" Rudolph would never have said it aloud, but he didn't believe the dark spirit.

"*IT WAS THE ONLY WAY … DO NOT WORRY, I CAN RETURN YOUR POWER AND MORE BESIDE IT!*"

"I don't want power! I want my daughter back!"

"*GO BACK AND BRING THE OTHER BOY AND YOU SHALL HAVE HER BACK AND MORE!*"

"Wh-what other one?"

"THE BOY YOU BROUGHT … HE HAS THE TRUE ONE'S PRESENCE INSIDE OF HIM. IT IS SOMEONE CLOSE TO HIM … FIND HIM AND CONSUME HIM. I GIVE THIS CHARGE TO ALL WIZARDS!!! CONSUME THIS BOY!!!"

"All?" whispered Rudolph. He knew the spirit could speak to people great distances away.

"DO NOT WORRY … YOU HAVE BEEN FAITHFUL. THIS PLACE IS NO LONGER SAFE FOR ME. I WILL DWELL IN YOU AND YOU IN ME. TOGETHER WE WILL RULE TWO WORLDS!!!"

With a loud rumble, the monster threw itself from the pool and into the open mouth of Rudolph. Jerking and shaking, Rudolph stumbled back as the dark spirit somehow, impossibly, shrank itself and vanished inside his parted lips. For a moment, he looked stricken and about to explode. Then a wicked smile spread across his face as his eyes turned the color of blood. They practically dripped red.

PART III—*The Babysitter Returns*

Chapter Forty

Sarah Watkins sat next to Samantha in the shadow of the sand dune, staring miserably past the crowded beach to where the waves continued crashing down. It was the picture of her life—endless crashing without reprieve or any good reason.

Even with the hot sun beating down and the sounds of laughter and joy carrying across the beach, Sarah felt cold and miserable. She pulled her shirt tighter to her shoulders. She wished she could completely disappear inside of it and be gone. It did little to hide the new green swimsuit covering her bloated body. Everyone called her a big ball of snot. Beside her, Samantha had her face buried in her hands and was trying hard not to cry. They called Samantha something much worse.

Beach week had begun …

Under a giant umbrella that shaded enough space for a table and three beach chairs, Trent Long leaned against Jennifer's shoulder and whispered in her ear. Laughing, Jennifer gave Trent a playful slap on the arm. She glanced back at the sand dune where Sarah and Samantha sat very alone and smiled wickedly.

On the other side of Trent, Brett Bufford belched and stood up from his chair. "Man, I feel good today." He flicked his head toward the sand dune and smirked. "Yo, Sam, come here!"

"Don't call them over here!" Jennifer said sharply. "I don't want them sharing my umbrella."

"I'm not calling the fat one, Jen, so chill!" Brett said. "Samantha, you coming?"

Trent laughed. "Forget her, dude. We got enough hot babes to keep us busy for a while. Just look at them." He waved an arm vaguely toward the water.

As advertised, over half the senior class had made it to beach week and now covered a large portion of sand—mostly by lying in the sun. Few were in the water, but sunbathing dominated. The smell of sunscreen and beer filled the air.

"Of course," Trent said quickly, "the only babe that I see is the one next to me." He flashed a smile and clicked his teeth next to Jennifer's ear.

"Gee, thanks, Trent," Brett said, cracking up.

Jennifer snorted. "Just get me another beer. I'm hot and thirsty and you guys are being stupid."

"You're always hot," Trent said.

"For that," Jennifer purred, "Brett, you get the beer."

In the shadow of the dune, Sarah ducked her head. Samantha blinked back tears. Neither girl looked at each other. From day one, the girls had been treated as objects of amusement by Trent and Brett ... which meant everyone else treated them the same way.

It all started on the first morning—after an exciting car trip down from Virginia where Samantha and Sarah spent the entire time saying what a blast the week would be.

Instead it was almost immediately blasted in their faces when Sarah first walked from the beach house in her two-piece bathing suit.

"Hey, look everybody, I found a spare tire!" was Brett's first comment at seeing her.

"What does she think this is, Grossville?" was Jennifer's comment, almost immediately after.

It went downhill from there.

Samantha got it even worse. While Rachel was the "fat girl" and "beached whale" to make fun of, Samantha became an object to ogle at. When she started for the beach, Brett came behind her and tried to grab her around the middle. Pulling away, the girl slapped him across the face.

Calling her a choice name, Brett backed off. It had been in front of a large group of their peers and almost immediately Samantha became ostracized. Jealous, the girls refused to speak civilly to her, and the guys started to see who could get the "closest" to her without getting slapped. Only Sarah stood by her friend.

And now they had three whole days left before the awful week would end …

"I feel like crawling in those waves and never coming back," muttered Samantha. "I mean it."

Sarah swallowed and stared back at the water. Then she gasped. "L-look in the water," she said.

Under the umbrella, Trent suddenly pulled away from Jennifer and also stared into the water. His eyes became saucers. Brett joined him. Soon the entire beach stopped what they were doing to gape.

"Lisa! Steven!" Rachel ducked under as another wave swept over her. Coughing, she staggered forward. The waves battered her back, but didn't take her down. She had been through too much to fall so easily. "Where are we?"

Lisa, her red hair plastered over her eyes, surfaced next to her and coughed. "I forgot. Darvy is from North Carolina! I bet he sent us there!" She ducked under as another wave came. Spluttering seawater, she then lunged forward to shallower water.

Groaning, Rachel struggled to follow. "Did it have to be the ocean?"

On her right, Jason grabbed Jakey and hefted him up in his arms. Courtney hung on to his shoulder. Just beyond them, Steven stumbled toward shore.

"At least we have everybody," wheezed Rachel. Then a lithe brown body exploded from the water and latched on to her back, sending her under.

Sputtering, she managed to regain her footing just as another wave sent her staggering. "Jak!" she cried in horror, looking back to see the familiar face. "What are you doing here?"

Frightened, the boy wrapped his arms around her waist and squeezed tightly.

"Don't worry," Rachel said worriedly. "We'll take care of you. Come on. Let's just get to the beach before anyone else shows up."

Every single eye on the beach watched in amazement as two teens and five kids staggered to shore. They seemed to have appeared from nowhere—where had they come from and what were they doing? Really, dressed like *that*?

The first to reach solid sand was the guy about their age with thick, dark hair. He wore a white ruffled shirt with tight brown pants. Plastered to his skin, the clothes revealed a muscular build to accompany his handsome face, mostly hidden under a dark scraggly beard and mustache. In his arms he carried a young skinny boy of eight or nine years. A young girl a few years older clung to his right elbow. Both children were dressed similarly to the guy—fancy clothes meant for a ball, not a beach.

Behind them came a slender boy about nine or ten. Dark brown eyes timidly viewed the beach. He wore only a pair of pants and as his brown skin soaked in the sun, it appeared to glow. Many were struck by his handsome features and cool expression. They thought the beach was being invaded by movie stars.

Especially when they saw who emerged from the ocean next.

Trent's and Brett's jaws dropped.

"Who's that hot babe?" breathed Trent.

"I don't know," muttered Brett, "but we need to find out. Wow!"

Sarah Watkins rose unsteadily to her feet to get a better look.

A girl about their age stood in the water with a small browned boy clinging to her waist. Beside her, a young skinny girl wearing an outlandishly purple dress grabbed her hand and spoke softly.

Nodding grimly, the teenage girl lifted her head and made for the dry sand. Her stunning, chiseled beauty drew all eyes from the beach … and something about her seemed very familiar.

"Everybody is looking at us," Rachel stammered as she reached dry sand.

"Don't worry, we're used to it," Lisa said, flashing a small smile. "We're rich."

"I-I'm not," Rachel managed to say.

"Yes you are," Lisa said cheerfully. "That boy Jan gave us a handful of gold rings and rubies before we left—as a thank you to Steven for leaving his ripstick. We both decided that you get them all. Well, at least half."

Rachel coughed and then suddenly broke into laughter. All her nervousness vanished. They were home … they'd made it back to their own world. Breathing deeply, she looked around and saw a glorious beach on a beautiful day. Best of all, she saw houses with wires over the dunes. An airplane flew overhead.

"We did it!" Rachel said all at once. "We're back, Lisa!" Throwing back her head, she let out a yelp of happiness. She'd always wanted to do that.

Giggling, Lisa stepped away from her. "Careful, Rachel, now you're starting to be embarrassing."

"We're back where?" Jason said to them, frowning. Shaking water from his ear, he seemed oblivious to all the people staring from the beach.

Rachel grinned at him. "King Darvy grew up in North Carolina."

Jason winced and then groaned. "Wonderful. Just great. My parents are going to kill me."

Steven wiped sand off his chest. He smiled wanly at Rachel. "I guess Jak still belongs to you."

Seeing him, Jason groaned again, this time even louder. "I don't suppose you can send him back, can you?"

"Not on your life," Rachel said. She put a protective arm around him and smoothed back his wet hair. "I'm still his babysitter."

The boy, still looking like a frightened puppy, hugged her waist even harder.

The people on the beach were starting to edge closer. None of them were speaking and all kept staring.

Looking toward them, Rachel all at once gave a jump and turned to face the water. Back rigid, she gasped for breath and started to tremble.

"What is it, Rachel?" asked Lisa anxiously.

"Don't tell me you see some wizard," Jason growled, pulling Courtney behind him.

"N-no … it's just that …" Rachel gulped. "I, uh, I think we just crashed my high school's beach week."

"Yo, who are you and where did you come from?" Brett asked loudly. He walked by the gawkers and headed straight for Rachel. Everyone naturally gave way to him. "You all shooting a movie or something? Did your boat wreck?"

Jason frowned at him. "Why do you say that?"

Brett shrugged his tan shoulders and tried to flex his muscles without appearing to do so. "Your clothes are funny, and, well, you look like movie stars or something. Seriously, what's going on? Where did you all come from?"

Jason rolled his eyes and dismissed him almost immediately. Taking Rachel by the arm, he tugged her away. "Why don't we find some intelligent life around here and see about getting a phone."

"And, you," Brett continued, ignoring Jason and looking at Rachel, "are the star that shines the brightest!"

Rachel gave a start. Her shoulders tensed. *Could Brett Bufford be talking to her?* Gulping, she turned to face him.

Brett's eyes widened in appreciation, but not in recognition. "Wow …" he said in admiration.

Rachel became aware of Lisa and Steven standing at her side watching her. Jak's grip loosened but remained attached to her waist. Even Jakey and Courtney stood as silent witnesses. All the horrors of Panterra had vanished. Rachel was suddenly thrust back into being a teenage girl. And a babysitter. People like Brett couldn't take her focus off her job.

Jason glared as Brett stared way too long. "Hey, back off, hot shot," he said rudely.

"Jason, it's okay," Rachel said. She put a hand on his shoulder and took a deep breath. "I can handle this. I know him."

"You know me?" Brett grinned toothily. "Really? I mean, I'm Brett."

"I know that," Rachel said coolly.

"She just said she knew you, moron," Jason said, narrowing his eyes.

"No kidding?" Brett winked at Rachel. "Must be my lucky day!" He pointedly ignored Jason and leaned toward Rachel. "Let me guess, we met in your dream, or was it mine?" He laughed. "Seriously, what's your name? I think I would remember meeting you. More importantly, what's your number?"

Rachel gently loosened Jak's grip and patted his hair. Then she stepped close to Brett Bufford so the top of her head nearly touched his chin. Looking up, she stared straight into his eyes. Thinking she was about to kiss him, Brett's eyes went goopy. His lips actually parted.

"My name is Rachel Pugsley, Brett Bufford. And my mom beat up your dad. My number is three. As in, you have three seconds to get out of my face before I slap you."

Brett was so startled, he jerked back as if he was already slapped and ended up falling on his backside.

"Okaaay," Jason said, hiding a grin. "Where were we?"

"Trying to find some intelligent life," Rachel muttered. "Come on. There's none around here."

Jak kicked sand in Brett's stunned face as he hurried to catch up with Rachel.

Gasps raced across the beach as the news spread. The "hot babe" was Rachel Pugsley and she'd just knocked Brett down a few notches.

Sarah and Samantha stared at each other when they heard the news. Not able to breathe, Sarah stared as the gorgeous girl strode across the beach without looking to the left or the right. No fear or doubt accompanied her steps. An amazing-looking guy was on her right and five children followed.

"Where did you say Rachel went this summer?" Samantha asked in a hushed voice.

"To-to Florida to babysit," Sarah answered.

Samantha whistled. "Wow …"

Rachel walked by Trent's umbrella without noticing the golden-haired boy gawking at her. Jennifer scowled and pinched Trent's side as his eyes turned to follow Rachel.

"R-Rachel?" asked a timid voice. "Rachel?"

Near the stairs leading over the sand dune marking the end of the beach, Rachel paused. She recognized that voice. Whirling, she saw Sarah Watkins walking to her, almost in a daze. Rachel's face immediately softened. Wrapping a towel around her as if hiding behind it, poor Sarah looked to be seeing a ghost … but more than that, her eyes were desperate for kindness. Blinking, Rachel smiled at her.

"Hi, Sarah—I didn't see you," she said. "Uh, how's beach week?"

Sarah's lip trembled. "Oh, um, great," she said with a strained voice. "Really great. What are you doing here? I thought you were babysitting in Florida."

"Uh, yes, I was." Rachel shrugged. "We, uh, decided to take a trip to the beach. You know, just for fun."

"Yeah," muttered Jason. "And we took a shortcut. Now we have to get home the long way."

Sarah looked so confused that Rachel reached out and grabbed her arm. "Don't worry, Sarah. I'll explain everything one day. I promise."

"Rachel," urged Jason, "we really have to figure out a way back to Florida."

"In a minute, Jason. Here, I want you to meet Sarah. Sarah, this is Jason Richardson."

"Is-is that who you babysit?" Sarah asked.

Rachel's eyes widened. "What? Jason? No! He's the neighbor."

Jennifer snorted from the umbrella, where she watched everything with undisguised interest. "Stupid fatso," she muttered loud enough to be heard.

Rachel visibly jumped. Then she realized Sarah trembled before her—Jennifer hadn't been referring to Rachel, but to Sarah.

Jason noticed, and his mouth jerked slightly. "Nice to meet you, Sarah," he said loudly, reaching out to touch her arm. "A friend of Rachel's is somebody special. And," he nodded toward the beach, "it's nice to finally meet somebody with class on this beach full of stuck-up airheads."

Jennifer audibly gasped, and Sarah ducked her head, blushing.

Rachel bit her lip. "Sarah, can you do us a huge favor?"

"Oh, sure. What do you need?"

"Jason and I have to figure something out … can you watch the kids for a couple of minutes?"

"I can help," Samantha said shyly, shuffling next to Sarah.

"Great!" Rachel said. "You're Samantha, right? You're a big help, both of you. Uh, I guess they can go in the water … if they like. Just don't go too far out."

Lisa looked down at her ruined dress and frowned. "This isn't exactly swimwear," she muttered.

Courtney put an arm around her shoulder and smiled. "I think a swim at the beach is just what we need to catch up. Boy, have we got a lot to talk about!"

"Well, maybe I'll just sit in the shallow part." Lisa twisted her mouth. "Why not? Let's go swimming!"

Steven and Jakey steered Jak back to the crashing waves, each explaining the best way to bodysurf. After a long, stressful couple of days, swimming at a beach seemed like a perfect thing to do.

Samantha and Sarah followed with their sole focus on babysitting. They had to do everything to ignore all the stares … but by now they were used to them. Besides, now the stares held more envy than ridicule.

Steven and Jakey managed to coax Jak toward the bigger waves, and soon the boys were doing their best to bodysurf with Samantha. Sarah stood watching wistfully near where Courtney and Lisa sat in the shallows, each wearing the most ridiculous clothes. Dresses fit for a lavish ball, only found in British movies, did not belong in seawater, at the beach, in North Carolina. She sighed.

Rich people …

Slowly the others on the beach resumed what they had been doing, but with frequent glances at the newcomers.

Back at the sand dune, Rachel and Jason were in serious discussion.

"Okay," Rachel said ruefully. "I left my purse back with my horse Bolder. I don't have a phone or anything."

Jason patted her arm apologetically. "Lucky for you I used to keep Shawna's picture in my wallet—so I never lost it. The wallet, I mean."

Rachel swallowed. "Uh, oh … um …"

"Yeah, I actually have everything *but* her picture." Jason licked his lips and toed the sand. "Remember that night back when Lineus was giving Jak riding lessons?"

Rachel squeezed her eyes tight and nodded. "Yeah, I was so stupid."

"No you weren't, Rachel. You were right … I really was jealous. I, I went off in the woods and, well, that's when I lost

Shawna's picture. I," he swallowed, "guess things happen, you know."

Rachel frowned and then her eyes widened as she understood what Jason was trying to say.

That was when Trent coughed and hurried over from the umbrella.

"Hey, Rachel," he said brightly. "It's me, Trent Long."

"I know who you are, Trent," Rachel said tightly, not wanting the moment to end. She turned away from him.

Jason sighed. "You're the most popular girl in your class, aren't you?"

Rachel was saved a response when Trent nervously tapped her shoulder. Brett Bufford, meanwhile, sulked under the umbrella.

"Ah, cool," Trent said. "Listen, um, what's going on?"

Rachel bit her lip. "Are you trying to help us?" she asked tightly.

"Uh, yeah. Yeah." Trent smiled broadly. "Anything you need, you know, you just ask your friend Trent."

"Do you have a van?" Jason suddenly asked. "Something that holds eight people?"

"You bet," Trent said enthusiastically. "We got a nice one just for this trip—it easily holds eight. And there're plenty of other cars for the others, so I can give you all a lift anywhere."

"Good. I'll buy it," Jason said, searching his clothing for his wallet. "I should have a check with me."

"Uh, what?" Trent looked lost.

"We'll take it. I mean I'm buying the van." Jason had fished out his wallet and winced. It was soaked. "Is there an ATM nearby?"

"Jason," Rachel started, but the dark-haired teen cut her off.

"Relax," Jason told her. "I've been sitting on my allowance for years. I always wanted my own van."

"It's a minivan …" Trent mumbled.

"Perfect," Jason said. "Let's work out a deal. Cash now and we'll work out the details later."

Trent just stared.

Two hours later, Jason took the wheel and started the engine of a five-year-old minivan with tinted windows and bumper stickers for rock bands he'd never heard of. Despite a floor covered in old wrappers and a faint sour smell, it was in fairly good condition. In the backseats, the kids were busy stuffing chips and ham sandwiches in their mouths. Bottles of soda rolled at their feet. Clearly overwhelmed by his new surroundings, Jak sat next to Steven with his eyes wide and directed out the window. Then Steven introduced him to cheese chips and cola. The boy began to believe he hadn't woken from his fall but had finally died and crossed over to heaven.

Rachel leaned against the passenger seat and groaned in great comfort. "Air-conditioning," she murmured.

"And the radio." Grinning, Jason slipped a pair of sunglasses on, another purchase from Trent. "You ready?"

"You bet." Rachel lowered the sun visor and yelped. On the other side of the visor was a small mirror. For the first time since leaving Florida to enter Panterra, she saw her reflection …

Smooth lean cheeks browned by constant sun, thick chestnut hair, and dark red lips—she only recognized her eyes. Her riding combined with being sick for two weeks, all the running, and the lack of heavy eating had melted away her girth. Underneath was something she never thought possible. Toned muscle and curves … Rachel squirmed. She'd been so busy worrying about the kids that she'd never realized her transformation. Sure, she noticed how running and riding became easier and how her belly stopped being in the way, but her mind couldn't comprehend the change. In her head she'd always been the fat girl. Now …

"Now you know why your boyfriend Trent sold us everything so easily," Jason said, watching her marvel at her reflection. "And why all those guys are out there still staring at us with drool running down their faces."

Rachel felt her face grow warm. "I, uh, Trent isn't my boyfriend."

"Good. Then I won't have to punch him in the nose. Come on, Rachel. Let's go home."

"I actually live in Virginia," she murmured.

As the van exited the beach parking lot, Samantha grabbed Sarah's arm.

"You know, I kind of miss Virginia," she said wistfully.

"Yeah." Sarah looked at where Trent and Brett stood scratching their heads and asking if anybody knew Rachel's number. "Let's leave this creep show."

"I'll get the car started. You know, Sarah, when we get back home, I bet we can find some good babysitting jobs."

It took driving the rest of the day and through the night … with several stops to let Jak throw up on the side of the road (which led to all the kids throwing up eventually) and more stops to teach Jak about the proper toilet facilities, but as dawn broke the next day, the minivan turned down a familiar street. They were once again in Camelot Acres.

"We're home!" Jason sang out, rubbing his grizzled chin. Having looked in the mirror, he was anxious to shave … and then sleep for a week.

"I wonder what our welcome will be like," he muttered. Nobody had a phone in the van. When he'd borrowed Trent's in North Carolina, he hadn't been able to contact any of his family. His parents' phones had been off, and he'd only gotten the answering machine for his house. The same was true for the Winters' house.

Rachel stirred beside him and smacked her lips. On the first bathroom break, they had pulled in at a thrift store and traded their Panterra clothes for shorts and T-shirts.

"What time is it?" Rachel groaned. She'd slept a lot of the way.

"No idea, but it's just about sunrise."

Rachel looked back at the sleeping children and couldn't help but smile. All five had managed to curl up in the first row of seats. Lisa rested on Courtney's shoulder, with Steven's head resting in her lap. Courtney's lap supported Jakey. Poor Jak had curled into a ball on the floor. "I almost don't want to wake them."

"I do," Jason grunted. "I need a shower, a bed, and then a pizza. Large with everything on it."

"Sounds good," Rachel yawned. "Can you imagine making the trip we just did on horseback?"

Jason shuddered. "I wouldn't be able to walk for a week." Then he frowned. "I just don't know what I'm going to tell my parents … I wonder if they have the cops out looking for us."

"We'll find out …" The van pulled up the long driveway. "Steven, Lisa? You're home."

Looking lost, Steven lifted his head from his sister's lap. Seeing the familiar white house, he sat up with a start.

Lisa rubbed her eyes and shoved her brother toward the door. "Hurry up and get out. Just don't get too excited," she growled. "I remember how we left the place—it's going to be a mess inside with a broken door and everything."

Rachel was just stepping out the door when she froze. "You're right … every time it rained while we were gone … the house is probably flooded!"

"And moldy," Lisa nodded.

"Want me to come in?" Jason asked, his eyes drooping.

"No-no. You go home and take care of Courtney and Jakey. Uh, I'll keep Jak here for now." *Later we'll figure out what to do with the poor kid.*

"Okay … I'll call you later."

"Thanks, Jason. For everything."

Jak staggered from the van and once again stared in awe at his surroundings. Then he went to his knees and promptly threw up on the driveway.

"I'm going to sell this van as soon as I can," Jason groaned. "All it smells like now is vomit."

Courtney and Jakey mumbled their goodbyes, and then Rachel was left with the three children and one large, empty house.

"Come on," she murmured. "We'll see how bad the damage is and get Jak cleaned up." Her red Toyota remained parked as normal. "Worse comes to worst, I'll call your parents and we'll get a hotel … I just don't know what to tell them."

The door was closed but unlocked. Running ahead, Steven opened it and peered in tentatively. Looking back, he shrugged. "Seems okay."

"Careful," called Rachel. "It might be dangerous!"

The shattered door … poisoned food … fallen furniture—that was how they'd left the house. What would it be like now? How long had they been gone? Weeks, at least.

Rachel followed Lisa inside while tightly holding Jak's hand.

Inside turned out to be as clean and elegant as the first day Rachel arrived.

Rachel stared in wonder. "What the …"

Lisa ran from the kitchen. "Rachel," she exclaimed. "Come and see! Everything is fixed up! It's like nothing happened!"

Amazed, Rachel took in the spotless walls, floor, and then the kitchen. Then she gasped.

"Oh, but something happened." She let go of Jak's hand ran to the table. Her purse sat there, right next to her notebook. Beside it was a large pitcher of ice water with four glasses set up.

"Wh-where did my purse come from?" she asked, dazed.

"I brought it," said a voice coming from the living room. "I thought you might want it back." It was a voice Rachel had thought she would never hear again.

Rachel stared in shock. "M-Marcal?"

"Hello, Rachel … When searching for you, I found Bolder wandering the trees." The warrior walked calmly into the kitchen and started pouring glasses of water from the pitcher. He offered the first two to the boys.

Rachel found it hard to even breathe. "What, what are you doing here?"

"I had to see you again … to make sure you made it back in one piece. I've been waiting all night." Marcal grunted. "Here, take some water and relax."

Rachel gave the offered glass to Lisa. "But how did you know? How did—"

"It's a long story, Rachel."

"In here, Dearie!" crooned Vikki Rosa's soupy voice. "We have lots to talk about, Rachel."

"Wh-who else is here?" Rachel demanded, looking around wildly.

"Just us, Rachel. Relax." Marcal smiled but did not look happy. "I made a promise to help you. I haven't broken it yet."

Rachel nodded slowly. "Lisa, when you're done with your water, take Jak upstairs and show him how to wash his face. Uh, actually, take Steven too and see if you all can start turns in the shower."

"What about you?" Lisa asked worriedly.

Rachel shot Marcal a look. "I'll be fine. Trust me."

Marcal nodded.

Lisa trusted Rachel. Once she and the boys had finished their water, she hurried them up the stairs. But at the top step, she put a finger to her lips and took a seat. Jak and Steven crouched behind her. Each strained their ears to listen.

Entering the next room, Rachel tried her best not to feel cowed. Vikki Rosa had always unnerved her before. Could it be possible that the rich woman knew about Panterra? Something felt very wrong. Rachel took a deep breath and made sure to be on guard. It was time to find out what was going on.

Vikki Rosa sat in the large easy chair in a long, flowing evening gown. An empty glass next to a bottle of wine sat on the table near her. Coming in from the kitchen, Rachel moved to cautiously face the wealthy woman.

Vikki Rosa smiled lazily when seeing her. "Come, Rachel, take a seat. Welcome back. My, how you've changed …" As she took in Rachel's new beauty with a smile, her eyes narrowed in anger. "I guess the new world did you some good."

"Wh-what are you doing here?"

"Waiting for you, dear. I arrived late last night when the word of your arrival reached me … I left a very rich date to wait for you, dear. Tell me, how was Panterra?"

"H-How do you know everything?" Rachel didn't sit. Standing before Vikki Rosa, she did her best to remain in control. Her mind worked furiously to make sense of what was happening.

Marcal stood back near the kitchen, very willing to leave the women alone. He looked uncomfortable in a blue suit and a tie. He kept searching for a sword hilt at his side.

"Wait just a minute, Rachel," Vikki Rosa purred. "First you should be thanking me."

"What for?"

"Why, for fixing up this house and keeping it clean! When Jane Lovington left, or should I say Isabella, I had to go and hire a new housekeeper." She pouted and spoke as if Rachel had done something naughty. "And fixing that door took a few calls too. Besides, who's the one e-mailing Elizabeth Winter and reporting how well you're doing?" She chuckled at Rachel's startled reaction. "Yes, every night I've contacted her … she really wants to talk to you, you know, but I keep saying you're so busy with the neighbors and having a thrilling blast. And oh, yes, I arranged for the parents of the Richardson brats to stay in Europe an extra month. Some friends of mine invited them to spend two weeks in the Alps. I've taken the liberty of visiting their house and sending them text messages from Jason's phone."

"I-I don't understand."

Vikki Rosa nodded. "I know, and that is why I am being ever so very lenient with you." She pouted again. "You have caused me a great deal of stress, you know. You just can't stay out of the way, can you?"

"You're the one who got Jane Lovington hired in the first place." Rachel swallowed. "It was you who set this whole thing up, wasn't it?"

"Bravo, Rachel," Vikki Rosa said dryly. "Finally, you give me credit. I'm not just some dumb, rich floozy, am I?"

"B-but why?"

Vikki Rosa sighed and smoothed out her hair. "Rich people have everything, don't they?" She reached behind her and withdrew a fistful of bills. Rachel's eyes widened when she saw they were all hundreds. "Money is what makes the world turn, Rachel." She shook the wad of cash at Rachel. "This is life, dear. You can accept it or not. But it doesn't change the fact that without money you're nothing in this world. But with it … with it you can buy anything. Even a wizard."

Rachel backed up and thumped onto the couch. "What did you do?"

"Oh, come, you know what I did." Vikki Rosa slapped the money down beside her in agitation. "This money is for you, Rachel. You won, okay? All I ask is for you to forget about me and let me talk to the children one last time."

Staring at her like she just grew two heads, Rachel could only shake her head.

"Look, Rachel, I'm trying to bury the hatchet!" Flustered, Vikki Rosa brushed her hair back with her hand. "I'm not going to hurt them, only say my goodbyes … and ask a few questions."

"Wh-why?"

Vikki Rosa glared. "Because money can buy anything except youth!" she snapped. "Don't look at me like that! No matter how many face creams I use, I still get wrinkles! I have my hair dyed every month and still get gray hairs! You don't understand, you stupid girl. You have your youth, and even your beauty now, but when you're old and worn, then you'll understand! Then you too would do anything, I mean *anything* to regain what you lost! And what is wrong with that? I'm too young to grow old!"

Rachel shook her head. "You risked the lives of children … children of your friend."

"I regret nothing except agreeing to let you be the babysitter! You were supposed to be a fat lazy cow who kept out of the way!"

"Get out!" Rachel growled, leaping to her feet.

Taking a breath to compose herself, Vikki Rosa didn't budge. "I'm not going anywhere, Rachel." Her voice turned ice cold and she hissed like a snake. "If you won't take the money, it is your own affair. I have to talk to those children. As it turns out, Steven is not the boy we're searching for. It's one of his friends, so he's perfectly safe. We just need to know his closest friends and where they live. Of course, this boy will be found sooner or later, mind you, but you can save us a lot of trouble."

Rachel froze. Her eyes found Marcal. "What is this?"

"Oh, I'm sorry," drawled Vikki Rosa. "I forgot to introduce the new captain of Isabella's Guard. But wait, you know Marcal, don't you?"

"B-but …" Rachel's eyes grew wide as Marcal bowed stiffly.

At the top of the stairs, Steven shook Lisa's shoulder. "Lisa," he hissed.

"Shh! I need to listen!" The redhead leaned forward and hugged her knees tight.

Frowning, Steven slowly stood and slipped away.

Rising to his full height, Marcal pulled at his collar. "When I found Bolder, Rachel, Isabella had the reins. Wolves had decimated most of her men and she didn't know how to fight them … so she asked me to guide her to safety and I agreed." He grimaced. "When morning broke, we started to gather the survivors. She let the men from Durnwirk go, but only if I agreed to return to her guard. I couldn't say no, Rachel. In any case, it wasn't long before Borbu charged into our camp with the news of Rudolph's power. That was when Isabella had me contact you through the mirror—she used a lot of magic to find you, Rachel. She did it to help you."

"You mean to help her." Rachel's throat was dry. "I, I had my doubts about you … I'm sorry I was right."

"Remember when I told you to trust nobody? I meant that." He stepped toward Rachel. "Especially those who are closest to you."

Lisa drew in a sharp breath from where she listened. "Steven," she whispered, "we have to help—" Turning, she realized that she was alone. Steven and Jak had quietly left her.

Chapter Forty-One

Rachel looked for a weapon. Before she could make a grab for the lamp, Marcal drew level with Vikki Rosa's chair and stopped.

"Now that you told Rachel the truth, I will tell my truth." He reached over, grabbed Vikki Rosa's long silky hair, and pulled up. "I will do nothing to harm this girl!" Shrieking, Vikki Rosa covered her face with her hands. "This babysitter is worth many times more than you, woman. Your whole existence is meaningless." Letting go of the hair, he turned and bowed to Rachel. "I mean it, Rachel. I will never harm you."

"No!" screeched Vikki Rosa, grabbing at him. "Isabella said for me to find the child! You're supposed to help me!"

Marcal drew back a hand to strike, but Rachel screamed for him to stop.

"I believe you, Marcal, but let's not do any more damage." She walked over to where the hundred-dollar bills had fallen to the carpet. When she bent down to gather them, Vikki Rosa flinched from her.

"Get back!"

Instead, Rachel offered her the money. "Being rich does have its benefits, *Vikki*. You can always go somewhere far away and start over. Take this money and leave. Never come back and *never* harm another child again. If I ever hear of you again, I will tell Elizabeth and Doug everything. *Everything*!"

With her face going pale, Vikki Rosa trembled as she took the money. "Th-they didn't tell me the kids would be harmed … you must believe me."

"You didn't ask, I bet," Rachel said. "Now get out."

Vikki Rosa stumbled for the door, whining as she went. "I-I need a cab … I didn't bring my car … Come, dear, you can't do this! I had too much to drink …"

Rachel followed her with smoldering eyes. "Walking will do you good."

Rachel slammed the door behind the woman, hopefully to never to see her again.

"Is it wise to let her go?" grumbled Marcal. "A bad egg is still a bad egg even if cracked and fried. She can come back to hurt you."

"I'm not afraid of her," Rachel said, shutting her eyes and leaning against the door. "Oh, I feel sick …"

"You are a strange young woman, Rachel."

Who feels like she's about to throw up. Never before had she felt so confused, angry, and certain all at the same time. Rachel opened her eyes. "Right now I'm just tired … What happens next? Is-is Isabella, is she coming here again?"

Sighing, Marcal wiped his brow. "I think it is over for you, Rachel. Isabella knows her power is weak here. Also … she knows you defeated the dark spirit once already. Sending that woman here was a last grasp at power, but it's finished."

"B-but what about Steven's friend? Is he in danger?"

"Doubtful …" Marcal grimaced. "About the time you left Panterra, the dark spirit's image appeared to Isabella and Borbu. It told them the boy brought was the wrong one, but the chosen boy's presence was on him. It wants them to search for this chosen boy near this area, but I think both wizards understand the dark spirit has already double-crossed them once. It has secretly given power to Rudolph, and this has made them wary. Besides, the dark spirit mentioned that you were here and had to be left alone. This means the dark spirit fears you and knows you can hurt it, maybe even destroy it for good."

"H-how? I can't do anything … it nearly killed me and Steven before. I thought it'd gone …"

"I don't know …" Marcal rubbed his chin. "Tell me what happened on the mountain after you left the mirror."

"Let's go to the kitchen … I think I first need a drink of water."

Lisa found Steven in his room curled on his bed without any covers and fast asleep. Jak lay on the floor by his bed like a watchdog. When Lisa had entered the room, his eyes had flashed open and he gave her a look that sent shivers down her spine. Then, seeing who she was, Jak had yawned and put his head back down, closing his eyes. Lisa still shivered slightly. Jak hadn't been formally introduced to her yet, but she knew he couldn't speak and had been hurt badly in a fall. Watching the sleeping boys for a long moment, she felt a twinge of jealousy. Steven seemed to have had bonded with him pretty tightly.

Then she had a thought. What had Steven wanted to tell her? She had ignored him because she'd thought Rachel was in danger … but the strange man turned out to be a friend, and Steven had gone off and had fallen asleep … Lisa wished she knew what was going on. Being home was great, but she felt as if she was almost a stranger. Rachel and Steven had both changed. They were browner, leaner, and … wiser?

Lisa looked closely at her brother. He still had his little-boy good looks, but his face now seemed even gentler. All his tension had vanished. Just now, he appeared to be deeply relaxed in sleep. No nightmare. Murmuring softly in his sleep, he snuggled against his mattress. Not wanting to wake him, she quietly slipped out. As she did, she missed seeing her brother's hands start to tremble.

Feeling more than a little lonely, Lisa went to her room and closed the door. Hours later she would shower and make a fresh start at resuming life.

Rachel struggled to believe her own words, but successfully told Marcal all that happened. When she was finished, the warrior stroked his beard.

"The question is, what happened to Rudolph …"

"He, he probably ran after the priests. I think those people from the village were pretty mad at being treated so badly."

"Yes, perhaps …" Marcal got up from the table and pushed back his untouched water glass. "I'd better get back. Isabella will want to know what happened … then we'll both return to Panterra and leave you in peace here."

Rachel lifted her eyes hopefully. "She really won't come back?"

"Rachel, believe me. You single-handedly reduced the dark spirit and its pet wizard to almost nothing. She will not try to harm you. She and Borbu are done with your world."

"Oh, I hope so. Th-thank you, Marcal."

"No, it's thank you. I tried to lead you to Isabella to destroy the power of the wizards. Instead, you ended up destroying the power of the dark spirit and showed us that we can choose our own paths with or without wizards. No longer will we follow the dark spirit because of fear. That is something you taught us, Babysitter. With great joy and sadness, I say goodbye."

"Wh-where are you going to go?"

"I'll report to Isabella, and then we'll go back to Panterra." He cleared his throat. "I'll return to Durnwirk. Tell Jak that he may soon gain a brother … if his sister shares the same feelings as I."

Rachel blanched. "W-wait, what about him? What do I do with Jak? He's here with me."

Marcal's eyes widened. Then he grinned. "You're his babysitter, Rachel, remember? He is better off with you for a time."

"But—"

"Goodbye, Rachel."

Rachel watched Marcal leave and shook her head tiredly. "What a summer," she groaned. "But boy, do I have a lot to write about …" First she needed a nap … Too tired to check on the kids, she made her way to the couch and just about collapsed. She dreamt of riding Bolder in a great field of flowers … with Jason at her side.

A blue Ford Mustang met Marcal on the road. Isabella rolled down the passenger window and grinned. "Did the fat babysitter buy it?"

Marcal nodded tersely. "She said Rudolph lost his power and that the dark spirit had vanished."

The wizard snorted. "Serves the traitor right! Then our path is clear … the spirit will return once we find the proper boy."

"Wh-what about Rachel?" Vikki Rosa mumbled miserably from the passenger seat. "She's, she's not fat anymore! She's changed." Her shoulders shook. "Shouldn't we do something to her? I put my sleeping drops in the water pitcher as you said and they should all be asleep by now."

Isabella gave her a nasty look. "Rachel will be going back to her home soon enough. Let her rot there! Besides, she saved me a lot of trouble by stopping Rudolph. You, on the other hand, are past your usefulness and way past your prime. Didn't you tell me that Rachel wants you far, far away? Then I suggest you take her up on that, before I do it myself."

"B-but, I, I—"

"I'll send you to my world!" Isabella's nostrils flared and her eyes started to change colors.

Letting out a strangled yelp, Vikki Rosa grabbed the door handle and tumbled out to the street.

"Remember," Marcal growled, climbing into the car, "if Rachel sees you again, you're a ruined woman. I suggest going someplace very far from here indeed."

The Mustang backed up and spun to face the opposite direction. In a squeal of tires, it tore off, leaving Vikki Rosa in the midst of tears, coughing on fumes and gripping her torn dress.

A cool morning breeze blew through Dougar Circle under the cloudless sky.

Away from the events of Camelot Acres, Geoffrey Brown enjoyed the gentle gust as he stood in his small front yard, tossing the football up in the air. To him, the wind sounded like thousands of cheers blending into a roar as he made a spectacular catch in double coverage during a tight play-off game.

"Geoffrey Brown reaches up and catches another touchdown!"

He no longer imagined his problems to be a battle in the midst of war. Instead, they were now defensive backs in a great football game that he had to juke or bowl over the best way he could.

"Hey, you looking for a star quarterback?" asked a voice behind him.

Caught in the midst of another leaping catch, Geoffrey landed lightly and turned to where Tommy Hunt cruised into his yard and hopped off his bike. "I got one already." Grinning, Geoffrey fired a bullet pass that Tommy barely managed to catch. "Me. Ain't you a little early, dude?"

Tommy shrugged. "I couldn't sleep. I had the feeling you were out here playing football by yourself."

Geoffrey snorted. "It ain't even seven yet."

"Well, what are you doing out here then?"

"Hunting a rabbit. It comes out in the early morning, but I haven't seen it yet. One day I'm going to catch it with my hands and we'll have rabbit stew."

Instead of laughing, Tommy nodded. "That would be cool. Did you set any traps?"

"No way! I said I want to catch it with my hands like I told you."

Tommy tossed the football back. "Is it okay if I watch?"

"Sure, but I don't think it's out right now."

"We can just play catch then. Just pretend the football is the rabbit and let's see your moves."

"You're on!"

Ever since Steven had mysteriously gone on vacation with his babysitter, the two boys had started hanging out. At first they would meet in front of Steven's house and just stare silently. Geoffrey had been convinced the school janitor had kidnapped the boy, but nobody would believe him … except for Tommy. Then one day, a car pulled up next to them and their old teacher Ms. Fathomb stuck her head out.

"What are you boys doing here? Didn't you hear that Steven is vacationing with his babysitter in the Bahamas? I've been hired to keep the house clean for them, so unless you want to help, go enjoy your summer!"

Startled, the boys had nodded and had immediately run off. That was the first day Geoffrey had invited Tommy over to his house. Soon after, the two boys were inseparable. Sometimes Rosco and Oliver would come out and play football with them, but mostly they did fine by themselves. In a week, Steven had become a distant memory that neither wanted to bring up.

From under the bush, the brown rabbit twitched its nose in fear. The early morning was supposed to be free of humans. Instead, two of them loudly occupied the largely barren yard and blocked the path to the green grass. Its nose twitching, the rabbit stared at the paved river of death, just beyond the two humans. Many furry critters had met their demise on that hard, dark surface. To get to the better food, the rabbit had to cross. Danger filled the air.

Suddenly the bushes crashed above the rabbit.

"Sorry," yelled Tommy, working out his arm after his errant pass sailed into the bushes.

Geoffrey hooted with excitement. "There's the rabbit!"

Springing from cover, the startled animal raced for the road.

Tommy leapt in the air. "Get it, dude!"

Diving at the streaking ball of brown fur, Geoffrey just missed.

Tommy rushed to head off the rabbit, but the terrified animal cut between the boys and streaked toward safety.

"It's going for the road!"

"I got it!" Pushing himself off the ground, Geoffrey got to his feet and sprinted after his quarry. For months he'd been waiting for this moment … when he'd finally catch a rabbit barehanded! Just as he reached the road, Tommy suddenly shrieked in terror. "Look out!"

A small green car had appeared on the hill overlooking Geoffrey's house and approached at a normal speed. Suddenly it sped up and swerved straight at where Geoffrey entered the road.

Time stopped as Geoffrey's eyes went as big as two footballs. Barely seeing the car from the corner of his eyes, he managed to throw his weight to the right while pivoting on his foot. His worn sneakers slid on the road as he turned sharply. Without hesitating, he gave a desperate lunge back into his yard. The car's bumper brushed his shoe as he crashed face-first into the hard-packed dirt littered with brown grass.

Stunned, he could barely move. His right thigh and arm burned with pain. Dimly, he was aware of the car screeching to a halt behind him.

"Th-that was cl-close. Is that guy crazy?" Tommy had just regained his breath when the driver's door opened.

Geoffrey could only hear his pounding heart. Then he looked up and saw a horrified look on his friend's face.

"P-Pastor Smith," Tommy choked out.

The rabbit had made it safely into the green grass and had never looked back. It had survived the river of death.

Chapter Forty-Two

The single bulb again hurt the boy's eyes. Once again he lay on an examination table in a small room. This time, no straps held him down, and he appeared to be alone. Blinking, he sat up and looked around. The room appeared to be empty—white walls and a white floor. Then he saw the other examination table—and the blades hanging from the ceiling. Narrowing his eyes, he made out a shadow looming above the other table. A small body lay on the table and did not move.

"Who's that?" he asked, sliding from the table.

The shadowman moved to the other side of the table to block Steven's view. "*Leave us, boy,*" it hissed. "*I'm done with you. I founds a new meals to eat! Go aways or I'll be backs to haunts you*!"

Clenching his fists, Steven shook his head. "Who's on the table?" he whispered.

"*None of your concerns! He is mines*!" The shadowman jerked back, and Steven caught a glimpse of the boy's face. Then the shadowman threw itself headfirst into the boy's chest.

Steven woke with a start. He lay on his side, curled into a tight ball and slick with sweat. Rolling over, he sat up and gasped for breath. Jak lay curled just below him, gently snoring. It all came back—he was back at home and out of danger. He had faced the monster and won. Nightmares would no longer frighten him. Except the wizards were no longer after him—they wanted one of his friends … When first hearing the news, he had started to panic. Which one did they want? How could he warn them all? But then an overwhelming tiredness had dragged him to his bed.

Now, thanks to the shadowman, he knew. Careful not to wake Jak, he crept off his bed and slipped from his room. This was something he needed to do alone.

Jak raised his head just after Steven left. Without making a sound, he followed.

Borbu nudged the back of Geoffrey's leg with his foot. "Are you okay, boy? I saw a rabbit in the road and swerved—I didn't see you until too late." He sounded shaken. Relief spread across his face when Geoffrey nodded and rose shakily to his knees.

"I-I'm okay."

"Good." Breathing a sigh of relief, Borbu reached down and grabbed a hold of Geoffrey's right arm before yanking the surprised boy to his feet. "Now, if I'm not mistaken, you know Steven Winter, correct?"

"P-Pastor, Sm-Smith," Tommy asked, wiping his shorts nervously. "What are you doing?"

"Ah, yes," purred Borbu. "Tommy Hunt. You're one of Steven's good friends, too. Aren't you? What a surprise to find you both together."

"Y-you left our church," babbled Tommy.

Borbu's voice dripped with false sympathy. "Yes, what a shame."

"Let go of me!" Geoffrey, realizing the man hadn't pulled him up to help him, began to struggle.

"None of that, boy," chided Borbu. Moving his other hand to the back of Geoffrey's neck, he squeezed tightly.

"Arrggh!" Geoffrey's face twisted in pain.

"Let him alone!" Tommy cried.

The door crashed open, and Rosco stumbled out in his boxers, wiping sleep from his eyes. "Yo, what the—" Staring at the green car parked almost in their yard, his gaze moved to where a pudgy man gripped Geoffrey by the scruff of the neck.

Immediately the man released Geoffrey and stepped back. "The boy nearly ran into my car!"

Rosco's face tightened and a dangerous look entered his eye. "Keep your hands off my brother!" he said with menace.

At that instant, another car screeched to a stop next to the small green one. Everyone turned to look as Ms. Fathomb swung her ample lower body from the driver's seat.

"Borbu!" she cried. "What are you doing, you fool! Get away from those boys! Now!"

Borbu blinked. "Fatbottom? What are you doing? Where were you when I needed you?"

"Watch your mouth!" Ms. Fathomb said in her teacher's voice. "You said you would never call me that!"

"You're my apprentice—you said you'd never leave me!"

"Boys, keep back. I need to chat with this hunk of stupidity, and we haven't much time."

"What's going on around here?" Rosco demanded, stepping into the yard. "I'm about to call the cops, and I don't even like cops!"

"Relax," snapped Ms. Fathomb. "There's just been a misunderstanding."

"Mess with my brother and there'll be a big misunderstanding when I bust your face!"

Ms. Fathomb never flinched. Used to unruly students, she put both hands on her hips and glared. "There'll be none of that! Young man, you keep back! Borbu, get in your car."

"I'm the wizard! You're the apprentice. I'm sure one of these boys is the one we need!"

"Borbu, you're a fool. I'm a teacher now. I gave up my magic."

"You're the fool!" Borbu pointed a finger at Geoffrey and then Tommy. Both young boys stood as stone statues. "This is all we worked for! We're almost there!" He immediately flinched and retreated several steps when Rosco charged into the yard.

"You get off our property, now!" The angry teen stopped in front of his brother and made a fist.

"Borbu, it's over for us." Ms. Fathomb ignored Rosco and sighed. "When we came here, I chose the teaching profession in this world. You chose to be a spiritual leader. Together we thought we had the plan to find the chosen child and rule Panterra … It was a good idea but a terrible plan. Borbu, neither of us really have it in us to kill a child." She spoke softly as if to one of her students. "I saw Isabella earlier … she told me about

Rudolph. If you continue on this path, you'll only end up like him."

Contorting his face, Borbu started to sneer, but thought better of it when seeing Rosco's muscles ripple as the teen flexed from only a few feet away. While not the biggest guy, Rosco looked to be one of the strongest. In his boxer shorts, he looked like a boxer ready to go into the ring. Looking once more at Tommy, Borbu winced. "P-perhaps you're right … I, I guess there're better things to do with my time."

"Come, Borbu. Follow me and we'll discuss it over some coffee." Ms. Fathomb looked over at Rosco. "You keep an eye on these two boys, you hear? There might be another looking for them."

Rosco frowned. "What the—"

"Watch your mouth, young man!" snapped Ms. Fathomb. "I did you a favor, but this is the last I'll help you. I said watch the boys, and I mean it!"

As the two cars pulled away, Rosco whirled on Geoffrey.

"You gonna explain to me what just happened?"

Shaking, Geoffrey looked back at where Tommy still stood frozen. "I-I don't know," he stammered.

Tommy gulped, finally relaxing a little. "That guy … he was our pastor. He disappeared almost a month ago. My mom says he's a bad man and a liar."

"Well, if he comes back he's a hurt bad man. What about the fat woman?"

"She is, um, was our teacher."

Frowning, Rosco shook his head. "It's too early for this, man."

Tommy suddenly gasped. "Look! There's a guy watching us. From down the street …"

Whirling, Rosco started to glare. Suddenly his eyes popped wide and his mouth dropped wider. "Th-that's the homeless dude," Rosco finally croaked. He rubbed his eyes, but the man didn't disappear. Standing with his arms folded, dressed in a long black coat, he stood seven houses down on the side of the street. White hair glinted from the top of an otherwise clean-shaven face. Rosco would recognize that man anywhere—especially in his nightmares. "He-he's Red."

Geoffrey went deathly still. "I'm scared."

"Get inside the house, both of you. Tommy, bring your bike. Does your mom know where you are?"

"N-no, but she won't be up for another few hours." Ever since the Pastor Smith incident, his mom had stopped interfering with her son's life. His dad, who lived upstate, had threatened to take Tommy to live with him if she ever tried again. At this moment, though, Tommy really wished his mother was standing next to him.

Seeing Rosco's reaction to the man known as Red brought the icy hand of fear back around Tommy's heart. This day, which had started so promisingly, had turned nightmarish very quickly.

Weeks ago, when Geoffrey had talked about Red kidnapping Steven, Rosco blew up and demanded that Geoffrey never mention it again. But, Tommy now realized, Rosco never had contradicted his younger brother.

Steven reached the end of the road and slowed to a walk. He entered the wooded path cautiously. Over the past few weeks he'd grown even leaner and developed tougher skin. Not bothering to stop for shoes, he'd slipped from the house and had broken into a run as soon as he hit the driveway. Now he slowly went forward into the trees. He had a real problem. He'd no clue where Geoffrey lived. The two had only met at school and had never visited each other's homes.

Biting his lip in frustration, Steven breathed deeply to relax. That was when he realized … the monster never stirred from within. Looking down at his blue and white-striped T-shirt, bought from the thrift store, he ran both hands over his stomach and felt nothing. Yanking up the elastic band of his loose athletic shorts, he breathed deeply. The monster was gone. Instead of relief, Steven felt uneasy …

Overhead, the sun continued to rise, but no birds sang as a strange quietness covered the landscape like an unwanted blanket.

Reaching the cracked road of Dougar Circle, Steven tugged at his hair. Which way should he go? Just as he decided to go right, the same direction he and Lisa had gone when getting her bike, he heard something from behind him. Turning, he was surprised to see two girls coming around a bend on bikes. Seeing him, they squealed as one and pedaled faster.

"Steven!" they called together.

Caught in the open, Steven could only stare and wait.

Susie Perkins and Callie Edwards braked their bikes in front of Steven. Both stared in amazement.

"We thought you were in the Bahamas!" Susie said.

"Yeah," chimed in Callie. "Swim coach was real mad that you didn't tell him and had that rich lady call instead."

"What are you two doing here?" Steven asked in genuine confusion.

"Well, when our friend, meaning you, ditched us for the summer, we decided to save the world," Susie said, grinning.

"Yeah, we're part of the bike recycle team. We ride every morning looking for bottles to recycle."

The girls both turned to show him half-full backpacks slung across their backs.

"Oh." Steven looked distractedly past them. "Do, um, you know where Geoffrey lives?"

"Geoffrey Brown? Sure we do." Susie frowned. "I thought you stayed away from him, though."

"It's really important. I need to find him."

The two girls exchanged nervous looks. They vividly remembered the day Geoffrey had led Steven out of school into the trap. None of the teachers believed it, but all the kids knew Geoffrey had turned on Steven and helped set it up.

"Okay," sighed Susie. "Take my bike. Just cut between those houses. It's a shortcut. Turn left at the road and go until you reach a hill. Geoffrey's house is at the bottom, the first on the right. We'll catch up with you there."

"The small one with all the dead grass in front," Callie told him, nodding.

"Okay, thanks." Taking Susie's bike, he pointed it in the right direction and started pedaling without looking back.

"Why is he barefoot?" Callie asked, frowning.

"I don't know, but we'd better hurry and follow him. Put down your bag and let me on the handlebars. We'll save the world later."

As the girls struggled to get on a single bike, Jak dashed from the trees and went after Steven.

"Rachel? Hello? Rachel? I can't believe I'm talking into this thing … Rachel?"

"Let me try, hag!"

"Watch your manners, boy! I'll use this mirror to paddle you!"

"Ah, you're hogging it!"

"Go back with your sister and break your neck on that foolish board."

Rachel blinked and opened her eyes. "Who's there?" she groaned. "Is it time to ride again?"

"Rachel! I hear you! Come and pick up the mirror! I can't see anything and we need to talk to you!"

That sounded like the woman's voice …

"Yes! Hurry up! We want to talk to Steven!" And that was definitely Jan …

"And Courtney!"

"Joe?" muttered Rachel. The voices sounded muffled and far away. Sitting up, she saw she was on the couch back in the house—far away from Panterra, right? "Wh-where are you?" she asked more loudly.

"*Pick up the mirror and hurry*!" said the woman's voice. "*You might be in danger*!"

"Danger … when am I not in danger?" Still half asleep, Rachel half walked, half stumbled into the kitchen. She started blinking rapidly.

"You there, Rachel?"

Nobody was there, and her purse sat on the table. The voices were coming from her purse. "I knew it … I've gone crazy."

"Rachel? Are you there?"

"*I'm sure she heard you the first million times, hag*," Jan's voice said.

"Shut up! Rachel?"

Shaking her head clear, Rachel ran to her purse. "This happened to me before," she muttered.

Sure enough, deep in her purse, under the nearly empty sunscreen bottle and by the lip balm, she found a familiar-looking mirror. *This must have been the one Marcal used to contact me on the mountain.* He'd either left it by accident, or possibly on purpose put it in her purse. Looking into it, Rachel saw the woman's old familiar face looking worried.

"Wh-what are you doing in there?" Rachel said stupidly.

"Thank goodness I reached you! Listen, Rachel. We're still on the mountain. The people here drove out all the priests and are treating us like heroes. Little Darvy is about to be crowned official king."

"Uh, okay, that's great."

"*I don't know, Rachel.*" The woman sounded worried. "*I found a library here, and I've been doing a lot of research … you know, for the book I'm starting to write.*"

"*I found it,*" Jan's voice said from behind the woman. "*Not you.*"

"I don't understand—"

"Shut up! Oh, not you, Rachel, just the stupid boy. Anyway, I found some books in English. That's how I found out how to use this mirror thing … but more importantly, it turns out you were right."

"I'm always right!"

"Not you, stupid boy! Rachel!"

"I was right? About what?"

"Remember what you said about the priests' power coming only from the people giving it to them? Well, the spirit in the cave is the same way. The only power it has is the power the wizards give it. It feeds off of fear and evil—things they do for it, like sacrificing people, make it stronger. The wizards gain their power by allowing the dark spirit inside their souls to live with them. The more fear and evil they cause, the stronger they are. Not only that, but the spirit lies to them. There's magic in this land that the spirit can't control. For one, according to this book, water portals can be created by anyone who has the right belief and mortal blood of the first comers to Panterra."

"Uh, I don't understand …"

"Believe me, neither do I."

"Because you're stupid."

"Shut up, stupid girl! Rachel, whoever wrote the book studied this matter for a long time. And Rachel, he claims to be from New York."

"Huh?"

"Some guy who calls himself Aerrius wrote all this down—he says he wanted to find a way to destroy the dark spirit and free Panterra or something or another. I tell you, Rachel, this is pure crazy."

Rachel gulped. "Aerrius …" She thought back to the robed figure at the pool that could change faces and ultimately was eaten by the spirit—did the first wizard of Panterra actually start as somebody who sought to destroy the dark spirit? She shuddered. She remembered something her mother told her. Good intentions could easily turn into terrible actions that come back and bite you if you're not careful. "Yeah, uh, I agree," Rachel said, talking to the mirror. "It's crazy. But it's over, right? We beat Rudolph."

"No! That's why I contacted you! This Aerrius guy says the spirit gains power by possessing people who let it inside them. It only loses power in the presence of pure love. It gains power by turning that love into hate."

"What does that have to do with me?"

"*Rachel, the dark spirit has vanished. And so has Rudolph. There's a good chance, I think, that it now lives inside Rudolph. According to the book, Aerrius allowed himself to be possessed by the spirit in order to gain its thoughts. According to him, the dark spirit must have a pure boy willingly sacrificed in order for it to gain full control and power of a human body. Until then, even if possessed, the human has some control. However, once the dark spirit has complete control of a human body, there can be no stopping it. Spirit powers combined with human powers would create a monster that could not die or be destroyed. Love would weaken the spirit, but strengthen the human. Hate would weaken the human, but strengthen the spirit. Rachel, weapons could hurt the human, but not the spirit. They would not work. And …*" The woman paused. "*If the sacrificed boy is from Earth, the monster would be able to have power on Earth and on Panterra. That's the dark spirit's plan.*"

"I-I don't know how this can be possible …"

"Rachel, I think anything is possible. This Aerrius must have been tricked by the dark spirit. Eventually, instead of being against the dark spirit, he became more and more in love with it … the dark spirit took him over. And now it has Rudolph."

"No …" Rachel shook her head. "This can't be happening."

"Rudolph was in the great hall, remember? That means he had access to the dark spirit and to a water portal. The dark spirit cannot be destroyed unless it doesn't have a home to rest in—then it must return where it came from. The spirit could very easily have hidden and then entered Rudolph after you left. Now they're probably both after the boy that would give them supreme power. And then they'll be after you next."

"Oh, no," Rachel groaned. "Why didn't I destroy him when I had the chance?"

"Because you're a good person, that's why! Much better than these brats here! Jan, you can't ride on the walls with that!"

"But what do I do?"

"Serves you right for falling! You're not even properly healed, idiot! Sorry, what was that?"

"What do I do?"

"You have to protect whatever boy Rudolph is going after and watch out for Steven and Lisa. Remember, if Rudolph can get you to hate, he can only gain power. Hurting those kids would be a great way to make you hate. And that's not all. There's news of a babysitter army marching in this direction. They're after all the wizards, Rachel. That means the people here have lost their fear of the spirit and of wizards. The only way for wizards to survive is to help the dark spirit get the child. So the wizards will all be out helping the dark spirit."

Rachel found it hard to breathe. "But-but, Marcal … he said Isabella had given up."

"I wouldn't count on it. I think everyone here is tired of being under wizards and their dark magic. She would have no life without the dark spirit in power."

"Why can't this nightmare end?"

"Rachel?" Lisa called from the stairs. "Rachel, who are you talking to?"

Swallowing, Rachel lowered the mirror. "L-Lisa? Can you get Steven and Jak down here?"

"Aren't they already down there? I just finished a shower and went to tell them to wash up, but they're gone."

"*Oh, no,*" gasped the woman's voice. "*It may have already started*!"

Steven slowed the bike to a stop and went still. No monster had warned him, but after spending hours in the woods with Jak, he'd developed a sense for reading nature. While he couldn't pinpoint why or how, he knew something or somebody was following him. Looking around, he saw nothing … and heard nothing—not even a bird. He stood on a rough patch of a dirt trail between a drainage ditch on his left and the grassy backyard of a small rundown house on his right. Past the drainage ditch was a steep drop-off covered with trees and brush. The path ended just past where the ditch directed the water down into the patch of woods. There, Steven could see the road that led down to Geoffrey's house. While he could see the pavement ahead, something told him he wouldn't reach it.

"Who's there?" he asked suddenly.

A faint chuckle came from behind a tree on the other side of the ditch.

"Clever, Steven. You have the sense of a wolf." Lineus jumped lightly over the ditch and stepped onto the path three feet behind Steven. "I see you ride metal horses in this horrid world. Nice color … pink is what they call it, right? Isn't that a color for little girls?"

Steven gripped the handlebars tightly as he looked toward the voice. Lineus still bore the marks of their last meeting. His eyes were puffy and blackened, and an ugly bruise covered his chin. He wore a twisted smile and held a six-inch blade in his right hand.

"You always were a clever little boy, weren't you?" he said scathingly. "You never trusted me with riding lessons … but perhaps I can give you a different lesson. One similar to the one I gave Jak."

Steven immediately stomped a foot on the pedal and tried to escape. Starting from a full stop, he had little chance.

Growling, Lineus easily caught up with him before he could gather speed. "Got you, you little pup!" He grabbed the back of the boy's shirt and yanked back. Jerked from the seat, Steven landed painfully on the back tire and barked his shins on the pedals. Next, he lost his grip on the handlebars and tumbled to the side. The bike fell just in front of him.

Lineus breathed heavily as he stood over the stunned boy. He sneered, "You were a little monster last time, but now I got you where I want you!" Lineus knelt next to the boy and grabbed the back of his neck. He cruelly shoved Steven's head into the path. "Tell me where you're going and who your friend is!"

Twisting and kicking, Steven managed to throw a foot back into Lineus's stomach and crawl free. Lineus's hands made a desperate grab that caught the bottom of the boy's shorts. Steven desperately pulled free, but tripped in the process.

Immediately Lineus pounced on the boy's back. He snarled in triumph as he held him down. He leaned close to Steven's ear and hissed, "I'll stick this blade in your spine if you don't cease your struggles!"

Then all of a sudden Steven was free again. Unleashing a strangled yell, the traitor had fallen away. Not knowing what happened, Steven rose to his feet and yanked up his shorts. Snatching up the bike, he ran down the path without looking back. At any moment he expected Lineus to grab him again. It never happened.

He reached the road and managed to hop over the bike's seat. As he pedaled, he heard Lineus's screaming reach a new octave. Then it was cut off by the deep-throated growl of a large and angry dog. It sounded as if one of the neighbors didn't like prowlers in their backyard.

It hadn't been a dog that had jumped on Lineus.

When the young man from Panterra had knelt with his knife poised over Steven's back, he'd felt another presence. Before he could process what it could be, a brown blur leapt from his right and slammed into him, knocking him free of Steven. Sharp teeth sank into the arm holding onto the knife and sharp claws latched onto his back.

Landing hard on his side, Lineus lost his breath and knife at the same time. He also lost the boy he'd been following … Isabella would not be happy—already she'd threatened to turn him into a toad when he'd awoken in the inn with Rachel and Steven gone.

"I can't lose again," he gasped, trying to shake off the animal on top of him.

Then he heard the growl in his ear.

"W-wolf," he whispered, growing very still and very fearful. Turning his neck carefully, he looked over his shoulder and received the shock of his life. Not a wolf, but something far worse stared back at him.

Screaming, he kicked and shook his body with a frenzied panic. The thing above him growled and roared, slashing at him with sharp nails. Suddenly Lineus rolled free and into the ditch. Finding his feet, he screamed and ran as if death pursued him. He couldn't help but look back to see if the thing pursued. The last glimpse Lineus had before leaving the ditch was of a small boy baring teeth and hissing at him … The same boy Lineus had killed not a few days before. Something went loose in his pants as the first tree rose up and bashed him in the head. Darkness rescued him as his body fell.

Chapter Forty-Three

Lisa stomped her foot and glared at Rachel. "We're just going to sit in here while Steven is out there, probably in danger?"

"No, we're not." Rachel grabbed her purse and stuffed the mirror back inside. The woman said she would continue to search for ways to defeat the dark spirit and would contact Rachel as soon as she had news. Lisa and Rachel had spent the past ten minutes searching the house and then the garage for any clue of Steven's and Jak's whereabouts. They found Steven's shoes and his bike, but nothing else. "Where do you think Steven went?"

"Dougar Circle," Lisa said after a brief pause. "I know he has a friend there … Oh, I can't believe he didn't get me! I bet he's going there to warn him." She remembered that Steven got up just after Vikki Rosa said the wizards were searching for one of his friends.

"Do you know where on Dougar Circle?"

"No, but I know how to find out."

Lisa stepped past the old twisted oak tree and approached the rundown house with more than a little fear. Only Rachel and Jason at her side kept her going … that and knowing this might be the only way to find Steven.

Jason yawned. Rachel had called his cell phone just as he left the shower, to tell of Steven's disappearance. Hair still wet, he wore an old T-shirt and sweatpants. Courtney and Jakey were asleep in their beds … and he wished he could join them.

Knocking on the door, Lisa waited. She heard movement on the other side and was glad to know she hadn't woken up the house.

The door opened, and Macie, the girl who had nearly stolen her bike, stared at her in surprise. "What are you doing here?" Macie demanded, suddenly wide awake.

"We need your help," Lisa said to her. "Please."

Seeing Jason and Rachel, Macie immediately tried to shut the door.

"Wait!" Lisa said, jamming her foot in the way. "We're just trying to find my brother!"

Macie stared at her. Then she asked, "Why you got the cops with you?"

"We're not cops," Rachel said quickly. "I'm the babysitter, and this is my neighbor."

Jason nodded tiredly.

Macie then frowned. "What you want me to do about it?" she asked, sounding confused.

Lisa spoke in a rush, "Just tell us where Geoffrey Brown lives. I promise, he may be in danger with my brother. We just want to help him!"

Macie bit her lip as if deciding something. "Is this about the bullying?"

"Huh?" Lisa asked. "No, it's extremely urgent!" She stomped her foot in frustration. "Hurry and just tell us!"

The girl shrugged. "Rosco don't hang with us no more. You remember the house I chased you to and your brother burned his little behind? That's where the Browns live."

"Oh, thank you!" Lisa gave Macie a quick hug and ran from the steps. "Come on, we have to hurry!"

Jason and Rachel rushed to keep up.

Behind them, Macie quietly closed the door.

"Who was that?" Toothy called from his bedroom.

"Don't know … Friends, I guess."

Steven jumped off the bike and ran to the front door of the house at the bottom of the hill. The bike had just fallen by the time he knocked.

Inside, Oliver grunted from where he slumped on the couch watching an early baseball game on TV.

"Anybody order pizza?" he asked lazily. "Or did we forget to pay a bill?"

Nobody smiled. Rosco, on the edge of the couch beside his brother, immediately shot to his feet. Sitting on the floor, Tommy and Geoffrey looked at each other.

Nana had just left for work, and the four boys were alone. The homeless man had since disappeared from sight but remained very present on their minds. Before allowing Nana to leave, Rosco had checked all the windows to make sure the guy wasn't waiting outside. They hadn't told the old woman anything, but she had sensed their anxiety.

"You boys just sit tight inside until I get back," she had said. "Tommy, if you want, you can go call your mom and ask if you can stay the day. You can even spend the night, if you like."

"Yes, ma'am," he said with feeling. "Thank you."

Now somebody was at the door …

Dancing nervously, Steven appeared to be in the need of the bathroom when the door cracked open.

"What do you want?" growled a deep, unfriendly voice. It sounded familiar, but Steven couldn't place it.

"Does Geoffrey live here? I need to speak to him."

A pause. Then the voice growled again. "He ain't talking to you." The door shut.

Steven immediately banged on the closed door. "It's important!" he called.

"Get off our property!" ordered the muffled voice. "We'll call the cops!"

"My, my, boy," purred a voice behind him. "I don't think they like you very much. Are you sure this is where your friend lives?"

It was as if ice water went down Steven's back. Freezing, he sucked his teeth. From behind him, Rudolph sauntered up the driveway.

"Maybe you're just not knocking hard enough. Let me try."

Steven narrowed his eyes as he turned. His lips went tight. "What are you doing here?" he asked.

"Boy, is that how you speak to your elders?" Rudolph's shadow fell over the boy as the tall man stood just in front of him. "You thought you beat me, didn't you? *DIDN'T YOU!*"

Steven jumped as his eyes grew wide. The voice rose from Rudolph like it came from the monster. "Nobody is home," he managed to say.

"Good, then they won't have to see this." Rudolph jerked out an arm and grabbed Steven's hair. Grinning like a maniac, he shoved the boy backward before letting go. Slamming hard into the door, Steven bounced forward and then fell to his hands and knees.

Stepping calmly over the boy, Rudolph slammed both his fists on the door. The whole house seemed to shake. "Open up before I get angry!" he bellowed. "Rosco, don't be a fool and open up! I just want to talk to young Geoffrey. That's all."

Twisting to his backside, Steven raised a foot and kicked Rudolph in the back of the knee. "Don't listen to him!" he screamed. "He's trying to kill you!"

"That's enough, you brat!" Rudolph spun around and tried to stomp on Steven's middle.

Rolling to his left, Steven dodged the foot and rose to his knees. He threw himself at the wizard, trying to grab the long legs.

"No you don't!" Rudolph stepped back and kicked the boy in the thigh.

Watching from the window, Geoffrey flinched. Once he had stood by and let his friend suffer because of this man. Now it was happening all over.

"No," he whispered.

Tommy stood behind him and gulped. "What do we do?"

Rosco and Oliver were shouting from down the hall, where they were looking for baseball bats. Both wanted the boys to stay put.

"We help Steven," Geoffrey said simply. "Let's go."

Rudolph grasped Steven by the collar and easily lifted the boy to his feet. "I no longer need you, do I, boy?" Suddenly his voice deepened and changed as he said, "*BE CAREFUL! THIS ONE*

CAN RESIST MY POWER." Then his voice went back to normal. "Ridiculous! I'm the most powerful wizard in two worlds!" It was like the man had two minds. His face twisted. "*DON'T BE A FOOL!*"

Flailing wildly, Steven did his best to break away, but the way Rudolph argued in two voices confused him momentarily. Suddenly his feet dangled from the ground.

"Witness my power!" Rudolph tossed Steven into the yard like he would throw an old pillow.

Landing hard on the seat of his shorts, Steven rolled backward and ended up on his side with very little breath. It suddenly seemed plain. His monster had left him and entered Rudolph … Only the man had no self-control and had let the monster completely loose. Rudolph, he thought, must be the real shadowman.

The door behind Rudolph opened, but the wizard ignored it. Leering now, he wiped his mouth as he stepped toward Steven. "You think I can't destroy this boy? Watch!" He raised both his hands and grinned. His brilliant blue eyes flashed a terrible red. Overhead, several feet above the small house behind Rudolph, a green mist formed against the blue sky. Bolts of energy flared from Rudolph's fingertips.

"Charge!" screamed Geoffrey. At first, shocked at seeing the frightful sight of the man he knew as Red standing with electricity coming from his hands, he now tore from his petrified state and launched himself in an effort to save his friend. Crashing into Rudolph's back, he sent the tall man staggering. Green bolts of energy blasted into the ground. One bolt reached Steven and then abruptly fizzled. Geoffrey bounced back as if electrocuted himself. He hit Tommy and both boys fell in front of the door.

"Wh-what happened?" Rudolph gasped, regaining his footing. He lifted his hands and tried to induce a bolt of energy, but nothing happened.

Geoffrey snarled and disentangled himself from Tommy. "I'll rip your face off if you hurt my friend again!"

Rudolph turned to him and all at once nodded approvingly. "*GOOD BOY! COME TO ME!*"

"No," gasped Steven. He struggled to sit up. He rubbed his shin where the green bolt had struck. A puzzled expression was on his face, and he had trouble coming up with words. "He wants you to go to him … just stay back."

Rudolph shook his head. "No. No!" He again tried to unleash an energy attack, only to fail once more.

"Wh-what's he doing?" Tommy cried, scooting back.

Geoffrey shook his head. "I-I don't know. That guy is nuts."

Screaming in frustration and almost fear, Rudolph ran to where Steven struggled to stand. Gripping the boy's shoulders, he bent to the boy's level. "What did you do to my power?"

"Leave him!" Geoffrey cried. Before he could run and attack, Rosco grabbed his arm and pulled him back.

"Stay back," his brother whispered. "We're in trouble." He wrapped both arms around Geoffrey's chest, keeping him firmly in place.

Steven shook his head as if trying to clear it. Looking fearfully up into Rudolph's eyes, he started to waver. "It's all in your head …" he rasped.

"You stupid!" Rudolph shook the boy like a rag doll. "Stupid boy!"

Steven's eyes slid shut and he went limp. Unable to take any more, his body shut down.

Rudolph's face strained with desperation as he held the unconscious boy. Then he let go and stepped back as if burned. Steven collapsed face-first and kept still. Somebody from the street clapped sarcastically.

Rudolph turned wildly to see Isabella leaning against a freshly parked blue Mustang. Just behind the Mustang was his old pickup. Both vehicles had arrived unnoticed. From the back of the pickup, a crowd of warriors from Panterra climbed out. These were members of Isabella's Guard.

"What is this?" he snarled. "*MY ALTERNATIVE PLAN,*" he immediately roared. "*YOU CANNOT BE TRUSTED!* No, no!" he wailed back. "Keep her back!"

"Rudolph, you always were a fool," Isabella sneered. "The boy you want nearly leapt into your arms, and yet you went after the useless boy we no longer need. Step aside and let your master finish the job!"

Rudolph looked desperate and elated at the same time. "No! *YES*!" he cried nearly in one breath.

"Marcal!" barked Isabella. "Lead the men. I want the boys alive. Kill the rest."

Rudolph's face twisted in pain when he saw the warrior climb from the passenger side of the Mustang. "You!" he seethed. "You're the one who killed my daughter!"

Marcal bowed his head and said, "It was a mistake, Rudolph." He crossed the road calmly. Only his eyes betrayed a deep sadness as he gazed at the tall, white-haired man trembling in the middle of the yard. "A terrible mistake."

The pickup's door opened, and a massive man oozed out. He joined the six warriors who had started to gather at Marcal's back. Fresh from the kitchens, Dosco's loose flesh quivered in anticipation. He looked ready to prepare a good meal. His eyes were on the children.

"The only mistake was letting you live!" screamed Rudolph. "I told you that my wife and daughter were still inside that building! I told you!"

"You did," acknowledged Marcal.

"Yet you still had the wizards destroy it!" Rudolph shouted. White spit flung from his mouth. "You murdered them!"

"I did not know they would obliterate it, Rudolph … I only meant for them to scare the villagers … We had just battled and were exhausted. We needed food and nobody would give us any."

"I needed my family!" Rudolph cried. "I *still* need them!"

"I know." Marcal closed his eyes. "After that day, I left and distanced myself from all wizards and their wars … I lost everything too."

Rudolph covered his face in his hands and shook his head. "You know nothing about loss!" he cried hoarsely. "And now you've come to finish the job. To slay me too. Is that it?"

"I don't want to hurt anyone," Marcal said calmly.

"Careful, Marcal," Isabella said coolly, standing up. "I gave you an order." She started to cross the street after Marcal but did so at a relaxed pace.

Marcal's shoulders slumped a little. "Isabella," he said, "the more bodies we leave, the harder it will be to leave quietly."

"Very well," Isabella said irritably, pausing at the grass. "Just grab the two boys at the door and get it done with!"

"No!" cried Rudolph. He reached in his cloak and withdrew a knife. "If anybody comes closer I'll kill the boy!"

Oliver slipped behind Rosco. "Man," he whispered. "What did you do this time?"

"N-nothing," he spluttered.

"Yeah, well, they ain't the cops and I don't think they're selling magazines." Oliver slid a baseball bat into Rosco's hand. "When whatever happens, happens, we'll step up to the plate, right, bro?"

Gulping, Rosco nodded.

When following Steven on the shortcut trail, Callie and Susie heard the vicious snarling of a dog and immediately retreated back to the road they had started from. Taking the long way around, they suddenly veered off the road when they saw a strange, green cloud emerge in the sky in the area of Geoffrey's house. Susie nearly flew off the handlebars. She jumped down and sprinted to the edge of the hill overlooking the green mist.

"Oh my gosh, Callie … We need to call the police."

Shaking, Callie nodded. "B-but how? I didn't bring my phone!"

"And I left mine in my bag with the bottles," groaned Susie. Then she snapped her fingers. All around the street, doors were opening and people were staring out. "Somebody will have a phone. Come on!"

As the girls hurried to the nearest house, Lisa raced around the corner and didn't stop until reaching the top of the hill.

"We're too late!" she said, pointing to the cloud. "Look."

"At least we found the right house," Jason said grimly, slowing up behind her with Rachel at his side.

Rachel looked down with horror. The entire time she had told herself it was all just a false alarm. Steven would be playing in the yard or something … Instead, Isabella stood near a small yard talking animatedly to Rudolph. Marcal stood beside her, looking very much a part of the conversation. Seven men in armor and wearing swords stood in the road, facing two teenage boys with baseball bats. Tommy and another boy hovered around the door of the house. And Steven … He lay yards behind Rudolph, motionless in the grass. He looked like a forgotten toy cast aside.

"Wh-what do we do?" Lisa whispered.

Rachel looked around quickly. "They haven't seen us yet …" she muttered. Then she spotted Callie's abandoned bike and slid her purse off her shoulder. "My mom used an ice cream cone," she mumbled. "This will have to do for me."

"Huh?" Jason asked with a perplexed look.

Lisa actually managed a smile. "I think I know the plan."

"Rudolph," sighed Isabella. "I said put that away. Despite everything, you're still my apprentice. And you seem quite adept at magic when you're not being a fool. Let's discuss this and work it out as wizards."

"I want my power back!" Rudolph waved his knife in Isabella's face, but without real intention. His eyes were red with tears, frustration, and anger.

"And you shall have it, but first we must finish this! Don't you understand that my power is also weak here? We must take the boy with us and finish the ritual in another place."

"How can I trust you?" wailed her former apprentice.

"We can do it together!" Isabella gave a slight nod toward Marcal and indicated Rudolph.

Marcal gave a brief shake of his head but stepped closer to the crazed man.

So intent were they on each other, none of them noticed the bicycle gliding down the hill, picking up speed.

Rudolph gave a maniacal grin and gripped his knife tighter. "Yes. Let's do this together!"

"That is what I said," Isabella said through gritted teeth. "Now let's do it!"

That was when the bike plowed into her back.

Wearing a determined look, Rachel guided the bike downhill to pick up as much speed as possible and then aimed the bike straight at the wizard. She refused to flinch. The front tire struck just between the wizard's feet, ramming the handlebars into Isabella's kidneys.

Grunting in pain, the wizard flew forward as if shot from a gun. Rachel helped her momentum by flying over the handlebars and slamming into the wizard's shoulders. Isabella went headlong into a shocked Rudolph, sending both into the dirt.

Rachel landed heavily on top and rolled clear. Her adrenaline roared and she didn't allow herself to pause. Pushing herself to her feet, she slid her purse from her shoulder and reached inside to pull out the last of the sunscreen.

Startled by what had just happened, the armed men stared at her in shock. Marcal was the first to react.

"Rachel!" he cried. "Are you insane?"

"Only for believing you!" she shot back. Staggering, she tried to run for the house. "Get everyone inside!" she yelled. "Especially Steven!" Her knee flared with pain and her left shoulder didn't want to move.

"Get her!" wheezed Isabella, picking herself off of Rudolph. Blood ran from a gash on her cheek. "Now!"

Marcal hesitated, but the other men rushed to cut Rachel off from the house. None, however, seemed too keen on attacking the young girl. Seeing what she just did to two wizards had made them wary. This, after all, was the feared babysitter.

Rosco and Oliver glanced at each other.

"Now or never, bro," Oliver said.

Rosco nodded. "Now. Geoff, you and Tommy grab your friend and get inside!"

Together, the two brothers brandished their bats and charged the men from behind.

Seeing their attack, Rachel raised her sunscreen bottle and, swinging her purse, also charged from the front.

One of the warriors tried to brandish a sword, but Rachel smashed his face with a heavy blow from her purse. Forcing her left shoulder into action, she sprayed another warrior in the face with a steady stream of sunscreen.

The man fell back with a bloodcurdling shriek, scratching at his eyes. Then the Brown brothers struck.

Rosco chopped a brutal blow into the back of the helmet of one man while Oliver swung for the legs of another.

Caught again by surprise, the armored warriors scattered in disarray. Before they knew what was happening, Rosco and Oliver were pelting them with blows without letup. These were men who had volunteered for the Wizard's Guard because it promised easy riches without much effort. With Isabella gone for long periods of time, their drilling had been less than par. Most had never faced real combat or even received proper training. To them, a battle meant terrorizing defenseless villagers for riches. In the face of real resistance, they just wanted to run.

"No!" screamed Isabella, now sitting on top of Rudolph. "Where's Bodin? He's to bring the reinforcements! Marc—" She stopped, her breath literally knifed from her. Jerking, she looked down and saw Rudolph's face twisted in hatred. In his hand he held the hilt of his knife. The blade had disappeared inside of her gut.

"I've waited a long time for this, Isabella," spat Rudolph. "Now your power is mine!"

Coughing, Isabella slumped to her side and could only stare in disbelief as her life started to leak away. Rudolph pushed himself to his feet and grinned evilly. A surge of power shot threw his body.

Marcal cried out in alarm. He immediately dropped to her side. "Isabella! No!"

"Now you know some of my pain," Rudolph snarled at him.

The two men locked eyes for a second and then with primal howls leapt at each other's throats.

Rachel staggered back as the man with burning eyes refused to go down. "Steven! Get to the house!"

The boy was beginning to stir as Tommy and Geoffrey grabbed his arms and pulled him up.

Before Rachel could offer help, the man swung a fist blindly toward her head. Ducking, she beat him off with her purse. Just as it looked as if Isabella's forces were beaten, Jason screamed from the hill. He and Lisa sprinted full speed toward the melee.

At first it looked as if he and Lisa were coming to join the fighting. Then from behind him, a host of warriors brandishing clubs and swords poured over the hill giving chase. A warrior in an open-faced helmet led the charge. He snarled like a wild animal through a brutally marked face lined with fresh scars.

Lisa gripped the mirror like a baton in a death relay as she stayed yards ahead of the charging mob.

Just as Rachel had set up to start her bike attack, the old woman had reappeared in the mirror. Rachel had shoved the mirror at Lisa and had told her to find out what was happening just before leaving on the bike. Jason, totally lost, had looked between the girls and then watched stupefied as Rachel went down the hill.

"She's coming back right?" he'd asked Lisa.

Lisa had shushed him. The woman had started talking to her in the mirror … and then from behind them in the street they had heard a terrible noise of marching. Soon after, Isabella's warriors appeared, running straight at them.

Chapter Forty-Four

Callie and Susie stared out the front window of the house closest to the top of the hill. A middle-aged couple had answered the door and let them in without questions. At first they thought the overexcited girls were crazy and they wanted to call their moms—not the police. But then the twenty men dressed in dark armor and carrying weapons rushed by.

Behind them, the middle-aged woman set the phone down. "Well, I called the police, but from the looks of it, they may be too late."

"Too late, my foot!" snapped the woman's husband, striding to the door. "If that bunch of wild hooligans thinks they can march into our neighborhood and raise a ruckus, they got another thing coming!"

"What are you going to do?" demanded the woman.

Her husband answered with a wicked gleam in his eyes. "Get out there and show them young pups a lesson!"

The man was not alone. Neighbors called neighbors, and soon the word spread. Dougar Circle was under attack—a gang of pasty-faced hoodlums were after the Brown boys. Suddenly, the street was filled with bodies. Men of all ages came out with chunks of wood, baseball bats, and in some cases, old military bayonets and rifles.

"I'm fine," Steven said, trying to free himself from his friends. "Besides, they're not after me."

"We don't care!" Geoffrey said hotly. He and Tommy still gripped Steven's arms. "We ain't leaving you."

Steven's eyes went wide. "Really? Then look out!"

Tommy and Geoffrey turned to see a massive man wielding a butcher's knife coming at them.

As the reinforcements charged down the hill, the tide of the battle quickly turned. Rosco and Oliver desperately fought for their lives as two armored men hacked at them with swords. Side by side, they steadily retreated toward the house. Caught in front of the boys and far from the house, Rachel continued to fight off the sunscreen-blinded warrior with her purse. Three of the men lay on the ground—one trying to pull himself up on his good leg. The other two were moaning as they gripped their ringing heads. Many more men would soon be coming.

"I don't know which one to grab, so I'll grab you all," muttered the enormous man. His cheeks quivering, his beady eyes fell on Geoffrey first. "Alive, yes, but not in one piece!"

Screaming in unison, the boys stumbled back as the knife sliced the air front of their faces.

Jason ran straight for the blue Mustang. "In the car!" he cried to Lisa.

"*What's happening*?" demanded the old woman's voice from the mirror. "*It sounds worse than Jan taking a bath*!"

"They're trying to kill us!" screeched Lisa. "A whole army is after us!"

"I can't see anything but blurs!"

Just as the reinforcements reached the bottom of the hill, Jason tore open the driver's door and threw himself into the seat. Lisa jumped into the passenger seat. Looking through the windshield, Jason's eyes popped wide as a line of cars, vans, and pickups drove from down the street straight toward him. A small green car led the way.

"What do we do now?" Lisa screamed.

"You have to make Rudolph reject the dark spirit—it's the only way!"

"*I don't think she was talking to us*," said the mirror in a new voice.

"Shut up, Joe! Haven't you broken your neck yet?"

Lisa ignored the voices. "Jason, we're trapped!"

The green car sped up and zoomed past them, heading straight into the charging crowd of warriors. Seeing the metal carriage hurtling toward them, the warriors scattered to the side and broke their charge.

Skidding to a stop, the green car started honking its horn. "The Lord's Army has arrived!" cried a voice. "Drive this spawn from these streets and sing Halleluiah!" Borbu stuck his head from the window and waved his arm. The convoy of cars behind him stopped, and a mass of men started pouring out. They went after the warriors without hesitation. At the same time, the residents of Dougar Circle attacked from the sides.

As the morning air was shattered with screams and shouts of battle, Dosco twisted to see what was happening and suddenly snarled. "I see the redheaded dog! When I'm finished with you three, I'll cut her into pieces too small for rats!" Turning back to the boys, he raised his eyebrows as Steven suddenly dove at his feet, howling with rage.

"Leave my sister alone!" he shouted.

Surprised, the large man stepped back and flailed both his arms to keep his balance.

"Get him!" shouted Geoffrey. He and Tommy charged at the same time and struck the fleshy belly with all their might. It was only enough to send the man reeling back, but not enough to topple him. Still, he lost his grip on the knife. Bellowing in anger, he slapped at the boys' heads. Geoffrey caught a blow on the top of his head and slammed face-first into the ground, inches from impaling his face on the fallen knife. His body jerked and he went limp. Tommy received a glancing slap that sent him flying backward. Steven rolled away from the giant feet.

"You're the red dog's brother, are you, boy?" spat Dosco. "She wronged me, boy. You can thank her for your death!"

Rachel had been pushed back by the blinded warrior and was close enough to hear Dosco. She looked back in time to see Dosco stomp at Steven's prone body.

Crying out, she blindly flung her purse at the blinded man in front of her and barged into him with her shoulder. He fell back with a cry. Then she went after the fleshy man who was bent on crushing Steven.

Steven had rolled just at the last moment, but the giant man's foot caught the bottom of his shorts, pinning the boy to the ground.

"Leave those kids alone!" Rachel screeched. For a moment she let all her fury and frustration turn into hate, all directed at the massive man. Yelling like a banshee, she ignored her hurts and flew at the fleshy lump. She dove into the back of his planted knee just as he raised his foot over Steven.

Crawling from his pinned shorts, Steven managed to lunge away as Dosco's leg crumbled and he fell awkwardly where Steven had just lain. Rolling, the boy grabbed the hem of his shorts and managed to pull them back up as the giant started screaming in terrible pain.

"My leg!" wailed the massive cook. "I can't get up!"

Rachel got to her feet and glared down at him. "Leave the kids alone!" She drew back her foot to give him a sharp kick.

"You are a fool, Marcal!" hissed Rudolph. A new energy burned within Rudolph, and nothing could stop him. With a grunt, he flung Marcal aside, sending the man crashing into the pavement next to the gurgling Isabella. "I am all-powerful!" he screamed. "Bow to me, or you will die!"

Marcal didn't get up. Wearing a shocked expression, all he could do was stare.

Rudolph looked around at the surrounding chaos with fury. Isabella's men were trying to regroup, but more and more Earth men seemed to be arriving at every moment. And they all helped the babysitter. Once again, the babysitter had messed up his plans. Searching the yard, he spotted the boys. They were with … the babysitter.

Double fury boiled into his red eyes. "You will not take my power … I have great power! You cannot comprehend it! Dark spirit, give me all that I deserve! I've done your will, have I not? *YOU HAVE DONE MY WILL … RISE!*"

Green light flashed upward into the sky, and green mist started to swirl. All around, men staggered to halt their fighting and look up in fearful wonder.

"BEHOLD MY POWER!" roared Rudolph. His dark coat flapped around him as he rose from the ground to enter the heights of the sky.

Cries of fear followed his ascent and some men from Earth and Panterra fell to their knees in wonder.

Rachel gasped and quickly lowered her foot that had been poised over the fallen man's head. "I'm sorry," she murmured to the whimpering pile of flesh below her. *I can't hate! That's what gives the spirit power!* It seemed like it was too late.

A green bolt sizzled and blasted into the ground near her.

"I WILL HAVE THE BOY NOW!" bellowed a voice from Rudolph. "NONE WILL STOP ME! GIVE THEM UP OR DIE!"

"No!" cried Rachel. Taking a deep breath, she did her best to clear her mind of all hate. Looking down at Steven and then over at the blue car where she could see Lisa's bright hair through the window, she managed a smile. *Those kids will remind me of what's good in life … I will not hate anybody.* "You have no power here!" she cried.

"DON'T BE A FOOL! LOOK AT ME!" Rudolph rose even higher. "I CAN STRIKE YOU DEAD IF I WISH!"

"Then …" Rachel swallowed. "Then do it!"

Several gasps swept through the men, and many more fell to their knees. Some covered their faces while others bowed their heads in fear.

Rudolph glared down at her—his eyes blazing red. "YOU ARE NOT WORTHY TO DIE BY MY HAND. LET THE UNDERLINGS DO THE WORK." He pointed a finger at the road in front of the blue Mustang. "ALL WHO WISH TO JOIN ME AND MY POWER MAY LIVE. FIRST THIS WOMAN MUST BE DEAD AND THE BOYS GIVEN TO ME!" A thin green light shot from his fingers, sending many to shriek and duck for cover. A great cloud of mist appeared and hovered.

"A water portal in the air," Borbu muttered nervously. Backing up to his green car, he eyed Rudolph and then Isabella.

Bodin rose to his feet and spat in the direction of where Marcal knelt by Isabella. The female wizard lay in a small pool of blood and appeared lifeless.

"My men are your men, Wizard," Bodin cried out. "They always will serve you."

"TENDL TELLS ME OTHERWISE, BODIN. HE IS WAITING FOR YOUR RETURN … DO MY BIDDING AND I WILL MAKE YOUR RETURN A PLEASANT ONE."

The scarred warrior's face turned ashen.

"And I, I have no quarrels with you either," Borbu said, swallowing. "I merely came here to protect against Isabella gaining all the power …"

The floating wizard said, "DO MY COMMAND AND I WILL DO YOU JUSTICE."

Borbu looked sick as he gave the briefest of nods.

Jason stuck his head out the window of the Mustang. "If any of you try to get near Rachel, I'll run you flat!" The keys had remained in the ignition. With a twist, he roared the powerful engine to life.

Bodin sneered and lifted his sword. "I will defeat a metal beast as easily as a human beast! Bring it!"

One of the residents of Dougar Circle rose on unsteady feet. "I'm with the kid." He gripped a long-handled hoe in two hands. "Evil spirits are at play here, and I ain't afraid."

Several men murmured their assent and joined him.

Bodin's men, now with time to prepare, raised their swords.

Before anybody could make a move, a long, deep howl rose in the distance.

Immediately everyone froze.

A second howl closely followed the first.

Bodin dropped his sword and touched the barely healed scars on his face. "W-wolves," he stammered. "The wolves are back!"

Rudolph faltered in the sky. "N-NO!" he roared. But his voice shrank. "It's impossible!"

But another long howl sent shivers down many spines. It sounded closer.

From across the road from Geoffrey's house, Lineus stumbled out of the trees and swayed like a drunken man. Only his face, battered and bruised, wore a look of horror.

"It's the Wolves of Nyanhelm!" he cried. "They're coming!"

Panic broke out from the men from Panterra.

"Run for it!" Bodin yelled.

Many, including Bodin, were fortunate survivors from only a few nights before. None would ever forget the terror and teeth that had ripped at them throughout the night. Without hesitating, they fled into the open portal created by Rudolph.

"No!" shouted the wizard. "You must get the boy and kill the babysitter first!" Nobody listened to him. Even Dosco, torn leg and all, managed to pull his heavy body up and hobble toward the portal.

Lisa climbed out of the Mustang as the men of Panterra fled from the wolves. "Rudolph, don't you get it!" she yelled. "You have no power here! Give it up and go back, too!"

"NO!" roared Rudolph. "I HAVE POWER! LOOK UP AT ME AND SEE IT!"

Rachel stared up at him in almost pity. "We're sorry for you, Rudolph. But we're no longer afraid of you. Wolves bring more fear than you do. Now, go away!"

"I WILL KILL YOU ALL!" A dark surge of green clouds started to form around the wizard, and energy crackled around his fingers. But then he stared over the terrified faces of the Earth humans and started to choke. Coming down the hill were three young girls—Courtney and … his daughter? Could it be? No. They were just two more Earth girls with Courtney and the boy Jakey …

"Layla," Rudolph cried out. "I need you! Hag? Where are you?"

"*Right here, you old fool*!" shouted the woman's voice from the mirror Lisa still held. "*Don't you get it? That dark spirit is inside you, twisting up your feelings! The only way to be free is to reject his nonsense*!"

"Only way to be free …" Rudolph gasped and shuddered. "I thought I had all the power … Why is nobody listening to me?"

"The only power out there that matters is the power of love! Everything else is just in your head! Don't you get it? That's why you can't use your power around here. There's too much love and very little of it is for you, you old fool!"

"But-but I am using power …" Rudolph's voice trailed off. He looked once more at Courtney. "I need to be free …"

In an instant, all his faith in the dark spirit fled. The portal slammed shut just as the last warrior made it into the mist.

"*NO*!" roared the voice of the dark spirit.

The woman also cried out.

But it was too late. Suddenly Rudolph was just an old man stuck high in the air. With a startled yell, he kicked and waved his arms uselessly as he fell. A terrible thud sounded behind Geoffrey's house.

The police soon arrived with screaming sirens and flashing lights.

Rosco limped from his yard to meet the first car that squealed to a stop at the bottom of the hill.

"Man, Officer," he groaned. "I never thought I would say this, but am I glad to see you."

"Looks like you'd rather see an ambulance, son." The officer nodded at Rosco's bloody arm and ripped shirt. "Was this a gang fight or something?"

Rosco shook his head. "Or something," he answered.

By this time, most of the Lord's Army had returned to their cars and had driven away with very thoughtful faces. The last to leave was Tommy's van. His mother had been the force behind their arrival and drove off with her son buckled tightly at her side. Earlier, Pastor Smith had come to her house to warn her that her son was in grave danger. Immediately, she had flown at the pastor, beating at him with her fists until he'd quickly explained it wasn't him behind it—he even had apologized for disappearing from church. Believing him, Mrs. Hunt had immediately put out the call for the Lord's Army to congregate at the old church. Pastor Smith had met them there. When confronted with the missing money, he had acted genuinely confused and promised he hadn't touched it. He'd suggested they ask Susan Proom … funny thing, but the youth pastor had vanished weeks before, in a brand-new car. In any case, when hearing of young Tommy being threatened, the men in the army barely hesitated in following their former pastor in the one and only physical battle they would ever face together. Sadly, their pastor had been one of the first to disappear in the green mist. Once again, they were left with many more questions than answers.

The police found dazed and confused residents wandering the area, but none were talking much. A few wild stories about a flying man and "Viking" warriors nearly led to public drunkenness arrests, but everyone tested sober. Besides, it became apparent that some battle had occurred. The Brown yard was scorched in areas and there were traces of blood on the road. About a dozen swords and an assortment of clubs were collected from the area and turned over as evidence—but who had carried them? They were made in a very unique fashion and full of intricate detail never seen on Earth before … Finally, the police searched for a gang of fantasy buffs who had tried to establish a homeless man as their prophet and formed a cult surrounding the execution of a local boy. The homeless man had either cracked under the pressure or was mentally unbalanced. After climbing to the roof of the Brown house, he'd leapt off and critically injured himself. Nobody knew his name, but he resembled a local janitor who called himself Red Deer and had been recently fired from a private school for clogging all the toilets on the last day before summer vacation. With his shattered bones and his being in a coma, the police wondered if they would ever be able to question the strange man. A screaming ambulance carried him to the hospital as they wrapped up their investigation.

Other injures included bruises and a few cuts, but nothing too serious. The residents of Dougar Circle had been through a lot in their time, and ultimately they decided to do what they usually did in times of trouble. They kept mum to the public and quietly gathered in small groups to discuss what really happened.

Among the residents was a bunch of kids from Camelot Acres … They raised a few eyebrows and made the police a little nervous. If anybody from that area was involved, it could be a big story. Instead, a young woman identified herself as the babysitter and said that they had just been curious at all the noise.

While some of the younger cops tried to catch her eye, an older one told her to get back to her house and take all the kids with her. One of the kids, a young redhead, even carried a mirror with her, for goodness sake! Rich people, the cops knew, were in a different world. Before sending Rachel on her way, the police warned her to be careful. There were reports of wolves … not that the police believed such a ridiculous thing.

Still, shortly after the police arrived, so did animal control services. Over a hundred reports had been phoned in from across the area, reporting the presence of wolves. Not one was ever found, and none were actually spotted. All in all, it had been a bizarre day.

Rachel leaned heavily against Jason as they stood across the street from where a police officer tried to question Rosco and Oliver. Geoffrey, still a little groggy, stood proudly between his two brothers.

"What a babysitting job," Rachel groaned. "If anything else happens before we get home, I'm asking for a raise."

Jason put an arm around her shoulder. "You deserve it, Rachel. I never knew babysitting could be so exciting."

Sitting on the curb by them, Courtney elbowed Jakey, and the younger boy covered his eyes.

Steven sat on the other side of Jakey, hugging his knees thoughtfully. Lisa stood over his back and watched him with a worried face.

They were waiting for Callie and Susie to retrieve their bikes. With the reports of wolves, Rachel had told the two girls to come with them and call their moms from the Winters' house.

Lisa couldn't stand it any longer. She dropped next to her brother and threw her arms around his back, squeezing tightly. "You idiot," she said fiercely. "Why did you leave without me like that?"

Steven grinned sheepishly and shrugged. "Sorry," he said. "I knew you would find me."

Lisa looked ready to hit him, but instead squeezed tighter. "Never again, Steven, will you go off like that without me! I'm your sister, remember?"

Then the mirror started talking in her ear.

"Is it over?"

"Yes, it's over, hag! Now let me see! You've been hogging that thing forever!"

"Wait your turn, Jan! I want to talk to Courtney!"

"I want to tell Steven I finally rode the ripstick without crashing!"

"Shut up, both of you! Murd? Where are you? Get these brats away!"

"We'll leave, hag, if you give us the mirror!"

"Yeah! Give it to us!"

Callie and Susie gave startled jumps as they approached, walking their bikes. The mirror clutched in Lisa's hand sounded off like a bad radio sitcom.

"I guess," Rachel said with a faint smile, "babysitting Jan and Joe could be worse."

Chapter Forty-Five

It wasn't until they reached the wooded path connecting Dougar Circle with Camelot Acres that Lisa suddenly clapped her hands together. "Where's Jak?"

Steven, being carried in Rachel's arms, turned and looked down at her in confusion. "I thought he was with you."

"We thought he was with you!" Lisa said back to him.

Rachel swallowed and pulled Steven tighter to her. "There're wolves around."

Jason grabbed her arm and said, "Look through those trees, was that the blue Mustang?"

"Where?" Rachel asked.

Marcal hadn't looked once at her after Rudolph had tumbled. Instead, he'd simply muttered his apologies and dragged Isabella to the Mustang. Jason and Lisa had moved aside, and soon the car roared up the hill with the injured wizard and her captain inside.

Jason answered worriedly, "Pulling out down the street—I think it just left your house!"

Steven slid from Rachel's arms as the babysitter clenched her fists. "Come on!" she cried. Telling Steven to stay with Lisa, she rushed from the path in the trees fearing something bad had happened. The others rushed to keep up. Poor Callie and Susie didn't know what was going on.

As Rachel reached the driveway and approached the familiar door, a brown flash shot from behind the hedges and ran straight into her arms.

For a brief moment, Rachel thought it was a wolf and nearly shrieked. But then thin brown arms wrapped around her neck and slight legs clamped on her waist.

"Jak!" she cried, wrapping her arms around his back. "Where were you?"

Sweaty, with his hands full of mud and smelling rather sour, the boy only grinned.

"I think this calls for a celebration," Jason muttered. The others quickly joined them. "Why don't we all go inside and take twenty-hour naps?"

In other news, a young woman arrived at the hospital just behind the homeless man. Carried from a dark blue Mustang by a tall, bearded stranger who gave no name, she was identified as Jane Lovington, but had no papers. Illegal immigrants were common in the area, and the hospital assumed they had another one. This one had a knife wound in her abdomen, which had been covered in a layer of mud and organic material that smelled strangely of urine … and amazingly, it had sealed the wound and started the healing process. More amazingly, only an hour after waking, Jane had a visitor—the strange Good Samaritan who had brought her in. Left alone only for a moment, the two then somehow completely vanished. The police officer sent to question the woman about her knife wound had been standing outside the room at the time. Yet when the nurses went in and reported the room empty, all they could find was a tub full of water in the bathroom. The IVs had been yanked out and the electrical equipment shut off. A blue Mustang sat abandoned in the parking lot. Truly, it was a mystery.

After Susie and Callie left with their moms, Rachel sank into the couch and rubbed her temples. Upstairs, the showers were running full force. Jak, after being shown how the shower worked, had woofed with joy. Closing the door, he had yet to come out. For almost an hour he could be heard jumping and dancing under the water. Rachel finally had Steven use his parents' bathroom while Lisa used the one in Rachel's room. By now they were no longer in a babysitting relationship. They were family. Her babysitting rules were not necessary.

Jason walked in and sat next to Rachel. In the kitchen, Courtney and Jakey were busy trying to set the table and put together a salad. While Vikki Rosa had done a tremendous job making sure the house was clean, all she had done with the food supply was stock it with expensive wines. Rachel had already dumped every bottle in the sink.

"So what's for lunch?" Rachel asked tiredly.

"Oh," Jason said, "I took the liberty of ordering three large pizzas."

Rachel gave a start. "You what?"

Jason frowned at her. "What's the matter?" he asked.

"Oh, uh, nothing …" Rachel smiled and shook her head. The last time she'd ordered pizza seemed like a lifetime ago … several lifetimes ago. "I'm sure the kids will love it."

"Yeah … uh, Rachel?" Jason asked.

"Hmm?"

"Um, remember when I told you how I didn't know what I wanted to do and was thinking of taking the year off from the university?"

Rachel nodded carefully. "Yes, I remember."

"Well, um, I just want you to know, that I'm going back. To the university. I, um, found out what I wanted to work for."

"Oh, that's nice … Wake me up when everything is ready."

Jason left with his siblings early in the evening. Flushed with happiness, everyone now just wanted to sleep. The pizza had been a huge success, and of the three large pies, only five slices remained. Jak had devoured four slices of his first pizza ever, but Jason proved to be the king by inhaling seven.

Before leaving, Jason sent his siblings outside and gave Rachel a brief hug at the door. Jak watched unabashedly from the stairs. Thankfully Lisa and Steven had been cleaning up in the kitchen so they didn't see Rachel turn beet red.

"I, um, might not be able to see you tomorrow," the dark-haired teen mumbled.

"Uh, okay … I guess you have a lot of catching up to do … Shawna …" Rachel's cheeks burned even more.

Jason stepped back and scratched the back of his head. He didn't appear to notice Rachel's embarrassment. "I called my dad this morning and they're flying in tomorrow afternoon. But I, I do want to call you after they arrive. Okay?"

"Uh, sure … That'll be great."

Walking out with Jason, she gave Courtney and Jakey quick hugs and then watched them walk down the driveway. Warmth flooded her heart.

Later, after taking another shower, just to make sure she was really back, she went downstairs to find Steven, Jak, and Lisa all curled up on the floor of the TV room, sound asleep. The three were just as close a family as the Richardson siblings. She didn't have the heart to wake them. Flipping off the television, she went back to the kitchen with her notebook. She had a lot of writing to catch up on …

Before she could get started, the phone rang.

"*Rachel? It's Elizabeth—what's happening down there*?" demanded a voice when she answered.

"Uh, uh, I, uh, I don't know," stammered Rachel, suddenly feeling like the fat kid with no social skills. "The kids, uh, are okay."

"I got a call that there was a riot at Dougar Circle and that you were there."

Rachel took a deep breath. "Uh, I can explain."

"Rachel, everyone is saying you're a hero! What was it, some crazy cult tried to kidnap one of Steven's friends and you stopped them?"

"Huh?"

Elizabeth Winter had heard it from the grapevine that Rachel had single-handedly stood up to a terrible cult and saved a child from being kidnapped.

"Oh my goodness, Rachel—you must have been so scared! Well, I just want you to know, we're taking the first flight out tomorrow."

"Oh, uh, okay—"

"Robbie and Margie miss Steven and Lisa terribly—and so do Doug and I. My goodness, Rachel, you wouldn't believe what we've been through!"

"Uh, yeah—"

"Oh, listen to me talk—Rachel, I know you're busy with the kids and probably want a rest. But I just have to tell you. You know Lisa and Steven were both adopted from Colorado, right? That's why we didn't really want them with us. You see, as part of the trip we searched for their birth mothers … well, to make a long story short, we found her. It's almost impossible to

believe, but Lisa and Steven do have the same mother! I can't tell you how much this means to us, Rachel! We really are a real family!"

Rachel had nodded and stammered. But now a smile spread across her face. "Elizabeth," she said very clearly, "that's great news!"

"Oh, it's been such a long time—I haven't talked to you in forever! Have the kids been treating you well? Your mom has been calling constantly and we've been talking nonstop about you and the kids. I knew you would do a great job. I have to go now—Robbie is trying to climb walls again. We all send our love and we'll see you tomorrow!"

Doug climbed out of the taxi van and grinned as Robbie and Margie shot from the back like two little rockets.

"Aren't you two going to help your dad with the luggage?" he called after them.

"Don't worry," said his wife. "Doug, I'm here. Just carry everything inside and I'll have you sort it out later."

Doug grimaced. "Why did we have so many kids when they don't do any of the work?"

"To brag about, of course." Elizabeth gave him a quick kiss. "Besides, I don't blame Robbie and Margie. They want to see the surprise Rachel has for us."

"Ah, yes." Doug smiled. "The two best times of vacation are leaving home and coming home."

Robbie raced back to the front door and poked out his head. He looked a little worried. "Dad, Mom, Rachel is gone!"

"What?" Elizabeth asked in surprise.

"Look in the pool," her son said. "There's some other girl there!"

Doug shoved a wad of bills at the cab driver. "Er, can you unload everything and just leave it on the driveway? Keep the change."

The driver speechlessly nodded, his eyes never leaving the bills.

"Well, the new housekeeper is doing a fabulous job," Elizabeth said as she hurried inside after her husband. "When Rachel told me Jane had left, I'd started to worry."

"Yeah, so did I—I worried—" Doug stopped short. "Lizzy, who is that girl?"

Margie and Robbie moved close to their father's legs and pressed against the glass door in silence. Elizabeth joined them and frowned.

Out in the pool, Steven stood in the shallow end and looked to be giving swimming instructions to a trim, tanned teenage girl with thick brunette hair. Lisa and Susie Perkins sat on the edge giving encouragement.

"You don't suppose Steven found his first girlfriend, do you?" Elizabeth asked worriedly. "She's over twice his age!"

"Where's Rachel?" growled Doug. He hurried out the door and nearly fell in shock.

"Daddy!" cried Lisa, pushing herself to her feet.

"Hey, Dad," Steven said, grinning shyly.

Both son and daughter waited expectantly as the teenage girl stood and flung wet hair from her face. Giving a shy smile, she slowly approached the pool's side.

"R-Rachel?" Doug stammered. "Is-is, I, er, that, what, you?"

The beautiful girl smiled shyly. "Hi, Mr. Winter, uh, Doug. How was your flight?" Rachel asked. Suddenly, a brown boy burst from the water next to her, gasping for a breath. Putting an arm around his shoulder, Rachel sucked in her breath. "This is the surprise. His name is Jak and he hasn't a home … I, uh, we, uh, kind of took him in."

Elizabeth moved beside her husband. "So, dear, do you believe Rachel is capable of babysitting now?"

Doug swallowed and shook his head in a daze. "Oh, um, er, well … yeah," he managed to say.

That night Rachel called home to tell her mom she would be coming home soon. The day had been hectic and crazy. As soon as little Susie Perkins said her goodbyes and left, the questions began to fly. Rachel had done her best to explain about Jak—a boy they had found and who had helped them tremendously.

Elizabeth barely heard her. She knelt down and took Jak's shoulders and smiled warmly. Doug shook his head and waved Rachel to be quiet. "I think we already have a new member of the family."

Very quickly, Elizabeth contacted the child services in Florida and managed to obtain temporary custody of Jak. Since he didn't show up on any records and seemed a complete mystery, the child services didn't know what to do with him anyway.

The boy had already been adopted by Margie and Robbie. The two gave him the tour of the house—accents and all—and then spent the rest of the day playing hide-and-seek. Jak won every time. While he didn't speak, he seemed very bright and had the nose of a bloodhound … or a wolf.

After scratching his head in wonder at it all, Doug had spent the rest of the afternoon with Steven in the living room. Father and son had a lot to talk about. Lisa stayed with Rachel in the kitchen and made dinner that night. When Rachel finally arrived in her room, a shiny necklace lay on top of her notebook. Before dialing home, Rachel had to wipe away a tear.

"Rachel, it's about time you called! Your father and I were getting worried!"

"Uh, hi, Mom."

"Tell me, have you decided on the fall yet?"

"Oh, uh, actually I've been kind of busy … babysitting was, uh, harder than I thought—but really worth it. I mean, I can't thank you enough for everything."

"Oh, that's great, Rachel. Well, um, I spoke to Lizzy earlier … how would you like to attend the university in Florida?"

"What?"

"Doug works closely with some of the board members and will get you in for the fall. He and Lizzy want you to stay at their house and work as their babysitter. They'll pay your tuition as part of the salary. Isn't that wonderful? I just hope you can meet somebody at the university, but I'm sure you'll do fine."

"Uh, Mom, I, uh … but I miss you!"

"Oh, don't worry. Lizzy and Doug invited your father and me down to visit. We'll be on the flight tomorrow. Oh, I hope you don't mind, but I already told Lizzy you accepted."

Rachel sat back on her bed with a thump. Her door opened and Elizabeth leaned in, grinning. "Sorry," she said, "but I've been eavesdropping a little … I hope you don't mind, but I sort of wanted to surprise you, too. I've spoken with Lisa and Steven—I think they would both die if you weren't around."

"I-I guess I am their babysitter … Thank you, Elizabeth."

"No, Rachel. Believe me. We thank you. I'm not sure what happened while we were away, but you really made a hit with the kids. It's like they came from another world."

Lisa shot up in her bed before her clock reached 6:00 a.m. She grinned at her reflection in the mirror. Lisa Winter grinned back. No longer did she imagine herself as a princess. Just thinking about it caused her smile to turn into a grimace. She was perfectly happy to be herself in a safe house with a wonderful family. Then her clock hit the hour and the alarm blared.

Minutes later, fully dressed, Lisa crept into her brothers' room. She slipped inside the door and paused. The blinds were closed, and she had to adjust her eyes to the darkened room. Glancing at her brother's bed gave her a start. The mattress lay bare, and her brother was not in sight. Then she saw two large eyes staring up at her.

She nearly screeched, but then relaxed. Jak stared up at her from the middle of the room. Only his head was visible as the rest of him lay under a sheet. Steven slept deeply on his right. Robbie snored on his left. The boys had emptied their beds of sheets and pillows and gathered them in the middle. Jak watched Lisa with an amused expression.

"Jak," she hissed when her heart started beating normally. "You nearly scared me to death."

Then she sighed. "Well, I guess it doesn't matter if everyone wakes up this time." Grinning at Jak, she put a finger to her lips and walked to where Steven's bare feet stuck out from the blanket. She'd learned her lesson.

With a loud whoop, she pounced on her brother and started a vicious tickle attack.

"Hey!" Steven yelped, jerking awake. He'd been having a wonderful dream about eating pizza in a toy store. Now he squirmed and resisted his sister. "What are you doing?"

Lisa flung back the blanket and sat on her brother's flat stomach. "No kicking me in the face this time," she said, grinning evilly. He'd grown since the last time she'd snuck into his room but was still too small to take her down. Or so she thought.

Suddenly Steven rolled to the right and sent his sister crashing to the ground.

Jak rose to his knees and watched curiously as Steven ended up looming over his sister.

"Sorry," Steven said, "but I'm going to kick you somewhere else this time."

The boys only wore shorts. This proved to be to Lisa's advantage.

Lisa grunted. "You mean, I'm going to do the kicking!" She reached up and tickled Steven's ribs and sent him twisting away. Following up her attack by pushing Steven back, she lunged at him and rolled him to his stomach. A forearm planted in the small of his back and held him down. Her hand raised and poised for a swat. "Say who's the best sister in the world," she cried in triumph. "Say it!" The hand blasted down.

"Ouch!" Steven cried. "Why don't you just say why you're waking us up?" The shadowman and monster were gone. They would never haunt him again. But his sister …

"For this!" Lisa said. She gave another swat.

Robbie sat up sleepily and blinked at them. "Hey," he said, "what's going on?"

"Lisa has gone crazy," Steven said, his face pressed in the carpet. "Find a tranquilizer." This earned him another swat.

Jak shook his head and put his head down to go back to sleep.

Seeing him, Lisa grunted a protest. "Oh, no you don't," she said to him. Shoving off her brother, she launched herself at the brown boy. "We have to get up. We have lots to do today. Right, Steven?"

Steven sat up and frowned. Lisa and Jak tussled next to a confused Robbie. "Like what?" he asked.

Lisa paused from trying to tickle Jak under the arms and said, "We have a party to plan!" Then Jak shook himself free and rolled away. At times he could be as feisty as a wild dog.

Steven blinked and then grinned his lopsided smile. "Right," he said. "I almost forgot. I have to do something."

"First get dressed," Lisa said, panting. She got to her feet and brushed back her hair. "But you'll have to wait until I'm out of the bath—*hey*!"

Steven took off like a shot with Jak following. Soon Robbie was left alone in a mess of sheets and pillows.

"I think I missed a lot of fun during the vacation," he grumbled.

From the hallway he heard a door slam and Lisa's agonized wail of "It's not fair! Rachel! Rachel, where are you? I need help!"

Few clouds dotted the bright blue sky later that morning. Birds sang and insects buzzed as a party was quickly scheduled at the Winter home to welcome Rachel's parents. The invitees included an old woman with her overgrown "son" and two bratty grandchildren. (Rachel had spent a long time the previous night talking to her mirror. Darvy couldn't make it but said he would be very happy to create a water portal if it meant a day of peace and quiet.) The odd group showed up promptly just after breakfast … in the backyard by the pool. After loud, boisterous introductions, Steven went off and delivered the first written invitation, which went to Geoffrey Brown. Lisa, Jan, and Joe (who took turns falling on the ripstick) went with him to deliver it straight to Geoffrey's front door. On the way back home, Lisa stopped and dropped a second written invitation in Macie's mailbox. Tommy had been invited by phone and would be arriving later.

Elizabeth and Doug Winter were bemused about the changes in their household but too happy to care too much … even after Jak brought them a live rabbit he somehow managed to catch … and let it loose in their bedroom.

While Doug escaped to pick up Rachel's parents, other guests kept arriving.

The sun continued shining brightly when Jason arrived with Jakey and Courtney, dressed for the pool. They just barely managed to beat Geoffrey to the front door. Macie arrived a little while after … and was greeted by a new friend presenting her with a new bike. Lisa never really used it anyhow.

Food, laughter, and lots of trouble filled the rest of the day. Rachel never felt happier … especially when she saw her mother and Elizabeth Winter meet again.

Being a babysitter wasn't so bad after all.

In a far off land, peace began to settle. A hero had come and gone. Monsters had been vanquished. Wizards had been humbled. And children were now protected. All would be well…

THE END

The Rules of Babysitting

(by Margie and Lizzy, presented to Rachel before being presented to Panterra)

One: Always keep calm. Never take things personally.

Two: Keep personal issues out of babysitting. Never take your anger or frustration out on kids.

Three: Be healthy. Never get sick on the job. You must have full attention and focus on the kids.

Four: Everyone must be your favorite. Never show individual favorites when babysitting and never purposely ignore a child.

Five: Respect children. Never invade the privacy of children you're babysitting unless it's an emergency.

Six: Always speak kindly. Never speak meanly in front of children.

Seven: Always be ready. Never make assumptions or take anything for granted.

Eight: Have energy. Fake it until you make it—if you don't feel energetic when on babysitting duty, pretend you do until you feel it.

Nine: Always be courteous to adults, even when they are rude and/or unpleasant—be the example for the kids.

Ten: Always look out the window before answering the door. Don't talk to strangers unless they're delivering pizza (that *you* ordered!). Talk from an upstairs window if you have to.

Eleven: Always be consistent in your actions and words.

Twelve: Trust children. Don't accuse anybody of anything without proof.

Thirteen: Play safely. Never encourage dangerous play or dare dangerous behavior.

Fourteen: Children should always wear shoes when outside.

Fifteen: Follow all the rules left by the parents, even if you don't agree with them.

Sixteen: Make safety your number one priority. You must earn children's trust, and they will become your friends once they know they are safe.

Seventeen: Never lower your guard when babysitting—that's when accidents happen.

Eighteen: Always be happy. Never be angry.

Nineteen: Always tell the truth and never lie to the children you're babysitting. Trust must be a two-way street.

Twenty: Rule with your head first. Never allow emotions to control your actions.

These rules are not listed in order of importance but in the order written by two young girls many years ago. While the wording has changed, the spirit remains the same. Please follow responsibly.

In the course of this story Rachel Pugsley managed to lose quite a large amount of weight. Please remember, this is only a story and *SHOULD NOT* be tried at home. If you ever want to lose weight, this is something you first need to discuss with your parents and then with a trusted doctor. The best way to begin is by doing what Rachel started doing at the Winters' home—exercising daily and eating a healthy diet. That means to cut back on fried foods and foods high in fat. Eating when you're hungry is good, especially if you're young and growing, but just make sure you're also exercising. The key for weight loss is consistent exercise paired with healthy eating. Slow and steady weight loss will tone muscles and provide a lifestyle that can last for life. What should *NEVER* be done is starvation. Too many people in the world suffer from not enough food. Let us help those in need while taking care of our own bodies.

For Rachel, she was constantly judged for her outward appearance and often ridiculed or ignored because of it. Thankfully for her, she found her courage and a way to rise above it—mostly by caring for others. She had her true inner beauty revealed by putting others before herself, even risking her life. All of us have strength for good inside of us. It is important we don't let others make us feel weak and powerless, no matter what. It is also important we don't put down others, especially for superficial reasons such as looks. Treating every person with respect and value is not just the way of the babysitter, it is also the way of life … that sadly many (including many adults) seem to have forgotten. Let's make sure we don't forget.

Acknowledgments

Thank you to all who made this book possible—my wonderful family, the editors of Kevin Anderson, and the great snowstorms of 2015. Special thanks goes to Ce-Ce Cox of Outside-Eyes Editing and to Diana Cox for taking on the terror without flinching and leading this story to new heights. Most of all, of course, thank you to all the babysitters of the world. You have an important job and I hope and pray you do it well.

About the Author

Gregory Saur is the author of several novels for young adults, including *Otherworld: Orcish Delight* and *Royal Pains and Angels in the Outhouse.* He lives in Virginia, but often visits strange worlds only found in his imagination. When not writing, he practices to become a wizard, but only a good wizard. Right now his best trick is making pizza disappear. You may visit him whenever you like, just as long as he's not home at the time.

You are still reading. Thank you, but the story is over. I mean it. Why are you still reading this? If you would like to read more, find another book by the same author. Then you wouldn't have to read this anymore. SO WHY ARE YOU STILL READING? *It's okay. I know. You're probably just bored. Well, in that case, here's free advice. Stop reading this.* Fine. *Be that way. If you ever have another babysitter, just remember: be kind. And if you ever happen to be a babysitter, just remember: be kind. Better yet, as the great philosopher from another planet once said, "Be good."*

Now stop reading this. Seriously.

Some people just never learn. Here you are again. Really?

If you're going to be like this then you probably have too much time on your hands. You may now go to a certain social media website and tell the author you read this. I'm sure he'll be very impressed. Most likely not. Make sure you ask your parents first, of course. Very likely they will be equally unimpressed and make you do some chores. So your best bet is to STOP reading this and read another good book. If you can't find one, just go back to the front of this one and find the list of books by the author... like I already said to do. Now for the last time... STOP READING THIS!

Sincerely, Warmpa Finkletoes

Yes... I'm back.

Now go away.

FINDING INNOCENCE TRILOGY

Book One: Strange Old World

From Saur & Saur

2019

www.ingramcontent.com/pod-product-compliance
Lightning Source LLC
Chambersburg PA
CBHW030429310726
48979CB00009B/1680/J
* 9 7 8 0 9 9 6 4 2 4 5 0 9 *